No Angel

No Angel

Penny
Vincenzi

'I want no angel: only she'
from a First World War poem, anonymous

THE OVERLOOK PRESS
Woodstock & New York

F

First published in the United States in 2003 by
The Overlook Press, Peter Mayer Publishers, Inc.
Woodstock & New York

WOODSTOCK:
One Overlook Drive
Woodstock, NY 12498
www.overlookpress.com
[for individual orders, bulk and special sales, contact our Woodstock office]

NEW YORK:
141 Wooster Street
New York, NY 10012

Cataloging-in-Publication Data is available from the Library of Congress.

Manufactured in the United States of America
FIRST EDITION
1 3 5 7 9 8 6 4 2
ISBN 1-58567-481-8

For Paul: with love. Not to mention huge appreciation
for some particularly crucial structural advice.

Acknowledgements

As always, a long list of people without whom this book would not have happened. Probably top of the bill should go to my agent Desmond Elliott (no relation to the villain of the piece) for his encyclopaedian knowledge of publishing, after a wonderful lifetime in the business. Stories, anecdotes, facts and figures tumbled down the wires from his office to mine; the book would have been much the poorer without him.

I owe a big debt too to Rosemary Stark who gave me an extraordinarily insightful view of twin-ness, as did Jo Puccioni.

I would like to thank Martin Harvey for taking me round the Garrick Club and acquainting me so patiently with its history and its connection with publishing, and Ursula Lloyd who once more guided me through the complexities of medicine in the early part of the century, and Hugh Dickens for an immensely authoritative over-view of military matters.

For legal and other advice, I owe, as always, huge gratitude to Sue Stapely who either knows whatever I need to, or someone else who does; and to Mark Stephens who adds zest and originality to his fearsome knowledge of libel law and publishing.

I have delved into some particularly wonderful books for information: most notably *Despatches from the Heart* by Annette Tapert, *In Society: The Brideshead Years* by Nicholas Courtney, *The Country House Remembered* edited by Merlin Watterson, *Mrs Keppel and Her Daughter* by Diana Souhami and the marvelous *Round About a Pound a Week* by Maud Pember Reeves. Huge thanks to my four daughters Polly, Sophie, Emily and Claudia who continue to endure my self centered and panicky ramblings as publication draws nearer with kindness and sympathy, never indicating for a moment that they find (as they must do) the annual repetition of the drama rather tedious. I am and always will be immensely grateful to them. And to my husband Paul who has to endure even more of it, and (almost) never indicates it either...

I owe everybody a great deal. It has, as always, in retrospect anyway, been tremendous fun.

Part One
1904–1914

CHAPTER I

Celia stood at the altar, smiling into the face of her bridegroom and wondered if she was about to test his vow to cherish her in sickness and in health rather sooner than he might have imagined. She really did feel as if she was going to vomit: there and then, in front of the congregation, the vicar, the choir. This was truly the stuff of which nightmares were made. She closed her eyes briefly, took a very deep breath, swallowed; heard dimly through her swimmy clammy nausea the vicar saying, 'I now pronounce you man and wife', and somehow the fact that she had done it, managed this marriage, managed this day, that she was married to Oliver Lytton, whom she loved so much, and that no one could change anything now, made her feel better. She saw Oliver's eyes on her, tender, but slightly anxious, having observed her faintness, and she managed to smile again before sinking gratefully on to her knees for the blessing.

Not an ideal condition for a bride to be in, almost three months' pregnant; but then if she hadn't been pregnant, her father would never have allowed her to marry Oliver anyway. It had been a fairly drastic measure; but it had worked. As she had known it would. And it had certainly been fun: she had enjoyed becoming pregnant a lot.

The blessing was over now; they were being ushered into the vestry to sign the register. She felt Oliver's hand taking hers, and glanced over her shoulder at the group following them. There were her parents, her father fiercely stern, the old hypocrite: she'd grown up seeing pretty housemaid after pretty housemaid banished from the house, her mother, staunchly smiling, Oliver's frail old father, leaning on his cane supported by his sister Margaret, and just behind them, Oliver's two brothers, Robert rather stiff and formal and slightly portly, Jack, the youngest, absurdly handsome, with his brilliant blue eyes restlessly exploring the congregation for any pretty faces. Beyond them were the guests, admittedly rather few, just very close friends and family, and the people from the village and the estate, who of course wouldn't have missed her being married for anything. She knew that in some ways her mother minded about that more than about anything else really, that it wasn't a huge wedding like her sister Caroline's, with three hundred guests at St Margaret's Westminster, but a quiet affair in the village church. Well, she didn't mind. She didn't mind in the very least. She had married Oliver: she had got her way.

'Of course you can't marry him,' her mother had said, 'he has no money, no position, no house even, your father won't hear of it.'

Her father did hear about it, about her wish to marry Oliver, because she made him listen; but he reiterated everything her mother had said.

'Ridiculous. Throwing your life away. You want to marry properly, Celia, into your own class, someone who can keep you and support you in a reasonable way.'

She said she did not want to marry properly, she wanted to marry Oliver, because she loved him; that he had a brilliant future, that his father owned a successful publishing house in London which would be his one day.

'Successful, nonsense,' her father said, 'if it was successful he wouldn't be living in Hampstead would he? With nowhere in the country. No, darling,' for he adored her, his youngest, a late flower in his life, 'you find someone suitable and you can get married straight away. That's what you really want, I know, a home and husband and babies; it's natural, I wouldn't dream of stopping you. But it's got to be someone who's right for you. This fellow can't even ride a horse.'

Things had got much worse after that; she had shouted, raged, sworn she would never marry anyone else, and they had shouted and raged back at her, telling her she was being ridiculous, that she had no idea what she was talking about, that she clearly had no idea what marriage was about, that it was a serious matter, a considerable undertaking, not some absurd notion about love.

'Very over-rated, love,' her mother said briskly, 'doesn't last, Celia, not what you're talking about. And when it's gone, you need other things, believe me. Like a decent home to bring up your children in. Marriage is a business and it works best when both parties see it that way.'

Celia was just eighteen years old when she met Oliver Lytton: she had looked at him across the room at a luncheon party in London given by a rather bohemian friend of her sister's and fallen helplessly in love with him, even before they had spoken a single word. Afterwards, trying to analyse that sensation, to explain it to herself, she could only feel she had been invaded by an intense emotion, taken hold of, shaken by it; she felt immediately changed, the focus of her life suddenly found. It was primarily an emotional reaction to him, a desire to be with him, close to him in every way, not mere physical attraction which she had experienced to some degree before; he was quite extraordinarily handsome, of course, tall and rather serious, indeed almost solemn-looking, with fair hair, blue eyes, and a glorious smile that entirely changed his face, bringing to it not just a softness, but a merriment, a sense of great joie de vivre.

But he was more than handsome, he was charming, beautifully mannered, clearly very intelligent, with a great deal more to talk about than most of the young men she had met. Indeed he talked about things she had never heard a young man speak of before, of books and literature, of plays and art exhibitions. He asked her if she had been to Florence and Paris and when she said she had, asked her then which galleries she had most enjoyed and admired. He also – which she found more engaging than any of the rest – had a way of treating her as if she were as clever and as well-read as he. Celia, who was of a generation and class of girls educated at home by governesses, was entirely charmed by this. She had been brought up in the only way her parents knew and recognised: to marry someone from her own social class, and to lead a life exactly the same as her mother's, raising a family and running a household; from the moment she set eyes on Oliver Lytton, she knew this was not what she wanted.

She was the youngest daughter of a very old and socially impeccable family. The Beckenhams dated back to the sixteenth century, as her mother, the Countess of Beckenham, was fond of telling everyone; the family had a glorious and quite grand seventeenth century house and estate called Ashingham in Buckinghamshire, not far from Beaconsfield, and a very beautiful town house in Clarges Street, Mayfair. They were extremely rich and concerned only with running their estate, conserving their assets, and enjoying what was mostly a country life. Lord Beckenham ran the home farm, hunted and shot a great deal in the winter, and fished in the summer, Lady Beckenham socialised both in London and the country, rode, played cards, organised her staff, and – rather more reluctantly – saw to the upkeep of her extensive wardrobe. Books, like pictures, were things which covered the Beckenham walls and were appreciated for their value rather more than for their content; talk at their dinner table centred around their own lives, rather than around abstract matters such as art, literature and philosophy.

Confronted by a daughter who professed herself – after only three months' short acquaintance – to be in love with someone who, by their standards, was not only a pauper, but almost as unfamiliar to them as a Zulu warrior, they were genuinely appalled and anxious for her.

5

Celia could see that they were entirely serious in their opposition; she supposed she could marry Oliver when she was twenty-one, but that was unimaginably far off, three years away. And so, staring into the darkness through her bedroom window late one night, her eyes sore with weeping, wondering what on earth she could do, she had suddenly found it: the solution. The breathtakingly, dazzlingly simple solution. She would become pregnant and then they would *have* to let her marry him. The more she thought about it, the more sensible it seemed. The only alternative was running away; but Oliver had rejected that sweetly but firmly.

'It would cause too much anxiety, hurt too many people, my family as well as yours. I don't want us to build our life together on other people's unhappiness.'

His gentleness was only one of the many things she loved about him.

Just the same, she thought that night, he would not accede to this plan too easily. He would argue that pregnancy would also cause great distress; he would not see that they deserved it, her blind, insensitive, hypocritical parents: hardly models of marital virtue themselves, her father with the housemaids, her mother with her lover of many years. Her sister, Caroline had told her about him, the year before, at her own coming out ball at Ashingham. Caroline had had too much champagne and was standing with Celia between dances, looking across at their parents talking animatedly to one another. Celia had said impulsively how sweet it was that they were still so happy together, in spite of the housemaids, and Caroline had said that if they were, much of the credit should go to George Paget. George Paget and his rather plain wife, Vera, were old family friends; pressed to explain precisely what she meant, Caroline said that George had been her mother's lover for over ten years. Half shocked, half fascinated, Celia begged to be told more, but Caroline laughed at her for being so innocent and launched herelf on to the dance floor with her husband's best friend. But next day she had relented, remorseful at disillusioning her little sister, said she mustn't worry about it, that it wasn't important.

'Mama will always keep the rules.'

'What rules?' Celia said.

'Society's rules,' said Caroline, patiently reassuring. 'Discretion, manners, those sorts of things. She would never leave Papa. To them marriage is unshakable. What they do, what all society does, is make marriage more pleasant, more interesting. Stronger, actually, I would say.'

'And – would – would you make your marriage more pleasant in that way?' Celia asked and Caroline laughed and said that at the moment, hers was fairly pleasant anyway.

6

'But yes, I suppose I would. If Arthur became dull, or found pleasure of his own elsewhere. Don't look so shocked, Celia, you really are an innocent aren't you? I heard it said the other day that Mrs Keppel, you know, the king's mistress, has turned adultery into an art form. That seems quite a nice achievement to me.'

Celia had still felt shocked, despite the reassurance. When she got married, she knew it would be for love and for life.

So – Oliver must not realise the full extent of her plan. She knew exactly how one became pregnant; her mother had instructed her with great and unusual forthrightness on the subject when Celia had her first menstrual period, and besides, she had grown up in the country, she had seen sheep and even horses copulating, had been present at the birth of lambs, and had spent all of one night in the sweet steamy stench of the stables with her father and his groom, as her father's favourite mare dropped her foal. She had no doubt that she would be able to persuade Oliver into making love to her; as well as being absurdly romantic, constantly sending her poems, flowers, love letters pages long, he was passionately affectionate with her, his kisses far from chaste, intensely arousing – to them both.

Celia had rather more freedom than many girls of her age. Having raised six children, her mother had become weary of the task, and was in any case extremely busy and inclined to leave Celia to her own affairs. When Oliver came for the weekend at Ashingham, invited to join one of the Beckenham house parties as Celia's guest, they were able during the day (Oliver being quite unable to join in any sporting activities) to roam the grounds on their own and after dinner to sit in the library on their own talking. The roaming and talking had led to a great deal of kissing; Celia had found she quite literally could not have enough of it, and was yearning for more – as, quite plainly, was Oliver.

She had not experienced passion before, either in herself or any of the young men she had met; but she found she could recognise it very easily now. As easily as she had been able to recognise love. He had been very respectful of her virtue, naturally, but she was absolutely confident that she could persuade him to take their physical relationship forwards without any difficulty whatsoever. Of course he would be anxious, not only that they would be found out, but that she would become pregnant. But she could reassure him about that, tell him some lie – she wasn't sure what; she believed there were times in the month when you were supposed not to be able to become pregnant, she had read it in some book in her mother's room – and then when it happened – well there would be nothing more to worry about.

She was very precise in her plans: she pretended to have acquiesced to her parents' views, to have come to see that Oliver was not the right man for her – although not too swiftly, lest she arouse their suspicion – and stayed at home dutifully for several weeks, while writing to Oliver every day. Then she went to London to stay with Caroline for a few days, ostensibly to do some shopping, and it had all been absurdly easy. Caroline had discovered that she was pregnant herself, and was wretchedly sick, totally uninterested in what her younger sister was doing, and unwilling as well as unable to chaperone her. Absences of two or three hours while Celia was officially shopping, seeing dressmakers, having fittings for the London Season, but actually discovering the raptures of being in bed with her lover, went almost unnoticed.

Celia had been right, Oliver was initially resistant to the risks of making love to her; but a mixture of emotional blackmail and a determined onslaught on his senses worked quite quickly. She would meet him at the big house in Hampstead, where he lived with his father, in the early afternoon; his father still spent every day at the publishing house, and it was easy for Oliver to pretend to be lunching with authors, or visiting artists' studios. They would go upstairs to Oliver's room, a big, light book-lined affair with huge windows on the first floor, overlooking the Heath, and spend the next hour or so in the rather narrow almost lumpy bed that swiftly became paradise for Celia. They found a physical delight in each other almost at once; Oliver was not exactly experienced, indeed his own knowledge had been gained at the hands of a couple of chorus girls introduced by his best friend at Oxford, but it was sufficient to guide him through Celia's initiation. She lay there, that first time, braced for discomfort, for pain even, looking at Oliver as he took her in his arms, promising to be very careful, and found herself discovering almost at once an acute capacity for sexual pleasure.

'It was wonderful, so wonderful,' she said, lying back, breathing hard, drenched with sweat, smiling at Oliver, 'I couldn't believe it, it was like – like a great tangle somewhere deep inside me being – being sorted out.'

He kissed her, surprised, at her pleasure and at his power to grant it to her; then he poured them both a glass of champagne from the rather warm bottle he had smuggled up from his father's cellar and they lay there for an hour telling each other how much they loved one another, before he had to return to the offices of the Lytton Publishing House in Paternoster Row, and she to her sister's house in Kensington (stopping off first to collect a bagful of fabric samples from Woollands of Knightsbridge). Two days later, they had another tryst and two days after that yet another; then she returned home, her head filled with happy memories, her heart with more love than ever before.

She calculated (having studied the subject carefully) that she was quite likely to have become pregnant that week, but she was disappointed; it took two more visits to London before her third period most wonderfully failed to arrive and, even more wonderfully, she began to feel sick.

After that there was, despite her happiness, dreadful retribution. She faced her parents with great courage and determination, and had to face Oliver's fear and shock as well. That was almost worse; he found himself confronting not only her condition, but a demonstration of her formidable will and what he was forced to recognise as her capacity for deceit. He had wanted to use contraceptives after the first time, but she had refused, saying they hurt her, that there was no need, she had taken advice on the subject, had talked convincingly of a douche (which she did not even possess). Oliver found her behaviour very difficult to come to terms with.

Nevertheless, through it all, through the rows, the raging, the threats of disinheritance, of banishment, of surgical intervention in the pregnancy, all of which she knew were not to be taken seriously, through the plans to which her parents finally agreed for a wedding ('small, very small, the fewer people hear of it the better,' Lady Beckenham had said) through Oliver's distress and the doubt in his eyes that came close to mistrust, through her own increasing physical wretchedness, through all these things she was happy. For the rest of her life she was to remember those afternoons in the small uncomfortable bed, in the big rather cold room, filled from floor to ceiling with books, when she soared into orgasm, and then lay in Oliver's arms, listening to him talk not only of his love for her and of their life together but of his hopes and plans for his own future within Lyttons. He told her of a wonderful new kingdom, a seemingly magical place where books were created; stories told or talked about, ideas mooted and discussed, then turned to pages within covers, authors commissioned, illustrators briefed. She felt an immediate understanding and something close to affinity with it all. Thus sex and work became permanently joined together in her heart; and were to remain so for the rest of her life.

Her father was very good at the wedding; she had to admit that. Having finally agreed to it, declared himself beaten, he had gone into it with whole-hearted generosity; he instructed the staff to prepare a lavish wedding breakfast, made a splendid speech, produced an enormous amount of champagne, and finally disappeared, ostensibly to sleep but probably, as Celia observed to Caroline, to rendezvous with the latest parlourmaid.

Lady Beckenham had behaved rather less well; she was icily courteous to the Lyttons, sat stony-faced through the speeches – particularly the one made by Oliver's best man and older brother, Robert, who had recently emigrated to New York for a career on Wall Street, commenting in a hissing whisper to Caroline, that she considered both him and it rather common. She ignored Jack altogether, despite all his efforts to be charming and friendly to her, and looked coldly on as he flirted tirelessly with every pretty girl in the room. She spoke insultingly briefly to old Mr Edgar Lytton, who was struggling to cope with what he clearly regarded as a painful and difficult situation, and to Oliver hardly at all. Finally she pointedly settled herself down for a long time with her two eldest sons and their wives, making it plain that was where she felt her proper place to be.

But to most of the guests, and certainly to anyone looking at the official photographs afterwards, of Celia in the exquisite lace dress her father had been unable to deny her, with the Beckenham tiara in her gleaming dark hair, and Oliver so extremely handsome, by her side, it was hard to believe that the day had been anything but exceptionally happy.

The young couple honeymooned very briefly – as befitted their income and Celia's rather fragile physical condition. At three months, she was at the peak of her pregnant misery, constantly sick, and plagued with headaches; so wretched in fact, that she was almost unable to enjoy her wedding night. They went to Bath for a week, and while they were there she suddenly began to recover, so that by the time they reached London again she felt almost well, had lost her pallor and regained her energy. It was just as well. Again greatly to his credit, Lord Beckenham had bought the young couple a house as a wedding present; it was in Cheyne Walk – he had insisted that it was not to be in Hampstead – charming, large, but in an appalling state of repair.

For the first few months of her marriage, indeed until the birth of the baby the following March, Celia was entirely occupied with restoration and refurbishment. Rapturously happy, she transformed it into something quite gloriously original. At a time when walls were heavily coloured, hangings dark, lamps dim, Celia's house was a brilliant statement of light, somehow a reflection of the river which she loved. They were white-painted walls, curtains in bright blues and golds, pale wooden floors, and several of the new impressionist-style paintings instead of the heavy portraits and landscapes so fashionable then.

Having worked on her house all day, she would wait impatiently for Oliver's return, and they would often dine in the morning room on the first floor, with its lovely view of the river, while she pressed him for every detail of his day.

Oliver was only able to afford the most modest staff: a very overworked cook-general and the promise of a nursemaid when the baby came, so she often made supper and served it herself, which gave her great pleasure. Quite often she insisted he brought his father home for supper. She adored Edgar Lytton; he had Oliver's gentle courtesy, his charm, his deep poetic voice. He had also, clearly, once had the same golden looks. He was an old man now, seventy-five years old, for Oliver and Jack had been late children, the result of a second marriage. His wife had left him a year after Jack was born. But he still worked all day at Lyttons, with Oliver and the daunting Margaret, still showing the flair and business skill which had brought the publishing house its admittedly rather modest success – and said it was there that he wished to die.

'I hope I shall be found in my office, entirely penned in by books,' he said to her more than once, and Celia would kiss him fondly and tell him she hoped nothing of the sort would happen for a very long time.

He took her to the Lytton building in Paternoster Row at her own insistence, and was surprised and charmed by her genuine interest in it and in his stories of how he had launched the company. Lyttons was now rising to join some of the great names in London publishing, Macmillan, Constable, Dent, John Murray, but its beginnings had been extremely humble and its success entirely due to Edgar's talents and foresight.

He had made a marriage in 1856, which was both happy and fortunate, to a Miss Margaret Jackson. Margaret's father, George, owned a bookbinding shop that was also a printing works, and when his ambitious young son-in-law professed an interest in printing a set of poetry books to add to the educational pamphlets he was already doing well with, George encouraged him. These were followed by a history of England and by the time George died in 1860, the publishing house of Lytton-Jackson had been launched. Its greatest success was based on Margaret's suggestion for a series of books to be published in serial form, after the style of Mr Dickens. A new and brilliant young writer was commissioned to write fifty-two weekly instalments of *The Heatherleigh Chronicles*, the story of a small town in the West Country, not unlike Mr Trollope's *Chronicles of Barsetshire*. These made a great deal of money. The next piece of publishing inspiration was a set of school primers and then an exquisitely printed and illustrated set of Greek and Roman legends. The first editions of those books were extremely valuable; three of the five volumes owned by Lyttons were kept in the company safe.

Margaret, however died in 1875, having borne Edgar Robert and Little Margaret. Broken-hearted and lonely, Edgar then made a disastrous second marriage to Henrietta James in 1879. She was a silly vapid woman and ran away with an actor five years later, leaving behind two sons Oliver and Jack. Her defection was almost a relief to Edgar, and this intrigued Celia considerably.

'Such a sad story', she said, when Oliver told her, 'but I'm so glad he did marry her, otherwise I wouldn't have you now.'

Little Margaret showed a great flair for publishing from her earliest years; it was considered inevitable that she should follow her father into the firm. In an age where women had no rights, apart from those granted them by their husbands, and few were educated beyond the age of fifteen or so, she was highly unusual not only in winning a place at London University to read English, an almost unimaginable achievement, but in holding a highly complex and difficult job, working alongside men as their undisputed equal. Robert, on the other hand, showed no interest in publishing at all, and became a banker, sailing for America and the heady delights of Wall Street in 1900.

But Oliver, like Margaret, seemed to have printing ink in his blood. By the time he was fifteen, he was working at Lyttons in his school holidays – his father was proud to have been able to send him to Winchester – and at the age of twenty-two, down from Oxford with a first in English, he moved into what was known as the second office, as Edgar's undisputed heir. If LM, as Little Margaret was now called (a most unsuitable name for a girl over six feet tall, with, a resounding voice and an imposing manner) resented this, she never said so or even hinted at it; she was in any case paid exactly the same salary as Oliver, and her influence was as broad as his. It was a highly successful partnership; LM's talents were for the business side of publishing and Oliver's for the creative.

As for Jack, he showed little interest in anything except pretty girls and certainly in nothing remotely intellectual; the army had been suggested as a career by his housemaster at Wellington, who had said he was, if nothing else, brave and extremely popular.

Celia loved Jack; they were the same age, and like her, he was a youngest child.

'Both of us spoilt babies, and isn't it nice?' he said to her once.

He was extremely charming, less serious than Oliver, amusing, irresponsible, always full of fun. Oliver doted on him, but at the same time worried about his tendency to play his way through life.

'Oliver, he's only nineteen,' Celia said, 'not an old married man like you.'

However Jack had slightly redeemed himself in the family's eyes recently; having joined the army, he had been commissioned into the 12th Royal Lancers and seemed set for a successful career. His commanding officer told Edgar that Jack appeared to have that rare combination of qualities, so essential to good soldiering which made him popular both with his men and his fellow officers. It was a long way from the bookish world of his family, but it seemed to suit him.

Celia also invited LM frequently to the house and sought her friendship. Despite her slightly daunting personality, Celia had liked her immediately. LM was almost fearsomely clever and articulate, could demolish anyone in argument, and appeared rather serious, but she was actually very good company, had a slightly quirky sense of humour and an intensely curious and ingenious mind. No one seemed to know much about her; she lived on her own, and kept her own counsel. Although she dressed rather severely, and wore her dark hair pulled starkly back, she had style and something that came close to glamour; in a crowd, she attracted attention, and men, almost to their surprise, found her attractive and even sexually disturbing.

She was very kind to Celia, if slightly sternly so, and appeared to like her, even inviting her opinion on the latest books from time to time; it also helped Celia in those early days, intellectually in awe of the family as she was that LM clearly regarded Oliver very much as a younger brother.

'Don't be ridiculous, Oliver,' she would say, or, 'Oliver I sometimes wonder if you have the slightest idea what you are talking about,' and would even occasionally catch Celia's eye and wink at her. She was already, Celia felt, a most valuable friend.

Giles was born in March 1905. To Celia's total astonishment, her mother (who had refused to have anything to do either with her or the house until then), arrived two days before the birth, with a large suitcase and one of the maids from Ashingham. She not only stayed with Celia throughout her labour but then remained – an immense comfort and help to her – for a month afterwards. Although she neither explained nor apologised for her earlier behaviour, Celia recognised the gesture for what it was, and accepted it gratefully.

Celia was in fact deeply shocked by the experience of childbirth. Although she bore it with stoicism, and not a sound reached Oliver's ears as he paced the house in an agony of anxiety, she suffered very much. It was a long labour, although straightforward. She felt the first contraction at dawn on one day and was not delivered of Giles until a brilliantly bloody sunset flooded the river the following evening. It was not even the pain which distressed her, nor the exhaustion, so much as the brutality of the whole procedure, the humiliation and what appeared to be the wrenching apart of her entire body. She lay in their bed afterwards, exhausted and exsanguinite, holding Giles in arms so weak she feared she would drop him, wondering why she felt so little for him. She had expected some sort of rapture, an echo of the flood of love which she had felt for Oliver, and found only a rather dull relief that the pain had stopped. He was an ugly baby, and a large one – eight pounds – and he continued to wail for most of the rest of the night. Celia felt he could at least have rewarded her with a smile, or a nuzzle of his surprisingly dark head. When she told her mother this, Lady Beckenham snorted and said there was nothing on God's earth as unrewarding as the human baby.

'Or so ugly. You think of foals, lambs, puppies even, all much prettier, and a lot more interesting.'

Celia had decided – having read a great many rather modern books on the subject – to breast-feed him, but he was a finicky feeder and she found trying to thrust an agonisingly tender nipple into his ungrateful mouth so unpleasant that she handed him over with great relief to the nursemaid after two days. At least that way she got some sleep.

'Very sensible,' Lady Beckenham said, 'so common, really, breast-feeding, the sort of thing the tenants do.'

But if Giles was something of a disappointment to Celia, he gave great pleasure to his father. Oliver would spend literally hours holding him, jiggling him on his knee, studying his face for family resemblances and even, to the nursemaid's horror, giving him the occasional bottle.

The arrival of Giles prompted a truce between Oliver and Lady Beckenham; she was a naturally talkative woman and not prepared to sit with him in silence at mealtimes during Celia's lying in. Moreover he had managed to find a topic on which he could ask her advice. Lyttons were to publish a book about the great houses of England, and since his mother-in-law had personally stayed in at least half of them, she was able to give him a great deal of information.

She had photographs sent from Ashingham of the shooting parties which she had attended and given. Oliver looked at them, at the men in their tweed suits, greatcoats and brogues, at the women in ankle-length gowns, with large hats on their heads, and realised the pictures encapsulated the 1900s, the decade already known as the Edwardian era: an era when the rich lived lavishly and with extraordinary self-indulgence. At the great houses, Lady Beckenham told Oliver, tea was a full dress meal, ladies in elaborate gowns, gentlemen in short black jackets and black ties.

'And at dinner, seven or eight courses, full evening dress of course with decorations.'

After dinner at Cheyne Walk one night, slightly drunk on Oliver's finest claret, she explained what she called the disposition of the bedrooms at house parties.

'One had to know who should be near whom. The card placed on each door wasn't just to let every guest know where to sleep, but to be a guide – if you follow me – for anyone else who needed that information.'

Oliver nodded courteously while Celia sat transfixed, waiting for further revelations, but they did not come. Her mother realised she was talking too much and retired to bed.

It was a measure of her warming attitude towards Oliver, that she actually offered to introduce him to a few owners of the great houses. Nevertheless she still did not invite him to call her by her first name.

'I can't think of anyone who does, except Daddy,' Celia said, 'and she calls him Beckenham, you know, even to this day' but she did at least begin to address Oliver by name for the first time.

'I still think he is a rather odd husband for Celia,' she wrote to Lord Beckenham, 'and a very odd father, far too involved with the baby, although one has to admit he is devoted to Celia and Giles and is certainly trying to do his best for them both. He does have a certain facility for conversation, and can be quite amusing, but I worry about his political views. He expresses some sympathy for the idea of the trades unions; I suppose that is his background and can't be helped. I'm sure he will learn in time.'

Giles was christened in Chelsea Old Church with at least some of the splendour that Lady Beckenham had wanted for the wedding. He wore the Beckenham family christening robe, a one hundred-year-old mass of frothing lace, received the family silver spoon and teething ring from his maternal grandmother, a large cheque from his paternal grandfather, and numbered an earl and a countess among his five godparents.

'Is it really necessary to have so many?' Oliver had asked, and yes, Celia said, it was.

'Caroline's baby had four and I'm not going to be outdone by her at the christening as well as the wedding.'

Oliver didn't quite like to point out that it had been entirely her fault their wedding had been such a low key affair; she had become slightly formidable since Giles's birth. Something to do, he feared, with the arrival of her mother in the household.

Edgar Lytton particularly enjoyed Giles's christening; he spent much of the time holding the baby, giving him his finger to suck, rocking him when he cried, and appeared in all the official photographs beaming with happiness. It was extremely fortunate that the day gave him so much pleasure, that it had been, as he remarked to LM later, one of the happiest of his entire life, for that night he had a heart attack and died just as dawn was breaking. Oliver was at his deathbed, summoned urgently by LM, but was never quite able to forgive himself for failing to stay and have a glass of brandy with his father after escorting him home from the christening.

'Do stay,' Edgar had said, 'I don't want the day to end.'

But Oliver had refused, said he must get back to Celia and the baby. What he was actually anxious to be getting back to was not the baby, but Celia, and moreover a Celia naked in bed, as she had whispered to him that she would be before he left Cheyne Walk. She had only just felt able to resume their lovemaking after the traumas of childbirth. To the relief of them both, it was as rapturously wonderful as ever; but it was a long time before Oliver was able to experience it without a sense of guilt and betrayal.

The other legacy of Edgar's death, delivered into Oliver's hands at the end of a hideously sad time, was the control and, indeed, the ownership of Lyttons.

CHAPTER 2

Celia picked up a silver candlestick (being the nearest object to hand) and hurled it at the nursery door which Oliver had just closed gently behind him.

'He's a beast,' she said to Giles, who was sitting placidly in his cot waiting to be taken out and dressed, 'an old fashioned stuffy beast.'

Giles smiled at her; she glared at him for a moment, then smiled back. He had an oddly radiant smile which transformed his rather solemn little face. He was a year old now, and while still not beautiful, he was a nice looking child, with large dark eyes and brown hair. He was also extremely good; after the first fretful few months he had suddenly become an angel baby, sleeping through the night and between feeds, and when he was awake, lying gazing at the teddies which Jenny, the nursemaid, kept propped up on his cot and at the mobile of tiny cardboard birds which Celia had made and strung across it, after reading that children should be stimulated from the earliest possible moment.

He had developed a little slowly, probably, Celia felt, because he was so placid and happy with the status quo, but at thirteen months, he was doing all the requisite things, standing, and crawling in a perfectly textbook manner and saying mum-mum and dad-dad and na-na which was his name for Jenny. Jenny had proved a great success; only nineteen years old when she arrived in the household, and virtually untrained, she had swiftly become a model nursemaid, adoring Giles, while not being foolishly indulgent with him, surviving the sleepless nights and noisy days with cheerful resignation, and managing the mountain of washing and ironing for her charge with formidable energy.

After Edgar Lytton died, and Oliver became modestly well-off, there was talk of hiring what Lady Beckenham called a proper nanny, but Celia had resisted this. She would rather have a proper cook, she said, and a decent housemaid; Jenny was more than competent, and pleasant to have around, indeed Celia had come to regard her as one of her closest friends during the first difficult months of motherhood. She said as much to her mother, who replied that she hoped Celia wasn't making the all too common modern mistake of thinking that servants could be

17

dealt with on a friendly basis. Celia, stung by this, said Jenny had done more for her sanity since Giles's birth than anyone else in the world, and she didn't know where she would be without her.

'Well, you are playing with fire,' said Lady Beckenham tartly, 'and I should know. Very tolerant with the first couple of Beckenham's housemaids and simply made a rod for my own back, even expected to give houseroom to a baby, which she swore was his. Of course it wasn't,' she added. 'You have to keep servants where they belong, Celia, which is at a distance, both literally and metaphorically.'

Celia said nothing more and continued to regard Jenny as a friend, and when Jenny asked her on her twentieth birthday if she could be called Nanny now, Celia was quite hurt.

'Jenny's your name, that's how I think of you, why do you suddenly want to be called Nanny?'

'It's the other girls, Lady Celia, the other nursemaids and the uniformed nannies in Kensington Gardens. They think it's very odd you call me by my name. And I'd like to be called Nanny, it would make me feel proud. As if I had a proper job, wasn't just a nursery maid.'

'Oh – all right,' said Celia, 'I'll try and remember.'

But it wasn't until Giles started calling Jenny by his pet name that she made a real effort, again at Jenny's request, and still felt hurt at what she felt was a rejection of her friendship.

The reason for the hurled candlestick that morning had been Oliver's second refusal to let her play even a modestly active role at Lyttons. Celia was bored; she found domestic life and motherhood intellectually unsatisfying. She was extremely intelligent and she knew it. Moreover she was becoming well-read; during the long days of her pregnancy she had pored over the works of Dickens, Trollope, Jane Austen, George Eliot; she also devoured the daily papers, *The Times* and the *Daily Telegraph*, and had persuaded Oliver to take out subscriptions to the *Spectator* and the *Illustrated London News*, so that she had a better grasp of current affairs. She also, with great daring, occasionally bought the *Daily Mirror*; among other things she shared with Oliver was a degree of social idealism. It was one of the first things she had loved about him and found fascinating.

She had read the writings of such people as Sydney and Beatrice Webb, George Bernard Shaw and HG Wells and found that what they had to say about social injustice made absolute sense to her. She and Oliver had agreed that they would vote for the Labour Party in the next election, and spent long evenings in the small downstairs sitting-room at Cheyne Walk discussing the rise of Socialism, the increasing role that the state should play in improving the lot of ordinary people, and how to combat the poverty which underpinned the wealth of the upper and middle classes. It was for Celia, at least, largely an emotional reaction; part of her stormy move away from her roots, a discovery of yet another new world which appealed to her idealistic heart.

But she also wanted to do more than run her household and care for her child; she found the company of her immediate circle dull at best. Gossip, except of a very high calibre, bored her; she hated cards, she even grew tired of shopping, and although she enjoyed entertaining and giving dinner parties, these hardly filled her days and certainly didn't employ her brain. Neither, for that matter, did playing with Giles.

Oliver's life, on the other hand, fascinated her; she read all the literary reviews in the papers and the magazines, and whenever Lyttons gave a party for an author, or to launch a new series, she felt herself in heaven. She loved talking to writers, liked their odd blend of self-confidence and self-doubt, never tired of hearing how they wrote their books, where their ideas came from, what inspired them. She found illustrators equally fascinating. She had a strong visual sense; changing fashions in design and colour particularly intrigued her. Often, rather than go to yet another tea party, she would wander round the Victoria and Albert museum or the Tate Gallery; she had books on the work of the great art nouveau masters, Aubrey Beardsley, Mucha, Boldini, and was au fait with the more modern artists such as Augustus John and Duchamp. And then she loved Lyttons itself; the big imposing building in Paternoster Row with its wonderfully grand entrance hall leading into a series of untidy dusty rooms, with battered old desks where Oliver, Margaret, and other senior members of staff worked. The place felt like a library and study combined from the huge basement where the books were stored and where a tiny wooden train whizzed truckloads of books around on a metal railway line, to the wrought iron spiral staircase at the back, which rose dizzily up the full height of the building.

Edgar had been well off rather than rich when he died; he had left only £40,000 to be shared between his four children, but the value of Lyttons was considerable. Assets consisted not only of the books themselves and the worth of the authors under contract, but the very substantial building which Edgar had shrewdly bought with the money left to him and Margaret by George Jackson.

Celia had become more and more fond of LM. Where she could have met with hostility and condescension, intruding as she did into a very tightly bonded professional and personal relationship, she found only friendship and a genuine interest in her. And LM, too, shared the new liberal attitude to society which had so charmed her in Oliver. Their friends intrigued her too: they were not quite part of the bohemian set so prominent in London at that time, their lives and concerns were a little too commercially based for that, but they were intellectual, free-thinking people, given to rich conversation and with attitudes and views which would have shocked the Beckenhams. It was meeting those people, writers, artists, lecturers, other publishers, that made her daytime friends, as she thought of them, seem so unsatisfactory and so dull; and that had led, indirectly, to the candlestick being hurled at the nursery door.

'I want a job,' she said to Oliver, 'I want to use my brain. I think you should let me come and work at Lyttons.'

The first time she made the suggestion he had been almost shocked; it surprised her, for many of the women she had met through him worked for their living.

'But you are my wife,' he said, his blue eyes quite pained as he looked at her, 'I want you to be in our home, taking care of our son, not out in the rough world of publishing.'

Celia said it didn't seem very rough to her, and had argued her case for some time. 'You don't have any women on the editorial side, and I think you should. I might not be much use at first, but I'd learn quickly. And I'd love it so much, darling, darling Oliver, working alongside you, being part of all your life, not just the dull bit at home.'

Oliver had said, even more pained, that he was sorry she found home life so dull; Celia told him he should sample it for himself and then he would see what she meant, and that she found it almost insulting that he should consider her suited to it. They had quarrelled quite badly after that, and only made up in bed, as they always did; she had left it for a little while, and then tried again, that very morning; Oliver's response had been exactly the same, the pain mixed this time with some irritation.

'My darling, I told you before, you're my wife. And the mother of my son. And—'

'So that excludes me from doing anything more challenging than seeing to the laundry and singing nursery rhymes, does it?'

'Of course not. You know I value you far more highly than that.'

'Then prove it. Let me show you my real value: working with you, making Lyttons even more successful than it already is . . .'

'Celia, you know nothing about publishing.'

'That's a ridiculous argument. I could learn.'

'It isn't quite as easy as that,' he said, and she could see he felt defensive; it amused and annoyed her at the same time.

'I suppose you think I'm not capable of it.'

'No of course I don't. But—'

'Then why not? Because I'm your wife?'

'Well – yes. Yes, that's right.'

'And that's the only reason?'

20

'I—'

'Is that the only reason, Oliver?'

'Celia, I don't want you working outside our home.'

'But why not?'

'Because I want you supporting me from inside it. That's far more valuable.'

'So a wife shouldn't work. Is that what you're saying?'

He hesitated. Then, 'Yes. Yes it is,' he said, very firmly. 'And now I must go.' And walked out, shutting the door rather loudly behind him.

Later that day, LM walked into Oliver's office.

'I want to talk to you,' she said.

'Oh yes? What about?'

'Celia.'

'Celia? If she's been talking to you—'

'She has, yes,' said LM calmly. 'Isn't that permitted?'

'About her working here? I've told her, I will not have it, she has no right to bother you about it.'

'Oliver, you sound alarmingly like Lord Beckenham,' said LM. 'I'm surprised at you. Celia has every right to telephone me if she wants to. You don't own her, and I hope you don't think that you do. Anyway, I don't know what you're talking about. Celia hasn't even mentioned working here. She simply telephoned me to say that she'd been thinking about the letters of Queen Victoria which John Murray are about to publish. I'd told her I thought it was a marvellous coup, so she suggested that we commission a biography of the queen, to coincide with their publication. It seemed to her that we might benefit from all their advance publicity. I think that shows a rare combination of editorial and commercial sense. It's a marvellous idea and I'm convinced we should go ahead with it. And if Celia did ever want to work here, I, for one, would encourage it greatly. We would be foolish to reject her. Now, you might like to consider who should write this book; in my opinion, it should be put in hand immediately. Oh I hope you're not going to turn the idea down because of some outdated idea about wives and where their place might be . . . yes, I thought so. I see I have struck home. Really Oliver! I'm shocked at you.'

When Oliver arrived home that night, Celia was not downstairs. She heard him moving from room to room looking for her; finally he opened their bedroom door, his expression a mixture of irritation and anxiety. It changed then; she was sitting up in bed naked, her long dark hair trailing loosely over her shoulders and on to her breasts.

'I'm sorry if I made you angry,' she said after a moment, holding out her hand to him. 'I only, truly, wanted to be of use to you. Please come and join me, I can't bear to be quarrelling with you all the time like this.'

He did what she said, as she knew he would; he was still completely unable to resist her. Later, over a rather belated dinner, he said slightly awkwardly, that LM had persuaded him that perhaps he had been wrong, and he should consider allowing her to work at Lyttons. She did not take issue with the word allow; her triumph was too fragile to risk.

Looking back, she saw the evening as the major turning point in their relationship: more important in some ways even than the one when she had told him she was pregnant. She had defeated him, just as she had defeated her parents, by a mixture of deviousness and determination. From then on, she had her way: both at home and, more importantly to her, at Lyttons.

Celia moved into Lyttons a month later; she was given a modest office on the second floor which she turned into her own small kingdom, with a large leather-topped desk, on which she installed several silver-framed pictures of Giles, an exquisite library lamp, and a small portable typewriter. The walls were hung with framed book covers and Mucha posters, and on either side of the small fireplace she put two leather-covered button-backed sofas.

'So that I can talk to writers in a relaxed atmosphere,' she said to Oliver.

Oliver, who was still not entirely comfortable with the arrangement, said rather stiffly that it would be quite a while before she was talking to writers.

'You have to learn the basics of publishing first, Celia, it's imperative you understand that.'

Celia said meekly that of course she did, and worked good-temperedly and patiently for some time on all the more tedious tasks which came her way: and a great many of them there were too, she had a suspicion that Oliver fed her more proofs to check and manuscripts to mail out for approval than he did to the other editors, but she didn't care. She was totally besotted with her new life; it was like a love affair. She woke up longing to be with it again, and left the office later and later, reluctant to part from it, often missing Giles's bedtime. She tried to keep this from Oliver; she knew it would upset him. He had only agreed to her joining Lyttons on the understanding that it would not come too seriously between her and Giles. Jenny, who had been given a pay rise and a rather grand new uniform in honour of the new arrangement, and was very happy indeed with it, was often obliged to cover up for her mistress, implying, where a conversation with Oliver required it, that Celia had arrived home far earlier than she actually had.

Celia was paid a salary: one hundred pounds a year, all of which she passed directly to Jenny. Both Oliver and LM had agreed that it was essential her position at Lyttons was on an official basis. The other staff, initially suspicious of her, irritated by her appointment, came swiftly to accept her; she worked so hard and so uncomplainingly, never pulled rank, made appointments to see Oliver and LM like everyone else in the building, agreed, publicly at least, with everything Oliver said, and made so many good suggestions that it was impossible for them not to appreciate her presence. Although Lyttons was an important publishing house, extremely well-regarded both for its innovative approach and its high standards, it was small, especially on the editorial side, employing only two senior editors and two juniors; an extra brain, and one of such high calibre, was very welcome.

Celia was a superb proof reader; she never missed a single typographical or grammatical error while remaining sensitive to every writer's style. She even quietly pointed out errors in detail or sequence, such as when a character left the house on foot and yet arrived at his destination by hansom cab, or had a father who died a few months before the onset of a fatal illness. The first time she noticed a mistake of this kind, she was shocked, surprised that a powerful creative intelligence could co-exist with such incompetence. Oliver told her it was extremely common.

'They get carried away with the excitement of telling the stories, and then can't be bothered, when the work is finished, to go through the tedious business of checking. We once had a two-year pregnancy in a published novel; carry on your good work, my darling, we need it.'

He came round quite slowly to her being at Lyttons; he still felt manipulated into it, and the knowledge made him angry. On the other hand, she did have an inordinate number of good ideas. Her most successful was a series of simply written medical books, aimed primarily at mothers, incorporating tips for diagnosis, first aid, and simple precautionary advice against infection. It was such a great success that LM went into Oliver's office, shut the door behind her, and told him that the annual profits of Lyttons would be boosted by at least five per cent and that Celia should be rewarded: 'Either financially, which I doubt she would value, or by increased status. Make her an editor, Oliver; you won't regret it, I'm quite sure.'

Oliver said there could be no question of Celia becoming an editor so soon, others in the firm had had to work there for years before attaining such a position, and she had only been there for just over twelve months. LM who told him he was being pompous and biting off his nose to spite his face (she was rather given to clichés) nevertheless conceded. However, when the biography of Queen Victoria went into its sixth printing, and Celia suggested a companion volume about Prince Albert, to be sold as a bound set with the first, as a Christmas gift, things changed. She found herself sitting in Oliver's office, with a glass of madeira wine in her hand, being asked it she felt able to accept a new position as junior editor with a special interest in biographies. Celia smiled sweetly first at her husband and then at LM, and said that she did indeed feel able, promised to work very hard indeed and hoped that they would not regret their decision.

Oliver said later that night, rather stiffly, that he would regret the decision on one basis and one basis only: if Giles were to suffer from a lack of attention.

He was devoted to Giles; fatherhood, despite its rather precipitant entry into his life, had made him extremely happy and given him a confidence that he had lacked before. He found watching Giles turning from baby into little boy and observing his development, extraordinarily fascinating. He loved to hear the shout of, 'Daddy, Daddy, hallo, hallo,' each night, which was Giles's special greeting to him (Celia only got a single, 'Hallo Mummy') and loved to have him on his knee, singing and playing with him, looking at picture books.

Celia promised him that Giles would continue to receive as much of her attention and time as he needed, and then proceeded to break her promise on an almost daily basis as she fell into her new world and work with a passion and a delight which surprised even her. Fortunately for her, and for the time being at least, Oliver did not notice and Giles was unable to complain.

CHAPTER 3

Four days late now. Or was it five? Yes, five. Five days without it. Without the wonderful, reassuring, blessed pain and mess and extra work; five days of a growing fearful worry; five days of trying to face what it meant; five days of trying to imagine what they could possibly do.

If only she'd said no; if only. She knew when it had been; that Saturday night, when he'd had the glass of beer and everyone had been asleep. She hadn't wanted to, of course she hadn't; but he'd been so good, he worked so hard, was so generous to them all, and uncomplaining.

'Come on old girl,' he'd whispered, 'just quickly now. I'll be very careful, I'll pull out.'

It hadn't seemed fair to refuse him. He didn't have many other pleasures in life.

Sylvia sighed and heaved the bucket of grubby water up on to the table to soak the baby's nappies. That was what she did, soaked them in the water she'd already used; she'd only washed a few things that day, in any case, just the baby's things and the boys' shirts. It would save her going out to the yard for clean water twice. It was hard work, that. And tonight Ted was going to want his bath. It being Friday. He needed more water than the children; it meant two more trips out to the tap, and then heaving the pans on to the stove to heat the water for the tub. Sylvia felt weary even thinking about it. Although maybe the strain might bring it on. It had happened before. She must try not to think about it, about her missing monthly. The more you thought about it, the more it could delay it. Once she'd been almost sure, then the baby had got a fever and she'd been so worried, she forgot and sure enough, next day, there it was.

She sighed, and looked at the clock which stood on the table. It had been her mother's, that clock; it kept good time in spite of being so old. It was already seven o'clock. Ted had been gone half an hour. She'd nursed the baby while he had his breakfast, and if she was quick now, she could sweep the floor before she woke the other children. And maybe get their bread and dripping on the table. The main thing was to keep the ex-baby in bed as long as possible. He was such a problem, was Frank, such a large, energetic child. Sylvia hated having to restrain him in the high chair, but it really seemed the only thing to do for most of the day. That or tying him to the table leg. It was just too dangerous, with the stove alight, and the hot water on it in the big pans, to have him crawling about. And he was trying to stand now, he'd pull it over on himself if she wasn't careful. She would really make an effort today, to finish her work by the time the children went back to school after dinner, so Frank could crawl round the front steps. Or maybe if she didn't manage that, perhaps one of the older ones would take him out down the street for her. Poor little chap. He cried a lot. It must be very dull for him.

Sylvia and Ted Miller lived in Lambeth, with their five children. They had one quite large room about twelve foot square, and one smaller one, in the basement of a house in Line Street, one of several like it off Kennington Lane. Steps in the front of the house from a tiny hall led up to the street. The back room led straight outside to the yard which housed the tap, the privy, and a hanging larder which kept the milk and dripping and so on cool – in the winter at least. In the summer, it didn't work too well.

Sylvia, Ted, the baby and Frank, the ex-baby, slept in the larger room which doubled up as kitchen and temporary bathroom twice a week. Frank shared their bed, the baby slept in the bottom drawer of the large chest-of-drawers bequeathed to them by Sylvia's mother. It stored their clothes, some food, and indeed most of their other posessions. On one side of the room, facing the bed, was the coal-burning stove, and there was just room for a small folding table under the window and the big old high chair that had been Sylvia's mother's.

The family ate in shifts; there was no room at the table for them all to sit at any one time and, anyway, there were only two chairs. The children usually ate standing up, or sitting on their parents' bed. The three older children slept in the small room, in a large bed, top to tail like sardines in a tin. There was room, Sylvia reckoned, for one more child in that bed, for Frank when the baby finally outgrew her drawer. After that – Sylvia resolutely turned her mind away from after that. It was possible to make a cot out of a banana crate, lots of the families did that, and there was just room for it in the back bedroom.

Ted worked in a city warehouse, an hour's walk away; he did a twelve-hour day, and was paid twenty-three shillings a week. It was said in the district that as long as you earned about a pound a week, you could manage; the minute you dropped under that, even to nineteen shillings and eleven pence, you were in trouble. The rent was seven shillings a week, and the family spent another shilling a week on coal. It was a lot, but then the basement was cold and damp; that was the drawback of the low rent. Sylvia's friend, Joan, who lived just beyond the Oval, had three upstairs rooms, seven children and managed on far less coal. Still, Sylvia wouldn't have swapped places with her; Ted was so kind and gentle, had hardly ever hit any of the children, and had certainly never hit her.

He had even given up smoking years ago, and scarcely ever drank. Although if he did, he changed a bit. Joan's husband had a terrible temper; he beat the children if they were naughty, or even cheeky, with a leather belt, and if Joan didn't have his dinner ready, or his breakfast, for that matter, when he came through in the morning, he hit her too. And although he earned more than Ted, as much as thirty shillings in a good week, he spent up to a shilling on drink.

Ted and Sylvia had been married for eight years now; and they were still happy. Life wasn't exactly easy of course, but their children were all healthy, and the three at school were doing well, could all read and write their names and the oldest, Billy, was really good at his numbers. And it was a nice street they lived in, very few troublemakers, everyone ready to lend a hand to everyone else. The landlord wasn't too bad either; twice when Ted had got behind with the rent, once because the baby was ill and they'd had to pay the doctor, once when Ted himself was ill and off work for three weeks, he'd given them time to pay. Being thrown out on the street was not something Sylvia worried about. Finding room for them all, within their few, constricting walls, keeping them healthy with the constant damp, keeping them clean with the high cost of soap and of heating water, keeping the housebugs at bay, those were the daily problems she had to cope with. Somehow, with Ted's kindness and patience, she managed, and managed to stay fairly cheerful as well. But she was very much afraid that if she was in the family way again, she might not be able to.

She couldn't be. She simply *couldn't* be. Not now. Not just when everything was so much better; not when her work was so wonderfully enthralling and satisfying; not when she was feeling happy and strong; she just couldn't be. Of course she wasn't. It was only a few days late. Probably because they'd been so busy lately. Yes that must be it. And worrying about it of course. That always held it up. But – well she knew when it had happened. If she was. The night after a literary dinner where Oliver had been the guest speaker. He had been terribly nervous, had rehearsed his speech for days. She'd listened patiently, making suggestions, admiring this turn of phrase, that literary reference, all the jokes. It had been at the Garrick, so she hadn't been able to go. He had got ready, dressed in his white tie and tails – it had been that grand – in silence. He had been white-faced, clearly felt sick.

'You mustn't worry,' she'd said, going over to him, putting her arms round him, 'you'll be marvellous. I know you will. And I shall sit here, thinking about you and just willing you through it.'

'Yes, yes,' he'd said, 'but you don't understand, so many marvellous people are going to be there, all the giants of our business, Macmillan, John Murray, Archibald Constable, Joseph Malaby Dent . . . it will be David and Goliath, Celia, I really don't know—'

'Oliver,' she said almost severely, 'that is an absurd thing to say. You know perfectly well David slew Goliath. As you will tonight. Now give me a kiss and let me do your tie. You know you can never do it when you're nervous. There. You look wonderful. So handsome. And more important, very impressive and – and literary. Now go along, my darling. And don't forget to pause at the end of each paragraph. Don't hurry it. Let them enjoy it, savour it.'

She sat, as she had promised, in her small sitting-room on the first floor, reading, thinking of him, when she heard the car pull up in front of the house – very late – after one. She ran down the stairs two at a time. He came in the door, threw his hat down on a chair, looked at her solemnly for a moment, then smiled.

'It was marvellous. I probably shouldn't say it, but it was. The whole thing was magnificent. What an occasion! If only, if only my father had been there to see it.'

'Come upstairs,' she said, taking his hand, 'I want to hear about every moment of it. Every single moment.'

'You're so good to me,' he said kissing the top of her head, 'to me and for me. I could never have done it without you. Never. And you've stayed up waiting for me all this time. You must be so tired.'

'I'm not a bit tired,' she said, 'and of course I couldn't have gone to bed. Now I mean it, every single moment—'

Later, empowered by happiness and triumph, he had made love to her. She had lain in bed, waiting for him, excited, both physically and mentally, had felt her body lurch with pleasure at the first touch of him. She had been impatient, hungry, the ecstasy had been huge, intense, straight away; she reached one orgasm swiftly, felt herself rise, crying out, to touch the next. Too good, too strong, too overpowering even to pause to think of the consequences, never mind take any kind of action, but as her body finally quietened, fell into peace, she did think, with a touch of panic, that it was exactly, exactly the very time she was most likely to conceive. And – well maybe she had. And if she had – Celia

28

wrenched her mind away from her biology and tried to concentrate on what was going on.

It was the weekly editorial meeting, and she had an idea to propose. A very good idea. She was nervous about that as well. Waiting for her turn to speak, her heart was thumping so hard she was sure that nice Richard Douglas, the senior literary editor sitting next to her, must be able to hear it. She always tried not to show emotion in the office. It wasn't fair. Apart from LM, she was the only woman, and if you were going to work as men's equal, then you must behave like one too. But this was very difficult. It would be even more difficult if Oliver turned the idea down.

He shouldn't; of course he shouldn't. If he did, it would only be because she had proposed it. He was still inclined to do that, even now. Even now that she had several successful books either out, or in the process of coming out. He seemed to feel he had to: not because he resented her success, he was very proud of that, but because he was so anxious to be fair. Not to favour her in any way. Not to abuse his position. She liked that in a way, but on another level it irritated her dreadfully. Because it actually wasn't fair. She tried to take it well, tried not to refer to it even, when they were at home together, or travelling back from the office, in the motor car Lord Beckenham had insisted on giving them for their last Christmas present.

Oliver had tried to resist it, but she had persuaded him it would be unkind and hurtful.

'He really likes you so much, Oliver, Mama told me so. Ever since Giles was born, he's thought you were wonderful. He wants to help. And it would be enormously helpful anyway, to have a car. I hate always having to catch the bus, especially in the evening. It makes me late for Giles.'

This was quite untrue, since if she was late leaving the office (supposedly never after half past four these days) and she couldn't find a bus, she simply took a hansom cab. She argued to herself that it was an entirely appropriate call on her salary, but she knew it would annoy Oliver, who was naturally careful with money, a legacy from a childhood when everyone had talked constantly about his mother's extravagance. It upset him, those references. Even though he couldn't remember his mother, he had felt in some way that her behaviour reflected badly back on him; and it had left him with a strong resolve to behave quite differently. He feared greatly, and sometimes even expressed the view, that Jack took after her.

LM, who was even more thriftily inclined, walked to work most days. She had sold the big house on Fitzjohns Avenue which her father had left her, bought a far more modest one in Keats Grove, and had

29

adopted a mode of dress on her thirtieth birthday - long skirt, white shirt, coloured cravat and neatly tailored jacket – which was never to alter for the rest of her life, and which saved her from having to keep up with (and therefore spending money on) fashionable clothes.

Celia, who adored clothes, and spent a great deal of money on them, mostly with the allowance from her father, found this almost impossible to understand, but she did feel that LM, rather perversely, looked very nice in her uniform. It flattered her tall but distinctly shapely figure, and the large, loosely knotted cravats in a range of brilliant colours set off her strong, dramatic features, her large dark eyes. LM clearly took after her mother, Celia thought. Oliver's golden looks came from Edgar. No one would ever have dreamed they were half brother and sister. Robert on the other hand, she remembered thinking at the wedding, could have been LM's twin. Celia had liked Robert; she wished they saw more of him. He had, despite his rather serious manner, a wonderful and rather wicked sense of humour. He was apparently becoming extremely rich, in his tall building in New York's financial district. Half the mothers in New York must be after him for their daughters.

'Yes, Celia?' Oliver was saying. She jumped. She really should concentrate harder in meetings. She found it rather difficult, even when she wasn't worrying about her biology. Her mind roamed around as they discussed costings and publication dates and the wording of Lyttons' entry in the *Writers and Artists Year Book*, a new work of reference for writers, illustrators and publishers.

She looked at Oliver and flushed; he was wearing his sternest, I-am-not-giving-you-any-special-concessions-just-because-you-are-my-wife expression.

'I think you had an idea to discuss?' he said.

'Yes. Yes, I have. Actually. I – well I was thinking about the Everyman series.'

'We've all been thinking about that,' said Oliver heavily. The new Everyman imprint, launched by Joseph Malaby Dent, was pledged to publish a cheap library of the greatest works ever written. And it was doing well; self-improvement was very much on the agenda in these times of social change.

'I think we should launch a series of biographies. Equally cheap. About the outstanding men – and women, of course, lots of them – in history. I think it would do extremely well. I don't think we should necessarily run it chronologically, because people are so much more interested in more recent figures. Disraeli, Florence Nightingale, Marie Curie, Mr Dickens himself, would all be wonderful subjects. Lord Melbourne even; everything to do with Queen Victoria still seems to attract great attention. Henry Irving, Mrs Siddons, there are so many.

And we could commission an original illustration for each one, as a frontispiece, and—'

She stopped; everyone was staring at her. Their faces were unreadable. She flushed, faltered, then went on.

'And maybe those illustrations could be offered separately with each book. As a promotional item. And each book could contain an advertisement for the next one at the end. And I thought we could launch the series through *The Times* book club, make a virtue of the beastly thing, perhaps offer a bigger discount than usual . . .'

'Oh no,' said Oliver firmly, interrupting her. 'Definitely not. Nothing would persuade me to do that.'

Celia felt rather sick; she looked at him. He was looking sterner than ever. She'd been sure, so sure this was a good idea. So sure, indeed, that she hadn't even sounded him out in private beforehand, as she sometimes did. She should have done. Saved herself this kind of humiliation. She looked down at her shoes. They were very nice shoes or rather short boots, in grey leather with black buttons at the side. She'd been really excited when she'd found them. They looked wonderful with her new grey skirt and jacket.

'Pretty shoes,' Giles had said when she'd gone up to see him, wearing them for the first time. 'Pretty Mummy.'

She'd been so pleased at that. Absurdly pleased. Maybe she should give up on her career, for a while at any rate, immerse herself again in the more normal business of life like buying clothes and playing with her child. Then it wouldn't matter if she – well if she was pregnant. Everything would be safer, easier. In fact—

'Absolutely brilliant idea,' Richard Douglas was saying, 'really quite, quite brilliant, Celia. What a clever girl you are. What do you think, LM?'

'I agree with you,' said LM. 'The market for biography is very large. It could run for years. Always new people coming along. Or rather, leaving.'

'What on earth do you mean, leaving?' said Oliver. He looked rather irritable.

'Dying,' said LM briskly, 'every obit is a potential new subject. I even agree about *The Times* book club, Celia.'

'I said no,' said Oliver.

'Well – maybe not.' LM smiled at him. *The Times* book club was not so much a thorn in every publisher's side as a dagger. Formed in 1905 to increase circulation of the paper, it offered books to members of their reading library – supplied at a discount by publishers – which were then sold on cheaply as used books even after only two or three borrowings.

'But we would certainly value the exposure they offer. Celia, it's a splendid idea. I really am most impressed.'

'I agree with you about launching the series with more recent subjects,' said Richard Douglas. 'In fact, we might even make the whole thing alphabetical. What about that?'

'Couldn't keep that up,' said Oliver, 'you'd get some new subject with a name beginning with A and then where would you be?'

'I do like the library idea though,' said Celia earnestly, 'so that it is something people collect. Build up. Maybe the spines could have letters on them, quite large, I mean, above the title. So that people could file them and find them easily.'

'Possibly, yes,' said Richard. 'I see this as having altogether a very strong graphic style. Don't you, Oliver?'

'What? Oh – yes. Yes indeed.'

Celia looked at him again; he was finding this difficult, finding it hard not to feel jealous. She must be careful.

'Fairly lyrical, I think,' said Richard, 'the style, I mean. Art nouveau, I would suggest. And the binding, possibly dark blue. I'll get the studio to mock some things up. We mustn't waste time on this. Definitely get the first two or three out for Christmas. I like the idea of selling the illustrations separately, Celia. My goodness. What a clever girl you are.'

He had a tendency to sound patronising; he did then. Celia knew he didn't mean to. And he had been more encouraging to her than Oliver had. But there was always an element of surprise expressed in any praise he gave her: that she, a woman, could have strong, clever ideas.

She felt clever: clever and strong. What had she been thinking of, ten minutes earlier: something about staying at home, giving up work? Absurd. Totally absurd.

'We must find a name for it,' said LM, 'the imprint that is. Any ideas for that, Celia?'

'Well—' she hesitated, looked round. She had of course: a wonderful idea. But they were most unlikely to like that as well, surely.

'Well, I thought – I thought – Biographica. What do you think?'

Another silence. Then LM said, 'I think that's marvellous, Celia. Very, very strong, simple, memorable. Moreover—' she hesitated – 'moreover, I think we should consider letting it be your responsibility. Your own imprint. Would you agree, Oliver?'

It was a bold suggestion; she was the only person who could have made it; being a Lytton, not being married to Celia, and of course not having any editorial territory of her own to defend. Celia stared fixedly at the grey boots again. Of course Oliver would never agree to that, to her looking after the series.

'Well – well, we could consider that, I suppose,' Oliver said. He cleared his throat. 'As long as other senior people are happy with it, of course. I wouldn't like the decision to be taken here and now in this room.'

'Why ever not?' said LM briskly. 'We three make all the major decisions. I don't recall you getting Mr Bond's agreement, down in accounts, to the launching of the new Heatherleighs, or Miss Birkett's to the medical series. That was Celia's, too. Good gracious, Celia, we shall have to look to our laurels, if we are not to see you in complete control of Lyttons soon.'

Celia smiled at her; she felt she could have flown through the air. But then she looked at Oliver again and he was patently struggling to smile, to look good-humoured. This was hard for him. She had to show him she still felt quite clearly that he was in charge.

'I absolutely agree with Oliver,' she said, 'this is not a decision to be taken here. Not while I'm here, even. But of course I'm really pleased you all like the idea so much. And I would love to be properly involved, with it. Please.'

She could feel Oliver easing, saw his face relax, and returned his swift, careful smile. It was a long time, she suddenly realised, since he had had a really strong idea of his own.

'Ted,' whispered Sylvia, 'Ted, I've got something to tell you.'

'What? What's that?' His voice sounded startled, confused. He was always so exhausted at bedtime, that he fell asleep at once. Except very occasionally. Pity he hadn't that night.

'Ted, I'm – well, I'm in the family way. Again. I—'

'What?' He sat up, shocked into wakefulness, forgetting to be quiet, 'Oh, Sylvia, no. Oh, dear, oh dear girl. How'd that happen?'

'Usual way, I suppose,' she said, managing to sound light-hearted, even in her anxiety and with the nausea which was always worse in the evening than the mornings. Probably just as well.

'But I was so – well, I thought I was any road – so careful. Oh dear.'

'I know, Ted. But – it does happen so easy. Doesn't it?'

'Seems to.'

There was a long silence. Then, 'When?'

'Christmas. Thereabouts anyway . . .'

'What are we going to do?'

'I don't know. Well, I've thought a bit. We can just manage – just this time. Put Frank in the other room, in an orange crate. Then Marjorie can come in with us. And the new one in the drawer.'

'I s'pose. Yes.' There was another pause. 'How you feeling?'

'Not too bad. Tired.'

'I'm sorry, old girl,' he said, 'very sorry. I won't let it happen again. I swear.'

Sylvia was touched; she leaned over and kissed him, trying not to disturb Frank.

'It was my fault as well,' she said, untruthfully implying that she had been as enthusiastic as he. She felt he'd earned that much at least. And they'd never be able to cope if they started quarrelling.

She was pregnant, as she had known of course that she must be. And having once got used to the idea, and despite the sickness and the lassitude, she was pleased. Of course it helped with Oliver; made him less touchy about her working at Lyttons. And very happy, of course: happy and proud.

He was not so foolish as to suggest Celia might consider staying at home, at least for a while, but he did say he thought she should take things a little easy, and perhaps work shorter days; Celia (rather to his surprise) agreed that it might be a good idea and then, entranced by her new job and its new responsibilities, anxious to prove herself worthy of it, proceeded to work harder and for longer hours even than before. Three months later, LM found her curled up with pain on her office floor; that night she miscarried the baby, a little girl, and lost so much blood that it was feared for twenty-four hours that she might not live.

Oliver, as angry with her for putting herself at risk as he was distressed at the child's loss, forbade her to work at all until further notice; Celia, weak and wretched, could only feebly agree. The doctor, having established to his satisfaction that there was no serious physical cause for the miscarriage, that she had not had a fever, and that there were no indications of any tumours, 'although she might have a weakness in the neck of her womb', said that in his opinion it was a simple case of what he called over strain.

'Nature intends you to rest while your baby matures,' he said sternly, 'not rush about putting an undue burden on your body.'

He prescribed a strong tonic for her, containing a great deal of iron, and complete bed rest for at least two weeks, had a quiet word with Oliver as to the danger of another impregnation taking place too soon, and warned Celia that once a miscarriage had taken place, there was a very real danger of it happening again at the same point in any subsequent pregnancy.

'Your womb may have a weakness; it will expand as long as its unhealthy condition will permit and than will relieve itself of the baby, unless you are very careful indeed. No lifting, even of books, no running up and down stairs. I always advise against opening windows, that sort of thing.'

Celia nodded dully at him and didn't speak.

She recovered physically quite quickly, but mentally suffered severe depression, lying in bed, in an uncharacteristic lethargy, crying a great deal, staring up at the ceiling with blank eyes, fearing, indeed knowing that this was the price she was paying for her crushing ambition. She was hostile to everyone around her – with the rather surprising exception of Jack.

He arrived home on leave while she was still in bed and spent many hours sitting with her. Being emotionally uninvolved, and in any case, cheerful and uncomplicated, he was simply sweetly sympathetic, which was exactly what she needed. He told her funny stories about life in the mess, played draughts and various uncomplicated card games with her and generally made her feel something like normal again. The night before he was due to leave, he found her weeping copiously; too upset to pretend, she told him she was dreading being without him again. Touched and sad, Jack got on to her bed and sat with her in his arms, promised to write regularly, and even offered to sing her a whitewashed version of a few barrack room songs, if she thought that would cheer her up.

That made her first giggle and then cry again, but less desperately; finally she fell asleep in his arms, her head on his shoulder, whereupon he crept away, leaving a funny message pinned to her pillow about being afraid of Oliver challenging him to pistols at dawn if he found them together. She often thought of that in the years to come, of his kindness and sweetness and what a good friend he had been to her – and of how extremely depressed she must have been, not to have found him attractive . . .

But once he had gone, she lapsed back into misery and into a growing difficulty with Oliver and with her marriage. She felt, indeed knew, that Oliver blamed her for the miscarriage; he was withdrawn from her, refused to discuss how he felt, and indeed when he did visit her room, was more inclined to sit making polite conversation or even reading, than showing her any kind of understanding or comfort. One night she found a book called *Women in Health and Sickness*, rather pointedly laid open on her dressing-table. Celia put down her hairbrush and read, 'Women's sphere is not to sparkle in the realms of literature, but to shine with a clear, steady and warm light in the home', then 'a healthy body with a fairly informed mind is preferable to an overstocked brain and a delicate frame'. Oliver had obviously left it for her; she cried almost all night and could hardly bear to look at him for days, so badly did she feel at his continuing hostility and her own remorse.

Eventually, though, Oliver became worried enough about her state of mind to consult not only the family doctor, but also a gynaecologist, then a psychologist, and even a herbalist. To no avail; Celia continued in her state of blank misery.

Finally, in despair, Oliver asked her mother what she thought he should do; Lady Beckenham arrived at Cheyne Walk, complete, as usual with her maid, and after a couple of days, told Oliver she thought the best thing Celia could possibly do was go back to work.

'She's just lying up there feeling sorry for herself, with nothing to do; she needs occupation. I always found a week's fishing up in Scotland put me right after one of these things. Don't look so surprised, Oliver, I lost at least four. Bloody miserable it is too, you couldn't begin to imagine it, being a man. Can't imagine much about anything, if you're at all like Beckenham. I'd rather thought you were a bit different, I must say. And she thinks you blame her; you shouldn't. These things happen. I've ridden to hounds when I was pregnant with no mishaps; lot more likely to induce miscarriage than bookwork, I'd have thought. Anyway, I don't imagine fishing would do Celia much good, but I hope you take my point. You let her get back to that work of hers, she really loves it, heaven knows why and I think you'll find she'll be as right as rain in no time. Only don't get her pregnant again yet, for God's sake. It happens horribly easily afterwards. She's not as strong as she likes to think.'

Oliver was so appalled by the picture she painted of him that he went straight up to Celia, took her in his arms, and said tenderly, 'Darling, I want you to know I do love you.'

'Do you?' she said, looking at him warily. 'You don't seem to.'

'Of course I do. I'm sorry you've had such a rotten time. And—' he paused, looking back at her just as warily, 'well, I want you to come back to Lyttons as soon as you possibly can,' adding, 'only part-time at first,' when she sat up in bed, her face flushed with excitement and said:

'Tomorrow?'

'No darling, not tomorrow. Next week, if you're good.'

At which Celia burst into tears again.

'Darling, please don't. I want fewer tears now. Perhaps it's not such a good idea,'

'No, no, it is. I just need to have something else to think about. I'm so, so sorry, Oliver, I feel so guilty, so bad. I should have been more careful, it's quite right what the doctors have all said; it was selfish of me, and it's hurt you so much as well as me. Please forgive me.'

'I do forgive you,' he said, kissing her, 'of course I do. And you – well you weren't to know,' he added with great generosity. 'But next time, well of course you must do what the doctor says. Rest, rest and more rest.'

'And you're not angry with me any more?'

'Not angry. Sad for us both, that's all. But next time we'll get it right. And that isn't going to be for quite a while,' he added firmly. 'We must be very, very careful. Now your mother thinks you should join us for supper downstairs. Feel up to that?'

'I do, yes.'

'Wily old bird, your mother,' he said, 'lots of common sense. I like her more and more. She told me she had at least four miscarriages herself. Did you know that?'

'Not till today,' said Celia, 'when she told me. I suppose it's not the sort of thing you'd talk to your children about. But I did find it comforting. It didn't stop her having more babies. So—'

'Darling, I told you, no talk of more babies.'

'Well – all right' said Celia with a sigh, 'but I have missed loving you dreadfully. It's one of the things that's made me most miserable. I thought you didn't want me any more, that you were too angry with me.'

'I want you terribly,' said Oliver, 'and if – well, as I said, we must just be very careful. I know you don't like that, but—'

'We will be careful,' said Celia, 'I promise. If I can have you loving me again, I'll promise anything.'

Biographica was launched in December 1907 with the first three volumes boxed together, the biographies of Florence Nightingale, Lord Melbourne, and William Morris, each one with a frontispece illustration by a new artist Celia had discovered, with the auspicious name of Thomas Wolsey. The series was sold out in days. An army of collectors – the young men who literally collected volumes from the publishers and delivered them to the booksellers – was kept fully employed right up to Christmas.

Celia was already working on the next set, in between performing (rather perfunctorily) her proper Christmas duties of present-buying and tree-trimming. She was almost, but not quite, too busy to notice how tearful she felt every time she saw a baby in a perambulator, or even the ubiquitous infants lying in straw-filled mangers with their mothers bent tenderly over them, hands clasped in prayer. It was especially bad when she took two-year-old Giles to a crib blessing at Chelsea Old Church, so bad, indeed, that they walked home together, hand in hand, he looked up at her and asked her why she had cried so much in church. Celia smiled down at him and said she hadn't really been crying, it was only that she was so happy and so lucky. And when they got home, and Oliver was waiting for them by the huge Christmas tree he had had set up in the hall, with presents for them both, a toy pedal car for Giles and an exquisite three-strand pearl choker for her, she did feel that to a large extent, she had spoken the truth.

Meanwhile, in her bed in Line Street, with the mattress carefully covered with layers and layers of newspapers, her children banished to a neighbour's house, her husband pacing wretchedly up and down the tiny corridor, trying to ignore the sound of her groans, a great pan of water boiling endlessly on the stove, and attended only by another neighbour who was unofficial midwife to the district, Sylvia Miller gave birth to a rather small but perfectly healthy baby girl. Lying in bed afterwards, pale and exhausted, but very happy, showing the baby to the other children, she told them her name was Barbara.

But little Frank, who had just begun to talk and was very excited by the new arrival, said, 'Barty, Barty, Barty,' while stroking her small silky forehead.

And Barty she remained for the rest of her life.

CHAPTER 4

'Well I'm going to. You have no right to stop me. I am not your – your chattel.'

'Oh, for God's sake, Celia,' said Oliver wearily, 'of course you're not my chattel. I hardly think urging you to take care of yourself, to take things very easily indeed, constitutes laying down some kind of diktat. I'm worried about you. You and the baby. We must not have a repetition of what happened last time.'

Celia met his eyes and flushed.

'No,' she said, quietly, 'no of course not. But I have given up work, Oliver. For the time being. Until the baby is safely born. All I plan to do now is join Mrs Pember Reeves's group, and observe one of these pathetic families. Once or twice a week. It will probably be marginally less exhausting physically than playing with Giles. It's important, Oliver. I'm surprised you don't support me more. Obviously your socialism is hardly even skin deep.'

'Oh, Celia, really. This has nothing to do with the depth or otherwise of my socialism. Or yours for that matter. It is concern for you and for our baby. You need absolute rest.'

'That's not what Dr Perring said. He said I should be careful and take plenty of rest. Especially at the stage when it happened last time. Which is still a long way off. When it comes, I shall take to my bed for a week or so, I promise you. I am doing what he said, I am sleeping for at least two hours every afternoon. This work is not going to prevent me doing that. Anyway, Oliver, unless you want to be branded as an outmoded, capitalistic-style husband to the whole of the Fabian society, you have to let me do it.'

Oliver looked at her. 'Tell me again,' he said, 'precisely what this task involves.'

'I knew you weren't listening. Mrs Pember Reeves, she's such a wonderful woman, Oliver, it was in her house the Fabian Women's Group was founded, she has come up with a scheme for helping poor families in Lambeth. Well poor families everywhere. Not by doing charitable works, raising money, taking them soup, all that nonsense.

39

Mrs Pember Reeves has a permanent solution in mind. She says the state must be obliged to realise its responsibilities, must understand exactly what the poor are condemned to unless they are given what they need. Which is decent housing, and a chance to raise their families without the constant fear of poverty and illness.'

'And how does she propose to make it realise that?'

'Well, by showing, in a properly informed, detailed report, exactly how poverty damages people, damages them permanently, it's a vicious circle, condemning the children, and especially the girls, to a life-pattern which repeats that of their mothers, only then can the state be persuaded to provide the basic human needs. And satisfy the most basic human right, that of decent living conditions and a chance for women particularly to better themselves.'

'Does this have anything to do that other subject so dear to Fabian hearts, getting the vote for women?'

'No, not really. Only very indirectly at any rate. Of course I care about that as well. But I can't start demonstrating, tying myself to railings and so on, or you really would lock me up.'

'True.'

'And I think I can do more good this way. Do you know, Oliver, there are families not two miles from here, large families, living on less than a pound a week, in a couple of rooms a quarter the size of this one. And the mothers, decent, intelligent women, simply can't make a tolerable life for their families within those homes. The infant mortality rate is dreadfully high, not because the mothers are ignorant or incompetent, but because they lack the money to provide for their own and their families' needs. They don't have enough food, they don't have enough clothing and they certainly don't have any facilities for recreation. And it won't get any better until they obtain those things. As a right. If Mrs Pember Reeves' scheme comes to fruition, there will be hope for these women. And I intend to help her see that it does.'

Oliver sighed. 'Well, I can't stop you, I suppose. I've never been able to stop you doing anything. Even,' he said, with the shadow of a smile, 'even from marrying me.'

'I don't see what you're afraid of, Oliver.' Celia said impatiently, 'What harm do you think this will do me?'

Oliver looked at her. 'I'm afraid of two things,' he said. 'One is that you will harm yourself and the baby. The other is,' and here he stopped, smiled again, almost involuntarily, at her, 'the other is that in spite of everything you've said, you will arrive home one day with one or more of these families, and inform me that they are coming to live with us.'

'Oh don't be so ridiculous' said Celia, 'we are absolutely forbidden to

40

make any kind of personal input. I could be expelled from the Fabian society if I did. That really is one thing you don't have to worry about.'

LM was taking the short cut up from the underground station towards her house; she was lost, not so much in thought, as in financial consideration. She had a remarkable facility for mental arithmetic, she could carry three or four columns of figures in her head, add them up, subtract them, make percentages of them: it was not only an enormous help to her in her work, it was also a pleasure, almost a recreation. Just as some people recite poetry in their heads before going to sleep, or on a walk, played with figures. Tonight though, she was not playing; she was calculating the precise profit Lyttons were making out of the three new volumes of Biographica. They had had to be priced at a higher level than originally planned; such considerations as the book club and library discounts, the new titles on approval scheme for the central London book showroom, the rising cost of binding – all these things had meant that the series had been launched at six shillings per volume. That had been all right the first year: just. This year, it looked as if they might have to be six shillings and sixpence, which hardly met with their original criterion of a cheap library of quality books. And even at that, they would do well to make a profit of half a crown a book; which meant that for their initial print order of five thousand, they would make a little over a thousand pounds. Not enough. Just not enough. But—

'Now what is a lovely lady like you doing walking out on her own at this time of night. And in a dark alley like this too? Eh?'

LM said nothing: just stood absolutely quiet and still.

'Going to come quietly? Much better if you do.'

Hands were on her now, strong hands, one gripping her shoulders, the other on the back of her neck.

'Come on now. Just along here. This way, that's right, on you go – no, no, don't you try biting me. I wouldn't like that at all. Not yet, any road—'

They had almost reached the street lamp at the end of the walk; one of the man's hands had moved down, was caressing one of her breasts.

'Very nice. Very nice indeed. Can't wait to see a bit more of those. Really can't wait. Hey, now, I said no biting. I get quite aroused when I'm bitten. Or scratched, so don't start that either.'

LM swung round swiftly, suddenly, confronted him; under the street lamp his face was very clear. A well-shaped face it was, with a strong jaw and a wide mouth; dark waving hair, thick black eyebrows and set quite deeply, a pair of very dark eyes. They were smiling, the eyes: smiling confidently.

'Like what you see, do you? I certainly like what I see.' He reached up, touched her mouth; she took his finger between her teeth.

'Now now. Temper temper. Come on now, this way. And get a move on. I haven't got all night.'

'Haven't you really?' said LM turning to face him winding her arms round his neck. 'well I have. And I really hope you're up to it.'

She had met him at a meeting of the Independent Labour Party in Hampstead; she had noticed him straight away, because he wasn't quite like most of the people there, the self-consciously middle class folk in expensive clothes; he was clearly working class, in his heavy tweed suit, a scarf knotted round his neck, his hair untidy. He had been leaning against the wall; he'd noticed her too, was watching her with a half-smile on his face.

Afterwards he told her he'd felt her, even before he looked at her; 'Felt you under my skin, getting at me.'

The meeting was badly attended; afterwards, there was been an invitation from Michael Fosdyke, a local party member, to come to his house up on the Heath, for tea and biscuits. 'Or beer, if anyone wants it. Or a glass of wine.' She'd been hurrying away from the hall and the crowd, not wishing to take any of Michael Fosdyke's hospitality, for she found his social conscience, worn stark naked on his sleeve, hugely irritating, when the man had stopped her. Quite courteously, but firmly: simply stepped in front of her.

'Not going up to the big house? To discuss how to improve the working man's lot over a glass of madeira? Shame on you.'

'I am not,' she said, meeting his amused dark eyes with her own. 'I happen to think I can do more for that than I could by eating a lot of expensive biscuits, baked by Mr Fosdyke's rather underpaid cook.'

'My goodness,' he put his head back and laughed. 'Well that's a novel view. And how would you then? Improve our lot?'

'I don't think yours needs improving too much,' she said, 'you seem fine to me. But I'm in the publishing business. And I have friends in journalism. The *Daily Mirror* and so on. I think a few well-expressed articles are worth a million words of waffle.'

She was aware she was talking too much to him: encouraging him. It was dangerous for a woman to talk thus to a young man. Whatever his social background. She didn't quite know why she was doing it; he just made her want to.

'And . . . you're all alone. You're not afraid of being attacked?'

'Of course not. It's greatly overrated, that fear, in my opinion. I walk all over London. I love it. Nothing's happened to me yet. Anyway—'

'Yes?'

'Well. I'm hardly a – a young girl.'

'So what? That's a stupid thing to say.'

'Why?'

'I hadn't noticed attacks being limited to young girls. Besides, you're a very attractive woman. If you'll pardon my saying so.'

'Thank you.' She looked at him; he wasn't being insolent, his expression was charmingly serious.

'So, why don't I walk you home?'

'Oh no. No, you mustn't do that.'

'Why not?'

'Well—'

He might attack her on the way. Or even burgle her house, at some later date, if he knew where it was. He might. But it did seem unlikely.

'Why not?' he said again.

'No reason really,' she said and realised he was smiling at her; a slightly knowing smile.

'Well then. Let me take you. Not far is it?'

'No. No, just down – down there.'

'You'd better tell me exactly where,' he said, 'I'm going to find out sooner or later. If I'm going to walk there with you.'

'Yes. Yes of course. It's in Keats Grove.'

'Very nice.'

'Yes. Yes it is.'

She could be making an appalling mistake; telling him all this. Then she thought that if he had been some well-spoken middle class Hampstead resident, she wouldn't have hesitated, and felt ashamed of herself. Just the same—

'Look, it really isn't necessary,' she said rather feebly.

'I know it isn't,' he said simply, 'but I want to do it. All right?'

'Yes,' said LM, 'yes all right.'

They walked in silence for a few minutes, then she said, 'So where do you live?'

'Oh, down the bottom. Near Swiss Cottage. Got a little house there.'

'Of your own?' she said, and then hated herself for sounding surprised.

'Yes. Belonged to my auntie. She left it to me. I was her favourite. I let half of it out, to pay for the outgoings, rates and that.'

'Yes, I see.'

'This printing business of yours—'

'Publishing.'

'What's the difference?'

LM chose her words carefully. 'Publishers sell the books; printers – well – print them.'

'Oh yes? What do you do there then? You a secretary or something?'

'No,' said LM who had always found honesty a most valuable and underrated commodity, whatever the circumstance, 'no I own it. With my brother.'

'You serious?'

'Yes. Absolutely. It was founded by our father.'

There was a silence; then the young man smiled.

'I knew you were quality,' he said, 'soon as I saw you.'

'Knew you were keen too,' he said several hours later. They were sitting on the sofa in LM's drawing room; he was kissing her. LM was responding with considerable passion.

She'd asked him in for a cup of tea. She told herself it was only polite, it had been quite a walk, and he had another, much longer one before he got home. They were engrossed in a political discussion by then: about whether the Liberal Party would manage to bring in enough social reforms to improve the conditions of the working class before the decade was out. It was quite a complex discussion. He was extremely well-informed. Anyway, her housekeeper, known as Mrs Bill, was at home; she had moved with LM from the big house, quite sure she was incapable of looking after herself. She now had a pair of pretty little rooms on the top floor. She was actually called Mrs Williams, but had been christened Mrs Bill by LM herself when she was tiny.

She really wanted to go on talking to the man: she liked him. Liked him a lot. His name was James Ford, 'But my friends call me Jago.' He was what Celia would call charming and what she would call easy. Easy and intelligent and with a quirky sense of humour. He talked well, he was articulate and opinionated, and although he had a London accent, his turn of phrase was surprisingly polished and confident. He drank two cups of tea, brought by a resigned Mrs Bill, who was used to what she called funny people coming to the house and then (as the debate on the Liberal party had still not been quite settled) she offered him a beer; he shook his head.

'No thanks. You having one?'

'No,' she said, 'I don't like beer. I might have a whisky.'

'You could offer me a whisky. Not suitable, for the likes of me, is that what you thought?' His expression was amused.

'No,' she said angrily, feeling her face flush, 'no I didn't think that. I think it's unfair of you even to imply it. I just thought – well, that you'd like beer. Most men do. Of course you can have a whisky. I'd like it if you did.'

'Your brother like beer?' he said, 'the one who owns the publishers with you?'

'No,' she said, 'he doesn't. But my father did. Very much. So can we drop this absurd disussion?'

'If you like. No need to get aerated. And I'll have a whisky. Please. Suits you though,' he added.

'What does?'

'Getting aerated. All rosy you look. Really pretty. Much younger. How old are you?'

'Thirty-two,' said LM after a brief pause, 'what about you?'

'Thirty. My word, you don't look thirty-two.'

'Well – thank you,' she said slightly awkwardly.

'You got a trades union at your place?'

'No. No we haven't.'

'Print unions are getting quite strong, you know.'

'I do know,' she said, 'printing costs are quite high. Quite rightly. In my opinion. Although it causes us problems of course.'

'Your brother think like you? A socialist as well, is he?'

'Of course,' said LM simply, and then added, her eyes suddenly amused as she looked at him, 'and so is his wife.'

'Oh yes? She another upper class lady is she?'

'Very upper class. Her father is an earl.'

'Oh God,' he said, 'bet she's a nightmare.'

'Actually,' said LM, 'she's not. She's extremely clever. And a very good, loyal friend. And she has done wonders for my brother, who used to lack self-confidence. I like her. She works at Lyttons with us. She's an editor.'

'She is? Unusual place it must be, employing women in positions like that.'

'We believe in employing women,' said LM, 'it's perfectly simple. Provided they're up to the job of course.'

'Yes, well, lots of women believe in being employed, too. Doesn't make it easy for them to get the jobs though, does it? Except in service of course. Helps having friends in high places I suppose.'

'Yes, I suppose it does,' said LM briskly. 'What do you do?'

'I'm a builder,' he said. 'A roofer. Not bad work in the summer. Horrible in the winter. And a lot of the time, you get laid off, especially if the weather's really bad. I've been out of work for weeks now. Nice new job starting next month though. Row of houses near Camden Town.'

'So – what do you live on?' she said, genuinely interested, 'when you're out of work?'

'Well, I've saved a bit. Get a bit off the dole if I'm lucky. They're not exactly forthcoming with it though. Then there's the rent from my tenants. Capitalist really, I am. Just like you.'

'Have you got a family?' she said, ignoring this.

'No,' he said briefly.

'You've never married?'

'I didn't say that.'

'Well—'

'Look,' he said, suddenly defensive, 'I'm not asking you a lot of personal questions, am I?'

'No. I'm sorry. Have another whisky.' It seemed important to win him back over.

'Yes I will. Thanks.' He drank it in silence, looked at her awkwardly.

'I was married,' he said suddenly, 'but she – well – she died.'

'I'm sorry. So sorry.'

'Yes. Bit difficult.'

'Did you love her – very much?' she said. She surprised herself: that she could ask him something so direct, so intimate.

'Very much. Yes, I did. She died having a baby. And the little one went with her. Bad business.'

'I'm so sorry,' she said again. She felt tears in her eyes. She blinked hard, took a large sip of whisky. He looked at her surprised.

'You mean it, don't you?'

'Of course I mean it. It's such a sad story. It – well it shocked me.'

He turned away, pulled a rather ragged, grubby handkerchief out of his pocket, and blew his nose.

'Sorry,' he said. 'sympathy gets to me. Can't help it.'

'When – when did she – did it happen?'

'Beginning of the year,' he said briefly.

She was shocked; that he had faced such grief so recently. She put out her hand, put it on his arm.

'That is so sad.'

'Yes, well. She was – she was everything to me. She was lovely. Gentle and good. And so brave. God, she was brave. I still can't believe it. Bloody doctors.'

'What happened?'

'Oh, it started coming too early. Only eight months she was. They said she'd be all right, didn't need any special care. That she was young and all that. Turned out the – the afterbirth, it came first. So the baby died. And then she – well she died. Loss of blood. Nothing they could do, they said. Well they would say that, wouldn't they?'

He sat there, his head bowed, looking at her hand, on his arm. Then he looked up and his dark eyes were full of tears. He managed a shaky smile.

'This is daft. I only wanted to see you home. Not tell you my life history. But you're nice to talk to. Helps a bit, when you can talk. Now I'd better be off. That woman of yours will think I'm up to no good.'

At the front door he turned, smiled at her.

'Thanks. Thanks for everything. It's been really—' he hesitated – 'really enjoyable. And I still don't think you look your age. Nothing like.'

'Thank you.'

There was a silence. Then, 'Well I didn't attack you did I?' he said cheerfully, 'And I won't be back to do your house either.'

'What?'

'I bet that's what you thought,' he said, 'when I first offered to walk you home.'

Anger shot through LM: anger threaded with guilt.

'How dare you say that?' she said. 'How dare you make such an assumption about me?'

'I dare,' he said, 'because it's quite likely to be true.'

'Oh is it really? I offer you hospitality, kindness, and you reward me with a hide-bound, class-entrenched attitude like that.'

'Oh, come along, Miss Lytton. You're giving yourself away. Of course you've been very nice to me. Very kind, done your duty, like the good socialist I'm sure you are. But listen to you, you're still spelling all that out.'

'Please leave,' she said, her voice shaking, 'at once.'

'All right,' he said grinning, slightly awkwardly now, 'No need to get upset. I'm only—'

'There is every need,' she said, 'and I am upset. Very, very upset.'

Fresh rage and a pang of fierce loneliness hit her together; the tears rose again in her eyes. She turned away.

'You're crying.'

'I'm not crying. And please go.'

'You are crying,' he said again, and put out his finger and wiped away the one tear that had escaped on to her cheek. 'What an emotional creature you are.'

'I am not emotional.'

'Yes you are,' he said, 'very.'

'I am simply,' she said, struggling for dignity, 'simply very angry. And insulted. That you should regard this evening as a bit of – of social work on my part. I'd like you to leave.'

'All right. All right, I'm going.'

47

Mrs Bill appeared. 'You all right, Miss Lytton?' she said, her voice loaded with meaning.

'Yes, Mrs Bill I'm quite all right,' said LM firmly. 'My guest is just leaving.'

'Yes I am,' he said. He opened the door, went out into the porch, turned, smiled at her differently, quite gently. 'I'm sorry if I upset you, very sorry. But you must admit—'

'Admit what?'

'Well, that it was what you thought,' he said, 'at the beginning. I know it was. I could see it in your face. That's what makes this so ridiculous. Why don't you just say so?'

And LM, confused with emotion, unable to keep up the lie, said, her mouth twitching at the corners, 'Yes, all right. I admit it. I did. I'm so, so sorry.'

'And that's why you were so angry? Because I guessed? And that made you feel bad?'

'Yes. No. Oh, I don't know.'

'So much for socialism,' he said and his expression was an extraordinary blend of contempt and amusement. 'I knew it was too good to be true.'

LM took a deep breath. 'Why don't you come back in,' she said, 'and have another whisky?'

Half an hour later, she had locked the drawing-room door, and removed most of her clothes.

Jago Ford was not her first lover. She was a woman of extraordinary passion. She had lost her virginity at the age of seventeen to her father's best friend. Precocious and self-confident, strongly attracted by him and eager to discover for herself the delights of an activity she had managed to glean only a very little information about, she set out to seduce him. It had not been difficult; he was not only charming, good-looking and rather vain, he had recently been widowed, and he found her enthusiastic advances irresistible. It had not lasted long, but long enough for LM to discover a considerable appetite for sex; at nineteen she had another affair with a young man at university. She was far more in love with him than he with her; astonished at her willingness to sleep with him, he had continued the relationship until they both graduated. There were only four women in her year; and she was infinitely more attractive than the other three. She was broken-hearted when he left her to become engaged to a rich, vapid debutante; desperately hurt that having shared much brilliant conversation and even more brilliant lovemaking and for quite a long period of time, he regarded her nonetheless as unsuitable to be a barrister's wife. That, above all, had shaped her attitude to men of her class and age; she was terminally suspicious of them, would have no more of them. She had no desire to be married herself, hated the idea of having children; she wanted companionship, good conversation, and above all physical fulfilment. It was hard for a woman to find.

There had been a few unsatisfactory relationships through her twenties; two of them with unhappily married men, who found in her not only the companionship and physical release they needed, but also complete discretion. Each time however, she was left hurt and freshly lonely, her sense of self-respect diminished.

In Jago Ford, she found absolute happiness. He was interesting, challenging, he liked and admired her; and he was a superb lover. As was she.

'You really know what to do, don't you?' he said, as they lay exhausted and smiling in one another's arms, the first wonderful, tumultous, noisy, astonishing time.

'I should hope so,' she said, half indignant, 'what did you think I was, some kind of Victorian virgin?'

'Now don't get aerated,' he said, kissing her tenderly, 'I didn't mean that quite. I meant you know it's about taking as well as giving. You need it don't you?'

'Yes,' said LM sighing, half rueful, half amused, 'yes, I really do.'

She found it hard that first time, not to think of his wife, of the gentle, kind Annie he had loved so much, and had so recently lost. It inhibited her, worried her; she felt she was robbing Annie of Jago as she took him into her hungry body, stealing memories, breaking trust.

But, 'don't,' he whispered to her as she held back, confused by those thoughts, recognising them for himself, in himself even, 'she's not here, she's gone. She'd want me to be happy. And you won't be the same.'

She wasn't the same: he told her that, too. Close enough now to talk about her, LM learned that Annie had been awed, even shocked at times by sex; raised by a strict mother, taught to keep herself safe, told she would find marriage something to be endured, she had nonetheless managed more than that. But her role had always been passive, anxious, seeking mostly to please; and Jago, recognising that, had held back too, afraid of hurting her, asking too often, giving too little pleasure. In time they had come to enjoy each other; but it was a careful, watchful enjoyment, and by then the baby which was to part them for ever had been conceived, and from the beginning Annie had been unwell.

'I loved her altogether,' he said simply to LM, 'but being with you doesn't hurt her. Nor remembering her. You don't have to worry about

49

her. You just worry about me,' he grinned suddenly, 'and do what you can for me.'

She seemed to be able to do a lot.

Jago's father had been a clerk in an insurance office and had been eager to see his only son educated. Jago had won a scholarship to a boarding school and had done very well there; there was even talk of teacher training college. But then his father died; Jago at fourteen was clearly old enough to earn a living and help to keep his five younger siblings. The easiest option was manual work; he had become apprenticed to one of the legion of builders covering London with houses. He had done well, and by the age of sixteen was earning half the family income; he had set aside, without too much bitterness, his dreams of a different kind of life. What he could not set aside, however, was the sense of injustice that had brought it about; that the widow of a man who had worked and died, as his father had, in the service of a large company, should have been left with almost nothing to live on. He was troubled, too, by another injustice: that the men who owned the companies drew from them large amounts of money on which they paid virtually no income tax, lived in great luxury in big houses, ate and dressed superbly well, and enjoyed the best of everything, while the men who made the money for them and worked a great deal harder, lived very often close to poverty.

He had been brought up by his father, a timid man, to accept such things, as an unalterable fact of life; but as he grew older, he became first puzzled and then angry, joined the trades union movement and the new Labour Party, and resolved to change the world. He even made speeches at a few political meetings and might have made a concerted effort to enter political life at least at a local level, had he not met Annie and fallen in love. Responsibility and the prospect of fatherhood had blunted such difficult ambitions; like his father before him, he needed his job and his salary; there was little room left for idealism. Grief and loneliness had reawakened it to a degree, but had taken away any real stomach he had for fighting; when LM met him, socialism was once again an interesting notion rather than a crusade.

'The buggers'll win whatever you do,' he said to her more than once, 'might as well grab what you can and make the most of it.'

Although he was clever, he had a certain resistance to further self-improvement. He said life was too short, that learning was for childhood, adulthood for living. He read the newspapers, followed politics and the progress of socialism, but that apart, pursued a rather self-indulgent intellectual road.

'So don't you try getting me to watch Shakespeare and read Dickens,' he said to LM, 'because there's other things I'd rather do. I need cheering up after a long day in the cold, not preaching.'

LM said Dickens had never preached, and indeed held views on society which she was sure Jago would sympathise with, but he said all he could remember was some nonsense about a little chap being sent to the workhouse and working as a pickpocket before being reunited happily with his high-born family.

'That wouldn't ever happen, Meg—' he called her Meg, said it was his own name for her, that LM didn't sound like the sort of woman she was. 'It would never happen, not in real life and you know it as well as I do.'

He had a certain passion for geography, dreaming of other places, other peoples and LM gave him, for their first Christmas together, a subscription to the *National Geographic* magazine, which he devoured, bombarding her with information about remote tribes in Africa, Eskimos, the Chinese and their astonishing early civilisation. He dreamed of travelling one day, if only to Europe; she promised him that they would do it together. She had travelled a little with her father, to Rome, Florence and Paris; she said it was indeed a most wonderful experience.

The more she knew of him, the better she liked him; even his considerable tactlessness was the result of an impeccable honesty which echoed her own. The only difference was that she had learned to stay silent, not to speak her mind.

He never said he loved her; but he told her he enjoyed being with her more than he had ever enjoyed anything. 'Except being with Annie of course.'

'Of course,' said LM, struggling not to feel hurt, and then he said that being with Annie was different, and she was not to mind.

'She was very young for a start,' he said, 'it was me telling her things, not the other way round.'

She could have talked to him forever; enjoyed their agreements, which were many, as much as their disagreements. On Sundays, they would go for long long walks, sometimes just over the Heath; sometimes they would take an omnibus out to the country, to the Hog's Back in Surrey, to Burnham Beeches in Buckinghamshire and talk endlessly, about politics, class, the countryside – in which he was surprisingly interested – about travel and religion. He was a passionate atheist, she was a modestly committed Anglican and liked to go to church.

'Although how you can look God in the face after what we've just been doing without His blessing, I don't know,' Jago said, the first time she left him on Sunday morning.

She told him she thought God had meant people to enjoy sex, and wouldn't care if they were married or not. 'And besides, I love the words. They're very beautiful. You should come with me.'

'Not me,' he said, reaching out to stroke her dark hair. 'If I did find God it'd be in a forest or on a mountain top, not in some grim church.'

LM said that was what all non-church goers said and that most churches were far from grim: 'Wait till you see Notre Dame Cathedral in Paris. Or St Peter's in Rome. Then you'll change your mind.'

Jago said he was quite happy to wait and turned over to go back to sleep.

They had been together now for three years; happy, odd years. They gave each other great contentment, saw one another at least three times a week, spent most Sundays together, shared one another's hopes, fears and pleasures, agreed that they were as happy as two people could be, and yet they told no one officially of their relationship. Jago feared ridicule from other people on the subject, and LM feared humiliation.

They occasionally discussed meeting one another's families, wondered whether it would make their lives together easier or more difficult, and always finally decided against it.

'They'd just be watching us, wondering how we got on and what might happen in the end,' Jago said. 'And not just yours, mine as well. Mine more so, I should say. So let's just keep ourselves to ourselves. It's worked pretty well so far. Might spoil it if we changed anything.'

It wasn't quite as difficult as one might suppose, this near-secrecy; their individual lives were perfectly self-sufficient. They both worked hard, long hours, albeit in rather different ways, and then LM's life had always been entirely absorbed by Lyttons, work, and to a lesser degree, her politics; they were hardly likely to find friends in common.

LM was quite sure it would not last, and if people saw her abandoned, left to her loneliness and singleness again, it would hurt twice as much. She was aware that Oliver and Celia suspected there was someone in her life, but they both respected her reticence: Oliver out of delicacy, Celia from a sense of sisterhood. Celia was an extraordinary woman friend; unquestioning, undemanding, untroubled by secrets. Her philosophy was based on the simple assumption that if LM – or indeed anyone – wanted to tell her something, then they would; if she did not, then Celia had no desire whatsoever to know it. LM was quite sure that if she had asked Celia to buy a white dress for her, recommend a priest and suggest some music suitable for a wedding (or, for that matter, to lend her a baby's cradle and a perambulator) she would do so without asking a single question.

There was, LM knew, no question of such a thing ever being necessary; Jago and she could be lovers, best friends, twin souls, but they could never be man and wife.

'It's unthinkable,' he had said once, adding, 'well, not unthinkable, but undoable.'

LM agreed with him, while crushing a pang of rather natural hurt. He had, not surprisingly, a dread of her becoming pregnant.

'I couldn't bear it,' he said, 'really couldn't stand it.' Every month he would ask anxiously whether she was 'all right' and would visibly relax when she told him she was. She was fairly confident that it would never happen; she had never been so much as a day late, even when she had been really young, and running appalling risks. At thirty-five, as she now was, it seemed extremely unlikely.

The only person who did know of course, was Mrs Bill; she had been with Edgar Lytton for many years, had watched LM grow up, and accepted what she saw as the extraordinary behaviour of her mistress with resignation and total discretion. She neither approved nor disapproved; it was LM's own business, and as incomprehensible to Mrs Bill as her insistence on working all the hours God sent, when there was not the slightest need for it.

One of the things Jago most liked and admired about LM was that she worked; it increased his respect for her. He never tired of hearing about it, not so much the details of the books they were publishing, that mostly bored him, but about the mechanics of the company, the cost of running it, the way books made a profit, or indeed a loss, and the number of people required to keep the operation going. He was also fascinated by the dynamics of her relationship with Oliver and Celia, how they could work together without strife.

'We do have strife, though,' LM said, laughing. 'We argue all the time. About what to publish, when, and how much it's going to sell at.'

'That's not strife,' he said, looking at her with genuine amazement, 'that's housekeeping, I mean who's the boss?'

'Oliver and I are the boss,' said LM, 'and Celia just works with us. Not for us, with us. It's perfectly simple.'

Jago said if that was simple, he was the Earl of Beckenham. He was much fascinated by Celia's parentage, by her life before her marriage, by her presentation at court; LM teased him about it and told him he was a social climber at heart. There were times when she really thought it was true.

'Now Mrs Miller, this is Lady Celia Lytton. Lady Celia, Sylvia Miller.'

Jess Hargreaves had been placed in charge of introducing various Fabian ladies to their subjects in Mrs Pember Reeves's survey. Her pleasant rather strong voice boomed through Sylvia's front room and into the room beyond, where the children, threatened with the loss of dripping for their tea if they misbehaved, sat listening enthralled.

'Mrs Miller has – what is it now, Mrs Miller – oh, yes, six children. Her husband works in a warehouse in the city. Mrs Miller is very happy for you to sit with her, and to tell you anything you want to know; but she is worried she may be rather too busy to give you much of her time. Also she is expecting again, and not feeling terribly well, especially towards the evening, so it might be better if you came in the mornings, while most of the children are at school. Only Barty, she's the baby, will be here then.'

Sylvia looked at the ladies anxiously; she had been worrying all day about their arrival, had scrubbed the steps specially, got the washing out, put Barty into a clean pinafore dress. Mrs Hargreaves had stressed that none of it was necessary, but it was all right for her, she didn't have to welcome a lady – and a Lady, what was more, they hadn't warned her about that – into a dirty house full of grubby children and pretend it didn't matter. She liked Mrs Hargreaves, but the new lady, she looked a bit – well a bit much with her hair piled up on her head and just a few curls escaping from a very large hat with an enormous bow at the side. She had lovely clothes, a loose cream wool coat over a long dress with a high lace collar, and very high-heeled shoes. Sylvia wished she could have had someone more normal.

She wished even more that she'd said no, right at the beginnning, that she'd got enough to worry about, without trying to remember what she spent on what, and which child had had which illnesses, without having someone watching her while she got on with her work. Ted had told her not to do it and she'd been going to refuse; but when Mrs Hargreaves came back to see what she'd decided, it had been the awful day when she'd realised she must have fallen again, and she was in such a state it was easier just to give in.

'Hallo, Mrs Miller,' said the lady, holding out her hand, 'it's so very good of you to let me do this. Can I hold your little girl? Just for a moment? I'm expecting myself, I've got a little boy already and I'm so hoping for a girl this time. Oh, isn't she pretty? And what lovely hair. It's the colour of a lion's mane.'

Sylvia hoped that the lady wouldn't notice the nits in the lion's mane. She'd spotted them herself that morning and hadn't had time yet to do anything about them.

'Well, I'll leave you to get acquainted,' said Mrs. Hargreaves, 'and you can arrange with Lady Celia which days would be best for her to come. I'm sure you're going to work together very well.'

Work together, Sylvia thought: that was a fine way of putting it.

But as time went on, it did get to feel rather like that. Lady Celia was

extremely tactful; she never pressed her for any information if she wasn't
certain about it, always asked her if she was sure she could spare the time
for her, and once or twice, when the evening sickness had been really
bad, had actually rolled up her sleeves and made the dripping
sandwiches for the children's tea. She wasn't supposed to do that, Sylvia
knew; she liked her for it. Nor did she ever make Sylvia feel
uncomfortable or inferior to her; indeed she always told her how
wonderfully she managed, that she could never do half so well herself,
and although she did have very nice clothes and arrived in a big
chauffeur-driven car, she chatted away to her in the most normal
manner about the children and Giles and her own pregnancy.

'I'm a bit worried, I'm so big already, only four months, I think I
must have a monster in there.' She often sent the chauffeur off with the
children for rides in the car, and although she was supposed to be
meticulous about getting every detail right in her notes, saying it was
important if the report was to be of any use, she sometimes would smile
at Sylvia conspiratorially and tell her she could always make it up if
Sylvia had forgotten whether she'd bought fourteen or fifteen loaves in a
week, or spent a shilling or elevenpence on the boot club. She clearly
found things like the boot club and the clothing club a bit difficult to
understand at first.

'Can't you just keep the money aside, and buy things when you need
them?'

Sylvia tried to explain that if the money was there it would get spent
on food. 'There's always a call on it. Important to have it where it can't
be touched.'

After a bit Lady Celia stopped asking about such things.

She adored Barty, and spent ages playing with her, or singing nursery
songs.

'I'd love to bring you some toys Giles has grown out of, and even
some clothes. His pinafores and so on would do wonderfully for her,
they're just like girls' clothes, but Mrs Hargreaves and Mrs Pember
Reeves both say it's absolutely forbidden. This whole thing is not about
charity, as I know you understand.'

Sylvia did know, and most of the time she wished it was; she would
have loved a few outgrown toys for Barty who was bored most of the
time now, being the ex-baby tied in her high chair for much of the day;
half her delight at seeing Lady Celia came from being released, taken
outside, shown books and played pat-a-cake with. Barty was so pretty
too, Sylvia could see why Lady Celia liked her. It was true about her
hair being the colour of a lion's mane, and she had a very long, delicate
neck; she was a clever little monkey, had learned to walk exceptionally
early, which was a pity, given her position in the family: better if she'd

been a pudding like Marjorie and Frank. As for clothes, Barty was dressed most of the time in what resembled rags; a few frilly pinafores from Lady Celia's nurseries would be very welcome.

Still the time and the attention were very welcome; from dreading Lady Celia's visits, she had come greatly to look forward to them. She wondered if Lady Celia enjoyed them as much. It really didn't seem very likely.

CHAPTER 5

It was almost Christmas. The Lytton house was filled with it, every downstairs room and the nursery decorated with garlands made of evergreen and bunches of holly. A vast tree stood in the hall, studded with wax candles, which were to be lit on Christmas Eve, the pile of presents under it growing daily. Wonderful smells of baking rose up from the kitchen, carol singers arrived almost every night, and Giles would stand at the door in his nightgown listening to them. Celia had taken him to see the giant Christmas tree in Trafalgar Square and the special shop windows in Regent Street and Knightsbridge, and they had sent a letter up the big chimney in the drawing-room to Santa Claus, carefully dated December 1909 to avoid confusion. Every house in Cheyne Walk was brilliant with lights, and the trees along the row were all strung with twinkling, star-like garlands. Celia had a child-like love of Christmas; this year, being pregnant, it seemed to her especially poignant. She remembered the Christmas when she had cried so unexpectedly and so often and felt the guilt ease away. She had planned Christmas surprises, bought and wrapped presents, organised a big Christmas dinner party and a children's party as well. Oliver, whose Christmases had been rather severe affairs, presided over by his overworked father, and without a mother to give them magic, teased her about her excitement, worried about her getting too tired, but became caught up in her starry happiness nonetheless.

Twice a week, though, the happiness faded, was replaced by guilt. The Miller house had no tree, no presents, and the street was dull and dark, apart from one tree in the window of the house at the end. Ted had promised to go and hack a branch of yew down from the park one night nearer Christmas; they could decorate that, he said, with a few sweets and chains of coloured paper, and they could set the two big candles he had been promised from the factory in the window. There wouldn't be much in the way of presents exactly, Sylvia explained to Celia.

'But Ted's doing overtime and we should be able to afford a ham on the bone, by way of a Christmas dinner. And some oranges and nuts.

And Ted's mum, she said she'd be over with some sweets for the children.'

Celia hadn't realised Ted had a mother; she'd assumed all four parents must be dead, or they would surely be helping their beleaguered children. It turned out that Sylvia's parents had both died, and so had Ted's father, but his mother lived with her only daughter in Catford.

'But they don't get on, her and Ted. She says he could do better in life. I'd like to know how. Anyway, we agreed years ago, it's better she stays away. Comes for Christmas Eve or thereabouts and that's enough.'

Celia had actually prepared a Christmas box for the Millers: little toys for all the children, a tin of pressed tongue, a small box of crackers, and some dried fruit. And a couple of warm shawls for the new baby. She had to be careful, if there was too much, the other families who were being observed might get to hear of it; there would be jealousy and she'd get into terrible trouble.

She was worried about Sylvia; she had almost two months to go, and hardly seemed able to drag herself about, she was even paler than usual, and apart from her large stomach, was wraith-thin. That was hardly surprising: Ted had been ill for a couple of weeks, unable to work, there'd been a shortfall in the money, and when there was less money, the children and the wife went without. The man needed the food to work; that was a given, an accepted precept, nobody questioned it. Even a pregnant wife. Even allowing for such problems, Sylvia was not herself. Normally brave and cheerful, she was much given to fretting, obsessed that there was something wrong with the baby.

'It's so small,' she said to Celia one cold, dark afternoon, 'and it's hardly kicking at all. I hope it'll be all right.'

'I'm sure it's all right,' said Celia soothingly, 'it's small because it's another girl, I expect.'

'Doesn't follow. I was huge with Marjorie. We've been lucky so far, not lost any. Most people have, out of six.'

Celia couldn't imagine how anyone in Sylvia's situation could regard themselves as lucky, but she smiled at her encouragingly.

'Well there you are. You're obviously a good, healthy mother, have good, healthy babies.'

'It's terrible when they die,' Sylvia said, her eyes gazing into space as she squeezed out the washing, 'really terrible.'

'Yes, of course it must be. Here, let me do that.'

'No, no you mustn't, Lady Celia. Not my washing.'

'Why not? I don't have to do my own,' said Celia simply, 'go and sit down, Sylvia, please. Give Barty a cuddle, she's been so good.'

She stood at the table, squeezing out the endless clothes. None of them looked very clean.

'What I mean is,' said Sylvia, stroking Barty's soft cheek, 'what I mean is, if the baby dies, there's a funeral to pay for. Over two pounds that can cost, and we only have insurance for thirty shillings.'

At least one shilling a week from a working class family budget went on burial insurance.

'Don't, Sylvia,' said Celia, distressed at this talk of babies' funerals, 'don't even think about it.'

'I have to think about it,' said Sylvia earnestly. 'And then if a child is born early and it's alive, and then it dies, you don't get no insurance at all. So it means a pauper's grave. We couldn't do that. We'd have to find the money somehow.' Her face was very drawn, her eyes heavy.

'Sylvia please! You mustn't distress yourself so much. Of course your baby won't die. It – she, I'm sure it's a she – will be lovely and strong. Just like Barty. There, shall I hang this up for you?'

'We'll leave it for now,' said Sylvia, 'till the children have had their tea. Nicer that way for them.'

The washing line hung in the kitchen, sagging over the small table; it was indeed much nicer without it.

'Anyway, Lady Celia, I shouldn't be talking like this, worrying you. You being in the family way as well.'

'Oh, well mine's a long way off,' said Celia, 'not till May. Only unlike you, I'm absolutely enormous. My doctor's coming to see me tomorrow actually. What does – what does your doctor say? About you being small?'

Sylvia looked at her, and her heavy eyes were almost amused. 'We don't see the doctor, Lady Celia. Not for a baby. It costs a lot of money, seeing a doctor does.'

Celia felt sick suddenly; she was always making these mistakes, saying stupid, thoughtless things. Here she was, over-cared for, over-indulged, her every ache and pain fussed over, her tiredness treated as an illness in itself, and Sylvia couldn't consult a doctor over a very real worry. It was terribly wrong.

'Sylvia, if you want to see a doctor,' she said quickly, knowing she was yet again overstepping the strictly drawn up boundaries, 'you could see mine. I would gladly arrange that. If you're really worried.'

Sylvia flushed, looked shocked. 'I couldn't,' she said, 'it's very kind of you, Lady Celia, but I really couldn't. It's only a baby. Not an illness. I'll be all right. Oh, now, here are the children. I'd best be getting on.'

Celia wondered miserably, as she was driven home, if she was actually making matters worse rather than better for the Millers.

'Good Lord,' said Oliver. He was reading a letter intently; he had been sorting through the post at the breakfast table, adding to the ever-growing crowd of Christmas cards on the sideboard.

'What?' asked Celia. She was buttering her third piece of toast; her appetite was enormous.

'My brother. He's getting married.'

'Well don't sound so surprised. He's twelve years older than you, I can't think why he hasn't been snapped up before. Who's the lucky girl?'

'Hardly a girl. She's older than Robert. She's – heavens. She's forty-two. A very elderly bride. How extraordinary.'

'Oliver, forty-two is hardly elderly. LM is nearly thirty-six. I shall tell her you said that, if you're not careful.'

'Oh, darling please don't. It was a slip of the tongue. But I am surprised. Robert so likes pretty girls.'

'Well maybe she's a pretty woman. Or a rich one,' she added thoughtfully.

'Celia, really! Anyway, Robert doesn't need to marry money. He's got more than enough already.'

'You don't know that, Oliver. Darling, don't look at me like that, I'm only joking. You know how much I adore him. I do hope they come to London to visit.'

'That's exactly what they are doing. As part of their honeymoon.'

'How lovely. When? I hope I'll still be able to move out of my chair.'

'You should be able to. Quite soon after Christmas. They're getting married just before, on Christmas Eve. Then sailing out of New York on January the first.'

'Of course we must ask them to stay,' said Celia. She looked at Oliver thoughtfully. 'All a bit sudden, isn't it? Maybe it's a shotgun wedding.'

'Celia, don't be ridiculous. Anyway, this was sent a while ago, it takes two weeks at least for a letter to come from New York.'

'I know. That still makes it sudden. What's her name?'

'Um – Jeanette. Mrs Jeanette Elliott. She's a widow. She has two sons. She has a house in New York City and – heavens, a house on Long Island as well.'

'There you are,' said Celia, 'a rich widow. How very intriguing. I can't wait to meet her. I shall start planning their visit today.'

It was extremely intriguing. Why should Robert Lytton, so good-looking and charming and rich, who had apparently always enjoyed his freedom so much, suddenly decide to marry a woman older than he was, with the added complication of two stepsons? There could be only two explanations, Celia thought, as she went upstairs to prepare herself for Dr Perring's visit; either Robert had fallen madly in love, or he needed some money. The latter seemed more likely. She was still pondering on it, and thinking how revealing the newly-weds' visit might be when Dr Perring arrived; what he had to tell her drove any thoughts about anything but herself straight out of her head.

He stood over her for a long time, first holding his stethoscope to her stomach, then probing it gently. He took so long that she began to feel anxious, that there must be something wrong.

'No,' he said, smiling down at her, folding the sheet back over her, 'nothing wrong. But I think I can hear two heartbeats. And you are very – large. I think you've probably got twins in there, Lady Celia. That is, if you are quite confident about the dates.'

'I'm quite confident,' said Celia. She was: she had conceived during a magical time she and Oliver had had in Venice the previous summer. In a vast bed in a vast room, the golden light on the water reflecting on the ceiling, at the Hotel Cipriani. She had absolutely no doubt about it. She managed to smile at the doctor, then lay looking down at her stomach in silence. She felt very shaken. Shaken and almost scared. Twins! Two babies: that was extremely strange. It was almost as if one of them was replacing the child she had lost.

Dr Perring patted her hand. 'You look rather pale. You mustn't worry, most women carry twins perfectly safely. The birth can be difficult of course, but you had no complications last time and you're still very young. Young and strong. I think I would like you to have them in a nursing home, rather than here, that would be my only advice.'

'Yes,' she said, 'yes of course. If that's what you think. Er – what makes twins Dr Perring, how does it happen?'

'Well, it's a division of the egg at the moment of fertilisation. Into two embryos. It's not that uncommon of course. But—'

'Yes, but what causes that, the division? Why should it happen?'

'Nobody knows,' he said, 'it's a mystery. Fun though, twins.' He smiled at her encouragingly. 'Most mothers enjoy them. They amuse each other and if they're the identical sort, you can dress them alike, all that sort of nonsense.'

'When will we know that?' asked Celia 'Not till they're born, I suppose?'

'No. They'll be the same sex, of course, if they're identical that is, but the real point is that they share a placenta. The afterbirth you know.'

'Yes. Yes, I do know. I've published a book about pregnancy and childcare.'

'I always forget,' he said, smiling at her, 'what a clever, well-informed young woman you are. It's very refreshing. Now there is one other thing, Lady Celia. I would advise extra rest. Extra care. Several hours a day with your feet up, early to bed, that sort of thing. The strain on your system will be considerable.'

'Yes,' she said dutifully, 'yes of course.'

After he had gone, she sat thinking. About all that it would mean. A big change, not just one more child, but two: a large family all at once. It was exciting: Dr Perring was right. It was also quite challenging. There was no question of the current nurseries being big enough: they would need to prepare a new day nursery and probably a new night nursery as well. And she would need more help: Jenny would have to have a permanent nursery maid. Possibly two. She'd like that. It would stand her in very good stead on the nanny benches in Kensington Gardens. And the maternity nurse would have to stay for longer than two months. The feeding would be very demanding. Giles's pram and cot wouldn't do either; she would have to buy a double pram, and another cot. Perhaps Sylvia would like her old pram. Just as a loan. The new baby could sleep in it. Then she thought, it was much too big; it would practically fill the little room, certainly take up all the available space.

She'd forgotten about Sylvia briefly; she started worrying about her again now. If she was to have this extra rest, she wouldn't be able to continue with her visits. If Oliver knew, he'd practically tie her to the bed. She had a feeling he'd welcome the excuse to do so: he was getting very weary of hearing about the Millers and their problems. But she must be around to help Sylvia when she had her baby. She couldn't fail her now. She'd need things like extra milk, extra food, clean sheets, napkins for the baby. The ones she'd seen had been in rags. She had already promised herself that she'd provide them; no matter what Mrs Pember Reeves said. She wasn't going to sit there, making her wretched notes, while Sylvia starved politely.

Celia made a decision. She would tell Oliver about the twins after Sylvia had had her baby. She would rest as much as she could until then, but she couldn't fail her new friend. And she would telephone Dr Perring and tell him she hadn't told Oliver yet, that he was very busy and she didn't want him worried until after Christmas. Or something like that. It only meant a delay of a few weeks.

'Of course I realise he probably doesn't love me as much as I love him.' Jeanette Elliott smiled serenely at her best friend, summoned to hear what she had described as some rather important news. 'I also know he probably likes the idea of my money. But I don't care, Marigold. I want to marry him.'

'You're mad,' said Marigold Harrington. She was well known in

New York society for her frankness. 'You really are completely mad. You'll regret it.'

'I don't think so. I really don't. I'm sure he's very fond of me. And I've been quite lonely since Jonathan died, you know. I actually rather like being married, that's the thing. I think Robert will be—' she hesitated, then said thoughtfully, 'an excellent husband. And the boys need a father. They are growing up fast, and—'

'Do they like Robert?'

'Oh yes,' said Jeanette quickly, 'very much.' She stood up, walked over to the window, and stood looking out across Central Park. 'Don't the trees in the park look beautiful, all lit up? I so love Christmas.'

'Jeannette—'

'Marigold, please! Let me enjoy being happy. Please. Robert wants to marry me. He doesn't have to. He's not a pauper, he has quite a lot of money of his own, he's very successful.'

'Which bank does he work for?'

'Lawsons. He worked for Morgans in London, and came to their New York office in 1902, moved to Lawsons eighteen months ago. He was well thought of there. Oh, I've checked him out, Marigold, have no fear. I'm not quite as stupid as you think.'

'I don't think you're stupid Jeanette. Not usually, anyway. I just think you're being a bit – blind. You know what they say about love.'

'Nonsense. I just told you, I have no illusions at all about Robert's feelings for me. But as I said, I think he'll make a very good husband. He's charming and amusing and good-looking.'

'Hardly the most important things.'

'In some ways they are. To me, at this point. And then he's very easy. Not the least like the standard stiff-necked Englishman. Most of my other friends like him very much; I don't see why . . .'

'Most of your other friends don't know you're going to marry him. And so soon. Anyway, I do like him. What I know of him. I've only met him two or three times, don't forget. I just don't see why you have to – well take such a big step. Why not just have him as your lover? For a while at least?'

'Oh, I've had him as my lover for a while,' said Jeanette cheerfully, her large blue-green eyes sparkling at Marigold with something close to malice, 'but now I want something more. We both do. And it would be very bad for the boys if that were to continue, if it became gossip. And with Laurence going off to Deerfield in the fall, everything has to be absolutely in order. No, I'm afraid you can't change my mind, Marigold. It's absolutely made up. Robert has written to his brother and sister and told them we are to be married, and now I am telling you. As my dearest and oldest friend. There will be an announcement in the

New York Times tomorrow. Then the whole world will know. And no doubt will have a great deal to say about it. Now won't you have a drink before you go. Tea, or a glass of wine?'

'All right, I can take a hint,' said Marigold. 'I'm leaving. We have to go to a concert tonight, at the Carnegie Hall. I should be on my way. Thank you for telling me anyway. Before the rest of the world.' She stood up, went across to Jeanette and kissed her. 'And I really do hope you'll be very happy.'

'I hope so too,' said Jeanette, 'thank you. And – you will come to the ceremony, won't you? You and Gerard?'

'Of course. Of course we will. Thank you.'

As her car joined the hectic traffic, Marigold looked up at the great Palladian-style house on Fifth Avenue, built by Jeanette's father-in-law as a monument to his money. Lights were blazing through the winter dusk, and there was a huge Christmas tree on the front lawn. Marigold thought that even if Robert Lytton did love Jeanette very much indeed, he would have to be a man of absolute innocence and unworldliness not to be at the very least aware of what he was acquiring when he married her. On the two occasions when she had met him, Robert Lytton had seemed to her very far from being either innocent or unworldly. But then of course, neither was Jeanette. Formidable was scarcely an adequate adjective to describe her. Marigold decided she could stop worrying about Jeanette; and began to wonder instead if Robert Lytton, for his part, knew exactly what he was taking on.

Jeanette Brownlow was only twenty years old when she married: it was a case of love at first sight on both sides. Jonathan Elliott had seen her across the room at a debutante ball two years earlier and decided he would like to marry her; she had accepted his invitation to dance, and before it was even half over had decided much the same thing. She had not at the time realised that Jonathan Elliott's father was Samuel Elliott, founder of Elliotts Bank, fast becoming one of the younger giants of Wall Street. When she did, it made him seem even more attractive.

Matters took a little time to settle; Jonathan was being pressed by his father to consider marriage to the daughter of an old friend, accomplished, but dull. Jeanette was not beautiful, but she was lively, stylish and very witty; she was also quite determined to marry Jonathan.

Three months later Jonathan told his father that he wanted to marry Jeanette. Samuel Elliott was not pleased: she had no fortune to speak off, her father was only a modestly successful businessman and she had a reputation for being wild. There was a story of Miss Brownlow climbing to the top of one of the statues in Central Park wearing nothing but her stays after a party, and another of her dressing up as a young man and going to a music hall. But Samuel reckoned without Jeanette's charm; she worked on him patiently and tirelessly for over twelve months, flattering him, amusing him, asking for his advice on her modest investments – thereby displaying, as far as he was concerned, not only her famous single-mindedness, but a certain shrewdness which he both liked and admired – and it was finally agreed that the young lovers should be allowed to marry when Jeanette was twenty.

After which she launched herself into the career of a corporate wife with extraordinary skill.

Her only failure was at child-bearing; for each of her two sons she had several miscarriages, and before Jamie, the younger, was born she had endured two stillbirths. It was agreed that there should be no more attempts at securing the large family she had longed for; and besides, as Jonathan, who was still deeply in love with her, pointed out, he had an heir and a spare and her energies could now be fully devoted to him.

Jeanette who had not enjoyed the torments of her child-bearing years, returned to her role of corporate hostess with some relief. When Jonathan was thirty-five, he became president of Elliotts; when he was forty, Samuel died; the family moved into the Fifth Avenue mansion and Jonathan took over the bank. He ran it superbly; his two greatest assets were a cool head, and absolute clearsightedness. In the panic of 1907, sparked off by a spate of overspeculation, while people fought to withdraw their money from their banks, he put out a statement saying that if they left it where it was, it would be safe. While other financial establishments panicked, he stayed calm, worked, together with JP Morgan and others, on persuading several of the major banks to put money into the stock exchange and joining Morgan in his warning that anyone on the stock exchange who panicked and thus exacerbated the problem would be, as Morgan famously put it, 'properly attended to' when the crisis was over. Eight banks did collapse and a great many financial institutions with them; but Elliotts was one which survived.

But also in 1907, Jonathan Elliott was diagnosed as having cancer and he died a year later. Jeanette was devastated; she had truly loved him, and he her, and not a day had passed since they met when they had not told one another so. Luckily, however, she had a brave and blithe spirit; she knew that a future either for her or her two boys, Laurence and James, could not be built on introspection and grief. Moreover she was a clever woman, with a clear grasp of the financial world; she demanded (and got) a position on the board of Elliotts, returned to her life as a hostess, and did her very best to see the boys were raised as Jonathan would have wished.

It was at a charity benefit in the summer of 1909 that she met Robert

Lytton. Recognising in him the same degree of looks, charm and determination, if not quite the financial prowess, that Jonathan had possessed, she moved swiftly into a relationship with him. After four months, he asked her to marry him; only a little – and not unnaturally – suspicious of him, she refused, but suggested that they should be lovers. Whether out of moral probity, or from a long-term shrewdness, Robert Lytton refused her offer until she had at least agreed to consider marriage; Jeanette, amused and charmed by this, as well as troubled by a certain sexual frustration, agreed that she would certainly continue to consider it. The discovery that sex with Robert was extremely pleasurable was only one of the factors which persuaded her to agree finally to his third proposal of marriage at the end of November.

She knew all her friends would be horrified. Marigold's view, that Robert was only after her money, was only the start of a huge and inexorable torrent; she would have to be very strong to stand against it. She did not mind, indeed the prospect quite amused her; as did people's naivety. She could look after herself; her own personal fortune was vast and she managed most of her stock and shareholdings with skill and pleasure. The two houses were in her name, and her role at the bank was an executive one, however much the new chairman might dislike it. When he tried to suggest that she should not attend major meetings any more, she reminded him gently that in less than ten years Laurence would be joining the bank, and it was important that the Elliott view and philosophy of banking was maintained for him. There was little, she argued, that Robert Lytton could do to move in on Elliotts and its assets; if he wished to work there, he would find it uncomfortable and quite possibly humiliating.

Robert was not Jonathan, she had no illusions on the matter, and she was certainly not blind to his faults. But he was clever and charming, she was physically and emotionally in love with him; her life as his wife would be a great deal more pleasant and amusing than it would be as Jonathan's widow. And besides, the boys needed a father figure: and they – well they would come to like Robert a lot. She was quite determined about that.

'I hate him,' said Laurence, 'I just hate him. He's so – so ingratiating. I don't know how Mother can. After Father.'

'What's ingratiating?' said Jamie.

'Slimy. Wanting to be your friend. Agreeing with everything, just so you'll like him. Ugh!'

'He doesn't seem so bad. He gave me that train set last time he came, said it wasn't even a Christmas present.'

'Exactly! Why do you think he did that?'

'Because I wanted it?' said Jamie hopefully.

'Of course not. To make you like him, think well of him. Well, I won't be bought by him, Jamie, even if you will. And if you are, I won't be your friend any more.'

Jamie said hastily that he wouldn't be bought by Robert Lytton either. He was quite frightened of Laurence. He took more after their grandfather than their father, with a tendency to go off into dark brooding silences. One day he said, he would be an even greater banker than Samuel Elliott: 'That's my plan. And Robert Lytton needn't think he can try and stop me.'

Jamie couldn't imagine why Robert Lytton should want to try; he seemed keen only that the two boys and he get along well. But Laurence was always right about things; so maybe he just didn't understand. Maybe he should try and like Robert less; only his mother had said she hoped they could all be friends, and it was very nice to see her happy again, hear her laughing. He loved his mother more than anyone else in the world; knowing how unhappy and lonely she had been after his father died had been worse than his own grief.

Anyway, Christmas was coming; he wasn't going to let any of this spoil it. And after Christmas, Grandmother Brownlow was coming to look after them while his mother and Robert Lytton went off to Europe on their honeymoon. They were going to see the London Lyttons, as Robert called them; and his mother had promised that next time they went to London, she would take him and Laurence as well. He'd asked if they couldn't go this time, but she'd said no.

'We're on our honeymoon, darling. We want to be on our own. Just this once.'

He didn't really know what that meant, but Laurence had explained. Or rather he'd told him that they'd be having sexual intercourse all the time.

'I think it's disgusting. At her age. She'd better not have a baby, that's all.'

Jamie wasn't entirely sure what sexual intercourse was, but the idea of his mother having a baby was dreadful. He was her baby; she was always saying so. She surely wouldn't want that to change.

Celia stood in the church, holding Giles's hand, wondering how she could be doing this: singing, actually singing *Away in a Manger*, listening to the choir, pointing out the crib: when only two hours before, she had – no don't think about it. Don't.

67

'Look,' she whispered to Giles, 'look, they're coming with the candles now.'

It was very dark in the church; it had been dark in the room. Sylvia's room. Too dark to see anything really. All those shadows. Impossible.

Giles squeezed her hand, looked up at her, smiled; Sylvia had squeezed her hand too, very feebly, whispered thank you. For what? For nothing. Nothing at all really. Just for – for comforting her over her baby. Her dead baby. It had been dead. Quite dead. Still and white and collapsed in on itself. On herself. A girl, it had been, as Celia had said. A tiny, sweet-faced girl. Too tiny. Born too soon.

The virgin's baby was enormous; rosy and smiling. Not tiny, not born too soon. Six weeks too soon. The virgin was smiling; Sylvia had smiled, finally, as she bent to kiss her goodbye, smiled through her tears.

'It's for the best,' she had said, 'poor baby.'

It had been for the best; the baby couldn't have survived. Even if she had been born alive. The midwife had said so.

She had a dreadful sort of wound on her back, and her legs were twisted together, literally wrapped round one another. But her face had been beautiful; peaceful and almost smiling. Celia knew she would never forget it, that face. As long as she lived.

She'd told Sylvia she would probably be coming that day, had been looking forward to it, to seeing her face when she opened the hamper. She'd sat in the car (having had the statutory rest) excited, like a child. It was going to be a lovely afternoon, and afterwards there was the carol service. She could really enjoy it this year. It was, after all, what Christmas was all about.

When she got there, had got out of the car, a man she'd never seen before – Ted she presumed – had been sitting on the steps. He was a big burly man; he looked at her and tried to smile.

'Are you Lady Celia?' he asked, as if there could be some doubt, as if people were always arriving in the street in large chauffeur-driven cars. Yes, she said, she was, she'd brought a few things for Christmas.

'She's having it,' he said, 'she's having the baby now. It's too early. She – she just started. A couple of hours ago. I had to get the midwife, she said, not just Beryl next door, it was all going wrong she said.' He looked dreadful, ashen, was shaking.

'Oh God,' Celia said, 'oh, God. I'm so sorry. I'll go away. At once. I'll come back tomorrow, when it's over.'

'No,' he said, 'no, she said, if you came, could you go in. She said it would – help.'

'But—'

'Please,' he said, 'she was so frightened this time. I don't know why.'
Celia looked at him. She felt rather frightened herself.

'Mummy – Mummy. Can we go and see the baby?'

'No darling, you can't. I'm sorry—'

'The other children are . . .'

What was she saying? She was thinking of the other baby again, of Sylvia's baby. Not the one in the crib. She took a deep breath, managed to smile at Giles.

'Yes, of course. Sorry, darling. Mummy wasn't thinking. Come on, we'll go and look at the baby. Bring your candle.'

They walked across to the crib; stood in the queue to put their candle by it. She looked down at the baby in the crib; at the smiling rosy baby.

She'd looked down at the other one; lying so still and white, in her arms. Only a few minutes old, only a few minutes dead. The midwife, Mrs Jessop she was called, had tried to revive her, massaged her chest, breathed into her little mouth, but it hadn't done any good. She had simply lain there, white and still and somehow broken. Like a doll. Mrs Jessop had handed her to Celia, had gone tutting off to her own house down the street to fetch more towels and newspapers.

'I told them to get plenty, they should know by now. You stay with her, she can't be left.'

'It's for the best,' Sylvia said, determinedly brave, looking up at her from the bed, 'it's for the best really. I knew there was something wrong. I knew. Can – can I hold her? Just for a moment.'

Celia handed the baby over tenderly; Mrs Jessop had wrapped her in a towel. She kept thinking of the shawl she had bought, thinking foolishly that the baby would be warmer in it. Sylvia looked at her, stroked her face.

'Oh, the poor poor little thing. Look at her, look at her legs, oh, it's so dreadful. I knew, I knew, didn't I say?'

And yes, Celia, said, she had indeed said. 'Well, thank God, thank God she died – oh dear God.'

Sylvia started to cry; quietly at first then more loudly. Celia felt absolutely helpless, not knowing what to do in the face of such grief, so she just stayed there, looking down at them, at Sylvia and the baby, half crying herself.

And then it happened. Or had it? It was so hard, so hard to see. But the tiny chest had moved, she thought. Or was it the lamp? Flickering, guttering, with the cold wind coming in the door. Did it just look as if it had moved? Surely, surely it couldn't have. But then it happened again.

The chest moved again. And this time Sylvia saw it. And then there was a tiny sigh. And, 'Oh God,' Sylvia said, 'oh dear God, no.'

And then she looked at Celia and said quite calmly, as if she was standing up, perfectly well, wringing out the washing, or cutting bread, 'Will you help me?'

And Celia had said, just as calmly, 'Yes, I'll help you.' All she had done was fetch her a pillow; that was all. She was sure that was all. To lay the baby on.

'Mummy, put your candle down. Go on.'

'Sorry darling.'

'Here, with the others.'

'Sorry.' She put her candle down. They were all flickering. Brilliant, golden, dozens of them.

The light had flickered like that in the room. Perhaps, perhaps they had both been mistaken. Yes, they probably had. The baby hadn't breathed at all. She couldn't have done. She had twisted legs and a damaged spine and she had been born dead. She hadn't breathed. To believe anything else was madness. The midwife had tried to revive her and she hadn't been able to. And anyway, she couldn't have survived, having not breathed for so long, her brain would surely be damaged too, starved, like the body, of oxygen.

Mrs Jessop had appeared rather annoyed that everything had changed, that Sylvia herself was holding the baby, that she was now wrapped in a shawl, rather than in the threadbare towel. 'I left you holding it,' she said to Celia, 'what's been going on?'

'Nothing's been going on,' said Celia. 'Mrs Miller wanted to hold her baby. That's perfectly natural. It – comforted her. I gave her the baby to hold. And wrapped her in the shawl. I brought the shawl, it was a Christmas present.'

'Well, I'll take it now,' Mrs Jessop said. 'I have to take it away.'

'It's she, not it,' said Celia. 'She's a girl. A baby.'

'Whatever it is,' said Mrs Jessop, 'it's dead. So I have to take it.'

'Yes,' said Celia, 'yes, that's true. She certainly is dead.'

'Why are you crying?' asked Giles.

'I'm not crying.'

'You are.'

'I have something in my eye.'

'Poor Mummy. Let's go back to our place.' He looked again into the crib. 'Is the baby asleep?'

'Oh yes, I think so.'

'His eyes are open.'

'I know. But I think he's asleep.'

Billy had said that, when she'd left: 'Is the baby asleep?' He was at the top of next door's steps waiting to find out what had happened.

It had been difficult to answer, but she knew she had to; it would be one thing that would help Sylvia and Ted, not having to break it to the children.

'I'm sorry, Billy,' she said, sitting down on the steps, taking him on her knee, big boy as he was, 'I'm afraid the baby's died. I'm so sorry. It was a little girl and she – she was very ill. But your mummy's perfectly well,' she added, 'and she said she'd see you later. When she's had a little rest.'

She suddenly felt she needed a little rest herself; she couldn't imagine feeling anything but utterly exhausted ever again.

CHAPTER 6

The doctor was wearing a black tie; his expression as he came into the waiting room was sombre. God, Oliver thought, dear God, something's happened, something terrible's happened. He wondered wildly if he kept a black tie in his rooms at the nursing home in permanent readiness for tragedy. Deaths of babies, deaths of mothers. Twice as likely, perhaps, with twins. He stood up, braced himself physically for what he was about to hear. Let it be the babies, dear God, please let it be the babies.

The doctor smiled: beamed, held out his hand and shook Oliver's enthusiastically. And Oliver realised. The black tie was for the king. The king had died that morning. In his anxiety over Celia, he had quite forgotten. The hard-living, pleasure-seeking, philandering king was dead: long live the king. But—

'Marvellous news,' said the doctor. 'Girls. Twin girls. Identical.'

'And my wife—'

'Very well indeed. She did splendidly. Very brave, very brave indeed. And now she is extremely happy of course.'

'May I go in?'

'You may.'

Oliver pushed open the door gently, looked in at Celia. She was lying back on a mountain of frilled pillows; she was pale and her eyes were shadowy, but she smiled at him radiantly.

'Isn't it marvellous? Aren't I clever? Look at them Oliver, look at them, they're beautiful.'

'In a minute. I want to look at you first. My darling. My dearest darling. Thank God you're all right. The doctor said you were very brave.'

'I was quite brave,' she said cheerfully, 'but it wasn't nearly as bad as Giles. Even though there were two of them. And I had some wonderful whiffs of chloroform.'

Oliver shuddered within himself; he was not physically brave, indeed he was not particularly brave in any way, he knew. And the thought of what Celia, any woman, had to go through to bring a child into the world filled him with a sort of sick awe.

'I love you so much,' he said simply.

'And I love you. Do look at them, Oliver, go on.'

He went over to the two cradles, set side by side. Beneath their mountain of blankets, two absolutely identical faces looked up at him: unseeing dark blue eyes, thick dark hair, tiny rosebud mouths, finely waving, frond-like fingers.

'They're lovely,' he said, His voice had a catch in it.

'Aren't they? I'm so, so proud. And pleased and excited and – well everything really. Shall I tell you what I think we ought to call them?'

'Tell me.'

'Venetia and Adele.'

He smiled at her. 'Why? Very nice, but why?'

'Venetia after Venice. Which is where they were conceived. And Adele because it was my grandmother's name. And she was named after William the Conqueror's youngest daughter, she was called Adele, and she married Stephen of Blois and became a saint. So good omens all round.'

'Yes,' said Oliver slightly feebly. He knew there was no point arguing with Celia; she had clearly made up her mind. And they were nice names: he might have chosen different ones, plainer perhaps, more English. But she had had the babies, after all.

'I was thinking, darling, as I was having them, we ought to do a book of names. A sort of dictionary. What do you think? Every single mother-to-be would buy it. I think it would do awful well.'

'Celia,' said Oliver, sitting down, taking her hand, smoothing back her hair, 'Celia, how can you possibly manage to think about books and publishing when you've just had twin babies?'

'Oh really, Oliver,' she said, 'I never stop thinking about books and publishing. You know that. Even when I wasn't allowed to work, and all the time I was pregnant, I was thinking about them. And I'll tell you something else. I can't wait to get back to it. Well, you know, in a month or two.'

Oliver looked at her doubtfully. He had rather hoped that she might have enjoyed the past few months so much that it would convert her to a life of domesticity. He was obviously wrong, if she was talking about coming back to work a mere hour after she had given birth. Of course she couldn't. She wouldn't. He was very anxious that she shouldn't rush back. Apart from anything else, Giles would need attention; the entry of an extremely powerful invading force into his safe cosy self-centred little world was bound to be difficult for him. And then Oliver was never quite sure if he really liked Celia being at Lyttons or not. She had a lot of

73

very good ideas, she had a strong visual sense, she seemed to possess an instinctive grasp of publishing and what would do well and what wouldn't, but he did feel constantly undermined by her presence, robbed just slightly of authority, of the mystique of being the person in charge. And she was so good at presenting her views, and at dismissing the arguments which opposed them (usually presented by himself) that she was almost irresistible. Which meant he knew he would lose almost before he had begun.

It wasn't working with women that he minded; he had always done that, always enjoyed it, and made use of LM's clear mind and talents. It was working with his wife that was emotionally difficult; it was so hard to ignore intimate knowledge, to set aside domestic disputes, to resist personal pressure. However, there was no point arguing with her about that either: she would come back when she wanted. He knew that very well.

'Twin girls!' said Jago. 'Very nice. God, I bet they'll be a handful.'

'I'm sure they will,' said LM, 'they're already in danger of taking over the entire household, as far as I can make out.'

'The one I feel sorry for is the poor little bugger who's there already. He won't get much of a look-in will he? One small nose properly out of joint there, I'd say.'

'Oh, I don't know,' said LM, 'Celia and Oliver are very good parents. I'm sure they'll be careful with Giles.'

'Twin girls!' said Jeanette. 'How very, very lovely. What are they called? Boys, you have two new cousins. Two little girls. Wouldn't you like to meet them?'

'I don't know,' said Jamie.

'No thanks,' said Laurence.

'No thank you,' said Jamie.

DOUBLY FANTASTIC NEWS STOP CAN'T WAIT TO MEET THEM STOP DOUBLE CONGRATULATIONS STOP WANT TO BE GODFATHER STOP LOVE JACK

'Darling Jack. Not sure about the godfather bit though . . .'

'Why not? He is their uncle.'

'Oliver! Godfathers are supposed to be a good influence. Oh, I'm only teasing. Of course he can be a godfather. As long as we have a really stolid one to balance him. When does he go out to India?'

'In August.'

'Well that's fine. Plenty of time for the christening.'

'Two babies!' said Giles. 'Why two? One is all we need.'

'Darling, it'll be fun.'

'No it won't.'

'Why not?'

'Well because they'll play with each other. They won't want to play with me. I think one should go back.'

'Oh Giles, don't be silly. Of course they'll want to play with you.'

Giles looked at her and his little face was wary. 'I don't think they will.'

'Well I'm sorry, darling, but I can't do anything about it. Two babies is what came and two babies are staying. And they're very sweet and very lovely, and we're very lucky to have them.'

Giles didn't say any more. Like his father, he had learned not to argue with his mother. But he didn't think he was lucky at all. The babies had already taken over the nursery and most of Nanny's time, there were two more nursery maids, neither of whom seemed very interested in him, and another lady who certainly wasn't. Everyone who came to the house, his aunt, his grandmother, his mother's friends, his own friends even, and their mothers and nannies, went on and on about how wonderful to have twins, how unusual, how special they were, how exciting, how beautiful.

The only person who had seemed to understand how he might be feeling was his grandfather; he had had a look at the twins and said, 'Very nice,' and then turned, winked at him, and said, 'pretty boring, babies, aren't they? And two are twice as boring. Let's go for a walk by the river and look at the boats.' Giles had really appreciated that.

All the stupid twins ever did was cry and want bottles. And his mother had far less time for him as well, was always exclaiming over them, saying how they were both crying or smiling or touching each other, and how even she couldn't tell the difference between them. They had to wear little ribbons pinned to their blankets and shawls and their cots, so that everyone knew which was which, white for Adele, yellow for Venetia. Giles had managed to swap them over once, it had seemed a nice little piece of revenge for all the trouble they were causing him; he'd liked the thought of them growing up from then on with the wrong names, but Nanny had noticed. Apparently Venetia had a thing on her bottom called a mole, so they were swapped back again.

75

Nobody actually said anything to him, but he was afraid that Nanny, for one, had suspected him. Nanny was the nicest about it, she actually seemed to realise there was more to life than having two sisters who looked exactly the same, but that didn't stop her being too busy to play with him most of the time. Nor him being bored, stuck up in the nursery, listening to the twins crying.

Thank goodness he would be going to school soon.

'Twins!' said Sylvia. 'Twin girls. Oh, Lady Celia, how lovely.'

She managed to smile; but actually she felt more like crying. She felt like crying most of the time these days. Ever since the poor little girl had been born and died. It was all too much for her. Barty was driving her mad, crying to get out of her high chair all the time, and if she did get her down, getting into terrible mischief, and she just didn't have the energy to cope with her. The other children just got noisier and noisier and ate more and more and made more and more washing.

Ted was bringing home a bit of money, which helped, but that was another thing, he'd started drinking. Not a lot, but enough every Saturday to make him behave differently. A bit less gentle. He'd hit Billy more than once, when Billy was being cheeky. And he was always wanting to do it, as well. Every Saturday. She was so frightened, so terrified of falling pregnant again. Every night, when she finally dropped exhaustedly to sleep, she saw the baby, the little peaceful face and the twisted legs, and woke up crying. And then she couldn't get back to sleep, what with Ted snoring and the worrying about everything. So she was tired, much tireder than she ever had been, all the time. It was awful.

'I'll bring them to see you,' Lady Celia was saying, 'if you like.'

Sylvia said that would be lovely and tried to imagine finding space for Lady Celia to sit with both her babies in the front room, and hearing what she said even, with Barty crying and struggling to get out of her high chair. She didn't like to complain, but life really was getting worse. She'd always thought it would get better. That was surely what it was supposed to do.

'I've been laid off,' said Jago.

'Oh Jago, no. Why?'

He shrugged. 'Usual. The boss wants to cut costs, get the houses up cheaper. So – it's fewer people doing more work. And I'm not one of the few.'

'I'm sorry,' said LM. She couldn't imagine anything much worse than being out of work: it wasn't just the loss of money, it was the idleness, the boredom, the sense of futility in life. On her long walk to work each day she passed men who were just standing about, waiting outside building yards or factories in the hope of a day's casual work; they all looked the same, not just gaunt and shabby, but depressed, hangdog. It seemed to her dreadful that people, willing and able to work, were refused the opportunity.

'What will you do?' she said.

'Oh, look for casual work. Till I find something solid again. At least I haven't got a family to worry about. They're the really unlucky ones. Bloke working on the houses with me last week, he'd been out of work for five months, ended up walking four hours a day to the one job he could get.'

'Four hours!' said LM. 'But that's ridiculous.'

'Didn't have a choice, did he? At least he kept his family fed. Four kiddies he's got and another on the way.'

'And has he been laid off?'

'Oh yes,' said Jago.

'My darling,' said Robert.

'Yes, my dearest?'

He hesitated. He had been rehearsing this conversation over and over in his head for weeks; he knew exactly what he wanted to say, had the exact arguments to present. And he knew there was no logical reason why she should not agree.

But—

'Dearest? Which do you think?'

She smiled at him; she was standing in front of the mirror over the dining-room fireplace, trying on earrings. He had bought her a pair of diamond ones at Tiffany's for her birthday; she was wearing those, and was holding up another pair to her ears. A pair that Jonathan had given her. Jonathan had given her most of her jewellery of course; a twenty-two-year marriage provided plenty of opportunity for generosity. And it was all beautiful. He had clearly had perfect taste, as well as being a brilliant financier and a wonderful husband.

Sometimes – quite often in fact, Robert felt he disliked Jonathan Elliott. Disliked him intensely. It was ridiculous of course; Jonathan was dead, Robert had never known him, and it was hardly reasonable to expect that he would not be a considerable presence in his wife's life. But the influence he exerted was still so extremely strong; over the house, the servants, the children, and over Jeanette. She never openly acknowledged it, never said Jonathan said this, Jonathan had liked things done like that; but where he had established a way of doing things, a set of rules, a view even, she was inclined still to conform to it. And so were the children. If Laurence was anything to go by, then Robert felt his dislike was justified.

Laurence was a nightmare: hostile, clever, extremely devious. He was never *actually* rude to Robert in front of his mother, just awkward, difficult. But if Jeanette were not around, he was openly insolent. And there was nothing Robert could do about it. He could hardly go running to her, telling tales of Laurence's rudeness. Apart from anything else, it made him look impotent and foolish. And they had agreed, from the very beginning, that disciplining the boys must remain her territory, although Robert's implicit back-up would clearly be a great help to her. And even if he did tell her about Laurence's behaviour, she wouldn't believe it. She knew he was being difficult, finding it hard to accept Robert, but she insisted that time would take care of it.

'The only way is to be patient, my dearest. Patient and understanding. He is only a child, only fourteen. He loved his father very much. We must try to see it his way.'

What Robert wanted to talk to her about though, was nothing to do with Laurence. It was about himself. He wanted her backing in an enterprise of his own. He wanted to found his own business. It wasn't that he wasn't doing well at Lawsons; he had risen fast, and was already vice-president of the private client division. He had a good salary, an impressive office, and a burgeoning client list. But he knew that having his own business was the only way, he would achieve the kind of success he had always wanted. It certainly wasn't going to happen at Lawsons: there were two further generations of the family rising in the hierarchy, and they would take the company over. Neither did he wish to work at Elliotts: under the eye and aegis of his new wife. That would not be a pleasant experience.

In any case, it was not further into the area of banking that Robert wished to move. He was growing bored with that: with the predictability of it, the ebb and flow of money, the rise and fall of the markets. He had developed a new passion, an interest in property. He had watched the high speed rise of New York over the past decade, the way that buildings, endless rows of buildings, were growing into a sturdy forest, covering what had been the outskirts of the city, converting them into an ever-growing centre, and knew he wanted to be part of it. That was where the future lay, that was where the money was being put down, that was where it could be harvested. He had a client who was in the real estate business; five years earlier Robert had helped him raise the capital for two modest buildings off Wall Street. Today he was a rich man. Not a millionaire: but rich. And he had suggested that Robert might be interested in joining him in his business. In helping him to expand. Robert wanted to do that very much. Every time he thought about it, he felt excited, emotionally as well as intellectually. It was quite a long time since he had felt like that. He had already done some research, investigated the potential of the area west of Broadway, down to the docks. It seemed limitless. One of the streets he had earmarked, in fact, was already being built on. That had given him confidence. He was convinced he could make a success of it. And it would be very nice to be a success. A proper success. In his own right. Not just a shadow of his wife's former husband, not just a shadow, indeed, of his wife.

Not that he was not very fond of Jeanette: of course he was. He was extremely happy with her. She was as warm, as amusing, as passionate, as he had hoped. She was also witty and very stylish; mostly bought her clothes in New York, but she shopped in Paris, too and patronised Poiret who was the first to introduce the narrow hobble skirt, in daringly simple moulded silks and satins, she had a wonderful collection of evening gowns, all cut very low to reveal her unarguably splendid bosom, and she was always first with every new hairstyle; her remarkable, still vibrant red-gold hair being one of her greatest vanities. Robert was truly and genuinely proud of her, and to be seen with her.

They shared a great deal, not only a love of good food – Robert had gained at least ten pounds since their marriage – but also art, music, travel, and good company. They sought people out; they entertained constantly. The magnificent house on Fifth Avenue with its ballroom, its music room, its drawing-room, its galleries and its superb grounds, had been designed as a show place; and Jeanette loved to show it off. She was tireless and tirelessly imaginative; she gave not only dinners and luncheon parties, but concerts and garden parties, and such novelty affairs as the treasure hunts and fancy dress balls which were so popular in London at the time.

She often said she wished she had a house in London; her honeymoon visit there, when she and Robert had stayed with Oliver and Celia, had made her love it more than ever. There was high society and a season in New York and Washington, of course: but they somehow lacked the careless arrogance of London, they were more watchful, more self-conscious. And New York was so far from Europe, from the exotic glittering play-palaces of France and the artistic treasures of Italy: nor did it have a King and Queen to grace it. Jeanette was obsessed by royalty. She was far more impressed that Celia had been presented to the King and Queen at Buckingham Palace, than by the fact that she was a senior editor at Lyttons and had published a great many successful books.

But the highlight of the visit was meeting Lady Beckenham, who had arrived at Cheyne Walk with a distinctly malicious light in her eyes, had talked about house parties at Sandringham and Windsor, revealed various bits of titillating gossip about the King and Little Mrs George as Mrs Keppel was called in royal circles, and told Jeanette that she had a box at Ascot. Jeanette was gently amused by Celia's socialism, sceptical of her claims that people like Jenny and Sylvia Miller were her friends; Robert told Jeanette that she was more of a snob than Lady Beckenham herself.

'Nonsense,' Jeanette said, but he persisted, adding that in his experience there was no more snobbish creature on God's earth than an over-privileged American, 'And you are very over-privileged.'

Jeanette accepted this with her usual good humour, adding that she had not noticed any particular reluctance on his part to share that privilege. He managed to smile; but he actually hated such observations. They were her revenge whenever he crossed her, in however small a way; he felt put in his place; diminished. It was a sensation he had learned to tolerate very early in their relationship.

'My darling,' Robert said again now.

'Yes, my dearest. I can see you're not interested in my earrings. And why should you be? I shall wear yours, in that case. Did you want to talk to me about something? Ah Laurence, there you are. My darling boy, you look so handsome. I'm looking forward to having you at our luncheon party today. I want you to sit next to me and impress everyone. Doesn't he look handsome, Robert, in that suit?'

'Thank you, mamma,' Laurence turned his dazzling smile on her, looked briefly and coldly at Robert and then picked up a book that was lying on the table.

'He does, yes,' said Robert with difficulty. And Laurence did: he was a handsome child, with his father's fine features and his mother's colouring; he was tall for his age, yet without any of the unpleasant physical characteristics of adolescence, his skin was clear, his voice unbroken, and he moved with grace and confidence. Robert frequently found himself wishing passionately for the first outbreak of pustules on that high, aristocratic forehead.

'Now Robert, what was it, my dearest? I'm sorry I interrupted you.'

'Oh – it's nothing,' said Robert. He had no desire to launch into a discussion about his prospects and a request for financial backing in Laurence's presence.

'No, I insist. It's not fair, you've been trying to talk to me all morning. Laurence won't mind, will you darling, if we talk grown-up for a bit?'

'Of course not,' said Laurence. He looked at Robert, his eyes amused.

He knows, Robert thought, he knows I don't want to discuss whatever it is while he's here.

'You see. Go on, Robert, do. I'm quite intrigued.'

'No really,' said Robert firmly. 'It's only about a client of mine I thought you might meet.'

'Yes? Which one?'

'Oh – name of John Brewer. Very clever, runs a real estate company. Look, it isn't important. I have to get ready for luncheon myself.'

'Yes, but dearest, why especially did you want me to meet him? I do want to know.'

'Jeanette—'

'Mama,' said Laurence, his voice more drawling than usual, clearly amused, 'I don't think Robert wants to have this discussion in front of me. That's perfectly all right. I understand. I have plenty of other things to do.'

'Well that's absurd,' said Jeanette. 'Why should Robert not want to have a discussion in front of you? I can understand you not wanting to listen to it, of course, client talk is very boring. But—'

'No, Mama, I can see it would be better if I weren't here. I'll see you at luncheon.' He stood up, walked out of the room, with the same malicious expression in his pale eyes as he looked at Robert.

Jeanette smiled after him. 'He's so sensitive isn't he? Which is precisely why he's a little difficult at times. I mean, I had no idea you would prefer to have this conversation in private.' She smiled encouragingly at Robert. 'What is it about? You have my absolute attention, and I am highly intrigued now.'

Robert took a deep breath. If he didn't tell her now, it would become a big issue between them. Jeanette couldn't bear to be kept from information – of any kind.

'I – have developed an ambition to – to have my own firm,' he said. Jeanette smiled at him encouragingly, her expression eager, interested, inviting. But her pale eyes were glassy-hard.

'Yes?' she said. 'That sounds very interesting to me. I've always liked your ambition, Robert. I am attracted by ambition. As you must realise. Jonathan was hardly a low-achiever.'

'No indeed. Well, I'm pleased to have your support at least. You see, I – I feel I have reached a plateau at Lawsons. I can't get much further there. It is very much a family-based firm. And I have been developing other interests.'

'Other interests?' Her expression was amused.

'Yes. Other business areas.'

'Which area precisely?'

'Real estate. The client I mentioned, John Brewer, has done extraordinarily well, from quite a modest base. He has built what amounts to several streets now, in the financial district.'

'That sounds most interesting,' she said, 'I look forward to meeting Mr Brewer.'

'I look forward to it, too. He's very amusing. The thing is, Jeanette, it is in real estate now that I feel my future lies. That I have a real instinct, a proper feeling for. There's something about bricks and mortar that I like, it's real, substantial, not some notional substance existing largely on paper.'

'Hardly,' she said coolly, 'we may not be quite on the gold standard like Great Britain – a huge mistake on their part, in my opinion, to cling to that – but the notional substance, as you call it, certainly exists. It can be called from any bank at any time.'

'Yes, of course. But I just feel a great sympathy for the property business. I feel I could get properly to grips with it. Make it a field of my own.'

'As you have failed to do in banking. Is that what you're saying?'

'No,' he said sharply, 'no I'm not saying that. I don't think I have failed in banking.'

She smiled suddenly. 'Neither do I, Robert. I know you are extremely highly thought of at Lawsons. Extremely.'

It was an arrogant, patronising remark. He didn't like it.

'Jeanette,' he said, 'I don't think you quite understand—'

She interrupted him. Smiled her sudden, brilliant smile, disconcerting him as she often did with a switch in emotional temperature.

'It's all right, I think I do. You are a young man.'

'Not exactly young,' he said, 'that's why—'

'Thirty-nine is young. In my view. Anyway, we won't argue about that. You want to make your own way. That is exactly as it should be. And I have some – sympathy – for your wishing to change fields. And I would have thought that real estate certainly has a great deal of potential. Yes, in principle, it sounds a splendid idea. Most commendable.'

Robert wasn't quite sure if he liked commendable, it smacked of a school report; but he was encouraged by her enthusiasm.

He looked at her; she smiled again.

'Is there any more?'

'Yes. Yes there is. I have naturally done some work on this. Budgets, forecasts, where one might look for the most growth, both geographically and financially.'

'Yes?'

'And of course we are in a period of rapid financial growth at the moment. A good time to proceed with such a venture.'

'Ye-es. Very possibly. I could ask one of the partners, if you like. Now, what would the next step be?'

'Well,' said Robert, taking a deep breath, both metaphorically and literally, 'well, John Brewer has suggested that we go into partnership.'

'I would be much in favour of that. He has an established business, he is familiar with all the areas you are not. And I imagine what you would bring to the arrangement would be, among other things, some financial input. Contacts, know-how, all that sort of thing.'

'Yes, indeed. But—'

'Yes?'

'John wants to expand. Naturally. That would be the basis for my joining him.'

'Naturally.'

'And so – we would be – that is, initially we would be looking for backing.'

'Yes?'

'Indeed I could not proceed without it.'

'Of course.'

'I have put out several feelers. Nothing more than that. But I – well, I wondered if you – that is, if Elliotts might be able to—'

'To what, Robert?'

He felt himself beginning to sweat. This was precisely what he had been afraid of; that the obtuseness which she could summon at will, which she had made an art form, would confront him at this stage. That he would have to make a long, painful journey of the conversation, say every single, difficult word: rather than be allowed to take a blessed short cut.

'To, well to put up some of the money. Not all of it of course. But a – a proportion of it. On a strictly business basis, of course. I wouldn't be looking for any kind of – of favourable treatment.'

There was a long silence; then she walked over to the window, stood looking out. He watched her: her slightly broad back, her long neck, her elaborate hair. She seemed to stand there for a long time. Then she turned round and faced him.

'Robert,' she said.

'Yes?'

'Robert, I am finding this very difficult.'

'If you find it difficult, then please, don't even think about it any further. Without talking to the board. I understand.'

'I don't think you do. It's not the concept that I find difficult, not the

83

idea of your having a real estate company, it's that you should have asked me for the money.'

'Not you, Jeanette, Elliotts.'

'Please don't be obtuse. However you dress it up, you are asking for the money from me. You would hardly be going direct to the loan department at Elliotts would you? Without asking me first?'

'No,' he said, 'that would clearly be ridiculous.'

'Indeed. But even if you did, then you would still be in an advantaged position.'

'Jeanette—'

'Robert, please. Just give me a moment. While I—' she stopped.

'While you what?'

'While I — calm myself.'

'Calm yourself? What about?'

'Surely you must realise — no obviously you don't — realise how — how distressed I feel.'

'Distressed? But why?'

'Because it seems my friends were right,' she said with a heavy sigh. Absurdly heavy, it seemed to him.

'What? What do you mean, what were your friends right about?'

'They said — many of them said — that you were marrying me for my money. I told them it was absurd, that there was no question of such a thing, that I was quite sure you loved me. I went into our marriage believing that. It seems I was mistaken.'

'Darling, this is ridiculous. Of course you're not mistaken. And of course I love you. Very much. But—'

'Yes Robert? But what?'

He was silent.

'Please do go on.'

'It just seemed foolish,' he said finally, his voice low, 'not to approach you about such a matter.'

'Foolish? Indeed?' She turned round; her eyes were full of tears. 'I'm sorry you would think it foolish to be honourable. Not to try to take advantage of me, not to try to benefit financially from our marriage.'

'Oh really!' he said, a rush of anger hitting him, 'you're being childish. Absurd.'

'I don't think so.'

'You are. I am not trying to take advantage of you, as you put it. I'm hoping, Jeanette, to become more independent from you, not less. So that I benefit less from our marriage financially. Not more.'

'Whatever your reasons or justifications, I find it very painful. And I could not agree to it,' she said, finally. She pulled a handkerchief from her sleeve, blew her nose, dabbed at her eyes. 'I'm more than delighted to support you in your new enterprise in any other way I can. Believe me. But financially – no. I'm sorry. I couldn't even consider it. Now – if you will excuse me, I have to repair my face and restore my equilibrium. I am going to my room for a while. I'll see you on the garden terrace at lunchtime.'

Robert stood looking after her; he wondered feebly how Jonathan Elliott would have dealt with such a situation. Not that, of course, it would have arisen.

Laurence came into the room; he looked at Robert.

'Is my mother quite well?' he said.

'Perfectly well. Why do you ask?'

'I passed her in the hall. She was looking – distressed.'

'She was not distressed,' said Robert. It was plainly a lie; and Laurence knew it. He looked at him, and his pale blue-green eyes, so exactly like his mother's, were contemptuous.

'She was distressed. Quite clearly.' There was a pause. Then: 'I think you should tell me why.'

'I have no intention of telling you why,' said Robert. 'It's nothing to do with you.'

'Robert,' said Laurence, 'when my father was dying, he told me to look after my mother. I intend to do that. If she is distressed I need to know the reason why. So that I can attempt to deal with it.'

Robert stared at him; then he pushed past him and walked out of the room.

In a small house in London, at almost exactly the same time, an interesting reverse of this conversation was taking place.

'I don't understand,' LM was saying, 'why you won't let me help you. If I lend you the money – lend, mind, not give – you can set up your own building firm. Put an end to all this uncertainty, to being pushed around by foremen, laid off. I have nothing better to do with my money, nothing that would give me more pleasure. Please, Jago. You can pay me interest, at any foolish rate you like.'

'No,' said Jago, 'I won't take it. And don't ask me again.'

'Oh really,' said LM, 'you are ridiculous. There are men everywhere who would give their – their right arms for an offer like this.'

Jago looked at her. 'Wouldn't be much good in the building trade with just the one arm, would they?' he said and grinned.

It was a very hot day: hot and somehow oppressive. London was not in good heart that day. It had not been in good heart since the old king died; nor had the country. It was as if England itself knew that the hedonistic, pleasure-seeking of the Edwardian age was over forever, that the extravagances, the self-indulgence, the endless party that had been the short reign of Edward VII were at an end. Those hoping for more details of that party were disappointed; Edward had directed that his private papers and letters, many of them no doubt deeply scurrilous, were to be burned. Mrs Keppel had been banished from court, rebuffed when she arrived at Marlborough House to sign the visitors' book. This was in spite of a promise from the queen that the family would look after her. The sterner virtues of the new king, with his equally stern-faced consort, so different from the saintly Alexandra – who had summoned Mrs Keppel to visit the dying king – were becoming already apparent.

The funeral was splendidly impressive, King George rode beside his brother-in-law the Kaiser, followed by Edward's favourite horse, riderless, boots reversed in the stirrups, and then the usual parade of military and political luminaries; but it was the sight of the king's little dog Caesar, trotting behind the coffin, an oddly touching sight amidst the pageantry, that touched his subject's hearts. Every village, every town held services, every street was decked in black. Weeks later, the country was still officially in mourning. The famous black Ascot took place with everyone dressed in black, even the race cards were black-edged.

But Celia was content, extremely happy indeed, enjoying life, her return to health and strength – and of course her twins. They were good babies, far better at sleeping, at feeding, at smiling, at cooing, even, than their brother. She had recovered quickly from the birth, and was planning a return to Lyttons in September. That had been the compromise between her and Oliver; he had wanted her to have a year of domesticity at least, she wanted as little as two months. There had been a bitter battle, when he had accused her of not loving their children; she had accused him of not loving – or understanding – her, of disliking her presence in the firm. They had fought before, but they had never struck at one another's soft underbellies, at Oliver's insecurity, and at Celia's slightly lukewarm maternal feelings. They had made it up, as they always did, but the scars had gone deep. There was, even now, a slight chill, a wariness between them; a lessening of the intense pleasure they had always shared in one another's company.

But – as Oliver was constantly being told, he was one of the luckiest men in London; and while he might at times think otherwise, he also knew better than to argue. As everyone could see, he enjoyed commercial success, critical admiration, a dazzling wife and a beautiful family.

★

86

'Don't cry! Dear, dear Sylvia, don't cry. Here, come here, please. Oh, dear—'

Celia opened her arms: like a child, Sylvia went into them. Just for a moment; then she pulled back, rubbed at her face with her fist.

'I'm sorry, Lady Celia. This is no way to behave, when you've brought me the girls to see. I'm sorry. So sorry.'

'Oh Sylvia, don't be absurd. Let me – let me make some tea. You sit there, hold the babies. If you can manage them both. Barty, you come with me. Then we can talk.'

Celia went out into the yard to fill the kettle; Barty followed her like a small, devoted puppy. She was endlessly energetic, scuttling about everywhere on her wiry little legs. Being strapped to table legs, and into high chairs for half her short life seemed to have done her no harm. Celia looked down at her, at her funny, wide-eyed little face, at her mop of golden brown hair, and at the huge bruise on the side of her cheek. Sylvia had put that there; she had pretended at first, had said Barty had fallen down the steps, then that Frank had hurt her while playing with her. Then suddenly she told Celia what had really happened: that she had done it.

'She gets on my nerves so much, Lady Celia. She's so restless, won't do what she's told. Always somewhere she shouldn't be, or crying to get out. I can't cope with her. She doesn't understand, I have to keep her in, it's for her own good.'

That was when she started crying.

Sylvia had a bruise on her own face: on her temple. She said that was from Frank slamming the door on her; Celia knew that wasn't true either. It couldn't be. Sylvia looked wretched, so exhausted and frail.

'I've fallen again. I knew it would happen, I knew it, I kept telling Ted, but he wants it, all the time, I can't keep him off.' It was a measure of her misery that she was talking about such things to Celia. 'It's the drink, Lady Celia, he's started drinking quite a lot. How are we going to manage, how – and suppose it's like last time, suppose—'

She started crying again.

'Oh Barty,' said Celia, holding the kettle out to the tap in the yard, 'oh Barty, what are we to do with you?'

And then, as Barty smiled up at her, picked up a stone, started kicking it around the yard as she had seen her brothers do, and pushed a grubby hand into Celia's, then, quite suddenly, Celia knew exactly what she was going to do.

'She's coming to stay for a while,' she said flatly to Oliver, 'just for a while, there's no more to it than that. We have to help them. You know that's what we believe in. Sylvia is pregnant again, the children are running wild, Ted's knocking her about, and she can't cope. And she specially can't cope with Barty. She told me so, said she didn't know what to do with her. And I love Barty, and she loves me. There's plenty of room here, she can sleep in the night nursery with the twins, or even with Nanny until they're a bit older.'

The more Oliver raged, said it was absurd, forbade it, said that he would not have such folly in his house, the more determined she became. 'It's our house, Oliver, it was a present from my father, remember? I cannot believe you are attempting to forbid such a thing. A thing that will do so much good to so many people. To Sylvia, to Ted, to the family. To Barty of course. What kind of a life is she having, tied to a table leg half the day, and now being hit by her mother?'

'And what did Ted Miller have to say about this?' said Oliver furiously, his face working with rage. 'This kidnapping of his daughter?'

'She is not his daughter, she is their daughter. He's very happy about it. Very. It will be a great help to them all.'

She did not say that Ted Miller had been so drunk that he had been incapable of marshalling any coherent words at all, save that Barty's was one less mouth to fill, and if Celia wanted to fill it she was welcome. Or that Sylvia, even in her doubtful gratitude, had wept tears of very real grief as she put Barty's few ragged clothes into a paper bag and held her to her for a long time before she kissed her goodbye.

'And the Fabian society, what do you think they will they have to say about this?'

'A great deal, I'm sure. I don't think I care. As far as I'm concerned, people like the Millers are going to have to wait an awfully long time to benefit from this report of Mrs Pember Reeves. Years, decades. By which time Barty's life will be quite ruined, and Sylvia will be dead. What I'm doing is practical, Oliver, it will help them all now. And really, what difference will it make to you? You hardly ever see the children, except at the weekends. The house is huge; it's selfish and – and wrong of you to keep it all for ourselves, for our family's benefit.'

'And have you thought what damage you may do to Barty herself? Estranging her from her family, making her confused, disoriented, discontented with her lot?'

'Oh don't be so ridiculous, Oliver. She's not going to stay forever. Just a few – months. I shall take her to visit her family every week. And I – well I have had one idea. That I think you will be pleased with. I can see that – well that there will be adjustments. All round. And more for

88

the nursery staff to do. So – I have decided to do what you want, what you asked me to do. I shall stay at home, taking care of the children, for another year. So if I do that for you, surely you will do this for me? And agree to Barty staying with us for a while?'

CHAPTER 7

'The *Titanic!* On the maiden voyage! Oh, Oliver how wonderful that would be. But do you think you could get tickets, I've heard it's terribly difficult. Oh, it would be wonderful my darling, do try. Heavens, I'd have to get an awful lot of clothes to buy, it's going to be the best-dressed ship ever, you know. I'd have to get new luggage too and – yes, Giles, what is it, darling? I'm talking to Daddy, I've told you so many times not to interrupt.'

Giles was standing in the doorway of the dining-room, the expression on his solemn little face a mixture of determination and anxiety.

'Will you come for a walk in the park?'

'With you? Oh, darling, I can't, I'm so busy, Nanny will take you, surely she's going anyway, with the twins and . . .'

'She can't take us all,' said Giles, 'it's too many children for her to manage. She said so.'

'Well, then Lettie can go too.'

'It's Lettie's day off. Please, Mummy, I do want to and it is Saturday—'

'Giles, darling I can't. Not today. Maybe tomorrow. I've got such a lot of work to do and then—'

'You don't go to the office on Saturday.'

'No, darling, I know. But I have to work here. I'm sorry. And then – Giles, darling, don't look like that, come here, I have something so exciting to tell you.'

'What?' said Giles. His voice was heavy.

'You remember Uncle Robert? And Aunt Jeanette; they came to stay with us just before the twins were born.'

'Ye-es,' said Giles.

'Of course you do. He's Daddy's big brother. Anyway, they've had a little baby. Isn't that exciting? She's called Maud. And we're going to America to see her, in a few months' time. On a huge new ship. Look I have some pictures here, Daddy is going to try to get us tickets on her first voyage.'

'Can I come?'

'No, darling, I'm afraid you can't.'

'Why not?'

'Well, because it's partly work, our trip. We want to publish some books in America. And anyway, you'd be at school. And if we took you, we'd have to take the twins.'

'Why?'

'Because it wouldn't be fair otherwise.'

'They wouldn't know. They're only babies.'

'Not really babies any more: they're nearly two.'

'They still wouldn't know.'

'Of course they – Giles, no I'm sorry, you can't. One day perhaps. When you're a bit older. Now look, do you want to see some pictures of the ship? *Titanic*, it's called.'

'Ships are always called she, not it,' said Giles. He walked out of the room. Celia looked after him.

'Oh dear—'

'We could take them all, you know,' said Oliver, 'it might be fun.'

'Oh, Oliver, darling, no. It would mean taking Nanny, and possibly Lettie as well. And then what about Barty, we couldn't leave her behind.'

'Why not?'

'Oliver, you know why not. She's part of the family. You know she is.'

'I don't know anything of the sort,' said Oliver, 'actually. But we had better not enter into that particular discussion just now. It might spoil a nice day. Anyway, I suppose you're right, Barty or not, it would turn into a mammoth undertaking. Not to mention a very expensive one. Anyway, I'm pleased you're so delighted with the idea.'

'I'm thrilled with it. I do hope you can get us on *Titanic*, that's all. But anyway, another ship would do just as well. And Oliver, it'll be lovely to have a little time on our own. Just the two of us. It doesn't often happen these days, does it?'

'It doesn't. Well I'll leave you to your organisation. I presume you're busy with the proofs of the Browning book?'

'Terribly. It's going to be late if I'm not careful. And we'll miss the centenary. Not to mention the shopping. I must get something for the baby too. Oh it's all so exciting. You were wrong about Jeanette being past child-bearing age, you see. I'm glad they're so happy together.'

'Now what makes you assume that?' asked Oliver, smiling just a little heavily.

'Well – they must be. If they're having babies. I do wonder what she looks like.'

★

91

'She looks just like you,' said Robert, 'exactly. Same hair, same eyes—'

'Oh, dearest. I'm not nearly that beautiful.'

'Of course you are. And those little hands, look, so graceful and – heavens, Jeanette, she's just been sick. What should I do, call the doctor, get the nurse, what do you think—'

'Oh Robert,' said Jeanette, laughing, 'babies are sick all the time. It's called possetting. Give her to me and that muslin napkin. Come along, little one. Oh, Robert I can't believe it still. After all the trouble I had with the boys.'

She really hadn't been able to believe it. When the doctor first diagnosed her pregnancy, she had simply laughed. Of course she wasn't pregnant, she couldn't be, she was forty-three years old, she always had terrible trouble conceiving, she'd been ill constantly . . .

'Mrs Lytton,' the doctor said, 'Mother Nature's a clever old lady. Very frequently, women of your age find themselves pregnant. It's what we call the last-chance baby. There is a sudden surge in fertility. No, there's no doubt about it, you are pregnant, about five months I would say. I can hear the heartbeat and it's very strong.'

'But I feel so well,' said Jeanette almost plaintively.

'Good,' he said patting her hand, 'be grateful. Now you must tell your husband. I imagine he'll be delighted.'

Robert was: delighted and immensely proud. He had given up any hope of fatherhood when he married Jeanette; he had not thought it of any great consequence to him in any case. He had never liked children and his experience of Jeanette's boys had not changed his mind. But the emotions which filled him that day, when she told him that she was not only pregnant, but healthily and happily so, were overwhelming. He sat staring at her, asked her twice if she was quite sure, and found his eyes filling with tears.

Pregnancy, this time around, suited her; she was well, happy, confident. She seemed to ripen, her voluptuous body became proud and full and she was serene, less awkward and proprietorial with him. It was as if their positions had shifted, as if he had in some way assumed some sort of authority over her, rather than the rather uncomfortable reverse he was used to.

The day the baby was born, he suffered agonies of fear: but Maud arrived shortly after Christmas in what the doctor described as an indecently short time,

'No difficulty of any sort,' he said cheerfully, 'and the whole thing was extremely easy for her. Congratulations.'

It was altogether the happiest time Robert could ever remember; his new real estate company, founded two years earlier in partnership with John Brewer, and financed by Lawsons bank at a very competitive rate, was doing well. Several streets on the west side of Manhattan island were being built by Brewer Lytton, and they had just been successful in their bid to build a medium-sized, luxury hotel on the upper East Side. This too had had the effect of stabilising the marriage; of making Robert feel less like some uneasily manipulated puppet with strings pulled this way and that at Jeanette's whim. In fact the only cloud on his particular sky that summer, a dark, brooding angry one, was Laurence.

'He won't even speak to me,' he said to Jeanette, a week or so after they had broken the news to both the boys. Jamie had been initially pleased, flushed and beaming with excitement; then catching Laurence's furious, forbidding gaze he had carefuly switched off his smile, stiffened in his mother's embrace.

Laurence said politely, 'Congratulations, sir,' and shook Robert's hand, as his mother had bidden him; but afterwards, meeting him in the corridor on his way to the garden, Laurence said, 'If anything happens to my mother, I shall never forgive you. Never.'

It was said with such venom Robert was shaken; later, he told himself he must have exaggerated it, that it was natural for Laurence to be worried. His mother's obstetric problems were not unknown to him, and he was old enough to recognise the danger of her condition, particularly in view of her age.

'And dearest,' Jeanette said, when he told her, 'you must realise it is difficult for him. He is old enough to understand what has brought this pregnancy about, he has to confront the fact that we are making love with one another. That's uncomfortable for a boy of his age, who is coming to terms with his own sexuality. We must be understanding; don't be too hard on him.'

Robert said it was Laurence who was being hard on him, not the other way round; but Jeanette said that was absurd, and that they were two mature and very happy people and must make every allowance for an immature and anxious boy.

'And Jamie is delighted, he came and whispered to me last night, as he went up to bed, and so that is wonderful, don't you think? Laurence will come round, my dearest, you mustn't doubt it. We just have to be patient.'

But so far he hadn't done anything of the sort; he came in dutifully to his mother's room to meet his sister on the day she was born, bent over her cradle solemnly and looked at her, then kissed his mother and again, shook Robert's hand. But he refused the offer to hold her, to give her his finger to grip, to comment on her appearance, or even to take any part in choosing a name. Jamie, initially excited, begging to hold the baby, covering her small face with kisses, eventually took his lead from his big brother and visited the nursery less and less, except when

93

Laurence was out; Jeanette, amused by this, used it as an illustration to Robert of how Laurence, too, would grow accustomed to his small sister's presence.

'We mustn't rush them, dearest. There's plenty of time.'

Robert doubted it greatly; but he didn't say so. Laurence was sacred territory for Jeanette: beyond criticism, beyond doubt even.

'Mum, Mum, oh Mum—'

Barty hurtled down the steps, into Sylvia's arms. Sylvia held her absolutely tight, partly because she was so pleased to see her, partly because she didn't want Barty to see she was crying. She missed her so much; more and more. Every visit – and Celia had kept her word, Barty was sent in the car every two weeks to Line Street – was more painful than the last. Sometimes Celia came too, sometimes she did not. The visits were for the most part agony; at first Barty screamed when it was time to go back to Cheyne Walk, clung to her mother, had to be prised off. That made Celia angry, Sylvia could tell, although she struggled not to show it.

'Now Barty,' she would say, stroking the back of her head as she buried her face in her mother's shoulder, 'now Barty, you mustn't behave like this. It's not fair on your mother. She has so much to do and to worry about, it's such a help for her, to have you taken care of, and to know you are happy.'

Sylvia knew Barty couldn't possibly understand this; but she did, and it made her feel bad, ungrateful herself. Of course it was better for Barty, she had only to look at her, putting on weight, her face no longer white but rosy, her hair silky and well-combed, her grubby, threadbare clothes and worn-out boots replaced by lace-trimmed pinafores and fine leather shoes. And nobody was going to hit her at Cheyne Walk, nobody shout at her. She had become one of the privileged few, safe, protected, cocooned by money from the real world; it must be better for her. And if Sylvia missed her, longed to have her back, longed to have her babbling away again, getting up to mischief, fighting for her freedom, struggling to be free of the high chair, of the table leg, giggling at her brothers as they teased her, saying Mum and Dad and Marjie and Billy in her rather deep husky little voice, then that was wrong of her. She mustn't even think of it. Barty was one of the luckiest children in London, in England, probably in the world. She had escaped the certainty of poverty, the risk of brutality; it would be a crime to force her back into it. Of course one day, she would come back. Of course she would. She kept telling Barty so. When things were better, when her dad was back in regular work – he was doing casual at the moment.

When his temper had eased, when the new baby – little Mary, so sweet really, but so demanding and noisy, crying such a lot – was older: then Barty could come home again. But until then, she must stay with the Lyttons. She was lucky to be there. So lucky.

'Go way.' Adele's imperious little voice rang across the day nursery. She pushed Barty: pushed her hard. 'My dolly. Mine.'

Barty stood her ground; she didn't want the doll, and anyway, she had dolls of her own. Plenty. Aunt Celia, as Celia had instructed her to call her, often bought her toys: she had dolls, teddies, a dolls' cot, nearly as much as the twins in fact. But not quite. At Christmas – and she had gone home for her first Christmas day although not the second (her mother had said she wasn't very well and nor was her dad) the twins and Giles got toys from everyone, from their grandparents, their uncles and aunts, from Nanny even; Barty just got them from Aunt Celia and Wol. She loved Wol; he was so kind and gentle, had more time for her than Aunt Celia, often came to the nursery and played with them all.

She had given him the name: Aunt Celia had told her to call him Uncle Oliver, but of course she couldn't, and after the first few faltering attempts, had managed Wol. He had liked that, had smiled at her and said it was a very nice name, and in future that was what she was to call him. She couldn't say Aunt Celia very well either, but she kept trying. You did keep trying when Celia told you to do something. She'd learnt that. Her mother called her Lady Celia; Barty had asked soon after her third birthday, if she could call her that too, But Celia had said good gracious no, of course not, Barty was part of the family and it was much too grand a name.

'Giles doesn't call me Lady Celia does he?'

Barty didn't really understand what being part of the family was, but she knew she was different from Giles and the twins. Nobody treated them the same: certainly not Nanny. Or Lettie, who helped Nanny. Or Cook. Or Truman, who drove the car. They all – except for Nanny – called the twins Miss Adele and Miss Venetia and Giles was called Master Giles. They called her Barty. And not always nicely either. 'Barty take this up to the twins, Barty, don't sit there, that's Master Giles's place, Barty, don't shout at Miss Adele like that, Barty, how dare you take Miss Venetia's bricks.'

She really didn't think any of them liked her. They certainly didn't like her being there. Sometimes Lettie, for instance, would make a great show of giving her a cuddle if Aunt Celia was in the nursery and then the minute she'd gone, she would push her away, tell her to go and tidy up the toys or fetch the towels from the laundry room in the cellar so she could bath the twins. Barty didn't exactly mind, it seemed quite all right, really; everyone at home had to help, but she couldn't understand why Giles never had to do anything like that. And she didn't like the way she'd find Nanny and Lettie talking in low voices, but when she came into the room they'd stop suddenly; in fact Nanny would often scold her for trying to listen to things she had no business to hear.

Much worse than any of that was missing her mother and missing her father and missing her brothers and sisters; and worst of all was her brothers and sisters not being so pleased to see her any more. Billy was kind, and let her play with him, but the others were – well, they were rude. Told her she wasn't one of them any more, when she wanted to be one of them again more than anything. Sometimes as she was leaving she would look at the room, with all of them jammed round the table, eating bread and dripping, talking, shouting, laughing, and pushing each other, and she would think of the nursery, right at the top of the great big house, where there was just the twins, who were so horrid, and Giles who didn't talk to anyone much, and Nanny and Lettie, telling her to eat up her supper quickly, or to stop talking with her mouth full, and where after tea each day the twins went to bed and Giles went to his own room to do his homework, and she just had to sit quietly so she didn't disturb the twins, not play with the toys, even, until it was her bedtime, and she couldn't bear it.

She did have her own room; it was very small, of course, not nearly as big as Giles's, but it was nice, and she really liked it. She could do what she liked in it: look at books, or do some drawing, or just think quietly to herself without worrying about doing the wrong thing. It was very easy to do the wrong thing: to interrupt the twins if they were saying something – although they could interrupt her and everyone listened – or ask Giles to look at a book with her, or say she felt sick. For some reason, they didn't like her to be ill. It made them cross.

'I've got enough to do, looking after the other children, without this as well,' Lettie had complained one night, when she had been coughing so much she had woken her up. And then when they discovered she was hot and had to stay in bed, she heard Nanny, saying to Lettie, 'It just isn't fair. Why should we have to wait on her? She's not one of their children, not properly. Just come off the street really.'

That made Barty cry. But the worst thing of all was being told all the time, over and over again, how grateful she should be and how lucky she was. Everyone said that: not just her mother, who was bound to, of course, but Nanny and Lettie and Truman and every now and again, even Aunt Celia.

'You're a very lucky little girl, Barty,' she said one night, quite sternly, when she had found her crying on the stairs and Barty had told her she wanted her mother, 'you should be grateful instead of miserable. How do you think your mother would feel if she knew?'

Barty felt quite sure that if her mother did know, she'd take her back in spite of her dad being out of work; but she had been told so often she mustn't worry her, that she would have found it almost impossible now to get the words out. She just had to be brave and good, and one day she would be allowed to go home again. One day.

'I'm always surprised you don't get more mixed up with them,' said Jago. He was sitting in LM's drawing room, reading Saturday's *Daily Herald*; it carried on its front page a photograph of Mrs Pankhurst and some of her ladies, pressing a petition on some politician who was attempting rather unsuccessfully to ignore them. 'I've said it before, and I'll probably say it again. There you are, perfect example, a successful working woman, college-educated, and you don't throw your weight behind them. You ought to.'

'You have indeed said it before, and as I've said before, I don't have time,' said LM slightly stiffly.

'That's no excuse. Suppose Mrs Pankhurst said that. Where'd you all be then?'

'We're still nowhere much yet, anyway.'

'Meg! I'm surprised at you. You might not have got the vote yet, but everyone's certainly thinking about it. Look at that demonstration last June, forty thousand women. All demanding the vote.'

'Yes, and I was one of them.'

'I know, I know. But that was about the beginning and the end of it, far as you were concerned. I think you should do more for them, I really do.'

'I'm never quite sure why,' she said, 'why you care so much.'

'It's what politics is all about,' he said simply, 'to me. The underprivileged getting help. Getting their rights, getting what they need. Women are underprivileged, you must see that. Regarded as second class citizens. Paid shockingly. Kept down by men by a kind of divine right. It's not right.'

'I know it's not right,' said LM, 'but I don't feel I can do anything about it, Jago. Not personally. The very fact I *am* a working woman means I don't have time to chain myself to railings and smash windows, all that sort of thing. I'm proving myself and my sex in other ways.'

'Well,' he said, 'doesn't speak much for your sense of sisterhood, that's all I can say. I think I'm going to join them anyway. Go to some meetings and that. Not the suffragettes probably, the suffragists. More peaceful, not so aggressive. Probably because a lot of men belong.' He grinned.

'Of course you must do that,' said LM, 'if that's what you want.'

'It is. And I will. I've been thinking about it for quite a while now. Anyway, what about your work? Couldn't you publish some books about it? That would be something you really could do to help. Half the problem is hardly anyone agrees with women getting the vote. Men say women are incapable of making a political decision, that they'd stop marrying and having children, all that rubbish. You could change all that. Well some of it, anyway.'

'We run a publishing house, not a newspaper,' said LM briskly. 'It's not our job to publish propaganda. Now are we going for this walk, or not, before it gets dark?'

'I think we're not,' he said.

'Why not? Because I'm not a good suffragette?'

'No,' he said, 'because I can think of a better thing to do. On this very nasty cold afternoon. Even better than chaining yourself to a railing.'

She looked at him; he had thrown the paper down, was sitting back in his chair, a lazy grin softening his rather fierce features. LM's senses lurched; she smiled back at him and stood up.

'Come on then,' she said, 'let's not waste any more time.'

But later, lying happily sated in his arms, his words came drifting back into her head. Perhaps there was something she could do for the suffragettes through Lyttons. Perhaps with Celia's help . . .

'I think it's a wonderful idea,' said Celia, 'really wonderful. Of course we can't publish propaganda as such. Although we could possibly do a biography of Mrs P. Or the Gore Booth sisters, they're really interesting. Rich, aristocratic, clever and yet they believe in it all, work terribly hard. People would be fascinated by them, I'm sure. But I actually think the way to push the female cause is through fiction. Too much popular literature supports the notion of the little women at home, taking care of their menfolk. And when I think of women like Sylvia, of what they have to endure and go on enduring for the rest of their lives and their daughters after them – well . . .'

'What does your Mrs Pember Reeves think about women's suffrage?' asked LM.

Celia's face closed in on itself. 'I – don't quite know,' she said quickly. 'We never really talked about it.'

Celia and the Fabian movement had parted, extremely stormily, after the removal of Barty from her family. Mrs Pember Reeves had told her that, quite apart from making a serious mistake from the point of view of the movement and its aims (thereby forcing them to request Lady Celia's immediate resignation) she had done something wrong and extremely cruel.

'You have turned that child into a social experiment, Lady Celia. She will suffer for it all her life.'

Those words haunted Celia; two years later, when she was tired or dispirited, the memory of them could still reduce her to tears. She crushed them hastily now.

'What we should do I think,' she said slowly, 'is find a really splendid woman novelist to write a book for us, with the suffragette movement at its heart. That would do a lot of good I'm sure. I'll think about it really hard. Mind you, I haven't got much time at the moment. We sail for America in two weeks. Oh LM, I'm so excited. On the *Titanic*! Her maiden voyage. How many people will be able to boast of that in years to come?'

Lyttons were riding high early that year. The publishing business was generally booming, the actual number of books published had increased from six thousand in 1900 to over twelve thousand in 1912. People wanted to read and the leisured classes had been joined in that by the working man – and woman – better educated now and eager to extend their personal horizons. Lyttons had somehow caught precisely the mood of the age: its new fiction was intelligent and challenging, not merely entertaining. Celia's Biographica list fed the hunger for knowledge, and a new series of books that Oliver had proposed on popular scientific subjects, such as astronomy, meteorology and botany, were flying out of the bookshops.

'We love your books, Mr Lytton,' the proprietor of Hatchards, Piccadilly told him over lunch at the famous publishers' table in the Garrick Club one day. 'They have such a style of their own. However different the subject matter and indeed the design of the dust jackets, they all have – how can I express it – they all have such an air of quality. I never hesitate to recommend anything from the house of Lytton to anyone. I trust them. Let us raise our glasses to Lyttons and to quality.'

Such accolades had given Oliver the confidence to expand the company, increase print runs, hire extra staff. And to look at the American market – where already several of his English competitors were publishing. The forthcoming trip would be much more than just an opportunity to visit his brother's home and meet the latest small Lytton. His working relationship with Celia had also settled into something more comfortable, less threatening than it had been in the early years; Oliver's own self-assurance, his many personal successes, the fact he was now regarded in the literary world as one of the lions of publishing, had meant that he could see her not only as part of his winning team, but as important, essential, even, to it. He found himself able to consider her suggestions, to welcome her talent for innovation, to praise her, to criticise her, all with an easy disregard for the fact that she was his wife. Which in turn had its effect on their personal relationship, made it stronger, more robust, more pliable even. He still sometimes wished she was at home, running the household, caring for the children, but he could see that if he achieved that ambition, he would fail in another, equally precious: the growth of both the financial and literary success of Lyttons.

Celia had also become one of London's literary hostesses: an invitation to a dinner party at the Lyttons was something to be angled for, talked about, treasured. There in the dining-room at the back of the house, overlooking the exquisitely designed, carefully wild garden, the great and the good would gather: writers, publishers, artists, actors, the occasional politician, anyone, indeed, with something interesting and original to say. The Longman cousins, Robert Guy and William L were favourite guests; so was John Murray, Sir Frederick Macmillan, William Collins IV and his younger brother Godfrey, and − perhaps Oliver's greatest friend in the industry, Joseph Malaby Dent. They would be joined by the most famous literary names of their day, Macaulay, Yeats, George Bernard Shaw, Hugh Walpole, Kipling, Harold Nicolson, and bringing grace and glamour to the occasion, the Sackville Wests, Mrs Patrick Campbell, Lady Diana Manners, the dazzling Grenfell brothers, Julian and Billy, and on one particuarly glorious occasion, the greatest dancers of their day, Nijinsky and Karsavina.

It was said that if Celia Lytton had ever wished to write a gossip column for her friend Lord Northcliffe (another frequent guest) she would not have had to stir from her own dining-room. She presided over these occasions with charm and skill; her placements were challenging and interesting, one publisher's bestselling author seated next to another, an old establishment figure opposite a revolutionary preaching trades union rights, state pensions or, of course, equal rights for women.

Celia, her beauty illuminated by candlelight, dressed always in black, would sit at one end of the table, arguing, challenging, charming, and at times outraging; Oliver, all grace and old-style courtesy, sat at the other. It was an unbreakable rule of the Lytton dining-room that the ladies never left the gentlemen to their port and doubtful stories, but stayed to share in them, and so there was never the sharp division of male and female conversation. The talk would travel endlessly, unbroken, from gossip and chatter to literary argument to political debate and back again; the parties continuing well into the not-so-small hours, sometimes until three or four in the morning. One August, indeed, Celia had thrown a birthday party for herself that had only ended with a champagne breakfast as dawn broke. For anyone with social or literary pretensions, an invitation to the Lyttons was a delight: the lack of one was little better than a disaster.

But it was her trip to New York which was absorbing much of Celia's energy that spring; she was inordinately excited about it. With only six weeks to go, she had bought an enormous number of clothes for the voyage: day dresses, dinner dresses, sports clothes – she was much taken with the idea of deck tennis and all the other sporting activities available on this wonderful ship. She had invested in a set of new luggage, including a cabin trunk, which was actually a small portable wardrobe and would not even need to be unpacked. She and Oliver had a stateroom on Two Deck, and were promised calm seas and a record speed for the voyage. Robert would meet them at the docks on their arrival in New York, they would stay at the Elliott mansion on Fifth Avenue, and apart from the social delights of the visit – Jeanette was insisting on giving a large dinner party for them, and on taking them out to Long Island for a weekend in East Hampton – there would be plenty of time to meet American publishers and bookshop owners; and for Celia to partake of such New York pleasures as Saks Fifth Avenue and Henry Bendel. She was so excited she was literally unable to sleep.

'I have been thinking,' said Jeanette.

'Really, my darling?'

'Don't mock me, Robert. You know I don't like it.'

'I'm sorry.' It was true; she liked, indeed demanded, to be taken seriously. 'Are you going to tell me about it?'

'Yes. Because it could affect you. I am thinking of investing in Lyttons.'

Robert felt a stab of irritation. When he had needed investment money, she had refused; now that he was doing well, she was seeking to join in his success. And to rob him, to a degree, of his personal achievement.

'I think it's a little late for that, my dear,' he said, trying to keep his voice light, 'Brewer Lytton are doing very nicely.'

'No Robert, you misunderstand. Of course they are. I'm so proud of you. No, I mean the other Lyttons. The literary Lyttons.'

'What? I don't understand.'

'I am so very impressed by them all. Oliver and Celia, and his rather terrifying sister. It seems to me they are extraordinarily talented. Moreover I find what they are doing quite fascinating. I have always been drawn to the arts, as you know. Here is my chance to be personally involved.'

'In – what way would you see that involvement?'

'I thought I would like to help them establish a presence in New York. Oliver mentioned that he was thinking of it when we went over there, but that he lacked the finance, and I know that several English publishers are moving into the city.'

'I see.' He felt shocked, almost outraged. That she should bestow upon Oliver what she had refused him; that she should think of it herself, without any prompting, any request. It was monstrously unfair: not to say arrogant.

'Yes. I thought I could provide some capital: on a strictly business basis of course.'

'Of course.'

'So that they could obtain premises, hire staff, all that sort of thing. I should enjoy it enormously.'

'And would you be looking for an – involvement in this venture?' asked Robert.

'Oh – a little, obviously. I should want to know what they were publishing and why, should like to go to board meetings, I would be on the board naturally.'

'Naturally.'

'But mostly, I would like to learn about publishing, first hand. I think it would be a most interesting experience.'

'Yes, I daresay.'

'You don't look altogether pleased. Why is that, my dearest?'

She knew as well as he did. But there was no point spelling it out.

He looked at her. 'I just wondered, Jeanette, if you had considered the possibility that Oliver might not welcome your proposal.'

'Not welcome it? How absurd. Why ever should he not?'

'He is a fiercely independent person. And Lyttons is very much a family firm. I don't know that he would welcome outside interference.'

'Now that is absurd, Robert. If he was so independent, he would have founded his own firm, not merely taken on his father's. This would actually be a chance for him to do that. And I am family, or so I had supposed. I am a little hurt that you should consider me otherwise. No, I have made up my mind. I shall write to him, so that he has time to consider the suggestion before they arrive here in April. In fact if you will excuse me, my dearest, I shall go and do it now. There is no time like the present; Jonathan taught me that.'

Damn Jonathan, thought Robert, walking out of the room, closing the door just a little too firmly; damn him and damn his money. He didn't like this; he didn't like it at all.

Jago stood in the entrance to the hall in Camden High Street, one of very few men in a turbulent ocean of women – and wondered just for a moment what he was doing there. He was tired, and really needed to get to bed early. He had to be up at five the next day, to get to a job in Clapham, but – well, he had just felt he ought to. He was more than concerned at the exclusion of women from the franchise, he felt actually outraged. And he didn't understand how LM, who was, after all, a prime candidate for the battle could continue to regard it as in some way beneath her. Well, not beneath, but certainly outside her immediate interest.

He supposed it was because she had never had to fight for her rights. Or indeed for anything really. Her father had obviously been half a century ahead of his time in his attitudes, sending her to university, and then employing her in a proper position, equal to that of her brother, rather than in some kind of token job, looking pretty in reception or typing letters. So she took it as her due. But then surely she should feel she had to campaign for other women, who had not had such opportunities. It wasn't her background: lots of the famous suffragettes came from quite privileged homes. Christabel Pankhurst herself had hardly had to fight for her position in the world. They cared for other women, they wanted to extend their good fortune. LM should too. They had had words about it: not exactly angry with each other, but certainly annoyed. Well, it was too bad; he felt he had to come and he had said so; and now he was here. And didn't quite know what to do with himself, or where to sit or—

'If you don't want to miss the beginning, you'd better sit down. Plenty of room, over there look.' It was a light, slightly amused voice, with a London twang to it: a pretty voice.

Jago swung round to look at its owner: she was pretty too, young, with fair hair and large grey eyes, surprisingly well-dressed, in a pale green dress and hat. (Jago sometimes got rather tired of LM's uniform, although he would never have said so to her, thought how much nicer she would look in softer, more feminine clothes.)

'Come on,' she said, smiling, as he continued to stand there, 'you can sit with me if you like.'

He followed her in; to his embarrassment she led him to the front row. He looked round; the hall was full. There were several men, a good twenty or so; that was encouraging. His companion saw him checking them out and smiled.

'You're not alone, you see. No need to be frightened.'

He smiled back at her.

The speaker raised her hand for silence: a tall, striking woman with black hair and piercing dark eyes.

'Thank you all for coming,' she said, 'it's good to see so many new faces as well as the more familiar ones. I would urge any newcomers to join the NUWSS; we need all the supporters we can muster. You will find enrolment forms at the back of the hall; please take one as you leave. Now, I want to talk to you first about violence.'

Lord, thought Jago; surely this lot weren't going to turn to violent protests as well. They must realise it didn't do their cause much good.

'As you know,' the speaker went on, 'we at the NUWSS have always eschewed violence; we favour peaceful means and the gentle persuasion of such parliamentary figures as Mr Lloyd George and Mr Balfour, rather than the more militant methods of our sisters. The Labour Party has come round very strongly to the idea of supporting votes for women. So what I want to talk to you about next tonight is the establishment of an Election Fighting Fund. This would finance candidates for the Labour Party, at the next election, probably in 1915. If we can get enough candidates elected, then our own battle will be won.'

Jago sat listening intently, wondering if in fact she was right; if a continued peaceful campaign would be more successful than the extremely belligerent one favoured by the suffragettes. To work from within certainly seemed more sensible; on the other hand it required a certain faith in politics and politicians, which Jago personally lacked. Just the same, at the end of the meeting, he found himself signing up, not only for membership of the NUWSS, but as a volunteer for the Election Fighting Fund.

'Although I don't know what I can put into it,' he said to the pretty girl, whose name, he had discovered, was Violet Brown. 'I haven't got a penny piece to spare.'

'No more have I, nor have many of us,' she said, smiling at him cheerfully, 'doesn't mean you can't help us find people who have. You know anybody who might know anybody with money?'

Jago said, rather too hastily, that he couldn't think of any off-hand.

He didn't mention it to LM for a few days. She was – well she was a bit odd about her finances. Protective. Almost secretive. Refused to talk about them. He could never quite work out why. She had so much money: what seemed to him an unlimited supply. He supposed it was partly because she was innately tactful and saw it as an area of difficulty between them, but also because she was, and always had been, completely independent in every way: her money, like her life, was her own, to manage as she wished, and she was answerable to nobody. She once revealed to him, rather uncharacteristically, that she had lost quite a large sum speculating on the stock market, not enough to cause her problems, exactly, but certainly to give her pause for thought. But when he asked her for details, offered her sympathy even, she became edgy, almost truculent.

'It's my own business,' she said, clearly regretting she had mentioned it at all, 'and if I've been foolish then that is for me to worry about, it has nothing to do with anybody else.'

After that he had never mentioned money again.

It wasn't that she was tight, quite the reverse. Not only had she, over the years, continued to offer him money to start his own firm – which he continued to refuse – but she always bought him splendid presents for his birthday and for Christmas, clothes, books, pictures and ornaments for the small house he was so fond of. At first, being as proud and independent as she was, he had found them difficult to accept; but he had come to see that this would in itself have been mean, that in allowing her to give him presents, he could give something back to her. For his last birthday, she had given him the most generous present yet, an extremely nice silver pocket watch on a chain. That had been almost too much, in fact; he liked it very much, but he hardly ever wore it, except when he visited her; it seemed to him likely to invite hostile comment from his friends and workmates and even the possibility of assault and robbery as he walked home late at night through the mean streets of Kilburn, or sat drinking in public houses. At times it also represented a considerable temptation. It was all very well being the owner of something so splendid, but when he was out of work he would look at it, lying in its dark blue velvet-lined box, and think that if he sold it – or even pawned it – he would have no problems for several weeks, could buy food, coal, a great deal of beer. He could even take LM out for an occasional meal rather than endlessly accept her hospitality. So far he had resisted, aware, of course, that it would be a dreadful betrayal of their relationship, but he sometimes wondered if it had ever occurred to LM that she had bestowed a burden as well as a gift upon him. He rather thought it had not.

'Well – I suppose so,' she said, when he finally suggested a donation. 'I certainly approve of the NUWSS more than the suffragettes. Their approach seems more intelligent to me. Working with the Labour Party seems a much more positive position to start from. I'll – well I'll certainly think about it, Jago.'

Jago knew better than to press the matter.

A week later, he went to another meeting; Violet was there at the door again. She smiled at him; he smiled back at her, appreciating her friendly, flirtatious prettiness. She was dressed in the same green coat but a different hat, a jaunty brown affair, with a feather in it. It suited her.

'Hallo,' she said, 'nice of you to come back. Brave enough to go in on your own this time? Or would you like to sit next to me again?'

'Brave enough,' said Jago, 'but I think I'd like to sit next to you anyway.'

'In that case,' she said, 'you can earn it. Stay here, tick off the names, make sure you write down any new ones. I'll be back in five minutes, just got to check on the leaflets.'

Jago said it would be a pleasure.

After the meeting she asked him if he'd be good enough to help her check through the evening's donations.

'Normally Betty Carstairs, our treasurer, does it, but she's poorly. Would you mind? It won't take more than fifteen minutes, twenty at the most. And there's a couple of beers round the back.'

Jago said he wouldn't mind at all, even as he wondered if she really needed his help, or saw it as a good excuse to detain him. Either way he was quite happy. It was a long time since anyone had flirted with him. Harmless stuff, flirtation. Harmless and fun.

'Good God,' said Oliver.

'What?'

'This letter. It's from Jeanette.'

'Really? I shall have to look to my laurels, Oliver, if you're going to start getting unsolicited letters from ladies.'

'Don't be rididiculous,' he said. He always found it hard to realise when she was teasing him. 'She's offering to invest in Lyttons.'

'Invest in it? Surely not.'

'She is. She says she would like to encourage me to open a New York office, and to provide the necessary financial backing.'

'Good God,' said Celia, 'that is extraordinary. Just out of the blue – or had you mentioned anything to Robert?'

'I talked about it when they were over here. You may remember. But certainly never since. I wonder why – well it's a most interesting notion. I would certainly like to have an office over there. It would be marvellous. On the other hand, I don't know that taking her money—'

'If I read Jeanette right,' said Celia briskly, 'there would be no question of taking her money. It would need to get back to her, increased, many times over. But – well I think it's a very interesting idea. Personally.'

'Do you? I think it would worry me.'

'I can see why it might worry you having Jeanette involved,' said Celia, 'which of course she would be. But not about the money. She is immensely rich. Croesus looks quite impoverished by comparison. She can afford to invest a great deal, and lose it.'

'You think she'd want to be involved do you?'

'Well of course. Why else should she be doing it?'

'I have no idea,' said Oliver.

Celia was right. Jeanette's sole motivation was self-interest. To begin with, she was an intellectual snob: although a genuinely cultivated one. She liked the idea of having a publishing company she could call at least partly her own and partly to Jeanette meant a great deal more than half. She was intrigued by the notion of a new career in her mid-forties; by new contacts, new interests, new concerns. And then she was bored; her children, even the small Maud, only absorbed so much of her time. Her role at Elliotts was limited; she felt ready for new challenges. And Lyttons would provide them, she could see. A letter from Oliver, indicating at least a strong interest in her proposal, had both pleased and encouraged her. She could hardly wait for his arrival in New York. To Robert's clear unhappiness with the whole thing she gave hardly a moment's consideration.

CHAPTER 8

'Lady Celia, Miss Adele isn't very well. I think perhaps we should call the doctor.'

'What sort of not well?'

'Well, it's that cold Master Giles had, I'd say, only worse. She's hot. Temperature up a bit, just over a hundred. And she's got a cough, Very wheezy. I've been putting embrocations on her chest all day, but it hasn't really done much good.'

'Oh dear.' Celia hesitated. She had come home from the office to see the children quickly and change for an evening at the theatre. She'd been longing for it, Sarah Bernhardt in what was supposed to be one of her greatest roles, Lady Macbeth. And before she went, she'd planned to do some packing. She had an awful lot to do: only two weeks now before they sailed.

'I'll come up and have a look at her, of course,' she said after a brief struggle with herself. 'See what I think.'

'She'd like that, Lady Celia. She's very fretful.'

Adele was indeed fretful: flushed, restless, clearly uncomfortable. She wailed as soon as she saw her mother, and held out her arms to be picked up. Celia sat down, took her on to her knee, then nodded at Nanny over the small dark head.

'Yes, I think we should call the doctor. Tell Brunson to get him on the telephone.'

The doctor came within half an hour; he spent a long time listening to Adele's small chest through his stethoscope, looking inside her mouth and at her throat.

'You were right to call me,' he said finally, 'her chest sounds very congested. She must be kept in bed, of course. Carry on with the embrocations, Nanny, and she must inhale as well. And get this for her,' he scribbled out a prescription 'first thing in the morning. It should loosen the cough, ease her lungs. We don't want croup developing.'

'No indeed,' said Celia. 'You don't think it's dangerous, what she has?'

'Oh no,' he said, carefully hearty, 'not dangerous. But it could be unpleasant. She's very small.'

'Yes, of course. Oh, dear. Poor angel.' She dropped a kiss on Adele's head. 'How – how long would you expect it to continue, Dr Perring?'

'Impossible to say. Sometimes children throw this sort of thing off in hours, sometimes it can go on for days. There's no real danger, but she does need careful nursing. Ideally by her mother, of course,' he added, smiling just slightly heavily at Celia: 'they always make the best nurses.'

Celia went downstairs to see him out and to telephone Oliver to let him know that she would not be at the theatre that evening.

In the morning Adele was better: tired and fractious, but her temperature down and the cough looser. Celia, weary herself from a night of nursing – for she had taken Dr Perring's words seriously – went to the office for an important meeting with some booksellers, but promised to come home immediately if Adele took a turn for the worse.

'Just telephone me, Nanny, I can be back in half an hour. Less, probably.'

Nanny didn't phone; that evening, Adele was clearly well on the way back to her normal bouncy health. Celia started to pack. She'd been afraid even to contemplate what she might have had to do if Adele had been really ill. Of course, a mother's place was with her child – her sick child. But not being on the *Titanic*! Missing the maiden voyage! it would have been the biggest disappointment of her entire life. Unbearable. Professionally, too, it was becoming important; she had already promised to give a talk about it at a literary evening at Hatchards, and had discussed with LM the possibility of a book, not only about the *Titanic*, but about the other luxury liners which were becoming so popular. She had to be on it; she simply had to.

'Another meeting?' LM raised her eyebrows.

'Another meeting,' said Jago. He crossed his fingers in his pockets. Which wasn't necessary. It was quite true. He was going to another meeting. It just happened to be a small one; just him and Violet and Betty Carstairs, the treasurer. And why not? All right, it was in the small house where Violet lived with her widowed mother – conveniently out for the evening – but he wasn't going to be unfaithful to LM, just spend the time listing names and subscriptions, and sticking stamps on envelopes containing letters to sympathisers and supporters.

And he'd told Violet he had some news. Which he did. LM had told him that Lyttons were proposing to do a book about Mrs Pankhurst and her daughter. Of couse they weren't members of the NUWSS, but it was wonderful publicity for the cause. And it would undoubtedly mention the NUWSS, LM had said so. They would be so excited. And he would gain a lot of prestige in their eyes. Violet would probably be very impressed. He liked the thought of that. Impressing LM was virtually impossible. Of course there was a drawback, once they discovered he knew someone connected with a publishing house, they'd be looking for money, for donations from it as well. They were very demanding when it came to their cause, turned the tiniest pebble over and over again. LM had given twenty pounds, but that was all. She'd got quite difficult when he'd suggested a proper, formal subscription from Lyttons.

'I really don't want to be that involved,' she said, 'it simply isn't the sort of thing I feel Lyttons should be doing.'

When he asked why not, she hedged for a bit and then said slightly reluctantly that many of their customers were unsympathetic to the suffragettes, indeed actually hostile to them. 'It could do us a great deal of harm, Jago, you must see that.'

Jago said he didn't see that at all, and she said well, that was unfortunate, but it didn't alter the situation.

'I think doing the book will be far more useful in the long run. And Celia has also expressed an interest in publishing a work of fiction based around the movement, indeed one of our editors has been briefed to look for a writer. That will be extremely valuable as well. So please don't try and imply, Jago, that Lyttons or I don't have the interests of the suffragettes at heart.'

Jago, sensing danger, said he wasn't trying to imply anything of the sort.

'Venetia isn't so well this evening, Lady Celia. The same thing I'm afraid.' Celia laid down the sets of lace-trimmed negligees she had just bought from Woollands and was folding gently in tissue paper ready for packing, and sighed.

'Oh, Nanny. Is she as bad as Adele?'

'Worse, I'd say. Very nasty cough.'

'I'll come up.'

It was exactly the same story; the doctor was summoned, he prescribed the same treatment and care, and departed. This time they had to call him back in the morning. Venetia, always the more delicate of the twins, was clearly worse, her temperature soaring almost to a hundred and two, her little chest rising and falling rapidly, her cough rasping. A second night of anxiety followed the first; at midnight, as she lay in her small bed, coughing endlessly, the inhalations and embrocations apparently impotent against the endless painful cough, Celia looked up at Oliver who had come up to sit with her as well, and said, 'At this rate, Oliver, I may not be on the *Titanic*. I can't leave her if she is as ill as this. I wouldn't know a moment's peace. It's dreadful but – well anyway, of course you must still go.'

At which, Nanny, coming in with a fresh bowl of steaming inhalation, was touched to see him bend down and kiss the top of Celia's head with great tenderness.

'My darling,' he said, 'if you don't go, then neither shall I.'

'Oliver! You've been looking forward to it so much.'

'Of course I have. But I wouldn't enjoy it in the least without you. And I have to tell you, my darling, that I am deeply touched by your devotion to our children. I know what missing the voyage would mean to you.'

'Oliver really!' She said, smiling at him wearily. 'Any mother would do the same.'

'Not so,' he said, 'I can think of a great many mothers who would do nothing of the sort.'

Nanny, who had heard a great many horror stories about other mothers while sitting on the nanny benches in Kensington Gardens, felt bound to agree with Oliver.

However, two days later, Venetia was better, pale and rather hollow-eyed, but still with enough energy and strength to make her small presence felt strongly once more in the nursery. The Lyttons' presence on the *Titanic* seemed guaranteed again.

'This is Sarah Parker,' said Violet. 'She's come to help this evening. You ought to introduce your publishing friend to her, Jago, she could tell her a few stories. Just out of prison, aren't you Sarah? Sarah, this is Jago Ford. He may be a man but he's harmless. Well, better than harmless, matter of fact. Got friends in high places, he has, getting a book published about Mrs P.'

'Really?' Sarah Parker smiled at Jago. She was a tall woman, very thin and pale, with a rather misleading air of exhaustion; her voice was deep and well-educated, her presence authoritative. 'Which publishing house is that, Mr Ford?'

'Call me Jago. Place called Lyttons.'

'Oh, yes?' The lovely voice swooped suddenly with interest and a touch of amusement. 'Lady Celia Lytton's empire.'

'You know about her, do you?'

'I do. Emmeline has dined with her. And Christabel, too, I believe. She's a very interesting woman. Highly successful. Of course being married to Mr Lytton makes just a little difference.'

'Yes?' Jago was confused suddenly by this outsider's view of the Lytton empire. Thus far in his life it had been only a shadowy background to his relationship with LM.

'Of course. But I'm being unfair. She has had a great many clever ideas. So she's doing a book about Emmeline is she? Well that will help a little, certainly. Violet, pass me those envelopes would you? I may as well make myself useful.'

As she sat sticking stamps on to envelopes, Jago noticed how thin and clawlike her hands were, how gaunt the lines of her jaw.

'What's it like in prison, then?' he said abruptly. He knew it was a crass question, but he felt it was worse not to ask it at all.

'Fairly dreadful,' she said calmly. 'The worst thing is the isolation. It's hard to feel the power of the sisterhood when you're with your own thoughts and fears twenty-four hours a day.'

'Fears?' said Jago.

'Oh yes. Of the warders, their brutality. The hard labour is not exactly insupportable, but if a warden finds fault, say with the scrubbing you've done, you're put on bread and water. And then the force-feeding is a dreadful experience. For the first time I understood, seeing my cell door open as they came for me, what it meant when people spoke of their bowels turning to water.'

Jago felt uncomfortable; he was not used to such conversation. Violet put her hand out and covered Sarah's with it.

'How often did they do it to you?' she asked.

'Half a dozen times. Then I became too ill, and I was admitted to the prison hospital. Your throat is lacerated, you see, with the feeding tube. It's very wide, and it's four feet in length, rammed down you with great force. And you vomit at the same time. I still can't eat anything but the most sloppy food. My doctor says I probably never shall.' She smiled cheerfully round the group. 'But never mind. I'm not actually going to subject myself to it again. That's why I'm throwing in my lot with you. It's not really cowardice, I hope. I've become extremely doubtful about the good that all the violence does. The public sees our more militant members as troublemakers. Christabel and Emmeline don't agree of course. I'm afraid they're not very pleased with me.'

After Sarah Parker left, Violet looked at Jago thoughtfully. 'So who is your friend? What's – his name?'

'It's a her,' said Jago, 'and her name's Margaret Lytton.'

'Never! You're kidding me. You know one of them, one of the Lyttons themselves?'

'Yes.'

'Well?' The grey eyes were sharp now, sharp and piercing.

'No,' he said hastily, 'no, not well. Not well at all.'

'Oh come on. You wouldn't have that sort of influence over someone if you didn't know them well.'

He said nothing, looked down at the rather genteel cup, filled with weak tea which Violet's mother had brought in.

'Well who'd have thought it?' said Violet. She looked at him, under her long lashes, and half smiled. 'you've obviously got a lot to offer. Having a lady friend like that.'

'She's not a lady friend,' said Jago, 'not like you mean.'

'She isn't?'

'Well no. Look I've got to be going now. It's been really interesting meeting Mrs Parker and everything. But I've got to be up at five.'

'Wasn't it interesting being with me? No, I thought not. Knew it couldn't be. Dead uninteresting I am.'

She looked dejected, her small shoulders drooping. Jago felt a pang of remorse.

'I don't think you're uninteresting,' he said, 'not at all.'

'Course you do. Most people do. I meet all them clever people through the cause, and I can see them all thinking oh, she's just a bit of nothing. Oh dear, oh I'm sorry.' She pulled out a lace handkerchief, blew her nose on it.

'Violet—' said Jago gently.

'What?'

'Violet, I don't think you're at all uninteresting. I think you're very sweet. And—' he cleared his throat, 'very attractive. Very. And – well and – interesting.'

This was dangerous; he knew it. He had no illusions about Violet Brown. His sexual instincts were extremely acute. At the same time it was exciting. And it was a long time since he'd been in an exciting situation.

Mrs Brown suddenly appeared in the doorway: a fierce cottage loaf of a woman.

'Violet, it's getting late,' she said, 'time we was locking up.'

'Yes, all right, Mum. The gentleman's just going.'

On the doorstep, Jago turned, said, 'Thank you for a very nice evening, Violet. And I really did enjoy talking to you. Not just to Sarah.'

Suddenly she leaned forward, just for a moment, her small body pressed against him; he could smell her perfume, cheap and cloying but still sweet and arousing, felt her lips move under his briefly, before she pulled back, hearing her mother in the hall.

'There's still a lot of work to be done,' she said, 'if you wanted to help us some more.'

★

113

'I have the theme for our novel about the suffragettes,' LM said to Celia next day.

She had been fascinated, inspired even, by the stories Jago had told of Sarah Parker; had felt the familiar uncurling of professional excitement as she recognised their power. He had appeared, quite late on her doorstep, said he'd felt he had to see her, had to talk to her. She'd known what he really wanted, but she was tired, and still slightly irritated by what she saw as his over-enthusiasm for the suffragette cause, had been unable – or unwilling – to match his desire with her own, had sent him home after a short while. But the information he had brought with him, imparted over a couple of bottles of beer, had been invaluable.

'Yes?' said Celia. 'What is it, the theme?'

'It's quite unusual, I think, and very powerful. It's about conflict within the ranks. The battle between a militant leader and her non-militant lieutenant. If you follow me.'

'I think so.'

'Apparently there's quite a lot of it. The hunger strikers have a dreadful time in prison, have to endure appalling suffering, feel isolated and disillusioned. I think it would be marvellous stuff for fiction.'

'I agree. How clever of you to think of it.'

'Well I didn't exactly think of it.'

'No?' Celia looked up at her. Her eyes were heavy and she was drawn and pale.

LM felt a rush of sympathy. 'More night-time nursing?'

'Yes. It's hard being a working mother, LM. But at least they're all better now. Our trip on the *Titanic* is quite safe. Thank goodness. I was so afraid we'd have to miss it. Imagine how dreadful.' She smiled. 'But I can have a couple of good nights' sleep before we sail. Now, I like this idea for the book. How did you come across this storyline?'

'Oh, from a – a friend of mine,' said LM, 'who's been to a few meetings.'

'And would she come in and talk to us about it, do you think?'

'Oh, I don't think so, this friend is very busy. A working person, you see.' LM felt herself flush, turned away quickly to look at some papers she was holding.

'Yes, I see,' said Celia gently, 'yes of course. Well, we certainly mustn't trouble her. Perhaps you could write a few of the stories down yourself. Or even ask your friend to put us in touch with this Sarah Parker.'

'Yes, Yes. That might be possible. I'll certainly ask – ask about that.'

'I've even found someone who might write the book. Clever woman called Muriel Marchant. She's coming in to see me tomorrow. Any chance of speaking to your friend before then?'

'Oh, I should think so,' said LM, 'we're going to have a meal together tonight, as a matter of fact. I'll make some notes then.'

Only when she got home, there was a note pushed through the door from Jago to say he had a bad cold and wouldn't be able to come. That cold! It was a brute. Probably the same one the twins had had. He must be feeling wretched. Not a lot of fun, taking care of yourself under such circumstances. She decided to go down to his little house and take his favourite beef broth and some of the red wine he had taken to drinking lately; that would do him good. And she could get some notes about the Sarah Parker woman while she was there.

'Tomorrow!' said Giles, 'I thought the boat went on Thursday.'

'It does. But we have to travel to Liverpool tomorrow night. That's where we get on it.'

'Can't you get on it in London?'

'No, darling. It doesn't come to London. That would be difficult.'

'I don't see why. It could come up the river. I could see you get on it then.'

'Oh, darling!' Celia laughed, hugged him. 'What a wonderful idea. But I'm afraid not. It's too big.' They were up in the nursery; she took him over to the window, pointed at Albert Bridge. 'It wouldn't nearly fit under that. And even if it did, it would be late getting to New York.'

'Oh, I see.'

He looked very dejected; Oliver picked him up, hugged him.

'We won't be gone very long, Giles. Promise. Only a few weeks. Back for the twins' birthday.'

'I don't care about the twins' birthday,' said Giles. His voice was small and rather distant.

'Darling! That's not a very nice thing for a big brother to say.'

Giles was silent.

'Anyway,' Celia said, 'we're going to have to say goodbye to you tonight, at bedtime. All of you. When you wake up we'll be gone. And then you can start ticking off the days till we're back. Only twenty-one altogether. And you have to look after the girls, as you're the oldest.'

'I don't want to look after them. They've got Nanny and Lettie. I don't mind looking after Barty,' he added. 'I like Barty.'

'Good,' said Celia briskly, 'where is Barty?'

'Still in bed, Lady Celia. She slept badly, got a bit of a cold,' said Nanny.

'Oh, dear!' said Celia, 'not another one.'

'Oh, no, Lady Celia, not the same thing at all. She's just a bit snuffly that's all.'

'Thank heavens for that. Goodness, look at the time. We must go. So much to do today.'

After they'd gone, Lettie looked at Nanny. 'I'd like to see her give up her trip for Barty,' she said, 'for all her talk about her being one of the family.'

'LM,' said Celia, 'LM are you all right? You look terrible.'

LM was hunched over her desk; she appeared smaller and thinner than usual, and when she looked up at Celia, her eyes seemed enormous, etched into her white face. They looked sore too, red-rimmed and swollen; her mouth looked odd too, blotchy and somehow swollen as well.

She sat staring at Celia as if she wasn't quite sure who she was; then she said, and her voice was very slow, 'Yes, I'm fine. Well, bit of a cold. Everyone's got it, after all.'

'But LM, you should be at home, you should—'

'I'm perfectly all right.'

'Well, you don't look it. You don't look it at all, you should be at home in bed.'

'Celia,' said LM and her voice was very hard, almost threatening, 'Celia, I am absolutely capable of deciding whether or not I'm all right. And I have no wish whatever to go home. Now I imagine you have a great deal to do, this being your last day. And no doubt a great many things to brief me on, so can we get on with that please?'

'Yes,' said Celia, 'yes, of course we can.'

'Something dreadful's happened to her,' she said to Oliver, 'I know it. She looks appalling. Someone has upset her terribly. A man if you ask me. The man, whoever he is. Anyway, don't mention it, whatever you do.'

Oliver said he had no intention of mentioning it, had no idea what he might mention, in any case. They both went into an editorial meeting with bright, calm smiles on their faces and tried to treat the pallid, exhausted LM as if she was her normal competent self. The only clue came at the end of the meeting when she said she would like to detach herself from anything to do with the prospective novel about the suffragettes.

'It's a subject for which I feel very little sympathy, and really cannot make any contribution to. I'm sorry if I gave the opposite impression.'

'But LM,' said Richard Douglas, 'Celia gave me to understand you had a contact who had actually been in prison, who could provide information about the force-feeding and so on. It would be of great help to Muriel Marchant if that were so.'

'I'm afraid I was mistaken over that,' said Celia who had noticed an increased deadening in LM's voice, a swift and intent study of the papers on her desk as she spoke. 'Entirely my fault, very stupid of me. I'll try and find someone else for Muriel to talk to, as soon as I get back from America.'

She looked up and met Oliver's eyes; he was looking puzzled. He leaned forward slightly in LM's direction, obviously about to question her further; Celia struck out in his direction under the table, the pointed toe of her boot catching his ankle. She could tell from the slight gasp of breath that she had hurt him; she reached out and touched his arm gently.

'Shall we go on to the next item?' she said. 'The print run for the new edition of the Dictionary of Names? LM, I think you have the figures?'

LM's exhausted face, softening just slightly as she looked at her, told her she had not misread the signals.

'It hasn't done as well as we hoped this year,' she said, 'I think I'd recommend bringing it down to two hundred.'

'Disappointing wouldn't you say, Celia?' said Oliver coldly. He was still clearly suffering. 'You were so convinced that it would be a continuing bestseller.'

'Yes, and clearly I was wrong,' said Celia.

Sick children, wretched adults, a professional misjudgement. She would be extremely glad to escape to the luxurious tranquillity of the Atlantic Ocean and the *Titanic*.

Barty felt absolutely horrible. Her head throbbed, she ached all over, and her chest hurt dreadfully. Every time she took a deep breath, it felt as if knives were going through it. And then she started coughing, and couldn't stop. This hurt her chest more and made her throat really sore. It had been a bit tickly when she went to bed; now it felt as if someone had been at it with a razor. And she was hot: so hot. Lettie had told her to get up and get dressed. It was a windy day and they were going for a walk after breakfast, so she must put on her bodice as well as her vest and her long combinations; each item of clothing felt like some kind of a tight, hot oven. She couldn't really quite imagine going for a walk over the bridge to Battersea Park which Giles had told her was the plan, even though it was her favourite place. Her legs felt weak and wobbly, and every so often everything started swimming round her until she had to sit down. As always when she wasn't well, she longed for her mother.

'Barty do hurry. You're holding everyone else up. Have you got a stone in your shoe or something?'

'I just don't feel very well,' said Barty.

'Oh, nonsense,' said Lettie, 'you look perfectly all right to me. Plenty of colour in your cheeks. Bit of fresh air, that's all you need. We've been indoors too much lately, with all these coughs and colds.' Barty knew better than to argue; she struggled to keep up with them as they crossed Albert Bridge. Standing by the pond while the twins fed the ducks, she felt as if her lungs were going to burst, they hurt so badly.

'I really don't want any. Please don't make me eat it.'

'Don't be silly, Barty. That's extremely good chicken. You're a lucky girl, you should be grateful to be getting it, not having to make do with bread and water.'

Lettie loved these reminders, these digs at Barty's background. Barty was beginning to learn at least to pretend to ignore them; but today, sick and wretched, she couldn't. Her eyes filled with tears; the chicken on her plate blurred.

'I don't want it,' she said again.

'You eat it,' said Lettie, 'or else.'

'Don't, Lettie,' said Giles. 'She doesn't have to eat it. She isn't very well.'

'She should eat what the Lyttons are good enough to give her,' said Lettie. 'Barty, you just finish what's on that plate.'

Barty picked up her spoon, slowly filled her mouth, and managed to swallow the chicken. Halfway down her throat, it seemed to swell, to gain a horrible consistency; she retched, deposited it back on her plate.

'You disgusting little urchin,' said Lettie, flushed with anger. 'What a thing to do.'

'Gusting,' said Adele.

'Urchin,' said Venetia. Neither of them had the faintest idea what the words meant, but they could tell Lettie was cross with Barty; that was enough to please them.

Something snapped inside Barty.

'Shut up,' she said, 'shut up all of you. I hate you.'

Lettie stood up. 'Barty,' she said, 'you go straight into the bathroom and wash your mouth out with soap. I'll be along to make sure you've done it properly. And then I shall give you a dose of castor oil; it's very good for naughty ungrateful children.'

Barty stood up; the room really was swimming now, and the floor heaved under her feet.

'I can't,' she said. The next thing she knew she had crumpled on to the floor and Lettie was looking frightened and calling for Nanny.

'Bronchitis,' said Dr Perring, 'quite bad I'd say. Temperature over a hundred and two. Far worse than the twins. It could turn to pneumonia. Where's Lady Celia?'

'At her office,' said Nanny.

'I think she should be told.'

'I don't think there's any necessity for that.'

'Why not?' He sounded fierce.

'Well, the other children got better. I just can't see any reason why this one shouldn't.'

'This one is much worse. As I just said.'

'Yes, but she's not too bad. And Lady Celia is going away this evening. To America. I don't want her worried.'

'I'm sure she'd want to know that one of her children is as ill as this,' said Dr Perring.

'It's not one of her children,' said Nanny firmly. Dr Perring looked at her.

'I don't think that's a very wise judgement,' he said. 'What's she been doing today, this little one? Kept in the warm, I hope?'

'Well – most of it, yes.'

'As long as she hasn't been out in this bitter wind.'

'Only – only very briefly.'

'She went to the park,' said Giles. He had been reading in the corner of the day nursery; no one had really noticed him.

'The park!' said Dr. Perring.

'Yes. To feed the ducks. We all did.'

'Very unwise. Well, I shall certainly come back in the morning. And ring me at once if you're worried. Now who is going to telephone Lady Celia, Nanny? You or I?'

'I will,' said Nanny.

Celia was rather wearily scooping papers into the large leather satchel she used to transport work from Paternoster Row to Cheyne Walk and back again, when the telephone on her desk rang.

'Yes?'

'There's someone here for Miss Lytton, Lady Celia. A gentleman. I told him she'd gone, and now he's asking for you.'

'What is the gentleman's name?'

'Mr Ford. He's very pressing, Lady Celia.'

'Let me speak to him.'

Nanny put the phone down with an expression of great relief on her face. It wasn't her fault if Lady Celia didn't answer the phone when she rang. She would try again of course, but just for the moment, she'd have to leave it. She hadn't left a message because the girl at the office would probably get it wrong. And Barty seemed better, she was lying quietly, half asleep. Coughing now and again, but probably by the time Lady Celia got home, to change and collect her luggage, she'd be asleep. And there'd be no need to worry anyone with it. She was obviously all right. Just a cough, like Giles and the twins had had. They'd been right as rain in a couple of days. Barty would be too. She really couldn't have Lady Celia missing that ship, just for a cough. And being worried because Barty had been upset, and because the doctor had thought she shouldn't be taken out. It was ridiculous. She had thought of ringing the doctor again, but now Barty was quiet, it seemed better to leave it for a bit, just let her go to sleep. That was the sensible thing to do. Definitely. Lettie thought so too. And Giles seemed to have forgotten about it, and anyway he'd gone out to tea with a friend. So really it had been a blessing that Lady Celia hadn't answered.

'It was just a mistake,' said the man, 'a stupid mistake. What she thought. A – a misunderstanding.'

He looked nearly as dreadful as LM, Celia thought. White-faced and unshaven. He was clearly a working man; even though he was wearing a rather nice tweed coat; the heavy boots and muffler and cap told her that. And his accent of course. But he was extremely attractive. There was no doubt about that. Celia felt what she could only define as a stab of admiration for LM. If she could engage the attention of a man like this, not exactly good-looking, but powerfully – well, sensual looking, she must have some extremely interesting depths. Celia thought of LM, of her rather severe clothes, her carefully controlled face, her neatly bound hair, her passion for order, and felt astonished. She had always imagined that any man friend of LM's would be a rather prissy, intellectual, old-maidish person. Then she remembered the ravaged face of that morning, the voice throbbing with misery, the burning dark eyes, and realised they were symptoms of violent feeling in themselves. Well, good for LM.

'What sort of misunderstanding?' she said.

'I don't think I could tell you.'

'Well then I don't think I can help you,' she said.

He hesitated. Then he said, 'I was at my house last night with a − a young lady. I'd told Miss Lytton I wasn't well. She came round and found us—'

'Found you?'

He nodded.

'That doesn't sound like too much of a misunderstanding to me. I would certainly have reached the same conclusion as she did. With good reason I would have thought.'

'No,' he said, 'not good reason. We − we were only working.'

'Working?'

'Yes. Well, sort of working. Checking leaflets. For the suffragettes.'

So she'd been right. That had been the link.

'In your house?'

He nodded miserably. 'Yes.'

'Mr Ford,' said Celia, 'forgive me. But if all you were doing was checking leaflets, why tell Miss Lytton you weren't well? Why not invite her to join you, to help with the leaflets?'

'I didn't think she'd be too pleased,' he said.

'Why not?'

'Well − the young lady is very pretty. And sort of − well, sort of a bit cheeky. And she implied to Miss Lytton that—'

'Yes? What did she imply?'

'That more was going on than there had been.'

'So something had been going on?'

'Not − not really.'

'But something?'

He hesitated.

'Mr Ford,' said Celia severely, 'I can't help you if you don't tell me everything. What exactly had been going on?'

'Well, she was after me. I did know that.'

'Really?'

It was hardly surprising. Any young lady worth her salt would have been after Mr Ford.

'How − why were you so sure about that?'

'Because − that is, I thought − well, the other night she − she did kiss me. Just goodnight, really, of course.'

'She kissed you? I see. And did you kiss her?' Celia was becoming rather engrossed in this; it was hugely intriguing. She saw him looking startled, said quickly, 'I'm sorry. It's just, as I say, I need to have all the facts.'

'I—I suppose so, yes, I did.' Humour briefly crossed his face. 'Didn't have much choice really. And she had been making it clear she liked me.'

'So then you invited her to your house?'

'Well, in a manner of speaking, yes.'

'Mr Ford, that's a fairly clear manner of speaking, I would have thought.'

'Yes. I suppose so. But it was only to do the leaflets.'

'Oh really?'

He hesitated. Then 'I suppose I did want her to come, I liked her. But it was only – oh, dear God, I'm stupid.'

'It does seem as if you might be. What are your feelings for Miss Lytton? If I might ask?'

'Oh,' he said simply, 'oh, I love her.'

'You love her?'

'Yes. Very much.'

'So you lie to her. You invite another girl to your house, a girl who you know perfectly well finds you attractive, who, I would guess, you in turn find attractive, who will probably cause you trouble . . .'

'Yes,' he said, his voice very low, 'yes that's all perfectly right, I'm afraid.'

'But why?'

Jago looked at her.

There was a long silence. Then, 'For – for fun I suppose,' he said.

'Fun? You risk a relationship that's important to you, for fun?'

'I – suppose I did. Yes. I – well, I think that's just about the size of it. She's – well she's a wonderful woman, Miss Lytton, but she isn't exactly fun. And—' he hesitated.

'Yes?'

'Oh, nothing.'

'No, please tell me.'

'Well I'm always the underdog,' he said finally, meeting her eyes, his own half amused, half embarrassed, 'she's got everything, Miss Lytton has, the money, the – the class, the education, the position. I can never win. This other young lady, she thought I was wonderful. It might have been wrong of me, but that was really nice. Just for once.'

She looked at him, suddenly and sharply touched with sympathy. 'Yes,' she said slowly, 'yes, I can understand that. I really can. But it was still very wrong. What you did. Wrong and terribly hurtful for LM – for Miss Lytton. And I don't see what I can do.'

'Lady Celia,' he said, 'Please. I do need your help.'

'Yes, I daresay you do. But—'

'Haven't you ever done something,' he said suddenly, 'quite different of course, but still something that you felt you couldn't help? That you knew you were going to regret?'

'Possibly,' she said carefully, 'but I really don't think we need to debate that now. It's hardly going to help you.'

He was silent.

'What you have to do,' she said slowly, 'is go and see her. Tell her everything you've told me. Even about – well about feeling you couldn't help it. Try to make her understand.'

'She won't see me,' he said with a shuddering sigh, 'don't think I haven't tried. All last night, I just sat on her doorstep. And this morning, I was still there. She just stepped over me. She won't listen to me.'

'Well I'm hardly surprised,' said Celia, 'I'm afraid.'

'No,' he said, 'neither am I. But – well I do love her. And she loves me.'

'Oh really?'

'Yes, she does. And she needs me,' he added after a moment.

Celia thought fast. That was probably true. LM did need him. He had clearly been making her happy. It might be a long time, if ever, before she found someone else. And she felt instinctively that, in spite of some rather regrettable behaviour, he was actually a good man. Probably because of it. It was a rather sad, poignant story. She didn't suppose LM was much fun. In the way he meant. He was obviously younger than her, and hungry for pleasure. And it must be very hard, being a man in so subservient a position. There was – or had been – an echo in her own situation, with Oliver.

'Look,' she said suddenly, 'I'll talk to her. I'll try and get her to see you.'

'Oh,' he said, 'Oh, Lady Celia, would you? I'd be so grateful to you.'

'Well don't start being grateful yet. She hasn't even listened to me. Let alone you. But I'll do what I can. Only I have to be quite quick because I'm going away tonight, on a trip.'

'Yes,' he said, 'I know, she told me. On the *Titanic*. What an adventure. What I wouldn't give to go on that.'

She looked at him and smiled for the first time.

'I hope you'd give up this other young lady,' she said, 'for a start. But yes, it should be wonderful. I do know how lucky I am. Now you go and sit downstairs, and I'll telephone Miss Lytton and see what I can do for you. I'll come down when or if I have some news.'

It was twenty minutes later that she found him, with his head in his hands, sitting in reception. She put out her own hand, touched him gently on the shoulder.

'If you go up to Hampstead straight away, she will at least see you. I can't promise any more than that. Now I must go. I have a boat to catch.'

'She's dreadfully hot,' said Lettie, 'and her pulse is that fast. Breathing funny too. I don't know that we shouldn't get the doctor back.'

'She's perfectly all right,' said Nanny, 'she's asleep isn't she? Best left. We shouldn't worry Lady Celia. It wouldn't be right. Spoil her trip.'

'But Nanny—'

'Lettie, she's no worse than Venetia was. Look what happened to her. Forty-eight hours, and right as rain. You've really got to trust my judgment on this.'

'Yes, all right, Nanny. Oh, there's her car now. You don't think we should tell her?'

'No, Lettie, I don't.'

'You may come in, just for a moment,' said LM, 'but I have only five minutes. I really am extremely busy.'

Her voice was cold, detached; she looked at Jago as if he was a stranger, a travelling salesman come to waste her time. He stepped inside.

'Could we – could we sit down somewhere?'

'I don't see any real necessity for that. Since it will be such a short conversation.'

'Meg—' His voice was heavy, shaky with emotion.

'Yes?'

'I'm so – sorry.'

'Indeed?'

'Yes. Very, very sorry. I don't know what came over me.'

'I should have thought,' said LM, 'that was rather obvious. From what I saw, at any rate. A young, rather attractive woman. Overcoming you to a considerable extent. Well, I suppose it was natural, after all.'

'Yes,' said Jago, taking a deep breath, 'yes, it was. Natural, I mean.'

LM physically blenched. She went very white.

'I think you should leave at once,' she said, 'if that is all you can offer me. By way of explanation.'

'It is,' he said, 'yes.'

She stood up, walked over to the front door, opened it.

'Good evening,' she said.

'Meg! Meg, don't. Don't be like this.'

'Oh, for God's sake,' she said, a red flush rising now in her pale face,

124

'how do you expect me to be? Forgiving? Understanding? I'm sorry, Jago, but you read me very wrongly if that is the case.'

'I don't expect that, of course,' he said, 'but I – hoped for it.'

'I daresay you did. Well, you are to be disappointed, I'm afraid. Please leave.'

'No,' he said, 'I won't leave. Not till I've had my say. Then I'll go. Shut the door, Meg. If you will.'

She looked at him; he seemed more authoritative suddenly, less demeaned. She shut the door again. 'Go on then,' she said, 'have your say.'

'It was – natural as you say. None the better for it. I don't feel any less ashamed. But that was what it was. She was pretty and scheming and she got the better of me. It didn't change how I feel for you, Meg. It didn't make me love you less.'

'Oh, for pity's sake,' she said, 'what am I supposed to do now? Give you my blessing, send you off to see her whenever you want to?'

'No,' he said, 'no, of course not. Just – see it my way. Not the – the being unfaithful. It was only a kiss and a cuddle, mind.'

'Jago, I don't want this sort of detail.'

'You do,' he said, 'well, you should. It's important. I would never bed another woman, never ever. I couldn't. Not after you, not after knowing you. It would be unthinkable. Horrible.'

'I see,' she said. She sounded grim; but there was a gleam of something forming in her dark eyes: humour? Understanding? He took courage from it.

'No. But I can't help finding someone – attractive. That's what's natural. No one can help that.'

'Indeed?'

'Well – no one but you,' he said and risked a grin. She stared back at him, stony-faced. Too soon to grin. He hurried on. 'But what I did, inviting her to my place, the lying, that was unforgivable. I could help that. And for hurting you, making you so unhappy. I feel so ashamed, Meg. So very ashamed.'

She looked at him, said nothing.

'I love you,' he said, 'hard for you to believe it, just at the moment, but I do. I love you like I never loved anyone. Well, there's not been many of course. But – more than – more than anyone. Ever.'

He didn't say Annie's name: clearly feeling it would be the ultimate disloyalty. LM felt deeply moved; tears rose behind her eyes. She blinked hard, she couldn't afford that. Not tears. Not now.

'And there could never be another. Never,' he said, 'not after what we've had, what you've shown me.'

'I have to say,' she said, and her voice was softened, despite her efforts to prevent it, 'your behaviour hardly illustrates that.'

'Meg! You're not listening to me. I'm talking about love. Not – not a bit of nonsense.'

'That bit of nonsense,' she said, 'was very bad. For me.'

'I know,' he said, 'I know it was. You don't have to keep telling me. But I want it to be over. For both of us. I want us to be together again. So much.'

'How can I trust you?' she asked, and she could feel herself softening, almost against her will, 'that's the thing, Jago. Ever again?'

'You'll have to,' he said simply. 'There's nothing else you can do. Either trust me, or say goodbye.'

She was silent.

'Thing is,' he said, 'what I haven't said, it's not always easy for me. You being so clever and so on, and having everything.'

'I don't have everything, Jago,' said LM coolly. But she allowed herself now to smile.

'Yes, you do. Money, education, your career. That's what I call everything. I never realised, till I talked to those women, how important Lyttons was, how important you must be. It made me feel pretty small. Feeble. With – well with her, just for a while I had more. I was the one in charge. I think that had a bit to do with it. Quite a lot, matter of fact.'

LM stared at him; it was her turn to feel small, demeaned. She had never actually considered that: how difficult it must all be for Jago. Not within the confines of their relationship, at any rate. She had enjoyed being in charge as he put it; not in an arrogant way, perhaps, but enjoyed it, nevertheless, always the one to give, to offer, to – well, to have. Never to take, never to feel gratitude. She looked down the years, saw it as he must surely see it, saw herself inviting Jago into her house, giving him fine food, good wine, presents, always giving, and suddenly felt ashamed.

She took a breath, to tell him – what? How? But he spoke first.

'Thing is, except in bed, it never is me. In charge that is. But no, that's wrong, isn't it? Then it's both of us. Which is how it should be, of course.'

LM gave in to the tears. They flowed, unstaunched, down her face, silent, aching tears; she stood there, quite still, crying, looking at him, across the hall. Finally she stopped, held out her hand; he stepped forward and took it.

'I'm so sorry,' he said again, 'so sorry I made you unhappy.'

'Well,' she said, 'Perhaps I – well perhaps I can understand a little now, at least. Which is not to say I ever want anything like it, anything—' she smiled again, 'anything natural happening again.'

'No,' he said, 'no, it won't.'

'And I'm sorry, too. About – well about how you feel. I hadn't considered it before. I don't know what I can do about it, but I will try.'

'Oh no,' he said, 'I don't want any of that. Not you changing, Meg. I love you how you are. If you can believe it.'

'I—think I can,' she said, 'and I love you too. Shall we – that is – would you like to – stay for a while?'

'Yes,' he said, 'yes, that'd be nice. Thank you.'

Brunson let Celia in, told her Mr Lytton was upstairs, packing.

'Truman is ready with the car to take you to the station, Lady Celia. You have to leave in just over thirty minutes.'

'I know, Brunson, I know. Goodness knows how I'm going to manage. Where are the children?'

'The girls are all asleep as far as I know, Lady Celia. Master Giles is out at the house of a friend.'

'Yes, of course. I'd forgotten. But he'll be back in time to say goodbye?'

'I imagine so, Lady Celia.'

She ran upstairs to their room. Oliver looked at her; he was flushed and exasperated-looking. 'Why on earth are you so late? We have to leave in—'

'In thirty minutes. I know. I was doing something. God, Oliver, I shall be glad to get on that train tonight. Then nothing and no one can stop us. How marvellous. Don't worry, my darling, I can be ready. I'm almost all packed. Just my vanity case. I really think when we get back I shall have to see about getting my own maid. It's too much for me to do, especially when we're so busy socially. Anyway, give me twenty minute's peace, and why don't you go up to the nursery. Say goodbye to the girls?'

'I've already been. They're all asleep. Nanny was very anxious that I shouldn't wake them.'

'But – oh well, perhaps it's for the best. Look, just leave me alone and I'll be ready much more quickly. Do you know, in spite of everything, I'm terribly excited.'

'Me too, my darling. Me too.'

Barty was trying to stifle her coughing in her pillow. She wasn't sure where she was, sometimes she thought she was back in Line Street, in the bed with her brothers, and then she felt she was falling through the bottom of her bed, down and down to the bottom of the Lytton house, in a kind of hot swirling darkness. During the times she thought she was in Line Street, she kept calling for her mother; but she didn't come, only Nanny, looking fierce, to spoon more cough mixture down her. She'd had so much now she'd started being sick with it. Nanny had begun to threaten her now with more castor oil if she bothered Lady Celia.

'I don't want her worried if she comes up here, knowing you're ill. It would be very wrong of you. There's nothing seriously the matter with you, in fact you're getting up in the morning, I'm not having you lying here, being waited on another day. Now you just get to sleep and stay that way; that's what the doctor said you had to do.'

Barty knew quite well the doctor had said more than that but her tongue felt swollen and her throat was so painful, she couldn't possibly have said so. She couldn't have made the slightest sound of any sort; she had no idea why they were so worried about her bothering Aunt Celia. She did try to get up once because she wanted to go the lavatory, but even sitting up made her feel so ill she lay down again. She would just have to wet the bed. She was past caring.

Packed, dressed in her travelling outfit – a beige, tailored suit, in the style favoured by Queen Alexandra, with a wonderful wide-brimmed hat – Celia ran up to the nursery floor. It was silent; she opened the door of the day nursery stealthily. Nanny was sitting by the fire, mending. She rose, raised her finger to her lips.

'They're all three fast asleep, Lady Celia,' she said, 'I know you wanted to say goodbye to them, but I really think they're best left. They'll only be upset if they see you now.'

'I suppose so,' said Celia, 'but I wouldn't wake them, Nanny, I just want to look at them. I'm not going to see them for more than three weeks.'

'Well – be all right if you went in to the twins, I suppose,' said Nanny, 'but maybe not Barty.'

'Why not?'

'She was crying earlier. For her mum. You know how she does sometimes. I gave her a cuddle, read her a story, and she went off fine. But if she woke – well. Best not risk disturbing her.'

'Yes. Yes, I suppose you're right. Oh, dear, poor little Barty I do wonder sometimes—'

'Don't you worry about her. She's happy as a sandboy most of the time.'

'I hope so. Oh, goodness, look at the time. I'll just pop in, look at the twins—'

She slipped into the night nursery; the twins lay, sleeping sweetly, in their side-by-side cots. They could only sleep where they could see one another. One night, when Adele was ill and the doctor, wrongly fearing scarlet fever, had prescribed isolation, her cot had been moved to another floor. They had both wailed dismally far into the night until Nanny, in a flash of inspiration, had put a small mirror in each cot. Each twin gazed in grateful surprise at the image of herself jammed against the cot bars and fell asleep.

Celia smiled, her eyes filled briefly with tears, blew them each a kiss. She hated leaving them. Anything might happen.

'Darling, do come along. We're going to miss that train.'

'I'm coming. I am. Goodbye, Nanny. Thank you for being so absolutely wonderful. See you in three weeks. Oliver, where's Giles? We can't go without saying goodbye to him.'

'He's downstairs, waiting to wave us off.'

'Is he upset?'

'No, he's fine.'

'I'll come down,' said Nanny, 'make sure he's all right.'

'Very good of you, Nanny. Come on, darling, please.'

'Giles, my darling, goodbye. Be the best boy. We'll bring you lots of presents from America. And arrange for Maud and her brothers to come and stay. Give Mummy a big hug.'

Giles obediently did so.

'Have a nice time, Mummy. And Daddy.'

'We will, old chap. Now come along, darling, into the car. Truman's loaded everything up. I'm not joking, we really are in danger of missing the train.'

'I'm coming, really I am.'

'Have you really got to go?'

'Yes, of course we have. You know we have. Now Giles, no crying, there's a good chap. You'll upset your mother.'

Giles bit his quivering lip. He walked with them to the door, stood between Nanny and Brunson, holding both their hands. 'Have a wonderful trip, Sir,' said Brunson. 'And you, Lady Celia.'

'Thank you, Brunson. We'll be back before you all know it.'

Giles suddenly broke free, ran forward. His small face was anxious. 'Have you said goodbye to Barty and the twins?'

'Yes, of course. Well – I looked at them. They were all asleep.'

He looked at her. Then he said, 'Lettie was right about Barty, then.'

Celia stopped, very still, then she bent down to Giles's level. 'What do you mean, darling?'

'Celia for the love of God, come along. Please.'

'No Oliver, wait. This is important. Giles, what was Lettie right about?'

'She said – she said—'

'Celia!'

'What did Lettie say?'

Nanny ran forward, grabbed Giles's hand. 'Giles, don't upset your mother. She doesn't need to be worried just now.'

'What did Lettie say, Giles?'

He ignored her, looked up at Nanny, very shrewdly. Then he said, 'She said you wouldn't give up your trip for Barty.'

'What did she mean?'

'Master Giles, I said don't.'

'Giles, what did she mean? Why should I give up my trip for Barty? I don't understand. Did she say anything else?'

'Celia, I'm going. I'll see you at the station.'

'Giles—'

'Master Giles—'

'Did she say anything else?'

'She—'

'Giles, tell me, please.'

'She said you wouldn't give up your trip for her. For all your – your talk about—' his voice shook then steadied – 'about her being one of the family.'

'Giles,' said Celia, and for more reasons than one, she felt as if she was falling into a deep, dark abyss, 'I don't understand. Why did Lettie say that? Why should I give up my trip for Barty? There's no reason to. She isn't ill, after all . . . is she?'

Part Two
1914–1918

CHAPTER 9

'Dead! Oh, Oliver how dreadful. What can we do, should you go – what happened?'

'Apparently she had a – a miscarriage,' said Oliver, looking up from the telegram which had just been delivered. 'I don't know any more than that. The funeral is next week. I would like to go, of course, but it is quite impossible. There's no way I could get there in time.'

'Of course not. Poor Robert. Poor, poor man. A miscarriage! But it all went so well last time. I suppose she was – what – forty-five. But even so . . .'

'Well, the only thing we can do is write to Robert,' said Oliver. He sighed. 'And go and see him as soon as we can. How very sad. I liked her so much. And respected her, she was really extremely clever. I – we – owe her a lot.'

'I know it,' said Celia, who had actually, at times, resented the strength of Jeanette's involvement in Lyttons, and Oliver's overt admiration for her, and now felt guilty about it. 'She was marvellous to us. And I liked her too. That visit last summer was such fun, with all the children. She was so full of life, I can't imagine her – oh God. How cruel. I'll write to Robert at once. And those poor boys . . .'

'Yes, indeed,' said Oliver, 'they've had an appalling time, both parents lost. Oh, Celia, what a dreadful week this has been, the archduke murdered, war looming, and now poor Jeanette.'

'She is a little older of course,' the doctor had said cautiously, when confirming the new pregnancy, adding with slightly false jocularity that nature knew what she was doing. 'Only you mustn't place too much faith in her. Your blood pressure must be kept down, so plenty of rest, Mrs Lytton, in fact bed-rest at certain times, a long sleep every afternoon, no early rising, no strenuous exercise and of course absolutely no—' he cleared his throat '—no further intimacy. And I shall call to see you every week.'

'Don't look like that, Robert, my dearest,' Jeanette said, when the doctor had gone. 'It will be perfectly all right, I know it will. Look what a model obstetric case I was with Maud. I feel wonderful. And so happy and excited.'

'I know, my darling, I know. But – well I can't help worrying.'

'You mustn't. And besides, it's all my fault. I should have – well I should have insisted we were more careful. But it's so difficult in the heat of the moment. And they're such wonderfully heated moments, aren't they?'

He smiled at her, touched by her happiness. 'You really must take things more easily' he said, 'no more large-scale entertaining. No visits to Elliotts or—'

'I know, I know, Robert. Or Lyttons. I won't. I promise. This is much more important. Even I can see that.'

Well, at least she was acknowledging that. He had been miserable lately; she had been so absorbed, so busy with her new important literary life, as she put it. She had loved it; loved going into the Lyttons office – rather a smart office, a brownstone near Gramercy Park, built in the French style, but as she pointed out to Oliver, important that it should be prestigious, a good shop window for him. Robert had hated it all so much: feeling, ironically, estranged from her, in her involvement with his family. He had actually found the office for them; after that he was allowed no part of it. She took it over, showed it to Oliver, discussed leases, decor, staffing levels; he had been completely over-whelmed by her, by the whole thing. Robert watched him, and worried. Jeanette was very good at overwhelming.

It was not a large organisation, Lyttons New York, but it was quite a powerful one. It was run by an impressive young man called Stuart Bailey, whom Oliver had poached from Doubledays and appointed as editorial director. A managing director in charge of the business side had been found by Jeanette.

'He runs one of the charities I'm involved with, immensely capable, and very much in sympathy with the arts generally. I would suggest he and Stuart report jointly to you. Rather than ask either one of them to report to the other. They are both high-fliers in their field. It wouldn't work.'

Oliver, impressed, as always, by her grasp of company structure, agreed. In the event, as Robert had known they would, they both reported to Jeanette. Initially, the company published only what Lyttons in London did; after a few months, Stuart Bailey began to acquire his own books and authors. He was both shrewd and imaginative; Celia, particularly, had adored him.

'He's perfect. We ought to have him in London, really.'

'I think,' said Oliver, looking at her rather quizzically, 'there would not be room in London for the two of you.'

By the end of the first year, the company was doing well; not quite showing a profit, for the investment had been heavy, but certainly breaking even was within its sights. Jeanette was excited, deeply absorbed in it, constantly on the lookout herself for talent, for ideas. She seemed to Robert to be increasingly like Celia: absorbed in her work, becoming detached from her family. It troubled him and not only because he was jealous and resentful. She had formulated plans for the next year, for expansion, had proposed an art book division, was talking of making a solo trip to London, to discuss acquisitions with Oliver. It was all becoming absurdly grandiose. Or so it seemed to Robert.

But now she was to have another baby. And was promising that this new game of hers – for that was how he saw it – would cease. He was surprised she had acquiesced so easily: surprised and relieved.

'Of course the baby is more important,' she said, 'and certainly until he is safely born, he will be my prime consideration.' She smiled at him. 'And I'm sure, this time, it is a boy. An heir for you. Don't look so worried, my dearest. I will be good. And I'm sure, as Dr Whitelaw always says, that nature knows what she is doing.'

Only nature didn't of course; and at six months exactly, she went into premature labour, gave birth to a stillborn boy and died twenty-four hours later.

Robert Lytton was sitting alone in his study, trying to finalise plans for the funeral when Laurence came in without knocking.

'I want to talk to you,' he said.

'Yes? If it's about the funeral, I'd welcome any suggestions, of course.'

He was actually pleased to see Laurence; since Jeanette's death he had scarcely left his room, had had his meals served there, had left it only to go for long solitary walks in Central Park. He had been holding his mother's hand when she died, had sat by her unmoving on her long, last, dreadful day, refusing to move, even when Robert had asked him for a few moment's alone with her. A few minutes after the doctor had confirmed her death, he stood up, kissed her forehead and left, dry-eyed, his face blank. Jamie, crying helplessly, had run after him, but had come back almost at once, banished from his brother's grief, and hurled himself into Robert's arms.

Robert, struggling to cope with his own wretchedness, faced with the nightmare of caring for a young family on his own, including a little girl of two, had been concerned for Laurence, had gone to his room several times, knocked gently on the door, and been told to go away.

'He wants to be by himself,' Jamie said, his large blue-green eyes, so like his mother's smudged and swollen with crying, meeting Robert's half-embarrassed, half-bewildered. 'he told me to tell you not to – not to try and talk to him.'

'Well, that's perfectly natural,' said Robert carefully. 'I think we should respect that, don't you Jamie?'

Jamie nodded, tried to smile. Still only thirteen, he was too shocked, too distressed by his mother's death to maintain any kind of hostility towards Robert. He liked his stepfather, he couldn't help it, he had always thought he was kind and funny and fun; and when Laurence went away to school the autumn after Maud was born, he had relaxed into an acceptance of him. It was difficult when Laurence came home of course, and at first he had tried to pretend he was still not really having anything to do with Robert, and then to persuade Laurence that Robert was really all right, but Laurence fixed him with his cold eyes and said, 'You can be disloyal to our father if you must, Jamie. I find it impossible. Perhaps you'll understand when you're older. Don't worry about it. I know it's difficult for you.'

'That's not fair!' Jamie staunchly said, but Laurence shrugged and told him he was only speaking the truth as he saw it.

After their mother died Jamie woke one night to hear a dreadful rasping sobbing in the next room: it was Laurence. Jamie had gone in, climbed into his bed, tried to comfort him. But Laurence lay there, stone-still, and refused to talk about it; except to say, as Jamie finally turned away from him, 'You know he did it, don't you? He killed her, it's his fault.'

'Don't be silly,' Jamie said, and half-frightened by the rage in Laurence's voice, went back to his own room to grieve on his own; in any case he didn't really know what Laurence meant.

But Robert had.

'She died because of you,' Laurence said to him now, 'she died because she was having your child.'

'Laurence! That's a terrible thing to say.' But guilt stirred in Robert's blood; the same thought had not only occurred to him, it haunted his days and filled his dreams.

'Your mother died through a loss of blood,' he said firmly, fighting the tremor in his voice. 'I understand your grief and even your anger, but please don't imagine anything sinister.'

'Nothing sinister,' said Laurence, 'a simple case of cause and effect, wouldn't you say? You fucked her—'

'Laurence! How dare you speak to me like that. Apologise at once.'

'I apologise for using an obscene word,' said Laurence and his voice was very calm, very cold, 'but not for the act which it describes. You impregnated my mother when she was too old and not in good enough health for such a thing, and as a result she died. I fail to see how you can avoid taking responsibility.'

Robert was silent.

'Anyway,' said Laurence, 'after the funeral, at which clearly the niceties must be observed, I hope we shall not meet again. I have no desire to see you or to speak to you.'

'I'm sorry Laurence,' said Robert, so buffered by shock against this that he hardly felt anything at all, 'but of course we shall have to meet again. We share a house, a family.'

'We don't share a family,' said Laurence, 'Jamie is my brother and we are both the sons of my mother and father. And Maud is nothing to do with me.'

'Of course she is. She's your half-sister.'

'Well let me put it this way. I have no desire to see her again either. So I'd be grateful if you would leave my house as soon as it's feasible and take her with you.'

'Laurence, I think perhaps your unhappiness has driven you a little mad,' said Robert. 'This is not your house, it is – well it is the family house.'

'It belonged to my parents. It's now mine.'

'I'm afraid that is incorrect. It's mine, as a matter of fact. And—' he struggled to remain courteous and reasonable, 'and of course you will live in it too.'

'Are you sure about that?' said Laurence and his voice was odd, his eyes cunning. 'My father's will dictated specifically that the house was to come to me. After my mother died. It is the Elliott family home, built by my grandfather.'

'I'm aware of that. And of course when I myself – pass away – the house will be yours. In the meantime, I repeat, it is the family home. And I am presently the head of the family.'

'You are not the head of my family,' said Laurence, 'and I think you will find that the house is mine.'

'And you would propose to live in it on your own? Do I interpret the situation correctly?'

'You do indeed.'

'And your brother?'

'He will live here too. He belongs with me. That is what my father would have wished.'

'Well, that's quite absurd. Jamie is only thirteen. You are three years from being of age. It is quite out of the question that you should live here on your own.'

'We shall have the servants. They'll take care of us.'

'Laurence, this is an absurd conversation,' said Robert finally, 'not least because this house is mine. And there is no question of my leaving it.'

'I think,' said Laurence, 'that you should talk to the lawyers.'

'Will you have to go, if there's a war? Will you have to go and fight?' asked Giles.

'I don't know,' said Oliver, whose mind had been swerving around this possibility for months, 'I suppose – yes I probably will. But we must all pray that it doesn't happen.'

'Not much hope of that,' said LM briskly. 'It not happening, I mean. We can all pray as much as we like.'

She had come to supper with the family; partly to discuss when and if they might go to see Robert. He and she had been very close: born within a year of one another, they had grown up virtually inseparable. Oliver, born late in their childhood and to their stepmother, while much loved by them both, had never quite broken through that bond.

'Poor little boys,' LM said, 'it must be so hard for them.'

'Terrible,' said Celia, 'and poor little Maud too.'

'Yes, but she still has her father, at least. The boys are twice orphaned.'

'I didn't like Laurence,' said Giles. 'He wouldn't play with me at all.'

'Well he's a lot older than you are,' said Celia, 'although I have to say he did seem quite difficult. Jamie was a sweet little boy. I wonder how they're coping.'

'I'm sure that with Robert's help they're coping very well,' said LM. 'Anyway, I had thought I might go out and visit Robert. But now, of course, with war being imminent, it seems unlikely. Ships will hardly be ploughing across the waters on pleasure cruises will they?'

'Oh I don't know,' said Celia. 'America is hardly in the same direction as France and Germany. Or is it?' Her geography was famously weak.

'Not quite,' said Oliver, smiling at her, 'but I fancy the waters anywhere around this island could become pretty hazardous if war is actually declared. More to the point, the liners could be called into service, I'd have thought. And then there could be fuel shortages, heaven knows what. Either way, I wouldn't advise it.'

'On the other hand, it could be years before I see Robert again,' said LM, 'that saddens me greatly. It's all so very dreadful. I did like Jeanette, she was such a *good* addition to the family I felt. Well, life is very cruel. Very.'

'I would say,' said Giles, 'it was death that was cruel. Not life. Will I still go away to school if there's a war?'

'Of course you will,' said Celia, smiling at this rather precocious observation, 'especially since St Christopher's is right in the middle of the country. It will make me feel much happier.'

'Why? What's so special about the country?'

'It's always safer in the country, when there's a war,' said Celia and then seeing Oliver's warning expression, added hastily, 'lots of lovely fresh food and no nasty tanks driving about the roads.'

'I'd like to see the tanks. What about you? What will you do? To get away from them?'

'We'll stay here of course. We've got work to do.'

'What about the girls?'

'Giles, there is absolutely no certainty that there'll be a war yet.'

'But if there is—'

'I shall probably send them to stay with Grandmama. So they'll be in the country too.'

'But not near me,' said Giles hopefully. He was looking forward to getting away from the twins.

'Nowhere near you, no. Now Giles, it's nearly your bedtime. Off you go. I'll be up in a minute, tell Nanny.'

There was a new nanny in the nurseries; Jenny Paget and Lettie had been sacked immmediately on that dreadful day when Barty had been found to have pneumonia, and the voyage on the *Titanic* had been sacrificed.

'She saved our lives,' Celia had said, looking up at Oliver from Barty's bedside three days' later, when the news came through about the sinking of the *Titanic* and the appalling death-toll. 'Imagine, Oliver, if Giles hadn't told us about her being ill, we'd have been out there somewhere in that icy water, drowned – oh it doesn't bear thinking about. And she would have died too, I should think, with that dreadful pair not even calling the doctor again. How tenuous life is, isn't it? Just one tiny thread, pulled out of the fabric and everything changes.'

'Thank God for it,' he said, moving over to her, stroking her hair. He was dreadfully shaken by the news, by the thought of how close they had come to death, and for months afterwards he dreamed of drowning, of dark freezing suffocation, of separation from Celia and the children he loved so much. Even Barty now, he realised; in the first forty-eight hours when she was so close to death that they had fetched her mother, had kept a nearly hopeless vigil through the nights and days, he had looked down at her small, ferociously fevered body, listened to the fast rasping breathing, the dreadful cough, and been literally terrified at the thought of losing her. Not just because Celia, certainly, and he, to some extent, would have borne the blame for it, but because she had worked her way into his heart, with her courage, her sharp little brain, and her clear affection for him, her invariable delight at seeing him.

Giles was distraught, frantic with fear that he would lose her; 'She was my friend,' he kept saying, 'my best friend, my only friend really. She can't die, she can't.'

Even in her anguish, Celia felt worried that he should regard Barty as his only friend.

He was an odd little boy; she had to face that fact. Solitary, serious, overtly obedient, but deeply awkward, resistant to any attempt to be drawn out of himself. He was clever, but not quick; he needed time. Once his brain had grasped something, it went to work on it; he learned to read late, but within a year was reading quite complicated stories to himself. His tables caused him dreadful trouble until he worked out a logical pattern for them; after that he had the lot learned within a day.

He was not popular at school; he entirely lacked his parents' golden charm. Seldom invited to birthday parties, never picked for any team games, with only one or two friends, he was happiest in the holidays, when he and Barty invented elaborate fantasy games which they would play right through the long, easy days. They would be travellers in some distant country, working their way homewards across difficult territory; or soldiers in an army fighting to defend their land; or the king and queen of a kingdom, working out laws and systems and ruling their subjects (the twins when they would cooperate, and the new, much loved nanny) with solemn authority.

'It's against the law,' Giles would say, 'to walk on the pavement lines. You have to step in the middle. Otherwise you get fined.'

'In this country,' Barty would pronounce, 'we have to salute the boats. And pay a forfeit if we don't.'

Barty, at seven, was very quick; she grasped concepts and ideas, or learned by rote, all with equal facility. She went to school in the mornings; to a small establishment just off the King's Road. She was, her teacher told Celia quietly, the cleverest child in the class. She worked hard, not out of a sense of duty, but because she loved it. Like Giles, she was not popular; if only because she was different. The other children, with their unerring instinct for such things, noted a slightly different intonation in her voice a reticence in her dealings with them, a reluctance to talk about herself. She was brought to school by a nursery maid as they were; but the difference was that the beautiful woman who came to concerts and other school events, was not her mother, but a so-called aunt. When pressed, she would talk of someone else, someone she stubbornly called her mum; a fierce loyalty prevented Sylvia from becoming Mummy, or Mama. That, to Barty, would have been the ultimate betrayal. She tried not to talk about any of it but when driven to it, she spoke the truth. And with the truth, once they had it, the other children tormented her.

They then proceeded to do some research; nursery gossip provided most of what they wanted to know. The tactful reticence of the new Lytton nanny on the subject came too late; Jenny had talked with great relish on the nanny benches, and the story was a good one.

'Our nanny says she was living in the gutter when Lady Celia brought her home. She had to be scrubbed clean.'

'My nanny says she had lice. And ate with her hands.'

'Our nanny says her father was a drunk.'

'My nanny says there were six children all in one bed.'

She was nicknamed Snipe, short for guttersnipe; like Giles, she received no invitations to parties, nor did she ever have a partner to walk with in school crocodiles. She hid her unhappiness – a familiar feeling behind proud silence, which isolated her further, and sat working over her books while the other children played. Her success at lessons became a further excuse to torment her. Snipe the Swot is what they all called her now, and she became increasingly isolated. But she preferred school to home, just the same. At least the twins weren't there.

The twins, at four, were monstrous; Giles called them the fiends. Beautiful, fascinating, wilful, and with strong personalities working at double power, it was inevitable that they should be dreadfully spoilt. Not only at home, but wherever they went people would smile at them, point them out, say, 'Oh, look, how sweet'.

Exquisitely and identically dressed, they loved nothing better than to go out; it was like stepping on to a stage with an endlessly appreciative audience. Total strangers stopped them, asked them their names, how old they were, told them they were pretty; they had only to do the most ordinary thing, jump off a pavement, walk along a wall, holding Nanny's hands, and people would watch them, remarking how clever they were. By the time they were three they had appeared, photographed with their mother, in most of the society magazines and in the court pages of *The Times* and the *Daily Telegraph*.

Oliver protested at this, saying it was bad for them, but Celia, never slow to court publicity, laughed at him, told him they were too young to understand. Celia adored the twins; they possessed all the virtues – beauty, charm, sociability – that Giles did not. Accused by Oliver of favouring them, she laughed again, said it wasn't favouritism, just a natural pleasure in having girls.

'Rather than a boy who is – you must admit it, Oliver – very quiet. And Giles would hate to be photographed and taken about to shops and out to tea, you know he would.'

Oliver said rather feebly that he supposed she was right. In any case, he adored the twins as well; they were so irresistibly warm and affectionate, like small, silken-haired puppies, climbing on to his lap, kissing him, whispering they loved him. In their own social circle, they were famous, everyone wanting to be their friends, claiming close association with them. From the moment they were launched into child society, at dance classes in Knightsbridge at the age of two and a half, they were social stars. There was no shortage of birthday party invitations for the twins.

'Nobody knows how awful they are,' whispered Giles to Barty one day, watching the twins, sweetly smiling in identical white lace dresses, waving goodbye to some friends who had come to tea. Barty nodded sympathetically.

But it wasn't quite true. Two people, at least, had the twins' measure: one was Nanny, who was extremely strict with them, and the other was their maternal grandmother.

'Beautiful they may be,' she said to Celia at the end of a visit, as the twins entwined themselves on her lap, and covered her face with kisses, ignoring their mother's instructions to go up to the nursery, 'and very sweet. But they're getting out of hand. All very well when they're tiny, but later on, it will be less charming. You should be much firmer with them, in my opinion. Otherwise you'll be sorry.'

Celia laughed and said she knew they were naughty, 'But so enchantingly so. And they're only tiny still. Plenty of time to be stricter later.'

Lady Beckenham said that was quite untrue, as anyone who had trained dogs or horses knew: 'You have to be firm from the beginning. Otherwise they don't know where they are. And then you get nasty habits developing.'

'Mummy, the twins are little girls, not dogs.'

'No different,' said Lady Beckenham, 'no different at all. You send them down to me and I'll get them licked into shape.'

'I don't think that's a very good idea at all,' said Celia laughing.

But she was about to change her mind, for a rather more serious reason. On the 4th of August, 1914 when Great Britain declared war on Germany, and one hundred thousand telegrams went out to every reservist in the land, bearing the one dreadful word 'mobilise', her first thought was of the danger to her children and of the safety of Ashingham. A fortnight later, as the first British force entered France, she instructed Nanny to start packing the children's clothes and warned her mother to expect them all within forty-eight hours.

'My darling, I think you are being a little precipitate,' said Oliver. 'I see no great danger to any of us in the immediate future.'

'Oliver, don't be ridiculous. That's exactly the point. We have to act now, before it's too late. I want the children out of London quickly.'

'But why?'

'Everyone says there will be bombs raining down on London.'

'Everyone says the war will be over by Christmas,' said Oliver soberly, 'neither is very likely, in my view.'

She turned to look at him; they were in the drawing-room, sitting by the window. Below them, across the Embankment, the Thames flowed peacefully past; people walked along, arm in arm, or leaned on the wall, watching the boats. The sky was clear, the sun setting in a blaze of drama; it was all very tranquil and still. Celia felt calmed, soothed; then suddenly, as the reflections of the sunset, orange and blazing red hit the water, she thought of shellfire and felt afraid.

'Oh Oliver,' she said, getting up, standing behind him, her hands on his shoulders, her head resting against his, 'It's going to be so dreadful. Why can't people see it? The way everyone's rushing to enlist, people walking all night, apparently from remote villages; that march down Whitehall with people cheering, the headlines in the paper, all these For King and Country posters – you'd think there was some huge party about to begin. Instead of death and misery and slaughter. It's begun already, all those poor wretches from the *Amphion* drowned when they hit that German mine—'

'I think they do know. In their hearts,' said Oliver, putting up his hand, covering hers, 'certainly the men do. They pretend for their womenfolk. And for themselves to an extent. Not thinking about it all too much. It protects them from fear. And then, in a way, I think the country wants a war. Or thinks it does.'

'Oh, Oliver, how could it? How could anyone want a war?'

'My darling, it's a basic instinct. It goes with patriotism. Of which lately there has been a vast wave. It's almost a new religion. It's everywhere, in the meanest street, the most modest school, the dingiest factory.'

'The only people with any sense, as usual, who seem to see it all for what it is, are the women,' said Celia, 'that march on the fourth of August by the International Women was so incredibly powerful. Calling war the last great violent outburst of evil. Not much talk of patriotism then.'

'Didn't do much good though, did it?'

'I suppose not.'

'And there's another thing. With the improvement in communications, the newspapers and the wireless, people feel more – more one. More united. Which fuels the patriotism. Add that to the sense of empire, of glory and—' he sighed – 'and of course, in Britain we think

143

we can't lose a war. But I fear this time we may be wrong. Germany is very powerful. Very powerful indeed.'

She looked down at him. 'And – will you go? I've kept not asking you. I'm frightened to hear the answer, I suppose. It's bad enough knowing that Jack will certainly be there, but—'

He was silent for a long time. Then he said, 'I'm afraid I shall have to. I couldn't live with myself if I didn't.'

Another silence; then Celia said, 'Oliver, let's go upstairs. I want to – be with you.'

She knew why she wanted it suddenly, and so badly; it was for her what the cheering and the laughter were to the young men, a fence against reality. Against the unspoken rider to what he had said, which was that if he went, he might no longer live at all, never mind with himself.

Jack Lytton arrived at Cheyne Walk in the middle of the afternoon a week later; he had been due for a long leave, after his four-year tour of duty in India, but that had been cancelled and he had been granted only a week. After that he was re-joining his regiment for a month's training, before leaving for France. Well a week would be something, he thought; you could do a lot in a week. In London.

Brunson greeted him, took his coat and his luggage. 'Lady Celia and Mr Lytton are both out, sir. At the publishing company.' He always referred to it as the publishing company, as if it were a rather surprising place for them to be.

'Yes, I thought they would be. I told them I wouldn't be here until dinner time. Never mind. Could I have a whisky and soda, Brunson? I'm a bit travel weary.'

'Certainly, sir. I'll bring it into the drawing-room.'

'Any of the children about?'

'They're all out with Nanny, sir. For a walk. They should be back shortly.'

'Good. I can't wait to see them. The twins were babies last time; well it was the christening. Giles must be quite a big chap by now.'

'He is indeed, sir. going off to school in September.'

'Poor little bugger,' said Jack cheerfully.

Brunson looked at him doubtfully and disappeared into the pantry, only to reappear with the whisky tray.

'Perhaps, Sir, you might prefer this in your room.'

'Yes, that might be better, 1 – oh hallo hallo. You're all back. Know who I am?'

The children had come into the hall; they stood staring at him.

'You know me, Giles, surely. I'm your Uncle Jack. Don't you remember me?'

'I think so,' said Giles uncertainly, and then, holding out his hand. 'How do you do, sir.'

'I do, I do,' said Venetia.

'So do I,' said Adele.

'You don't,' said Giles, 'you were only babies. He was at your christening.'

'We do remember. Don't we Adele?'

'Yes we do.'

'Well it's very good news if you do. Do I get a kiss?'

The twins flung themselves at him; he stood up, laughing, one on each arm. They were very jolly little things. Pretty too. Extraordinarily pretty. Like their mother. Gorgeous girl, Celia. He could never quite work out how dull old Oliver had managed to nab her. She should have waited for him. He noticed Barty, standing politely quiet at the bottom of the stairs and grinned at her.

'Hallo. You're Barty aren't you? You've grown a bit, too. Can you give me a kiss?'

He bent down, released the twins; Barty came forward, kissed him dutifully on the cheek. She was quite pretty too. Wonderful hair. Funny little thing she'd been, he'd thought at the christening. Terribly shy and quiet. Hardly surprising of course. Jack was not an imaginative person, but even he could see that finding yourself, at the age of three, dumped down with a lot of strangers and told you were going to have to live with them from now on, must be a bit difficult. He'd sort of understood from Oliver that it was intended as a temporary arrangement; it seemed to have become permanent.

'How old are you?' he asked her.

She fixed him with her large, hazel eyes and said, 'Seven.'

'My goodness, that is grown up. And what's it like, living with this lot? Murder, I should think.'

Barty flushed, looked at the twins nervously. They were watching her, their dark eyes sharp.

'It's — very nice,' she said quickly.

So that was how it was; a bit difficult. The others probably resented her like mad.

'We like living with her,' said Giles firmly.

'I'm sure you do.'

The twins exchanged glances and started running up the stairs, giggling, their dark heads together.

'They're so silly,' said Giles, giving Barty a quick smile and then, 'how long are you here for, Uncle Jack?'

'Only a week. Planning to make the most of it, though.'

That night at dinner, he outlined his plans for making the most of it.

'I hope you won't mind, but I shan't be around much. Got some friends to catch up on. See a few shows, that sort of thing.'

'We won't mind at all,' said Oliver.

But Celia said, her eyes dancing with mild malice, 'and why shouldn't we want to see some shows too?'

'My darling Celia,' his blue eyes, darker than Oliver's, but exactly the same almond shape, with exactly the same almost girlishly long lashes, moved over her face, 'You can come to a show with me any time.'

'Good. Then I shall. What do you fancy most?'

'Oh, you'll have to tell me. I'm dreadfully out of touch. The music hall, I suppose. I long to see the Gibson Girls. Oliver, what suggestions do you have?'

'Now let me see,' said Oliver looking at him, his expression absolutely deadpan. 'There's a new production of *Othello* I'd rather like to see. I could take you to that. And perhaps *Rigoletto* at Covent Garden. How would you like that?'

'I think I probably wouldn't, thanks very much all the same,' said Jack, 'I can't seem to quite get the hang of Shakespeare. I remember you getting terribly excited about something by him, saying it had changed your life. I thought you'd gone a bit bonkers.'

'He probably had,' said Celia, 'now, I'll tell you what we should see, and I promise, Jack, I won't interfere with the rest of your leave at all, it's the first full length colour film. It sounds madly exciting. *The World, the Flesh and the Devil* it's called. There now, you can take me to that.'

'With the greatest of pleasure. Sounds very exciting. Does that appeal to you, Oliver?'

'No, I think I'll duck out, if you don't mind,' said Oliver. 'Now tell us about India, Jack, have you enjoyed it?'

'Absolutely loved it. Bit of action, lot of fun. Ended with a staff job you know, stayed behind as ADC to the Viceroy when the regiment went out to South Africa. Did I tell you that?'

'No,' said Celia smiling at him. Modesty was one of his most endearing characteristics. But she could see exactly why he should have earned such a prize: he had charm, he had social grace, and he was by all accounts a brilliant soldier.

'Yes, well, I did enjoy it. I tell you what was marvellous, the Durbar. The Coronation out there, you know in 1911. Magnificent. Fifty thousand troops, at the ceremony in Delhi. Bloody – beg your pardon Celia – absolutely fantastic. The viceroy led the Indian princes into the ceremony of homage, dozens of 'em, and the king emperor's train was carried by six pages, all either maharajas themselves or the sons of maharajas. Say what you will, they know how to put on a good show out there. The king and queen both looked wonderful, the king had a special crown created, you know. The people went mad, of course. Did a lot for increasing their enthusiasm. Not always as grateful as they should be, I'm afraid.'

'And have you done all those exciting things, big game hunting and so on?' asked Celia.

'I have indeed. Got rather good at it, as a matter of fact. Bagged quite a few tigers in my time. You go on elephant back, you know. Jolly exciting.'

'I'm afraid London will be rather dull for you after that.'

'Oh – I don't have any fears about dullness', said Jack, 'I intend to have a great deal of fun, and then it's off to France to deal with the Hun. Shouldn't take long. You're not worried about it, Oliver, I hope?'

'Oh – just a bit,' said Oliver.

'Well I'm going,' said Jago. 'Try and stop me.'

LM stared at him and felt terror literally churn in her stomach; she thought she was about to vomit. She clutched the arms of her chair so tightly that she could see the knuckles white when she looked down.

'You mean you've volunteered?'

'I certainly have. Today. Went with the lads.'

'What lads?'

'The brickies. You must have heard about the pals' battalions. Lord Kitchener's just given the nod to them. Volunteer together, serve together. That's the promise. You haven't been reading the right papers, Meg. Twenty thousand men in Manchester all volunteered together, formed fifteen battalions. City Tramways in Glasgow, that's another one, whole battalion in just sixteen hours, Boys' Brigade—'

'The Boys' Brigade?' said LM faintly. 'Boys?'

'Yes, well obviously only the ones old enough. It's a great idea. All together going out there, doing your bit for king and country. Anyway, so down we went to the town hall, lunchtime, three dozen or so of us. Off for training in a week or two, they said. Do you know, even the Australians are sending a force. Defending their empire. You can't help but be moved by that, Meg.'

'Oh Jago,' said LM, and her iron self-discipline deserted her, so fast that it surprised even herself. 'Oh Jago, I don't want you to go.' Fear and misery reduced her to helpless tears; she sat there staring at him, sobbing quietly. He looked at her, first almost amused, then concerned. He went over to her, knelt in front of her, took her face in his hands.

'Hey now. Don't be silly, Meg. This isn't like you. I'll be all right.

Course I will. I can't not go, let the old country down. You wouldn't want that, would you, feeling ashamed of me and all?'

'I'd rather be ashamed of you, than be without you,' said LM quietly.

'Well, you won't be without me for long. It'll be over by Christmas. Then we'll be back, right as rain. You see. Oh, Meg, don't, don't cry like that. Please don't.'

He took her in his arms, felt the sobs shaking her body, felt moved to tears himself.

'Hey,' he said, 'come on. You've got to be brave too, you know. Not just me. That's how I'll get through.'

'I can't think why you didn't talk to me about it,' she said, 'ask me how I felt.'

'Because,' he said, with simple logic, 'whatever you felt I'd have had to go. Simple as that. Now then – upstairs? Now? Take your mind off things.'

'You couldn't,' she said, 'really you couldn't.'

'I'll have a damn good try.'

They went upstairs; she lay in bed, naked, still crying. He got in beside her, took her in his arms.

'I love you,' he said, 'I love you so much. Still. Much as ever. You know that don't you?'

She nodded.

'And you love me. Don't you?'

'Yes,' she said, 'yes, I do.'

'Well then. That's all that matters.'

He started to kiss her. She felt his penis rising against her, sweetly familiar, felt the other familiar things, the urging within herself, the deep softening. She had thought it wouldn't happen, that misery would dull her, but it seemed to have sharpened her, made her want him more. She drew him into her, urgently hungry, felt him filling her, felt love filling her too; and memory with it: all the times that had mattered. The wonderfully shocking first time, on the floor by the fire at her house, the first time he had said he loved her, that she was special, unlike anyone else, all the glorious Sunday mornings, their own particular time, the night she forgave him for Violet Brown, when he had been so gently, so abolutely and tenderly remorseful and she had been so angry, and somehow the two emotions had exploded into something so sensual she still felt the memory physically, felt her body tighten and tauten whenever she thought of it, in her office, at the dining table, even in church. And tonight, this was another special time; she felt herself beginning to climb, a hot, dark ascent, felt her body clenching and unclenching, loosen and tauten round him, felt not only her physical self but her emotions gathering, pulling her around her centre, felt the flaring out, the spreading, the fanning of her orgasm begin, pushed, fought into it, let herself fall, felt first the breaking, the fierce peaks of it, and then the circles, lapping out and out, bigger and brighter each one, and finally, resting on the edge of it, sweetly at peace, felt fear and love for him fill her in equal parts and began to weep once more.

'I'm not going,' said Robert.

'I'm afraid you'll have to,' said Laurence.

'I've told you, Laurence, I won't.'

He was finding it hard even to sound strong. He still felt utterly shaken, by the discovery not only that Laurence was right, had, theoretically at least, the power to order him from the house, his house, but that Jeanette had not loved or trusted him sufficiently to change her will, the will that Jonathan had instructed her to make, had watched her sign, had had his lawyers file away.

Why, why had she not done so, why? He supposed – he hoped, he prayed – because she had thought it unnecessary, that they would live in the house together for a long, long time, until they were both old people and it would be right and proper for it to become Laurence's. But he feared it was because, in the unlikely event of her dying earlier than him, she had not wanted him to have it. Had not wanted him living there, as master. Otherwise why pretend, why dissemble?

Looking back examining the conversations, he could see the assurances were all double-edged. Yes, my dearest, of course everything is in order; no, my darling, you have nothing to worry about. Never actually saying she had changed the will, made the house over to him. Made anything over to him. It was all still for Laurence.

He might never have entered her life, might never have married her, for all the record there was of him in her papers, her official affairs. So – had she from the very beginning seen him as an adventurer, after her money? It was a dreadful thought. His mind ranged endlessly over the conversations about money, the time she had refused him even a business loan, the time she had set aside his suggestion that they should buy a house in London so that he could see his brother and sister more frequently, the many, many times he had suggested joint purchases of shares, of stock, of works of art.

'I will ask the trustees,' she would say vaguely, 'a wonderful idea, my dearest one,' and that would be the last he would hear of it.

He felt grieved, saddened, angry even, the memory of her shadowed, his love for her – and it had indeed been love – tarnished.

'Look, Laurence,' he said now, struggling to sound reasonable, light-hearted even, 'look, you can't really want to live here alone.'

'I won't be alone, I shall have my brother.'

'Your brother cannot possibly live here with you, without adult supervision. I simply can't even countenance that.'

'You have to countenance it,' said Laurence, 'I have the law on my side.'

'But I'm your legal guardian, as your mother's widower.'

'I think I would dispute that as well. The trustees play that role.'

'That is also open to legal argument,' said Robert, his temper beginning to lash, 'and I shall certainly pursue it.'

The financial implications were not too serious; his company was flourishing, he was a modestly rich man now in his own right. Thank God, he thought, thank God she had not loaned him the money to start Brewer Lytton; Laurence would be calling that in as well.

But to be banished from what he had come to regard as his own home, along with Maud, like some kind of disgraced servant, to have to find somewhere else to live, was insupportable. Not only for him, but for Maud. That was one of the things which made him most angry with Jeanette. Her own daughter's future, her place in the family home set at risk. How could she have done that?

Perhaps she had loved Maud less dearly, had regarded her in some way as less important than the boys. The Elliotts. Maud was a Lytton. But could a mother really think, act like that? Maud's family, her entire small world would crumble. It would make losing her mother far worse. She adored Jamie, who was very sweet with her, and displayed a kind of dog-like loyalty to Laurence, following him round the house whenever he was home, scurrying on her small legs, calling to him to wait for her. He never did, of course; he clearly disliked her almost as much as he did Robert. Maud was too small to notice; at least if they moved out of the house she would be spared the discovery.

But Robert had no intention of moving out. There was Jamie as well as Maud to consider; he needed a great deal of love and care, he had adored his mother, missed her dreadfully. The thought of leaving him alone in the house with the servants and his brother was inconceivable. So he would have to come too, wherever they went, and that would deprive him of his own birthright. Surely the whole thing was unsustainable in any court of law. Robert lay awake night after night thinking about it, his mind ranging frantically from legal boundary to moral frontier. He had taken preliminary advice from his own lawyer, who had expressed total astonishment at the terms of the will and at Laurence's determination to uphold it.

'What on earth have you done to him Robert?' he said, laughing. 'He's only a boy. This is Hamlet re-enacted, or something very close to it.'

Robert said it was not a laughing matter and that what Laurence thought he had done was murder his mother.

'Rather than his father. Just like Hamlet. All we need is a crazy sweetheart and—'

'It's me that's going crazy,' said Robert. 'The point is, can he get away with it, does he have the law on his side?'

'If he has a legal guardian,' said his lawyer, 'if he does, and that person is as determined as Laurence to get you out, then you might be in trouble.'

'There is no one guardian as such,' said Robert, 'there are only the trustees. Of the Elliott estate.'

'And they are not precisely defined as Laurence's guardians?'

'They are.'

'Well then, in theory, they could ask you to leave. But only if they felt it was in the best interests of both boys. You say the younger one, Jamie, is fond of you?'

'Very.'

'Then you have a strong moral case. You were an excellent husband, a devoted father and stepfather, and the status quo is on your side. They might examine your management of the household, make sure you are not absconding with any funds, indulging in any great personal extravagance, but provided they are satisfied with that, they are most unlikely to go along with the propositions of a clearly disturbed boy. I should stop worrying about it, if I were you.'

'I may be able to stop worrying,' said Robert, 'but I can't stop being distressed by it.'

It was true; Laurence's continued hostility was not pleasant to live with. He took his meals in his own room, stayed out a great deal and was altogether a seething, hostile presence in the house. If Robert went into the library or the drawing-room or even out into the garden, and found him there, Laurence would immediately leave; he never spoke to Robert, except to impart the most essential information, such as the date of his departure for Harvard, or to ask him whether or not he would be at the house at Long Island for the weekend, in case they should coincide.

It was difficult for the servants, and impossible for Jamie. 'I hate it,' he said, his face flushed, watching Laurence as he stalked out of the dining-room one Saturday lunchtime, having said that he had not expected Robert to be there, 'I don't know what to do.'

'I don't think you can do anything,' said Robert, adding carefully that he thought Laurence's behaviour was largely due to grief. 'He'll get over it. And it will be easier when he's gone to Harvard next month. I'm sure that by Christmas he'll be much more himself,' he added, mentally shrinking from the complexities, not only of Christmas, but also of Thanksgiving.

'He won't speak to me much either any more,' said Jamie, sadly, 'only to tell me things. I hate it,' he said again, 'it's so miserable. It makes missing Mummy much worse.'

'I know, Jamie, and I'm sorry,' said Robert, 'really I am.'

'It's all right. It's not your fault. You won't go, will you Robert? I'd really hate it if you did.'

'I won't go, no,' said Robert, 'but if I did, I'd take you with me. Of course. But there's no question of it. Not for a long time anyway.'

In the end, obviously having consulted the lawyers, Laurence came to see Robert one evening as he sat in his study.

'I have decided' he said, 'to allow you to stay here for the next three years. But as soon as I'm twenty-one, and have full authority to do so, I shall insist you leave my house. Is that quite clear?'

'Quite clear, thank you, Laurence. And perhaps we can now be a little more civil to one another,' said Robert.

Laurence stared at him. 'I never found you uncivil,' he said finally, 'simply unacceptable.' And walked out of the room.

Jago had gone: for four weeks' basic training at a base camp in Kent. He would be allowed home on leave after that for a few days, before sailing for France. LM felt utterly desolate and bereft, to her own surprise. Her usual firm disciplined optimism entirely left her; she was like another creature, frail and intimidated by fate. Worst of all, she had no one to discuss it with; after Jago had talked to Celia at the Lytton offices, he had never been mentioned again by either of them; LM because she was too embarrassed, too mortified by the incident, Celia because of her intense respect for emotional privacy. She had not even asked LM if everything was all right; LM, surprised and grateful for this, simply greeted Celia with a large bunch of flowers which she laid on her desk on the Monday morning, and assumed, correctly, that she would understand its message.

But now she longed for a confidant, someone with whom she could not only share her misery and fear, but from whom she could seek reassurance, however hollow, someone who would say, 'Don't worry, it'll be all right,' or repeat the favourite refrain of the day, 'It'll all be over by Christmas.' But there was no one. She longed for Oliver to volunteer, so that she could at least communicate with Celia about it; but the days and weeks went by and he did not.

'He is going, I'm afraid,' Celia said to her one day when she inquired as tactfully as possible about Oliver's plans, 'but I just live from day to day, until he finally enlists. I think he'll probably go into my father's old regiment. That's the plan anyway. Papa is raging away down there, because he's too old to go himself. Mama says it's given him a new lease of life, just writing endless letters and rushing up to London every other day to see this general and that. Even Kitchener has had to put up with a session with him. Well he was a brigadier, bless him. He feels dreadfully set aside. I'm sure they'll find him some kind of desk job. Mama is praying that they will anyway.'

LM nodded. 'They're all mad,' she said, 'these men. Wanting to go, wanting to fight.'

'I know, but it's in their genes,' said Celia. 'Even if women were allowed to fight, we wouldn't. Look at the Women's Peace Movement. We'd find some other way.' She looked at LM. 'But I'm sure,' she said carefully, 'that the war will be short-lived. Everyone says so.'

'I'm sure they're wrong,' said LM briefly, 'and so are you.'

She went back to her office, locked the door and indulged in the luxury of a short weep. Misery was making her ill; she was unable to eat, her stomach was permanently acid, and quite often she was actually sick. Every time she thought of Jago in uniform, boarding one of the hideously crowded troop ships which left the ports daily, she felt a pain not just in her heart, but in her head, violent, sick pain. She had often heard of people saying they didn't know how they would be able to bear things and felt impatient; you bore what you had to bear. Now, suddenly, and rather shame-facedly, she understood.

The country being caught up in a fever of patriotic sentimentality didn't help; she felt enraged by it. From every house, at every street corner, people seemed to be waving flags, and there were military bands playing constantly. Soldiers walking about in uniform inspired almost hysterical excitement. The endless posters of Lord Kitchener pointing his finger and telling her that her country needed her − or rather her man − made her want to scream. She didn't care about her country, she didn't care what it needed. She simply knew it was taking away the only man she had ever loved, and the only man who had ever loved her.

'Of course I'll have the children,' said Lady Beckenham, 'as long as you send some staff with them. I can see this war is going to cause us problems. Two of my girls are already talking about working in munitions factories.'

'Of course I will. Nanny's a country girl anyway, and Jessie's terrified of bombs.'

'The whole thing's absolutely appalling,' said Lady Beckenham, 'do you know they've taken four of our horses. The ones that work on the farm that is. And I was reading in the paper yesterday that in some cities the trams have stopped running because so many horses have gone. Poor beasts. They'd better not try to get any of my hunters, that's all I can say.'

'I'm sure they wouldn't dare, Mama,' said Celia, who would have pitted her mother against the Hun any day.

'I don't know. The cavalry are after good horses. And then they're transported in the most dreadful way, not boxed, just put into the hold tethered, swung up on cranes by slings at the docks, poor beasts. I heard of one chap, obviously decent, a groom, who stayed down in the hold with them the whole way, watering and feeding them, then had a heart attack himself and died on arrival in France. Still, saved all the horses. Jolly fine, I thought.'

'Possibly,' said Celia storing this up mentally for LM, who was fascinated by Lady Beckenham's greater excesses.

'If Beckenham doesn't get some kind of a job, I don't know what I'll do,' said her mother, 'he's in an absolute raging ferment, it's had the usual effect on him, of course. I hope your nursemaid isn't a virgin, knows how to look after herself.'

'I'll warn her,' said Celia hastily. Poor Jessie; she was very pretty. She must warn Nanny at least to keep an eye on her. She felt that the danger from her father was infinitely greater than anything the Hun might rain on her from the skies.

'Anyway, Mama, I'll keep them all in London for a bit. Nothing's hapening, and I don't want to be parted from them unless I have to. And Giles is off to school. He's so nervous about it, poor darling. I sometimes wonder—'

'You shouldn't wonder,' said Lady Beckenham briskly, 'he needs to go away. It's a year late anyway. He'll turn out soft if you're not careful.'

'I know, but he's so – so gentle.'

'Exactly. That's what I mean. Needs it knocked out of him. Won't do him any good at all. Pity the twins can't go. Get a bit of discipline.'

'Oh, Mama, really. They're only four.'

'Well, Beckenham was five when he went off. His father sent him early, thought he was getting soft.'

'There's nothing soft about the twins,' said Celia, 'I thought you said that was the problem.'

'What about Barty? Still doing well at school?'

Barty's academic success baffled Lady Beckenham, who regarded the lower classes as intrinsically unintelligent. Fascinated by, as well as disapproving of what she called Celia's experiment, she had expressed huge surprise at Barty being able to learn her letters or remember the simplest thing.

'Extraordinary,' she said, as Celia, with a mixture of pride and irritation at her prejudice, pressed Barty into reciting *Who Killed Cock Robin* one afternoon soon after her third birthday, 'Quite extraordinary. I'd never have believed it possible.'

'Mama, you're ridiculous. Half the women in the suffragette movement are from the working class, hugely intelligent and articulate. Look at Annie Kenny.'

'Yes, well they're all completely mad,' said Lady Beckenham with a sublime lack of logic. Any sympathy she might have had for the suffragettes had died along with Emily Davidson, who had flung herself under the king's horse at the Derby in 1913. 'All very well,' she had said at the time, 'but she might have killed that horse.'

'Barty's doing terribly well, yes,' said Celia now. 'The cleverest child in her class.'

'Ah, but does she have any friends?' said Lady Beckenham with piercing perspicacity.

Celia said Barty had plenty of friends and knew her mother didn't believe her.

'And how is this war going to affect your business?'

'I don't know,' said Celia, 'naturally we're a little worried. But the accepted view is that it will make very little difference. Certainly the country's mood at the moment is for business as usual; the theatres are still full and so are the picture houses, people need entertainment more at times like these, they need distraction. And we are in the entertainment business, I suppose. Also an awful lot of the soldiers are taking books out with them apparently.'

'How extraordinary,' said Lady Beckenham.

Even putting up with the twins must be better than this, thought Giles miserably, stuffing his mouth with his fist as he burrowed under the bedclothes, trying not to cry. He had been at school for a week now and every day had been worse than the last. He had graduated from being an object of mild interest to one of total derision; despised for a lack of prowess on the games field, teased for a (very slight) tendency to tubbiness, mocked for his slowness to grasp new subjects like science, sneered at for leaving home a year late, and tormented for being a less than satisfactory fag to the sixth former he had been assigned to.

Of all these, the late arrival had been the most serious; his nickname was Baba, and one of the more unpleasant forms of teasing he had to endure was having a small towel tied round his parts each night. 'Baba's nappy' was removed each morning to exclamations and mockery about the smell, the size of his penis, the shape of his testicles – indeed a second nickname 'skew balls' had been added to the first. He was so frightened of actually wetting the nappy that he woke constantly through the night and was becoming exhausted; He was also dreadfully homesick, missed his mother and father more than he would have believed, and Barty, of course and Nanny. And even, unthinkably, the twins.

Jago had gone: after four days' leave, during which LM clung to her self-control with a courage and determination which had only failed her on the final morning. He dressed in his uniform, picked up his bag and bent to kiss her while she lay in bed watching him. Until then she had managed to be quite cheerful for him, listening to his stories of basic training with genuine admiration, encouraged by the sense of camaraderie that clearly existed, amused by a letter which had been issued to every enlisted soldier by Lord Kitchener.

'You'll be glad about this Meg,' he said, as he showed it to her.

After a preamble about courage, energy and patience, the pamphlet informed the men solemnly that they must guard against excesses, 'particularly temptations both in wine and women', urging them to remember that while they should treat all women with courtesy, they 'should avoid intimacy'.

'That gave us a few laughs in the barrack room, I can tell you.'

LM felt sure it had, and marvelled at the stupidity and complacency of an officer class that could talk to the men as if they were virgins going off on a foreign holiday.

And so the four days had passed in some sort of happiness, but on that last morning she cracked; felt and heard grief and loss sweeping through her on a great, noisy tide, flung herself out of bed and into his arms, crying and calling his name, begging him to stay just a little longer, telling him she could not bear it, that she would die herself if he was killed. Afterwards she was ashamed of her lack of courage; if he could face the miseries of war, then she could surely face the worst that she would be called upon to bear, loneliness and anxiety and even terror. He had been clearly baffled, unable to cope with her misery; almost embarrassed, he had pulled away from her, said he had to go, that he would be late and court-martialled before he began.

'I love you Meg,' he said, 'remember that. Remember it always. That's the only certainty I can offer you.'

And then he was gone, walking down the street to Swiss Cottage railway station and thence to Victoria and the boat train to Calais. She knew a lot of the wives and sweethearts would be at Charing Cross, waving their flags and smiling bravely; he had forbidden that, had said he wanted to remember her lying in bed, their bed, smiling at him, that was all he asked of her. And she had failed him even in that, failed him already.

LM turned her head into the pillow and wept for two hours.

Oliver, too, was afraid. Courage was not one of his gifts; he was afraid of physical pain, of any kind of public humiliation, of conflict, and, most of all, of having to witness the pain of others. The days when Celia had borne Giles and the twins, he had been in an agony of wretchedness, dreading that he might be asked to see or even hear something that would illustrate what she was going through. She was so brave, in every way; almost nothing frightened her, and if it did, she gritted her teeth and confronted it. She was like Jack, whose courage was formidable. Oliver had fought his lack of courage as best he could, had struggled to master public speaking, had learned to ride for Celia's sake, had even once, but only once, hunted (lying awake all night before and imagining fearsome fences, broken limbs, social disgrace after falling from a bolting horse). He submitted himself to the dentist's drill, in order to inspire courage in his own children, and from time to time and most terrifyingly of all, confronted and even opposed Celia.

But all these things were nothing, nothing at all compared to the horror, the bowel-melting terror, of going out to the battlefields of France. And horror there would be, he knew; he had read in the papers reports of the first big battles of Ypres and Mons, and knew that despite the triumphs, the assertion that the Germans had been routed, the appalling casualty lists told a different story. There had been heavy casualties and very little gained. He would, he knew, have to see and face things that he could scarcely begin to contemplate: death, and worse than death, mutilation, continuous pain. Moreover, he would have to inflict those things himself, would have to give orders to shoot, to kill, to destroy. He would have to conceal his terror while living with it constantly, day after day, find courage, or simulate it – somehow.

Conversations with his father-in-law, veteran of both the Boer war and the Sudan with Kitchener, did not help.

'Nothing like it,' he said sorrow fully to Oliver, as they sat on the terrace behind Ashingham one golden October day, 'nothing like battle. Something takes you over, some extra force, gives you the strength, the taste to do things. I couldn't kill in cold blood; find it difficult to shoot my own horses when the time comes. But out there, my God, with the noise and the earth shaking with the guns, and your men all mobilised, obeying orders, and some enemy soldier in front of you, staring you in the face, and it's him or you, it's bloody wonderful. Can't really describe it. You'll find out. That young brother of yours, fine chap, he knows what it's like. We were talking about it the other day. He's gone hasn't he? Lucky young bounder. Wish I was going with you both.'

Oliver was leaving to do his basic army training at Colchester at the beginning of November. He had been told that it was unlikely he would go out to the front before Christmas, and that he would begin his army career as a lieutenant. The week before he left for Colchester he gave a dinner for all the staff at Lyttons; he took a private room in the Savoy Hotel, and after a lavish meal which showed very few signs of any shortages whatsoever, he stood up and made a brief speech. He said that heading Lyttons for the past ten years had been the glory of his life, and that he hoped and prayed for many more.

'I see my service for king and country as a brief interval between publishing cycles.'

Everyone laughed.

'But the firm must go on. And for the foreseeable future, it will be a different place. Very. Richard Douglas and William Dean have already enlisted, James Sharpe will be following them shortly. So Lyttons will be largely in the hands of women. Now I know this not an entirely satisfactory situation—' more laughter, which Celia and LM struggled politely to join in – 'because for some of you, the only satisfactory arrangement would be if there were no men in the house at all. That, ladies and gentlemen, is a situation I will personally never welcome. I shall be back, we shall all be back and examining closely – and critically – what has been done in our absence.' More laughter still. 'But I would ask those of you who remain, very seriously and from the bottom of my heart, to place your trust and your allegiance in my wife, and my sister. They are charged with the safety and the future of Lyttons and I know that with your help, they will assure it. Please be upstanding and drink a toast to them: Lady Celia Lytton and Miss Margaret Lytton.'

The staff rose obediently to their feet, raised their glasses, dutifully said, 'Lady Celia, Miss Lytton.' A few were subdued, but most of them were flushed, excited, clearly caught up with the drama of the moment. A bit like battle Oliver thought suddenly, smiling at Celia whose dark eyes looked dangerously brilliant and at LM, whose thin, drawn pallor had momentarily been replaced by a rosy, flush. If only battle possessed such safe excitement, granted such easy victory. . .

'That was very charmingly done,' said Celia, collapsing on to their bed, holding out her arms to him. 'Thank you my darling. I know your saying that will be the greatest help. And LM felt it too, I know.'

'She doesn't look well,' said Oliver, 'I worry about her.'

'Me too. I think her – her friend being at the front is destroying her. She so clearly loves him very much.'

'What's she told you about him? About their plans for the future – if—' he stopped.

'Of course they have a future. We all do,' said Celia firmly, 'but the answer is nothing. Nothing at all. And I would never ask. But she misses him dreadfully. It's quite clear. And is afraid for him, every moment of the day.'

'Is he in France?'

'Yes. Yes he is. As you will be, so very soon. Oh, darling Oliver, I simply can't imagine how I am going to bear all this.'

'You will bear it,' he said smiling at her gently, crossing over to her, taking her face in his hands, 'as I will. Because we have to. Because there is no choice.'

She looked at him. 'You're very frightened, aren't you?'

A long silence: then reluctantly, 'Yes,' he said, 'yes I am. To my shame.'

'You shouldn't be ashamed of it,' she said, 'of being frightened. Or of admitting it. To me I mean. If it helps. I don't think any the less of you. More in fact.'

'Why?' he asked, his voice very low.

'Because, my darling, the more frightened you are, the braver you are. I think you're wonderful. I love you so much.'

'I love you too,' he said, 'more than ever before, more than I would ever have believed possible.'

Somewhere in France. October 19th.

Dearest Meg,

That's all I am allowed to tell you; all our letters are censored, so don't expect detailed war reports. Not that you'd want them, but still . . . I love you too, Meg. I think of you all the time and it is such a help, knowing you're there, knowing you're safe. It really isn't too bad out here, and you must try not to worry. The journey here was really good. We came by train from Le Havre, in cattle trucks, and every station we passed through was ready with coffee or wine and bread and people shouted '*Vive l'Angleterre.*' You know what they say about fortune favouring the brave. We are all very brave here! We have to be: there isn't any choice. They're a good group of lads, I'm with. It's very good to be with others you know from the old days. It helps with the homesickness. The news from the front, for we are not there yet, is good. Our side is winning. Taking territory, winning battles and we'll win the war. That's for sure, definite. Take care of yourself, Meg. Don't work too hard. I'll be home very soon. For Christmas with a bit of luck.

All my love,

Jago

My dear Kitty,

Just to let you know all is pretty fine here and I'm enjoying it no end. We're well stuck in and have had a few chances to get at the Hun already. One particularly satisfactory skirmish. Arrogant lot, but we'll bring them down. Worst thing is the weather – pretty awful, cold and wet. The heat of India at its worst seems like heaven in comparison. Shan't forget that evening with you in a hurry. You were really marvellous. Only complaint, why aren't you the star of that show? Tell the producer I said so. Home for Christmas I hope. Keep the home fires burning and all that.

Love,

Jack

My darling,

I am becoming a fine soldier very fast. I can march, salute, and shoot, all as well as the next man, and I am enjoying it to a surprising degree. There are a lot of fine chaps here, including, rather wonderfully, John Dukes from Blackies. So we spend what little free time we have talking books and illustrators and putting the publishing world entirely to rights. He is doing a new series of children's picture books, which sounds very fine. I do feel we should try to develop a children's list. Perhaps you could put your mind to it, see what LM thinks. Last night we went on a route march, across the flats at Mersea. It was most beautiful, the light shining on the water, and the sky very clear. I looked up at the stars and thought of you and of how much I love you. Take the greatest care of youself, my darling, and I shall see you in – what is it now? – two weeks and three days. I am sure the reunion will be very sweet. And we are still hopeful of not being sent to France before Christmas. My love also to the children. Tell Barty to write to me, letters are so precious. I have written a brief note to Giles. I do hope he is getting on all right, poor little chap.

Most of all, my dear one, my very best love to you. Not a moment passes, but I don't think of you and how impossibly dear to me you are.

Oliver

Dearest Meg,

Just a brief note as I don't have long. I am well and safe and things are not too bad. The food is lousy, and we're a bit tired, otherwise nothing to complain about. The quarters aren't too bad. Quarters! Barns mostly, in a muddy farm, outbuildings, tents in the woods. We march to the front, the trenches, six or seven miles away, finishing with a long walk across dreadfully muddy fields. Yours truly fell in a ditch full of water up to the waist. So much for my new boots! The last bit out to the trenches was tricky, an open field studded with shell pits and although it was night-time, there was a full moon. When we got there it wasn't much better, some of the trenches were very shallow, and you have to lie down in the water and mud to get cover. I got down the deeper end, so was lucky. We were supposed to be there for two to three days, but the men in the shallow trenches could not stand it for more than two, and the CO said we should all go back, specially as many of our party weren't well with diarrhoea. That I have escaped too. We are also erecting miles and miles of barbed wire against the Germans. It is a lot better than roofing in November, I can tell you.

I love you.

Jago.

PS We are hopeful of coming home for Christmas.

Dear Meg,   Very very good news. Definitely home for Christmas. Be ready for me.

Love

Jago

If he was coming home, LM thought, clutching this letter literally to her heart, she must indeed be ready for him. It would be wonderful. She would get a tree, decorate the house, buy him such presents. And this time be happy and strong for him. If only she felt better herself. Perhaps now she knew he was coming home, she would begin to feel better. She'd never known ill-health before, not this dreadful constant sickness and lassitude and heartburn. And now her monthlies had stopped as well. She knew what it was of course; it was the change. She'd been half expecting it to happen for some time; she was, after all, forty. Her mother had had it early; but then she'd had cancer. LM stopped dead on her brisk walk down Haverstock Hill. Suppose that was it; suppose it wasn't the change, suppose it was cancer. Then she shook herself. Of course it wasn't. It couldn't be. But she would see the doctor. Soon. Very soon. That very day if she could.

'I'm pregnant. What do you think about that?'

'Pregnant! Oh, Celia, I – I don't know what to say.'

'Nor do I, LM. I don't know what to say to Oliver, either. He'll only worry. Say I've got to rest and all that nonsense. And of course I can't.'

'Oh Celia. I'm – I'm sorry,' said LM helplessly, hoping that was the right thing to say.

Although Celia was clearly anxious, she looked perfectly cheerful. But then she would; she met everything head on, nothing daunted her. She would cope with it, whatever happened. Her courage was immense. LM was brave too, very brave indeed about most things, but pregnancy frightened her. It was linked ineradicably in her mind with death: largely because of Jago, and the sad history of his Annie, but also because poor Jeanette had also died. And she had never forgotten finding Celia on her office floor that day, miscarrying, lying in a pool of blood. She thanked God almost daily she had never had to undergo it.

'I'm sorry, LM,' said Celia, 'I shouldn't have worried you. And what does it matter, really, with all these men dying every day. Oh I'm sorry, LM, I mean – oh God – don't cry, don't—'

'It's all right,' said LM hauling herself into self-control with a great effort, managing to smile at Celia, 'please don't concern yourself about me. It hardly matters.'

'LM, of course it does. Is – that is – have you – has he—' her voice tailed away. 'I'm sorry, LM I shouldn't have asked.'

'You have every right to ask,' said LM, 'you more than most. I should have told you, it was wrong of me not to. My friend, Mr Ford, whom of course you met.'

Celia nodded politely, as if she had met Jago at a literary luncheon party.

'Mr Ford, is out in France.'

'France—'

'Yes. At the front.'

'Oh LM, I'm so sorry. So very sorry. Is he – that is, what a stupid question, oh dear—'

'He's quite safe and well,' said LM firmly, 'and he writes regularly. But I have to admit I have found it quite worrying. But he's perfectly safe and well. And, I hope, coming home for Christmas. I'll keep you informed in future,' she added,

'LM, you don't have to.'

'I'd like to. You were so very – helpful that day. A good friend to us both.'

'I'm just glad it was helpful. One never knows. And I did like him very much, LM, I thought he was extremely—'

'But to return to you,' said LM cutting into this smoothly. Giving Celia the facts about Jago's war service was one thing; discussing him more personally was quite another. Celia flushed, recognising that she had said too much.

'Sorry, LM. Yes, me and my pregnancy. Oh dear.' She thought for a

162

moment, then said, 'I think I won't tell Oliver. Not before he leaves. He'll go off far more happily if he's not worrying about me. Then, with luck, I can just get on with it after that. I might not even see him again until after—' her voice crumpled slightly, then steadied, 'after the baby's born. That would be clever wouldn't it?'

'It would. When is it – that is when do you—?'

'Expect it? Oh, let me see. July. Long way off. Nothing to show for it at Christmas, except perhaps a bit of sickness, which I'm sure I can explain away. Oh, dear LM, I do wish I wasn't quite so fertile.'

'It must be difficult,' said LM politely. And thought yet again how fortunate she had been not to have that as one of her problems.

11th November

Dearest Meg,

The fighting is over for the time being, we're told. No more big pushes for a while, so you can stop worrying about me. We are in what they call a rest camp, after what I can now tell you was some pretty bloody fighting. Some officers have been killed; they're a good bunch I must say, the officers, brave and very good to us men. I wouldn't hear a word against them. I was a bit doubtful at first, to be honest, hearing how they came out in the first class trains and so on, while we were herded in like cattle, but you put your life in their hands and they do their best for you. Anyway, yours truly has come out of it without a scratch. I seem to be lucky. Sergeant major says there's no such thing as a lucky soldier, just a good one. If that's so, I'm bloody good. Christmas more or less assured. Don't know how long we'll be here, only that it's a relief.

I love you Meg.

Jago

Dear Celia,

I'll be home for Christmas. Hope you can offer me a place at your table. Or at least under your tree! I could do with a good old-fashioned family Christmas with your brood. I think about them a lot. Jolly fine they are. Tell Oliver it's perfectly all right out here, good fun in fact, but he'll need plenty of warm underwear.

Love

Jack

'Hallo, Mum.'

'Oh – Barty! I didn't hear you. How are you, dear?'

'Very well, thank you' said Barty politely. Of all the things she hated, becoming a polite stranger to her mother was the worst. That and the boys teasing her. Calling her a posho. That was horrible.

'You're looking very well. Is Lady Celia with you?'

'No. She drove me here, but she's gone to the office for an hour or so.'

'Will she be coming in then, when she collects you? Oh, dear, I must get the place tidy, wash the floor.'

'Mum! Don't be silly. It doesn't matter about the floor.'

'It does if Lady Celia's coming.'

'I think,' said Barty, 'she's got more to worry about than your floor. Wol's gone off to the war.'

'Oh no! Oh dear, how dreadful, I am sorry. Is he at the front?'

'No, training somewhere in England. She'll tell you about it when she comes back I'm sure. Is – has Dad said anything about going?'

'Oh no, dear. He feels he's needed here more. Keep the home fires burning, that's what he says. So many have gone, and he's getting on a bit now, over thirty, they probably wouldn't take him anyway, no need for everyone to rush off after all.'

'No,' said Barty, 'no, of course not. Where is he? I'd like to see him.'

'He's out, dear. At the working men's club. He spends a lot of time there now.'

'What does he do there?' asked Barty anxiously. She hoped it wasn't somewhere you could get beer.

'Oh, plays snooker. Cards. That sort of thing.'

'Yes, I see. Did he – did he know I was coming?'

It hurt, that her father never seemed to want to see her.

'Well, he wasn't sure of course,' said Sylvia carefully. 'He'll be sorry to have missed you though. Oh dear, I really want to clean the place up, Barty. Marjorie, come and help me. Barty's here, look, and Lady Celia's coming later, and I want the place clean.'

'She can help you, can't she?' said Marjorie indicating her sister. She didn't even say hallo to Barty; she was a large lumpen child, the image of her father, and of all the children she was the most overtly hostile to Barty. The boys might call her posho, go on about her voice and her clothes, but they were still intrinsically good-natured. Marjorie hated and resented Barty's good fortune with a passion. More than once she had asked her mother if she and Barty could change places.

'Why should it be her, why not me, if the idea was just to save space here and help you?'

Sylvia said as firmly as she could that Lady Celia had always favoured Barty, and wouldn't want to change the arrangement now. 'And besides she's got Barty turned into a young lady now, she'd have to start again with you.' This distinctly tactless explanation went no way towards reconciling Marjorie with the situation.

'Yes, I'll do it, of course. How are you, Marjorie?'

'Oh, very well thank you, your ladyship,' said Marjorie in mincing tones. 'I'm so sorry, but I have a call to make. Do please excuse me, your ladyship.'

'Marjorie,' said Barty, 'don't be silly. I want to be your friend. You're my sister.'

'Yes, and who'd think that, looking at you with your fine clothes and your posh voice, who'd think I was your sister? Well I'm glad, I don't want to be your sister, and I certainly don't want to be your friend. I'm going out Mum, down the shop, meet Doreen.'

And she was gone, after making a face at Barty.

'Oh dear,' said Sylvia, 'I have tried to make her see sense, Barty, but I can't.'

'Doesn't matter,' said Barty, blinking back the tears. 'So where are the boys?'

They were seldom there when she came home these days; they made themselves scarce, torn between embarrassment and hostility, and a guilty knowledge, in the older ones at least, that the huge gulf between them was not Barty's fault.

'Out playing. But Billy said he'd be back.'

'Oh good. Did Frank like the book I brought for his birthday?'

'He did, dear, very much. I explained it was one of Lady Celia's own firm's books, but he didn't seem that interested. He's good at school, Frank is. Might make the scholarship they said, only there's no point. I couldn't possibly get the uniform together if he passed.'

'Mum, Aunt Celia would pay for the uniform. I know she would,' said Barty earnestly, her large eyes anxious.

'Oh, no. I couldn't take any more from the Lyttons. It wouldn't be right.'

'It might help me,' said Barty quietly.

'Now, how could it help you? Pass me that bucket, dear.'

'Make the others hate me less.'

'They don't hate you.'

'I think they do. Let me ask her – Mum, is your arm all right? Doesn't seem to work too well.'

'Oh it's all right,' said Sylvia hastily. 'Hurt it lifting the washing last week.'

'Dad knocked her down the stairs.' It was Billy; he had come in the front door.

'Down the – Mum, that's so bad. You can't let him do that.'

'Barty,' said Billy, and the expression in his eyes was scornful as he

165

looked at her, 'living with those people has turned your brain. How do you think she's going to stop him?'

'Well I—' Barty's eyes filled with tears, partly because of Billy's reaction to her, partly out of fear and anxiety at her mother's plight. 'I – don't know. But I could tell Aunt Celia—'

Billy stepped forward, and gripped her arm in his hand. He was a big boy now, almost sixteen; it hurt. She winced.

'You tell your precious Aunt Celia about our troubles, and I'll break *your* arm. We don't want her here, interfering in our lives. She's done enough damage, taking you away.'

'She hasn't taken me away,' said Barty staunchly. But she knew it wasn't true. Celia had taken her away; and however much she might want it, she could never go back.

'I know it's the change,' said LM, 'I just wondered if there was anything you could give me to help.'

'Ah.' Dr Pitts looked at her carefully. 'Any hot flushes, sweats at night?'

'No,' said LM, 'but—'

'Any – any flooding?'

'No, I told you, the – the monthlies have stopped.'

'Yes, I see. Er – Miss Lytton—'

'Yes, Dr Pitts.' She had known him most of her life, he had looked after her father.

'Miss Lytton, forgive me, but I think – I can see this may come as a shock to you—'

He was looking very solemn, almost stern; it is cancer, thought LM, that's what it is, I have cancer, I'm going to die, like my mother, before I see Jago again. She screwed up her courage, took a deep breath.

'Yes?' she said faintly. 'Please tell me. Whatever it is. I would prefer to know.'

'Yes, well you certainly have to know,' said Dr Pitts. He almost smiled at her, then hesitated, as if hoping he would still not have to proceed. Then he took a deep breath and said rather quickly, 'Miss Lytton, there is absolutely no doubt, I would say, no doubt at all, that you are pregnant.'

CHAPTER 10

Why was it always at Christmas, Celia wondered fretfully, stabbing her fingers endlessly on pine needles as she tried to fix the candles on the tree on Christmas Eve, that life became so emotionally difficult for her? This one was proving particularly so. Oliver was home, but he had to leave on the evening of Boxing Day, and so the happiness was short-lived, the effort to appear cheerful and festive immense.

He had made a huge effort to be cheerful himself, but was obviously wretchedly anxious; 'They've given us some idea of what we have to expect,' he said to her, 'doesn't sound too good. To put it mildly. But—' he smiled at her rather weakly – 'but we have to make the most of it. At least I'm home.'

'Yes,' said Celia soberly, 'at least you're home. We're very lucky.'

LM had come into her office three days earlier and said, her voice extraordinarily unsteady, that Mr Ford would not, after all, be coming home for Christmas.

'Oh LM,' Celia said, 'I'm so terribly sorry, why not?'

'It seems that there aren't enough forces out there to defend the French front until further battalions arrive, and it has been decided, naturally, that married men must take priority with the allocation of leave,' said LM, rather as if she were reciting something learned by heart.

'Yes, I see,' said Celia. 'How very, very sad for you. But you must come to us for Christmas Day, you can't spend it on your own.'

LM had said she didn't think she would come, that she would prefer to spend the day in Hampstead, and disappeared into her office for several hours. But two days before Christmas she asked Celia if it would inconvenience her greatly if she changed her mind.

'My thoughts are not very good company at the moment' she said, with an awkward smile, 'I think I should get away from them for a few hours.'

Celia said she thought so, too, that she was delighted, and that Jack would be home and he was enough to cheer anyone up; but in fact she was a little worried about the effect of LM's gaunt misery on the general family mood.

And then there was the strain of keeping her pregnancy from Oliver; he had remarked that she was very thin, that she was clearly not eating properly, had asked her how he could possibly go away with any peace of mind if she wasn't going to take care of herself?

'Oliver I'm fine. Really. I've had a bit of a tummy upset, that's all. Sickness and all that sort of nasty thing. So if I am thin, that's what it is. But I'm much better now.'

'Are you sure?'

'Quite, quite sure. I feel wonderful.'

That was not quite true, for she was sleeping badly, as she always did when she was pregnant, and consequently was very tired; but the sickness had stopped, and she felt perfectly well enough to pretend. And mercifully she was indeed very thin. She had not wavered in her resolve not to tell him; but it was not easy, just the same.

Giles was causing her anxiety; he had come home from school in an odd state. She went down to fetch him, and he came out to the car perfectly composed, hugged her briefly and then climbed in beside her and sat, huddled very closely to her, not speaking much through the entire journey home. Once there, he shot up to the nursery where Nanny was greeted rather more enthusiastically than Celia had been. She told herself this was because at home he wasn't being watched by his peers. He disappeared for a long time into Barty's small room, and was quiet but cheerful at supper. But the next morning he came to find Celia.

'Mummy, can I talk to you?'

'Well, not for long, darling. I'm late already.'

'Oh. Perhaps tonight then.'

'Yes, that might be better.'

That evening he sat with her for a while, not saying very much at all, clearly nervous; but finally he took a deep breath and burst out, rather pink-faced, 'Mummy, can I please, please leave school?'

'Leave! But why? You're doing so well, you had a splendid report, and you sounded so happy in your letters.'

'They read our letters,' said Giles.

'Oh, I see. Well, what's wrong?'

'It's the other boys. They're horrible to me.'

'What sort of horrible?' asked Celia.

'They tease me. All the time.'

'Darling, everyone gets teased at school. It's horrid but it doesn't mean anything.'

'It means a lot to me,' said Giles. His voice was heavy.

She looked at him. 'Tell me about it, what do they do?'

'Call me horrible names.'

'That doesn't sound very serious.'

'They're really horrible names. And the prefect I have to fag for shouts at me and – and—'

'What does he do, darling? He doesn't ever hit you, does he?'

'No,' said Giles quickly.

Jarvis had made it clear to him that if he ever let on what they all did to him, his life would be hell. 'And I mean hell, skewballs. Know what I mean?'

'Well then. Shouting can't be too bad. And you're in the choir, I see, and starting the recorder. So it isn't all bad. What do your friends say, do they find it difficult, too?'

'I—' Giles stopped. To say he hadn't got any friends was too humiliating. It would brand him as a complete failure in his mother's eyes. 'They don't like it much either,' he said.

'There you are then. You're all in the same boat.'

'Yes, but Mummy, I hate it, I'm so miserable and homesick and I miss you and Daddy so much – and—' Perhaps he should tell her, perhaps he could. Risk the consequences from Jarvis; his mother was so clever, she would know what to do, how to manage it all, and if he didn't tell her how bad it was, she couldn't be expected to try to help.

'It is quite bad,' he said cautiously, 'the other boys – they – they make me—'

'Giles,' said Celia. She felt rather weary suddenly. All the way home in the car she had been reading reports in the paper about the dreadful total of casualties just in those first few months of the war: there was talk of ninety per cent, if the injured and captured were counted in. One battalion alone had sent out eleven hundred men and had eighty left. Her mother had phoned that morning with grim news of deaths amongst their own friends: from the Grosvenors, the Gordon Lennoxes, the Crichtons, the Wellesleys. And she was having to say goodbye to Oliver, to send him off to what was beginning to seem almost certain death. A small boy's homesickness at school seemed rather unimportant.

'Giles darling,' she said firmly, 'we all have to learn to be brave about things. It's part of growing up. There is a dreadful war on, and Daddy is going away to fight in it for us. Now, the last thing I want is for him to be worried about anything as he goes away. Anything at all. So I want you to be brave and cheerful, and certainly not mention any of this to him. It will get better, Giles. Daddy and your grandpapa, and just about everyone we know went through a bad time when they first went to school. They survived. Try to remember that.'

He looked at her solemnly for a long moment, and then without another word left the room, and went upstairs to the nursery. Later, mildly remorseful, she followed him, but heard him giggling with Barty. Obviously it wasn't too bad.

Barty would not be with them; she was to spend Christmas Day with her family and she had been fizzing with excitement, choosing presents for everyone, wrapping parcels, helping Celia to do up a hamper with food and crackers and a bottle of port for her father. But as Celia set the last candle in place and turned her attention to the parcels, there was a knock on the front door. She opened it herself and saw Billy Miller standing there, stern-faced.

'She's not to come tomorrow,' he said. 'Barty's not to come.'

'Oh Billy, but why not? She's looking forward to it so much.'

'She can't come,' he said, 'me mum's not well.'

'What sort of not well, Billy?'

'She fell down the stairs. Doctor had to come. She's broken her wrist and bumped her head, she's in bed.'

'Billy, that's dreadful. Should I come and see her, can I get her anything?'

'No,' he said his face flushed, shifty with awkwardness, 'no, don't come. We're best on our own.'

'But is your father managing to look after her? And all the little ones?'

'He's fine,' said Billy. 'I'm helping him any case. Thanks,' he added as a careful afterthought.

'Oh Billy, I'm so sorry. Please give your mother my love. Did you walk here? It's a long way.'

'No it isn't,' he said sounding almost surprised, 'only took me a bit of a while.'

'I know, but it's so cold. Look, let me send you back in the car. I've done a hamper for you all for Christmas Day, you can take it. Oh dear, Barty will be so disappointed. She's not here, she's gone to a carol service with Nanny and the twins. Anyway, let me call Truman, organise the car.'

'Yeah, all right,' said Billy.

He stood waiting for the car to be brought to the steps, gazing round him; clearly transfixed by the size of the house, the hall, the vast tree. Finally he said, 'You live in the whole house do you?'

'Well – yes,' said Celia, slightly uncertainly, and then struggling to justify herself, 'but there are a lot of us. Four children and my husband and me, and then there are—' the servants, she had been going to say, and stopped, appalled at her own insensitivity. I'm getting like my mother, she thought, and hurried on, 'my parents and my brother-in-law, and – well. Ever so many people. Ah, Truman. There you are. This young man, Billy Miller, Miss Barty's oldest brother, wants you to take him home to his house in Kennington and I would like you to take the hamper which Barty and I have prepared. It's down in the kitchen. Cook will give it to you.'

The hamper was being loaded into the car and Billy was having a glass of lemonade as Barty arrived home; she flung herself at him, starry-eyed.

'Oh Billy, how lovely to see you. Have you come to fetch me early, I can be ready in a minute . . .'

'You can't come,' he said gruffly, 'Mum's ill. She says she can't cope. But to tell you happy Christmas.'

'Oh. Oh I see.'

Celia never forgot that moment; for Barty did not cry, nor even argue, but, 'Yes, very well,' she said, 'I understand. Happy Christmas, Billy.'

She stood on tiptoe, gave him a kiss and then ran, very quickly, up the two flights of stairs to the nurseries without another word. Looking up after her, Celia felt awed that a little girl of seven should be capable of such iron self-control. But later, when she went up, Barty was lying face-down on her bed sobbing endlessly; Celia sat down beside her and took her in her arms.

'Barty darling, don't be so upset,' she said, 'I know it's disappointing, but it couldn't be helped, your mother is clearly very unwell. After Christmas we'll go and see her together. And—' she gave her a kiss, 'and I can't help being a bit glad, I was going to miss you tomorrow.'

'You don't understand,' Barty said between hiccups, 'they don't want me. If they did, they'd manage somehow, and anyway, I could have helped, it would have been easier for Mum. They don't want me any more, they think I'm not part of them.'

Celia went rather heavily down the stairs, her heart aching for Barty, and her head tight with panic at what she seemed to have brought upon her.

Christmas lunch was tense, in spite of the large party round the table. The Beckenhams had joined them; and to her mother's amusement, Celia always insisted that the staff sat at the table on Christmas day. Celia had placed Lady Beckenham next to Jack who was in high spirits, full of tales of victories in France and seeing off the Hun; Lady Beckenham liked and approved of him, and often said how extraordinary it was that he and Oliver were brothers.

'He's such a decent chap, seems to like doing all the right things, ridden a lot out in India you know, Beckenham thinks the world of him.'

LM, pale and gaunt, was seated between Barty, who was quiet and solemn, and Nanny. LM had not spoken very much, although she was gallantly wearing a paper hat and had read out her motto and Nanny's.

She had eaten quite a lot of goose and ham, but now that the pudding had been brought in flaming to the table, by Oliver, she was simply pushing it round her plate. Celia watched her; poor LM, she really did look wretched. And then LM pushed her chair back, said, 'Excuse me,' rather quietly, walked through the door and collapsed in a limp heap on the hall floor. Oliver leapt up, picked her up in his arms like a child and started up the stairs with her, instructing Nanny to call Dr Perring; but not before Celia had seen, with a thud of shock, as the loose jacket which LM had been wearing slipped open, that the neat broad waistband of her skirt was unfastened, and that the stomach just beneath it domed upwards in the unmistakable shape of pregnancy.

'You saw, didn't you?' said LM. She was too exhausted, too wretched to pretend any longer; lying listlessly on her pillows, waiting for Dr Perring, she had greeted Celia with a half smile and then turned her face to the window in silence. Celia sat down beside her and took her hand.

'Yes,' she said gently, 'yes I saw. But nobody else did. LM, when – I mean—'

'In May,' said LM, 'early May, I'm told.'

'And why didn't you say anything, why didn't you tell me?'

'I didn't know myself until a few weeks ago,' said LM. 'I thought – thought it was the change. And then – I felt so ashamed, so foolish—'

'Oh LM, you shouldn't. Feel either of those things. And besides – well, it's wonderful. I think so anyway. What does – does your—'

'Jago. He's called Jago,' said LM. The shadow of a smile crossed her face. 'I really don't feel I can go on referring to him as Mr Ford.'

'What a marvellous name. Is it in our dictionary?'

'I don't think so, no.'

'It should be. Well, what does he say?'

'He doesn't know.'

'He doesn't know? I thought letters got out to the front very quickly.'

'They do. I haven't told him. I'm not going to tell him.'

'What?'

'I can't. You don't understand. He couldn't take it, he would find it unbearable.'

'Unbearable? LM, why? You're right, I certainly don't understand, why should he feel that?'

And she sat there, holding LM's hand, listening to the sad story of Annie, of Jago's terror of pregnancy and childbirth, of LM's own. 'He would be horrified and so afraid. It would add to his burdens. You must know that, you haven't told Oliver about . . .'

'I know, I know, but of course, I will. Once he's gone, isn't so – worried about actually leaving, and isn't going to make me promise to stop working, all that nonsense, I shall write and tell him, he'll be happy then.'

'Oh, Celia,' said LM helplessly, 'I don't know what to do. I simply don't.'

'You have to tell him. You can't make that sort of decision for him. It's – well it's wrong. It's his child, as well as yours. He has a right to know about it.'

'No,' said LM after a long silence, considering this 'I can't tell him. Maybe afterwards, when the child is safely delivered and I've survived. If I do.'

'Of course you'll survive,' said Celia briskly. 'Childbirth is painful and uncomfortable but with proper care it's not really very dangerous. I realise that Jago's wife died in childbirth, but there were special reasons. And a good doctor would probably have identifed them, been able to deal with them.'

'I am rather old, don't you think,' said LM, 'to be having a first child?'

'I don't know. What are you – forty? Yes. But you're very well and very strong. The way you hump those books about – you'll have to stop that, you know. What does your doctor say?'

'Exactly that. That I am well and strong.'

'So – are you pleased at all? You must be.'

'No,' said LM, 'not really. I'm not. I don't want a child, my life isn't geared to having a child, I don't like children.'

'You like my children.'

'Only in small doses' said LM, managing to smile. 'I cannot imagine being with one twenty-four hours a day.'

'Well you won't have to be', said Celia just slightly stiffly. 'Obviously you'll have a nanny.' She found it difficult to hear that her children were less than adorable to anyone. 'What – what do you think you are going to do? Afterwards, I mean.'

'Heaven knows. I've tried not to think about it.'

'Well I'm afraid you'll have to think about it. It isn't going to go away, your little baby.'

'No,' said LM, 'Unfortunately, it's not.'

The baby was about the size of a small puppy, the doctor had said. In spite of everything, of the shock the horror, the dread, she had found that strangely touching. The thought of it sitting there inside her, growing. She would feel it kick soon, the doctor had also said; this seemed less attractive. Something wriggling, moving about inside her. An invasion of her, of her body.

'I am quite, quite sure of two things,' said Celia standing up. There was the sound of voices on the stairs; Dr Perring had arrived, summoned from his Christmas dinner. 'Don't worry, I'll tell the doctor, you don't have to do it. You have to tell Jago. It amounts to – to theft, not doing so. And you will – you will love that baby. When it arrives. I promise you that. Ah, Dr Perring. How kind of you to come. Merry Christmas. If I could just have a quiet word . . .'

Leaving the house was terrible for Oliver. His departure had been delayed and he was allowed to stay a further day. He got dressed in his uniform.

'Oh, you look so handsome', said Celia, determinedly positive as always, 'years younger and desperately dashing, like Jack. If you're not careful I shall tear that off you again, and make you late for your train.'

They had agreed that she would say goodbye to him at the house; he would find that easier, he said. They had said their own personal private farewells the night before; he had made love to her more gently, more tenderly than she could ever remember, moving in her so slowly and carefully she could scarcely feel it. She knew why and said so.

'You know you have to change now, don't you? Become aggressive, harsh, inflict pain. This is your last chance to be the real Oliver. Isn't that right?'

'That is right' he said, kissing her; she tasted salt, realised he was crying, and felt her own tears rise to join his. 'It frightens me, Celia, how well you know me. How am I going to live without you? Am I going to change, so you don't know me any more?'

'Of course not,' she said, 'you won't change for me. I know you won't.' But she lay awake for much of the night, staring at the window, dreading the dawn, and thinking that however perfectly she knew him, he could not read her one tenth as accurately. And that given her circumstances, given her secret baby, that was just as well.

'Bye, Giles, old man. Look after Mummy for me,' said Oliver.

He picked Giles up, noticing how thin he was, how frail he felt in his arms. Giles clung to him, burrowed his face into his chest.

'I can't,' he said.

'Why not? I need you to.'

'I won't be here,' said Giles with childish logic. 'I'll be at school. I could come home again,' he added, his voice light with hope. Oliver pulled back, looked at him. The small face was very intense, the large, dark eyes burning.

'I don't like it, Daddy,' he whispered, 'I don't like it at school.'

'You don't? That's not what you said the other day.'

'I know, but—' Giles hesitated, they looked at his mother. She smiled at him, but her eyes were hard. 'I do really,' he said finally.

'Good,' said Oliver, setting him down, 'that's fine, I don't want to go away worrying about you. And anyway, you are the man of the family for now, you have to be very brave and strong.'

'I – will,' said Giles. 'I promise.'

'Barty, my darling, goodbye. Take care of yourself, work hard at school, and I shall expect a long story ready for me to publish when I get home.'

Barty had started writing stories; very short, a page at the most, but unusually for so young a child she gave them structure and a point. One about a robin that lost its wing, but found another bird to carry it on its back, another about a fairy whose wand didn't work magic any more and had to take an exam at fairy school before she could have another. No one else had been allowed to see them; he had been touched by the honour and impressed by the stories themselves.

'I will,' she said, biting her lip, managing a smile, clearly determined not to cry. Her self-control was remarkable, he thought, for so young a child.

'And as for you two—' he said, scooping up the twins, one in each arm. No such considerations for them; carried away by the drama, by the chance for attention, unable to understand more than that he was going away for a while, they both buried their heads in his neck and bellowed, clinging to him with their small arms until they were prised off by Celia and Nanny.

'They're so tender-hearted, poor little things,' said Celia.

Nanny said nothing.

Oliver bent and kissed Celia briefly, very briefly, he could not bear to do more, picked up his bag and walked to the gate; Truman was waiting by the car. Oliver looked back, at the small group, at Celia and Nanny holding the twins, with Barty and Giles in front of her, all waving the small Union Jacks Celia had bought them. Celia was smiling bravely, radiantly. He focused in on her, removed the children from the picture, saw only her lovely face, her brilliant eyes, her tall slender body, the body which gave him so much pleasure, and then focused in further, just to her mouth, her smiling, beautiful mouth. It moved, silently as he looked at it, one last lingering time. It was that picture and above all that mouth, telling him she loved him, that Oliver carried with him through the next four, dreadful years.

'I have thought about what you said,' said LM, 'and I've decided you are right. I have written a letter. With my news.'

'Well I'm very glad,' said Celia, 'very glad indeed. I just know he'll be pleased. Anyone would be.'

LM wished she felt as sure.

She had actually been out three times to post the letter; had stood at the letterbox, dreading knowing that the news was irrevocably on its way, that it was no longer under her control. That she could not stop it. Twice she brought the letter back again; finally, sick with terror, on 3rd January, 1915, she let it drop, then stood there staring at the box, wondering if she waited, the postman would give the letter back to her when he came to empy it.

While Jago did not know, she was safe, their relationship was safe. She did not have to picture him filled with fear, or filled with distaste; not knowing what to say to her, how to react. Pretending he was glad, pretending he was happy. All kinds of morbid imaginings filled her: that he no longer loved her, that he had never loved her; that he had never loved her after Violet Brown; that he had actually continued with his relationship with Violet Brown, had been waiting to tell her. That he would picture her, not tenderly, not proudly, as she hoped in her more optimistic moments, but with pity, as someone old, too old for motherhood, a slightly ridiculous figure; that he would be horrified, repulsed, ashamed of her. That he would feel he would have to marry her, while not loving her, not wanting to; that he would look for excuses, even now, to end their relationship. And enduring all this, she waited.

She told herself that he would write quickly if he was pleased; that a long silence would indicate his distress. Letters went back and forward quickly; it was considered vital for the morale of the troops. She knew that she could get a reply to her letter within four days of its arrival; just over a week then from her posting. 11th or 12th or even 13th or 14th January should bring it; all those dates meant the message would be hopeful, happy. She was up at dawn each day, waiting restlessly for the postman; she saw him in the distance, down the street, watched from the window, waited until she could hear him on the path, counted his footsteps, heard the letterbox open, the letters drop. Or not drop. On the 11th there were none, the 12th just one, from a friend, the 13th, none; on the 14th, sick with terror, she saw a small pile on the floor. Surely one of them must be from Jago; it must be.

She knelt beside them, fumbling through them: a bill from the butcher, a letter from a rather depressed woman poet she had befriended, a note from another friend.

And – yes! A letter from France; in the military envelope with the military stamp. Her fingers shook so much, were so clumsy with fear that she literally could not get it open. She ran, half crying, into the kitchen for a knife, slid it under the flap of the envelope, pulled the letter out. And sat on the kitchen table, staring at it, hating it, hating the sender, hating what it said. Which was kindly, affectionate, well-intentioned; but not in the right handwriting, not expressing the right emotions, in not the right words. And was not from the right person, not from Jago, saying how happy he was about their baby, but from Oliver, saying along with other such platitudes, how much he hoped she was better, and that life at the front was after all not so bad.

Despair overtook her; quiet, dreadful despair. January turned to February, and still no letter; she went to work, went home again, ate the suppers Mrs Bill had prepared for her, went to bed and tried to sleep. Nothing could lift her mood or distract her. It was in those weeks she said afterwards that she finally began to lose her faith in God. He provided her with no comfort, no strength. She cared about nothing and no one, and she developed a great hatred for the child she carried inside. It was kicking now, vigorous and uncomfortable; she loathed the sensation, the feeling that her body was not her own, that it was invaded by an alien, unwelcome presence which had destroyed Jago's love for her. She was hostile and uncommunicative to Celia, who she blamed for persuading her to write to Jago, short-tempered with her staff, abrupt and cold to poor Mrs Bill, who deserved it least, and would have lain down her life for her. She looked back on the person she had been a year before, confident, in command of herself, in control of her life, with a man she loved and who loved her, and found it almost incredible that everything should have changed so dreadfully much.

'Your dad's gone,' said Sylvia to Barty one Saturday.

'Gone where?' she asked.

'To fight in the war, of course. Went on Tuesday, just like that. Said he couldn't stand it no longer, that he had to do his bit. He thought they might turn him down, being a bit chesty and that, but they took him at once. He was really chuffed.'

'Oh mum. Mum, I'm so sorry.'

'Yes,' said Sylvia, 'yes, it's quite hard.'

It was; Ted might have got a bit difficult over the last few years, but she still loved him; and after Christmas, when he had hurt her so much, he had signed the pledge, never touched another drop, and they had been really happy again, like the old days. Only worry had been falling again, but she'd escaped. And now he had gone; just when things were getting better.

'It was that poster,' he said to her, when she asked him why he'd finally decided to go.

'What, Lord Kitchener?'

'No,' he said soberly, 'worse than that. Picture of some bloke sitting in a chair, little girl on his knee, saying, "what did you do in the war, Daddy?" Made me realise, the kids want to be proud of their dad, want to know he did his bit.'

'You're such a good man, Ted Miller,' she said kissing him. 'I'm lucky to have had you.'

'Don't start talking in the past,' he said smiling at her. 'I'll be all right. Lucky I am, always have been. I've had you for a start. I don't deserve you, Sylvia, and that's a fact. And when I come home, things'll be better, I know they will. Now, you going to be all right without me? Should be, there'll be the army pay, coming in regular, only twelve and six, but I'll have it all sent to you.'

'I'll manage, Ted, course I will.' She couldn't think how, but nor could she say so. In fact, 'You should keep a bit, for your tobacco and that,' she said.

'Oh we get that, Syl. With our rations.'

He wasn't yet at the front, he was training somewhere in Kent, Sylvia said, but he'd be off in a few weeks. 'I don't think we'll see him before he goes.'

'Did he – did he say anything about saying goodbye to me?' asked Barty in a small voice.

'Of course he did,' said Sylvia, 'but he couldn't, could he? He said to give you a kiss.'

She hoped Barty would believe this; in fact Ted hadn't mentioned her. He had seen her very seldom over the past two years, disappearing whenever she was about to visit, probably Sylvia thought, because he was so ashamed of himself, afraid of what she might discern, perhaps report him to Celia.

'He could, you know,' said Barty, 'have said goodbye. He could have come to the house. Or written, at least.' She blinked back the tears. Every time one of her family displayed a loss of love for her, it hurt more, not less.

'Now Barty, he'd never have come to the house. Of course he wouldn't.'

'I don't see why not,' said Barty, and then stopped. She was beginnning to see why not; and beginning to realise why they regarded her as they did. Billy's goggle-eyed report of the house, the servants, the huge Christmas tree even, had done her no service. 'Well anyway,' she said, 'I'd like to write to him. How do I do that?'

'Give it to me,' said Sylvia, 'and then there's a special address. But don't expect anything back,' she added warningly, 'you know he can't write that well.'

That was an understatement; Ted could hardly write at all; Sylvia was by far the more literate of the two.

'No,' said Barty, thinking this was not the only reason her father wouldn't write to her, 'no, I won't expect anything back.'

'I did wonder,' said Laurence thoughtfully, 'if you would feel compelled to go and fight for your native country.'

Robert looked at him; the tone was particularly cold, the expression especially derisive.

'No,' he said, 'no Laurence, I don't. The war in Europe is dreadful, and my brother has enlisted, but this is my home now. And even if I did, I am far too old to be accepted. I'm sorry to disappoint you.'

Laurence shrugged. 'It's of no importance to me either way. I was just a little – surprised that's all. I would have thought it was the gentlemanly thing to do.' He paused, then said, 'No, perhaps surprise is the wrong word. Under the circumstances.'

With extreme difficulty, Robert said nothing. He was beginning to wonder how much longer he could endure this war of attrition. And how much it was worth enduring in any case. If Laurence hadn't been away two thirds of the year, not even the charms and beauty of Elliott House and the gratification of keeping up appearances, would have made up for the discomfort and misery of the other third. With two years to go before Laurence came of age, he had already begun to look out for a site for his own house.

The telegram came on 7th February. LM was getting ready to go to work, dressing herself carefully in the long loose coat she wore to conceal the quite small bump. When she got to work, she put on a loose pinafore, making the excuse that she needed it to protect her clothes down in the cellars, where she spent much more time now, with so many of the clerks gone to the front.

She heard the footsteps on the pavement, then on the path and heard the doorbell go; she heard Mrs Bill's voice, frightened, urgent, calling her name. And watched herself go down the stairs and take the yellow envelope, saw herself open it, and observed herself reading the words, the absolutely meaningless words.

Regret to inform you . . . report dated 5th February . . . Corporal Ford . . . killed in action . . . sincere sympathy. Under Secretary of State.

She heard herself saying to Mrs Bill, 'Mr Ford has been killed,' went upstairs, finished dressing, and quite dry-eyed, walked to the station as usual. She arrived at Lyttons, went into Celia's office and said to her in an absolutely steady voice, 'Jago has been killed,' and walked out again.

And although it was dreadful, very dreadful indeed, knowing she would never see him again, that he was lost to her forever, terrible knowing that he had probably died some hideous death, far away from her, by far the worst thing of all was knowing that he had died not loving her any more, not wanting her any more, and not wanting the child they had conceived together in an earlier, happier life.

'I'm thinking of offering Ashingham as a convalescent home,' said Lady Beckenham. 'Just for officers, naturally. I think one should do one's bit. Several friends have gone out to drive ambulances, that sort of thing. I have thought of that as well. With Beckenham out of the way, it's so easy down here suddenly. What do you think?'

'I should think with you out at the front, the war would be over much more quickly,' said Celia, smiling at her. 'You'd have the Hun on the run in no time.'

'Don't joke, I'm perfectly serious. I heard the most marvellous story the other day. Absolutely true. Some woman called Blanche Thirieau, who lived in Paris, knew that her husband was involved in the Battle of the Marne, and decided to go down there and visit him. And she actually managed it. Charmed the captain, who sent off a soldier to fetch her husband. It just shows what can be done if you won't take no for an answer. Still, I think I'd probably be as much use here. Now, when do you envisage sending the children?'

'I don't know, Mama. Still no bombs are there? But at the first hiss, then down they'll come. Is Papa enjoying life at the War Office?'

'Immensely. I can't imagine he's doing anything remotely useful, but he seems happy.'

'I must have him to dinner again,' said Celia, 'I feel bad about being so inhospitable. But what with one thing and another, I haven't got around to entertaining much lately. It's difficult without Oliver and—' she looked down at her burgeoning stomach.

'Don't worry about your father. He's perfectly happy. How do you feel?'

'Oh, tired. But all right. Five months is quite a good time. Don't you think?'

'I can't remember,' said Lady Beckenham vaguely. 'Whole thing's a bit of a blur, thank God. Have you told Oliver yet?'

'Yes. I thought I'd better. In case someone else did. He was thrilled, although a bit worried of course.'

'Any real news?'

'No,' said Celia soberly, 'only that he was alive four days ago. That's all you know. You get a letter and you think, thank God, and then remember that in the four days since it was sent anything could have happened.'

'Jolly tough,' said Lady Beckenham. 'I do know, I've been through it.' There was a silence, then, 'Was he at the last big one, do you think?'

'Mama, I don't know. I don't think so.' The reports of the attack on Neuve Chappelle and its attendant huge casualties had frightened her severely, not least because she had no idea if Oliver had been there or not. That made things infinitely worse.

His letters were determinedly cheerful, but still told of horrors: 'We are shelled the whole day long, the noise is dreadful and carries on in one's head the whole night. My main problem is lack of sleep, yesterday we were moving up a hill, having been ordered to reinforce another Division, lovely day, sun shining, blue sky, I have to admit to a flash of happiness and was thinking of you rather intently, when there was a rain of shellfire from concealed machine guns and snipers. So much for daydreaming. We lost quite a few men, and were starting to dig ourselves in at our destination, when the shelling started again and went on all night. But don't worry about me, my darling, I am not even scratched.'

She slept badly, visions of Oliver mutilated, dead, dying, and perhaps most hideously choked and blinded by the new terror, poison gas, waking her constantly from restless sleep; only going to Lyttons kept her sane. She was working feverishly, long, long hours, doing not only her own work but also that of Oliver, Richard Douglas, and James Sharpe, the art director. She particularly enjoyed the design work; she had a quick, innovative eye and some of the jackets she was commissioning were more interesting and arresting than anything Lyttons had done before. She had replaced James and his assistant, Philip, with two clever young women; the three of them worked together extraordinarily well. The more senior of the two, Gill Thomas, was a great admirer of the look and ideas to be found in the weekly magazines; she had designed a range of jackets of the women's fiction list which were strongly reminiscent of the covers of *Women's Weekly*. They were selling in thousands.

LM was still working hard, overseeing everything from budgets to shipments, promotions to stock control. Knowing she would have to leave for a while at least, and in the foreseeable future, was frightening Celia. She could not imagine how she would be replaced. LM had recruited and trained an excellent assistant – who had been told in strictest confidence the terms of her engagement – but she would be in no way a substitute.

Which reminded her. She looked at her mother.

'Is – is the dovecot in use at the moment?'

The dovecot was a small, exquisite building, reputedly designed by the third Earl to house his mistresses. It was called the dovecot because of its construction; it was circular, with a slate roof topped by a small glass rotunda, and stood about fifty yards or so back from the terrace, next to the sunken rose garden and close to a side door, which allowed discreet access to and from the main house. Inside there was a small panelled drawing-room on the ground floor, and a bedroom above it. It had no kitchen, but a bathroom, with primitive but perfectly efficient plumbing, led from the bedroom. Most wonderfully of all, it had its own tiny walled garden; it afforded, in its own way, perfect privacy.

'No, why do you ask?'

'I think LM might have need of it.'

'LM? What on earth for?'

Celia took a deep breath. 'To live in for a while with her baby' she said.

Lady Beckenham looked at her. She prided herself on never expressing surprise at anything; she considered it common.

'I see,' was all she said now 'well, yes, tell her, any time.'

'Thank you,' said Celia, 'I will.'

'You all right, Mum? Without Dad?'

'Yes, dear, I'm fine. Really I am. A few headaches still, but nothing to complain about. Billy's being very good, acting the man of the family as your dad said he should. Only problem is money. We're very short. I'm thinking of getting a job. In a factory or whatever. There's plenty of work. Not like at first, with all the firms closing down.'

'I know, Aunt Celia told me. Up to forty-four per cent unemployment, she said. It was partly because of there being no trade with Germany any more.'

'Fancy you knowing that,' said Sylvia admiringly, 'you're getting so clever, Barty.'

Barty ignored this. 'Where's Billy?'

'Queuing. With Frank.'

'Queuing?'

'Yes. For food. The queues are so long, an hour's nothing for a bit of meat. I send them to stand there instead of me. Everyone does it now. And Frank being so small, he can often wriggle towards the front and nobody notices.'

'We might be going away soon,' said Barty suddenly in a small voice.

'Going away? Where to?'

'The country. To Aunt Celia's mother's.'

'But why?'

'Because there might be some bombs, Aunt Celia says.'

'Yes, I'd heard that, too,' said Sylvia. 'They've started somewhere, haven't they, not in London though.'

'No. In Newcastle. The docks.'

'Well, you'll be one worry off my mind,' said Sylvia with a sigh.

'Mum, I don't want to go. I won't be able to see you so often.'

'Barty, you must go. You can't stay here.'

'Why not? I'm older now, I can be a help to you, I want to be at home again, with you all, please, Mum, please—'

'Barty, no. You're being silly. You're lucky, going somewhere like that, nice and safe. I wish the others could come with you.'

Barty looked at her. 'Perhaps they could,' she said.

'No Celia, I'm sorry. I'm perfectly happy to have your children, and Barty of course, she has very nice manners, but I shall be very busy with my convalescents soon, I really can't take in a houseful of urchins.'

'But Mama, don't you see, it's difficult for me. Keeping Barty safe, when her brothers and sisters are in danger in London.'

The Countess looked at her. Then, 'Celia', she said, after a long pause, 'this is precisely the sort of thing you should have taken into consideration when you decided to make that child part of the family. Now I'm afraid it's too late, and you have to live with the consequences.'

Celia looked at her in silence. Then, 'I'm afraid you're right,' she said, and sighed. 'I – I think I'll go and see LM.'

LM had submitted with surprising ease to Celia's suggestion that she move down to Ashingham.

'You can't stay here, LM, no one has guessed yet. I know they haven't, mostly because—' she stopped.

'I know,' said LM with a touch of humour, 'it's so extremely unlikely. A pregnant old maid.'

She was so brave, Celia thought: so uncomplaining, never railing against the cruelty of Jago Ford's death, just accepting it. A letter had come to LM from his CO; he had died a hero's death, he said, on a night raid, and more important, Celia thought, had died instantly from a German bullet, would have known nothing about it.

'That has to comfort you, LM. Suppose he had died slowly of injuries, in hospital or something.'

LM was more cyncial. 'I'm surprised at you, Celia. Have you ever heard of a soldier not dying instantly, and a hero, to boot. Jago might have died that way and of course I hope so, but I have no illusions. It might have been rather different.'

'Well,' she said, 'well, let's think about you. Much more positive. I think you should come down here, you would have complete privacy. Mama certainly wouldn't bother you, she's busy converting Ashingham into a hospital – a very aristocratic hospital naturally – and you can have your baby either there or at the local nursing home. Then you can decide what you're going to do.'

'Oh I have decided,' said LM. Her face was very hard, very set. 'I shall have the baby adopted. I don't want it.'

'Adopted! LM, you can't do that!'

'Why not?'

'Well because – because you can't. It's your baby, yours and Jago's. You can't just give it away.'

'Of course I can. Jago didn't want it, I don't want it.'

'How do you know that?' said Celia.

'He would have written and told me if he had. Of course he would. He was clearly horrified, and didn't know what to say. And it will be far better with some nice woman who will care for it, look after it, give it a good home.' She sounded as if she was talking about a puppy or a kitten rather than about a child.

'LM, you can't make that sort of decision now. Believe me, you'll feel quite different when you've had the baby.'

'I shan't feel any different,' said LM.

She didn't. The staff at the nursing home thought she was inhuman. They admired her courage during the birth, which was long and arduous, but then when they tried to give her her son to hold, she refused.

'No thank you. I'm really not interested,' she said and turned away and slept for the first time in three days.

'Shock,' said Sister, 'she's had a bad time. She'll be all right tomorrow.'

But the next day was the same. 'I really don't want him,' she said, 'I wish you could understand. Now please leave me alone.'

A junior nurse fed the baby, changed him, cuddled him; she felt very sad for him. He was such a beautiful child, with a lot of dark hair and huge, very dark blue eyes, which would undoubtedly turn brown. He was good, too, he took his bottle so well each time and then went back to sleep.

She took him in to LM later.

'Mrs Lytton.'

'I do wish you wouldn't go on with this tiresome fiction that I am Mrs Lytton,' said LM. 'I'm not married, and I would like you to respect my condition and address me as Miss Lytton. Anyway, what is it?'

'I just wondered – that is – Mrs – Miss Lytton – are you sure you wouldn't like to hold your baby? He's so beautiful.'

LM turned as violently as it is possible to do on a pillow, and said, her face stiff with rage, 'I wish you people would leave me alone. How many times do I have to tell you, I want nothing to do with him? I hope I shall be going home at the end of the week, and he is going to the adoption society. Now please leave me alone.'

The nurse, who was very young, shed large tears over Baby Lytton as she changed his nappy.

'I've been to see her,' reported Lady Beckenham to Celia, who was unable to get down to Buckinghamshire before the weekend, 'and she is in a very curious state. Wants nothing to do with the baby, can't wait to have it taken away and adopted. Well, no doubt for the best, since she's just not interested in it at all. Perfectly understandable of course, but it's difficult for the staff. And then she insists on them calling her Miss Lytton which they naturally dislike. The matron is a dreadful woman, although she likes to regard herself as a friend of mine. I have told her to respect LM's wishes, but I do see that she is not helping her own cause there in the least.'

'Yes,' said Celia, 'Yes, I can see that. Oh dear. When – when is the baby going?'

'Oh – next Tuesday I believe. And LM will come back here then.'

'Have you seen him? Is he – what does he look like?'

'Like a newborn baby,' said the Countess and put the phone down.

They had found a good home for Baby Lytton, the lady from the adoption agency told LM when she visited her on the Friday; a very nice family from Beaconsfield, 'An older couple, so the husband will not be going away to the war. They have a delightful house, and will be excellent parents, I'm sure. They are coming to see him, and all being well, will take him home on Tuesday.'

'Good,' said LM, 'the sooner the better.'

She felt very miserable; it was the third day after the birth, she was sore and uncomfortable, and her breasts were aching with undrunk milk. They had bound them up, which hurt even more.

'You have to expect some discomfort,' said Sister, who, not surprisingly, had taken a strong dislike to LM, 'but in a day or two it will dry up. Baby certainly is doing very well without it. He doesn't seem to need you at all.'

'Good,' said LM. For some reason she felt very near to tears.

Mrs Bill was doing the dusting on Monday morning when there was a knock on the door; it was the postman. He held out the letters to her; one of them was a large envelope, from the woman poet, Mrs Bill recognised the writing. She would never send her work to Lyttons, LM had explained, in case they lost it. Mrs Bill put the letters down on the table to sort through later and went back to her dusting.

Celia wasn't feeling very well. She had a throbbing backache, and felt sick and desperately tired. Hardly surprising, she supposed; she was running the household single-handed, as well as Lyttons and now Truman was talking about enlisting. She would miss him dreadfully if he went; he did so much for her. Deliveries of foodstuffs had fallen off and he collected all the grocery and meat orders, as well as ferrying everyone about, and driving her to and from work every day. She'd visited LM at the weekend which had distressed her. LM was so hostile to the baby, hostile to her as well. She knew LM blamed her to a degree – she wasn't quite sure for what – and she knew she was terribly unhappy, although she had been dry-eyed and insisted in a harsh voice that she hadn't even looked at the baby since his birth, and didn't want to. That was distressing too; Celia had looked at him and held him, and thought how much she would like to take him home. But she couldn't; she knew that. Her mother had read her mind over tea later.

'You are not running a home for waifs and strays, Celia,' she said sharply, 'And I'd have thought you might have learned your lesson.'

All in all it hadn't been exactly rewarding, trundling all that way in the car, when she could have been in bed, resting. She was just embarking on her current pet project, the new children's list, and thinking how ironic it was that something she had long proposed and had rejected, should have been indirectly brought to birth by Oliver joining the army, when her telephone rang.

'Yes?'

'There's a Mrs Bill on the phone, Lady Celia. Says it's urgent.'

'Oh yes. Yes, of course. Put her through.'

Mrs Bill sounded breathless. Breathless and upset.

'Lady Celia, good morning. How are you?'

'Very well thank you, Mrs Bill. And you?'

'There's been a letter,' said Mrs Bill.

'A letter?'

'Yes. From – from Mr Ford.'

'Mr Ford? But, Mrs Bill, there can't be, he's – he's dead.'

'I know. Must have got held up. Anyway, it is, most definitely. Postmarked France, and his writing.'

'You're sure? It's not from his CO? They do always write, you know.'

'No,' said Mrs Bill, 'no, definitely not. I'd know his writing anywhere.'

'Oh,' said Celia, 'well – well I – I think you'd better . . .'

'Lady Celia, I couldn't. I simply couldn't.'

'In that case,' said Celia, thinking hard, 'bring it down here to me. I'll send Truman for you. No on second thoughts, can you get a taxi? It would be quicker. I'll pay.'

'Yes,' said Mrs Bill. 'Yes, all right.'

She handed the letter to Celia; Celia looked at it. She felt absolutely certain that she should open it, decide what it was best to do. The circumstances were so extreme, and if it said the wrong thing, then it was best, given LM's mental state, that it should remain lost for ever. On the other hand, if it said the right thing—

'I'm going to open it, Mrs Bill,' she said. 'I know it might seem wrong to you, but—'

'No, Lady Celia,' said Mrs Bill, 'no, not for you to open it. That doesn't seem wrong at all.'

Celia ripped open the letter. She felt dreadful doing so, as if she were breaking into, plundering, LM's most intimate private life: Half way through unfolding it, she stopped, an almost physical fear gripping her. But she went on, sat there reading it very slowly and carefully. At first she couldn't take it in; quite literally, her mind as well as her eyes blurred with emotion, it was a meaningless jumble of words. Then the lines steadied, and she began to read. Mrs Bill watched her. After a few minutes Celia put it down on the desk and looked up at Mrs Bill, her eyes streaming with tears.

'Is it – is it bad news, Lady Celia?'

'No,' said Celia, 'no, it isn't. And we've done absoutely the right thing. Mrs Bill, I have to go. At once. Down to Beaconsfield. I must telephone for Truman – no, is your taxi cab still there? We can go together to Cheyne Walk, that would be much more sensible. There's really no time to lose.'

She stood up and winced; the backache hit her quite hard. Mrs Bill noticed.

'Are you all right, Lady Celia?'

'Oh yes. Just a bit of backache. Quite usual, under the circumstances, wouldn't you say?' She smiled at her. 'Come on, let's go.'

She walked rather slowly up the steps to the house; her back really hurt. She rang the bell: Brunson came to the door.

'Are you all right, Lady Celia? You don't look very well, If you don't mind my saying so.'

'I'm perfectly all right, Brunson. Really. But I need Truman.'

'He's not here, Lady Celia. He's gone down to see about enlisting.'

'Oh no. Oh, dear. Well – well never mind. The car's here, I'll just have to take it myself. I need something delivered urgently and—'

'If only I could drive, Lady Celia, I would take it.'

'I know you would, Brunson. Oh, dear—'

Her back stabbed again; differently, harshly. She was terribly afraid of what it meant.

'Brunson, would you go and see if Mrs Bill is still outside? In her taxi cab? I told her to wait a few minutes.'

But Mrs Bill had gone, and the cab with her.

There was nothing for it; she would have to drive to Beaconsfield herself. She knew the way, and she would, after all, be sitting down. Not haring round the office, as Dr Perring put it. Anyway, she must get this letter to LM, she simply must. It was more important than anything at that moment, than anything in the world. Two people's future depended upon it; and in an odd way another person's past. She owed it to LM. She would be all right. Of course she would.

LM was lying down, trying to sleep, trying to put the thought of the next day out of her mind, when the junior nurse came in.

'Supper, Miss Lytton? You have to eat, you know, you have to keep up your strength.'

'I don't want any supper,' said LM. 'I'm not hungry.'

The nurse looked at her; then she sat down on the bed, and took her hand. She had been told by Sister not to get involved with this strange patient, but she felt so strongly that she was making a mistake, that she wanted to keep trying. She also felt very sorry for the baby; he might be going to a good home, as Sister also kept saying, but he would be much better with his mother. And if his father had been killed in the war, she needed him even more. She just didn't realise it. And she was quite sure that if Miss Lytton only held him, just once, saw how beautiful he was, she would change her mind.

'Miss Lytton' she said, gently, 'are you quite sure you don't want to hold your baby? He's so lovely and—'

LM sat up abruptly. 'Get out,' she shouted. 'just get out. When will you get it into your cretinous head that I don't want that baby. I don't like it, I'm not interested in it, now just bloody well get out.'

The little nurse looked at her and burst into tears. She stood up and fled to the door; Sister, who had heard the noise, intercepted her.

'Miss Lytton,' she said, 'how dare you speak to one of my staff like that? How dare you? You have no right, no right at all. I appreciate that you are upset, but there is a limit, even to my tolerance. Now please apologise to her.'

LM looked at her. 'I apologise,' she said in a stiff, harsh voice, 'for upsetting your staff. But she upset me.'

'Well fortunately for you,' said Sister, 'you will be going home tomorrow. So we won't be upsetting you any longer. Nurse, run along, get on with your duties. Baby Lytton is crying. Poor little mite,' she added severely. She handed LM some papers. 'Mrs Burton from the adoption society brought these in. They are for you to sign. She says it will help make things go smoothly tomorrow.'

'Very well,' said LM.

LM took out her pen and started to look at the papers. They were very straightforward; in essence resigning all claims to Baby Lytton, promising never to try to contact him or his adoptive parents for the rest of his life, or to place any restrictions on his upbringing.

'I can't tell you who the adoptive parents are, or where they live,' Mrs Burton had explained, 'obviously it is far better that you don't know. And he will never know who you are, or how or where to contact you. His name will be that of his new parents, and—'

'Yes, yes,' LM said, 'I understand.'

She should have just signed the papers there and then; she knew she should. Get it settled; then she could relax, return to her former life. Rub him out of it. Never think of him again. She was glad she had hardly even looked at him, never held him; it made it so much simpler. He would be gone, as if he had never been. That was what she had wanted.

'I'm afraid there is no question of your seeing Miss Lytton now,' said Sister severely to Celia, 'visiting hours are long over, she's had her supper and is asleep. And if I allow one person in, I have to allow many more.'

'Sister,' said Celia, 'this is very important. I have to see my sister-in-law.'

'And nursing routines are also very important. Whatever it is must wait until the morning.'

A pain shot through Celia like the tightening of a rope. It frightened her; she remembered that pain, she knew what it was. It also made her angry.

'Sister,' she said, 'I want to see my sister-in-law, tonight, and I intend to do so. Now please let me go through to her.'

Sister hesitated. 'I shall have to ask Matron,' she said.

'Oh don't be so ridiculous,' said Celia impatiently. 'I'm not interrupting vital surgery or a difficult delivery, as far as I know. And I would remind you that Matron is a friend of my mother's, Lady Beckenham, and she would be most unhappy if she thought I was being kept from my sister-in-law.' Sister glared at her; she had already been ticked off twice by Matron, over what she described as her unfortunate attitude to Miss Lytton: Matron was hoping for an invitation to Ashingham House to discuss Lady Beckenham's plans for a convalescent home there, and even to be involved in the enterprise.

'Very well,' she said, 'I will go and see if Miss Lytton is prepared to see you.'

'I'll just come along with you,' said Celia, 'If you don't mind.'

'Miss Lytton. Miss Lytton wake up. You've got a visitor.'

'A visitor. Oh, no, it's much too late, I'm so tired.'

It must be Lady Beckenham: dreadful woman. But at least she had understood, had been the only person who hadn't tried to persuade her to reconsider her decision to have the baby adopted.

'Animals do it,' she had said, patting her hand rather awkwardly, 'take on other animals' young. You see it with sheep, mostly. Once a ewe takes to the new lamb, gets its smell, she accepts it just as well as the original mother. You don't have to worry.'

LM hadn't been quite sure she wanted to be compared with a sheep, but it had been strangely comforting. Just the same, she didn't really want to see Lady Beckenham now. And she hadn't even signed the forms. That really had to be done. She struggled up in bed, took a sip of water.

'I really don't want to see anyone now,' she said, 'whoever it is. Tell them I'm sorry. And if you'll wait I'll give you these forms.'

'LM, hallo.'

It was Celia. She looked strange; pale and wide-eyed. She was holding something out to her, a letter.

'LM you have to read this. Please. I wanted you to have it as quickly as possible. Sister, could you get me a glass of water please? I feel – not very well. And I'd like a chair, if you wouldn't mind.'

Sister gave what could only be described as a snort, and went out of the room.

Celia sat down rather heavily on LM's bed; she was clearly not well, and in considerable pain but LM was oblivious to it. She was oblivious to everything. She sat, reading the letter Celia had handed her, her lips moving as she did so. She read it several times, and when she had finished, she put it down, threw her head back on the pillows and smiled.

'And at the same time she was crying, crying her eyes out,' the junior nurse reported later to the others, 'and then she said, after quite a long time, a minute or two at least, she said, "please bring me my baby, straight away". And Sister said she couldn't have him, he was asleep, and I told her that, and she said she didn't care if he was asleep, she wanted him, and she'd go and get him herself if she had to, so in the end, I went and got him. Sister was furious. And she just took him and started stroking his head, a bit awkwardly to be sure, and kissing him as well, and just crying and saying she was sorry and she loved him, over and over again. It was really lovely. And then the poor other lady who'd brought the letter passed right out,' she added soberly, 'and Sister sent for the doctor, and apparently she'll probably lose her own baby. So sad isn't it?'

CHAPTER 11

'Come along, Maud my darling. Daddy is going to show you the lovely new house he's built for you.'

'Just for me?' Maud's large eyes, pure green, not a touch of blue, looked up at her father, very wide.

'No, I shall be there too, if you'll have me. And Jamie sometimes, too. And Nurse of course, and some of the other servants. I think you'll like it, it's in a really great street called Sutton Place. Right on the East River.'

'On the river! Can we have a boat?'

Robert laughed. 'Maybe not for the East River. But I'm also looking out for a weekend place for us on Long Island. We can have a boat there, of course.'

'Why do we have to leave this house?'

'It's too big for us, darling. For just you and me.'

'And Jamie.'

'Yes. Now go and see Nurse, ask her to get you ready to go out. I can't wait for you to see it.'

Maud was four now; quite enchanting, not exactly pretty, but very attractive, and rather unusual looking, with her red-gold hair and serious little face. She and her father were absolutely devoted to one another: but while she was certainly a little precocious, she was not spoilt. Robert was too afraid she would become like her half-brother to allow it; from the very beginning he had been firm with her, had briefed her nurse to be the same.

'I know it's hard, when she has lost her mother. But she could so easily become a brat, as we all try to make it up to her. And that won't do her any service in the long run.'

The most difficult time was, he believed, over for her. Jeanette was a loving and much-loved memory, which he worked to keep alive for her; but she was a fragmentary one, and Maud had lived for nearly half her small life now without her mother.

Her world was bounded very happily by Robert, by her nurse, and by Jamie, whom she adored. The Brewers formed a very satisfactory

192

extended family, John and Felicity both doting on her, and their son, Kyle, taking Laurence's part as big brother. Not that he could hold a candle to Jamie in her eyes; nobody could. So Robert was happy about Maud and happy about her future, especially now that he had built the house, and Laurence couldn't hurt them any more. He only wished that she could meet the rest of the Lytton family. In the early days of the war he had still toyed with the idea of taking her over to London, but the torpedoeing of the *Lusitania* by German U-boats, and the drowning of over a thousand passengers had plainly made it impossible. People said it was only a matter of time before America joined in the war; uneasily aware of their patriotic obligations and grateful for every day that it didn't happen, voters had re-elected Woodrow Wilson that year as the man who kept them out of the war. Robert, more torn in his attitudes to the whole thing than most, wracked with concern for his younger brothers, was guiltily grateful nevertheless, to be spared what they were going through.

'I want you to come and live with me here in Cheyne Walk,' said Celia.

LM stared at her; nothing could have appealed to her less. She hated the idea of losing her independence, leaving her home; she was famously solitary, and, indeed, Jago's refusal to move in with her had been an important factor in the success of their relationship.

'Oh, I don't think that's a very good idea,' she said quickly.

'But why? Or rather why not? It's only sensible, we can pool our outgoings on things like coal and food and so on, and especially when the children have gone, it will be ridiculous to have one of us in one large house and one in another.'

LM said hers was not a large house, and Celia said it was by most people's standards, and certainly large for one person. 'Nobody's suggesting you sell it, you can go back the minute the war's over. And it will be nice for Mrs Bill to have some company during the day. It can't be much fun for her all alone, just waiting for the zeppelins to come. I won't bother you at all, I promise, you can have all your meals in your room if you like.'

LM asked for time to think about it, but finally agreed, swayed not so much by Celia's arguments, but by a sense that she owed her a great deal. She knew that Celia's long, gruelling drive to Beaconsfield with the precious letter from Jago, had been, if not entirely responsible for the loss of her baby, at least partly so. She would never forget that night, she knew, as long as she lived; sitting there, holding Jay, clinging to him as if she could never let him go, while reading over and over again the wonderful words.

My beloved Meg.

I could never have believed I could feel so happy. Just to think of you carrying our child makes my eyes fill with tears; of course I am afraid for you, but I know that when I see you together, when I come home to what will be at last my own dear family, it will be worth anything either of us might have to endure. I feel so proud and so joyful, Meg. I love you more than ever and thank you from the bottom of my heart for this wonderful gift from you and from the God I feel suddenly I can believe in.

Your loving Jago.

PS I would like us to be married as soon as possible. I cannot have my son (for I'm sure he is a son) growing up a little bastard! Jago XXX

PPS. I think we should call him Jay.

Joy had filled her, poured into her, and love too, and in some strange way poured into the past few dreadful months, turning the wretchedness and despair into happiness and hope. Jago was still dead; but he was not, after all, lost to her, had not turned away from her as she had thought. He had loved her and he had wanted her to bear their child thus he was hers again. And when she thought of how nearly she had lost the small Jay, given him away without even having held him, this tiny piece of Jago, how if Celia had not arrived in time she would have done so, she felt overwhelmed with both fear and gratitude. But – and it was a dreadful but – Celia had lain in pain and grief, losing the baby which she had so wanted, which Oliver had so wanted, as a symbol of life continuing, of their life together, in spite of the war. Celia had risked that baby for her, with her usual defiant courage; and the risk had been too great.

'Don't be ridiculous,' she had said to LM the next day, as she lay, white-faced and exhausted, after the long night when the tiny girl had been born and died within an hour. 'It would have happened anyway, I was doing all the wrong things, Dr, Perring told me weeks ago I should stay in bed. I knew when I first got up yesterday that it was inevitable. I just kept ignoring the signs; if anything did it, it was all those books we humped up last weekend. Please don't feel responsible, LM; I'm so happy for you, at least.'

But she had not stayed so brave; later, after the necessary misery of registering the death, of the funeral, and writing to Oliver, she had cracked, had cried for days. Her mother cared for her at Ashingham. with her usual brusque sympathy, and LM had settled into the Dovecot with Jay, careful to keep him out of her way, feeling that seeing this other large, healthy baby would be more than Celia could bear.

She had been wrong there; Celia had arrived one afternoon, palely determined, and demanded to see him. 'I want to really get to know him, he's so important to us all. Give him to me, LM, I want to hold him, please.'

And LM had slightly tentatively handed over Jay, who was already gaining weight and doing what she personally knew was smiling at her, although everyone else said it was impossible after only three weeks.

Celia had hugged him to her and looked at LM over his small dark head and said, 'LM, he's very special to me. I promise you. I know I'm crying and I can't help it, but I didn't know Jago and this way I can. There's no point in me not seeing this little chap, when the whole point of that day was keeping him with us. Oh, look at him, he's so beautiful. I can't wait for the others to see him.'

She remained outwardly brave; but LM had found her several times, even after they returned to London, weeping helplessly.

'Don't start sympathising,' she said, quite fiercely, 'it's the last thing I need. I'll get over it. Let's just work and work till we drop. That's always been my salvation. It stops me worrying about Oliver so much, as well.'

Recognising that grief, and Celia's courage, LM finally agreed to join her in Cheyne Walk, with little Jay and Mrs Bill and Dorothy Jenkins, the cheerful, uncomplicated young woman LM had employed to care for Jay. It didn't last for very long.

There were several raids on the coast in early 1915, but the first air attack on London was not until the early summer. Celia had seen them, had watched, awed as zeppelins hung high over London, their great cigar shapes caught in the searchlights. Their lumbering, apparently gentle movement totally belied what happened next, something hitherto unknown and unimaginable, the violence of bombs falling on to the city in a dreadful explosion of noise and fire. They did not do a great deal of harm to human life, only killing a handful of people, but a great many buildings were damaged, and clearly they would be back. Everyone was very frightened. The very next day, Barty and the twins and Jay, together with the nannies, were all dispatched to Ashingham.

My darling,

It amuses me now, looking back on what we were told at Colchester about trench warfare. Four days in the front line, four days in support, eight days in reserve and fourteen days resting, that was the theory. It sounded grim but bearable. Now, with the acute shortage of men, any length of time can be spent there. A battalion of the Black Watch regiment is said to have spent 48 days in the front line. We have spent, this time around, 20 so far. The men are exhausted but amazingly, morale is good. They are a splendid bunch. We are in rather terrific new trenches, which helps, we actually have a wooden floor. And a brazier which is lit at dusk in the officer's quarters. Luxury. Also we are ten feet down at least. So we feel rather safer.

The worst danger, at night now at least, is from gas. God, that is a dreadful thing. The stuff of nightmares, as you yourself said. But, again, so far, so good. The conditions in the last trenches were so appalling, day after day waist deep in mud, no chance of dry clothes for the foreseeable future. And of course the hideous trench foot, several of my men got it, and the worst cases were invalided out. Their feet simply rotted with the permanent wet, and developed gangrene.

The squalor is in many ways the worst thing. It saps at the spirit and at courage. You simply would not believe it. Oh, my darling, those other days, when I moved about in a dry clean house, took baths, wore clean clothes every day, and had only worries about Lyttons and its new list to disturb my sleep, did they really ever happen? Only thinking of you makes me able to remember them.

I love you my darling, so very much. Write again, very soon. Tell the children to write, I love their letters, they keep my faith alive. And I loved getting the photographs of them all; wonderful to see little Jay. He certainly doesn't look like a Lytton. But it is with a part of you, my darling, that I go into battle every day: the locket with your curl of hair and your photograph are always, always in my breast pocket, and I touch it every time I go over the top. It's my lucky charm, and has kept me safe all this time.

I have to go now, it's late and we start the day early here. No need for an alarm clock at least!!!

My best love,
Oliver

Celia read this letter once quickly, and once slowly, as she always did, and then kissed it, stuffed it into her leather bag and went downstairs to the morning room, where there was a tray of tea and toast set out. The memory of breakfasts in the old days, with their endless dishes of eggs, bacon, kidneys and sausages, lined up on the sideboard under their silver covers, the fruit, the coffee, the hot rolls, the piles of butter, pots of different marmalades and jams, was more unbelievable than almost anything. Food shortages had become quite severe, and prices were very high; there was constant talk of rationing as the only equitable solution. Women stood in food queues for hours.

Cook reckoned to spend most of every morning in one queue or another. She had been splendidly magnanimous over her position since the housemaids had left to work in factories; remarking cheerfully that as she really didn't have a great deal to do in the kitichens, she might as well take over some of the cleaning. She was unusual in this: many of Celia's friends had cooks who became mutinous at similar suggestions. Cook and Brunson did it together, and together the three of them kept the garden looking neat and cared for. It was an oddly happy arrangement; Truman was at the front, and Celia drove herself around on the occasions when public transport did not meet her needs. She had acquired a Peugeot Bebe which she loved, and which used far less petrol than the Rolls, which was stabled at Ashingham for the duration of the war.

Celia's maid had also left, and gone to train as a nurse; Celia let her go without an argument, on condition that she kept a diary which could be published after the war. Celia looked after her own clothes, and did her own laundry. She found ironing, hitherto an almost mystical skill to her, rather soothing, and would stand for up to an hour at a time, pressing her dresses and skirts and lace-trimmed blouses; she still loved clothes and refused to adopt anything as utilitarian as LM's uniform. She liked the new, shorter skirt length, as much for its look and the fact it showed more of her undeniably good legs, as for its practicality, and she admired the simplicity of the new coats and jackets; but on the rare occasions when she went out in the evening, she wore her long dresses trimmed and layered in lace, her velvet cloaks, her high-heeled slippers, and spent time doing up her hair.

'You have to go on doing what matters to you,' she said firmly, 'as well as you can. Otherwise life becomes completely unrecognisable.'

The fact that life, for the most part, was completely unrecognisable was something she refused to dwell on; it did not suit her stubborn optimism.

School was no better: in fact it was probably worse, Giles thought. The bullying went on, he still had no friends, and he found himself as useless at cricket as he had been at soccer. The food, always bad, had become terrible, and perhaps worst of all, the teaching staff had changed. The young male teachers had nearly all departed for the front. They were replaced by much older men, or spinsterish middle-aged ladies, who not only made lessons far more boring, but appeared to be even less aware of what was going on under their noses. This led to a breakdown of formal discipline, and an increase in the power of the prefects and of the fagging system. Giles was getting desperate; his misery was exacerbated by a constant terror that his father might be killed, and that if the Germans won the war, they would bayonet all the children and eat them.

Nobody really thought the Germans would win; but late at night, when all the lights were out, it was hard not to remember stories told by the likes of Clarke, one of the more unpleasant prefects, stories he had actually heard, he told them, of the Hun bayonetting Belgian children and tearing their tongues out, before roasting them alive.

Giles was actually frightened of going to sleep, for fear he would dream of these dreadful things, but lying awake staring into the darkness with the horrors going round and round in his head was worse. And then he would think of his own father, fighting these terrible people, and wonder what would happen to him if he was captured rather than killed, and subjected to torture.

And then something else dreadful happened; they were all called into the hall one morning, and told by the headmaster that he had some very sad news for them. The boys glanced at one another in terror. A few had already been summoned singly into the head's study and emerged weeping, a few minutes later, having been told that their fathers, or occasionally their elder brothers, were dead. Could this mean that all their fathers had been killed? In some inexplicable mass murder? Or that the Hun had won the war and was on his way over?

'I know you will all be extremely sorry to hear,' said the head, 'that Mr Thompson, who taught most of you, and was very popular with you all, has been killed. He was an officer in France and died a hero's death; I have at least the comfort for you that the battle in which he was killed was a victory for England. So his death was not in vain and we must seek comfort in that. We will observe two minutes' silence; later today special prayers will be said in the chapel for Mr Thompson and for his family.'

Giles walked out of the hall in silence; he was crying, as many of the boys were. For once no one was mocking anyone else. Mr Thompson's lessons had been fun, he had made history into a wonderful story, and he was never sarcastic or impatient, in fact if anyone had a problem answering a question, he would go through it with them after the lesson and make sure they understood. And then he was a wonderful sportsman, a marvellous coach on the soccer field, building up strong first and second teams, persuading them to practice and train on the coldest winter mornings, not by bullying them but by setting a cheerful example himself. And every Sunday he would hold tea parties in his study, and serve hot toast with anchovy paste, and fruit buns; for many of the boys, who were miserable and homesick like Giles, he was the only person who made life worth living. And now he was gone: gone forever. It was Giles's first taste of real grief, and worse, of experiencing the finality of death. He found it almost unbearable.

★

'I think,' said LM, walking into Celia's office, 'when the war is over—'

'When?' said Celia wearily. She was feeling particularly tired.

'Yes, when,' said LM firmly. In some perverse way, Celia envied her. She had already survived the worst; her lover had been killed, and although her grief was dreadful she had faced it, coped with it, and it was over. And she was so happy with her little boy, so unexpectedly and wonderfully happy; while for Celia every day began and ended with a crawling, awful dread. Sometimes she would stand at the window in Cheyne Walk, see a telegram boy walking along the Embankment. She would watch him, her stomach seized with horror, anticipating the pause at her gate, the glance up at the house to check the number, the walk up the path, the knock at the door. And when he passed on by, she would sit down weakly, released from fear, and wonder how much longer she could take it. Oliver had been home only once since his departure for France; a strange, almost surreal time. He had been so exhausted that for two days he had simply slept; after waiting for him so long, filled with desire as much as anything else, she had lain frustrated beside him, wondering if he would ever make love to her again. He did, but only once in the seven days; and then with a kind of desperation which seemed to have no joy in it. He did not talk much to her, preferring to sit in silence, just being with her. He was eager for details of domestic life, and of the children, but he did not want to hear about Lyttons.

'I dare not even think about it, Celia, it would just frustrate me, make me miserable.'

When she asked him to tell her about life at the front, to share with her at least some of the horrors which she knew would have been censored out of his letters, he simply said he was trying to forget them for a blessed few days. She suspected that it was more likely he thought she would not understand; and she felt hurt by it. Finally on the night before he left, he did begin to talk to her and with passion, of many things: of a life that was scarcely endurable.

'No, it's unendurable, living in the mud where men and horses had died, with the noise and the stench, with the lice and the rats and the flies – sometimes so loud the buzzing of those flies, that it confuses the noise of approaching aircraft.'

He spoke of a dreadful confusion on the battlefield, of smoke and noise separating men from their commanders, with orders lost, of senior commanders miles away from the trenches refusing to accept that battles were not going the way they planned, of emergency field hospitals, little better than First Aid stations, of a growing sense of disillusionment with the direction of the war.

'There is a dreadful stalemate going on, it seems to me, with both sides defending themselves fiercely and successfully at the front. When a few inches are gained here and there, it is claimed as a great victory. Of course it is nothing of the sort. Some other strategies will have to be employed.'

She sat listening, appalled, frightened, but knowing there was nothing that she, nor he, nor indeed anyone could do but endure it. And when he went back, she felt dully, miserably aware that he had not enjoyed his leave as they had both hoped, that it had not brought the expected dazzling happiness, but formed a scarcely credible contrast to the conditions he had left behind, and thereby made returning to them worse.

'So what is this idea?' she said to LM now.

'I think we should do a book about the art of war. It has produced a remarkable outpouring of creativity. The paintings and the poetry, of course.'

'Those poems by Francis Grieg are so lovely,' said Celia, 'I keep reading them over and over again. I'm sure we shall do well with them. There's something really special about them, patriotism tinged with regret, a kind of slightly more realistic Rupert Brooke. Clever of you to find him, LM. Anyway, sorry to interrupt. I agree with you. And I don't see why we should wait to publish.'

'Well – two reasons. I came to the idea while thinking about the posters; I think they have to be part of it. They're remarkable works of art, some of them, and they've great power to evoke emotion. But I think people need a bit of distance to appreciate them as art. It would also be an expensive book to produce, and we can't afford good paper and so on at the moment. Mind you, some of them are extremely unpalatable. The less subtle propaganda is very unattractive. I saw one yesterday, showing a German nurse pouring the water on to the ground while an English soldier was begging for a drink; frankly unbelievable.'

'Oh I agree with you, I'm afraid,' said Celia, 'I saw another one – of a German bayonetting a child – horrible. My own particular hate is that one addressed to the young women of London. You know the one? Does your "Best Boy" not think you and your country are worth fighting for? And something about if he neglects his country, he may one day neglect you. It made me very angry. There are perfectly good reasons for some of these young men not to go; common sense being one of them,' she added briskly. 'I suppose the men running this war know what they are doing; but one does begin to wonder. Hundreds and thousands of dead and only a few yards of mud to show for it. I cannot believe it makes sense, that there isn't a better way. Now look, why don't we cheer ourselves up and go to the pictures? *Birth of a Nation* sounds so wonderful even if it is all about war, and I think we deserve a treat.'

The twins often said, once they were old enough to articulate the thought, that their view of men, formed as they grew up at Ashingham in their grandmother's convalescent home, was a rather sorry one.

'No one under fifty, unless he was blind, or had lost a limb, or was suffering from shellshock,' said Adele. 'It really was very strange.'

Initially people tried to protect the children from some of the more tragic sights; but it soon proved impossible. Apart from the fact that they roamed the grounds unchecked, they were fascinated by what they saw. They would stand staring at the poor men sitting on the terrace or the lawns, in their wheelchairs, their stumps tucked neatly into their trousers, their empty sleeves pinned to their chests, and would ask them in genuine fascination if they were going to grow some more legs, or if they would have wooden ones, or how they could eat without their arms. The first time this happened, Nanny heard them and seized their hands, horrified and flushed, pulling them away, apologising to the soldier; but he smiled at her and said it was quite all right, he really didn't mind, and it was extremely nice to be an object of such interest to two pretty young ladies. Nanny had an anxious conversation with Lady Beckenham, who said that if the soldiers didn't mind, then it could do no harm.

'Probably cheer the poor wretches up. And they're all decent chaps, from good families, they won't upset the girls in any way.'

Barty, being older, was more distressed by what she saw, but at the same time, could be more useful and she enjoyed that; she liked to sit with the soldiers who had been blinded and read to them, or simply chat, and she would run errands for the nursing staff, taking the men their cups of tea, leading or pushing them in their wheelchairs out into the garden, taking their visitors to them, and even helping with the making of beds and tidying of rooms when everyone was really busy. There were, at any one time, twenty or so men at Ashingham; mostly amputees or blind, very few with the much dreaded shellshock, for it required more skilled nursing, and presented problems that the slightly genteel staff there could not cope with. But one man came for a few days and then had to be sent away again; Barty watched, horrified, as he sat, shivering violently, staring ahead of him, apparently unable to hear or speak; every now and again he started clawing at his mouth, and mumbling incoherently.

'It's a horrible thing,' said one of the other men, watching her face. 'Poor chap.'

'But what is it, what's wrong with him?' asked Barty, her own eyes huge with horror.

'It's – well it's having been out there for too long,' the man said carefully, 'the noise from the shells, you know, going on and on endlessly and having to go into battle every day, and losing some of your friends.'

Barty said nothing, but she thought of Wol who had been gone for a long time now, and of her own father, of whom she had heard so very little, and dreaded the same thing happening to them.

'Oh my God,' said Celia. She was very white; she stood in the hall, looking at the telegram which lay on the silver letter tray, 'oh, dear God, Brunson when did this come?'

So it had happened. It was over. Oliver was dead.

'Lady Celia, please don't be distressed. I was hoping to intercept you before you saw it. The telegram is—'

'Brunson, of course I'm distresed, what do you expect, why on earth didn't you get in touch with me, it's unforgivable of you, oh God—'

She had picked it up now, not noticing that it was already open, pulling it out of its envelope. And then looked at Brunson, smiling slightly shame-facedly.

'Sorry, Brunson.'

'That's quite all right, Lady Celia. It was natural you should be upset. I have asked Cook to make Major Lytton's favourite meal for tomorrow night. Steak and kidney pie, as I recall.'

'You recall correctly, Brunson. Thank you. Dear Jack. It will be so good to see him.'

Jack looked at least five years older she thought, studying him as he lounged in a chair in the drawing-room, still in his uniform, with one long leg crossed over the other. Even so, he was still incredibly handsome; more so than Oliver, she thought, unwillingly disloyal, and then firmly stifled the thought.

'It's so wonderful to see you, Jack,' she said.

'It's pretty wonderful to see you, Celia. You're looking marvellous, as always. I've thought of you so much out there.'

'Me! I thought you had – what was her name – Kitty to think about.'

'Kitty's history, Celia. You should listen more carefully. It was Sally last leave. Terrific girl. Wonderful dancer. Did a solo in that revue at the

Duke of York's. Can't remember its name. We had a lot of fun. But 'fraid she's forgotten about me. Never wrote, anyway.'

'So you thought about me instead! Well, I'm very flattered.'

'Celia, my darling, you are far more beautiful and desirable than either of them, actually. God, Oliver's a lucky chap.' He was rather drunk already, she thought; and he hadn't had any wine yet.

'Jack! Old lady like me!'

'You're not an old lady, Celia. You're exactly the same age as me, if you remember.'

'Yes, that's true.'

She was always surprised by this; he seemed far younger than she was. She supposed that was what a lack of responsibility did for you. Except that being at the front under those appalling conditions, defending your country, could hardly be described as irresponsible.

'Let's go down and have dinner,' she said, 'it's your favourite, steak and kidney pie.'

'Celia! I'm more touched than I can say. Fancy you remembering that.'

'I didn't,' she said, laughing, 'Brunson did.'

'Marvellous chap, Brunson. Every household should have one.'

'It certainly should. Now come along. And you can tell me all about France.'

'I'd rather you told me about London,' he said, 'do you still go out all the time?'

'Oh Jack. If only I did.'

He kept her and LM entertained throughout dinner with stories of life at the front: funny, cheerful stories about trading tobacco and chocolates for the books she sent him, 'Sorry Celia, but I never was much of a reader.' He told tales of how a fellow officer had nearly got shot one night in the trenches 'Doing the tango with his rifle, and wearing nothing but a German helmet, you know, with the spike on top. One of the men saw him, and thought he really was Fritz.' Of how he had tried to conduct a love affair, 'Rather a short one, with a very jolly nurse, one night in the field hospital. I'd escorted a chap over there who'd collected rather a lot of shrapnel, and got caught by Sister in the dressings tent, she noticed it rocking a bit. She was fearfully cross, sent me straight back to my quarters with a flea in my ear. I heard the nurse got into fearful trouble.'

'Jack, you are dreadful,' said Celia, wiping tears of laughter from her eyes; even LM had begun to laugh.

'Well,' he said, 'you have to keep your spirits up somehow. It's not quite the Cafe Royal out there in the evenings.'

'I don't suppose it is,' she said sombrely; later, when LM had gone to bed, she said, 'You don't have to, Jack, but if you want to talk about it all, stop pretending it's fun, I'm quite prepared to listen.'

'I don't think I do,' he said carefully, 'it's safer, pretending. Protects you from the reality.'

'Bad?'

'Quite bad. Hard to enjoy soldiering, just at the moment.'

'Even for you?'

'Even for me. It's not the battles, it's not the huge casualties even, not even the discomfort. It is ghastly, the mud and the squalor, I have to say, worse for the men of course, we do get a bath from time to time and even to take our boots off. It's the sense of frustration. I shouldn't say this, and it's Oliver's claret talking really, and not for repetition, but you do get a feeling the generals don't know what they're doing. They're operating miles from the front line and a lot of it doesn't seem to make sense. I've never known anything quite like it, and nor have chaps who've seen a lot more fighting than I, out in the Boer War and so on. We have to obey orders of course, and accept the consequences, but – well—'

He saw her face, carefully adjusted his own, smiled at her quickly. 'Oh, don't take any notice of me, Celia. I'm just tired. A few days' leave and I'll be right as rain. And taking a much more optimistic view of it all.'

'Good,' she said quickly, picking up on his mood, his fear. 'Now how about a brandy?'

'A brandy would be fine. God, he keeps a good cellar doesn't he, old Oliver.'

'He does indeed. It's mostly empty, but Brunson has been conserving what's left.' She got up; as she walked past him, he put out his hand, and caught hers.

'You're such a wonderful girl, Celia. Oliver's a lucky chap.'

'Oh, Jack,' she said, telling herself that to withdraw her hand would be unkind, an unnecessary rejection when he was so unusually downhearted, 'you're always saying that.'

'And always meaning it,' he said, and lifted her hand and kissed it. First the back, and then, turning it over, he kissed the palm, slowly and very tenderly.

She stood there, looking down at his head, his golden head, so like Oliver's and felt desire shoot through her so strongly that she was startled; he met her eyes, recognised the desire, pulled her down and kissed her hard. On the mouth. Just for a second she gave in; felt her own mouth, soft, hungry, yearning for him. It had been so long, she missed Oliver so much and Jack was so – so beautiful. Just for a second, she let her mind carry her forward, let it visualise what she knew she wanted, watched herself lying with him, softening to him, taking him to herself. But then, reality returned; reality, and loving Oliver, keeping faith. She stiffened, stood up, and pulled her hand away.

'Jack. No. Don't. Please I'm hugely flattered but—'

He smiled at her: a rueful smile.

'I know. But we mustn't. Mustn't betray Oliver. Of course not. Not a brotherly thing to do.'

'Or a wifely one,' she said, and bent and kissed him lightly, gently on the forehead.

'You'd like to though, wouldn't you?' he said, grinning at her.

'No, Jack, of course I—'

'Celia, I know you would. It's all right. I'm not about to ravish you. I probably wouldn't think much of you if you let me.' He grinned. 'I'd sure as hell like it, though.'

'And I probably would, too,' she said, smiling back. 'Now I'm going to get your brandy, and then I'm going to bed.'

'With me?'

'No Jack, not with you.'

But it was safe, the danger had passed; this was the old Jack, the teasing, flirting Jack, the young brother. Her husband's brother, with whom anything other then friendship would be the ultimate disloyalty.

The next night, anxious that their relationship should return to its old ease and friendship, she insisted he took her out; they went to the Savoy, and afterwards to a rather seedy nightclub he knew, where they danced. He was a wonderful dancer, much better than Oliver; they stayed for hours.

'I could fall in love with you so easily,' he said into her ear, as they stood, only halfmoving on the tiny floor.

'I don't think you could,' she said, laughing up at him, 'not if you really knew me. I'm terribly bossy. I drive Oliver mad.'

'He needs bossing about,' said Jack, 'he's a bit of an old woman.'

'Of course he isn't,' she said.

'Of course he is. And unless you admit it, I shall storm your room tonight and ravish you mercilessly.'

She laughed, said that her room had a very strong key, and refused to admit it – of course. But she never forgot that moment; or Jack's words. And there were many times over the years which followed when they came back to her.

As well as looking after the horses, with only one girl groom whom she constantly denounced as useless and bone-idle, despite the fact she worked an eighteen-hour day, Lady Beckenham was working extremely hard in her convalescent home.

'I have become,' she announced to anyone who would listen, eyes gleaming with amusement, 'a cook general.'

This was a slight exaggeration; but she did do a fair amount of cooking for the men, her own cook having departed for the munitions factory in Beaconsfield, along with several of the other domestic staff. The kitchen maid who was actually older than cook, had stayed on, and she did her best, but she needed a great deal of direction and it was easier, Lady Beckenham said, simply to put on a pinafore and do a lot of the work herself. She even did some cleaning.

'I quite like it as a matter of fact,' she said to Celia, who stood incredulously watching her one day. 'It's rather satisfying. At least it's under your control. Although I do sometimes wish I'd done something a bit more adventurous. My friend, Bunty Hadleigh, you remember her?'

Celia did: the terrifying Duchess of Dorset, almost six feet tall with a booming voice, and a courage on the hunting field which even men envied.

'Well, she's gone out to drive an ambulance at the front. Got a letter from her this morning. It sounds terrific. She's living in a cellar with another woman, actually drives men from the front line to the field station. Marvellous. Says I wouldn't believe what she's seen. Tough though; apparently they have to sleep in their clothes, can't wash much and sometimes have to scrape the lice off themselves with a blunt knife. I can tell you I was very tempted to go out and join her. God, just look at that girl,' she added, pointing out a particularly pretty young nurse, who was patiently feeding a man without arms. 'Thank God Beckenham isn't here. It would be a complete nightmare.'

Lord Beckenham was enormously enjoying his war: Employed at the War Office in the recruitment department, he felt more useful and happier than he had for many years. He was a little sobered by the endless stream of young men – growing younger now, and shorter too, as the height regulations dropped – eager to go out and show the hun what they were made of, with no idea of what they were facing. But he would sit talking to them as they filled in forms, or he filled forms in for them. He told them how much he envied them, what a privilege and a thrill it was to be on the battlefield, defending their country, and they listened, their eyes shining, their courage bolstered, his words still ringing in their ears as they marched out to the troopships taking them to what was an almost certain death.

★

Sylvia had been struggling since Ted went. The money she got was not nearly adequate, the rent had increased, food was in scarce supply, and she spent much of her life in queues. For a while she sent Marjorie and Frank, but they would come home after waiting for two hours, and tell her there was nothing left. She knew that if she had been there herself, she could have argued and almost certainly secured something, even if it was not what she had actually been queuing for. So there was nothing for it but return to the queuing herself. She got no letters from Ted personally, because he couldn't write them, but, regular as clockwork, would come one of the printed cards, bearing various carefully ticked messages, such as 'I am quite well', 'I have not been wounded', 'I have received your letter.' And then the painfully printed TED and several crosses.

So far, it seemed, Ted had been right; he was lucky. Not a scratch. Her new worry was Billy, who was dead set on enlisting himself. He was only seventeen and a half, but the need for men was so urgent now that ages were not always checked. Bill was a big boy, he could easily be taken for sixteen. Sylvia had forbidden it of course, but she might as well have saved her breath; he wanted only to get out to France and join his father.

Very occasionally Sylvia would go and see Barty; Celia and LM would take her down for a weekend in their car and she would stay with LM, who she found less daunting than the others, in the Dovecot. She was terribly impressed by Barty; she was nine now and seemed so grown-up, with such a beautiful speaking voice and such good manners. She was pretty too, well not exactly pretty, not like the twins, but nice-looking, rather unusual, with her big eyes and her thick mane of curling hair. She was always delighted to see her mother, and when Sylvia was there, never left her side, dragging her from place to place to meet her friends among the men and the nursing staff, or to play with little Jay and even the twins. In the school holidays they would talk to Giles, who was, she told her mother, her special friend among the Lyttons.

'He's so nice to me,' she said simply, 'He doesn't think I'm different.'

Sylvia asked anxiously if the others were nice to her, and Barty said yes they were, really, these days, and added that she much preferred Ashingham to London.

'We have lessons in the old schoolroom with Aunt Celia's old governess, Miss Adams. She's very nice, but she's quite old and she has a bad limp. One of her legs is a lot shorter than the other, and she can't really cope with the twins, but she sends them off with Nanny after the middle of the morning, and then she and I have really nice lessons; she likes history best and English, and so do I. We're doing a book together about the ancient Greek and Roman legends, I'll show it to you, if you like.'

Sylvia said she didn't think she'd be able to understand much of it, but she admired it anyway, awed by Barty's beautiful handwriting, by her obvious skill with words; she often wondered what on earth would have happened to her if she had stayed at Line Street, and had to go to the Elementary. Although, of course, Frank had done well there; not so well at the Secondary, but then what school was any good these days with half the teachers gone to the war? She didn't tell Barty about Billy's military ambitions, knowng they would worry her, but she did reveal one night to Barty and LM, as they sat in the small circular drawing-room after supper, that she was having terrible trouble making ends meet.

'Well, why don't you get a job?' said LM, 'in a factory. You'd enjoy it, it's good money and they're crying out for people.'

Sylvia said she couldn't possibly do that, Ted wouldn't like it, and LM said what Ted's eyes didn't see, his heart surely wouldn't grieve over. 'Besides, you would be doing your bit for your country, especially if you worked in a munitions factory. Wouldn't that be a good feeling? And you'd make friends too, and don't you think you'd worry less, with something other than your own thoughts for company?'

Barty said earnestly that she, too thought it was a very good idea. The very next day Sylvia went nervously along to the labour exchange. Within three hours she was working at a munitions factory in Lambeth; a small place with white-washed walls and a stone floor. It made fuses for shells and apart from the foreman, the staff were all female. Sylvia loved it; the work, and the camaraderie, standing with the other women working on the machines; it was hard, she stood for long hours at a machine which honed the fuses into shape, and the work was more than a little dangerous. They all had to turn their collars up to stop the hot brass hitting their necks; there had been talk of explosions at other factories and it was possible to contract a disease from the TNT they worked with, and end up with yellow skin. But it was worth it, not just for the companionship and the money – fivepence halfpenny an hour – but to feel she was contributing to the war effort. It was shift work, with three eight-hour shifts, working on a six-week cycle; the night shift suited her best, although she became terribly tired, because she could be at home for the children, and also they were all allowed to sing as they worked. Her pay worked out at eighteen shillings a week.

'More than your dad gets in the army,' she said to Billy, 'fancy.'

Billy was grudgingly impressed, but said he was sure his dad wouldn't approve.

'Well he doesn't need to know, Billy,' said Sylvia firmly, 'and if you don't tell him, nor any of the others do, how will he? And if I don't do it, we'll starve, the prices they're asking for food these days.'

Billy said nothing more about her job, but started to complain about his, at the brewery in Lambeth where he had been working now for two years.

'It's that disgusting, and the smell gets worse every day. I'll be glad when I get out to France, I tell you that.'

Celia sat looking at the balance sheets LM had given her. They weren't good. Profits had fallen; along with sales. There was a paper shortage which meant, inevitably, rising costs. Meanwhile overheads had risen: rents, food prices – one third over pre-war levels meant higher wages. There was no good news.

'Except sales in certain areas,' said Celia, pointing at the sales ledgers. 'Novels, look. I suppose people are looking for escape.'

'Yes, but only the cheaper editions. Well that's inevitable.'

'Of course it is. LM, if we're feeling the pinch, what about ordinary people? Our customers? Heaven knows how this new magazine *Vogue* is going to do. Who's going to buy it?'

'Well you have,' said LM.

'I know, but there aren't many people like me. It is wonderful, I must say. And you know Chanel—'

'Not terribly well—' said LM.

'Don't be difficult. You know about Chanel. Well, she's started using jersey for dresses and skirts and things. Never been used except as underwear fabric before. The clothes look beautiful. What wouldn't I give – oh well.' She saw LM's blank expression and laughed. 'Back to books. The other thing that's doing well, you know, are the war books, the poetry, speeches, the novels. We must find more of them. And funnily enough, those children's books are succeeding. So more of them. And more of the cheap editions of the fiction.'

'Celia, Lyttons has never gone in for cheap fiction,' said LM. She looked anxious. 'It's not in the house tradition. We have such a commitment to quality and—'

'I know that, LM. But there won't be a house soon. Not at this rate. Popular fiction is going to save us. Well it'll go a long way towards it. Those books we put out last year, with Gill's new dust jackets, have made more money than anything else. We need a whole new range of those. The only trouble is, even those covers are getting terribly expensive. We may have to make them simpler still, rely on the typefaces for decoration. We want lots of fiction, with a war theme obviously; women are lapping it up. And historical romances, too. Anything to take people out of themselves. Then some more children's books: and more poetry I'd say, the market for that's insatiable. Lots of it. More of Francis Grieg; thank God we put him under contract. And anyone else good that we can find. A woman poet might be good. What about that one of yours?'

'I don't think so,' said LM hastily. 'We'd be lucky to sell more than the two copies she and her mother would buy.'

'All right. But let's see if we can find one. I'll phone round the agents today. So how does that all sound? And we'll just have to stop trying to preserve physical quality. Everything will have to go out on cheap paper. We don't have any choice.'

'I do agree with you, of course,' said LM, 'but I don't—'

'Yes?'

'Oh it's absurd, forget it.'

'I know. You were going to tell me you don't know what Oliver will say. Well he's not here and, as you said to Sylvia, what his eyes don't see won't hurt him. Let's worry about his commitment to quality after the war, when he gets home. Oh dear, I must write to him. Honestly our letters to each other would paper a wall. I suppose that applies to everyone, just reams and reams of paper and hundreds and thousands of words.' She stopped. 'You know what? Letters would make a marvellous theme – and form – for a novel. We could do a simple exchange from wife to husband; or father to child; or even – all those things and more. It would be brilliant, moving from story to story. It could contain everything, humour, sentiment, heartbreak. Oh, LM, it would be marvellous, we must commission it today. Do you think it would be one for Muriel Marchant?'

'Possibly, yes,' said LM. 'I agree, it's a wonderful idea. The only thing is that Muriel's got rather expensive lately. With her success.'

'Well, she owes most of that success to us,' said Celia, 'if we hadn't given her the suffragette book to write and it hadn't been such a huge seller, she'd still be an unknown. I'll remind her of that, if necessary. Anyway, she could regard this as part of her war effort. I'm really excited about it already. I'm going to telephone her straight away. And let's agree we won't worry about Oliver. And certainly not tell him. Anyway, he's lost interest in Lyttons for the moment. It's hardly surprising, poor darling. It's very hard,' she added cautiously, 'to keep on and on writing cheerful letters. When there's hardly anything cheerful to say. And I haven't heard from him for over two weeks now. The flow of letters has slowed right down.'

'Have you any idea at all where he is?' asked LM.

'Well, yes. He told me just before he went back. He shouldn't have, of course, but anyway, he did. He's somewhere in the area of the River Somme.'

CHAPTER 12

30 June 1916

It is my painful duty to tell you that a report has been received from the War Office, notifying the death of—

It had to happen; it would have been impossible to think it wouldn't, for all his bravado his boast of luck, but Sylvia took a deep breath, and read on. No 244762 Private Edward John Miller . . . the rest was a blur. A horrible senseless blur. Most senseless being the bit about the message of sympathy from their gracious majesties the king and queen. Who cared anyway, what did they care? It was an insult, a bloody insult. Gracious majesties, she'd give them gracious if she got the chance, sitting there in their castles, safe and sound. Sylvia was usually a royalist, but that phrase angered her; it shouldn't have been there, it didn't mean anything, they didn't know her, they hadn't known Ted or what his death meant to her.

But at least it was Ted. Not Billy. Just very, very slightly more bearable, better. Ted had had a life. Of sorts. A life of hardship, to be sure, but they had shared happiness, had loved each other, had seen all their children – well all except one – grow up healthy and happy. Had shared a lot of fun, of closeness, as well as heartache, in the two crowded, poky little rooms; it hadn't all been bad. It hadn't all been bad at all, thought Sylvia putting the letter down; she felt oddly calm now, her brief rage gone, remembering Ted. Seeing him as clearly as if he was standing in front of her, smiling at her, just come home, grimy from the day's work, saying what's for tea, or it's good to be home, or turning to her in bed, taking her in his arms, when in spite of the anxiety it had been so nice he still loved her and wanted her, her being so thin and plain and pale.

There'd been the violent time of course, but it had only been the drink, and she'd forgiven him straight away for all of it, even the concussion, when he signed the pledge, and he'd never broken his word. Well, maybe when he got out there, of course. He had said he might weaken. She remembered him the day he'd enlisted, and the reason he'd given, that the children needed to be proud of him, needed to know he'd done his bit. Well they had been proud. And so had she been, in spite of everything. Bob King down the road was still not gone, making the excuse of his gammy leg. Mavis King was embarrassed, she knew that, even though she went on and on about the pain Bob was in all the time.

The children were proud of Billy too, of course, amazed by his courage, that one of them should do something as brave as going out to fight real soldiers with real guns. Sylvia wasn't proud of Billy at all. She had hardly been able to bear it, the reckless ignorant stupidity of it, and the callous ruthlessness of an army that took children of seventeen out of their homes and into battle and let them die. It was a crime, a crime against humanity. This whole war was, all war was. Sylvia realised suddenly that she was crying, crying hard now; and she had yet to do the worst thing and tell the children. All the children. Including Barty.

'But I didn't even say goodbye to him.' Barty's voice was very quiet; she sat staring at Celia across the room, resisting Celia's efforts to take her in her arms, to hold her, to comfort her. 'And he didn't even write to me. Not once.'

'Barty, he couldn't write to you. He – he couldn't write very well at all, you know he couldn't,' said Celia, anxious even in giving the comforting explanation, that she shouldn't denigrate Ted in Barty's eyes.

'He could have sent me one of those cards. One of those pretty postcards, like Billy sends. Now he's gone, for ever and ever, and I never even said goodbye. Or good luck, or told him I loved him, all the things . . .'

Celia was silent. Then. 'But Barty, he did love you. Very much. I know he did.'

'Once he did,' said Barty and the words struck Celia like a lash, 'when I was his, he did.'

And she got up and walked out of the room.

She was crying in the schoolroom, her head buried in her arms, when the door opened. 'Just go away,' she said, 'I don't want to talk about it.'

'We don't want to talk either. Well, only to say we're sorry,' said a small voice, and she looked up and saw the twins standing there, hand in hand, their faces white and solemn, their large dark eyes filled with tears of grief and sympathy. And they walked forward very slowly, and took one of her hands each; Adele stroked her hair with infinite gentleness, and Venetia reached up and gave her a kiss. It was the first time they had ever shown affection, or any kind of tenderness towards her and it was the sweeter for being so unexpected. Barty managed to smile at them, and say thank you, then the tears rushed back, and she buried her head

213

again; the three of them stayed there a long time, the twins' small arms around her, and not one of them said anything at all.

'Now, Jamie. I want you to think about this very carefully. In a few months, Maud and I will be leaving this house. With Nurse and my valet and the chauffeur.'

'Why?' asked Jamie. He knew the answer, but he didn't want to hear it, wanted to postpone the terrible moment when he was forced to make a decision.

'Well, because,' Robert paused. He had struggled so hard not personally to threaten Jamie's relationship with Laurence. Laurence could do what he liked, tear his young brother apart with guilt and remorse; but somewhere there had to be a safe haven for the boy. Jamie was fifteen now, and in a turmoil of emotion for every reason, not just because of the conflict between his brother and his stepfather. He was not as clever as Laurence, who was exceptional: his entire scholastic career had been blighted by comparisons with his brother. He had hit adolescence in a rush, his hormones were raging, and he could think of very little except girls and what he longed to do to them.

He had no idea whether he hated Laurence for his troublemaking and unpleasantness, or liked and admired him for his loyalty to their parents, but was forced to accept that what he probably felt was a mixture of the two, and he had no idea how to deal with it. He was plagued by spots and sweaty hands, and by a hideous tendency to blush, and was altogether physically awkward and clumsy. He was still growing, had already reached six foot and was clearly going to be taller than Laurence: all of which which made him painfully self-conscious. And at any moment now, he was going to have to make a horrible decision; in January, Laurence would be twenty-one; he had already said he was going to make sure Robert left Elliott House, and that this time he would have the law on his side.

'And then you'll have to stop this nonsense, Jamie, playing box and cox, cosying up to dear Uncle Robert when you think I won't know about it, and then trying to ignore him and pretend you don't like him when you know I will. Well it's up to you, I really don't care. If you want to play the traitor, that's absolutely all right with me. There will still be one son true to our father's memory.'

The ridiculous thing, of course, was that Jamie knew perfectly well Laurence had allowed his emotions to get out of hand. Had he been more reasonable, more sensible even, had he taken a more honest view of events, then by now he would have been, if not fond of Robert, at least perfectly able to accept him. But some evil streak, some warp of emotional energy had driven him close to madness.

'I'm moving out,' Robert was saying carefully now, 'because really I think it's high time Maud and I had our own home, instead of living in someone else's.'

'That's silly,' said Jamie with awkward honesty. 'It's your home. When you married Mother, it became yours.'

'Well, not quite. It remained hers really. And now it belongs to the family – her family that is. It is, after all, called Elliott House. And while I didn't want to rush out of it, I think I would feel more comfortable now in a house of my own. So—' he paused. He's going to say it, thought Jamie in a panic, he's going to ask me what I want to do. 'So I thought you might like to see it,' said Robert, 'I'm very proud of it. I built it myself. Well my company did. Doing much this afternoon?'

'No,' said Jamie. 'No I'm not doing anything.'

Maud clung to his hand as they walked round the house. It really was very nice indeed. Not as grand as Elliott House of course, but large and beautifully designed, built high over the East River, with an unbelievable view of the water and the Queensbrough Bridge, a wonderfully graceful bow-windowed drawing-room, and a dining-room above that.

'This will be my room,' said Maud proudly, pulling him into the room over the dining-room, on the third floor of the curve, 'look, you can see right down to the Singer Tower. Isn't it lovely? Where will your room be, Jamie, where would you like to have it?'

'I – well – that is – I don't care,' he said quickly, terrified of commitment, trying to sound casual, succeeding only in sounding ungracious; Maud looked hurt, but Robert came forward and put his arm round his shoulders.

'Of course you care,' he said, 'and even if it is only for visits – in the vacations and so on, of course you must have a room here. Two rooms, in fact, I thought, a bedroom and a sitting-room. Now, I wondered if the garden floor would be a good idea for you. Come on downstairs, we have a fine garden, and two rooms open directly on to it; you would have your own front door, in a manner of speaking, come and go with reasonable privacy, no one would bother you.'

'I would bother him,' said Maud firmly, 'I would bother him a lot. He'd be lonely otherwise. Let's go and look where Daddy means, shall we, Jamie, and you can see if you like it.'

Jamie knew he would like it, and knew he would want to come. But he still had to tell Laurence, and he wasn't sure if he was brave enough.

Giles had had a breakthrough; he had discovered he could run. Run very fast and steadily and for a long time. The boys had been sent out on a cross-country run by one of the elderly teachers, who had had the inspiration at the end of an exhausting morning's teaching, when faced with the prospect of twenty small boys bursting with energy.

Giles had changed into his games kit, listening to everyone grumbling, and thought it would be rather nice; nothing difficult, no balls to catch or kick or throw in the right way, just running along, following whoever was in front of him. Only there never seemed to be anyone in front of him; he found himself at the front of the field, gloriously unpuffed, after the first fifteen minutes, forced only to stop when Miss Hodgkins, who was leading them, called out to him to wait.

'This is not a race, Lytton, slow down.' She was very puffed, Giles noticed, and scarlet in the face. Reluctantly he waited for her, tried to stay behind her and outstripped her again in minutes; she told him, now that they were on the home track in the woods to go ahead. He got back to school ten minutes before anyone else.

The run became a twice-weekly event; after the second week, Giles was allowed to run at his own pace. It was glorious, all alone across the fields and the woods, thinking his own thoughts, nobody teasing him or shouting at him. At half term, Miss Prentice, who was a sporty, rather jolly girl, engaged to a captain in the artillery, suggested athletics training to the headmaster: she knew St Christopher's had not gone in for this before, she said, but her fiancé had won the gold medal at Oxford for running and said it was refreshing for both body and spirit. The headmaster looked at her rather doubtfully, thinking privately that the bodies and spirits of the boys scarcely needed refreshing, but was persuaded by her second argument that the training would help to fill the sports afternoons.

'I think it would be better than Mr Hardacre taking them for cricket yet another day; he really isn't very – vigorous, and they're getting bored. I'll gladly do it; I know what's required. I used to watch my – my brothers.'

Her voice shook at this; both her brothers had been killed, one at sea, the other in France. More to divert her from her grief, than because he thought athletics would actually do the boys or the school very much good, the head agreed.

Giles loved athletics, too; he soared over the hurdles, and was as fast over the short distances, the one hundred and three hundred yards, as he was over the long. At two end of term athletics meetings with another prep school, he won every race, and experienced the unimaginable pleasure of being cheered by his fellow pupils at the prize-givings. The worst was over; he went home to Ashingham for the holidays with an air of something close to happiness, and spent the long, golden days holding race meetings with Barty and the twins. Jay, who was now two, would stumble along after them on his plump little legs, his face scarlet with concentration, refusing to cry, even when he fell over for the tenth time in one afternoon.

Jay was a large child, full of energy; he adored Barty particularly, and followed her everywhere she went, insisting that he sat next to her at meals, often creeping into her room at night and sleeping on the sofa which stood at the end of her bed, rather like a devoted little dog. He did look, as LM was always saying, exactly like his father; he had his brown curls, his dark blue eyes, his wide jaw, his way of observing things very seriously and then breaking into a sudden, almost surprised, smile.

'I wish one of my children looked like Oliver,' said Celia wistfully, 'it would really help you know, but look at them all, dark as can be: Beckenhams every one. It's not fair.'

It amused her, watching LM with Jay; LM was rather like a woman with a lover, her eyes lingering on him in adoration, distracted the moment he appeared from whatever she might have been doing or talking about before, introducing him as a subject into whatever conversation might be going on. But she did not spoil him, she was not silly with him; in fact she was rather more strict with him than Celia was with her own children, particularly the twins. If he was naughty or disobedient he would be severely reprimanded; there were things LM would not tolerate: temper tantrums, rudeness, physical aggression.

For this reason, Jay was never smacked; Dorothy, his nanny, was forbidden to do it, and LM would have been incapable of it. But she also said that she felt that smacking was counter-productive: she watched Celia giving Venetia a slap on the hand one day when she caught her pulling one of the cats' tails.

'You tell the child not to hurt something and then you hurt the child. Doesn't really make sense, does it? What does she learn?'

Celia, taken aback by this, said briskly that she thought it made a lot of sense, and that Venetia had learned how unpleasant it was to be on the receiving end of pain, adding that if LM had four children to discipline rather than one, she might find her ideas put rather severely to the test; but thinking about it afterwards, she had to admit that there just might be something in them.

'I expect you're wondering what I might like to do about Lyttons,' said Laurence.

He and Robert were having one of their rare meetings: it was Jamie's birthday and with unusual courage and determination, he had told

217

Laurence he wanted both Robert and Maud at the luncheon which Laurence had arranged at Elliott House. Laurence had objected briefly and then, rather surprisingly, given in. He was genuinely fond of his brother; it was the one healthy relationship in his life.

'Not really,' said Robert coolly. 'The arrangement was nothing to do with me. As you very well know.'

'Of course it was. It was an arrangement made with your brother. With my mother's money.'

'Exactly. It was an arrangement between your mother and my brother. I was not involved in any way.'

'Oh, for God's sake,' said Laurence impatiently, 'you are splitting hairs.'

Robert looked at him, and thought – surprising himself, for he was a gentle man – how much he would like to thrash him. And then thought he would undoubtedly come off the worse for it if he tried. Laurence was extremely fit: he had taken up boxing as a hobby, and his long lean body had become more solid and powerful-looking as a result, although there was not an ounce of fat on it.

He was undeniably handsome: with his green-blue eyes, his red-gold hair, and his tanned skin, unusual in a man of his colouring. He had a valet now, who dressed him superbly, his suits were beautifully tailored, his shirts and collars perfectly cut, his ties discreet, yet interesting. His shoes, so clearly hand-made, were light brogues; and he wore a gold wristwatch, and a signet ring on the little finger of his left hand.

It had belonged to his father, that ring. He told everyone who cared to listen that Jonathan Elliott had given it to him on his deathbed, had said he must never take it off. In fact, Robert happened to know the ring had been taken into Jeanette's keeping and Laurence had removed it from her jewellery box himself when she had died and appropriated it.

He often longed to pass this information on, but it would have sounded vindictive and petty, and like much of his other inside knowledge of the Elliotts, he kept it to himself.

'Laurence,' he said now, 'if you have anything you wish to say about Lyttons New York or indeed anything else, please do so. Otherwise, I think we should give Jamie our undivided attention.'

'I'm not sure if you would consider this anything or not,' said Laurence, 'but since forty-nine per cent of Lyttons has become mine, I would be surprised if you found it of no interest. I intend simply to hold on to it for the time being. I am getting no return on the money yet, nor would I expect to. But since it is a considerable sum, I would want it to work for me at least as well as it might elsewhere.'

'That's absolutely—' Robert stopped. Absolutely absurd he had been going to say; but there was no point. No point whatsoever. 'All right by me,' he finished.

The blue-green eyes looked at him in a sort of amused derision.

'But it's nothing to do with you,' he said. 'Or so you said. You appear a little confused. Anyway, if I do decide to call in the loan, no doubt your brother will tell you about it. Such a shame that your daughter has no share in it. Her being a Lytton and so on. But – clearly my mother didn't want that. I wonder why. Yes, Robert, you're right. We should get back to Jamie's celebration. I can hardly believe he's sixteen. It seems only a very short while ago that he was born and my parents were so wonderfully happy. I wonder what on earth my father would say now, if he could see us both, alone in the world. I'm afraid he wouldn't be very happy. What do you think, Robert, eh?'

My darling,

Well I am still alive. Battered, bruised even, with a gash running up one arm from an argument with a bit of barbed wire, but that is the worst. My luck holds. Forgive me for not writing for so long, but we have been very occupied. The great push continues. We are advancing on the German lines here, slowly but steadily, day by day. Yes, there are casualties, and the fighting is very hard, but there is no doubt that we are making progress at last. We have taken several villages and some strong German positions, and a great many prisoners, as many as 3,500 on the first day of fighting alone. The men are, rather amazingly, still in fine spirits, and many of them are saying they have never felt so well prepared for battle. There is no doubt we have finally got the Hun on the run. I love you, my darling one, so much. I will try to write again more fully soon.

Years later, in his celebrated history of the battle of the Somme, Oliver Lytton told the truth about this mighty battle, the 'great push', the advances. He told how Haig had wasted endless ammunition shelling empty trenches: how the Germans, having observed from the air the arrival of thousands of soldiers, the building of new roads, the delivery of guns, or ammunition and supplies, hurriedly moved back their troops from the front line. He told of his rage at the propaganda film the government had released: a silent film filled with silent lies, showing a massive artillery bombardment, an awe-inspiring build-up of weapons, but not a single corpse, and told how Haig had ordered attack after attack after the first dreadful day of battle, July 1st, when over fifty thousand Allies were killed. He told how the troops were told that artillery fire would break through the barbed wire defences, when any

Tommy could have told them that shellfire would lift the wire up and drop it down again, entangling the soldiers trying to get through it.

He told how, against military advice, Haig sent in a new weapon, the tank, fifty tanks, in fact twenty-nine of which broke down before reaching the battlefield. The rest got stuck in the mud. He wrote of how men were ordered out of the trenches to certain death, how he watched whole lines of them throwing up their arms under machine-gun fire and falling to the ground, never to move again, only to be replaced by other lines, equally doomed. He told of how generals discussed tactics over fine wines in warm chateaux while their men died in the mud, and how men with trench foot literally crawled through the mud to the dressing stations, rather than take precious stretchers away from the seriously wounded; and he told how by November, when the battle was finally declared over, and a great victory won, 460,000 British soliders had been killed or wounded, and less than ten miles of territory gained.

But once home on leave, sitting in the drawing-room at Cheyne Walk, his head in his hands, gaunt and somehow colourless with exhaustion and misery, he did tell Celia something else: how one morning, finally sick with exhaustion and despair, he had been standing, after a sleepless night filled with shells and fire, ordering his men out of the trenches, out into the line of fire. The last man had gone up, and Oliver had found himself staring up into the grey air, thinking of the ghastly dead landscape out there, full of noise and horror and death, quite literally petrified, unable to move. And that last man, a difficult, sullen character called Barton, had looked back down at him, and said in a tone of absolute derision, 'Not afraid are you sir?' and Oliver had moved at once, dragged to his senses, had climbed out behind him.

But in the second of that hesitation, a shell had come; had ripped off the soldier's arm, his leg and half his head, and Oliver stood there, staring at him, thinking that if his courage had not failed him, it would have caught him, that shell; he would have been lying there, screaming in agony. He had done the only thing that could be done under the circumstances, had gone on, into the grey hell, had fought bravely, had seen another of his men hesitate and run up to him urging him on, running beside him.

'But for as long as I live I shall remember Barton, and know that it was my fear that killed him. And it should have killed me. And—' his voice shook, he tried to meet her eyes and could only do so for a moment, 'all I could feel for a while was gratitude that it had not. And then, do you know what I did that night? Sat down and wrote to Barton's widow, told her how her husband had died a hero's death, how he had died instantly, when he actually lived for hours; when I should – I should have said—' and he started weeping helplessly.

'No,' said Celia, putting out an arm to hold him, drawing it back, unable to touch such misery, 'no, you should not have said that. What good would it have done? It would have made Mrs Barton's grief far greater, and it wouldn't have brought him back. My God, Oliver, you've been so brave for so long, you've led your men all this time, you mustn't crucify yourself for one break in your courage.'

But Oliver continued to crucify himself; he spent much of the leave alone, taking long walks along the river, or reading in his room, and even refused to go down to Ashingham to see the children. 'Don't make me Celia. I can't face them, can't be brave and tell them wonderful stories of valour and glory on the battlefield.'

He was home for ten days, and he did not once ask Celia any questions about Lyttons, about how she was managing with her own difficult life; nor did he make love to her or even express any desire to do so. She struggled to be patient, to leave him be; but when he went back, she sat staring at the river, on a dull, heavy February day, and wondered how her marriage, how any marriage, could survive so dreadful an onslaught.

As Oliver returned to France, Billy Miller was brought home: not dead, at least, although he frequently wished that he was, in those first dreadful months. An enemy bullet had struck him when he was within inches of safety, returning from a night raid, and badly injured his right leg. After weeks in a field hospital, gangrene developed, and the leg was amputated just below the knee.

CHAPTER 13

'You surely wouldn't enlist, would you?' Jamie's face was anxious, frightened, almost.

'We shall have to see,' said Laurence, 'I'd like to go, of course; any man would. Well any man except a coward. But there's no question of it at the moment, they won't take men who are at college. I may get my chance in the fall, but, in any case, they will be enlisting experienced men; I don't imagine I shall get my chance for a while.'

This was not strictly true, but Jamie was not to know that.

'Thank heavens,' he said and smiled awkwardly at his brother. 'It does all seem to be getting horribly near. Do you know I saw a whole lot of women, wearing khaki, coming out of a house in Madison Avenue today. Surely they aren't joining the army?'

'Oh no. But I've heard about it, it's some kind of centre for women and the war effort. They're volunteering to do some sort of work, either here or over there, driving or nursing or whatever. Very commendable. I don't see our revered stepfather doing anything to defend the country he speaks so sentimentally about.'

'Robert! That's ridiculous, Laurence. How could he go? He's far too old, surely.'

'How naive you are, Jamie. I'm quite sure that if he volunteered, a job would be found for him. But he prefers to stay. I suppose one cannot entirely blame him. He's safe here, after all. One must try to put oneself in his shoes – however difficult. Cowardice is a very unattractive characteristic, I always think.'

Jamie looked at him uncertainly. And then went back to his study, to do some more work. But he couldn't concentrate. The whole conversation had upset him considerably. First Laurence – of whom, despite everything, he was very fond – talking about volunteering to go and fight in Europe, and then a new conflict set up over Robert, the idea planted of his cowardice. He wanted and needed to admire Robert, not despise him. And he was quite sure he wasn't a coward. But Laurence did have a point. Sometimes Jamie felt he was in a maze, and every time he found the way out, Laurence was there, telling him to go in the other direction, getting him lost again. If only, if only his mother hadn't died. Life would be so wonderfully simple.

'Can we get him down here?' said Barty, 'Please, please? Mum can't look after him, and there are lots of men here without legs, he'd feel better about it maybe. And I could help, well I do anyway.' Her lip quivered.

'Oh Barty,' said Celia. She put her arms round her, hugged her tight; unusually Barty responded, clung to her. She was not physically demonstrative with Celia, rather the reverse; it was as if she knew she didn't really belong to her, or with her. Perversely though, she had loved to sit on Wol's knee, kissed him goodnight fondly rather than dutifully. It had annoyed Celia once; now, like so many other things, it was a distant memory.

'Darling, I'll see. I'll ask – well, I'll ask Matron. But, I do agree, it would be lovely to have Billy here.'

'Celia, no,' said Lady Beckenham. 'This is a convalescent home for officers. It's simply out of the question that a Corporal should be allowed here.'

'But Mama, Billy is family. Surely—'

'Celia,' said her mother, her face very hard suddenly. 'Billy Miller is not family. You still seem to have trouble accepting that. And we can't make exceptions. Now you must excuse me. I have to see to the horses.'

Barty didn't believe that there was no room for Billy at Ashingham. There seemed to her to be endless room. None of these people knew what no room meant. They should see Line Street. She was fairly sure why Billy couldn't come. It was because he wasn't an officer. But that was so awful, so wrong and unfair, when he was her brother, that she hardly dared even think it. And she certainly didn't dare discuss it with Aunt Celia, simply because it was so horrible, and if that was right, she would have felt she would have to – well run away or something. Leave Ashingham. Go home. Home to London and be in danger like the rest of them, from the bombs and everything.

Last time Sylvia had come down, she'd brought Marjorie with her. It hadn't been very nice, because Marjorie had been horrible and unfriendly, and rude to everyone, even to Nanny and Dorothy; but Barty had felt in a way it was understandable, listening to Marjorie's stories about life in London now. There was hardly any food, and the queuing was worse than ever, although there was going to be something called rationing, her mother said; everyone would be allowed at least a bit of everything which would make it more fair. The bombs were awful and terribly frightening, with noise and fire in the sky and they all had to go under next door's table, which was very strong, when there was an air raid, and say prayers, it was the only thing to do, although it wouldn't help much if a bomb actually hit the house. Some houses a few streets away had been hit, and five people killed. Half the men in their street had been killed, or badly injured like Billy; it was awful to see them Marjorie said, sitting around, some of them blind, some of them without arms or legs. At least everyone had to go now and fight, it was the law, even Bob Carter with his bad back, and actually it had turned out there was nothing wrong with his back at all.

Aunt Celia and LM didn't come down to Ashingham so often now: only about once a month, instead of every weekend. They couldn't get petrol for the little car. The twins and Jay hated not seeing them, and they all cried dreadfully on Sunday evenings when LM and Celia had to leave again, and Barty worried a lot about them too; in spite of everything, she was terribly fond of them both and the thought of Cheyne Walk being bombed was dreadful. It was so big and strong, though, she somehow thought a bomb would just sort of bounce off it.

And she felt so guilty, living safely down in Ashingham, in the lovely house, in the middle of the countryside with plenty of food; she loved playing with and looking after Jay, too, and was fiercely proud that he would only go to sleep if she read him a story. And the previous summer she and Giles had had a wonderful time, helping with haymaking and the harvest, and picking beans and peas until their arms ached. Most of the farm labourers had gone off to the war, there were only a couple of the older ones left and a few boys; a lot of the work was done by landgirls, rather jolly most of them. They were as grateful for help as the nurses were in the convalescent home; even the twins were pressed into service the summer they were six, and had to help picking peas.

The twins were much nicer now; ever since her father had died they had been kinder to her, and they weren't so spoilt either, their grandmama, as they called her, was very firm with them, sent them to their room if they showed off or were cheeky. They'd made an awful fuss at first, and said they'd tell their mother, or refuse to come out of their room again, but when they discovered that meant missing a meal because Lady Beckenham was quite happy to leave them there all day if necessary, they quite quickly started to do what she said. There had also been one dreadful occasion when she smacked them both very hard indeed: that had been when she discovered them stealing strawberries from the strawberry beds, after they had all been expressly forbidden to do so; and another time, when she found them walking behind nice old Miss Adams, mimicking her limp, Lady Beckenham had got her horse crop and made them pull down their knickers and had given each of their small bottoms a hard whack.

Barty had been quite sorry for them, it had obviously hurt a lot and they howled with pain; but she observed that they never did tell their mother as they had threatened, presumably beause they were so ashamed of themselves. When they had to apologise, as part of their punishment, to Miss Adams and Nanny and Dorothy, and Giles, who had been at home at the time, they seemed genuinely sorry and cried.

She overheard Aunt Celia saying to Lady Beckenham that they seemed very happy, and Lady Beckenham had said she had told her before, a disciplined child was a happy child. For the previous Christmas, the twins had been given a dog by their grandparents: a black labrador they called Soot. They had to look after him themselves and feed him and brush him. Barty had thought they'd try and get someone else to do most of it, but they were extremely conscientious, and when Soot was ill after eating a decomposing rabbit, they insisted on sitting up nursing him all night in the gunroom.

'Quite right,' said their grandmother when Nanny came to her anxiously, wondering if it should be allowed, 'he's theirs and they should look after him. Won't do them any harm.'

But none of this happiness made Barty feel any better about Billy.

Dispatches, the novel written by Muriel Marchant, at once touching, sad and patriotic, and even with flashes of humour (inserted for the most part by Lady Celia Lytton, its editor) was a huge success: despite being published on inferior paper, with a simple jacket, it had sold almost five thousand copies. Second, third and then fourth editions had been rushed out, and Celia had proposed a sequel. Muriel had written this in record time, and three months later, *Further Dispatches* reached the bookshops.

'Wonderful,' Celia said happily, when news of the books' sales reached her, 'I think we should embark on a third straight away. It's bound to sell. Don't look like that, LM, it's paying the beastly rates increase. If that goes up one more time we're going to be in genuine trouble.'

'Those books are what our father would have called below stairs stuff,' said LM.

Celia said briskly that she was surprised at her talking like that, given her radical views on the social structure of the country, and LM said it was nothing to do with social structures, it was intellectual ones she was worried about.

'We have never compromised on those. I can't feel comfortable with this. Or that terrible poetry,' she added. Celia had discovered that poetry did not have to be good to sell; whatever it was like, it seemed to reach out to women particularly, and to comfort them.

'Well that terrible poetry is paying the wages. LM, surely you should be grateful that Lyttons is surviving. Plenty of time after the war to raise standards again. And you must be pleased with the children's books, they're very good, and doing well. Respectable enough for you?'

'I suppose so,' said LM warily.

'My dream, you know,' said Celia, 'is to find a children's writer. A really, really good one, creating classics, like Lewis Carroll and Louisa May Alcott. But I don't hold out a lot of hope for it. God, I'm tired. Couldn't sleep last night. The noise of those zeppelins – I'm sure they're getting closer. Thank God we don't have to risk our children's lives.'

'Indeed. Although I sometimes wonder if Jay quite realises who I am,' said LM soberly. 'And actually, if we shouldn't move the whole enterprise out of London, whether it's not just foolhardy, staying on, risking our lives, and the lives of the people working for us. They're all so loyal and—'

'Oh LM, so do I. But then I think of all the work involved in moving, and decide it's not worth it. The war surely can't go on much longer. And it would be difficult, far away from printers and the delivery vans and so on. Yes, the staff are loyal, but then you have to remember we've given lots of them great opportunities, jobs they'd never have got if men had been around, chances to develop their talents and skills. I do often wonder what Grandpa Lytton would say if he knew the entire editorial department and almost all the art department is staffed by woman. You know this war's certainly done one thing. It means that women will definitely get the vote. No one would dare push them back into the home and under their men's jurisdiction now.'

'I hope you're right,' said LM.

'Of course I'm right. You just wait and see.' Celia looked at her. 'LM, are you ever – well—'

'Frightened? Terrified. Quite often,' said LM cheerfully, 'but it's like not being able to sleep. You just get used to it, don't you? Shall we go home now?'

'Yes, let's. Cook managed to get some beef yesterday. Tough, I'm sure, but I've been looking forward to it all day. It really is much better now, she says, with meat rationing. She hardly has to queue at all. I hear they're going to persuade farmers to use more land for growing food as well. I don't know how Mama will feel about that. Ploughing up her precious paddocks. Anyway I want to ask your advice about something. It's really, really difficult, and please don't give me a lecture, because it won't help.'

'I promise I won't, said LM. 'I'm much too tired.'

'Barty darling, I have some good news,' shouted Celia down the telephone. 'Billy can come to the nursing home in Beaconsfield, the one where Jay was born. Next week. I've arranged for a private ambulance to bring him down. He really needs nursing anyway, at the moment, it seems, not just what he'd get at the convalescent home, and he'll get it there. And you'll be able to see lots of him, and – what, Barty? On Thursday. Ask my mother to find out what time they want him. Got to go now. Love to the twins and Jay. Bye darling. See you soon.'

'Lady Celia, can I talk to you?'

Gill Thomas was standing in Celia's office doorway; she looked nervous and rather flushed.

'Of course. Come in. Would you like a cup of tea? I'm afraid we've long since exhausted this week's biscuit ration.'

'Yes, that would be very nice.' She sat down. She was a pretty girl, with shining dark hair and rosy cheeks; she looked as if she should have been living in the country, milking cows, rather than doing her genuinely innovative design work.

'It's not about Barry?'

'Oh no. No, nothing still. I suppose that's good news really. I have to tell myself that, anyway.'

Barry, Gill's fiancé, had been taken prisoner almost nine months earlier, and was in a German camp somewhere near Metz. That was all she knew.

'Yes of course it is. In spite of all the hideous propaganda, the Germans are pretty good about their prisoners, I believe. He's probably much safer there than in the front line.'

'I think he probably is,' said Gill. There was a silence; then she said, 'Lady Celia, I have to give in my notice.'

'What? But Gill why? You're happy here, you told me that only the other day, and you're doing such wonderful work and we appreciate you so much—'

'I know. I mean – well the thing is, I've been offered a job at Macmillan.'

'At Macmillan! Oh, Gill, you can't. No, that's a stupid thing to say.

Tell me why you want to go. They're a wonderful house, of course. It's a great feather in your cap. More money, I suppose?'

'A bit. But – well, it's a more senior position. That's the most important thing. And I'd have more people working for me. I just feel it's a great opportunity.'

Celia looked at her. She simply could not afford to lose Gill. She was so clever, and she worked so hard.

'How much are they paying you?'

'Lady Celia, that really isn't the main thing.'

'I know, but it's still important. I'd like to know anyway, in case one of our other people gets approached. If we're underpaying everyone—'

'You're not! Your salaries are perfectly generous. They've only offered me another five shillings a week.'

'So you'll get . . . what? Sorry, I ought to know, but I don't have the files here.'

'Three pounds ten shillings.'

'I can give you that,' said Celia promptly.

'Lady Celia, it really isn't the most important thing. As I said. I'm quite well off.'

'It's the position. All right, what are they offering you?'

'Well—' Gill looked increasingly uncomfortable. It had taken her all day to screw up her courage for this interview; she had hoped so much Celia would just accept her resignation, shake her hand and say goodbye.

'What will your job be there?'

'Senior Art Editor.'

'Yes, I see. Well – that is very impressive. But—' she paused, thinking fast. 'Gill, how would you like to be Art Director of Lyttons? With complete authority over the art department?'

Gill was silent; the offer far exceeded anything she might have hoped for. At the beginning of the war she had been a junior illustrator at Blackie's; now she could be in charge of the entire visual side of Lyttons, one of the major, most admired publishing houses in London. She felt slightly dizzy. The offer from Macmillan faded into insignificance.

'Look,' said Celia, 'you don't have to decide now. Think about it. Let me know tomorrow. Only—' her lips twitched, 'I would advise you for your own personal safety, to accept. I might just come and put a bomb under Macmillan's building if you go there.'

'I – no I don't want time to think about it,' said Gill after a moment. 'That would look as if I was simply trying to get the best offer.'

'Very sensible of you,' said Celia. 'I would. In your position.'

Gill looked at her. 'I don't think you would,' she said, 'I'd say loyalty was one of your outstanding characteristics, Lady Celia. Both to your staff and to the house of Lytton.'

'Well, I'm married to the house of Lytton,' said Celia briskly, 'So I don't have much choice. As for my staff, I value them totally. Simple as that. Now then, Gill, come on, put me out of my misery. What's your answer?'

'My answer is yes please,' said Gill. 'I accept with great pleasure. And I really do appreciate your trust in me.'

'Gill, we wouldn't be where we are today without you,' said Celia. 'Of course I trust you. Now then, somewhere I've got the best part of a bottle of sherry. I think that's more appropriate to the occasion than tea. And we must get Miss Lytton in. I know she'll be pleased.'

LM did appear to be pleased, and toasted Gill's future success with enthusiasm and the rather musty sherry. But when Gill had left, she looked at Celia, unsmiling.

'I don't think that was very wise,' she said.

'Why on earth not? LM, we couldn't manage without her. I really couldn't bear to let Macmillans enjoy the benefit of her talents. I'm sorry if you feel I should have consulted you, and of course I should, I got a bit carried away, LM, I'm so sorry—'

'Yes, you should, I think,' said LM, 'for such a senior appointment. In Oliver's absence.' She paused. 'But you do have overall editorial discretion, so that's not what's troubling me. Well not seriously.'

'You don't like what she does, do you?' said Celia, 'You think it's too populist. LM, she got the new fiction list off the ground, with those jackets. And she does wonders with the restrictions we have to cope with these days, no colour, no decent paper—'

'Oh, I know. I don't really admire it, of course, and I do think it's populist. But she is superb in her field, and we need sales. I have come round to your way of thinking entirely on that one. A good publishing house should have a complete range of titles. Certainly at the moment.'

'Then—'

'Celia, that was a very permanent appointment. And a very senior one. One which would be virtually impossible to unscramble at the end of the war.'

'But why should we want to unscramble it? She has an eye for more quality work as well; she won't want to put populist jackets on the classics, or anything like that. In fact she was saying the other day how much she'd like to publish some folders of watercolour prints, maybe limited editions, really high quality, which people could collect and frame, together with biographies of the artists. Of course that's out of the question at the moment. But I really don't think you need to worry about it, LM.'

'Again, that's not my concern. But Celia, what do you think is going to happen when people like James Sharpe come back? Their jobs are after all pledged to them; they will be expecting, and rightly, to pick up where they left off. How do you think they'll feel about finding a woman in charge? How will she feel, at having her wings clipped?'

'They won't be,' said Celia, 'she is young, she has ideas, she's moved forward. James won't have done that. He can't expect just to come back into a position of total authority. He—' she stopped. 'I see what you mean. He will, won't he?'

'He will indeed, I'm afraid. He'll have gone through years of hell defending his country and Lyttons with it, and he'll expect a reward. Not demotion. If he comes back at all,' she added soberly.

'Oh dear. But LM, surely Lyttons is still important. As important as James Sharpe. Are we really supposed to take a great step backward and pretend nothing has changed?'

'I think you'll find that is what James, and, indeed, Oliver will expect. Demand even. With some degree of justice. And that will be terribly difficult for Gill. Given her new position.'

'Well—' Celia poured herself another glass of sherry, 'well, LM, I do see that what you say has a great deal of truth in it. But right now, we have to keep Lyttons going, somehow. God knows it's difficult enough, without having our hands tied by considerations which don't even apply yet. I think I'll worry about it all when—'she stopped, sighed, 'when Oliver and Richard and James all come back. Meanwhile, we have to keep the home fires burning, as we are being constantly told to do by every songstress in the land. And they'll burn a lot brighter at Lyttons if Gill stays. I'm very sorry, LM, that I didn't consult you. It was wrong of me. It's a senior appointment and you're on the main board, senior rank and all that, and—'

'Oh, for heaven's sake,' said LM, 'Do stop going on about that. You're quite right, we won't have a main board if Lyttons doesn't survive. And I do assure you, my position in the company is the least of my worries. I really don't think anyone can possibly be too concerned about their position in life at the moment.'

'He's a corporal,' said Sister Wright, 'that's all. I really don't like it. He shouldn't be here, and nor would he be if matron wasn't so in awe of Lady Beckenham. He should be in an ordinary hospital somewhere.'

'I absolutely agree with you,' said Staff Nurse Price. She spent much of her time telling Sister Wright, whose bad temper was legendary, that she absolutely agreed with her. It made up for some of the inadequacies which had landed her at a private nursing home in Beaconsfield, rather than out at the front as she had hoped. She was not a good nurse, clumsy, forgetful, inefficient, even, at times, squeamish. She would never have reached the grade of staff nurse in peacetime.

'But it's so he can be near his little sister,' said a junior nurse, who had come in on this conversation. 'I think it's nice for him. And she's lovely. She cycles here, you know, it's a long way, five miles, to see him and—'

'I am perfectly aware how far Ashingham House is from Beaconsfield,' said Sister coldly, 'and nobody asked your opinion, Nurse. In fact you have no right to be listening to our conversation. You can go and empty Corporal Miller's bedpan since you're so enthusiastic about him; he's been ringing that bell of his for some time. No manners at all.'

'Yes, Sister.'

'I don't quite understand the connection with the countess anyway,' said Staff Nurse Price when she had gone. 'he's surely not related in any way. Perhaps someone in her household—'

'It's her daughter,' said sister, 'she's adopted the child, Corporal Miller's sister. A very odd woman, in my view, extremely high-handed, just like her mother. Anyway, she's paying for Corporal Miller to be here. More's the pity. Now, Staff, you go and see to Major Fleming's dressings, and be sure to take them to the sluice afterwards. I have paperwork to do.'

'Yes, Sister.'

'Hallo Billy. How are you? I brought you some buttercups. I picked them on the way.'

Barty laid the large bunch of buttercups down on Billy's bedside table. She smiled at him, leaned over and gave him a kiss. He looked back at her, his eyes dull.

'Any better today? The leg?'

'No. Bloody agony still. And they won't give me enough to help with the pain. Specially not at night. Old witch that Sister is. I hate her. I hate it here, Barty, it was better at the field hospital, I tell you. Someone to talk to at least.'

'Oh Billy, don't say that. I come and talk to you nearly every day. And I'm sure the nurses talk to you, and the other patients.'

'Never see the other patients,' said Billy, 'There's a chap down the corridor lost an arm and a leg, I hear him groaning sometimes, apart from that it's like a bloody morgue. I'd rather be in a morgue,' he added.

'Billy, please! It's only till you're better, and you're lucky to be here. At least you're well looked after. And it's lovely for me to see you so much.'

'They're horrible to me,' said Billy, 'they don't like me. Other day, they left me, long past my dinner time, when I wanted – well never mind what for. Then that Sister come in, told me to stop making such a fuss. I can't help it if I need – things. Can I?'

'No, of course not,' said Barty. She felt dreadful; it had seemed such a good idea, having Billy here, near her, so she could help look after him. And it was true, he did still need nursing, the wound wasn't healing properly, there was even talk of further surgery.

'So I'll have even less leg,' Billy said bitterly. 'Nobody thought that in the other place.'

He complained a lot; and he was truculent and argumentative, but underneath, Barty could see, he was desperately miserable. Quite often, when she arrived, she could tell he'd been crying; his eyes would be swollen and red and his nose running. Well, she'd have cried if she'd been him. Eighteen years old, and only one leg. Stuck in a wheelchair for the rest of his life. And however much he hated the nursing home, what was going to happen to him when he left it? Who would give work to a man with only one leg? The brewery wouldn't take him back, they'd already said so.

She'd asked him about life in France, but he wouldn't talk about it. He said she wouldn't want to hear and he was trying to forget.

'It wasn't all bad though,' he said staring unseeingly in front of him. 'Mostly, but not all. We had a lot of laughs. Believe it or not. You had to, really. Only way to keep sane.'

Barty didn't tell Celia what Billy had said about the nursing home, because it would have seemed so ungrateful. But she did tell her he was bored and that the days were very long.

'Of course. Poor boy. Well, let's see – he can read, can't he?' said Celia. 'Yes, of course he can. I'll get some books and papers together for him, Barty, send them down later in the week. I'd like to get over myself, but – not this weekend. Maybe next time we come.'

Barty said that would be very nice, and hoped Billy wouldn't complain to Aunt Celia about things as much as he complained to her. Everyone kept saying how grateful he must be to be there. She sometimes thought if she heard that word once more, she would scream.

'I've had such a nice letter from Robert,' said LM, coming in to Celia's office. 'He says he feels so much better now that the Americans are in the war. He'd enlist, he says, if they'd take him, in fact he tried, but he really is too old. Forty-four. Oh dear, and I can remember him going away to school and crying. Anyway, he said he rejoiced the minute he knew they fired the first shot, whenever that was, and opened a bottle of champagne.'

'He's lucky to be able to get it,' said Celia, 'I can hardly remember what it tastes like. October 27th, it was they came in. Oliver said in his last letter it was so marvellous to know they were there, in France, at last. God, this really has become a world war, hasn't it? Russia, Japan, Italy, Australia and Canada, of course, where will it end? Sorry. Go on LM, Any news of that dear little Maud?'

'Yes. Robert and she have moved into a different house – he wanted to have somewhere of his own, he says, and the younger boy, Jamie, spends a little time with them there. But mostly he's at college or stays with his older brother. What an extraordinary arrangement. Here we are: "Maud is five now and starting school. She is very bright and beautiful, and looks just like her mother. As soon as the war is over, I shall bring her over to meet you all again."'

'How lovely,' said Celia. 'I would adore that.'

'Yes. He's sent a photograph of her, look, she does look rather sweet.'

'Let me see. Oh, goodness yes, she does. What a dear little thing. Lovely eyes.'

'Robert's business is doing very well, apparently; whole streets owe their existence to him, he says. Imagine that.'

'Well, whole authors owe their existence to us,' said Celia just slightly irritably. She had always found LM's adoration of Robert difficult to cope with. Oliver thought he was wonderful too. As, most unfairly, had Grandpa Lytton. Of course he'd made a lot of money, but it was hardly on a par with building up a publishing house that was the envy of the literary world. He was very charming and she liked him; but he lacked Oliver and LM's fearsome intellect. Still, he was the oldest in the family, maybe that had a lot to do with it; not that her own oldest brother, Henry, impressed her very much. She saw him very clearly: as someone neither very bright or very competent. He was fifty now; he'd followed his father into the army, never managed to rise higher than the rank of major, and had left military life to run Lord Beckenham's Scottish estate. He had a rather dull wife and several extremely plain children; it depressed her to think of him inheriting the title and Ashingham. Anyway, that was a long way off, judging by her father's rude health and zest for life.

'And then he says – this is the bad news—' said LM with a grim smile, 'his partner's wife, her name is Felicity, has written some poetry and he wants to send it to us for our opinion.'

'Oh heavens,' said Celia, 'how absolutely dreadful. Yes, I did meet her. Very pretty, but rather – wifely. Oliver thought she was wonderful. The sort of woman he should have married, I suppose. I'm sure it will

233

be quite awful and we shall be duty bound to write at least a page of admiring appreciation. Do tell them when you write back that we don't publish poetry, won't you?'

'Too late. Robert read an article in one of the papers about the explosion of poetry being written at the moment in England with a list of all the poets, and who their publishers were.'

'Oh God,' said Celia.

In just a year now, Giles thought, he would be leaving St Christopher's and going to Eton. It seemed unimaginable, and equally unimaginable that he would be quite sad to go. After the first wretched two years, he had really begun to enjoy it. And now he was house captain, he had his own study, he had a fag of his own – who he was usually very nice to – and he still won every race at every athletic meeting in which he competed. In fact he could fairly claim to have turned St Christopher's into an athletics school. Standards at rugby had continued to fall; although Miss Prentice had turned herself, by sheer determination and a refusal to let St Christopher's become a laughing stock, into a soccer coach.

'I've seen photographs of women's football teams, mostly at the factories where they work, so don't tell me it can't be done.'

She had sought the help of the bigger boys in this and had formed a games committee; training was twice a week, and she ran up and down the pitch in a football jersey and a pair of shorts, blowing her whistle and shouting instructions. At first it was fairly chaotic, but old Mr Hardacre, who was over sixty, but knew the rules, had helped from the sidelines, and so did the bigger boys, and gradually the team had shaped up. The head had been most unhappy about it, particularly Miss Prentice's shorts, and had asked her if she couldn't possibly wear something more seemly, but she had suggested briskly that he try running up and down in the mud in a long skirt, and he backed down.

All the boys adored Miss Prentice; like the dead David Thompson, she was a caring and thoughtful influence in the school, and like him, gave Sunday afternoon tea parties, organised treats for the boys' birthdays, kept a kindly eye on the small new ones, and generally made the rather bleak school life warmer and more bearable. The thought of leaving Miss Prentice behind was another source of sadness to Giles. Although she was so old, twenty-three now, she was more like an older sister than a teacher, and actually talked to them all over the Sunday tea and toast.

'What I really want,' she said one day, 'is to have a school of my own. A bit like this, only for boys and girls.'

'Girls!' someone said incredulously. 'Girls in a school?'

'Yes, why not. Well, I'm a girl aren't I?'

'Not quite,' said someone else, and they all giggled; Miss Prentice laughed too.

'All right. Well I was a girl once. Anyway, that's only one idea, I've got lots more, most of which would horrify the head and Mr Hardacre.'

'Like what?' asked Giles.

'Well – it would have lots of scholarships for a start. So that poor children could benefit as well.'

'I don't know that that would work,' said Giles.

'Why ever not?'

'The other children, the ones who weren't poor, might not be nice to them.'

'Oh Lytton, what a ridiculous thing to say. Of course they'd be nice to them. We're talking about children, not a lot of prejudiced adults.'

'I know we are,' said Giles soberly.

'You can just stop snivelling and pull yourself together. And you can't need the bedpan again, I've only just emptied the last one.'

'I can't help it,' said Billy. His voice was low, his face flushed with embarrassment.

'Of course you can help it. You seem to me to lack self-control in every way. I don't have Major Hawthorne calling out for bedpans all the time. I can only imagine it's—'

'Sister, please fetch Corporal Miller a bedpan at once.' Celia Lytton's voice, at its most ice-edged and autocratic, cut into Sister Wright's monologue. 'And when you have done so, and he is comfortable again, perhaps you would like to come and inform me. I shall be in matron's office?'

'It was so awful,' she said to her mother, 'poor Billy has some problem with – well with his stomach. It's the morphine, apparently. Binds them up and then they need medicine to unbind them. So of course he needs the bedpan a lot. And that witch of a sister won't let him have it. Makes him wait and suffer. And when I got there, he'd obviously been crying.'

'Crying!' said Lady Beckenham.

'Yes, and she was vile to him about that as well, told him to stop snivelling. Well, wouldn't you cry, if you were little more than a child and only had one leg, and it hurt you all the time, and you had no prospect of any kind of future in life? I certainly would.'

'No you wouldn't,' said Lady Beckenham. 'You'd buckle down and get on with it. As you have over the past three years. Can't have been easy. Only thing to do of course, but I've admired you for it.'

'Oh.' Celia stared at her mother. She couldn't ever remember being praised by her for anything in her entire life, except once, when she had fallen off her pony out hunting, broken her wrist, had to have it rather painfully set and insisted on going out again the very next day.

All her mother had said, even then, had been 'Thank heavens you didn't make a fuss in front of the master,' but Celia had recognised it as approbation nonetheless; this was effusive by comparison, almost shocking.

She rallied. 'Well anyway, he's so wretched. In pain and utterly miserable. And the staff are just taking it out on him.'

'Taking what out on him, Celia?'

Celia ignored this. 'I reported Sister's behaviour to Matron. She was horrified, said she would speak to her.'

'She probably wasn't horrified at all. But I daresay a few brisk words will be said. Anyway, I agree, there is no excuse for unkindness. I might go down there and visit him myself. He seems a pleasant enough lad. And it would keep Matron on her toes, let her know I'm aware of what's been going on. Dreadful woman.'

'She's better than Sister Wright.'

'No she's not,' said Lady Beckenham. 'She's extremely common.'

Three days later she arrived in Billy's room. Barty had begged to be allowed to come too, but she refused. 'I want to talk to your brother alone. Tell me a bit about him, Barty, what does he like doing?'

'Oh – well, he likes playing cards. And he used to be good at drawing. But he does quite like reading. Those adventure stories Aunt Celia took him really cheered him up.'

'Yes, but what are his interests?' asked Lady Beckenham impatiently.

'He—' Barty stopped. She really didn't know what Billy's interests were. She had left Line Street when she was far too tiny to be aware of such things, and they had effectively cut her out of their lives soon after. She didn't want to admit that though. And – what was it he'd been looking at in the *Daily Mirror* the other day, and talking about? Oh, yes, horses. Saying how he'd hated seeing the horses suffering out in France more than anything. 'Poor beasts. At least we know why we're there. They don't.'

'He likes horses,' she said quickly.

'Horses? Does he now? I'm surprised he knows anything about them at all.'

'Well, there were a lot in France. Apparently.'

'Yes. Yes of course there were. Well, that'll give us something to talk about.'

Billy was lying staring at the window when she got there. He turned his head to her, said, 'Good afternoon,' and then went back to the view.

'Good afternoon, Corporal Miller. How are you?'

'Bl – pretty awful.'

'Really? Leg hurting you?'

'A lot. Got to have some more off.'

'Oh, I'm sorry.'

'Not as sorry as I am,' said Billy, and burst into tears.

Lady Beckenham passed him a handkerchief and sat in silence, while he composed himself.

'Why is it necessary?' she said.

'Ain't healing. And they can't make it. So it's got to come off above the knee, the doctor says.'

'I see. Well – I'm sure he knows what he's talking about.'

'He'd better,' said Billy. He blew his nose. 'Sorry.'

'There's no need to apologise. I can understand you being upset. But the only way is to be positive, you know.'

'Positive!' said Billy. 'Positive, when me life's over before it begun. Who's going to give me a job, eh? What girl's going to look at me? I don't think you know what you're talking about. With respect,' he added, after a pause.

'Oh yes, I do' said Lady Beckenham. 'My grandfather lost a leg as a young man. Out in India. During the Mutiny. Know anything about all that?'

Billy shook his head.

'Well I'll tell you about it one day. It's a good story. But he fought at Delhi and had to have his leg amputated on the battlefield. Not pleasant. Anyway, he came back, got the Military Cross and won my grandmother's heart. She was a great beauty too. They had a wonderfully happy marriage, and she had thirteen children. And he rode to hounds until he was sixty. So let's have no more despair. Now then, Barty says you like horses. Is that right?'

Billy nodded silently; he was altogether beyond speech.

'Where did you get to know anything about them?'

'They had them at the brewery. Where I worked.'

'Oh, the dray horses. Beautiful creatures.'

'Yes. I used to give 'em apple cores sometimes. And once I helped hold one while it was being shod. Shoe come off, just as it was going out. Stood like a rock.'

'And in France?'

'Yeah, well, that was horrible. Seeing them there, in the mud, struggling. I see a mule drown once, in that mud. We all tried to drag him out, but wasn't no good. And then hearing them scream in battle,

237

watching them lying there, dying. Officers always shot 'em if they could of course. That was something. But still horrible for them. And they're so nice-looking, horses are. And so brave.'

'Yes. Yes they are. Well now look. When that leg is on the mend – and I'm sure it will be, I'll have a word with the doctor myself – you can come out and see my horses one day. Would you like that? Not that there are many of them now. Just a couple of hunters, and they've been on nothing but grass for years, terribly out of condition. We don't get out much these days, of course.'

'Out?' said Billy.

'Yes. Hunting. And then we've a few farm horses still. And I thought I might try and get a pony for the children. So we have a few for you to meet. How does that sound?'

'All right,' said Billy. 'Yes, thanks.'

'Fine. Now, you mustn't allow yourself to despair. It's very important. Half the battle is being positive, you know. Keeping your spirits up. Not brooding. At least you're not blind. So many of those poor chaps are. That would be far worse now wouldn't it?'

Billy nodded.

'Good. As soon as you're up to it, I'll take you over. You'll enjoy it. Good to have someone to talk to about horses. Know anything about bloodlines?'

'Not a lot, no,' said Billy with the shadow of a smile.

'Well you must learn. Half the trouble with you, I'd say, is you've not got enough to think about. And it's a fascinating subject. I'll send you some books over with Barty. How would that be? I think she said you could read.'

'Course I can read,' said Billy indignantly. But he didn't really mind. He was transfixed by her.

'Good. Right then. And I'll send some stuff on the Indian Mutiny as well. There are some terrific yarns about that, you know. Including my grandfather's diary. You'll enjoy that enormously. He couldn't spell too well, but you won't mind that, I don't suppose. Good heavens, look at the time. I must get back. Dozens of animals waiting to be fed. I came on my motor bike, it's my new toy. Uses less petrol than the car.'

'A motor bike!' said Billy. 'Cor!'

'Yes, it's jolly good. It's got a sidecar, thing you can sit in. You could come over to Ashingham in that, now I come to think of it. Goodbye, Billy. Chin up.'

From that day on, Billy was Lady Beckenham's slave.

'You know,' said Celia, 'these aren't bad. In fact they're quite good.'

'What?' asked LM.

'That woman's poems. Felicity Brewer. You know, Robert's partner's wife.'

'Oh – oh yes, I remember. Really? I'm very surprised.'

'So am I. Although I don't know why we should be. She's as likely to be able to write poetry as anyone else, after all. Here, have a look at them. I think we could include a couple in that anthology we're doing. Wouldn't that be nice?'

'The standard's hardly high,' said LM.

'I know. But it's not exactly low, either.'

'That's a matter for debate I'd say.'

'Oh LM, do stop it,' said Celia wearily.

'Sorry. Let me have a look. What are they about?'

'Oh – what I'd call landscapes. There's one about the skyline in New York, being like – what was it – oh, yes, 'petrified poplars'. I like that don't you? And people are much more sympathetic towards the Americans at the moment, now they're fighting for us. Anyway, I won't do anything if you don't agree.'

'No, no,' said LM, 'you go ahead. Robert will be terribly pleased. And poetry isn't something I can make a judgement on anyway. Heavens it's cold.'

'Not as cold as it is out in France, I daresay,' said Celia sombrely.

Dear Mum,

Worse thing now is the cold. We work nighttime quite a lot which makes it worse. Being moved up to the line and so on, so Fritz doesn't see us. All in our gas masks, horses included, they don't like it at all. A cup of tea ices over in a minute . . . And the poor horses get frozen into the mud where they stand. It's not much fun sometimes, but we're quite cheerful and looking forward to Christmas. Keep your fingers crossed I'll be home.

Love to all, don't worry about me,
Frank

Frank did not come home for Christmas; but Oliver did. Gaunt, pale, exhausted, full of anger at what was being endured.

'Passchendaele will go down as one of the most dreadful and disgraceful episodes in the history not just of this war, but of all wars. I tell you, Celia, the men are beginning to hate the armchair generals as they call them. They suspect, quite rightly in my opinion, that a lot of the time they don't know what they're doing. I'd like to put Haig down in the mud for a week, I can tell you. Those frightful letters he writes to the troops: the boys take a very dim view of them, talking about the

239

need for self-sacrifice and so on. We had quite a few deserters after Passchendaele, you know, and who could blame them. Poor chaps.'

'What happened to them?' asked Celia.

'Oh – caught and shot, most of them. Boys, they are, no more than boys.'

He was often morose, frequently angry; but she comforted herself that at least he was talking to her more. On the other hand, he did not even attempt to make love to her.

Christmas at Ashingham in 1917 was a surprisingly cheerful affair; not only all the Lyttons were there, but several Beckenhams as well, two of the boys as Lady Beckenham still called her sons, and Caroline, all with their children. There were some empty places of course, Caroline's husband and one of Henry's sons were both in France and so was one of the girls, nursing with the Red Cross, but the family had been lucky, had endured no casualties.

'Yet,' said Caroline, touching the table and closing her eyes briefly: Celia joined her in her silent prayer.

Jack was not home this year: 'Had a bit of luck,' he wrote to Celia, 'been made up to full Colonel, invited to one of the chateaux with the generals for Christmas. I'll try and rob the cellar to stock up Oliver's. Best love, thanks again for the last leave, it was marvellous. Jack.'

'He stayed with you, did he?' asked Oliver when she showed him the letter.

'Yes,' said Celia, 'he did. We went out on the town one night, it was indeed marvellous.'

'He's always had a bit of a soft spot for you,' said Oliver, smiling at her. His attitude towards Jack was so indulgent that Celia knew if she'd told him Jack had tried to seduce her, he would never have believed it.

Christmas lunch was comparatively lavish: two geese, and several only slightly tough chickens – they had to be kept into old age these days on egg-laying duty and Lady Beckenham had made two deliciously rich and alcoholic puddings.

'There wasn't really enough fruit, so I added extra suet and a lot more brandy. You'd have had a fit, Beckenham, literally pouring it in I was.'

She liked making Christmas puddings, it was part of the family tradition and before the war this had been the only time in the entire year she visited the kitchens; now she did rather more.

To Barty's intense joy, Billy joined them: not for lunch, but for the tenants' Christmas tea, presents and carol singing in the great hall at Ashingham. Afterwards Lady Beckenham took him to the grooms' quarters over the stables, insisting he could manage the steps, and producing an old crutch which had belonged to her grandfather.

'Come along, now, you can do it. You can do anything if you want to – there now, you see. Perfectly all right.'

He and Barty spent the rest of the evening there with the two girls, until he had to go back to the nursing home for the night. He was still in a lot of pain but the further surgery had been pronounced successful and the wound was healing well.

'Doctor says I should be able to have an artificial leg,' he said to Barty, 'might even get me job back, in that case. You never know.'

Barty agreed that indeed you didn't.

'Well,' said Oliver, mellowed into something approaching cheerfulness by the best part of a bottle of port that he and his father-in-law had shared after dinner, 'well, let's hope and pray that this is the last Christmas of the war.'

'Do you really think that's likely?' asked LM.

'I think it's possible. In spite of everything, I do believe the tide has turned. We've had some genuine victories at last, rather than just gaining the odd inch of mud; we owe a great deal to the Australians, they're a fine bunch of men, and the Americans of course. You must show me your letters from Robert, LM. I'd like to read them. God, I wonder when we'll see each other again.'

Robert and Maud spent Christmas Day with the Brewers:

'You can't be on your own in that house,' John Brewer had said, after Jamie announced, flushed with distress, that he was to go to friends of Laurence's.

'I don't actually know them very well,' he said, 'but Laurence seems to think it will be fun.'

Clearly he didn't know them at all and it was unlikely to be fun: fun in any case was not a concept with which Laurence was over-familiar. But Robert smiled at him, told him he was sure he'd have a great day, although they would miss him, and spent the next hour trying to console Maud, who had been planning her Christmas with Jamie for weeks and had lovingly wrapped at least half a dozen presents for him already.

'We'll have a good day,' John said, 'Kyle's here and Felicity's sister and brother-in-law, and their two, and besides, we have to drink a toast to Felicity and her literary success. Your sister seems confident that several of her poems will be published. It's so marvellous. I'm so very proud of her.'

Robert liked Felicity Brewer; she was a pretty woman, with a mass of golden-brown hair, large, rather pale blue eyes, and a gentle manner, which concealed the fact that she was steely and extremely determined. She was from a very old Boston family, her grandfather had been a general in the Civil War, her father was a most distinguished and successful lawyer, her mother was one of the queens of the New York charity circuit, and Felicity herself had grown up in a large house in East Hampton, been educated by a private governess, presented both at the Junior Assemblies and the Junior League Ball, the mark of a truly successful social season, and had been unarguably debutante of her year. Her family had not been exactly thrilled when she had fallen in love with the impoverished, if charming, John Brewer; but her father who had a shrewd eye for a good man and a promising investment, had given his permission and had never regretted it. Robert found interesting echoes in this of Oliver's marriage to Celia.

Kyle Brewer, their eldest son, looked exactly like his father, indeed was rather more handsome, but took after his mother in other ways. He had a rather greater interest in music and literature than in bricks and mortar; he had graduated in English literature from Yale the previous summer and was now desperately trying to persuade himself that the attractions of moving into Lytton Brewer as heir apparent to the company could really outweigh a career in journalism or something like it. Even publishing.

It was a very difficult decision; his father told him almost daily that he did hope he would join the firm, how lucky he was and what a great future he had in front of him; Kyle told him almost daily that he wasn't sure if real estate was for him, and that he wanted to explore other options. His father, in some exasperation, had now given him three months to make up his mind and embarrassed Kyle dreadfully over pre-lunch drinks by suggesting that if he didn't join Lytton Brewer, perhaps he could join the other Lytton firm at the opposite end of Manhattan.

'I'd love to think he could,' said Robert, 'but as you know, John, that firm is nothing to do with me. It was Jeanette's baby, and now, of course, Laurence has a large interest in it. Which means my own influence is nil. But perhaps when Felicity is published in London, she could talk to Oliver about it.'

'I wouldn't dream of bothering Mr Lytton,' said Kyle, 'please don't even think about it any more. And let's talk about something else,' he added, glaring at his father.

'Like playing clumps?' said Maud hopefully. Jamie had taught her clumps during the last few weeks, and she had been hoping for a game on Christmas Day.

'What's clumps?' asked Felicity, intrigued.

'Oh, well, you're in two teams and you're both given something to draw, and the other people in your team have to race to guess what it is. It's so much fun,' she added.

'It sounds wonderful,' said Felicity, 'we'll play it after lunch. Right now we'd better go in, or Cook will have a tantrum. She's dying to serve ours and then get home.'

'Then come along,' said Robert, smiling at her. 'Nothing could spoil Christmas more quickly, in my opinion, than a tantrumming cook.'

The day was a great success and Maud told her father at the end of it that she thought she would like to marry Kyle Brewer.

'He's so handsome and so good at drawing.'

'Right, well you'd better let him know in good time,' said Robert, smiling at her, and allowing his imagination to contemplate just for a moment and with intense pleasure, how neatly such an arrangement would outflank and enrage Laurence, particularly if Kyle was indeed working for Lyttons. And then reminded himself sharply that Maud was only five, and that the last thing he wanted for her was to be ensnared in his family feud. Only – only of course it was going to be impossible for her not to be.

CHAPTER 14

LM looked down rather helplessly at Celia. Every so often she put out a tentative hand to touch her, to stroke her hair, to caress her back, and withdrew it again. What use were such gestures in the face of such pain? She had only seen Celia cry once in all the years she had known her, and that had been when she had lost her baby. Even then they had been brave, almost optimistic tears. But this helpless, hopeless Celia was shocking in her despair.

'Celia – please,' she said finally, 'listen to me. Oliver is not dead. He's injured, in hospital. Arguably safer, better off. You must try to—'

'Try to what?' said Celia turning a grief-wrecked face to her, 'yes, LM, try to what exactly? Do go on, I'd like to know, tell me what I should try to do.' Her voice was angry, ugly in its passion; LM looked back at her steadily.

'Try to be hopeful,' she said.

'And what should I hope for? That he will have one or two limbs left? That he won't be entirely blind? That he won't have gone quite mad? I'm afraid I don't find that very – helpful, LM.'

'Celia, you don't know anything yet. Only that he has been wounded.'

'I think that's quite a lot,' said Celia quietly, 'quite a lot. Minor wounds don't take you to hospital, minor wounds don't get you away from the front even.'

'But—'

'LM, would you mind leaving me. I appreciate what you're trying to do, but I don't think you can possibly understand how I feel. I would really rather be on my own.'

There was a silence; LM looked down at her hands. 'Very well,' she said, 'of course. I shall be downstairs, if you need me.'

'You had far better go to the office,' said Celia, 'there is a great deal to be done.'

'Yes, of course.'

She went down the stairs and was putting on her coat and hat before she realised she was weeping. Mrs Bill emerged from the dining-room,

244

coal scuttle in hand.

'Miss Lytton, what is it? It's not – Colonel Lytton hasn't been –?'

'No, no, Mrs Bill. Well, he hasn't been killed. But he has been wounded and taken to a field hospital. We don't know where, or how bad it is.'

'Oh poor Lady Celia,' said Mrs Bill. 'Poor, poor Lady Celia.'

'Yes indeed,' said LM, 'perhaps you could take her some tea later. Not just now, she wants to be alone,' and hurried out of the door and down the steps, shocked, as always, by the ease with which her own still-savage pain and grief could be resurrected.

Two hours later she was correcting some proofs when her office door opened; Celia stood there, perfectly dressed, her hair in order, her face resolutely set.

She looked at LM and said simply, 'I'm sorry. So very sorry for what I said. Of course you understand. Just for a moment I forgot.'

And LM stood up and held out her arms to her as she would to little Jay, and Celia went into them and they stood there together for a long time, not speaking, not crying even, simply drawing comfort from one another.

'It was just thinking about Billy that really panicked me,' said Celia later, over their customary lunch of bread and Beckenham cheese. 'His missing leg, you know, thinking of Oliver without a leg. Just a stump. Or an arm, his sleeve pinned to his chest in that dreadful brave, ugly way. Or – suppose it was gas, LM, suppose he was blind, how would he bear it, how would I bear it for him?'

'Well, you would,' said LM, 'both of you would. But it may not be. It may be something which you can cope with rather more easily.'

'It might be shellshock,' said Celia, 'think of that. They never recover from that. He's had a long war, LM, he was – well he was very—' she stopped.

'Afraid? Yes, I'm sure. He was never a very brave little boy. So different from Jack, who was born reckless. Rather like Jay, I'm afraid. But he's been magnificent, right through this dreadful thing. He has so clearly learned courage. It must have cost him very dear.'

'Yes, I'm afraid it has,' said Celia sadly, thinking not even of Oliver's damaged body at that moment, but of his dreadfully changed and damaged spirit. 'But he's not the only one. Millions and millions of young men, all with their lives ruined. When, in the name of God, is it going to end?'

'Now Barty, you mustn't cry. It won't help anybody. Especially not Lady Celia.'

Lady Beckenham had never subscribed to the Aunt Celia label; she considered it foolish and misleading, and had told Celia so. 'You have to be brave, hope for the best for Mr Lytton.'

'I'm not crying for him,' said Barty, rubbing her eyes, blowing her nose dutifully on a very grubby handkerchief. 'I'm being as brave as I can about him. I know I have to be.'

Lady Beckenham looked at her. She had grown very fond of her over the years; she seemed to her to be a rather remarkable child. Barty was eleven now, tall for her age, and very thin, not exactly pretty but extremely striking, with her great mass of golden-brown hair, and large brown eyes. She was highly intelligent; more so than the twins, Lady Beckenham sometimes thought and she also worked very hard. This could certainly not be said of the twins. Miss Adams said she considered Barty to be quite exceptional, and although Lady Beckenham was not altogether convinced by this, she was impressed by the fact that Barty was already reading the works of Jane Austen and the Brontë sisters, and could recite most of Shakespeare's sonnets. She was not an intellectual woman, indeed she had hardly read any of Miss Austen's work herself, and hated Shakespeare, but she did accept that they were a yardstick by which one could judge a child's intellectual development. Even more impressive to her was the fact that Barty could do quite complicated algebra, and could draw maps of most of the major countries of the world freehand. She was a nice child too: all the nurses loved her, often said her help with the men was genuinely valuable.

'Well, what are you crying about, then?' she said now.

'Billy.'

'Billy! But he's much better, back with your mother, doing well with his wooden leg I thought—'

'Yes, he is, but he can't get any work. He went to the brewery and they won't take him, said they weren't taking any amputees – such a horrible word – and that he wouldn't be able to cope with the work. He tried some factories, but they all just sent him away. He wrote to me today about it. He says he wished he'd been killed. It's not fair, when all he's done is fight for his country.'

'What's he living on? Get a pension does he?'

A pension, she thought: at the age of eighteen. What kind of a world had this war created?

'He will do. I'm not sure what you get for a leg.'

'What on earth do you mean?' asked Lady Beckenham.

'You get sixteen shillings a week for a right arm. Unless it's below the elbow, then it's only eleven shillings. One of the nurses told me. But she wasn't sure about legs.'

Lady Beckenham was, for once in her life, silenced. The pragmatism of it was literally shocking. But she supposed the money available had to be apportioned somehow.

'I'll speak to Beckenham about it,' she said finally. 'He'll know.'

'But the thing is, he doesn't want a pension. He wants to work. How can he sit around for the rest of his life, doing nothing? I'm sorry—' her voice tailed off, she was crying again, 'sorry, Lady Beckenham.'

Lady Beckenham looked at her, then rummaged in the pocket of her breeches for her own handkerchief.

'Here you are, use this. It's a bit cleaner than yours.'

'Yes. Yes, I'm sorry. I will try not to – it's just that I can't see any hope for him. Ever again.'

There was a long silence. Then Lady Beckenham said, 'Barty, how's Billy doing on that wooden leg of his?'

'Oh – all right I think,' said Barty, 'very well really. He's practising up and down Line Street, he says. He can walk a few steps without the crutch even. He says every time he falls over he thinks of your grandpa and gets up again. Dot and carry one, they call him in the street.'

'Good lad,' said Lady Beckenham, 'that's the sort of thing I like to hear. Now listen. I've got a problem in the yard. One of those wretched girls is leaving, says she'll get more money in a factory. It's beyond me, I must say, ghastly work, but still. I can't stop her. I think Billy could manage mucking out, watering, that sort of thing. I'm not making any allowances mind, he's got to be able to cope with the work. But if he could – good gracious, Barty, you'll have me over in a minute. There, there, don't start crying again, for heaven's sake.'

'Still no news, Lady Celia?'

'No,' said Celia briskly, 'no news. But I tell myself that has to mean good news.'

'And you don't know which hospital he's in, even?'

'No idea. Not yet. But you know, my mother says you can get used to anything, and it does seem to be true. I just coast along from day to day. Gill, forgive me for saying so, but you look dreadful, rather as if you've slept in your clothes, what on earth have you been doing?'

'Sleeping in my clothes. Travelling on the tube all night,' said Gill cheerfully.

'All night? Why?'

'There was a raid starting when I left here. Have you ever taken shelter in one of the tube stations?'

'No,' said Celia, 'I haven't. Mostly we take our chances at home. We once spent a night in the crypt at St Martin's-in-the-Fields, that was bad enough. There were so many people cooking their supper on primus stoves that the condensation was running down the walls.'

'Well, the underground is worse. The smell is quite awful, and the snoring! Hideous. So I just sat on the tube, which keeps going round and round, and slept. Much nicer.'

'Good Lord,' said Celia, 'how very enterprising of you. Keep that story for our war diaries. Is that the artwork for the poetry anthology?'

'Yes. It's very simple, I'm afraid, but I wanted to conserve the budget for the third volume of *Dispatches*. So just graphics – again.' She sighed. 'Did we really ever have colour on our jackets? Or was that some kind of hallucination?'

'We did,' said Celia firmly, 'and we will again. That looks really nice, Gill, thanks.'

'Good. I'll tell them to go ahead then. How are the orders going on?'

'Oh, not bad. You know.' She smiled at Gill. 'Certainly they're going to be marvellous for *Dispatches*. I don't know what we'd have done without those books.'

'Your idea, Lady Celia.'

'Was it? I'd forgotten.'

It hadn't been true what she'd said to Gill; she didn't think no news meant good news at all. She knew that with so many casualties, the letters and telegrams were dreadfully delayed. Oliver could have been dead for days and she wouldn't have known. Nor was it true that she was getting used to it; her sense of dread, of almost physical terror, of shrinking from what the reality might be, was increasing. She no longer had bad dreams; she scarcely slept at all, merely dozed fitfully, surfaced endlessly, as with illness or pain. Indeed she felt both ill and in pain; she had constant nausea and a leaden ache in her stomach. Whatever she did, wherever she was, the visions rose before her: of the dreadful final telegram, or of an Oliver mutilated beyond recognition. She had thought nothing could be worse than the first shock; in fact the long days and nights – which followed six of them already – had proved infinitely more terrible. Without her work to concentrate on, to escape in, she would have gone quite mad; as it was, she felt very nearly so.

Work was, in any case, appallingly difficult: two of the girls she had hired as sales clerks-cum-representatives had given in their notice, in order to work in munitions factories, and now she had only two clerks left. Writing out the invoices was yet another thing she and LM had had to do more and more of recently.

Often they sat all evening in the cellar at Cheyne Walk, half-listening to the bombs falling while they worked.

'As if it mattered,' LM had said more than once, and Celia said nonsense, they couldn't start thinking that way. If they did lose the war, it wasn't going to be with James Thin of Edinburgh or Blackwells of Oxford owing them several hundred pounds. Occasionally the treacherous thought drifted into her head that they could just pack up Lyttons until the war was over and then re-open; but she always dismissed it sharply. Other houses were fighting on; it would be Macmillan or Collins or Blackwood who would truly benefit from their absence, and indeed when the time did come to open Lyttons' doors once more, it could well be to no customers at all. And besides, Oliver had entrusted her with Lyttons, her and LM; they could not fail him. She owed him that, at the very least, in return for all he was doing for them. Them and the rest of the country.

The frequency of bombing had greatly increased. The old zeppelins had been replaced by far superior machines which could fly distances of up to a thousand miles, so that a round trip from Berlin to London for a bombing raid was perfectly feasible. Often she, LM and Mrs Bill and Brunson, who joined them in the cellar, would emerge at the end of a raid and go out into the night together to try to discover what harm had been done. One night there was heavy bombing particularly close; they could not see a great deal of it in the dark, but morning revealed a huge hole in Green Park, just by the back entrance of the Ritz, the windows out in half the buildings below Piccadilly, and a shower of shrapnel in the courtyard at Buckingham Palace.

They were all desperately tired. The long drive down to Beaconsfield to see the children was becoming less and less inviting. She knew that when she got there she would be confronted by further problems: the naughtiness of the twins, the difficulties Miss Adams was having teaching them all, Barty's anxieties about Billy, Jay's persistent bed-wetting – not her responsibility exactly, but one which LM fretted over and shared with her endlessly – it went on and on.

And she missed Oliver so badly; she would never have believed how much. She missed hearing his voice, seeing him smile at her as he came into the room, all those happy, rambling conversations about the children, the more purposeful ones about Lyttons, even the battles over authors, budgets, promotion, publishing strategy. The thought of having him there to share her problems was almost unimaginable now. And keeping Lyttons afloat financially was more and more difficult; sales were falling, costs rising, and the premises were falling into disrepair. There was a hole in the roof caused indirectly by bomb damage. It wasn't a large hole, but it let the rain in; every morning and evening they replaced the bucket which stood beneath it, but it was filling up faster all the time. The whole roof really needed to be replaced, but they simply could not afford it, and anyway, there was no one to do it. Builders and roofers were in terribly short supply; even the chimney sweep was a woman, who had taken the business over from her husband. She was astonishingly cheerful and brave; they always gave her tea when she had finished, and some toast if there were no biscuits. 'Lot better now, it is,' she would say, slurping tea out of her saucer, 'rather be halfway up a chimney any day than halfway down a washtub.'

'We should do a book about women in the war; we could call it *New Lives for Old*,' Celia said, and LM agreed, adding that she often wondered if there were any circumstances in which Celia would not want to commission a book. Celia said she couldn't think of any.

The cleaners had all left, and they had to do the work themselves. Some of the more junior girls had refused, had said they hadn't come to work in an office to do cleaning; Celia said firmly that if they couldn't do it, she would, and swept and dusted so ostentatiously around their desks that they gave in and said they would help after all, as long as it was reflected in their wages, otherwise they'd be doing two jobs for the same money. Celia said she was doing about a dozen, but she knew it was hardly a fair comparison. She and LM were, despite punitive taxation – six shillings in the pound now – still rich by absolute standards, still went home to a large comfortable, if cold, house, and a cooked meal, often with fresh meat and vegetables brought from Ashingham. The food shortage was much worse again, despite rationing; there were reports that January of up to four thousand people in a queue at Smithfield, and as many as one million people queuing every week in London alone.

But there was an additional anxiety which haunted her most hopeful days, and that was over the viability of her relationship with Oliver and the fact that he no longer seemed to desire her physically. She would lie awake, staring into the darkness each night, alone in her bed, remembering how she had lain with him, being loved by him night after night, felt his mouth on hers, welcomed him into her, into her greedy body, ridden him, ridden her pleasure, heard herself crying out with it, lain afterwards, gratefully sated, listening to him telling her he loved her.

That last time he had come home, he had scarcely kissed her, apart from a grazing on the lips now and then; she could scarcely bear to think about it now, knowing she might never see him again. He had turned away from her in bed each night, and fallen exhaustedly asleep; in the morning, hopeful that he would welcome it, that he was not so tired, she would put out a tentative hand, a hungry mouth, but he hurried out of bed with some excuse or another and went to the bathroom, to emerge dressed, and avoiding her eyes. He repeatedly said he loved her still; but he didn't seem to want her. As well as feeling hurt and rejected, she felt physically frustrated and irritable. She would wake from other dreams, sexually explicit rather than horrific, her body throbbing with desire, or worse, a half-orgasm which left her more wretched than before. She had tried to talk about it, to ask him what it was, but he cut her off.

'Don't, Celia, I beg of you. I simply cannot bear it. I am sorry: I don't want to say any more about it than that.'

She had begun to find herself over those past few months, indeed, until the news of his being wounded had reached her, looking at other men with a predatory eye: seeking reassurance, if nothing else, that she had not become ugly, unattractive. She half-wished, half-feared that Jack would come home again; this time it would not be so easy to resist him.

Some of the men at Ashingham were charming, and one in particular, tall, dark and extremely handsome, had lost an eye at Passchendaele and been a successful barrister in that dreamlike former life they had all led. He loved to talk to her, and he made her laugh; she would sit with him occasionally if she had the time, and could escape from the children. One evening she found a bottle of claret in her father's cellar, and took it to his room. They drank it over exchanged confidences; he had loved his wife very dearly, had come home on leave and found her in bed with someone else.

'I thought I would like to kill them both and then myself; and I could have done, I had got very used to killing, I was not the civilised fellow who went away in 1914. But – in the end I walked away, I didn't have enough passion left in me.'

'It seems to kill passion, war,' Celia said sadly, 'sexual passion that is,' and then looked hastily into her glass, realising what she had said.

He looked at her for a moment and then said very gently, 'It does, you know. You are out there, thinking of your wife and how you love her, remembering loving her, and somehow the brutalisation that has taken place comes between you and that memory. It's hard to explain. Don't despair, Celia. You are all we have left, you know. We need you so badly.' He smiled suddenly. 'Oh dear, this is the claret talking, I'm afraid. Sorry.'

Somehow that conversation calmed her, restored her loyalty and her faith in Oliver. A few days later her mother teased her about it.

'I know what you're up to. I haven't been watching Beckenham for forty-five years for nothing. Don't blame you either, he's extremely good-looking.'

'Don't tell anyone will you?' said Celia laughing.

'No, of course not. I've learned to keep my counsel. And not telling anyone anything whenever possible is the secret of a happy marriage, in my experience.'

Celia, remembering suddenly the story of George Paget, looked at her. 'Mama? Was it true – about—'

Lady Beckenham put her head back and roared with laughter. 'George? Oh yes. Absolutely. Kept me sane, through all the housemaids. And the Beckenhams born on the wrong wide of the blanket—'

Celia had never considered this. 'No! Really?'

'Oh yes. Your father was never very keen on birth control. Dotted about the county they are. We've had to support at least three of the little buggers. Well, not so little now. One girl threatened a lot of trouble. We had to buy her off. Couldn't actually admit it of course, not openly. Said we liked to take care of our staff, that sort of thing.'

'Oh. Goodness, I never realised.'

'Good. I hope not many people did. No, I was very fond of George. And he of me. His wife knew, of course, but she hated sex, so it suited her. Perfectly good arrangement all round.'

'Yes. Yes, I see.' Celia was silent; the pragmatic approach to marriage of her mother's generation had always intrigued her. She wondered what she would do, if she found someone else overwhelmingly attractive; or indeed if Oliver failed ever to desire her again. Both were unimaginable, of course. Absolutely unimaginable.

'I think he must be dead,' she said flatly to LM on the tenth day. 'He would have written himself by now, got news to me somehow. It's the only explanation.'

'Is it? Is it really? I imagine things must be very confused out there, so many battles, so many casualties—'

'Yes, yes, I know. But one of the things the VADs do is write letters. It's one of their jobs. So even if he was – very sick,' she hesitated, took a deep breath – 'or really very badly injured, he would get one of them to write. I know he would.'

'But, Celia he might be too ill for that.'

'LM, if he was too ill for that he would be dead by now. Conditions out in those hospitals are dreadful. Simply because they are so overworked, and ill-equipped.'

'How do you know that?'

'I was talking to a VAD the other day. She'd been sent home because she had been injured herself, driving an ambulance. She says it's appalling out there. She's not supposed to talk about it of course, it's bad for morale and it upsets people. But she was visiting someone at Ashingham, and she just started telling me, and then quite clearly she couldn't stop. I – well I didn't tell you before. She said they were often confronted by dreadfully injured men at the emergency station, but could offer them little more than first aid. Bandages, a little antiseptic, a drink of water. That was until they got to the proper military hospital, an agonising two-hour drive away or more. She said sometimes she was overcome with panic, wanted to run away. Even at the hospital, the men often face a long wait before they're treated. The surgeons are working round the clock. Literally, sometimes dropping with exhaustion.' She giggled suddenly. 'Do you know, she told me about one surgeon who operated permanently with a cigarette in his mouth. Every so often some ash would drop down on to the patient, and he would say, "Don't fuss, it's sterile." We must get all that into the war diaries, too. Anyway, that doesn't bode too well for Oliver's chances.'

'God, how dreadful,' said LM: thinking of another soldier in another field hospital, praying as she did almost every day that he had truly died instantly, had known nothing.

'Yes. So don't try and make me think he's all right, LM, because I know he can't be. It's impossible. I'd rather not hope, quite honestly. It's better for me not to try. Oliver's dead. I know he is.' There was a silence: she looked down at her wedding ring, twisting it on her finger. Then she took a deep breath, and looked at LM, her eyes full of tears, but managing to smile. 'How would you fancy a night out?'

'A night out? Well – well yes, I suppose it would be—'

'We could go to the Old Vic. You know it's never closed. Apparently it's worth going just to hear Lilian Baylis's speech if there's a raid. She just won't have anyone walking out. She comes on to the stage and says, "Will those who wish to leave please do so at once. *We* are carrying on." Of course hardly anyone leaves. We certainly wouldn't would we? Let's go, it would cheer me up. Sybil Thorndike's playing in *Richard the Second*. I'd so love to see her. Are you game?'

LM said she was game.

'Good. I'll try and get tickets at lunchtime. Now I must do some work. These proofs have more and more mistakes in them. Typesetting does seem to be one thing men are better at than women.'

Barty thought she had never been so happy. For the first time in her life, she felt she belonged somewhere. She loved living in the country, loved walking across the fields and through the woods, making up stories in her head which she then wrote down and sent to Wol, loved her duties on the estate, collecting eggs, haymaking – it had been a good summer, there had been a lot to do – loved her lessons with Miss Adams. The twins were really quite nice these days: a healthy terror for their grandmother kept them under control, and they took their duties very seriously, caring for Soot, and the small dish-faced New Forest pony called Horace. He was ostensibly for all the children but actually only ridden by them and little Jay, since neither Barty nor Giles had any interest in horses.

The twins were extraordinarily beautiful children, with gleaming dark hair and huge brown eyes, small and almost doll-like; still almost eerily identical and absolutely inseparable. They always spoke in the First person plural: 'We don't like porridge, we hate arithmetic, we didn't fall off Horace today, we have brushed Soot.' The patients adored them; the twins cheered them all up. Long acclimatised now to the men's injuries, they would stand by legless or armless men, tell them what they had been doing that day, sing them songs, ask them about the war and whether they had known their father. Even the poor souls suffering from shellshock were cheered by their blithe unself-consciousness; Lady Beckenham stood one afternoon, watching from the house, as Venetia held one hand of a violently shaking man and Adele the other, both of them smiling encouragingly into his face and telling him he would soon feel better.

'Jolly good, what you did for that poor chap this morning,' she said to them later, and the next time Celia came down she told her she could be proud of them. 'It'll stand them in good stead in life all this,' she said, 'you see if it doesn't.'

Barty and Giles were still great friends; he was getting very grown-up now, he seemed to have grown inches every time he came home. He liked school now, he told her, he would be quite sad to leave.

'Well why do you have to, can't you stay?' she asked, and he looked at her in a slightly superior way and said surely she knew that when you were thirteen you went to your public school. Barty said no she didn't know and she wouldn't have asked the question if she did.

Giles looked at her again and then put his hand on her arm and said, 'Sorry, Barty, sorry. Shall we go for a walk, and dam that stream we found the other day?'

She said she'd like that and jumped up and said she'd race him to it. Then they dammed the stream, their friendship ostensibly quite restored; but such episodes, rare as they were nowadays, did remind her, that she was not quite like he was, that there was still a gulf between them, and nothing could ever close it.

But best of all was having Billy with her: all the time, another member of her family, a person of her own. She no longer felt estranged, lost to them all, but confident and happy. Billy was happy, too, working extremely hard, although with great difficulty; the wooden leg was ill-fitting and uncomfortable. He fell over constantly in the slippery yard, either when he was struggling to walk without his crutch, or when the crutch itself slipped. Consequently he was always covered with bruises and grazes, but he never complained, clambering up again, refusing help.

'I won't be a charity case,' he would say fiercely, 'if I can't do me job, I'll have to leave again.'

Lady Beckenham respected this, criticising his work quite harshly if it was not up to her extremely high standards. 'That horse is still muddy there, look, behind his withers,' she would say, 'I don't call that grooming, Billy. Do it again.' Or 'That headcollar still isn't fastened properly, I've shown you twice, for heaven's sake, what's the matter with you?' And he would stand there scarlet-faced, biting his lip, but he never made excuses, never asked for special treatment, even when he sprained his wrist and had to wear it in a sling for a few days.

'I can manage,' he said furiously to Sheila, the groom, when she offered to do the water troughs for him. 'I can manage perfectly all right.'

And Barty could see that indeed he could.

'Oh dear. These are awful,' said Celia aloud.

She was sitting at her desk, looking at the sales figures for the previous three months. They were indeed awful. The only successes were *Dispatches* and the new poetry anthology: everything else, the dictionaries and reference books, the reprints of the classics, even the children's books, were doing badly, hardly breaking even. They hadn't done any popular fiction this quarter of course, that would have helped: but – these figures would only just cover their overheads, never mind make any kind of a profit. What on earth was she going to do, what could she pull out of her extremely threadbare hat that would save Lyttons? Perhaps, she thought, with something that was closer to a sob than a sigh, perhaps it was as well Oliver wasn't coming back. What would he think of her, having entrusted her with it, leading a successful business straight downhill to bankruptcy? Well she hadn't – yet. She just had to find a way through this. Somehow. Stupid to neglect the popular fiction. She knew why: it was because she'd been so busy, doing everything herself, she hadn't had time to sit back and plan. Well, that must change. Now. At once. She would spent the rest of the morning simply working out strategy. She picked up the telephone on her desk.

'No calls, Mrs Gould. Nobody at all.'

'Very well, Lady Celia. But—'

'No buts. No calls. No visitors.'

'Sorry,' said a voice. A most beautiful, musical, resonant voice, an actor's voice, 'too late. You have one.'

Celia looked up; in front of her stood the most glorious looking man she had ever seen. He had dark gold hair and brilliant, very dark blue eyes, with surprisingly thick eyebrows; he was not especially tall, not quite as tall as Oliver, and quite heavily built, with very broad shoulders. His features were absurdly perfect: he looked, indeed, rather like a film star, a cross, she thought wildly, between Douglas Fairbanks and a blond version of the new Latin sensation, Rudolph Valentino. He was wearing an officer's greatcoat, over what appeared to be an ordinary dark grey suit, and when he walked forward, holding out his hand, she noticed that he limped quite badly.

'Sebastian Brooke,' he said, smiling at her, a most wonderful, wide, generous smile, 'my agent tells me you are looking for a children's book. I have written one. May I tell you about it?'

For the rest of her life Celia remembered that morning: not just because of Sebastian Brooke's spellbinding presence, nor because of the magical tale he had written, a fantasy called *Meridian*, a work of such charm and humour and originality that she could not believe someone else had not already bought it; nor even because of the extraordinary moment when Janet Gould rang through, and said: 'Lady Celia there's—' and she had cut her short and said, 'Mrs Gould, I told you no calls, no matter who they are from,' and Mrs Gould said, 'But Lady Celia this is from your mother,' and she had said, thinking it was about Billy or Barty or the twins, 'Oh God,' and asked Sebastian Brooke to excuse her, and picked up the phone, and her mother had said, talking very fast, rather like a telegram, lest the crucial part of the conversation should not get over fast enough, 'Celia, it's Oliver. He's all right, in hospital, recovering, no loss of limb, shrapnel wounds to the stomach, coming home as soon as he can be moved'. Nor even because of the way she burst into tears and then started laughing helplessly, almost hysterically, and had stood up and asked Sebastian Brooke to excuse her, while she went to her sister-in-law's office, nor even because of seeing LM in tears of joy and relief herself, and feeling even in her happiness a sense of poignancy at her courage and generosity. She remembered that morning forever afterwards because, for the first time since she had set eyes on Oliver, all those years before, another man had driven him, albeit briefly, absolutely out of her head and her heart, and even managed to make her forget, just for a while, her grief at his presumed death.

Part Three
1918–1920

CHAPTER 15

'Oliver! Oliver, my darling, don't, don't cry. Didn't you hear what I said, I said the war is over. LM just telephoned, saying had we heard, Oliver don't, please don't—'

'I'm sorry,' he said, wiping his eyes on the back of his hand, blowing his nose hard. 'Yes, I did hear.'

'But—' she stared at him, 'but Oliver—'

'Celia it's wonderful news, of course it is. But I find it hard to rejoice, I'm afraid. Look at me, look at all these chaps here, look at young Billy, think of Jay's father. All for what? Well, at least there won't be any more dead, any more wounded.'

'No. No, of course there won't.'

She felt upset at his reaction, confused; LM had said London was in uproar, the king had come out on to the balcony at Buckingham Palace, strangers were joining hands and singing Rule Britannia, in Trafalgar Square huge crowds were dancing, shouting, 'Have we won the war?' and then, 'Yes we've won the war'. It sounded so exciting, such fun, making some kind of sense of all the misery of the past four years. And here, in her mother's house, her husband was in tears.

She sighed, struggling for patience, as she did so often these days. Later, she heard from Sylvia that young Frank had reported a very muted reception to the ceasefire on the front. Told to maintain their position for the remaining few hours, the men had waited silently for news. At eleven a.m. the Germans laid down their arms.

'It was weird. A few of us got together, us and Fritz, exchanged ciggies, till the officers stopped it, said it wasn't allowed. I don't think any of us could quite believe it.'

Her brother-in-law told much the same story. 'All I could think of, all most of us could think of, was the millions of men who'd died. For what? It was hard to rejoice.'

Oliver had come home to Ashingham in late September; he could be cared for there in comfort. He was still very frail; he had sustained a serious wound to his stomach, and had had three separate operations to remove all the shrapnel. The wounds were only now beginning to heal.

He was grateful to be home, quietly pleased to see her and the children, but beyond that interested only in himself and his recovery. Celia took a few days off to be with him and settle him in; it was a strange, happy time, but looking back, everything seemed to be slightly out of focus, nothing as it had been or even as she might have expected. She had met him in London at Victoria, watched, shocked, as his stretcher was taken off the ambulance train, to see his emaciated form – and ashen face, with his blue eyes, which seemed somehow paler and more sunken. He was helplessly weak, scarcely able to lift his hand to take hers and smile at her. She had hired a private ambulance and travelled in it with him; he had hardly spoken during the journey, not even to complain, although he was clearly still in considerable pain. Later that night, when he had been settled in his room, given some medication, had a sleep, she had gone quietly in, sat down beside him.

'I can hardly believe you are here,' she said, and then, when he did not answer, 'I love you, Oliver. I love you so much.'

Still silence: then, 'May I have some water?'

Absurdly, she felt resentment: that he could say this and yet not respond to her; then she shook herself. He had been repeatedly to hell and back; she had no right to expect anything from him at all.

She gave him some water, said quietly, 'How are you?'

'All right,' he said, 'yes, all right. Glad to be home.'

And that was all she got from him for twenty-four hours.

The next night he seemed stronger; he had slept well, the pain was easier. The twins and Barty had been allowed in, just for a few minutes each; he had smiled at them, appeared pleased to see them, managed to kiss the twins, to hold Barty's hand. He told her he had enjoyed her stories, they had helped him a lot; it was more than he had said to anyone since he got back. Again irritation, and an odd resentment stirred in Celia; again she stifled it, shocked at herself. Later she went in with a cup of warm milk for him; he was on a liquid diet, and being given fluid intravenously. She helped him to sit up, held the cup for him; he sank back on the pillows exhausted, and suddenly smiled at her.

'Thank you, my darling. I'm – sorry.'

'Oliver! For what?'

'Not to be more of a husband to you.'

'Oliver, that's absurd. I don't expect anything from you, anything at all.'

'I do love you,' he said, and went straight to sleep.

She felt better after that, better able to cope with his irritability, his self-obsession, his silence. It was difficult; the children were disappointed, had expected hugs, kisses, an interest in them and in what they were doing. As I did, thought Celia, struggling to explain to them why

260

he was as he was, to lower their expectations. The twins were not impressed, but Barty was.

'He's had such a horrible time,' she said to them, 'and he's just dreadfully tired. He can't think about anything else till he's better.'

The twins stared at her; then, 'He's not your daddy,' said Adele, and, 'It's nothing to do with you,' said Venetia, and they both ran off; Barty looked after them, her eyes filling with tears. It was so long since they'd been unkind to her, she'd forgotten how it hurt.

'Don't take any notice of them,' said Celia, putting her arm round her, 'you know what they're like. And thank you for trying to explain. What you said was exactly right.'

Barty didn't answer, managed a rather weak smile, and walked off towards the library. Next afternoon Celia found her reading to Oliver from the *Just So* stories. She felt irrationally irritated.

'Barty, you know Wol is supposed to sleep in the afternoon.'

'Yes, but he—'

'Now run along. My mother was looking for you.'

'That was unkind,' said Oliver mildly, when Barty had gone.

'Not at all. She knows perfectly well this is your rest time.'

'I was wide awake, the door was open, she offered, and I thought it would be nice. I was bored.'

'Oliver, I would have read to you, if you'd wanted me to.'

'Yes, but Barty offered. Oh darling, it doesn't matter. Anyway, it's a good sign, don't you think, that I was bored?'

'Yes. Yes, of course.' She looked at him; she wanted to talk to him, this might be a good time. 'Oliver, after the weekend, I really have to get back to London. To Lyttons.'

'That's all right,' he said, closing his eyes. 'I'll be all right. I'm well looked after here.'

Nothing about her, nothing about missing her: only himself . . . Stop it Celia, stop it, you're being childish. She bent and kissed his forehead.

'Good. I'm glad you feel that.'

'I do.'

'Shall I sit with you for a while?'

'Oh no, darling, I don't think so. I'm very tired, I might sleep now, after all. You did say it was my rest time.'

'Yes I did,' said Celia and left the room quietly.

When she left on Sunday night, she kissed him goodbye tenderly. He seemed stronger, sitting up, reading.

'Goodbye, my darling, I'll come down again next weekend. As long as I can get the petrol, of course.'

'Yes, well, if you can. I feel so much better this evening. It's been a lovely day.'

'Hasn't it? I'm glad you enjoyed it.'

'Yes. Yes, I have.'

'I'm afraid the house in London is in a bit of a state. And the office. What with the—'

'Really? Darling, could you possibly bring me some books down when you come? I'm reading more now, and your father's library is a bit limited. Nothing more recent than Mr Dickens.'

'Yes of course,' she said happily. 'I could bring you some manuscripts and some of the things we've been publishing, if you like.'

'Oh,' he said, 'oh no, that sounds rather too much like hard work. I was more thinking of things like Conan Doyle, this fellow Dornford Yates. That really would cheer me up.'

'Oh,' she said, 'yes, all right.'

'I'm tired now, darling. I wonder if you could draw the curtains, let me have a sleep. Goodbye. I'll hope to see you very soon.'

Nothing about missing her, nothing about driving carefully, nothing about what problems might confront her at the other end. Of course, she must expect that. Of course. But it was difficult just the same. Unbidden, the words of Sarah, Duchess of Marlborough, came into her head: it was one of her favourite quotations. 'The duke returned from the wars today, and did pleasure me in his top-boots.'

That was what she had dreamed of through the years: an impatient, joyful, glorious reunion. Reality was proving very far from that.

The next weekend he looked far better; the weather was beautiful still, and he was in the garden when she arrived, just before Saturday lunch. Barty was sitting with him; she ran over to Celia.

'Aunt Celia, hallo. Wol is much better, he's got his drip out, and he's eating some soup. I fed him myself last night,' she added proudly.

'How lovely,' said Celia, kissing Oliver. 'I'm so glad. Hallo, darling. It's marvellous to see you in the garden.'

'Isn't it? I'm so enjoying it. And Barty is a wonderful nurse. And she's been playing the piano for me as well. Darling, did you bring me some books to read?'

'Yes, lots. And also a new book I want you to—' She was dying to show him Sebastian Brooke's astonishing work; it had absorbed her totally through the week, reading it, thinking about it, planning when and how they could publish it, what it would be worth, how much she should offer his agent.

'Oh, darling, nothing new, please. I told you I really couldn't manage it. Something light, I did say. I meant to ask you if you could get something by Warwick Deeping. And Conan Doyle, as I—'

'Oh,' she said, 'yes, of course. Well, that is what I've brought. Actually. Here.'

'Wonderful. I shall start immediately after my lunch. My soup. How long will that be, Barty? Would you like to go and find out?'

Barty ran off. Celia waited. Waited for him to say he was pleased to see her, ask her how the drive had been, the week had been. How she was, even. None of it came. Nor did it for the entire weekend.

'How is your husband?' asked Sebastian Brooke the following Monday. They were lunching at the Savoy Hotel, waiting for his agent; she had already made an offer for the book. Otherwise she knew someone else would. She had actually asked Oliver if he would like to discuss it, and he had said flatly that he wouldn't. 'I'm not up to it, darling, sorry. I just have to leave it all to you for the time being.'

The offer had been accepted; four hundred pounds. An enormous amount of money. Then Sebastian's agent, Paul Davis, had phoned her again. Macmillan wanted the book, had offered more. Was she still interested? She said yes, she was, but didn't think she could go any higher; in that case, said Paul Davis, she might have to wave it goodbye. Celia took a deep breath, said would five hundred pounds secure it? Davis said he would put it to his client. He came back to her later that day, and said five hundred and fifty would see it safely hers. These were enormous sums of money: the standard advance against royalties (of twenty per cent) was twenty pounds. Oliver had always said that if it was enough for A E Housman it was enough for anyone. Very occasionally there would be an item in *The Bookseller* saying that some extremely famous author had been offered two hundred pounds, but it was rare. And Sebastian was hardly famous. Although of course he would be, and Lyttons would be more famous with him. Celia closed her eyes, gripped the edge of the desk and said all right, five hundred and fifty. It would, after all, be money recouped from Sebastian's sales. The lunch was to settle the deal and celebrate the association of Lyttons and Sebastian Brooke.

'Oh – he's much better,' she said to Sebastian now. 'Yes. Still very weak, of course.'

'I'm sure. Poor chap. But glad to be home. Glad to see you.'

He smiled at her: that wonderful, brilliant smile.

'Well,' she said, 'well yes, he is glad.' And then for no reason other than that she wanted to tell someone, had to tell someone, added, 'I suppose.'

'Now what does that mean, you suppose?'

'Oh – I don't know. He's very – down.' Even as she heard the words she thought how absurd they sounded, how ridiculously inadequate; she met Sebastian Brooke's eyes, smiled awkwardly. 'What a stupid thing to say. Of course he is.'

'Yes,' he said, 'of course he is. But that doesn't make it any easier, does it?'

'No,' she said startled, 'no, it doesn't.'

'It's awfully difficult,' he said, 'all round. These reunions.'

'You – that is—'

'Oh I had one,' he said smiling again, 'a disastrous one. I've recovered now. As you see. I'll tell you about it another time if you like.'

She looked at him, wondering, not for the first time, about his personal affairs, aware suddenly how much he and his life intrigued her. 'That would be . . .' she said, then stopped.

Paul Davis was being shown to the table. He bowed over Celia's hand. She disliked him; he was excessively sycophantic: an oleaginous shark, as Oliver had once called him. She was surprised that he was representing Sebastian, that Sebastian should have taken on such a man; on the other hand he was extremely successful.

'Lady Celia. How beautiful you look, and what a very nice treat. Not many publishers buy me lunch in such style these days.'

'Well, we know about style at Lyttons,' said Celia.

'Indeed you do. How is Oliver? I heard he was home.'

'Yes. Yes, he's much better. He's down at my mother's home, convalescing.'

'Well, I hope he will be back in London soon. Putting us through our paces, driving hard bargains. I daresay a spell in the trenches is good for that sort of thing.'

'A spell in the trenches isn't good for anything,' said Sebastian Brooke quietly. 'except taking away your zest for life.'

'You've heard about Sebastian's war, have you?' said Paul Davis.

'No. No I haven't. We've only talked about *Meridian*.'

'Well, no doubt he'll tell you about it. His great claim to fame was enlisting as a private. Didn't you, Sebastian?'

'I did indeed.'

'Why on earth did you do that?' asked Celia in genuine astonishment.

'Oh – I entirely lack leadership qualities,' said Sebastian lightly. 'I thought I'd rather be told what to do. I also greatly admire the British working man, and came to admire him even more out there. I don't think I would have enjoyed being in the officers' dugout nearly as much.'

'But – but it must have been so much harder,' she said, 'the conditions, the—'

'In some ways, perhaps. Physically yes. But emotionally, mentally it was easier. I just literally obeyed orders.'

'Where were you?'

'Oh – two of the big ones. Etapes, the Somme—'

'Oh. Well—' she stared at him, unable to think of anything to say.

'Then he got lucky,' said Paul Davis, 'got wounded. Got sent home. And had time to write this wonderful book. Let's talk about that shall we? Now I've had a further offer, Lady Celia.'

'You have?' She felt sick. She really could not, dared not, offer any more.

'Yes. Collins phoned me just before I left.'

'Paul,' said Sebastian, 'I'm not sure that I—'

'Sebastian, let me do this will you?' said Paul Davis, visibly struggling to sound cheerful and firm. 'I don't know why I let you come to this lunch. Very irregular.'

'It was because I insisted,' said Sebastian lightly, 'as you do actually very well know.' Celia looked at him; his eyes met hers in absolute complicity. And something else. Something she pushed to the bottom of her mind.

'OK, all right. Anyway, that's the situation, Lady Celia. They're very anxious to buy it. Talking about some quite large sums of money.'

'Well,' said Celia firmly, 'I understood that my offer had been accepted.' She didn't feel very firm. She knew the five hundred and fifty was far more than Lyttons could actually afford at that time, that it was an outrageous amount of money for a new author. But she also knew she had to have *Meridian*, had wanted to put down a sum that would guarantee the book for her. If necessary she had decided to do the unthinkable, and fund the offer from her own private income.

'It was. But I have to do my best for my client. I'm beginning to envisage some kind of an auction, as a matter of fact. Starting with your final bid, of course.'

'I'm afraid it is my final bid.' She felt sick; she could see *Meridian* moving away from her. She looked out of the window at the river, envisaged the book drifting down towards Greenwich, to the meridian line which was so central to its concept, taking Sebastian with it. Well, perhaps, it was for the best; she should never have made such a huge offer without Oliver's agreement; or at least LM's.

'In that case,' said Paul Davis regretfully, 'I'm afraid you're in danger of losing it. Because – ah, Lady Celia do you want to order?'

She nodded, picked up the menu. She felt terribly disappointed, near to tears. It was ridiculous; she'd lost books before.

'Sebastian, I think you said the oysters. And then—'

'No, just a moment,' said Sebastian, 'come back in a minute, would you?' he said to the waiter. 'Paul, I'm very unhappy about this. Very unhappy indeed. Lady Celia has already made a very generous offer and I am happy with it. She wants to publish the book. Provided that her ideas agree with mine, which is what I had thought this lunch was about, I want her to publish it. Can we please settle on that?'

'No,' said Celia sharply, 'no, I want to get this book on the right terms. For all of us. I don't want any favours – however kindly offered. What has Collins offered?'

Paul Davis looked at her. 'Six hundred. I have their letter here. Just in case you want to see it—'

'I'll pay that,' said Celia after a glance at the letter. She felt very sick. Six hundred pounds. About – she was good at mental arithmetic – thirty times the usual figure. Oliver's figure. What was she doing?

'Well – a higher figure would secure it. Collins are very keen. As you see—'

'Five hundred and fifty will be quite enough,' said Sebastian. 'That settles the matter, Paul.'

Paul Davis looked at him, and his eyes were very cold.

'Yes, all right,' he said finally, 'of course. You're the client.' He managed to laugh. 'It's your book, after all.'

'Yes,' said Sebastian, 'it is. And now it's Lady Celia's as well.'

They sat for the rest of the meal discussing publication dates, promotion, editing; illustration; Sebastian seemed extremely happy with all her proposals.

'Good,' said Paul Davis finally, pushing back his chair, wiping his rather blubbery mouth on his napkin. 'I'd better get back, draw up a contract. Thank you, Lady Celia. A delightful meal. I'll speak to you later, Sebastian.'

He walked out of the restaurant; they sat looking after him.

'Odious,' said Sebastian. 'I must find someone else.'

'He's a very good agent.'

'Is he?'

'Oh yes. But certainly not my favourite person,' said Celia.

'I'm glad to hear that,' he raised his glass, 'here's to our association.'

'Our association,' she said and smiled at him. 'That was very good of you. Letting Lyttons have the book. When you could have made even more money.'

'I would have let you have it for less,' said Sebastian.

'I know. But it never works, you know. I couldn't have you losing out. You'd have come to resent it. Resentment sours the best working relationship.'

'Hardly losing out.'

'Well – we'll get it back I'm sure. In sales. But meanwhile I'm extremely grateful.'

Sebastian Brooke smiled at her quickly: then his expression became serious, almost intense.

'I think you know why I did it,' he said.

'We've all got to go back to London,' said Barty, 'to live.'

'When?' said Adele.

'Why?' said Venetia.

'What's London?' said Jay.

'Anyway, how do you know?' said Adele.

'Your grandmother told me. After Christmas, she said.'

'Why should she tell you?'

'Why didn't she tell us?'

'Why didn't Daddy tell us?'

'Because I was talking to her about Billy,' said Barty, 'and she said I'd miss him when I went back to London. Which I will,' she added, and burst into tears.

The twins looked at her in silence and then at each other.

'We probably don't want to go,' said Venetia.

'Nor do I,' said Barty, blowing her nose, 'but we have to. The war is over, no more bombs.'

'Well, we can still stay here. Daddy is here.'

'He won't be soon. He'll be better and he'll want to go home.'

'How do you know?' asked Adele.

'Who told you that?' said Venetia.

They were fiercely jealous of Barty's relationship with their father.

'He did.'

'He didn't.'

'I don't believe you.'

Little Jay, sensing the hostility to Barty, his heroine, slipped his hand into hers. 'Will I like London?' he asked.

'I don't know,' said Barty.

Jay didn't: he hated it. He was utterly miserable. From the moment the taxi cab rolled away from Paddington Station and the excitement of being on the train was over, he could think of nothing but going back. He hated the grey streets, the noise of the traffic that drowned out the birdsong, the endless rows and rows of houses, with hardly a speck of space between them, the tiny patch behind the house in Keats Grove which was called a garden, the lack of things to do, the loss of his freedom.

At Ashingham he had run more or less wild; all day long he had followed Barty and the twins about from the house to the stables, out to the fields, back across the lawns to the house. While they had their lessons, he would go and talk to Billy, or to some of the men at the house, or he and Dorothy would go and look for eggs, or walk down to the village, or she would make him a fishing line and he would sit by the stream, waiting patiently for fish that never came. And when Giles came home for the holidays, he would follow him around instead of the girls, and Giles would give him and Barty cricket lessons and helped him to ride the old tricycle he had found in the stables which had once belonged to Aunt Celia. All the children ate their meals in the big kitchen at Ashingham; in the evenings he slept in a small room in between Barty's and the twins'. He was never lonely, never alone.

Now suddenly, he was alone all day with Dorothy: His mother, who was, in any case, a somewhat remote figure to him, left the house early in the morning, and usually returned after he had gone to bed. He was too young to go to school, so he and Dorothy went for walks to the Heath and to the shops, and sometimes to the public library, and that was the end of the entertainment. Once or twice a week he was allowed to go to tea with the twins, but even at their house, larger admittedly and with a bigger choice of toys, there was not a lot to do. Anyway, they had changed. They had all changed, even Barty. They wore smart frocks instead of the loose smocks they had all worn at Ashingham, or something called school uniform, skirts and jerseys and funny flat hats. They all went to school together and the twins had lots of friends who were also at the house, and didn't want to play with him, or else they weren't there at all, which was worse. Barty had lots of what she called homework to do, and although she did still read to him and play with him, he could see she was very busy herself.

Aunt Celia wasn't there either, she was at work with his mother, except at the weekends; the only person who still seemed to have time for him was the twins' father: Wol, as he and Barty called him. He still wasn't well enough to go to work, so he often read to Jay, and told him stories and helped him draw pictures. He didn't seem terribly happy; he often looked at Jay very sadly and sighed, and seemed to be thinking about something quite different. Once he said, 'We don't quite have a proper place here, do we, old chap?'

'I don't want a place here,' Jay said. He didn't quite know what Wol meant, but he could see that he felt lonely too. 'Can't we go back to the other one?'

And Wol had smiled rather sadly, hugged him close, and said he was afraid that wasn't possible, and they had sat there in silence for quite a long time.

'This is simply perfect,' said Sebastian. 'Marvellous. Exactly right. She's a clever girl, that art editor of yours.'

'Art Director. She's very proud of that.'

'Sorry. She's very clever, whatever she's called.'

They were in Celia's office, studying the design Gill had done for the dust jacket of *Meridian*. It was extraordinarily striking: a swirl of art nouveau-style graphics in the shape of a clock, all spelling out the word *Meridian* in different sizes and directions. The face of the clock was small: absolutely conventional, except that when you looked at it carefully, you saw that the numbers on it were not numbers but letters, spelling the word *Meridian* both backwards and forwards, with M replacing 12 and N 6. The hands of the clock were two androgynous figures, arms raised, palms together, set at six o'clock.

'Or rather N o'clock. And—' Gill had said happily, as she set it down in front of Celia the night before, 'we'll have colour, won't we? So I thought a wonderful greenish blue, interwoven with gold.'

'Marvellous,' said Celia, 'absolutely marvellous. And I presume the illustrations are in the same style.'

'Yes, only more directly illustrative, obviously. I've briefed the artist already. Full colour, I hope, and roughly one for each chapter?'

'Yes, and full colour, of course.' The more Celia read *Meridian*, the more she loved it, fell under its spell, became convinced of its truly enormous potential. And it was not just one book: Sebastian had already told her that he had many other stories with the same setting. She still had not told Oliver, or LM for that matter, what she had paid for it; either they would agree that it was worth it, or they would not, and since it was too late, there was nothing to be done about it.

The book was not just an enchanting story, but a brilliant fantasy, utterly original; set in a time zone which was at once parallel to, but out of reach of, our own. Everyone who read it, young and old, fell under its spell; even Jack, home at last from France, and staying temporarily at Cheyne Walk while he decided what to do with his life, said he found it impossible to put down.

'And he's only read about three books in his entire life,' said Celia, reporting this to Sebastian.

'Good. I can't wait to meet him. An illiterate Lytton. What a contradiction in terms.'

'You'd love him. Everyone does. Anyway, back to *Meridian*. One of its great joys, I think, is the way it assumes a certain literacy on the part of the children reading it. So the parents will approve, and the children will learn through it. And it has such humour, I love that the most. No, I think I love the small individual strands of the story the most.'

'Shall I tell you what I love about it the best?' said Sebastian, his extraordinary eyes on hers.

'Yes, what?'

'That you are going to publish it.'

'Oh, Sebastian,' she said, misunderstanding, for these were early days in their association, 'I'm so glad you like everything we are doing for it, I—'

'No, no,' he said, 'not that, although of course that is important. No, what I am most happy about is that it has led me to you.'

'Oh,' she said and stared at him, 'oh, I see.'

He smiled. 'And don't you love that about it, too, Celia?'

'Well,' she said, looking back down at the book, 'well, of course it's wonderful to be involved in such a work, a privilege—'

'I'm not talking about work,' he said, 'as you very well know.'

Flustered – a new condition for her – Celia pressed the buzzer on her telephone, and told Janet Gould to get Gill Thomas to come in.

'Mr Brooke is here, and wants to discuss the jacket.'

Sebastian's eyes met hers as she put the phone down.

'I don't think I do,' he said, 'but if that is what you want—'

She was in absolute denial about the whole thing, of course. Telling herself day after day that none of it was happening. That she was not looking forward intensely to the days when he would be at Lyttons, not becoming the kind of woman she disapproved of, watching herself as she moved and spoke and looked and laughed, concerned that she must be as graceful, as amusing, as desirable as it was possible for her to be. She did find herself thinking about him a great deal, but that was only because of his brilliance and the brilliance of the book he had brought to her. He did have an extraordinarily engaging and original mind, immense charm and exuded a most potent and impatient energy, seemed almost incapable of sitting still for more than a very short while, of keeping silent even, would constantly interrupt whoever was speaking to express a view, propose a new thought. And then of course he was extremely handsome, no one could deny that; neither could she deny his peculiarly intense sexuality. Nobody could. It was very powerful. But it didn't actually disturb her, it didn't divert her from whatever she was thinking or saying or doing – she just had to acknowledge that it was there. It would be foolish to do otherwise.

No. He had provided her with a wonderful professional opportunity, and she was enjoying that, along with his admittedly rather agreeable company. Besides, she needed a certain amount of distraction from the rest of her life, just at the moment. She could even argue that she deserved it.

'That was a very heavy sigh,' said Sebastian as he pulled on his coat, and she slid the edited manuscript of *Meridian* into her drawer.

'Oh – was it?'

'Yes. Anything wrong?'

'No! No not really. Well—'

'Want to tell me about it? Over lunch, perhaps.'

'There's nothing to tell.'

'Want to tell me about nothing over lunch?'

'I'm terribly busy.'

'So am I. But you are my editor, as well as my publisher. There must be many things which we could discuss over a plate of that rather good beef at Simpsons. Come on. You look tired. It'll do you good.'

She went. He was right; they did have a lot to discuss.

She was editing the book herself; not only because she felt no one else at Lyttons could possibly handle it, or appreciate its subtlety, but because she was afraid that no one else would realise how little editing it actually needed. The grammar was at times quirky, the construction of the plot just a little chaotic, but both suited the slightly anarchic nature of the story. She could not bear the thought of some earnest editor shortening Sebastian's long, untidy, yet entirely coherent sentences, or hauling one sequence before another, into strict chronological order when the whole charm of the tale was its higgledy-piggledy timespan. Those were the reasons she was doing it. No other.

'There's just one thing I thought I might suggest you changed,' she said to him, when they were settled into a table in the corner of the restaurant, 'and that's—'

'Are you tired?' he asked.

'What? Oh, yes. Yes, I am a bit. I think the war made us all tired.'

'It did. But now it's over, I feel very good.'

'Even your leg?'

'Oh no,' he said, and smiled at her, 'my leg is not very good.'

He had been shot in the leg while he was out in France in 1916; some rather brutal surgery had made it worse; he had developed an infection and finally been sent home to several more operations and a permanently damaged and painful knee.

'What's your knee?' he said now.

'What?'

'I said what's your knee? What's still hurting you?'
She was silent.
'Your husband?'
'No,' she said quickly. Too quickly.
'Your husband.' He smiled. 'Tell me about it.'
'No.'
'Why not?'
Again, silence.
'Tell me. Is he depressed?'
'He – not exactly. No. He seems quite cheerful. No, not cheerful. But not miserable either. Just—'
'Detached?'
'Yes,' she said, 'yes, that's exactly it. He doesn't seem interested in anything. Except himself.'
'Not even you?'
'Certainly not me.'
'Well that sounds perfectly normal,' said Sebastian. He sat back and looked at her. 'I did it myself, to a degree. He's had a hideous time, after all. He's probably just cut himself off from everything. Retreated into himself. Defence mechanism and all that.'
'I know. Of course I know. And I have been – tried to be anyway – very patient. But he doesn't want to talk about anything. Except himself. Not Lyttons, not the children, not the house, which is in a terrible state, needs a lot of work on it, as does the Lyttons building come to that, and most certainly not me. Not even what he's been through. It's – well it's difficult. Because I have to carry on doing everything, making decisions which really he should be sharing now. Very difficult.'
Sebastian looked at her and smiled.
'Dare I suggest, dear Lady Celia, that you might find it even more difficult when he does start taking an interest in everything again.'

'Hallo Marjorie.'
Barty stood in the doorway of the house in Line Street, and smiled rather tentatively. It was Saturday; she was allowed to come on her own now, on the bus. Celia encouraged it, encouraged independence of any kind. Barty and the twins came home on the bus from school together most days, the twins sitting in the front with their friends, giggling, Barty sitting behind them, pretending not to care. It wasn't exactly easy; she was supposed to be responsible for them, and they would never do what she said.
'Don't go on the top of the bus,' she'd say, 'it's raining.'

'We want to,' they would say, running up the stairs.

'This isn't our stop,' she'd call, another time, seeing them on the platform, waiting to get off.

'We want to get off here with Susie. We can walk the rest of the way.'

So she'd have to get off too, and walk behind them, watching their identical heads together, talking, shutting her out. They had got much worse again since they'd all been back in London.

And then Nanny would upbraid them for getting their uniforms wet, or scuffing their boots, but she would upbraid Barty more. 'You're supposed to be in charge of them, Barty, you're older than they are, do try to be more sensible.'

Useless to say anything: quite useless.

They all went to the same school: Helen Wolff's School for Girls in South Audley Street. It was a good school, and quite famous. Both Violet, Mrs Keppel's daughter and Vita Sackville West had been pupils there. Celia was less concerned with this than with the excellence of the education. She was determined that her girls should have exactly the same chances scholastically as Giles.

Barty, benefitting from her years with Miss Adams and from her own natural abilities, went straight to the top of her class; the twins stayed comfortably near the bottom of theirs. They were clever, but very lazy, and life was too much fun to be spoiled by reading books and learning mathematical tables. Within days they had become hugely popular, sought after by all their peers; consequently they were over-confident, disobedient, cheeky to Nanny, impertinent with their teachers, and overbearing with Barty; the happy, ordered discipline at Ashingham might never have been.

At first Barty had no trouble with the other girls in her class; they liked her, and she had become more like them, her background converted into something very close to theirs, both by the years with the Lyttons and by her experiences during the war. She was good at games, too; her prowess in the gymnasium and on the netball court helped to make her popular. But then the teachers began to tell the twins that they should be more like her: should work hard, pay attention, do their homework, learn their tables.

'Your sister sets you such a good example,' said their form teacher one day, when they, had both done spectacularly badly in a spelling test, 'why can't you follow it?'

The twins looked at one another and something passed between them.

'She's not our sister,' said Adele, 'she just lives with us.'

273

'She's someone our mother brought home when she was little,' said Venetia.

The word spread fast through the school: that Barty was some kind of foundling, rescued from the street by the bountiful Lady Celia Lytton, forced on her own children, who had to be nice to her, share their toys, give up a bedroom even. It was the sort of story little girls love: romantic with great scope for manipulation. Within days Barty had become an object of curiosity: of admiration to a few kinder girls, of derision to most of them.

'Is it true,' one of them said, 'you slept in a box with three of your brothers?'

'I slept with them when I was very small, yes,' said Barty. She was not about to betray her family, 'but in a bed, not a box.'

'And you all lived in a cellar?'

'Not exactly a cellar.'

'Not exactly? What does that mean?'

'Our rooms were at the bottom of the house. In – in the basement.'

'Your rooms? How many did you have?'

'Two,' said Barty steadfastly. She opened her desk, pulled out some books. She knew what lay ahead of her now; the game was up.

It wasn't as bad as before; she did have a few friends, was asked to a few other houses. But most of the time she was either ostracised or tormented. As before, she sought solace in work, in doing well. For the most part it didn't help her; she was nicknamed Swot, 'At least it's better than Snipe,' she said to Giles. When her name was read out, almost always at the top of the class, or as a prizewinner, the other girls would raise their eyebrows to the ceiling, make faces at one another, whisper behind her back. She pretended not to care: she cared dreadfully.

'Oh – hallo,' said Marjorie now, 'what are you doing here?'

'I came to see you,' said Barty, 'of course. It's Saturday. And next week we're all going down to Ashingham for Easter, so I'll be seeing Billy. I thought you might have some messages for him.'

'Shouldn't think so,' said Marjorie, 'he's gone posh too, hasn't he? What's he want to hee – ar' she stressed the h, elongated the rest of the word, 'hee–ar from us for?'

'Marjorie, that isn't fair. Of course he wants to hear from you. Don't be silly. Where's Mum?'

'Down the shop. With Mary. Trying to get some bread.'

'Trying? Why is it difficult?'

'Because, your ladyship, we ain't got no money. So she has to get yesterday's bread. Queue for it.'

'Oh. Oh, I see. Well, I'll go and find her then. Thanks. Is Frank about?'

'No. No he's gone out. With his girlfriend.'

'Oh. Oh, well, that's nice. Do you like her?'

Marjorie shrugged. 'She's all right. Bit stuck up. You'd get on with her allright, I s'pose.'

Barty gave up and went to find her mother.

Sylvia was standing in the queue. Mary had disappeared, gone to play with another child. She looked exhausted and very thin. Every so often she coughed.

'Mum! Hallo. Are you all right?'

'Oh, hallo, Barty dear. You've grown again. What a lovely frock.'

'Oh – thank you. Yes it's new.'

She looked down at the frock; she supposed it was pretty. Navy blue wool, with a tucked bodice and a dropped waist, the hem just below her knees. Aunt Celia had taken her and the twins shopping a week or so earlier, ordered dozens of things for the spring and summer for them from Woollands, pressing them to say what they wanted, saying how lovely it was to have some choice again. Barty thought it was awful, just made life more difficult; she never thought about clothes, she had no interest in them. The twins, on the other hand, had spent hours in the various departments, picking out dresses, skirts, blouses, light coats, white socks, ankle-strap shoes, straw bonnets. It had been dreadfully boring. When she grew up, Barty thought, she would be like LM and wear the same clothes every day.

'Wish I had some new frocks,' said Sylvia, 'all mine are worn right through.'

'I could—' Barty stopped— 'could ask Aunt Celia,' she had been going to say. But she knew her mother wouldn't like it. Wouldn't take any more what she called charity.

'It's enough for me to know you've got plenty of everything,' she was always saying, 'nice clothes, good food. Something less to worry about.'

Barty supposed she was pleased about that; but she hated hearing it, really. It simply spelled out that she could never, ever return to her family and be an expensive extra worry to them all. That was the worst thing really: knowing that she didn't belong to the Lyttons, and that the people to whom she did belong didn't want her.

'You all right, Mum?' she said again.

'Oh – yes. I suppose so. Life's a bit difficult. But then, when wasn't it? Nothing new in that.'

She sighed, then suddenly put out a hand on the wall of the shop to steady herself. Barty looked at her, alarmed.

'Mum! You look awful.'

'I'm all right,' said Sylvia, 'just a bit dizzy.'

'Look, you go back to the house, I'll wait here.'

'Would you, dear? That's kind. Two loaves if you can get them. Mind they're yesterday's, though. Here's the money.'

Mr Phelps at the baker's was one of the few people in Line Street who treated Barty as if she was perfectly ordinary, still belonged there. Most of them stared at her as if she were some scientific specimen to be studied.

'Hallo Barty. My, you've grown again. Where's your mum, then? Could have sworn she was in my queue.'

'She went home. She didn't feel very well.'

He sighed. 'No, she's not too good. Doesn't eat properly and that's a nasty cough she's got. Not enough money, that's her problem. Her and all the widows. Pensions are an insult. Shocking. Be surprised if she gets more 'n ten bob. I don't know how she manages at all. Here, take a couple of these rolls as well. No I don't want nothing for them. They're stale, but they're all right.'

Barty took them back to the house, made her mother some tea, spread some dripping on one of the rolls for her, and sat with her for a while. Later that night, lying between her freshly laundered sheets, in one of her lawn nightdresses, with her new frocks hanging in her cupboard, she worried about her mother buying stale bread because she couldn't afford fresh, and coughing endlessly, even in her sleep, according to Marjorie. And she thought, too, that it was really no wonder her brothers and sisters all resented her so bitterly.

'You seemed to enjoy that.' Celia smiled at Oliver across the dining table.

'Yes. I really did. I'm a little weary of fish, but that was particularly nice. The new cook is very good. Although I notice Jack is out more and more frequently. In search of good red meat, I daresay. I can't say I'm sorry. It's nice having the house to ourselves. Does it bother you, him living here?'

'Not at all. I like it. Honestly. But he must be awfully bored.'

'I'm sure he'll find something to do soon. I must say I'm absolutely astonished he's so determined to leave the army. It always seemed his natural habitat.'

'I think he's just totally disillusioned with it,' said Celia. 'It was coming on during the war. He told me when he was home on leave that time.'

And was silent, remembering that night, when she had been so tempted, the first time, indeed, she had ever properly felt desire for any man other than Oliver. And now – well now, of course he was home, so she wouldn't. Couldn't. Wouldn't even consider it. She looked at Oliver and smiled quickly.

'Anyway, how do you feel generally?'

'Oh, pretty good. Yes. Thank you. In fact, you know, I was thinking today that I really would like to start reading some manuscripts. And even look at some publishing schedules. There. How's that?'

'Oliver, it's wonderful.' She was genuinely pleased, at the thought, not only that he must be feeling so much stronger, but also of having him even half way back with her at Lyttons.

'Yes. So obviously I'm properly on the mend at last. I'd better start with Mr Brooke's work, I suppose since it is clearly so important to our Christmas schedule.'

'Oh – yes.' She was still nervous about that: about the amount of time and money invested in it. 'But there are other, more pressing works for you to give your attention to, Oliver. A new collection of detective stories, and—'

'I'll read those too. How's that? No, I've definitely been getting bored. So it's a very good sign. I'm sorry, my darling, you've had to wait so long for me. But I did feel dreadfully ill and weak.'

'There's no need to apologise. I've managed. Goodness, you earned a rest. And you did nearly die, after all.'

This had only really emerged during the months he had been home; he had lost an enormous amount of blood, and had actually developed septicaemia and been given the last rites by an over-zealous Catholic padre. It was something of a miracle he had survived. His stomach was permanently damaged, would never completely recover.

'Yes,' he said now, 'yes, I did. And I often wished I had.'

'I know,' she said. She smiled at him, hoping disloyally that he wouldn't start on the reminiscences which were so painful to hear, but obviously so important to his emotional recovery. At first she had felt proud that he would tell her, infinitely glad that at last he was talking. More recently, their constant repetition had made them harder to bear.

'But just lately I've felt more – grateful. That I didn't die, I mean. Grateful to be alive, even.'

She was surprised; this was the most positive thing he had said since he came home. Obviously something had shifted in him, had made him feel differently. 'Oliver, that's marvellous. I'm so glad.'

'Yes.' He smiled at her again. 'So, before you know where you are, I may be back at Lyttons, being an absolute pest.'

'Of course you won't be a pest,' she said. 'It'll be marvellous to have you back again. Helping me—'

'Helping you! Darling, I hope I'll be doing rather more than help you.' His voice was quite suddenly stronger, and just tinged with a warning note. She remembered Sebastian's words and smiled involuntarily.

'Of course you will,' she said, 'Of course. But you know what I mean. It's been a very lonely struggle.'

'You had LM.'

'I did have LM, Oliver, we had each other. I don't know how either of us would have coped without the other. But our areas of expertise are so different, we both had to make decisions on our own. She about financial matters, I about editorial—'

'Yes, yes of course,' he said, She was losing him again; he looked exhausted. 'I think I've done enough work for one evening.' He managed a smile. 'But it's been a beginning. I look forward to a great deal more. Now I think I might go up to bed, If you don't mind. Good night, my darling.'

'Good night, Oliver.'

She went to the foot of the stairs with him, kissed him, watched him go slowly up.

They had slept in separate rooms ever since he came home; he was often awake and in pain during the night and liked to read. It was sensible, they had agreed, the only thing to do really. But he had not once suggested he might want to lie with her, hold her in his arms. Let alone make love to her.

CHAPTER 16

'No decision from Segal, then?' said Robert casually.

'No,' said John, equally casually. They smiled at one another: careful, slightly awkward smiles. They were waiting for a decision on a contract to build a department store for Jerome Segal on Sixth Avenue to rival Saks and Henry Bendel in size and splendour. All had been going well, and they had been given several nods and winks from Segal to suggest that the contract would be theirs, had indeed spent many hours with him, enduring a series of over-detailed briefings, knew exactly where the ladies' lingerie would be sold, and the soft furnishings and even where the restrooms might be found, when a sudden silence had fallen.

The day when Jerome Segal had assured them contracts would be exchanged had passed, and a tactful telephone call was met first with, 'Sorry Robert, just a hiccup from one of my directors,' and then a certain evasiveness, a failure to return calls, a polite note asking for a week's grace, 'Just to get the last i's dotted and t's crossed.'

The week was up that day, and the day had already reached afternoon; neither Robert nor John would have admitted it, but they were nervous. They had invested a great deal of time and money in the project.

'I think after this we'll go back to purely speculative development,' John said lightly, 'simpler.'

When Robert's secretary finally put through a call from Jerome Segal, it was not to give them the go ahead but to ask for a more detailed breakdown of costings:

'Mr Segal,' John said, struggling to keep exasperation out of his voice, 'the breakdown could hardly be more detailed. If you remember, I even quoted for flower holders in the ladies' powder room.'

There was a silence: then, 'Yes, I realise that, John. But I've had some questions asked by our backers on the cost of the raw materials – the overall cost of the cement for example – perhaps you could break that down further for me.'

'I don't like this at all,' John said to Robert, reaching for the Segal file, 'not one bit. Nit-picking at this stage. I sense trouble. Even if we do get the contract.'

'Well if we don't, we can console ourselves with the thought,' said Robert, 'that we've escaped a difficult client. Now, let me have another look at those figures for the steel. Yes – it is a little high. We could probably pare that down.'

'You're so bloody optimistic, Robert,' said John, 'your mother should have called you Pollyanna.'

'I don't think it had been written then,' said Robert. He grinned at John; it was true, optimism was one of his outstanding – and valuable – characteristics.

However, in this instance, it was unfounded; the contract to build Segal's department store went to another company, by the name of Hagman Betts which no one had ever heard of.

'New,' said Robert, 'hungry. Probably running at a loss. Don't despair, John. It's only one development, for God's sake. Three more dead certs in the pipeline. Let's go out for a drink, forget about it.'

However, one of the three dead certs also went to Hagman Betts, and a second to another young firm called Stern Rubin.

'Don't worry,' Robert said to John, 'they can't keep this up. Can't afford it. They'll have to start charging more realistically soon. Then we'll be all right. We're hardly on the breadline now. Got enough to see us through a lean few months. Cheer up.'

But, as he drove home to Sutton Place, he didn't feel particularly cheerful himself. In fact he felt – what? Uneasy best described it. Without being quite sure why: it was true what he had said, they had plenty of reserves to drawn on, plenty of other clients. He was probably just tired.

'You look gloomy,' said Maud, as he walked into the snug. She was drawing.

'Oh, I'm all right. What are you drawing?'

'A house. Look.'

He looked. 'More of a skyscraper, I'd say.'

'Maybe.'

'We'll have you running Brewer Lytton yet,' said Robert.

'I'd like that.'

'So would I.'

He often fantasised about it; she loved nothing better than playing with her dolls' houses, building with her bricks, and all her best drawings were of the Manhattan skyline.

'Specially my daddy's areas,' she said solemnly to her teacher, when she had admired them.

She was seven now, still enchanting, astonishingly unspoilt; she went to a girls' day school in Manhattan, where her favourite lesson, by far, was arithmetic. 'Very suitable for an architect,' her doting father would say. She was still small for her age, and very striking with her mass of red-gold die-straight hair, and her large green eyes.

She and her father were all the world to one another; they dined together each night, took it in turns to wake one another with a glass of orange juice in the morning, discussed their respective days solemnly over breakfast. Robert whose social life had never recovered from Jeanette's death, led a quiet life; most evenings he was at home.

At the weekends they went to the house he had built in Montauk, Long Island, a dazzling white creation called Overview, right on the beach; the site carefully picked to be not too near Laurence's mansion. He had written to Robert when he had heard he was looking for a property, suggesting that it might be more comfortable for them both if they were not close neighbours; Robert did not reply to the letter, but worried about its spirit, and the unpleasantness that might ensue for Maud. Just the same he loved Long Island and wanted for her the pleasures it could offer: the sailing, the riding, the walks along the shore. In the event, they very seldom met Laurence, and then only at an occasional luncheon party, where they exchanged distantly courteous greetings and moved on.

Jamie was a frequent visitor; now that he was older, he found it easier to ignore the psychological pressures Laurence put on him, and to be openly friendly towards his stepfather. He was eighteen, at last free of his spots, tall and athletic, he was a fine tennis and soccer player, and although less academic than Laurence, he was going to Harvard in September to read history. He was teaching Maud to play tennis on the court at Overview; she still absolutely adored him, would do anything for him, looked for no greater happiness than to spend time with him at the weekends, often sitting on the deck at the front of the house in silence, simply watching him as he read the paper, of dozed in the sun. He was very fond of her too: had been grateful for her uncomplicated love over the years, her refusal to be distressed by Laurence's behaviour. Often, now, he came to stay at Sutton Place as well, ashamed of his early refusal to move in, and occupied the small suite Robert had planned for him so carefully when he had built the house.

'I wish we could be married, Jamie,' Maud had said and he had laughed and said he thought she was going to marry Kyle Brewer.

'I was, but Daddy says he's got a girlfriend. Anyway, I think I'd rather marry you. I know you better.'

'Well, I'd like it too, but I don't think it's possible, we're brother and sister and that's that.'

'Well, I shall be very jealous of whoever you do marry,' she said, 'very jealous indeed,' Jamie said he had no intention of marrying for a long time and when he did, Maud could certainly have a hand in choosing the girl.

'This flu's a nightmare,' said Celia to LM.

It was a brilliant May morning; she was standing at her office window, looking at the extraordinary sight of people walking about the streets of London in the sunshine, wearing masks.

'I just can't believe it. And the worst thing, according to Dr Perring is that, it mostly affects healthy young adults. What the war didn't take, the influenza will. I'm wondering if we shouldn't send the children out of London again. I'm really frightened about it. Oliver says I'm overreacting, but there have already been a lot of deaths.'

'Well Jay would like that,' said LM with a sigh, 'going out of London again, I mean. He's so bored and miserable, misses the other children dreadfully. He doesn't look nearly so well, and he's wearing Dorothy out.'

'When can he go to school?'

'Oh, not for another nine months. Even then, only in the mornings. He's terribly lonely, and he's being extremely difficult. And the bed-wetting is worse than ever. I don't know what to do with him.'

'Poor little chap. If I had one that age, I'd suggest they joined up for lessons in the morning or something. But, I don't.'

'No.' LM was silent; they were both thinking of the lost baby girl.

'Anyway,' said Celia, with a quick, over-bright smile, 'I'm sure Jay will settle down soon. He's been through a big upheaval I know, but children are so adaptable. What does Dorothy think about it?'

'I think she's quite worried. He's started saying he's going to run away. I suppose I could spend more time with him, but – well, what use is a rather over-aged mother to a four-year-old?'

'A lot,' said Celia firmly, 'but maybe not for fun and games. He'll be fine once he's at school, LM. Try not to worry. Anyway, I'll ask Mama what she thinks about having the children down there, at least for the summer holidays, away from the germs. We can send the nannies. That would cheer Jay up, wouldn't it?'

'Short-term, yes,' said LM.

'LM, I've learned to think short-term. So should you. Anything else is too complicated. I can't bear to look more than a day ahead at the moment. Everything seems to have got worse rather than better since Oliver came home, I don't know why—'

'Is he being very difficult?'

'Very. He's like a spoilt, bored child, kicking the furniture.

Demanding I play with him – well talk to him – and then, when I do, not wanting to hear anything I say. Oh, I shouldn't criticise him behind his back. I know he's had a horrible time. But I could so do with some support, and instead of him being the life-raft I was longing for, he's—'

'Making an ever bigger hole in the bottom of the ship?'

'Bit harsh,' said Celia laughing, 'but – well – yes, something like that. Anyway, he's going to start coming in regularly, two days a week, starting next week. I'm sure that'll be better.'

'It might,' said LM, 'on the other hand it might be worse. To begin with, at any rate.'

'Yes, that's what Sebastian said. Funnily enough.'

'Did he? That's a very astute observation. For an outsider.'

'Oh, I don't know,' said Celia quickly. 'It's fairly obvious really, isn't it?' She started rustling through some papers on her desk. 'I mean, goodness, LM, you should see all those letters and diaries that have come in for *New Lives for Old*. One of the most interesting things is how angry and upset so many of these women are now, with the men coming back, and assuming they'll just step aside. It's an outrage.'

'I don't suppose the men see it quite like that,' said LM.

The men didn't of course: it was a new conflict facing the nation. The country fit for heroes, promised by Lloyd George, was actually seething with repressed rage, and social and sexual injustice. Women were expected to vacate the positions they had occupied so successfully during the war, and return meekly to their homes and their husbands. The fact that those aged over twenty-nine had at last been given the vote did not go all the way towards placating them. And men, who returned from the front severely disabled, found themselves being given pensions which were at best modest, and at worst an outrage.

There was a degree of racial tension and hostility, largely directed at the West Indian troops recruited during the war; the demobilisation programme was ill-planned; the Ministry of Reconstruction, set up to oversee a return to peace in all its complexity, was disbanded early in the summer of 1919 when the need for it was at its peak. Rocketing prices, the direct result of ending government controls, combined with an absence of any real rise in wages, led to serious industrial unrest; including, perhaps most seriously, in the police force in Liverpool. This led to looting, violence and at least one death. Added to that mixture was the hugely increased strength of the Labour movement, which had grown so strongly during the war, and made England socially a rather unstable place.

In Line Street, Sylvia Miller was struggling against ill health, and trying to manage on her widow's pension, with one son back from the war embittered and unemployed, and another employed but seriously disabled, was just one among millions who had sacrificed almost everything and now were asking themselves what it had all been for.

Oliver and Sebastian sat facing one another on the leather sofas in Celia's office: the sofas which, despite Oliver's remonstrances, she had put in place expressly for the purpose of entertaining authors in her first week at Lyttons so long ago. She had moved to another office since then, something rather grander, next door to Oliver's in fact; but the sofas were the same, their gleaming glossy surface turned rather dull and dark, scuffed and scratched in places, but still infinitely comfortable and making the office pleasingly club-like. They were part of Lyttons' history now, those sofas. This was where Celia sat far into the night, reading manuscripts, where she and LM had slept occasionally during the war, where she encouraged her staff to sit when she had news for them, good or bad, where authors and agents discussed terms, publication, or editing decisions, where manuscripts were sometimes piled so high that they towered over the sofa backs.

They were part of Celia's personal history, too: Jago had sat on one of those sofas the first and last time she had met him, the night he had come to her for help. Here too, she had comforted LM on the few occasions she had seen her weaken, here LM had done the same for her; here she herself had shed tears of loneliness and fear during the long years of Oliver's absence. Here she and Sebastian had sat on that magical day when he came in with *Meridian*, and in his beautiful, musical voice, quite literally, she often thought now, bewitched her; and this was where she had been when the call came through from her mother, telling her that Oliver was alive and safe.

She looked at the pair of them now, at Oliver and Sebastian. Oliver, leafing through the promotional plans for *Meridian*, was frail, thin, strangely colourless, palpably weary; Sebastian, strong, vivid was pushing his hands occasionally through his hair in the impatient way he had, glancing up at her with his extraordinary eyes from time to time, smiling at her encouragingly. She struggled hard, so hard, not to compare them: Neither them nor her feelings for them. Oliver whom she loved so very much; Sebastian who was – was just unsettling her, disturbing her equilibrium.

'It's a wonderful piece of work,' said Oliver, smiling gently at him, 'truly wonderful. We are very lucky to have it.'

'Thank your wife,' said Sebastian, 'she fought off all comers. Although,' he added, 'I looked at the publishing houses of London and thought that of all of them, I would feel most at home with yours.'

'Good,' said Oliver, 'I'm glad. We must be doing something right.

Well, what can I add to this discussion? The publishing schedule looks fine, and—'

'No need to add anything,' said Sebastian, 'except your approval of the book, of course. I'm so delighted you're happy with it.'

Oliver looked at him, and Celia, intercepting that look, saw just for a moment a faint glimpse of the pre-war Oliver, the one she had done battle with so many times, brilliant yes, innovative certainly, but quietly arrogant, intent on holding his own position. He would not like to be told he might have nothing to add.

'Oh, I have a few suggestions,' he said now. 'I wonder if you're quite happy with the jacket illustration? It's very adult. And—'

'I'm ecstatically happy with it,' said Sebastian, 'and besides, I do agree with you, it is very adult but that's because the book is for rather adult children.'

'I think that might be a mistake,' said Oliver, 'I personally think this will appeal to a huge range of children, but remember it will be mostly adults buying it. They may feel it looks a little alienating for a children's book.'

'Oliver, I don't agree,' said Celia, 'there's nothing alienating about the jacket, it's beautiful. Magical. Anyone would be drawn to it—'

'I understand everything you're saying,' said Oliver, 'that both of you are saying, indeed. But I also know that there is a danger in making assumptions about such things. I have a long experience in books and—'

'I do know that,' said Celia, 'of course. And so do I. But this book is unique, it's like no other, it breaks entirely new ground. And I certainly don't want some infantile illustration on the jacket—'

'I'm not proposing an infantile illustration,' said Oliver coldly, 'Naturally. But I would like to see some alternatives. Something less abstract.'

'I really doubt that I should like that as much,' said Sebastian, 'but we can certainly try, I suppose.'

'Yes, indeed,' said Oliver, 'I think we should. And of course we won't proceed without your approval. Mind you,' he smiled at Sebastian, then glanced at Celia, the smile fading, 'we don't usually allow our authors to make such decisions. You are very much in the minority.'

'Well, that's good to know,' said Sebastian. 'It's certainly one of the things I would have looked for in my publisher. To allow a writer no say in the design of his jacket illustration seems to me like allowing a parent no say in the name of his child. Heavens, look at the time. I must go. Thank you for your time, Mr Lytton. I appreciate your making the effort to see me. I know you've had a rotten time. But it's good to know you must be feeling a little better.'

'Yes, indeed,' said Oliver, 'I am. And nothing is proving better medicine that becoming involved in the company again. I have greatly enjoyed this afternoon. Goodbye, Mr Brooke. Thank you for letting us publish your book.'

'Thank your wife,' said Sebastian, 'as I said. She has been the architect of the whole thing. And is a most marvellous editor, too.'

'Have you experience of other editors?' asked Oliver, mildly. 'I understood this was your first work.'

'It is. But I have a great friend who is a writer. She has told me horror stories about editors.'

'I see. Well, there are no such stories about Celia. As far as I know. Are there, Celia?'

'No,' said Celia. 'no, I don't think so.'

She wondered why suddenly she felt so chilled; chilled and depressed.

'So you'll brief that girl to do some alternative jackets, will you?' said Oliver when Sebastian had gone. 'Less abstract, I think. They can still be very beautiful, in keeping with the book.'

'Oliver, I really don't think it's a good idea. Everyone loves that jacket, it's so sophisticated and original.'

'Precisely. And this is a children's book. Shall I talk to her — what's she called — or will you?'

'Oh — I will,' said Celia hastily. 'Gill is her name. Gill Thomas, she's exceedingly talented.'

'James Sharpe will be back with us shortly,' said Oliver, 'he's had a lucky war. Unlike Richard, poor devil.'

Richard Douglas had been killed at Passchendaele; Celia who had loved him dearly, despite many stormy editorial meetings and clashes of will and opinion, had been horribly distressed by the news.

'Yes. Er — Oliver, about James Sharpe. I know he was Lyttons' art director, but now—'

'Darling, if you will forgive me, I think I might go home now,' said Oliver, 'I feel dreadfully tired. But it has been the most marvellous tonic, coming in today. And I like Sebastian Brooke very much. Nice chap. Hugely talented, obviously. I look forward to working with him. Tell me, Celia, how much exactly did you have to offer to secure the book?'

'Well — quite a lot. I did try to talk to you about it, but you were still feeling very frail.'

'I presume though, you discussed it with LM?'

'No,' said Celia, 'actually, no, I didn't. I didn't get a chance. I had to make a fast decision. Paul Davis was saying that he had half London after it, and clearly that was true; several people have told me how lucky we are to have it.'

'I wouldn't trust Paul Davis if he told me night followed day,' said Oliver, 'dreadful fellow. I'm surprised Brooke is with him.'

'In that instance, Oliver, I had to trust him. I felt I had to anyway.'

'So—'

Celia took a deep breath and said, 'Well—' then salvation arrived in the form of Janet Gould.

'Daniels is asking if you want him to wait here, with the car, Mr Lytton, or if there's anything else he can do, either for you or Lady Celia.'

'Oh, no. No I want him to take me home.' said Oliver, 'tell him I'll be along imediately. Celia, we can continue this discussion at home. Unless you want to come with me now.'

'No I can't possibly come with you now,' said Celia, not sure if she was amused or outraged at this suggestion, 'it's only half past four. I have an incredible amount to do yet. I'll see you at dinner. Now be sure to have a rest, won't you? You do look exhausted.'

'Yes, yes. I will. Thank you, Mrs Gould.' He smiled at her; his frail, weary smile. It was beginning to irritate Celia, that smile.

'How are you Mr Lytton? It's good to have you back in the office.'

'Thank you. I'm feeling much stronger now, every day. And I shall be in at least twice a week, from now on. I can't tell you how much I'm looking forward to it.'

After he had gone, Celia sat staring out of the window, trying to analyse where her sense of cold and depression had come from. It wasn't from Oliver interfering in the jacket design; it wasn't the thought of James Sharpe coming back; it wasn't even the thought of having to tell Oliver what she had paid by way of an advance for *Meridian*. Suddenly she knew. It was Sebastian's casual reference to his great friend who had horror stories to tell about editors. A female friend. Well, it was quite absurd of her to feel that. Of course he would have a female friend. He would have a hundred probably. Ridiculous of her to even think that he might not. She knew so little about him. Whether or not he was married, even, had ever been married. He was a complete mystery to her. Well, that was all right. Perfectly all right. He was one of her authors, nothing more. His friends, male or female, were of no importance whatsoever. She decided to cheer herself up by going to see her dressmaker.

For the upper classes at least, England was returning to her former self; the seals on the cellar doors of Buckingham Palace had been broken on Armistice night and the court had been revived with all its pre-war splendour. The great London houses, including the Beckenhams' in Clarges Street, had been reopened, and the dust sheets shaken off, cellars re-stocked, domestic staff re-employed.

Celia needed day dresses, evening dresses, coats, shoes, and, above all, hats; the first Derby, followed by the first Ascot since the war were only a few weeks away and she had nothing to wear, absolutely nothing at all. She was going to both with her parents and her sister Caroline – Oliver having a marked aversion to horses in general and race meetings, however glamorous, in particular. She was looking forward to it enormously, desperate for some fun. She and her father were also going to one of the first post-war royal garden parties; Lord Beckenham particularly enjoyed those, and would wander round happily, teacup in hand, studying not only the young female guests, but the female palace servants, who were often rather pretty. Lady Beckenham had also been asked to give a dinner party for a court ball towards the end of June. And then there would be Giles's first Fourth of June at Eton. That would be the best fun; the twins and Barty would come to that, she must get them something really very special to wear.

Serious as Celia was about her career, passionately as she loved her work, deeply as she still believed in, if not was quite able to adhere to, the socialist ideals of her youth, she also adored the official social scene, even while acknowledging its foolishness; she loved its colour, its glamour, its rituals. The fact that Oliver disapproved of it, was, this year at least, although she would not admit it, even to herself, an added factor in her enjoyment. He was happy for her to entertain at Cheyne Walk, indeed he greatly valued her skills as a literary hostess, but the pleasure she took in attending purely social events, her love of gossip and her mild addiction to such publications as the *Tatler* and *The Daily Sketch*, even her devotion to her wardrobe, all mildly distressed him.

Before the war he had reluctantly attended a few of the events, had even occasionally submitted to the rigours of court dress, with its velvet cutaway coat, knee breeches, silk stockings and cocked hat, but his experiences in the war, the horrors he had witnessed, had made such superficial formalities abhorrent to him, a betrayal of the person he had become, and he told Celia so. She had said she understood, and would not dream of forcing him, while adding that she did hope he wouldn't object to her own attendance. Oliver, knowing that an objection would be in any case overruled, said that of course he would not.

He was, however, furiously angry about the five hundred and fifty pounds advance. It was a long time since she had seen him so angry.

'How could you possibly commit that sort of money to one book, when by your own admission, Lyttons is in considerable financial difficulties? Without clearing it with anyone at all—'

'Oliver, there was no one to clear it with.'

'LM was there.'

'She was, but—'

'But what?'

'I told you. I had to make this decision very quickly.'

'Oh Celia, for heaven's sake. You should never be rushed on something like that. You know perfectly well.'

'Oliver, don't talk to me as if I was some junior clerk. And, with respect, you weren't there. You haven't been there for some time—'

'I hope you aren't blaming me for that.'

'Don't be ridiculous. Of course I'm not blaming you. I'm simply saying that I knew exactly the situation, the difficulties we were in. As you do not. And I knew we had to have this book. Well, a big book. A book which would sell in huge numbers and gain us prestige. It was essential.'

'I find it hard to believe that it was sensible give five hundred and fifty pounds to an unknown author, if we were in financial difficulties.'

'Oliver, don't over-simplify. He may be unknown, but you can see as well as I can that the book is extraordinary. The whole situation was extraordinary. The war was over, things were getting back to normal, everyone was fighting over properties. We had to be in there with a proper chance.'

'Well,' he said, after a silence, 'I am deeply unhappy about it. Deeply. I don't know how you can possibly justify it. Given the problems we have.'

'I think I can justify it,' she said, 'but you have to trust me. Let me prove it to you.'

'But, Celia, even if I did – even if you are right – the figures are very bad. I've been looking at them. The staff are going to be asking for wage increases. Prices are soaring. What you've given Sebastian Brooke represents two, or even three clerks' wages for a year. How can you justify that to LM and to me?'

'I – can't I suppose,' she said.

'Is it too late to withdraw this offer?'

'Oliver, of course it's too late. The book is being typeset now, the jacket has been designed—'

'It's being redesigned.'

She ignored this with an effort. 'Editing is under way, we would lose face, quite apart from it being an extremely unprofessional thing to do.'

'He seems fairly committed to us. Do you think he would take a lower advance anyway?'

'Oliver, no. I couldn't possibly ask him to do that. It would be an appalling thing to do. If—' she hesitated.

'Yes?'

'If you are absolutely set against this advance being paid, I am prepared to find it out of my own bank account.'

He stared at her; his face looked even more gaunt than usual.

'You would find five hundred and fifty pounds out of your own income, to pay Sebastian Brooke?'

'Yes. Yes I would. Doesn't that illustrate the extent of my belief in *Meridian*?'

He still stared at her. There was a very odd expression in his eyes.

'I'm not sure what it illustrates,' he said, 'but I am certainly not prepared to let you do it.'

That night, for the first time, he asked if he might come to her room. And haltingly at first, began to kiss her, to caress her; Celia, her body greedy, hungry for him, for sex, responded, felt herself liquid, achingly ready for him, began to move her hands over him, to kiss him harder, her mouth working on his. But then:

'Not now,' he said, pulling away from her, and turning back with a huge, heavy sigh, 'not yet. Please. I'm sorry.'

'But,' she said, 'but Oliver, I thought—'

'I'm sorry,' he said again, 'I can't. I wanted to hold you, to know you again. But that is all. For now. Please.'

She felt disappointed, and furiously angry too: the tangle of desire in her pulling, disturbing, almost hurting her. She turned on her back, lay staring at the ceiling, hot, fierce tears in her eyes.

'I don't understand,' she said. 'I really don't. Is it me, what have I done, what can I do?'

He reached out, tried to take her hand; she pulled it roughly away.

'Don't,' she said.

He turned his head to look at her and she saw there were tears in his eyes too. Remorse filled her; she took his hand again, said more gently, 'If you try to explain, Oliver, I will try to understand, to help.'

He sighed again, the same heavy, despairing sigh. 'I'm not the same person,' he said. 'The person who went out to France in 1914 was not at all the same as the one who has come home again. And cannot therefore be the same for you. It was the fear, you see: fighting the fear. That changed me more than anything. Anything I saw or had to do.'

'I – yes, I think I see.' She did not: not exactly. No one could who had not been there. But she had to try.

'It was disorientating. Sometimes I had no idea who I was, even. And then, when finally I was wounded, taken to hospital, I – I prayed that I would die, rather than have to go back. I prayed for it every night. Even in the torture of post-operative pain, I was just thankful. Thankful not to be out there any more. When they told me I wasn't healing, that there were complications, I smiled at them, thanked them. They thought I was crazy. Delirious. It was that bad, Celia. That bad.'

'Oh Oliver. I'm sorry. So sorry.'

'I was so absolutely terrified every day for the whole of the four years. Of failing again, as I did that one time I told you about. With that soldier.'

'But you didn't, Oliver. You didn't fail again. You went on and on. God knows how you did it. How any of you did it. Your men adored you, I'm always being told that—'

'And when are you told it?' His voice was amused again.

'Oh – at dinners. Things like that. At the regimental reunion we went to a few weeks ago. When we visited your batman, poor man—'

'Poor man, indeed.'

Oliver's batman had been blinded; he lived at home now with his elderly mother. Celia shrank from the thought of what might happen to him when she was no longer able to care for him.

'Well – anyway that was the fear. Of failure,' he said more quietly still, 'I failed that poor wretch of a soldier. If I can fail in one way, I can fail in another. With you. And I'm so afraid.'

'But,' she said, lifting his hand now, kissing it, 'you – we – have to face the fear, Oliver. Together. Drive it away.'

'I know. I know we do. But not yet. It's still too soon.'

She was silent.

'I'm sorry,' he said, and there was a break in his voice, 'so terribly sorry.'

'Oliver, don't! Please. Of course you're right. We have all the time in the world.'

'I hope so,' he said, kissing her gently, I hope you can be patient with me. I love you so much, Celia. I want you to know that.'

'I do know it,' she said, 'I do.'

He fell asleep after that, still holding her; but she lay wide awake, staring into the darkness, her body slowly quieting, happy that at least they had spoken of it, but aware just the same that she had not said she loved him, and wondering why. And aware too that there had been a reason he had chosen this night to ask if he might come to her bed; it was because of Sebastian, and of the place he might be taking in her life. She wasn't quite sure whether Oliver or herself was the more haunted by Sebastian's presence, lying in the bed between them.

'I'm sorry, Mr Lytton. Very sorry. But as I said in my letter—'

'Yes, I know what you said in your letter,' said Robert, 'that's why I'm telephoning you. To find out why you said it.'

'I'm afraid I can't give you any more reasons. The board considers the sum you are looking for exceeds the surety you can offer—'

'Oh for God's sake,' said Robert, 'the surety is on a guaranteed sale of those buildings. I've shown you the letters.'

'I realise that, of course.' The voice was carefully regretful. And if it were down to me, the money would be advanced to you. But I cannot act on my own. I have to take the advice of my board. I'm sorry.'

'Oh, very well.' Robert slammed the phone down; then regretted it.

At this rate he would have alienated half the bankers on Wall Street by the end of the week. Rea Goldberg was the third to refuse backing for the new construction Brewer Lytton were waiting impatiently to commence. He couldn't understand it. They had never had the slightest trouble before. And money wasn't exactly short: rather the reverse. The economy was extremely sound: wages were low, employment rising. There was a green light on enterprise. The city was growing: literally. Real estate was one of its biggest industries, and the people servicing it important to the economy. People like Brewer Lytton. Providing new housing, new offices, new stores: all crucial. But, suddenly, for Brewer Lytton, at least, the light had gone from green to red.

He walked into John's office. John was stabbing moodily at a sheet of figures with his pencil. He looked up at Robert.

'Any good?'

'Nope. The board turned us down.'

'Thought so. Bastards.'

'Yes. How about the hotel?'

Against Robert's instinct, they had put in a bid to build a new, small, but very prestigious hotel on the Upper East side.

'No news yet. But I have an insider there, who's going to get us a definite update this afternoon. I think this one will be all right, Robert. I know you said no more contract work, but I have a good feeling about this project. And they were impressed by your Elliott connections. Well, they want the hotel to look as much like Elliott House as possible.'

'More fools them,' said Robert wearily, 'let's hope my being impressive is enough to get us the contract. We certainly can't get a sliver off that price.'

It wasn't. Later that afternoon, John's insider told them regretfully that the contract to build the hotel was going to Hagman Betts.

'You're crying,' said Sebastian, 'what's the matter?'

'Oh – it's nothing.' She blew her nose, managed to smile at him.

'Just a personal advertisement in one of the papers. Listen. Lady, fiancé killed, will gladly marry officer injured in the war. Blindness, or other incapacity, not an obstacle. Poor, poor woman. She obviously feels that since her own life is ruined, she may as well devote it to helping someone else. Marry someone she doesn't love, doesn't even know. Isn't that so sad? And there must be hundreds, thousands like her. Their lives quite wrecked forever. Trying to be positive about it, to turn it to good effect. Oh, Sebastian I can't bear it. Sorry. So sorry.'

She started to cry again. He walked over to her desk, gave her a handkerchief. 'Use this. That one of yours is a bit of an apology for a handkerchief. Is that the only reason you're crying?'

'What? Yes, of course it is. Why else should I be crying? I'm perfectly happy.'

'Are you? Are you really?'

'Yes, of course I am. What do I have to be unhappy about?'

'I don't know,' he said. 'Let's go at it another way. What do you have to be happy about?'

'Oh, Sebastian, that's a ridiculous question.'

'Answer it.'

He sat down on one of the sofas, crossed his legs, smiled at her. He had come into the office to look at the new designs for the cover of *Meridian*.

'Well – I have just about everything anyone could want. Happy marriage. Marvellous career. Healthy children. Beautiful house—'

'That'll do. You've never seen my house, have you?' he said, interrupting, as he so often did.

'No. No, I haven't.'

'Would you like to? It's a very new toy.'

'I don't know. I suppose so, yes. I love Primrose Hill, it's so pretty.'

'You must come. Shall we go now?'

'Sebastian, don't be so ridiculous. Of course we can't go now. We're working—'

'No we're not. You're upset, I'm trying to cheer you up. We have to look at what I'm sure are some dreadful jacket ideas, then we could go and look at my house. It's very pretty. For a bachelor establishment. I'm rather proud of it as a matter of fact. Come on.'

'Sebastian, no.'

'Well, look, I tell you what,' he said, 'let's have lunch there. It's a lovely day, we can have some champagne in the garden and—'

'Sebastian, I can't have lunch with you. Certainly not in your house.'

'Why not?'

'Because I'm very busy. And – well and – it's not very – suitable.'

'Suitable for what?'

'For a married woman to lunch with an unmarried man alone in his house.'

'Lady Celia! I had no idea you were so conventional. Why should you care whether it's suitable or not?'

293

'Because others will care. Oliver will care, LM will care, the staff here will care.'

'And why should any of them need to know?'

'Sebastian I am not coming to your house.'

'Very well,' he said with a dramatically heavy sigh, 'another day. We could have lunch though, couldn't we? We still have a lot to talk about.'

'We do?'

'Of course. Well I do. It occurred to me that I know a great deal about you, and you know almost nothing about me. Aren't you curious?'

'Not – particularly.'

'Well you should be.'

'I really don't see why.'

'You know perfectly well why.'

'Sebastian—' she said, feeling herself flush, resenting it, 'I really don't think you should—'

'I'm your major author. You have the press release to think about. What other reason would there be? Ah now,' he said, laughing, 'you thought I was on quite a different tack didn't you? Shame on you, Lady Celia. Now come along, let's get these jackets over, quickly. Are they very bad?'

'It's not for me to—'

'They're very bad,' he said, 'I can tell.'

The jacket illustrations were very bad: so bad that they started laughing.

'Well at least we can say we tried,' said Sebastian finally. 'I can't believe Gill did, though.'

'Gill didn't do them. She was too upset. She asked one of her assistants.'

'Good girl. Tell Oliver – no I will tell him – that I think they're appalling.'

'He can still try to insist,' said Celia gloomily.

'Why?'

'Because he likes to have the last word on such matters.'

'Even if you don't agree with him?'

'Well – yes.'

'But he doesn't always prevail?'

'Not always. We have some terrible battles, though.'

'I see one coming up. I will not put my name to any of those jackets.'

'Contractually, I don't think you can refuse.'

'Bugger the contract. I don't imagine Oliver will want a dissatisfied author, publicly critical of his own book jacket, do you? Especially an about-to-be-famous author.'

'I don't—'

'Of course he won't. Now come along. Let's make our way to Rules. I feel a sudden need for some nice cold champagne.'

It was so hot: so hot and there was nothing to do. Jay had already walked round the garden about twenty times, and now he was back inside, because Dorothy told him he'd get sunstroke. When he asked her what sunstroke was, she said he'd know soon enough if he got it; she was always saying things like that. He didn't know how he was going to get through the day; it wasn't nearly lunch-time, they'd had lots of stories already, he was tired of drawing – maybe Dorothy would take him to the swings. That would be fun. He liked it at the swings, there were other children there. But, 'No Jay,' she said, 'not today. It's too hot and I've got too much to do. Maybe tomorrow. Now, you must let me get on and make your lunch.'

'Where's Mrs Bill?'

'She's gone to see her sister. She won't be back till supper time. Now your mother said she'd be back early tonight and maybe you and she could go for a walk before you go to bed. That would be nice wouldn't it?'

'Not very,' said Jay. He was very fond of his mother, but she wasn't exactly fun.

She didn't laugh much, or play games; Aunt Celia, or Grandma Beck (the nearest he could get to Grandmama Beckenham) were really fun, they played tag and hopscotch and hide and seek and all sorts of other games. His mother just wanted to read to him and talk. He sighed, and started to think about Grandma Beck. She had said, as she kissed him goodbye, that awful day, that he could come back to Ashingham whenever he liked. It would be lovely there today. He could have taken off his shoes and stockings and paddled in the little stream, or done some fishing, or maybe even had a ride on the pony.

Quite suddenly Jay decided to go. It was horrible here, and nobody took any notice of him, nobody cared how miserable he was. Grandma Beck and Billy, who only had one proper leg and was always kind to him, they'd care. They'd let him stay if he could only get there, he knew they would. But – could he get there? Dorothy certainly wouldn't take him. Nobody would. If he was going to go he'd have to do it on his own. He was sure he could remember how to get to the station. Down the main road for quite a long way – he'd often looked down it when they went for walks, remembering the journey up to Hampstead that horrid day – and then there was a station at the bottom. He was sure he could find it. But then he'd have to find the right train. How would he do that? Trains went all over the place, it would be awful to get on the wrong one. Then he remembered Dorothy asking the men who worked at the station where the trains went and where she got them. He could do that. He knew the station name: it was Beck something, like Grandma Beck. Fancy having a station named after you; one day he'd have a Jay station, all his own. With his own trains. He would live there, if he could. As long as it was near some fields and some streams.

He looked cautiously into the kitchen; Dorothy was singing to herself, and cutting up carrots for his lunch. That settled it really. Jay hated carrots. He went to fetch his money box, emptied the contents into his pocket, because you needed money for the train, he could remember that, and then walked very quietly through the hall and out of the front door, pulling it quietly shut behind him. Once clear of that, he ran as fast as his sturdy little legs could manage down the street towards the main road.

Sylvia felt very low. Low and not at all well. At least these days she didn't have to do anything much if she felt ill; the children got themselves up and dressed and walked to school, and as long as she gave them their breakfast, she could go back to bed for a few hours. Frank had some temporary work, with a builder: just mixing cement and humping bricks; he only got two pounds ten shillings a week, but it was better than hanging about at home feeling sorry for himself. It was awful about Frank: he'd been such a clever boy, could have got a job as a clerk, his teacher said; now he'd spent two years fighting for his country and been thrown on the scrapheap, as he put it, for his pains. It was wrong: it was terribly, terribly wrong.

'Now then. Here's to the right jacket.'

'The right jacket,' said Celia.

'Think there'll be any further trouble over it?'

'Oh yes, I told you. But don't worry. I'll see it through. Somehow.'

'I'm not worried,' he said, 'not in the least. I know that *Meridian* is in very safe hands.'

'Good,' she said lightly.

'Now then. Let's order and then we can begin our conversation. It's so nice here, isn't it? So – discreet – rather like a good gentleman's club. Do you come here with all your lovers, Lady Celia?'

'I don't have lovers,' she said firmly.

'None?'

'None.'

'Never?'

'Never.'

'I find that very hard to believe.'

'You must believe it. It's true.'

'But you are so desirable. How could anyone resist you?'

'Quite easily it seems,' said Celia laughing, 'and besides, if you are to take a lover, you have to feel desire. I have only experienced that for Oliver.'

'Indeed?' he said, and his gaze moved thoughtfully over her face, 'well, I find that rather intriguing, I have to tell you. I shall have to think about that. Was he your first lover?'

'Sebastian, that is a very impertinent question.'

'I know. I apologise. You don't have to answer it, of course.'

She sipped at the champagne; she felt confused, somehow nervous. Which was ridiculous.

'So – how old were you? When you and he were – conjoined?'

'Just nineteen.'

'Nineteen. Married at nineteen!'

'Yes,' she said briefly, alarmed at where this might be leading. She had no wish to reveal the slightly complex details of her marriage to Sebastian Brooke.

'And how old are you now?'

'I'm thirty-three. Another impertinent question.'

'I always think,' he said, ignoring her, 'that is the perfect age for a woman.'

'Why?' she asked, amused.

'Still very young. But – the bud has definitely opened. Not quite full bloom, though: wonderful things still to be revealed. I wonder what flower you would be.' He sat back, smiling at her. 'Not a rose, too predictable for you. A tulip perhaps, tightly self-contained things, tulips.'

'Do you see me as self-contained?' she said, pleased.

'I do. But you know, once a tulip begins to open, it blooms very fast. I await your blooming with great interest, Lady Celia. I intend to be there as it happens.'

'You do talk absolute nonsense, Sebastian,' she said, laughing.

'I know. I can't help it. Now then, I want to talk about me. As I said. There are a few things I think you ought to know. The first is that I am married.'

The road was much longer than Jay had remembered. On and on it went, down and down the hill; even after it joined another road, where he had thought he must be nearly at the station it went on as far as he could see. And it was terribly hot. And the cars were really noisy, hooting all the time. And when he had to cross the road, which he was sure he would, in fact he had just reached a place where he either had to cross or go in a completely different direction, not straight down any longer, he was afraid they wouldn't stop for him. It was a bit frightening. But it was still better than sitting at home, with Dorothy, eating carrots.

'Oh, dear heaven. Where is he? For the love of God—' Dorothy ran up the stairs for the third time since she had discovered Jay was missing. She had been up and down the street, calling him; she had asked the neighbours; she had checked the cellar, the attics – as if a four-year-old could pull down the loft ladder and climb up it – every bedroom several times, twice round the small garden, peering in the bushes: all a lot less likely, she knew, than the fear, too dreadful to contemplate, that he had been abducted. But the moment she faced that one, she must face the next two: phoning the police and then, of course, phoning Miss Lytton. At the thought of that, combined with the thought of what might have happened to Jay, Dorothy felt so frightened she nearly fainted and actually had to sit down and put her head between her knees. But it began to look as though it would have to be done. She would just make one last trip down the street calling him and then . . .

'Married!' she said stupidly, 'married! But Sebastian—'
'I know. I know. I should have told you. I kept putting it off. I – just didn't want to – I never do.'
She thought of all the times she had been curious that he had never married, wondered why not, imagined all kinds of romantic reasons for it.
'Like you, she was very young,' he said, 'as was I. She was eighteen, I was twenty-one. We were married in nineteen hundred and three. Just a year before you. I absolutely adored her; she seemed quite, quite perfect. She was pregnant,' he added, draining his glass, refilling it. 'Come along, you must drink up, Celia, or I shall have it all.'
'You can have it all,' she said. 'I don't want any more.'
Why was she so upset? It wasn't as if—
'Very well. Anyway, she lost the baby. Quite early on. And I discovered she wasn't perfect. Also quite early on. She—'
'What's her name?' asked Celia.
'Millicent. Such a silly name, don't you think? I always hated it. It

used to worry me, even when I was in the first flush of love for her. Millicent is too long, spinsterish, Millie is dreadful, a servant's name. Anyway—'

'So where does she live?'

She kept asking these questions, hoping while denying she was hoping it, that he would say she had died, that they were divorced, that he had left her long ago, that she had taken a lover . . .

'She lives in Suffolk. In a very nice house near Bures. I don't suppose you know that part of the world?'

'My nanny once took me to Frinton. I don't remember much about it.'

'Just as well. Horrid place, Frinton. Anyway – she lives down there. And I go and visit at the weekends.'

'Do you have any – other – any children?'

'No,' he said flatly, 'it didn't happen again. For some reason. It used to worry me, but—'

'But do you – that is—'

She had no right to be asking these questions, it was nothing to do with her. Absolutely nothing.

'I don't still love her, no,' he said, and there was a touch of amusement in his eyes, 'if that's what you mean. But I am – fond of her. And she is fond of me. And until now I have been rather dependent on her. Well, I still am. For the time being.'

'You mean financially?'

'Yes. She's got quite a lot of money. And I haven't got any at all. Unless you count the five hundred and fifty pounds you gave me.'

'I didn't give it you,' she said.

'No, of course not. But you know what I mean. Anyway, I can't even think about leaving her.'

Celia looked at him, and somehow managed to smile: a cold, dismissive smile.

'I'm sure that must be very reassuring for her,' she said, 'I'm very glad you told me, Sebastian. And as you say, it was something we definitely needed to know. Shall we order now: just one course, I think, I really don't have very long.'

'Oh stop it,' he said wearily, and for the first time since she had met him, he looked less glossy, less self-assured. He reached out and tried to take her hand. 'Do you think I'm enjoying this? Do you think I wanted to tell you? It took all my courage.'

'I can't imagine why,' said Celia. She pulled her hand free, 'you aren't admitting to some crime. Would you excuse me, I am just going to the lavatory.'

She walked across the restaurant, desperate not to appear upset, or even concerned, shrinking from the reason she felt both those things. Felt them very strongly. Absurd. Quite absurd.

'Now where do you think you're going? Eh?'

It was a man: quite a kind, nice-looking man. Carrying a rolled-up umbrella, wearing a hat, and with very polished shoes. Jay always noticed shoes, because they were down at his level. The man smiled at him. 'Are you all right? Not lost, or anything?'

'No,' said Jay firmly.

'How old are you?'

'Four.'

'Four! Little bit young to be out on your own.' He squatted down to Jay's level, smiled at him. 'Where's your mother?'

'At work,' said Jay.

'At work! Well, who's looking after you then? Or should I say, who isn't looking after you?'

'Dorothy.'

'Dorothy. And who is Dorothy when she's at home?'

'She looks after me,' said Jay.

'And does she know where you are?'

'Oh – yes.'

'Really? And she's quite happy for you to be out on your own on this busy road, is she?'

'Yes,' said Jay.

'What's your name?'

'Jay. Jay Lytton.'

'Right, Jay. Well now, it looks to me as if you must be going somewhere. You had that sort of a look about you. Want to tell me?'

'I'm going to see Grandma Beck,' said Jay. There was no reason why he shouldn't. It wasn't wrong. And if the man thought he was going somewhere sensible, maybe he'd just leave him alone.

'Right. And where does Grandma Beck live?'

'In the country.'

'In the country. Uh-huh. And you know your way there, do you?'

'Yes.'

'Well, good for you. Do you have to cross that nasty road?'

'Um – yes,' said Jay, trying to sound positive.

'Like me to help you across it?'

That wouldn't be a bad idea. It was a very big road. Maybe he should accept.

'Yes please,' he said.

'Right. Take my hand. Come on.'

★

300

'Gone!' said LM, 'how can he be gone? Are you sure?'

Such an absurd thing to say: Dorothy would hardly have phoned her, gasping with terror, if she hadn't been sure.

'Yes, Miss Lytton. I'm sorry, Miss Lytton, I just—'

'Have you told the police?'

'Yes.'

'And what did they say?'

'They said they'd come and take a statement. Told me to look again in the house. Asked where he might be.'

'Do they know how young he is?'

'Yes. I told them. Oh, Miss Lytton—'

'Don't start snivelling,' said LM, 'it won't help. How – how long was he gone before you noticed?'

'Not more than ten minutes, Miss Lytton. Definitely. We'd been looking at a book and I said I had to go and make the lunch and he—'

'Yes. yes, all right. Dear God, he's said he was going to run away often enough. Obviously he has.'

'Do you think so?'

'Well, use your brain, Dorothy. What else could he have done?'

'He might have been – have been—' her voice faltered.

'What? He might have been what?'

'Kidnapped,' whispered Dorothy,

'Oh God,' said LM. 'Dear God in heaven. Look – I'll come home. See the police myself. I'll get a cab. Just stay there, Dorothy. Don't leave the house, it's important.'

'No, Miss Lytton.'

'Under any circumstances.'

LM stood up; normally so calm in a crisis, she was in the grip of a hot, sick panic. She must tell Celia; tell her the police might phone, that Dorothy might phone, that anything might happen. She ran down the corridor to Celia's office. She wasn't there.

'She's gone to lunch with Mr Brooke, Miss Lytton.'

'Oh, I see. Well – oh God.' LM heard her voice shake, pressed her hand to her forehead.

'Is anything wrong, Miss Lytton, can I—'

'My son has disappeared,' said LM, 'that's what's wrong. Jay has disappeared.'

'Thank you for lunch,' said Celia, 'And I appreciate your telling me about your wife. I must get back to the office now and sort out the – the difficulty with your jacket.'

301

She smiled at him; it was extraordinarily difficult. Their lunch had lasted a little over half an hour, eaten over a laboured conversation. They were standing in the Strand; the traffic was heavy. Sebastian put his hand on her arm; she shook it off.

'Please Sebastian. I want to get back.' She was desperate to get away from him; from the new person he had become to her, no longer a dashing, romantic bachelor, with a somehow mysterious past, but a slightly seedy figure, concealing a marriage of convenience to a rich wife he did not love. It hurt: it hurt horribly. She stepped off the pavement, in order to cross the road; a taxi screeched to a halt.

'Look where you're going, lady.'

'Sorry,' she said, 'so sorry,' and then realising that a taxi was exactly what she wanted, opened the door. 'Paternoster Row, please.'

She would feel all right once she got back to the office. Where life was simple, where she was in control, where she was safe. Sebastian got in beside her. She looked at him.

'Please get out.'

'No,' he said, 'no I'm sorry I won't.'

'Get out!'

'No.'

She realised now that she was crying; furious with herself she dashed the tears away.

'Sebastian, please please will you get out of this taxi and leave me alone.'

Sebastian looked at her and then put out his hand and wiped away one of the tears. He smiled at her very gently.

'It's nice you're so upset,' he said.

LM sat weeping in her taxi as it made its way to Hampstead. She blamed herself entirely: not Dorothy. She had no business leaving Jay with her, leaving him with anyone. Jay, her precious, beloved child: all she had left of Jago, and of the strong, strange love they had had for one another. Jay, just a little boy, a sad, lonely, little boy, four years old, torn up from a life and a place he loved without scarcely a thought, abandoned to a strange, friendless life, with nothing to do, no one to do it with. And so wretched that he had run away, small and helpless as he was, in an effort to get back to where he had been happy. While she had been pursuing some pointless, senseless, selfish life of her own which offered him absolutely nothing at all.

She had been very wicked: wicked and irresponsible and treacherous. And this was her punishment. Dreadful, harsh, cruel: but absolutely just.

★

The man was pulling Jay along now; he hadn't let go of his hand when they had crossed the road, had gripped it much more tightly, was walking fast, much too fast for Jay to keep up. He was half running, and gasping for breath, struggling to get his hand free, pulling and tugging, but of course the man was much, much stronger than he was, and his grip was very hard, and tight.

Lots of people were staring at them, and every so often, if someone stopped, the man said something like, 'He's a naughty boy, ran away from school this morning, taking him back to his mother,' or, 'We've got a train to catch, going to miss it if we don't hurry. Excuse us, sorry, so sorry.'

After a bit, Jay began to cry; a lady coming towards them said to the man quite sharply, 'You shouldn't pull him along like that, he's much too small,' and the man said, 'I know, I know, but we have to get to my mother's house for lunch, nearly at my car, then he'll be all right, won't you, Jay?'

Jay was terribly afraid the man might really have a car, and that he'd lock him in it; he began to cry harder.

'Shut up,' said the man quite quietly, but it was frightening, just the same. 'Just shut up, you little brat,' and then more loudly, 'Now Jay, cheer up. Nearly home and then I'll give you some nice sweeties.'

And then ahead of them was a car, a big car and not even an open one, that perhaps he could have got out of, but one with a roof, and the man was fumbling in his pocket for the key, while still hanging on to his hand.

'Are you all right?' said one lady, to him.

'Yes of course he's all right, just a bit upset, his mother's had to go into hospital this morning. Now, Jay, come on, get in the car and we'll go and see Mummy.'

'I'm not upset,' she said for the third time. They were sitting on one of the benches in the Embankment gardens, 'not in the least. Why should I have been? I was just surprised, that's all. Surprised and well, I suppose – a little shocked.'

'Shocked? Why shocked? Because I'm married? I am after all, thirty-seven. Older than you.'

'Yes, I know that,' she said irritably.

'So—?'

'Just that you didn't tell me before. That's all.'

'I didn't want to tell you.'

'But why not?'

He was silent.

'And it's not the nicest story. Is it? That you are married to someone who by your own admission you don't love, but you don't leave because you can't afford to.'

'Oh, now dear Lady Celia, that is hypocrisy of the highest order.'

'Hypocrisy!'

'Yes, hypocrisy. Are you really going to tell me you don't have a single female friend in exactly my situation?'

'Well—'

'Of course you do. And you think none the worse of them for it. Even sympathise, quite possibly. So let's have no more of that. Now, will you please climb down from that bloody high horse of yours and listen to me. I need you to understand.'

'I don't feel there is a great deal to understand,' she said.

'Another arrogant statement. Of course there is. Have you never done anything, Celia, that you've been not entirely proud of? That has had lasting consequences?'

She was silent. Thinking that there were many of them: taking Barty from her family; not listening to Giles in his wretchedness at school; Sylvia's baby, and – well, helping her with that; even, she supposed, becoming deliberately pregnant by Oliver, presuming in all the arrogance of her eighteen years that it was what he wanted too, that he would be pleased, that he would want to marry her at once, even though he was little more than a boy.

'No?' His voice and his smile were gentle. Reluctantly she smiled back.

'Possibly,' she said carefully.

'Well then. I married Millicent, deeply in love. I had no money at all, I was the youngest son of a doctor who had crippled himself financially by sending me to public school. But at the age of twenty-one money doesn't seem very important, does it? Well – I don't suppose you know much about that. Anyway, it certainly didn't to me. I was a teacher, I taught at a prep school and pursued my dream of being a writer. Millicent was impatient of that, never believed I was capable of it. She was ambitious herself, in her own way, wanted to make her reputation as a society hostess. Her father was minor landed gentry, she was his only child and inherited everything, the house and all his money. He adored her, never really liked me very much. All very sad. Anyway – I did my bit. Tried awfully hard, stood at her side at endless boring balls and dinners and God knows what. And I think we were – tolerably happy – until the war. Then it all went dreadfully wrong. I came home on leave the first time to find her in the throes of an affair with some ghastly man. Well he probably wasn't ghastly at all, but he was what she should have married in the first place: upper class, fine shot, rode to hounds, all the right things. No doubt important to you as well,' he added gloomily.

'Not important,' said Celia, thinking of her father and his early objections to Oliver. 'Not important in the least. But I do – know about them.'

'Of course. Anyway, she said she wanted to marry him, was prepared to risk the ignominy of divorce and all that. I said fine. She said she'd make me an allowance, we all shook hands and I went back to France, feeling actually rather cheerful. You might be able to guess the rest.'

'He was killed?'

'Exactly. And she – well she had a nervous breakdown. Absolutely couldn't come to terms with it at all. It was terrible.'

'Oh, how dreadful,' said Celia.

'Yes. Anyway, I did my bit, as a gentleman should, stuck by her. By the time I was finally invalided home with my knee, she was much better. And terribly grateful to me, and said she wanted to support me while I wrote the book that I now knew I had in me. So I sat down there at Wychford, with my knee hurting like hell, and wrote *Meridian*. And you know the rest. Then I met you. Terrible shock that was,' he added, picking up her hand.

'What do you mean?' said Celia crossly. But she did not pull her hand away.

'I mean that was how I felt that day. Violent, quite extraordinary shock. Just at the sight of you.'

'Why shock?'

'That you existed. Looking as you did, being what you were, everything about you. Anyway, this is not the moment to go into that.'

'No,' she said, 'I agree,' thinking as she said it that she had felt the same, that her prime emotion had been exactly that, an intense shock, a bolt of sexual and emotional excitement. Now she tried not to allow herself to feel warmed and comforted by his words. Since there was nothing, after all, to be comforted for. Since she was particularly happy at the moment, her husband restored to her, and—

'Let's go for a walk,' said Sebastian.

'No,' said Oliver, 'Jay isn't here. Why should he be?'

'He's lost,' said LM, 'I don't know where he is. He's run away.'

'Oh LM, my dear! How dreadful – what can I do, is there anything the police, the hospitals?'

'No, no good. We've tried. Oh Oliver, oh God, I don't know what to do—' A series of visions, each one more dreadful than the last, was rising in front of her eyes: Jay locked in some dark cellar, under a tram,

305

in some squalid room, with some man, holding him down while he—
She suddenly felt very sick.

'Is Celia with you?' he asked.

'No. No, we can't find her.'

'You can't find her? Why not?'

'We simply can't,' said LM. 'Don't ask me why not. We thought she was at Rules with Sebastian, but—'

'With Sebastian?'

'Yes,' said LM, 'they went off to lunch and—'

'Well, she can't be at lunch much longer. It's well after three.'

'No. No, of course not,' she said, almost humbly.

'Tell her to ring me the moment she gets in.'

'I'm not in the office, Oliver. I'm at home.'

'I see. Yes, of course you should be. Well I'll phone Mrs Gould. And let me know at once if there's any news. About Jay. I mean.'

'Yes. Yes, of course I will.'

'Oh – Mrs Gould. Hallo. Sorry to have been so long. We had to wait forever to get a table, and then—'

'Lady Celia, could you ring Miss Lytton at once. At home.'

'At home? Why, what's happened, is she ill?'

'No. Jay is missing—'

'Jay! Oh, my God how dreadful. Mrs Gould, why didn't you—' her voice tailed away.

She met Janet Gould's eyes; then looked down, fumbling at her gloves.

'We tried Rules, Lady Celia, of course. But you had gone. Obviously – obviously you went somewhere else—'

'Yes. Yes that's right. We went somewhere else.'

'Could you ring your husband? Straight away, he said, the moment you came in.'

Even in her anguish about Jay, her emotional turmoil, her tangle of sexual excitement, Celia saw with complete clarity in that moment how tortuous and anarchic her life could become. Unless she stopped it now. At once.

Just for a moment the man loosed his grip on Jay's hand: just a moment, but it was enough. Jay was strong: fear and determination made him stronger. He tugged very, very hard, and got free. And ran, as he had never run before, away from the man, into the safe space in front of him. Into the road. And under a car.

CHAPTER 17

'Where on earth have you been?' Oliver's voice was sharp, unpleasant even, calling out from his study as she walked into the house.

'I've been at lunch.'

'So I was told. With Sebastian Brooke.'

'Yes.' She fought the defensiveness in her voice. 'He came in to see the new jacket designs. He doesn't like them at all, Oliver, he—'

'Celia, I really don't want to discuss jackets now. Jay is missing.'

'I know. Of course I know.'

'Well then, why on earth are you talking about jacket designs?'

Why indeed? Because they were uppermost in her mind. Pushing everything else aside. Even little Jay. The jackets. The book. The author of the book. What he had said to her. What she had said to him. How she had behaved . . . 'I – I'm sorry.' It seemed the only thing to say.

'I've been on the phone to the police. It seems everything that could be done is being done.'

'Poor LM,' said Celia, 'poor, poor LM. I'm going up there now, Oliver. To Hampstead. I'll be there if you want me.'

'Very well.'

'Where's the bloody ambulance?' said the woman. She was crouching by Jay, holding his limp hand. 'It's a disgrace, fifteen minutes it's been now, he'll be dead before it gets here. Poor little mite.'

'Where's his dad, anyway?' said her friend. 'Seems to have vanished into thin air.'

'He has,' said a man who had joined the group. 'I saw him driving off. Looking pretty worried. I don't think he was his father at all. Poor little chap,' he added.

The ringing of a bell announced the rather tardy ambulance; two men and a nurse jumped out, examined Jay's horribly inert form, and loaded it gently on to a stretcher.

'Is he . . . ?' asked the woman. Her voice tailed hopelessly away.

'Can't say anything,' said the driver, shutting the doors firmly. 'Mind the way please.'

'Well, I like that,' said the woman, 'after all we did. Fine thanks, that is. Wouldn't have happened before the war, would it? Ambulances came on time then, and you got a civil word or two out of the drivers.'

'Now then,' said the policeman who had called the ambulance and supervised the operation, 'move along there, let them through. Now I'll be wanting statements from you madam, and you sir, if you wouldn't mind. You say you saw what happened.'

'Must be dead,' said the first woman sadly, 'poor little mite. So tiny, he looked, just lying there all broken. That car wasn't half going some.'

The car that had hit Jay had actually not been going some at all; indeed it had been proceeding at a rather stately fifteen miles an hour down the Finchley Road, and could not have been expected to avoid a small boy rocketing out in front of it with absolutely no warning. Its driver, a most kindly and considerate man, who had been on his way back from visiting his elderly mother, was sitting in Swiss Cottage police station, his head in his hands, knowing that for the rest of his life, he would see that little body tossed in the air like some kind of stuffed toy before settling, with horrible finality, on the bonnet of his car.

'I would rather he was dead I think,' said LM, 'much rather, than abducted by some creature, tortured—' her voice broke; she began to cry. Celia took her in her arms.

'LM, you mustn't talk like that. I'm sure he's neither. I'm sure he's perfectly safe somewhere, probably just—'

'Just what? Walking happily along in the sunshine? Playing with some other children in a park somewhere? Arriving safely at your mother's house? Do tell me what else he might be doing, Celia. I'd be so grateful.'

Celia was silent. They were all in LM's small kitchen; Dorothy, white-faced, immobile, sat at the table, staring in front of her; Mrs Bill back from a visit to her sister, was pouring out a third brew of tea, destined to grow as cold as the first two, and Celia and LM were standing at the window, staring out. It was five o'clock: nearly five hours now since Jay had disappeared. A policeman was sitting on a chair in the hall, and another stood on the front path. It looked, Celia thought with sudden clarity, like a scene from a bad play. And in spite of her brave words to LM, she couldn't help thinking that, with half the police force of London looking out for him, if Jay was really all right, he would have been found by now.

★

'Now then. Let's have a look at him. Poor little chap. Let's get that blood off his face for a start, nurse. That's a very nasty wound on his head. Very nasty. Got a pulse yet? Let me try. And – ah. Hand me my stethoscope would you. Where are his parents?'

'There aren't any,' said the ambulance man, 'leastways, not with him. Seemed to be on his own. Bit of a mystery. Police were taking statements from the crowd.'

'Right. Well in that case, any reports of a missing child? Mr Jackson, go and check, would you? We must try and find who he belongs to.'

The phone rang loudly in the hall; LM picked it up.

'Yes? Yes, this is Margaret Lytton – yes. Oh I see. Yes. So is he – oh, I see. Yes. No. Of course. I understand. Goodbye.'

She put the phone down and walked very slowly into the kitchen. Celia never forgot how she looked at that moment: quite literally dead, grey-faced, somehow withered, her dark eyes sunken into their sockets. Dead. Like Jay.

'LM,' she said, 'LM sit down, here, come along.'

LM pushed her aside.

'I can't sit down,' she said, and her voice was hoarse, issuing from her somehow reluctantly. 'I have to get down to the hospital. Jay is there.'

'The hospital?' said Celia, still afraid to ask the crucial question, 'which hospital, LM?'

'St Mary's. Paddington.'

'And – and is he—?'

LM looked at her for another long moment. Then the faintest possible shadow of a smile formed on her white mouth.

'He's alive,' she said, and then clearly wishing to savour the fact, 'yes, he's alive. Shall we – shall we go in your car or in mine?'

'He's all right,' said Celia, 'well, he's badly hurt. He's got concussion, still drifting in and out of consciousness, and he has a broken leg and several broken ribs. But he's alive.'

'Thank God,' said Oliver, 'thank God for it. What happened?'

'Nobody quite knows. But he ran away from the house this morning, about twelve o'clock, and was brought in to St Mary's a few hours later. He'd been hit by a car. No one quite knows what happened before that. The driver was at the hospital. Poor, poor man, I felt so sorry for him.'

'I wouldn't feel sorry for him,' said Oliver grimly. 'What was he doing, why wasn't he looking where he was going?'

'I think he was,' said Celia, 'several people confirmed he'd been driving very slowly. Jay just ran out in front of the car. Came at him out of nowhere, he said.'

'The traffic is getting so dangerous,' said Oliver, 'I really don't think the twins should be allowed to go to school on their own. I never did like it and now—'

'Barty is with them.'

'Yes, and it's a terrible responsibility for her as well. She was very upset about Jay, they all were, we must let them know he's all right.'

'Yes, of course. I'll go up now.'

He looked at her; the expression on his face was odd.

'Are you – all right?' he said.

'Yes,' she said quickly, 'yes of course I'm all right.'

She wasn't all right. She felt she would never be all right again. Sebastian had taken her apart that day; the cool, contained whole which she knew so well, which she had so perfectly under control, had splintered into fragments. Sebastian had put her together again, in a different order, a different form, so that she felt confused, shaken, distracted by thoughts of a most dangerous and carnal kind.

'I'm in love with you,' he had said suddenly, into the silence, as they walked along the Embankment, while she still struggled desperately to appear cool. 'I'm in love with you. You do know that don't you?'

It was the most extraordinary moment: frozen, bleached in time, she had felt awed by it, almost afraid, afraid of what it would do to her, do to her life, and at the same time absurdly, ludicrously, joyfully happy.

'Of course you're not in love with me,' she managed to say.

Then he had stopped dead in front of her, halting her in her path, his face tense with anger, in a way she had never seen before, and said, 'Don't insult me, please, Celia. Don't. And don't play games either. This is very serious. Very serious indeed.'

'I am not playing games,' she said rather slowly. 'I really am not. I'm sorry if you think I am.'

He had become himself again, very quickly, his charming, overpowering self; 'Good,' he said, and took her hand, tucked it into his arm, and they walked along together in the sunshine, looking rather sober, she thought, rather – married even, not in the least like two people embarking on an illicit love affair. Which in any case, of course, they were not.

'And tell me now, please, what you feel about me,' he said after a while.

She said carefully that she felt all kinds of things for him, friendship, admiration, affection.

'Oh Lady Celia,' he said, smiling, 'what a liar you are. You feel a great deal more than that. Don't you?'

'No,' she said, and found herself smiling back just the same.

'Of course you do. An admiring, affectionate friend would not have reacted as you did to the news of my marriage.'

'Oh, you're wrong there, Sebastian. It was an extremely unexpected and not entirely pretty story.'

'Not more judgement, I hope.'

'No. But you must admit, you had led us all to believe that you were a bachelor.'

'I had? What did I say?'

'Nothing. That's precisely it. Most married people do refer to their spouses, fairly soon into a relationship.'

'I wasn't aware we had a relationship, Lady Celia. Yet.'

'Sebastian, don't be ridiculous. Of course we do. A very serious business relationship.'

'Oh,' he said, 'oh, yes, I see.'

'And now,' she had said, 'I really must be getting back. To work.'

To work. Her citadel. Where she was safe.

All night LM sat by Jay's bed, watching him, studying him, listening to his shallow breathing, willing her own strength into him, superstitiously afraid that if she ceased her vigil for a moment, he would drift away from her. They had told her he had been lucky, he was strong and should make a good recovery. Just the same, the sight of him, white and still, lying on the high bed, was a glimpse into what might have been, what might yet be, and she could not allow herself to trust them. She looked anxiously up each time a nurse or doctor came in, checked his pulse, his heartbeat, shone a torch in his eyes, and nodded sternly as they told her that he was doing well, was stable, that there was no change. He had come round from the anaesthetic and been violently sick; that, combined with the pain of the blow to his head, made him utterly wretched. He was crying a lot. He was also confused about where he was and what had happened to him, and complained that he couldn't see properly.

'That's the concussion,' the nurse said, 'it should pass quite soon. The important thing is that he regained consciousness fairly quickly. The longer it takes, the more serious, you know. Try not to worry too much. It could have been worse. Honestly.'

She smiled at LM; she was young and pretty, hardly out of the schoolroom, LM thought, with a soft, Irish voice. LM tried to smile back at her; it was very difficult. Apart from Jay's physical condition, there was another dreadful fear, ugly, sordid: that he had been in some way interfered with by the man he had been running away from, that his innocence was broken, his trust shattered. That was almost more frightening than the physical terrors.

She had settled herself by his bed when he was finally released from the doctors, from the operating theatre where the broken leg had been set and his broken ribs strapped up. But as she stood, utterly still, just looking down at him, the ward sister arrived.

'You can't stay there I'm afraid,' she said, 'parents are not allowed after visiting hours, it's against the rules.'

LM said firmly that it might be against the rules, but she was staying; Sister was looking at her, clearly nonplussed by this extraordinary piece of resistance, when the doctor who had first received Jay into the emergency unit reappeared.

'Mrs Lytton appears to feel she can stay here for the night,' sister said, with the look of one who knows she is finally about to get her way. 'I have explained that of course she cannot, it is quite impossible.'

'Sister, when he comes fully round, he'll be frightened,' said the doctor, who was young and imaginative and found much to question in medical attitudes towards patients, 'he'll need his mother. Let her stay. Besides, she can be useful,' he added, smiling, as Jay started to vomit again, 'I should be grateful if I were you, Sister.'

They did let her stay, but did not even provide her with a chair, certainly nothing to eat or drink; LM settled finally on the floor, just as Jay himself settled into a relatively normal sleep, oblivious to hunger and thirst, or even weariness, she simply felt infinitely relieved to be there.

She was woken from a fitful doze at six, when the morning ward round started; the young nurse came in, took his pulse and temperature, shone her torch into his eyes.

'He's fine,' she said, smiling at LM, 'little bit of a temperature perhaps, but that's to be expected, otherwise, he's going to be right as rain, I'd say. Why don't you go home now, Mrs Lytton, get some proper rest. You'll need it later, and there's nothing you can do now. When the doctor comes round, he'll say when he can go home and how soon, and you can telephone – do you have a telephone at home?'

LM nodded.

'Well, there now. And come back when you've had a nice sleep. Look at him, right as rain.'

LM looked at Jay; he did look much better. He was breathing a little bit fast, perhaps, but his colour was much better, and she was dreadfully tired and stiff.

'All right,' she said, moving reluctantly away from the bed, 'perhaps. Just for an hour or two. Then I'll be back.'

'Good idea. Doctor comes round about nine-thirty or ten,' said the nurse. 'I'll tell the day staff you'll be back later on. Besides,' she said with a conspiratorial smile, 'I think Sister will have a heart attack if you stay here very much longer.'

LM went back over to Jay, bent down, and kissed him tenderly on the forehead. He felt warm, soft, wonderfully and unarguably alive. He even managed a slight smile before drifting back into sleep. She tiptoed away.

As she left the hospital, walking through Out Patients, the nurse at the desk called out to her.

'Mrs Lytton?'

'Yes?'

'I have a note for you. Here. Left by a gentleman.'

'Really?' LM frowned. What gentleman would have written to her here? What about? Or was it – could it be – the dreadful creature who had tried to kidnap Jay? She ripped the envelope open; her fingers were clumsy with fear. Inside was a card with a name and address printed across the top. Hardly the action of a kidnapper . . . She stood in the sunshine on the street, enjoying the smell of the fresh air, reading it, half smiling.

Dear Mrs Lytton,

I am writing in the hope that you would be kind enough, in the fullness of time, to let me know how your little boy is. I am the driver of the car which hit him yesterday. I am quite sure you will never be able to forgive me; I shall certainly never be able to forgive myself. I can only assure you, although it seems rather too much to ask you to believe, that I was driving very slowly and carefully at the time, and that your little boy did suddenly appear, apparently from nowhere, into my line of vision. It is not something I shall ever forget. I understand from the hospital that his condition, although critical, is no longer considered life threatening, for which I thank God. However I would so very much like to speak to you personally, and express my remorse and to hear, with luck, of his continuing improvement.

Yours sincerely,

Gordon Robinson

What a nice note: what a very nice man. LM resolved to write to him and reassure him as soon as she herself had recovered from the incident.

The doctor was late on his round that morning; it was eleven before he reached Jay's bed.

'How is he?'

'Oh, not too bad. Still a bit drowsy. Perhaps a slight temperature.'

313

'To be expected, I suppose. But I thought he'd be more lively this morning. Let's see—'

He pushed up the bedclothes, placed his stethoscope to Jay's bandaged chest, listened to it for a long time. Then he stood back, looking down at him.

'I'm not terribly happy with this,' he said, 'where's Sister? I think we should get some further X-rays done.'

When LM arrived at the hospital just before lunch, bearing grapes, books, jigsaw puzzles, she was shown into Sister's office. The doctor was waiting there for her. He said he was very sorry, that he was sure there was no real cause for alarm, but Jay was not quite as well as he had hoped.

'In what way?' asked LM, her voice sharp, almost peremptory.

The doctor said, his voice very gentle, that he was afraid Jay had developed a chest infection, that he was developing breathing difficulties. 'It was the blow to the chest, you see. It didn't just break the ribs, it clearly damaged the pleura, as well.'

'What is the pleura?' said LM, still in the same rather threatening voice.

'It's a thin membrane, with two layers. One lines the outside of the lungs and the other the inside of the chest cavity. It provides lubrication and thus eases expansion and contraction of the lungs during breathing. That process has been upset. Now I have had a chest X-ray done, and we can only hope it is not too serious. I do assure you we are doing all we can. And he is a strong little chap.'

LM said nothing: she merely walked into the ward, and over to Jay's bed. He was drowsy, but awake, his breathing horribly fast, his eyes brilliant, his face flushed.

'Hallo, Mummy. Where were you, I wanted you.'

'I'm sorry, my dearest. Very sorry.'

'My chest hurts. Everything hurts.'

'I know. But it will soon be better. I promise. How's your leg?'

Jay licked his dry lips. 'Hurts too. And my head. So much. Hold my hand, Mummy. Don't go away again.'

'I won't, Jay, I won't. Just rest now, don't try and talk. I'll be here.'

'Bastards,' said Robert throwing the paper across the room. 'Bastards. Who's been feeding them that rubbish?'

'God knows,' said John wearily.

He picked the paper up; he had brought it in to show Robert. There was an item in the diary section of the business page: 'The real estate firm of Brewer Lytton is said to be in difficulty. It has failed to win

314

several crucial contracts, and two of the investment houses which have financed its projects in the past have recently withdrawn funding. A spokesman for Hagman Betts, the real estate company which has won the contract against Brewer Lytton to build the new highly prestigious Warwick Hotel on Park Avenue, said that this was not the first time they had beaten Brewer Lytton in a straight fight. "Our estimate was lower, it was as simple as that. Plus the fact that Warwick and their architects found our interpretation of their ideas imaginative, as well as compatible with their own." ’

‘In other words,’ said Robert, ‘we’re expensive and dull. Bastards. What are we going to do, John? This is the sort of mud that sticks. Badly.’

‘LM, hallo.’ Brunson had taken the call first thing next morning, had fetched Celia from the dining-room. ‘How are you? How is Jay today?’

‘He is – no better.’

LM had phoned the night before, briefly to say that Jay was not as well as had been hoped, that he had a high temperature, and she was at the hospital again.

‘Oh, God. I’m so so sorry. Is it –?’

‘He has pneumonia. In both lungs. The X-rays show that quite clearly.’

‘But how – why –? He was hit by a car, I don’t understand—’

‘It was a result of that. The chest injuries. It’s complicated, I—’

‘It’s all right, LM, you don’t have to explain. And the temperature is still high? Even this morning?’

‘Yes. Still a hundred and four. And he has trouble breathing, and – well, we can only wait, I’m told. He is being given oxygen, but there’s nothing else they can do.’

Her voice shook; Celia felt her heart literally stop in sympathy. She tried to imagine one of her own children, the twins, lying there, fighting death, how she would feel, what she would do. It was beyond her. ‘Would you like me to come and see you. Just sit with you? Would that help? You must be exhausted.’

‘Oh no,’ said LM, and her voice was quite surprised, ‘no, I’m all right. I have to stay, I have to be with him. Just – well, just in case.’

‘Yes of course,’ said Celia. ‘Is he – very distressed?’

‘Very. And has such trouble breathing, it hurts him so, that’s the worst thing.’ She sounded quite calm; stern, as she always was under duress.

‘Would you like me to come?’

‘Well—’

'I'm on my way,' said Celia.

She wasn't sure which of them looked worse when she got there, Jay or LM. He had been moved into a small room to the side of the ward; he was breathing loudly and laboriously. His face was flushed, a hard, dry colour. He was muttering, his voice fast.

'Home,' he kept saying, 'home, want to go home.' And then, 'Let me go, let me *go.*'

'He's delirious,' said LM almost briskly. 'Shush, Jay, shush. It's all right. Mummy's here. It's bad for him, you see, talking, it makes him cough.'

'Of course,' Celia looked at LM; she was grey with exhaustion, her eyes fever-bright. Her hair, usually so neat, hung in wisps around her face, her shirt was creased and slightly grubby-looking. Her hands, always thin, looked claw-like as she gripped the side of the bed, watching Jay.

'LM, have you had anything to eat or drink?'

She shook her head fiercely. 'I don't want anything.'

'You must at least drink. You'll be no good to Jay if you start fainting.'

'I'm no good to him anyway,' said LM, and her voice shook. 'I've been no good to him at all. That's why he's here, because I wasn't caring for him, I—'

'LM don't. You mustn't. Mustn't let yourself think like that, even for a moment. It was an accident, a terrible—'

'No! No, it wasn't. It was because he was unhappy, lonely, missing the other children, and because I wasn't with him. I can't let you say that, say – oh God.' She began to weep silently, her thin shoulders shaking, her face sunk in her hands. Celia stood there, feeling helpless, just listening, knowing there was nothing she could say.

'Jago would have been so shocked, so angry. That I had left him, our son, left him alone with someone even as careful as Dorothy. I am glad, for the first time, Celia, glad he's dead, that he doesn't know how I have failed him. Failed them both. It should be me lying there, dying—'

'LM, he is not dying.'

'He is dying. I'm sure of it. I know it. The doctors know it too. Don't – please don't—' Her voice rose in a wail: then she seemed to realise what she was doing, stifled it, controlled herelf with a vast, visible effort. 'I mustn't – it will upset him. If he can hear me . . .'

'Can he hear you?'

'I don't know. I think so. He responds to my voice. They say that's good. That he can . . . oh dear, I'm so sorry.'

'LM don't keep saying that. Look, go and get yourself a cup of tea at

316

least. There's a cafe opposite. You really must. I'll sit with Jay, don't worry, I won't take my eyes off him. I promise you.'

She didn't; it was a very long half hour. The small chest, uncovered except for its bandages, rose and fell painfully, the rasping breathing seemed to get faster and faster, the rapid, rambling little voice occasionally started, only to be stopped by a fit of coughing and desperate struggles for breath. A nurse came in, took his pulse and his temperature, half-smiled at her, went away again. Sister appeared, looking stern, followed the same procedures, ignored Celia.

'They resent me so much,' said LM when Celia told her this, 'they can't bear it that I'm here, not doing as I'm told, not going home. They've never come across anything quite like it. Now we're in this room it's a bit better, but I really thought Sister was going to spit at me when she came on duty this morning and saw me here again.'

'It's so ridiculous,' said Celia, 'so counter-productive. Children need their mothers. Sick children especially. I don't understand why they can't all see that.'

'If Jay was a poor child, with an uneducated mother, unable to argue her case, I certainly wouldn't be here,' said LM. Then she looked at Celia, her face stricken. 'On the other hand I would have been at home with him. He would have been safe. He wouldn't be here at all. Oh Celia, what have I done to him? What have I done?'

At Lytton House in Paternoster Row, Oliver sat in a state of mounting misery and anger. He had spent the entire morning poring over costings, royalty statements, publication schedules, past catalogues. It made almost unbearable reading. To see his beloved, prestigious literary house, so hugely admired and respected by the publishing fraternity, and that admiration and respect so hard-earned, so sweetly won, having apparently dedicated itself over the past four and a half years to so much rubbish made him want, quite literally, to weep. How could they have done it? Done it to him? For it did feel like a personal loss, worse than a loss, a robbery, something taken from him in his absence, while his attention and his care were elsewhere. As if his home had been entered by force, plundered of its treasures, replaced with cheap rubbish. Cheap rubbish: that was exactly what much of it was. The pap poetry, endless volumes of it, scarcely warranting the name, the cheap novels, with those dreadful jackets, reminiscent of women's magazines, the predictable second-rate detective stories, the appalling sentimentality of the *Dispatches* trilogy, page after page of nauseating, mawkish drivel. And the dictionaries, the literary works, the classics, all allowed to run down. Biographica, Celia's own beloved list, seemed to have ceased to exist altogether. And the look of everything, including the catalogues: vulgar, tawdry – it was truly distressing. How could Celia, with her pretensions to intellect, her aesthetic standards, how could she have allowed such vulgarity? And LM, who had grown up as he had, with the name of Lytton set as a standard of excellence, both literary and visual, how could she have stood by and allowed it to happen? It was appalling; it was not to be borne.

Celia arrived half-way through the afternoon; she was pale and looked exhausted. Oliver met her in the corridor.

'How is Jay? He's not—'

A long silence: then, 'No. But I fear the true answer is not yet. He has pneumonia. He's very ill indeed.'

'I'm – so sorry. Is LM bearing up all right?'

'Wonderfully, of course. She is so brave. But – if that little boy – well, if he doesn't survive, I don't know what she will do. He's all she has in the world. All she cares about. I fear for her, Oliver, I really do.'

'Well we must hope. And pray.'

'There is nothing else that will help him,' said Celia sombrely, 'and I don't set a great store by either of those things, I'm afraid.'

Oliver sighed. She looked at him.

'You look exhausted, Oliver. You'd better go home. Evidently a whole day is too much for you.'

'It is nothing of the sort,' he said shortly, 'and I do assure you there will be no more part-time attendance here by me.'

'What do you mean?'

'I mean,' he said, 'that I'm horrified by what has been going on here in my absence. Horrified. This is the first time I have been able to look at any of it—'

'That's hardly my fault, Oliver.'

'I realise that. On the other hand, neither is it mine. Nor that I was forced to leave Lyttons in your hands.'

'Lyttons has survived,' said Celia lightly, hanging on to her temper with a gargantuan effort, 'in fact it is in tolerable health. The same could not be said of many other houses.'

'Oh really? Macmillan, John Murray, Blackwoods, all seem to be thriving. And having taken rather less unpalatable medicine than you have forced down Lyttons' throat, if I might pursue your rather apt analogy.'

'Oliver, where exactly is this leading? And is it really so important that I must discuss it with you now, while LM's son is quite literally on the brink of death?'

'No, of course not,' he said irritably, turning away, 'and please don't imply that I don't care about Jay.'

'You implied that of me yesterday.'

'I most assuredly did not.'

'Oliver you did. When I started talking about the jacket of Sebastian's book.'

'Oh for God's sake,' he said, 'can we please have at least one discussion that doesn't lead us to that wretched book.'

She was silent.

'Look,' she said finally, struggling to sound level, reasonable, 'look, Oliver, we're both exhausted. I can see that there must be things you are not happy with. It was inevitable, I expected it. But wouldn't it be better to talk about them at home, over dinner? So that I can explain a little, give you the rationale for what I did? I think that's important.'

'No,' he said, 'I'm sorry. I'm dining at the Garrick tonight. With John Murray.'

'Oliver, is that wise? After a long day here. And you know how heavy the food is at the Garrick.'

'Allow me to make decisions about my own life, Celia, would you? As you clearly have been doing about your own.'

She stared at him, felt a flush rising. 'What is that supposed to mean?'

He said nothing, then walked into his office, pulled a stack of papers towards him. 'I have a great deal to do. I think it would be better to postpone this conversation for a day or so, when I have a few more facts at my disposal.'

'As you wish,' she said. She went into her own office and slammed the door. She suddenly felt very sick.

She went home early, read stories to the twins, put them to bed, sat looking at them tenderly as they lay there drifting into sleep, in exactly the same position, curled up on their left sides, their dark curls fanned out on their pillows, wondering again how she would feel, how she would bear it indeed, if it were they who were close to death; and then she went up to see Barty, reading in her little room, told her with sober truthfulness how Jay was, tried to comfort her as she wept. And then went downstairs and wrote to Giles: Giles whom she had neglected ever since he went to Eton, who wrote so dutifully every week to her. She did not deserve all the good fortune heaped upon her; just as LM did not deserve the bad.

LM was asleep in a chair in the corner of Jay's room when the night sister shook her awake. It seemed to her incredible afterwards that she should have been able to sleep so deeply; she supposed she must have been utterly exhausted.

'What is it?' she said, starting up, staring at her in terror, 'what, has he — is he—?'

'No, no, but he's very agitated. He wants something. I don't know—'

LM went over to the bed; Jay was tossing about, his fevered eyes staring unseeing in front of him.

'Barty,' he kept saying, 'where's Barty?'

'She's not here, darling,' said LM, putting out her hand, stroking his burning head, 'she's at home.'

'Want to go home. I want to go home. With Barty.'

He could manage no more for a while; lay there, staring in that same dreadful way, his breathing tortured, a torture to listen to. Then, 'Barty,' he said again, 'where's Barty?'

'He's very distressed,' said Sister 'it's not helping.'

'No,' said LM, 'no, I can see that. Barty is — well she's his cousin. He adores her. Could I — that is, would it be possible to — use a telephone?'

The night sister was rather different from her daytime counterpart. She looked at LM sternly. 'It would be absolutely against regulations,' she said, 'absolutely. Or for anyone to come here at this time of night, of course.'

'Of course,' said LM humbly. She had hoped she just might — but it was clearly completely out of the question. She began bathing Jay's forehead and neck again; she could feel his small body sending out waves of heat.

'I think the crisis will come soon,' said Sister, looking at him intently, 'very soon.'

LM had learned what that meant; it was the turning point in pneumonia cases, when the fever reached its height and, in medical language, broke, began to go down, and the body began to recover. Or — she looked at sister and saw that she read her face. Sister patted her hand.

'Now, I have the rest of my round to do. And — Mrs Lytton — the telephone is on my desk.'

With which she was gone.

The telephone rang: sharply and endlessly in the darkness. In the heart of the house in Cheyne Walk.

Brunson who might have heard it, had taken a sleeping powder; in his middle age, insomnia plagued him. There was an extension to the telephone in Celia's study, a greatly exciting innovation in the house; and her study was on the ground floor immediately underneath her bedroom.

'I shall hear the telephone if you ring,' she had said to LM, before leaving her that evening, 'and even if it's the middle of the night, don't hesitate, I shall come at once if — if you need me.'

She did, in any case, always sleep lightly; she had no fears that she would not hear it.

But technology is no match for man's – or woman's – folly; that very afternoon, the housemaid had pulled the extension telephone wire out of its socket by mistake, with her own much-prized piece of modern equipment, the Hoover electric vaccuum cleaner: and thus Celia's phone did not ring.

LM went back to the ward; Jay's breathing was worse. He was coughing helplessly, his little body wracked with spasms, and in between coughs, fighting for breath.

'He's still calling for his cousin,' said Sister, 'and saying something about home. Could you not get through?'

'I couldn't wake anyone,' said LM, 'I'm afraid.'

'Is it a big house?'

'Very big.'

'Oh dear.'

She looked again at Jay. 'He's not – good is he?' she said to Sister.

Sister looked back at her. 'Mrs Lytton,' she said, and her voice was very sombre, 'you must never give up hope.'

LM knew what that meant.

Barty had actually heard the phone without realising it. She had fallen asleep over her book, *Little Women,* had been weeping, indeed, almost as much over Beth's illness as Jay's, and woke up with a start, a crick in her neck. Something had disturbed her: what *was* it? She decided to go to the lavatory. As she made her way along the nursery landing, she looked at the grandmother clock which stood at the end of it. Half past one: very much the middle of the night. Everyone was fast asleep; Wol had been out for the evening, but he had arrived home at ten, she had heard him. There were no animals in the house, no dog that might have barked, no cats scuttering about, pouncing on mice. Well at least only in the cellar. Perhaps outside: yes, probably that was it. A car going past down the Embankment, a tugboat hooting, but she was used to those sounds, they wouldn't have woken her.

She was just walking back to her room when she remembered the telephone: you could just hear it up here, she and the twins often argued about whether it was ringing or not. The twins' ears were exceptionally sharp; awake they would have heard it, but they were very deep sleepers. Anyway, she had heard something. And it was most likely to be the phone.

Terrified of the news it might have brought, she raced down the stairs and across the hall, stood looking at where it stood, on a small table by the door, feeling rather silly. It was very silent now. It was hardly going to tell her anything. Then she remembered the operator. There was bound to be someone on duty, even at night. Otherwise the phone couldn't have rung. She unhooked the receiver from its upright base and started pressing the cradle up and down, to attract the attention of the exchange. After a minute or so, a bored female voice said, 'Number please.'

'Oh,' said Barty, 'oh, this is Sloane 589. And I—'

'What number do you wish to call?'

'I don't,' said Barty, 'I want to know if anyone has called this number. In the last few minutes. Is it possible to tell me that?'

'Are you a child?' said the voice suspiciously. Barty knew what that meant: lack of co-operation, at very best.

She took a deep breath, lowered her voice as she had learned to do in Miss Wolff's elocution lessons.

'Certainly not,' she said, 'this is Lady Celia Lytton calling. I would appreciate your co-operation.'

She couldn't believe it would work: but, 'One moment please' said the voice, slightly less bored, 'I'll see what I can do.'

She heard it saying, 'Anyone put a call through to Sloane 589 in the past few minutes?' And then a long silence. She was just giving up in despair, when the voice came back to her.

'Yes. One of my colleagues put a call through. I can't say who it was from, though.'

'No, of course not,' said Barty forgetting her Lady Celia voice, 'thank you anyway.' So it had rung; it must have been from LM at the hospital.

She looked up the stairs, and squared her shoulders: it took courage, for some reason, to go into Celia's bedroom in the middle of the night and shake her awake. It was forbidden territory, none of the children was ever allowed in: once the door was shut. Not even to knock at the door. She supposed Celia and Wol must want to be alone sometimes. Nevertheless—

As she opened the door, having knocked very gently and got no response, and walked across to the bed, the first thing she noticed was that Wol wasn't there. Aunt Celia was alone in the great bed. Maybe he was still out after all. Or else in the little room where he kept his clothes. There was a bed in there. There was the usual huge pile of books beside the bed. Including some that weren't even printed properly yet, just heaps of paper, proofs they were called. The one on the top of the pile was the wonderful *Meridian* book that Aunt Celia had allowed her to read a couple of chapters of. It had been so exciting and so special—

Stop it Barty, stop wasting time. She put out a thin arm, and rather nervously began to shake Celia's shoulder.

★

Jay had become very still. Stopped calling for Barty, stopped coughing; the only sound in his tiny room was his laboured breathing. LM had no idea what his temperature was now, but the last time Sister had taken it she had folded her lips together and put her thermometer back into its container at the end of the bed, before giving LM a quick, rather strained smile.

'I have to get back to my office,' she said, 'I'll be there if you need me.'

She patted LM on the shoulder, hurried out of the room. LM buried her head in her arms on Jay's small high bed, and began to weep.

'Quite right,' said Celia to Barty, coming back into her room. 'Clever girl, you are. Run upstairs and get dressed. Quickly. I spoke to the night sister, she said Jay had been asking for you. I'll see you down here in two minutes.'

'One,' said Barty, and she was back inside that time, wearing her school jumper and skirt and black stockings and boots. 'Let's take *Meridian*,' she said, 'I can read it to him. He'd like it.'

'Oh, my darling, I don't think—' Celia hesitated. Then she said, 'Yes, all right. Come along. Quickly now.'

Her car, one of the new small Ford Model Ts, was outside the house, standing next to Oliver's Bentley. Its press-button starter failed to turn the engine over.

'Damn,' she said, 'damn, damn, damn. Of all the times.'

'I'll do it with the handle,' said Barty. 'I know how, Daniels has shown me. You stay in the car, be ready to press the accelerator.'

'Barty!' said Celia. 'Is there anything you don't know?'

Barty smiled at her, and clambered out of the car. Three cranks of the starting handle worked; she smiled at Celia over the bonnet, gave her the thumbs-up sign.

They roared off, Henry Ford's rather noisy little engine breaking the silence. Other people in Cheyne Walk stirred, frowned into the darkness, muttered about the deterioration of the neighbourhood.

'Be quick now,' said Sister, 'and very quiet.' She had met them at the night door of the hospital. 'I could lose my job if this were to become known. You must be Barty. What a grown-up girl you are. I thought you would be much smaller, more like little Jay.'

'How – how is he?' asked Celia.

Sister looked at her. Imperceptibly, she shook her head. Then, 'He's holding on,' she said briefly. 'This way now. Up these steps. Now wait here one moment – just while I see—'

See if he's still alive, Celia thought, see if it's all right for us, specially for Barty, to go in. She closed her eyes, and prayed with a fervour which surprised her, to a God she did not believe in.

Jay was lying utterly still now. His breathing was no longer painful, it was too light and shallow for that. He had stopped calling for Barty, for his mother, stopped asking to go home. He seemed to have moved into another place altogether, LM thought, looking at him in despair; not death, not quite yet, but not life either.

She took the small hand; it was burning hot. She raised it to her lips and kissed it on the back and in the palm, and then laid it gently down again.

'I'm sorry, Jay,' she whispered, 'So sorry.'

The door opened: Sister came in. She looked intently at Jay's inert form, picked up his small wrist, checked the pulse; then put a finger to her lips.

'Someone to see you,' she said very quietly.

The doctor, LM thought; come for a final, useless check on Jay. Before he died. It had frightened her how little they had been able to do. She looked at him; he was quite peaceful now. She wasn't sure she wanted him disturbed again, have the stethoscope applied to his painful chest, his mouth forced open to clear the sputum, the oxygen mask pushed on to his little face.

'I don't think—' she began.

'But you must be quiet. Absolutely quiet.'

Perhaps it was going to be painful. Unpleasant for Jay. Perhaps she was going to have to watch while he was tortured quite senselessly.

'No,' she said, 'no really. I don't want any more—'

Sister turned round, beckoned, then stood back; a small shadow slipped past her, stood by the side of the bed, looked down at Jay for a moment, and then spoke.

'Hallo Jay,' it said, very softly, right into his ear, 'it's Barty. I've come to read you a story.'

Later it passed into the folkore of *Meridian* that it had saved the life of a small boy; as he lay most dangerously ill, with a fever of a hundred and five and pneumonia choking both his small lungs. The nursing staff and the doctor in charge of his case said (as of course they would) that he reached the crisis of his illness at the same time, and would have recovered anyway. But LM and Celia only knew that as Barty's soft rather husky voice read on and on through the long night, read the wonderful tale of the child-kingdom, with its oceans of clouds and underwater mountains, its flying fish and swimming beasts, its grown-up children and turned-back time, Jay became no longer torpid but calm, no longer burning with fever but drenched with sweat, struggled less to breathe and cried less with pain, and in the morning was to be found sleeping quite peacefully, propped up on his pillows with Barty's thin arms held gently round him.

CHAPTER 18

'I simply don't believe it,' said Robert, 'where is all this filth coming from?'

'What filth?' said Maud. 'I don't see any.' They were eating breakfast on the terrace at Sutton Place; Robert had to work through the weekend, said he couldn't spare the time to go to Long Island. Maud didn't actually mind; Jamie was coming to stay, and he'd said he'd take her to the zoo in Central Park. That would be wonderful fun.

'What my darling? Oh – nothing.'

'Daddy! Tell me. It can't be – nothing.'

'It is. Honestly.'

He folded the newspaper he had been reading, smiled at her. 'When are you and Jamie off?'

'Oh – not for a bit. He's going to be sleeping late, he said. He went to a party last night. Without me,' she added darkly.

'When you're grown up, darling, he'll take you to lots of parties. Anyway, you won't want to go with him then. With your brother. You'll have lines of young men waiting to escort you.'

'I'll always want to go with Jamie,' said Maud.

When her father had gone out of the room, she picked up the paper, turned it carefully to the middle where she knew he had been reading, and studied it to see what might have upset him so much. It didn't take long; she read remarkably fast for someone of seven.

'Further trouble at Brewer Lytton,' read an item half-way down the page. 'The real estate firm of Brewer Lytton is rumoured to be laying off half its work force next week. The firm has just failed to win a contract to build a new department store on downtown Broadway. Hagman Betts, who have recently completed work on one of the new, smaller hotels on East 62nd, put in the winning bid. Brewer Lytton have also been seeking finance from several hitherto untapped sources, but all the institutions thus far approached have turned them down, presumably wary of an association with a firm which seems set on a downhill course. The bankers, Rea Goldberg, who had apparently expressed quite a firm intention to back another Brewer Lytton project, a housing development, on the upper West Side, have now pulled out at the eleventh hour. No one was available for comment, either at Rea Goldberg or at Brewer Lytton.'

Maud wasn't sure what some of the words meant, but she got the general idea; it gave her a very nasty feeling in her tummy.

Jamie woke up at about eleven, and she sat watching him while he ate his breakfast; it was an awful lot. Six rashers of bacon, five eggs, a heap of hash browns, and four waffles with maple syrup.

'I have to build myself up,' he said, by way of explanation. 'I've been picked to row in the Harvard Eight.'

'Can I come and watch you?' asked Maud.

'Of course you can. But it'll be very cold.'

'I won't mind. Can we go to the zoo now?'

'Yes, of course.'

'That was so much fun,' said Maud happily, 'thank you for taking me, Jamie.'

'My pleasure entirely. Now I wonder if you'd mind very much if we popped into Elliott House. I've left some books there that I really wanted to study from tomorrow—'

'Um – well, no. I mean – will Laurence be there?'

'Nope. He's gone to Long Island for the weekend. With his latest girlfriend.'

'Poor thing,' said Maud with a shudder. 'I feel sorry for her.'

She didn't like Laurence; she had no idea of the full extent of his animosity to her father, but he certainly never talked to her, not even to say hallo. And he actually frightened her a bit with his ice-cold eyes and pulled-in mouth, and by the way he did everything so silently, suddenly appearing in rooms when you had no idea he was anywhere near. He was like one of the bad magicians in her fairy story books.

'Right. I won't be long, I promise. Come on, hop in.'

She hopped in: to his new car, a lovely dark green thing with an open roof called a Buick.

He had bought it the week before; 'Not quite a Bugatti, like my dear brother has,' he said to Robert, 'but it gets me from A to B. Or rather from New York to Harvard. Goes like the wind, Robert. You should get one.'

Robert said rather shortly he wouldn't be buying any kind of new car, or even a bicycle for the foreseeable future.

Elliott House was very quiet; only a couple of staff were about: the butler, who greeted them very warmly, and remarked how Maud had grown, and the housekeeper who asked her if she'd like some cookies and milk. Maud said she would, if they had time: Jamie said they had plenty, he had to find a few other things as well as his books.

'Sports kit and so on. You'll be all right Maud?'

Maud said she'd be fine, and followed the housekeeper into the kitchen.

Milk and cookies consumed, she wandered off in search of Jamie; he was nowhere to be seen. It was such a big house; she much preferred where they lived now. The only better thing about Elliott House was the indoor swimming pool – that was very special. She would like to have one of those at Sutton Place; maybe she could ask her father. There was lots of room. The dining-room was much too big and they hardly ever used it. She wandered out of the pool room and across the courtyard to where she had had her playroom. She wondered what it would be used for now. Nothing probably. It had been a lovely room. What a waste: all this house, just for Laurence.

The playroom was very much in use: Laurence had converted it into his own library and study. Books lined three of the walls, and a huge desk stood in the middle of the room, with – 'Oh boy,' said Maud aloud – a revolving leather chair in front of it. She sat in the chair, used the desk to push herself off, whizzed round and round, this way and that. It was fun.

Slightly dizzy, she sat still for a while, considering the desk itself. It was terribly neat: everything perfectly lined up. Pens and pencils in two parallel trays, a pad of pristine white paper, a telephone, at right angles to that, Laurence's diary, a much bigger tray of letters, and yet another tray with an assortment of things in it, which Laurence obviously felt must be neatly contained: a few invitations, a circular about an art exhibition, and a catalogue of books. She took a pencil from the tray, and a piece of paper, did a drawing of some of the animals she and Jamie had seen that day. A shaggy goat and a tiny little pony, no bigger than a dog, called a Falabella. She'd like one of those: it could live in the house with them. She drew it a kennel: a pony kennel. Rather than a stable. That would be fun.

How awful if Laurence came back here now and found her. In his creepy silent way. She hoped Jamie was right, that he really was away. She stood up, half-scared, carefully re-straightened the paper and pencils – and then her arm caught the edge of one of the trays and it crashed to the floor. There was nothing in it that might break, thank goodness; she scrabbled about, picking everything up carefully, packing it back as neatly and carefully as she could. One of the things was a cheque book and it had fallen face downwards, with something on top of it, so that it was open, with the top cheque creased. That was serious. Laurence

328

would surely notice. Maybe if she closed it, put some heavy books on it, it would flatten out again. She picked it up, turned it over, ready to fold it. The top cheque wasn't blank though, it had something written on it. In Laurence's very neat, black-inked handwriting, all the letters and numbers very upright and close together. She wouldn't have noticed it even then, if the name on the cheque hadn't been fixed in her head; a name from the article which had made her feel so horrid that morning and had upset her father. A funny name. Nathaniel Betts.

'Daddy.'

'Yes, darling.'

'I can't go to sleep. Can I come and sit with you for a bit?'

'No, Maud, you can't. I'm sorry. I'm busy and it's late. Now go on upstairs again. Read if you can't sleep, that's what I always do.'

'All right.' She sighed, her voice resigned, turned to leave the room again. Robert looked up; she was drooping, as he had known she would be. Maud was very good at drooping; her neck and shoulders drooped, her head drooped, even her back, in some strange way, managed to droop. He smiled suddenly, amused out of his anxiety.

'Come here, poppet. Sorry.'

'No, it's all right. You're busy, I can see.'

'Not too busy for you. Now you sit down there for just ten minutes while I finish this, and then we'll read a story. How would that be?'

'Good.' She smiled at him, came over, gave him a hug. 'I'll be very quiet.' She was good at that too; at sitting utterly still and silent, her large green eyes fixed on him. After a few minutes he threw down his pen.

'You're distracting me. You're being too quiet.'

'Miss Edwards says you can't be too quiet.'

'Well she's right in a way. But – well anyway, go and get a story.'

She sat on his knee, sucking her thumb as she still did when he read to her, listening quietly.

When he had finished, he said, 'Right. Do you think you'll be able to go to sleep now?'

She sighed. 'I'll try.'

'Is something the matter?'

She hesitated. Then, 'Ye-es. A bit.'

'What?'

'I'm worried. About Laurence.'

'About Laurence? Why on earth should you be worried about him?'

'I – knocked over something in his study today.'

'Oh dear. What on earth were you doing in his study? Not a good idea, poppet.'

'No, I know. Jamie took me to the house.'

'Well, he won't know. He's not psychic. And I'm sure you didn't do any harm.'

'But I did. And he might notice.'

'Oh, Maud.' Robert sighed. 'What exactly did you knock over?'

'A tray thing. His cheque book was on it, and a cheque got all bent.'

'Uh-huh. And did you put it back?'

'Yes. Well, sort of.'

'Oh, he'll think the housekeeper did it. Don't worry.'

'Do you really think so?'

'Of course.'

'Oh good. Daddy—'

'Yes.'

'There was writing on the cheque. It was filled in, you know, like you do them. Money and a name.'

'So—'

'I noticed the name. It was the same as in that article today, the one you folded into the paper.'

'The one what? Maud what are you talking about?'

'The name on the cheque. It was something Betts.'

'Hagman Betts?'

'Not exactly. Nathaniel Betts. And anyway—'

'Just a minute, Maud. Laurence had made out a cheque to Nathaniel Betts?' Robert swallowed. 'Maud, darling, I don't suppose you noticed what it said.'

'Oh yes,' she said, 'I did notice. Well, there were too many noughts in the number place to work it out. But I could read the words bit. It said fifty thousand dollars.'

'Oliver. Good morning to you.'

It was Jack, smiling, fit-looking, still somehow unsuited to his civilian clothes.

'I – missed you at the house.'

'Yes, well, we take breakfast a little earlier than you do,' said Oliver mildly.

'I know, I know. I'm a layabed. I'm just indulging myself after all those years in the army.'

'Well,' said Oliver wearily, 'you've probably earned it.'

'I don't know about that. But I intend to start getting up again much earlier soon.'

'Yes?'

'Yes. I clearly need to get a job. My army pension isn't very large and

I've only the small amount of capital Father left me. Worth a lot less than it was.'

Especially as he'd gambled away quite a bit of it, Oliver thought; and wasted quite a bit more on actresses and their needs – needs like jewellery and champagne. Still, even before France, he had been out in the stifling heat of India, helping defend the Empire. He deserved some self-indulgence.

'I expect that's true,' he said.

'Anyway, I've got a proposition for you.'

'A proposition?'

'Yes. I'd like to join the family firm.'

'Join Lyttons! But Jack—'

'I know, I know. Only ever read four books. Five now, enjoyed the children's story by that Brooke chap a lot. But – well, it does all begin to seem rather more interesting than I thought. And my idea was something you're not doing. Something you should be doing.'

'Oh really?' Oliver smiled. Jack must have been taking more of an interest in Lyttons than he thought. 'And what would that be?'

'Military books. Military history. The stories of the great regiments, the great battles. How we won the empire, how we won the war. All that sort of stuff.'

'Ye-es. And you think people would like to read it, do you? All that sort of stuff?'

'I certainly do. Wouldn't you?'

'Well – no,' said Oliver truthfully. Having come through four years of hell with the military life, he wanted only to escape from it.

'Oh rubbish. Look how fascinated people are by the great battles. Waterloo. Trafalgar. The Khyber Pass . . .'

'Well—'

'Look, ask Celia. I'm sure she'd think it was a good idea. I was in a bookshop yesterday, looking at the military books. Some of them are awfully jolly, lots of coloured pictures, and all that sort of thing. And I know plenty of people who could write the books for you, Teddy Grosvenor for a start, he'd love to do the Mutiny, I was talking to him about it, he brings it all to life just with a few words.'

'Really?' Oliver thought of General Edward Grosvenor, with his bluff manner and his fondness for port. Anything he wrote would be fairly brief. His vocabulary was extremely limited.

'Yes. And think of old Beckenham, full of wonderful stories. Bet he'd like to get going on something. And Lady B's grandfather's journals, young Barty was telling me about them; fascinating they sound.'

'Well—'

'Good man. I knew you'd agree.'

331

'Jack, I haven't agreed.'

'Well – say you'll think about it. I'd really love to do it. And I'd work terribly hard. I swear.'

'All right,' said Oliver, 'I'll think about it. And thank you. Where are you off to now?'

'Oh, going to a matinee. See a friend who's in it. Awfully jolly girl called Stella. You'd like her. I might bring her to meet you some time.'

'I'm sure Stella wouldn't want to meet me,' said Oliver wearily.

'I want to talk to you about something.'

Celia looked up at Oliver, made a determined effort to smile. It was a considerable effort; this was usually the signal for a long tirade of criticism, of complaints about her frittering away Lyttons' reputation, the lowering of standards over which she had presided. Or a painstaking appraisal of some very minor book which had come in, and whether they should publish it. He seemed to have entirely lost his capacity for taking an overview, for seeing what did and didn't matter, what Lyttons should and shouldn't publish.

'Yes,' she said, 'yes, what is it?'

'Jack came in this morning.'

'Jack! Into Lyttons?'

'Yes. He had a proposition for me.'

'For you?'

'Well – for Lyttons.'

'Oliver, really. When did Jack have an idea in his head that was remotely to do with publishing?' She smiled at him. 'What does he want to do, write a book about his regiment for us?'

'Something like that, yes.'

'What?' She stared at him; he was clearly serious.

'Don't look so astonished,' he said irritably, 'he's not entirely stupid, you know.'

'Of course he's not stupid. He's highly intelligent. But he's not – well very literate.'

'I think that's a little harsh.'

'Sorry, Oliver.' She always forgot how careful she had to be about Jack. Oliver could criticise him; she was not allowed to.

'Anyway, he's made a suggestion which I'm considering very carefully. I would like you to as well.'

'Yes?' she said. Trying to sound positive.

'It is that we should start a military list.'

'A military list!'

'Yes. A series of books on military matters. Histories of regiments, of battles, of traditions – all that sort of thing.'

'Oh.'

'What do you think?'

'I think—' she took a deep breath; this was going to be difficult, but it had to be said, quickly, before the idea took hold, 'I think it's an appalling idea.'

He looked at her levelly. 'And why do you think that?'

'It's so specialist, Oliver. Such a small section of the reading public would appreciate it. And those books are expensive to produce, otherwise they're not worth having and—'

'Not cheap, of course. Like *Meridian*.'

'Oh Oliver, please don't start on that again. It really isn't relevant.'

'It seems quite relevant to me.'

She was silent.

'Any other objections?'

'Well – I really don't think, even if we did such a thing, had such a list—' she hesitated, 'well, I presume you don't actually think Jack should be in charge of it.'

'Why not?'

'Oh really, Oliver, he has no experience. He wouldn't have the faintest idea what he was doing, wouldn't know about printing costs, illustrations, how to deal with the trade . . .'

'Well, obviously he would have people to help him on the practicalities. But the ideas and a lot of the contacts would come from him. That seems to me entirely sensible. Sensible and fair.'

'So you envisage – let me get this straight – a whole new department? Devoted to Jack and his military books?'

'Oh Celia, don't be absurd. Not a whole department. Obviously. Although I don't recall your objecting to a whole department, as you put it, being turned over to *Biographica*.'

'That is entirely different. As you very well know. The market for biography is vast and—'

'Oh yes, entirely different,' he said, 'it was to be your department. That was the real difference. Well, I like this idea of Jack's. Very much. At least a military list would have some – quality to it. The books would have class. Not a whole lot of rubbish.'

'Oh, Oliver please . . .'

'You simply don't seem to realise how much you've done to lower Lyttons' reputation. Putting a lot of rubbish out. Cheap poetry, trashy fiction which looks like *Peg's Paper*.'

'It was not—' she stopped. She must keep calm. 'We had to publish popular stuff, Oliver. The alternative was letting Lyttons go right under.

Going bankrupt. I told you. It was so tough. You don't understand. It was just – oh God. How I wish LM was here. She might be able to convince you.'

'I am very surprised at her allowing it all, I must say,' he said, 'even more than at you.'

She tried again. 'Oliver, you really don't understand. We had hugely increased costs. A falling market. No staff to speak of—'

'You seem to me to have done quite well in that direction as well. Hiring a lot of rather second-rate women. Who I would not personally have considered.'

'Is that so?' She was getting angry now; she couldn't help it. 'Well, let me tell you those second-rate women worked like slaves here all through the war. Each one doing the work of three. Often with bombs falling around them. Sleeping here, even, when there was a raid on. Doing their own cleaning. LM and I cleaned the lavatories personally, it might amuse you to know—'

'My heart bleeds for you, Celia. How dreadful. Life in the trenches couldn't possibly compete with that.'

'Oh damn life in the trenches,' she said savagely. 'I am sick to death of hearing about it. About the mud and the stench and the rats. Absolutely sick of it.'

'I'm sorry about that,' he said, his voice measured and very polite. His face was very white. 'I got quite sick of it myself, as a matter of fact. But I'll try not to refer to it again.'

Celia stared at him; she suddenly felt nauseous. That had been unforgivable. Absolutely unforgivable. She looked at him, went forward, tried to touch him. He shied away from her.

'I'm sorry, Oliver. Very sorry. I should never have said that. Please forgive me.'

He was silent.

'But – don't you understand. In my – our own way, we did have a hard time here, too. It was lonely. Worrying. Dangerous even. The responsibilities were huge – the children, the company—'

'You looked after the children very well,' he said with an emphasis on the word children, and this time his voice was very bitter indeed.

'Oliver—'

'I have to tell you, Celia, that I think a military list would do something towards restoring Lyttons' reputation, as a quality house. I am thinking very seriously of agreeing to Jack's proposition. And if I do, I shall expect your full co-operation.'

Celia looked at him, and then turned and walked out of the office. She couldn't take any more.

His criticism of her was endless: nothing was right for him. The way

334

the house was run, the new staff she had hired at home, the hours she worked, even their social life came under fire.

'You may go if you wish,' he would say as invitations came in, 'I would prefer to stay at home. I don't feel up to any of that sort of nonsense. Simply working is exhausting enough.'

She did go sometimes: at others she stayed with him, endeavouring to make their evenings together pleasurable. She bought gramophone records of the classical music he so loved, large sets so that he could play an entire symphony, or marked items in the newspapers so that they could discuss them at dinner, items about the things which had always so concerned them both, the growth of the Labour Party, the success of the suffragette movement, the social unrest, the plight of the disabled soldiers home from the war. She briefed Cook to make his rather bland diet as interesting as possible, and often suggested a gentle walk along the Embankment after dinner. Sometimes he seemed pleased, and went along with her plans, more often he did not, claiming a headache or indigestion, and disappeared into his study. Those evenings were almost a relief; at least she could get on with her own work.

But still he did not make love to her.

She could scarcely believe they had ever existed now, the wonderful sudden swoops of desire which had seen them hurrying up to their room in the evening, or shaking one another awake early in the morning, the smiling preamble, the verbal teasing, the, 'Surely not again, Celia?' the, 'I suppose I could if you really want me to, Oliver,' words that belied their on-going need for and delight in one another.

She struggled for patience, to remember what he had said to her, to understand; but it was hard. Hard in the face of her own desire and frustration, doubly so in the face of his criticism. Had he been loving in other ways, had he talked to her, listened to her, told her he loved her often, kissed her, held her in his arms, she could, she thought, have endured it more easily; but he retired to his study each night after dinner, leaving her alone, and it was very rare that he even came to her room. She could see he was wretched about it, embarrassed, ashamed, but she was trying so hard to understand him, to support him, and she got almost nothing in return.

But if home was not entirely happy, work was turning into pure misery, every day a call on wells of patience she had no idea she possessed, and when that failed, or her conviction that Oliver was wrong became overwhelming, there were noisy exchanges behind the closed doors of their respective offices, as he tried to reverse her decisions, questioned her judgement, demanded her acquiescence. She felt diminished, not only in the eyes of her staff, but in her very self, something she would never have believed possible. In the worst moments of the war, when she had been beleaguered and frightened, not only by the Germans but by soaring costs, diminished income, and a growing belief that nobody would never buy books again, she had still known precisely what she wanted and was trying to do. That sense had begun to desert her in the face of Oliver's interminable censure.

And then she would not have believed how badly she missed LM. Her calm, rather stern presence had been a support to her ever since she could remember, her sudden robust laugh, her oddly raucous sense of humour, her huge capacity for work, her shrewd judgement. But she was going to have to get used to being without her. She was not coming back. She had moved temporarily into the Dovecot with Jay and was in the process of buying a small house on the edge of Ashingham village. One day, she said to Celia, one day, perhaps, when Jay was away at school − 'and I am not at all sure I will be sending him away, not sure that Jago would have wanted that' − she would come back to work. Not before.

'I know I shall find it boring and frustrating and I shall miss Lyttons dreadfully. But Jay is more important. I have learned my lesson.'

Jay was recovering fast; already regaining his strength, the strange, white, thin face becoming round and rosy again, his leg mending well. He was sublimely happy to be back at Ashingham, and in the absence of Barty and the twins, had latched on to Billy; as soon as he recovered enough to leave the tiny garden of the Dovecot he headed for the stables on his crutches and followed Billy around until he was hauled home again to rest.

'Look at the pair of you,' Lady Beckenham roared one morning, arriving as Billy set Jay to work sweeping the yard, 'pair of cripples. It's like having the convalescent home all over again.'

She had arranged for Billy to have a more sophisticated artificial leg made; 'You'll be able to use it more like a normal leg, I'm told. It'll have a knee, so to speak. Much better for riding.'

She had also promised to give Jay riding lessons as soon as his leg was better; the very thought of him in a situation where he might fall off and fracture it again, or even break something else, sent LM into paroxysms of anxiety, but Lady Beckenham talked to her quite severely about it one night when she was close to tears. Jay had gone missing for an hour or more, and was then found in the woods, happily damming a stream, using his crutch to form the main structure.

'You can't wrap him up in cotton wool, you know. He's a boy and a damn fine one. I know he's had a bad experience and so have you, but he's over it now, and fussing over him like an old hen will simply make him anxious. He has to lead a normal boy's life, that's why you're here. You've done the right thing, getting him out of London and now you've got to let him benefit from it. He'll be all right, there's no danger here. Unless you count falling from the odd hayloft or horse, which all mine did without coming to any harm whatsoever.'

'Yes, all right,' said LM meekly. She was not used to being told what to do; it was rather soothing.

She had written to Gordon Robinson, thanking him for his letter, assuring him that she did not blame him in the least, and that Jay seemed to be making a good recovery; he had written again and asked if he might visit Jay, 'and perhaps bring some books to amuse him. It isn't much fun being laid up. I broke my arm as a boy, and can still remember the boredom of one whole school holidays, forbidden to climb trees and unable to play cricket.'

She had thought how kind and considerate he had sounded, had written back and said that would be extremely kind; but on the appointed day he had telephoned to say that he was not well himself. 'Only a gastric upset, but not ideal for visting an invalid.' LM had been almost disappointed, had suggested another day, but they had been unable to settle on one before she moved down to Ashingham.

'Some other time then,' he said; the next day a large box of books arrived by carrier, rather grown-up for Jay, some of them, but certainly of a standard she approved of, *Treasure Island, Robinson Crusoe, Gulliver's Travels.*

'I am not sure how old Jay is,' he wrote, 'but if these are too old for him, they can be kept. It is never too soon to start building up a library. I believe there is a wonderful new children's book about to be published, but I was unable to find it. Anyway, I hope he will enjoy these, and I look forward to making his acquaintance some time in the future.'

He was clearly a most suitable friend and mentor for Jay, even if he had come close to killing him.

'That's a very pretty dress,' said Sebastian.

'Thank you.'

'I like pink. Always have.'

'Really?'

'Yes. And it suits you.'

'Thank you,' she said again.

'Would it like to go out to lunch, do you think?'

'No,' she said, 'no, not today.'

'Are you sure?'

'Yes, I'm quite sure. I really can't come out today.'

She kept saying that; putting it off. She felt she had to: although of

337

course there was no reason why, really. It was only a lunch. A lunch to discuss all sorts of things. Publishing things. The launch of *Meridian* was timed for December, only a few months away. There really was quite a lot to think about, to arrange. Interviews with the literary papers, readings, meetings with the major bookshops. That was what she kept telling herself. And that self listened dutifully, then turned around and told her the actual truth: which was that lunch with Sebastian would lead not merely to a carefully planned publication of his book, but to an affair with him. There was no way she could avoid it: whichever path she took, whatever diversion she made, it would be there, confronting her. She was afraid of it, she shrank from it indeed; and yet, she felt, against her will, a hastening towards it, a growing impatience now to let it begin.

'Now,' she said, 'if you've come about the proofs—'

'I haven't come about anything,' he said, 'as you very well know. Except to see you.'

'Sebastian, I'm very busy. I really can't go out to lunch with you today.'

'What about tomorrow?'

'No. I won't be here tomorrow.'

'Where are you going? Lunching with someone else, I suppose. Tell me who it is, so that I can warn him of the dangers.'

'I am lunching with someone else, yes,' she said. 'Tomorrow is Saturday. It's the Fourth of June at Eton. We're all going.'

'How charming. Even the twins?'

'Of course the twins. They're wild with excitement. They have new dresses and coats and hats for the occasion.'

'And do you have a new dress and coat and hat?'

'Of course.'

'Well,' he said with a sigh, 'I shall just have to contain my impatience. But that particular dress is just made to go for lunch. In the garden.'

'The garden?'

'Yes. Of my house in Primrose Hill. I'm still waiting to show it to you. I hope you haven't forgotten.'

'I haven't forgotten,' she said, 'but—'

'Yes?'

'Sebastian—'

'Yes, Celia. Ah. Oliver good morning. I just came in to pick up my proofs. I have to leave now. Perhaps we could dine one night, discuss the publication details.'

'Yes,' said Oliver, 'yes, that would be delightful. Celia, we have to do something about these jackets—'

338

'He seems to spend a lot of time here,' said Oliver when Sebastian had gone.

'Does he?' she said, 'I really hadn't noticed.'

Giles was looking forward with something close to longing to seeing his family the next day. Even the twins. The twins were, in any case, much more bearable now. Not exactly sensible, but not so silly. And very pretty. It was nice to have pretty sisters, even if they were only nine. And it would be lovely to see Barty. She was getting really pretty now too. All that curly brown hair. And he liked her voice, sounding a bit as if she had a sore throat.

He was actually, and greatly to his surprise and relief, quite happy at Eton. It would have been much nicer to be at home; but compared with the early days at St Christopher's it was heaven. One of the best things was having his own room, tiny as it was, with a bed that folded up against the wall, and its own small grate, bookcase and writing desk. Even the housemaster had to knock before entering. You couldn't help feeling grown-up. And then the boys were all addressed as 'Gentlemen'. As in 'Gentlemen may wear half change (which meant a tweed jacket) after twelve', or, 'Several gentlemen have left their umbrellas in Chapel'. That made him feel really grown-up too. Grown up and important. He didn't even mind the clothes: he was tall, and knew they suited him. The first time he surveyed himself in the mirror wearing the striped trousers, tail coat and top hat, he felt quite different suddenly.

The food was horrible; but then it had been at St Christopher's. That was part of school life, although it was rumoured that when a boy had committed suicide recently at Eton, and when the housemaster had asked if anyone could throw any light on it, someone had said, 'Please sir, could it be anything to do with the food?' Tea was the best meal; you could cook it yourself, fried eggs, sausages, bacon, and, of course, toast, made at your own fire. The richer boys – Giles was not among them – ordered things like grouse and pheasant from Rowlands, the official café in the town. Of course you also had to cook for your fag-master, who came from the elite Library body, a group of senior boys; this could be arduous, but Giles was lucky again, as he had certainly not been at St Christopher's and had a pretty nice fag-master. His best friend, Willoughby, who had been at St. Christopher's with him, had a ghastly one; he was beaten constantly, usually in the presence of the head of house. There was nothing to be done about it, they both knew that; it was simply what happened.

The other thing which simply happened was harder to bear than the beating. Something that Giles had been warned about in the most veiled and peculiar terms when he had been about to leave St Christopher's, something that many fathers (although most assuredly not Oliver) had also hinted at, something that Willoughby suffered a great deal, and that Giles had so far escaped. Willoughby was small and blond and slightly girly-looking. After a very few days his fag-master, who was also a member of Pop – the society composed of the most exceptional and outrageous boys in the school – called him to his study, locked the door, and told him to pull his trousers down. Fearing yet another beating, Willoughby did so resignedly; what followed was far worse. Giles listened to the details, whispered to him behind his own locked door, with sympathetic distress.

'But why?' he kept saying, 'why should they want to do that?'

Willoughby said he didn't quite know, but they seemed to get a lot of pleasure from it. 'It hurts,' he said to Giles, 'it really hurts,' and started to cry.

Giles was deeply distressed, but knew there was nothing to be done about it, no one to complain to; he had already learned from his fag-master amongst others – that such things were part of the ethos of the school, and masters as well as boys were involved in it.

So far Giles had escaped, although he knew he was in the minority; the only encounter of a sexual nature he had had was with his housemaster, who insisted on the whole house being regularly inspected, naked.

'We have to make sure you don't have venereal disease,' he said; 'come on, boy, let's have a look at you.' Giles, who had no clear idea what venereal disease was, but could only suppose it was something extremely dangerous, submitted to some minor intimacies without complaint, and was grateful it wasn't any worse.

His prowess on the athletics field was of no immediate use to him, but he was very strong, and much better co-ordinated than he had been. He was developing a modestly good bowling technique, and running fast was an indubitable advantage on the cricket pitch. He knew he would probably never be in the first eleven, but he played for his house junior team and enjoyed it; and he was enjoying, too, the academic facilities at Eton, its superb classical traditions, and the extravagances and eccentricities of the various beaks or masters. The standard was set by the headmaster, Dr Allington, who stalked about the school, wearing an overcoat made of polar bear skin, and preached such superb sermons that people actually looked forward to going to chapel. Then there was CO Beaven, who drank a thimbleful of iodine before Early School, the lesson which took place before breakfast; John Christie who taught theoretical science, without appearing to know a great deal about it, and took Early School in his dressing-gown. Giles particularly admired Jack

Upcott, who taught Elizabethan history, and who was famous for saying that he would forgive any boy anything if he could make him laugh. Giles had no talent at all in that direction, but he found echoes of both his mother and his grandmother in Dr Upcott, something to do with a regard for any kind of excellence, and the view that it excused all manner of other things.

They all arrived at noon at Agar's Plough, in the new Rolls; the twins, in pale blue coats and shoes and flower-trimmed straw bonnets, fell out and rushed at him, Barty followed more slowly, smiling shyly. Then came his Uncle Jack, who said he'd been unable to resist and hoped Giles wouldn't mind his being there – which of course he didn't; he liked Jack a lot, he was always good fun, and full of stories about his own schooldays at Wellington and the terrible scrapes he had got into. And then his mother, looking staggeringly beautiful in a straight, dark blue dress in sort of shiny material, with a loose tie round the neck, and her dark hair cut much shorter, half hidden by a white hat with an enormous drooping brim and wide ribbon. Barty whispered to him that it was from somewhere called Chanel.

'It only arrived last night; she's very pleased with it.'

He saw a lot of the boys staring at her as she kissed him and felt very proud; most of the other mothers looked much older than she did, and wore baggy dresses, with shawls and furs round their shoulders.

'Hallo Giles, old man. How are you?'

It was his father: looking stronger than he had done, but very thin still, and dreadfully pale. His hair was almost completely grey; Giles thought of that morning when they had all waved him off to the war, so tall and upright in his uniform, his thick fair hair shining in the sunlight as he removed his hat and bent to kiss his mother, and thought how very much for the worse he had changed.

'I'm very well, sir thank you. It's good to see you. Do you want to watch the match?' The school was playing the Old Boys at cricket.

'Oh – not sure. What do you think, Celia?'

'Of course we do. I adore watching cricket. I was a frightfully good bowler myself once. Let's find a nice place to settle and enjoy ourselves. Giles, my darling, you must have grown a foot at least, and I love the buttonhole. I remember my brothers, there were three of them here at any given time for years you know, they all wore different colours.'

It was a wonderful day; Celia had organised a superb picnic, cold chicken, pheasant and salmon, salad, tiny fruit tarts, fruit salad, a platter of wonderful cheeses, and of course, champagne. And lemonade for the children but they were also, apart from the twins, allowed a small glass of the champagne. Barty didn't like hers; slipped it to Giles.

Half-way through lunch, a bus arrived, bearing a lot of old Etonians from Oxford, followed by another from Cambridge, all making a great deal of noise. Pretty girls wandered about kissing everyone – Jack seemed to think he knew a large number of them and kept bringing them over to the picnic for champagne, to try to establish exactly how – the sun shone most wonderfully, and the band played. Giles sneaked a third glass of champagne, actually belonging to his mother, who spent most of the meal jumping up to run over to this or that person to greet them; by the time they tripped over to the riverbank to watch the procession of boats, and listen to the strains of the Eton boat song, he was feeling very dizzy. Watching the boys stand up rather unsteadily in their boats to raise their flower-trimmed hats in salute to Windsor and Eton, made him feel worse; he had to sit down rather abruptly. His father came over to him, sat down beside him, and smiled.

'Bit too much of the bubbly eh? I didn't think that last glass was a good idea.'

Giles grinned at him sheepishly. 'It's awfully nice, though.'

'I know. It's been a superb day hasn't it? And it's so nice to see you looking so happy. Enjoying it, aren't you?'

'Yes,' said Giles, 'I really am. It's so different from St Christopher's.'

'You weren't quite so happy there?'

'Happy!' said Giles, his tongue loosened by the champagne, 'I was so miserable I couldn't believe it.'

'Oh now, it can't have been that bad, surely.'

Giles felt irritated.

'Father, it was dreadful. Honestly. I was terribly unhappy.'

'Well it can't have been too bad, or you would have told us,' said Oliver.

'I did tell you. Well I told Mother. You were away, of course.'

'And what was so terrible?'

He still looked mildly amused. He's patronising me, thought Giles. He felt angry suddenly, wanted to let his father know how bad it had been.

'Well,' he said slowly, 'I was beaten. Nearly every day Not just by the masters, but the big boys. They called me horrible names. And they made me wear a nappy. And—'

'A nappy! Why did you have to wear a nappy?' said Oliver. For the first time he looked properly concerned.

'Because they decided I should,' said Giles simply, 'they used to hold me down while they put it on. And then they all stared at my – well at me every morning when they took it off. And made jokes about it.'

'And you didn't tell any of the masters?'

'Of course not. It would have made things worse.'

Oliver was silent. Then he said, 'And you told your mother all this, did you?'

'No not all of it. Of course. But I did say I was dreadfully miserable.'

'And she didn't try and find out why? What was going on?'

'Well – no,' Giles began to feel rather alarmed suddenly. He shouldn't make too much of it; it was, after all, a long way in the past. 'But you were going away to the war. And she was very busy, and—'

'She didn't suggest you talked to me?'

'No. She said I wasn't to, that you had enough to worry about. That people were making all kinds of sacrifices, dying in the war, that it wasn't very important, me being miserable at school. I'm sure she was right in a way,' he added carefully.

Oliver was silent for a long time. Then he said, 'Well, I'm sorry, Giles. So very sorry. If I had known how bad it was, I would have considered it very important. Very important indeed.'

Celia sat and listened to Oliver as he castigated her for cruelty to Giles, for not informing him about his wretchedness, for not inquiring more closely into the reasons for his unhappiness, for not taking it up with the school. When he had finished she said simply, 'I'm sorry, Oliver, very sorry that you should feel like that. As I said to Giles at the time, there was a great deal of suffering going on, both out in France and here at home.'

'I don't feel that diminishes his in any way.'

'Of course it doesn't. But I felt it important that he should put it in perspective.'

'It's a great pity he didn't feel able to tell me about it. I would have felt quite differently.'

'You weren't here. Most of the time. You were away at Colchester, and then you went to France. How could I trouble you with a small boy's problems at school? I was encouraging the children to be brave for you, not to worry you.'

'Did you know exactly what those problems were?'

'Well, not exactly, no.'

'You didn't know he was being beaten, bullied.'

'No, I didn't. I thought just teased—'

'He was made to wear a nappy. Clearly there were some kind of sexual implications, as well. It was appalling, Celia, I can't believe you let it go uninvestigated.'

She looked at him steadily. Then she said, 'I had no idea it was as bad as that. Of course I didn't. If I had—'

'Then don't you think you should have known?'

'Yes! Yes of course I should. But there were a dozen reasons why I didn't. I was taking charge at Lyttons. The children were tiny. I was pregnant. You were leaving me for what seemed like an almost certain death. Of course I should have done more. But I was fighting a very lonely battle of my own here, Oliver. I would ask you to remember that, to take it into consideration. I am deeply sorry about it, and I shall apologise to Giles myself, of course.'

'And I suppose you think that will exonerate you, make everything all right?'

'No, of course not. But it will make Giles realise that I do care about him.'

'I think,' said Oliver, 'it is probably a little late for that. I am going to bed now, if you will excuse me. Goodnight.'

'Laurence, good morning. Robert Lytton here.'

'My secretary said – well, never mind. What do you want?'

'Yes, I said I was Henry Rea from Rea Goldberg. Sorry about that small deception. I wondered if we could meet for lunch. Just a few small matters I'd like to go over with you.'

'I really don't think we have anything to say to one another, Robert. And certainly not over lunch.'

'I have a great deal to say to you,' said Robert. 'You may not have much to say to me. Perhaps you would prefer to come and see me at my office.'

'I have no desire to come to your office. What is this about? I really would be grateful if you would—'

'It's about Hagman Betts, Laurence. And the mysterious way they keep winning contracts from us.'

'I really don't see what that has to do with me.'

'On the contrary, it appears to have a great deal to do with you.'

'What are you talking about?'

'It begins with a cheque. For fifty thousand dollars, made out to Nathaniel Betts.'

A miniscule pause: then, 'I have no idea what you're talking about, I'm afraid.'

'I think you do. I suspect – without being able to prove it of course – that this fifty thousand represents the difference between what they would have had to quote in order to make the last job profitable, and what they actually did quote. Something like that, anyway. And then there are all those nasty little items in the press. More or less implying that we are incompetent as well as expensive.'

'The press can only write what they know.'

344

'Correction. They write what they are told. And, my foolishly blind eyes having been opened by the news of that cheque – I don't know why I never thought of you before – I did a little research. I have contacts in publishing here, of course – through my brother. The reporter was asked where his information came from; about the refusal of finance, the particularly interesting quote about Hagman Betts being imaginative, and Brewer Lytton, by implication, much less so. It transpired that a young man from Betts had taken him out to an expensive dinner and plied him with bourbon, on the pretext of supplying him with an article on architecture in the city generally.'

'This is all so tenuous,' said Laurence. 'You're paranoid. It just doesn't mean anything at all.'

'Possibly not. In a court of law. But I am as capable of spreading rumour as you are, and I still have a great many friends in the banking fraternity. Your hostility to me is well known. It wouldn't be difficult to believe that you are out to do me down. And it would be interesting for people to know you have been paying large sums of money to Hagman Betts out of your own pocket. No doubt, filtered down from the bank.'

Another pause. 'I have never heard of anything quite so absurd. Clearly anxiety and depression have led to some kind of paranoid delusion. I feel almost sorry for you.'

'Not paranoia, Laurence. Nor a delusion. Fact. Absolute fact.'

'This is absurd,' he said, sounding slightly less sure of himself. 'You have absolutely no proof of any such thing.'

'Oh, but I do. Your cheque book came into my possession. Your personal cheque book. I have returned it now, delivered it myself to Elliotts, in an envelope marked for your personal attention. But I have taken the liberty of taking some photographs of the cheques. I have a small photographic studio in my house; it was quite easy to do. I printed them myself, in my own dark-room, you have no need to worry that any of this might leak into the outside world. But—'

'Celia, I must talk to you.'

'Of course. Oliver, I have some more poems by Felicity Brewer here. They're truly charming. I would like, if you agree, to publish a small collection of them. Illustrated, I think. They—'

'Yes, good idea. I like them too.'

'Oh.' Celia had been prepared for a long discussion, and then a long argument.

'Anyway, I can talk to Felicity about it myself. I'm planning to go to New York in a month or two—'

'Are you?'

345

'Yes. I want to visit our office over there, it's long overdue, and, of course, I want to see Robert.'

Jealousy stabbed her: it was both personal and professional, but especially that he should be excluding her from something so crucial to Lyttons' development as a major house. 'I didn't know. Can I come?'

'Oh, I don't think so, it will only be a very brief trip.'

'Oliver, I really would like to.'

'No, Celia, I don't want this turning into a major production. I'm sorry. Just a few days—'

She gave up; there was clearly no point in arguing.

'Now, it is on the subject of illustration that I really want to talk to you.'

'Yes?'

'I have had a letter from James Sharpe. This morning. He is much better, indeed quite restored to health, and—'

'Good. I'm delighted. He's had a bad time.'

James Sharpe had indeed had a bad time; shrapnel wounds to his spine had left him in considerable pain, with his mobility permanently, although not seriously impaired.

'I fear I shall never be able to tango with Celia again,' was how he put it to Oliver, but it was a little more serious than that. He could walk only slowly, with a limp, and leaned heavily on a cane: or rather canes. He was something of a dandy, and his blithely courageous spirit seized on the fact that canes could come with ivory handles, silver handles, could be made of ebony, mahogany, could be exquisitely carved, could be designed for town or country: he was acquiring a collection as extensive as his wardrobe of suits and overcoats.

'So – is he coming back?' asked Celia casually.

'He is indeed. He says he feels more than ready, and that it will hasten his recovery more than any medicine or surgery.'

'Well, of course. I am the last person to argue with that.'

'I know you are,' said Oliver. He hesitated, then cleared his throat. 'Incidentally I spoke to him about the military list. He thought it had considerable potential. He envisaged some large, quite lavishly illustrated books. He agreed with me that they would lend Lyttons extra authority at the present time.'

'Really?' said Celia. She did not dare argue any more about the military list. She was only thankful that Jack had not broached the subject with her himself. She expected it whenever he was at home for dinner; which was rarely. Perhaps an unusual streak of sensitivity was holding him back.

'Anyway,' Oliver was saying, 'when James comes back, there will obviously be no place here, for Gill Thomas.'

There was a silence; then, 'What did you say?' said Celia.

'Celia, it does irritate me the way you do that.'

'What?' she said, playing for time.

'Pretend you haven't heard me, when what I have said is simply something disagreeable to you, or that you wish to argue about. I said there would be no place here for Gill Thomas when James Sharpe comes back.'

'Well, that's ridiculous. Of course there is.'

'I'm afraid there isn't. James will be reinstated as art director and—'

'But that is so unfair. So terribly unfair.'

'I'm afraid I don't see that. James was our art director before the war. He will be our art director again now that it is over.'

'Oliver, that's impossible. I'm sorry.'

'Why?'

'Because Gill has been art director for years now. Very successfully.'

'I think that's open to debate.'

'It is not open to debate. Her work is renowned in the profession. It's original, distinctive, always relevant. And besides, she has been so loyal, worked so terribly hard.'

'I'm afraid that applies to many women who have been moved into men's jobs.'

'Oliver, it's not a man's job. It's a creative, difficult, demanding job, which Gill does superbly. Her sex has nothing to do with it.'

'It is a man's job here. And I always said that when the war was over, people would get their jobs back. I don't think you can deny that.'

'Well – no. But—'

'Did you appoint Gill Thomas art director?'

'Yes,' she said, 'yes, I did. Because she deserved it. And because – well because she had had another offer. From Macmillan. And we needed her here.'

'You appointed her art director to keep her from Macmillan. That was rather – irregular.'

'Of course it wasn't irregular. It happens all the time, in peace and war. You hear that a talented member of staff is leaving to take up another offer, so you move to keep them.'

'Not with a job belonging to some one else.'

'Oliver, James Sharpe wasn't here. He was in France. There was no one doing the job.'

'Then you should have made her, at best, acting art director. What did LM have to say about it?'

'She – she—' Celia stopped.

'I thought so. She was against it. I'm glad some sense prevailed here in my absence. Well anyway, whatever the rights and wrongs of the matter, Gill must go. Or step down, but I don't imagine she will be very happy about that.'

'She might. I shall certainly ask her. Or into a parallel position. Such as creative director or design director. Something that would keep them both happy.'

'I'd rather you didn't,' said Oliver. His eyes were very cold. 'I don't like Miss Thomas's work. I think it is vulgar and populist. I think it is in no small part responsible for the deterioration of Lyttons' literary standing.'

'Of course there hasn't been a deterioration in Lyttons' literary standing.'

'I think you must allow me to be the judge of that. Let us say its perceived literary standing then. She's certainly contributed to that.'

'Oh Oliver, really. She has won such praise for her covers. For the romantic novels—'

'Exactly. The trashy novels which we are no longer publishing.'

They weren't: the list had been closed after a bitter row.

Celia fought to keep her temper.

'As for *Meridian* . . . Everyone will be talking about that cover.'

'Ah but in what terms? You like it, and Brooke likes it, and no doubt the art department likes it, but I really doubt very much if the public will. Certainly if sales are not as good as you seem to think they will be, I shall have a very shrewd idea as to why – not.'

'LM loved it.'

'Well, she is hardly an arbiter on such matters.'

Celia was silent.

'Anyway, James will be back in a month. Will you talk to Miss Thomas, or shall I? I'm perfectly happy to do so if you feel you can't face it, I fancy you have made her something of a friend, always a mistake, I think.'

'And James Sharpe isn't your friend, I suppose?' said Celia. 'Oliver, this is appalling. I just don't know what to say to you. Except that what you propose is unfair, and unjust, not to mention a dreadful piece of professional misjudgement.'

'This is getting us nowhere,' said Oliver, 'I think perhaps I had better talk to Miss Thomas.'

'You dare!' said Celia. 'You just dare.'

She walked out of the office and slammed the door; when she got back to her office, she realised she was crying. She walked over to her desk, sat down and dropped her head into her hands.

'Celia,' said Sebastian's voice, 'Celia, whatever is the matter?'

He was sitting on one of the sofas; she hadn't seen him. She looked up at him, brushed her tears away impatiently, tried to smile.

'You look terribly upset.'

'I am terribly upset,' she said.

'What about?'

'Oh – it doesn't matter.'

'It obviously does. How about telling me about it? Over lunch?'

There was a silence. Then Celia said, very simply, meeting his eyes with hers in an implicit acceptance of everything, 'Yes, Sebastian. Yes, I'd like that very much. Thank you.'

CHAPTER 19

'Darling, I'm going to need lots of new dresses. Lots.'

'Really? Well you shall have them, you deserve them. But are you going to tell me why?'

'I'm going to London. Well, I have been asked to go to London.'

'London!'

'Yes. But not till the spring; it's all right, don't look so alarmed. I have a letter from Celia Lytton saying she wants to publish my poems. Isn't that wonderful? In a single volume, "obviously a slim one," she says, "but we would illustrate it, possibly with line drawings. I have briefed Gill Thomas, who used to work for Lyttons and has set up her own design studio, and she is very excited about it. Something rather in the style of Beardsley, she says, only softer." Doesn't that sound just too marvellous?'

'It sounds terrible.'

'Why?'

'I hate Beardsley,' said John, his face deadpan.

'Oh John! Not the illustrations, the whole thing.'

'I know, my darling. I'm only teasing. I'm wonderfully proud of you. It's marvellous news. May I come to London and meet your publishers, or would you prefer to go alone?'

'Of course I'd adore you to come. But actually—' she went back to the letter, 'they're coming here. Well Oliver Lytton is. He's coming out quite soon, he says: to see Robert and to visit the office here. Goodness, he must have changed since we last met him: that was before the war.'

'Yes, and I remember your being rather irritatingly taken with him,' said John.

'Was I?' Felicity's face was carefully blank. 'I don't remember.'

'Well I do. I got very tired of hearing about how romantic he was, how – Byronic I think was your description—'

'John Brewer, I would never have used such a word. About anyone.'

'Actually you did. Anyway, he seemed nice enough. Rather quiet.'

'Quietness is a rather nice quality I think,' said Felicity, 'especially when you live in a house full of extremely aggressive males.'

'Are we extremely aggressive?'

'Extremely. With the possible exception of Kyle.'

'Oh. Well anyway, I'd rather the aggressive male than the aggressive female. Celia seemed to me excessively so.'

'Well – she's a strong character, certainly,' said Felicity, 'but—'

'Strong! She's a nine force gale. Beautiful though. Anyway, my darling, this is all very thrilling news. We must go out and dine tonight to celebrate. Where would you like to go?'

'Oh, I really don't mind. Anywhere at all.'

'I shall take you to the King Cole Room at the St Regis. You'll like it there. Very fashionable.'

'I'd love that. And I can see the famous mural. The Maxwell Parrish one that everyone's talking about. I hear it's stupendous.'

'It's certainly very large. Not quite to my taste, but still. Now darling, I must go. We have a huge meeting with the architects at nine thirty.'

'For the new hotel?'

'For the new hotel. Work starts in a week and they're still messing about with the roof. That atrium, I told you about, remember?'

'Oh – yes. I still can't get over how marvellous it is that you got it after Hagman Betts had the contract.'

'Yes, it was indeed marvellous,' said John, smiling at her conspiratorially. 'But that's show business. As they say.'

'Some show. You don't think there'll be a problem, even now?'

'Absolutely not. Everything's in place, finance, construction workers, the lot. The only problem we've got, thank God, is finding the time and the men to cope with everything. That block on West 62nd is starting next week, and now Rea Goldberg are pressing us as well.'

'Rea Goldberg!'

'Yes indeed. They want a new prestigious building somewhere off Wall Street, and their architects have told us we can have the contract provided we can guarantee it will be ready by the Spring. I think,' he added, standing up and folding the *New York Times* in his usual over-methodical way, 'they're busy proving they never felt anything but warmth towards us. In case we might feel tempted to sling any mud at them. It's a small world down there.'

'I'm surprised you want to work for them.'

'Oh but we do,' said John cheerfully, 'very much. We've put in a pretty high estimate. Amazingly, they've accepted it. Goodbye, my darling. Work hard. I'll see you this evening at the St Regis. Seven thirty, and be sure to wear something really splendid. As befits a famous writer.'

★

'You've got a very clever mother,' he said to Kyle, as they waited for the architects to arrive, 'she is now officially a poetess. Lyttons are to publish an entire volume of her work. Illustrated even. In the spring. Isn't that marvellous?'

'Marvellous,' said Kyle. He felt a sudden, leaden depression. If only he were involved in that world. Books. Illustrations. Poetry. Prose. Instead of this one, of office blocks and reinforced concrete and roofing materials and planning permission.

He had finally decided he should join the family firm, in the absence of anything else; all his applications to newspapers and indeed publishing firms had been rejected, and his father was so extremely keen to have him on board. And of course, as even his mother had pointed out, it was a wonderful opportunity for a young man, going into a successful family firm, into a secure and lucrative future. 'Which journalism certainly wouldn't be, much as you might enjoy it.'

That had clinched it, really; that in spite of her own literary ambitions and talents, she seemed to favour real estate for him. She was probably right; he certainly seemed to lack demonstrable literary talent. And the one firm which might, of course, have employed him, had he asked them, Lyttons New York, was out of the question. He simply wasn't prepared to have them take on an embarrassment, simply because he knew the family. If he went into publishing, it would be on his own merits.

'I want you to tell me you love me.'

'I can't. I really, really can't.'

'Why not? You know you do.'

She did know it; she knew it very well.

Sebastian had invaded her, not only her body, moving in on it with a power and near-violence which had left her shaken, almost shocked by her response, and still physically stirred by it days later, but her mind, her emotions, all her senses. He absorbed her totally; she moved through the days feeling no longer herself, but some strange, disenfranchised creature, no longer the brilliant, cool, controlled Celia Lytton she had always known, but someone foolish, tremulous, half-coherent. She could not believe it did not show physically, this possession, could not imagine that, as she sat at her desk, in restaurants, in her own drawing-room, talking to editors, illustrators, having discussions with agents, conversing with Oliver about projects both professional and domestic, that people could not hear and see that she was quite different, no longer, completely herself, but half Sebastian, filled by his ideas, his words, his passions.

She had not expected that; she had thought that the affair which she had finally, and with such fear and joy embarked upon, would absorb her physically, possess her emotionally, even disturb her intellectually, but that she would be able to remain in control, to say yes, I am having an affair with Sebastian, say even that it was wonderful, face up to its consequences, to the lies, the emotional discomfort, the constant anxiety. But what she found herself in the midst of was an obsession; nothing she did or said or thought or felt had any interest unless it related to him. When she was not with him she could think only of the next time she would be; when she was with him, time stopped, she had no interest in anything beyond it.

Physically, the affair was astonishing; even allowing for long years of frustration, and for the intense pleasure she had always found in sex. But that first time with Sebastian, lying in his bed through the long afternoon, she had been taken to a new place entirely, a place of pleasure so violent that it was almost shocking, and yet also piercingly, intensely sweet. Afterwards, she would remember, remember her body and the things which it had done, how it had climbed, hung, hovered in suspension over the pleasure, now swooping, now flying, now feeling yes, yes, this time, it must be, it must come, yes now, now, yet able to wait, somehow quiet, somehow still, afraid to move lest the sensation became again too fierce, too much to bear. And when finally she did come, pushing, breaking, falling on the violence of it, over and over again, she did not shout or cry out as she had always done before, but remained absolutely silent, concentrating on the experience, an experience she could never have imagined, and certainly had never known.

'All right?' he said gently, a long time later, through the peace.

'Yes,' she said, smiling, opening her eyes to look at him finally, seeing him changed, absolutely different, no longer a man she desired, was intrigued by, wondered about, was afraid of, but someone totally familiar and important to her, converted by the unique power of sex.

'So, now what is to happen to us?' he said, and she replied that she didn't know, nor did she care, that the future was of no interest to her, nor was the past. She cared only about what they had accomplished in that hour or so, and in the hours preceding it when they had talked and been silent, discussed and agreed, uttered assurances and reassurances, laughed and even come close to tears, pursuing all the rituals of a yet-to-be consummated affair, before being unable to wait any longer and leading one another upstairs to bed.

In the end, of course, reality intruded; reluctantly, she dressed, went downstairs, and out to his car. He drove her to Swiss Cottage and there she got a taxi and went back, not to Lyttons, but to the house, constructing on the way an elaborate tale of an absentee author, an enraged agent, some missing proofs, and some tortuous traffic. In the event none of it was necessary, Oliver had been first at a conference and then dining with another publisher, and came home full of excitement at a scheme to introduce an award for literary excellence.

Celia, pretending to have been asleep – when she had been lying in the darkness, her mind and her senses still raking rapturously over her afternoon – sat up, smiling enthusiastically, interested. Oliver, surprised and grateful for it, went to bed contented himself; and Celia told herself, for the first time, the age-old lie beloved of adulterers, that being so happy could do her marriage no harm, indeed, on the contrary, it might do it some good.

But still she refused to tell Sebastian she loved him; it seemed the ultimate betrayal, the ultimate infidelity. Until she said that she was – emotionally at least – safe.

It had been Sebastian's idea that Gill should set herself up in a studio. 'You can give her lots of work, and she will get work elsewhere, too. Macmillan clearly thinks highly of her. It's a far better solution than having her stay on at Lyttons, irritating the hell out of this fellow, and him irritating the hell out of her.'

Celia had taken Gill out to lunch and put the proposition to her. 'And I will guarantee you enough work for the first year to more than cover your overheads. For a start there will be work to do on *Meridian*, Christmas showcards and things like that. And then I'm doing a biography of poor Queen Anne; I would terribly like you to get to work on her . . .'

Sebastian also made her feel better about Jack and his military list; 'It may fail, but if it keeps Oliver happy, gets him off your back, what does it matter?'

'Sebastian, of course it matters; it could lose Lyttons a lot of money.'

'Well – it might. And it might not. Publishing is altogether such a gamble, it seems to me. Anyway, I'm surprised you're so opposed to it, I thought you rather liked Jack.'

'Of course I like him,' she said irritably, 'I adore him. He actually keeps me sane a lot of the time at home. But he's hardly the right person to be in charge of a publishing venture.'

'My darling, I think you can only give in gracefully. Otherwise, it seems to me you intrude on two sacred areas: Oliver's view of his publishing company, and his affection for his younger brother. Probably in a few months, when and if he sees it's not working, he can sort it out for himself. Meanwhile let them all lose Lyttons a lot of money. It can afford it, I'm sure.'

She wasn't sure that Lyttons could; but she decided he was right and she should give in.

James Sharpe had moved back, and was driving her insane; she had forgotten how unoriginal his work was, or seemed to be, how steeped in the old traditions of book design and illustration, how reluctant he was even to try a new typeface, how often he said, 'We have never done that before'. It was odd, given his personality, which was fun; she supposed he had hidden behind that, and now had been overtaken by the war. But patient in her radiant happiness, feeling that she must pay for it, she stood beside his drawing board for hours, admiring his work, exclaiming over his ideas – before going off, half-guilty as if meeting a lover – to see Gill and brief her for other, more important books.

And visiting Gill did become, from time to time, a cover for her visits to her other, more important lover. As always in her life, love and work were inextricably interwoven.

There were considerable plans for the publication of *Meridian*. Even Oliver, irritated as he was by the fuss over it, and by another feeling he did not choose to examine, knew he had a star quality book; and felt, somewhat unwillingly, that this purchase of Celia's would go a long way towards restoring Lyttons as a prestigious house. It was a children's book to be sure; but in the mould of *Alice in Wonderland*, a book which adults would admire as much as children enjoyed it, a book which would be talked about and coveted, sit on grown-up bookshelves as well as in nurseries. The print order was considerable: seven thousand, with three thousand more to go out to the colonies, to India, South Africa, Australia. It was also priced quite highly, at seven shillings and sixpence.

LM had argued for this, before she left them; 'I know it's a lot of money, but it's going to be beautifully produced, the illustrations are lovely, and in colour after all, and it's on very superior paper, I think we can get away with it.'

Oliver, always more ready to defer to her than to Celia, agreed: Celia was not sure whether her prime emotion was gratitude or irritation.

Oliver was away for almost three weeks in New York that autumn: three wonderful weeks. Freed of criticism, of the daily discord, even of the daily deceit – although not of guilt, dear God, not of guilt – exploring Sebastian, exploring her increasing passion for him and his for her; discovering the intense, difficult happiness of adultery, Celia's prime emotion as the three weeks drew to an end, was dread. Oliver wrote twice, cabled several times; he was having a good time he said, Robert was a marvellous host, Maud enchanting, and the Brewers had been particularly kind. Felicity had taken it upon herself to show him a New

York he had never seen, the bohemian areas of Chelsea and the Village, the Seaport and of course the financial district.

'Quite extraordinary, those buildings are incredible, the creations of giants, making small ants of us as we scurry about. And of course Robert is responsible for several of them: I feel greatly in awe of him suddenly. I can see where Felicity gets much of her inspiration from; she is so interesting about it all.'

At the weekend they had all gone out to stay in Robert's house on Long Island. 'Marvellous, endless sheets of white sand and rolling ocean. A little over-social for my taste. I kept thinking how you would have enjoyed it, and felt sad that you were not there. Indeed I wish now I had agreed that you should come; everyone has missed you, myself most of all. I shall bring you another time.'

'I would much prefer that he didn't,' said Sebastian, kissing her, when she told him this.

'Yes,' she said, 'me too.'

'Well, we have had our honeymoon,' he said, and there was sadness in his eyes as he looked at her, 'and now we must return to real life. I fear it will be more difficult. For both of us.'

'I know it will,' she said.

The night Oliver came home, she waited for him at the house; Daniels had gone to Southampton to meet him. She sat in the drawing-room, wearing a dress she knew he liked, his favourite dinner had been prepared for him by Cook, a bottle of his preferred Sancerre rested in an ice bucket in Brunson's pantry. And Celia struggled to find some pleasure, some sweet anticipation somewhere, please please God somewhere, within her: and failed totally. As she heard the car, she flinched; as she walked down the stairs to greet him, she felt stiff with dread; as he waved from the bottom of the steps, ran up to greet her, she cringed. And watched the new, strange woman she had become smile, kiss him, put her arms round him, take his hand, lead him upstairs. That was the trick, she discovered; to watch herself. It made it all much easier. Not to feel, but to study how she felt, not to care, but to observe herself caring. That was how she could get through it. And he had changed. There was no doubt that it had done him good. He looked well, had put on weight, smiled more, told her she looked nice, that the wine was exactly right, the dinner delicious. He brought her a present from Tiffany's.

'I was told you would like that best.'

'And who told you that Oliver?' she said, smiling.

'Oh everyone,' he said, almost carefully vague, 'open it, try it.' It was beautiful, a fine gold bracelet, the clasp studded with diamonds; an extravagant present, something he would never normally buy her.

'Oliver it's lovely,' she said, 'thank you so much.' And watched herself kiss him again.

'I'm glad you like it. Tiffany's is the most wonderful shop, with what seems like acres of counters, or rather glass cases, all filled with beautiful things. And this was the most beautiful of all.'

'And did you choose it all by yourself?' she asked, teasing him. He flushed.

'Well – I had a little help.'

'From Felicity, I suppose?'

'Yes,' he said shortly, 'yes, she did make a suggestion or two.' He was clearly irritated; she supposed it was because she had teased him, implied that he couldn't choose her a present without help.

There was a silence; then he said, 'I did miss you, Celia, so much. It's so good to be home'.

'It's good to have you home,' she said. But she could not tell him she had missed him, could not get the words out.

After dinner they talked, he told her more about the trip, who he had seen, what he had done. 'They are such hospitable, easy people. I can see why Robert likes it there so much.'

'How is he? And Maud?'

'Both well. The elder boy is still a problem, but they seldom see him. Maud is sweet. You'd like her. So would the twins. Well, they'll all meet soon.'

'And Lyttons New York?'

'Doing very well. I'm delighted. Stuart Bailey is extremely clever. He's found some remarkable new writers, I've brought some of the manuscripts back with me. You must read them.'

'I'd like to,' she said. 'You don't think Laurence Elliott is going to cause trouble with Lyttons do you? He does own a large percentage, as I recall.'

'Forty-nine per cent. No, he hasn't been near the place, apparently. I think it's so far outside his area of expertise, he can't really interfere.'

'I don't think that ever stopped anyone interfering in anything,' said Celia drily.

And then it was time for bed; half afraid, she stood up, said, 'You must be tired. I hope you sleep well.'

'No, I'm not tired,' he said, and his face was a mixture of emotion: tenderness, nervousness, and near-amusement. 'I would like to come to your room. If I may.'

'Of – of course you may,' she said. Thinking that of all the things she had expected and worried over, this at least should have been spared her. And panic first hit her and then receded, as she reminded herself she had only to watch. She lay there, watching herself watching him as he climbed into bed, turned to her, took her in his arms. Watched herself lying there, hearing him tell her he loved her.

'I have missed you so,' he said. 'I was wrong not to take you. It has made me realise what I have in you.'

He began to kiss her; and then very quietly, pulling away from her briefly, said: 'I want you so much, Celia. So very much. But – help me. Help me, please.'

And then she watched herself again: and managed just a little more. But it was the hardest thing she had ever done.

Meridian was to be published on December 1st, and there were to be subscription dinners, running right through November, when the bookshop proprietors in major cities were invited to dine with the publishers and the author, and then placed their orders.

'We might even be able to increase the print order after that,' Celia said to Sebastian. 'And then Oliver is planning a wonderful dinner for you on publication day.'

'I hope you will be there,' he said, reaching out a finger, tracing the shape of her face.

'Sebastian, don't. Not here.'

She was terrified of any hint of their relationship coming out in the office; he was reckless, kicking the door closed behind him, producing flowers from behind his back, kissing her passionately as he leaned across the desk, sitting on one of the sofas watching her, and telling her he loved her. She sometimes feared he did it deliberately, hoping they would be caught, that their affair would come into the open. He took appalling risks.

'Of course I'll be at your dinner,' she said now, 'although at one point it was going to be at the Garrick and then, of course, I couldn't. I made a huge fuss.'

'Good. I would have refused to have gone otherwise.'

'Well that would have been really tactful wouldn't it? Anyway, it's at Rules now.'

'Rules! Our restaurant.'

'Sebastian, it is not our restaurant. In fact I have rather unhappy memories of lunching with you there.'

'Nonsense. That was where I learned that you loved me. Or rather that I might hope that you did.'

'What absolute nonsense,' she said, 'I was simply furious with you, no more than that.'

'And upset. And – well disturbed. I was hugely pleased,' he added complacently.

Celia was silent; she was still troubled by his wife, not by her existence but by Sebastian's extraordinary attitude towards her, his rather calculating assumption that there was nothing to be done about her.

'She is perfectly happy with the status quo. She wouldn't even mind about you, my darling. She has everything she wants from me.'

She was afraid, like all adulterous lovers, to ask whether or not he still slept with her; she told herself that of course he could not, that they must live like brother and sister.

In any case, she had no right even to inquire; there was Oliver, after all, and since he had come home, she had slept with him more than once. She had to. It was difficult: it got no easier, it was dreadful. She lay, submitting to him, trying to respond, usually managing it in the end wondering if he could in some way feel, tell a difference in her, in the way she moved, the way she was with him. And by sheer force of will she kept her mind closed to Sebastian, to being in bed with Sebastian, and his tumultuous, almost arrogant lovemaking, telling herself that until she had known him, certainly until the war, Oliver and she had been marvellously happy, that they had adored making love as they had adored one another, that it made no sense to set him aside however notionally. Sex with him must not become something inferior, a duty. It was different, that was all: and none the worse for it. None the worse for it at all.

The combination of guilt and happiness made her increasingly tender to Oliver: solicitous of his interminable minor illnesses, his faddiness over his food, his lack of energy. Although even that had eased since he had been in America.

'I think perhaps you are an American manqué,' she said to him, laughing one day, 'like your brother. Perhaps you should go and live there.'

She even welcomed his endless criticism; recommended now after the brief respite of his return. It helped in some strange way, made her feel less bad. There were days when she hardly felt guilty at all: days when she was particularly patient, especially generous – and welcomed him into her bed.

On other days, usually when she had been with Sebastian, not necessarily in bed, just listening to him, talking to him, making the kind of complex arrangements necessary to all lovers, thinking how much she loved him, how much she wanted him, comparing the monotone of her life before him with the dazzling brilliance of what she knew now, she felt dreadful, almost sick with it, ashamed of how she was behaving, how she was deceiving Oliver. She often thought of her mother these days, of her long-standing affair, of the explanation which had once so shocked her: that it did no harm, rather the reverse, provided that it was kept well contained, within the boundaries of marriage: and thought how what she was doing was worse. For this was not sex; this was love. Despite her refusal to admit it, she knew it to be so. She had taken the love which she had once felt for Oliver, just taken it from him and bestowed it upon Sebastian. Even though Oliver did not know, he must inevitably one day be the poorer for it.

They neither spoke of nor even acknowledged the future, she and Sebastian: they kept it at arm's length, a dreadful, daunting prospect that must be faced one day. Like childbirth, the pain of it was inexorable, and unavoidable. Either Oliver must go through it, or Sebastian, and in either case then so must she. But for the time being, it did not exist for them, they would not allow it to; for the time being they were savouring what they had, and it was extraordinarily sweet.

'And I would like you all to rise now and raise your glasses to *Meridian*. *Meridian* and Sebastian.'

'*Meridian*! And Sebastian!'

The champagne glasses were raised, shining golden in the candlelight. Everyone clapped. And smiled. A small and most exclusive gathering: Celia, Oliver, James Sharpe, a couple of senior editors, LM, who had come up for the occasion, Gill Thomas, at Celia's insistence, Paul Davis, behaving well for once.

Oliver raised his hand and said, 'I don't have very much to say about this book, except that it is undoubtedly one of Lyttons' greats. A superb piece of work, imaginative, original, truly enchanting. All my own children are completely enthralled by it – and given their different ages, I think that tells its own story. The subscriptions have far exceeded what I had expected, and as a result we already have a second printing – bringing the total up to nine thousand, with an additional five hundred for the colonies. Many, many bookshops have ordered showcards, in itself a rare distinction. There is already an excitement about it and with good reason. You must have seen the interviews in the papers, not only the literary ones, but personal profiles of Sebastian in *The Times* and the *Daily Mail*. I am told by my wife that this is entirely due to Sebastian's looks and charm, rather than to his literary skill; I am not sure whether he would wish to know that or not. All my colleagues in the trade envy me more than I can say. I am totally delighted and proud to be the publisher of *Meridian*, Sebastian, and I wish you every possible success. All I ask is that you write another book very soon.'

More applause. Sebastian stood up. He had come alone to the dinner, despite being instructed to bring a guest.

'I can't bring Millicent,' he had said to Celia, 'much as she would love it. Because of you.'

'Oh Sebastian, don't be absurd,' she said, (bravely, for she had dreaded that he would do so, more than anything). 'You must bring her, it's her moment as well as yours, you said yourself she has supported you through the writing of it.'

'I know. But I can't. I couldn't have you in the same room, I couldn't bear it. Looking at her, knowing I was married to her, and then looking at you—'

'But Oliver will be there.'

'I can endure that,' he said soberly, 'I'm accustomed to that. And so must you be.'

'My Lady,' he said now, with a gentle bow to her, smiling, 'Ladies and gentlemen. What can I say? I have dreamed of a night such as this. And yet never dreamed it would happen. I am so very delighted with everything, and Oliver, I have to say that being published by you is quite marvellous for me. For more reasons than one.'

His eyes rested on Celia; she looked away. This is dangerous, she thought, he is playing with a very big fire. She looked at him, standing there in the candlelight, so absurdly handsome, so full of energy, then looked at Oliver, still so frail, although undoubtedly distinguished that night, in his white tie and tails, and she struggled for the hundredth, the thousandth time not to compare them, thought how odd that they should be here, the three of them, so disunited as well as united by this book, this powerful, dangerous catalyst, with herself drawing them together as well as driving them apart.

'I would like to add my own particular thanks to Lady Celia,' he was saying now. Oh, Sebastian, don't, don't. 'Without her there would be no infinitely stylish publication, no sublime jacket – for which many thanks, Miss Thomas—' he bowed to Gill briefly, and she bowed her own head in return – 'no publication at all, perhaps.'

'Oh now, steady on, Sebastian,' said Paul Davis, and everyone laughed.

'No, it was she who spotted the potential of the book, she who bid for it so successfully, risked the wrath of her husband by the size of that bid—'

Sebastian! Stop! But Oliver was smiling, blew her a kiss. Thank God for champagne, she thought, thank God for it.

'And so I would ask you now to raise your glasses again. To the Lyttons, both of them, to the particular brand of brilliance they bring to publishing and the absolutely unique blend of their talents.'

★

'Well,' said Oliver as the car pulled up in front of the house, 'that was a very successful evening. The whole thing is quite marvellous. And Sebastian is right, he does owe most of it to you. Praise well-earned my darling. Well-earned.'

She was so overcome with shame and guilt, as well as the joy of the public accolade, that making love with Oliver that night was easy and almost joyful in itself.

'Tea would be very nice,' said LM, 'thank you.'

'Good. I'm sorry the little chap won't be with us, but at least I can meet you. Now I thought perhaps Fortnum and Mason—'

'That would be delightful.'

'Good. Four o'clock then. I shall be carrying a copy of *The Spectator*, and wearing a dark grey overcoat.'

As it turned out, so were several other men; but LM could not have failed to recognise Gordon Robinson. He was enormously tall, six foot five, rather distinguished-looking altogether, she thought, with thick silver hair and a thin, ascetic face. He bowed to her over the black homburg he had removed, and moved forward, smiling.

'Mrs Lytton. How delightful to meet you at last. May I—?' he indicated the chair beside her, which she had heaped with parcels.

'Of course.'

'Christmas shopping?'

'Well – yes. Mostly for Jay, though. I'm afraid I spoil him rather. I try not to but—'

'That's what children are for,' said Gordon Robinson, 'or so I've always thought. I haven't been granted the good fortune of a happy family myself, but I'm sure if I had, I would have been a most indulgent father.'

LM didn't like to ask why he had not been granted the good fortune; it seemed rather impertinent.

She enjoyed her tea with him more than she would have believed; it was very good to have some adult company, other than Lady Beckenham and Dorothy, and he was, although rather serious, very agreeable and certainly very easy to talk to. He was a solicitor, working for a City firm; he lived on his own in St John's Wood – which was why he had been in the area when he had knocked Jay down. He suffered constant remorse, he told her, at having placed his elderly mother in a nursing home.

'I struggled on at home, with the help of a nurse, for as long as I could, but in the end it became impossible. I think she's quite happy there, but—'

'I'm sure she is,' said LM firmly, 'and I'm sure she would not want to be a serious burden to you.'

'Indeed not. She is a rather – saintly person.' His eyes were amused as he spoke; she liked him for that, for so clearly having a sense of humour.

He was an only child, he said, 'A mixed blessing, but on the whole a good influence on a young life I think.'

'I hope so. Jay is an only child. But he has several cousins whose company he enjoys.'

'Oh really? Tell me Mrs Lytton, I don't suppose you are in any way related to the literary Lyttons?'

'Indeed I am,' she said smiling at him, 'and just to set the matter straight, Mr Robinson, it is Miss Lytton. Yes, my father founded the firm.'

'No! Oh, how marvellous. Well, it is they who are publishing that children's book I mentioned to you – oh how stupid of me, you would know that of course. Oh dear—'

He was so embarrassed that he flushed and stopped talking; LM was rather touched.

'I think it's very clever of you to know that at all,' she said, 'very few people have any idea who publishes books.'

'Oh, I've always taken a keen interest in the subject. My father was a great student of English literature, and I collect early editions.'

He talked easily and happily after that for quite a time: LM sat absorbing him, his kindness, his gentle manner, his careful courtesy. She liked him very much.

'I don't often come up to London these days,' she said as they parted at the front door of Fortnum and Mason, and he handed her carefully into a taxi, 'only for occasions such as this, or a board meeting at Lyttons. But the next time I do, may I contact you? I could give you a first edition of *Meridian* for your collection.'

He seemed delighted, said that would be charming.

LM's only concern, as she contemplated their future friendship, was what he would feel when he realised that she was not only Miss Lytton, but that there had never been a husband at all, that she had actually not been married to Jay's father. Gordon Robinson seemed a rather old-fashioned man. Perhaps she should have explained that day; but then he might have thought she was being presumptuous. Anyway, did it really matter? If such a thing was more important than friendship for him, then that friendship was hardly worth having.

Meridian was quite clearly going to be the kind of book which broke records and made reputations – the reviews were superb, especially in the hard-to-please *Observer* and even the *Manchester Guardian*, so much so that the book went into a third printing. All the bookshops had put in record orders for Christmas, and every set of parents and grandparents in the land seemed to be buying it for a Christmas present. It was even rumoured that several copies had been ordered by the Prince of Wales for his innumerable godchildren.

Oliver was happier altogether as Christmas approached; Lyttons' volume of war poetry had been acclaimed in all the review pages, the sales of the dictionaries and classical works were climbing again, enhanced by a two-volume edition of Greek myths, and they had also made an excellent acquisition of a biography of Queen Anne, at once a most learned and enchanting work by the famous Lady Annabel Muirhead. This was the latest in a series of brilliant biographies she had penned, but the first to be published by Lyttons. Celia had acquired it, after lengthy and painstaking negotiation, the point at issue not being, for once, the the size of the copyright fee, but Lady Annabel's need for reassurance as to the quality of the finished volume.

'I have finally decided to entrust Queen Anne to you,' she told Celia, 'poor woman, can you imagine, seventeen children, and only one surviving infancy. I feel that a house which can publish anything as superbly as you have done *Meridian* must be right for me. But I will insist upon approval of the finished manuscript; I have not had entirely happy experiences with editors in the past. I have learned caution.'

Celia said that of course she would have final approval; and the contract was signed. This did much to ease Oliver's criticism of her; he was grudgingly gracious about her role in the acquisition, although rather less so of the commercial value to Lyttons of *New Lives for Old*, her account of women's lives during and after the war, which had gone into a fourth edition.

'Of course,' he said, 'of course I'm pleased that it's doing well, but it is still not the kind of book I would have actually seen us publishing.'

Celia managed, with an enormous effort, to remain silent.

But, 'Oh really, Oliver,' said LM, who had come up to London for the monthly board meeting, something she had begun to attend regularly again, to Celia's huge relief, 'do stop banging on about what kind of book we ought to publish. Times are hard; provided the books are half-decent, and they sell well, we ought to be grateful to be publishing them.'

Oliver said nothing; but afterwards, in the privacy of her office, LM told Celia she thought he was becoming rather dangerously out of touch.

'Understandable, I suppose, with the war and so on, but he's been back a while now, I really think you have to stand up to him, Celia, or we'll end up publishing an awful lot of stuffy nonsense nobody wants to read.'

Celia went over to her and hugged her; 'I do miss you,' she said simply.

On the subject of Jack and his military list, however, she did not get LM's support.

'I don't think it's such a bad idea,' LM said, 'it's the sort of stuff people will buy for their libraries. Not a big sale perhaps, but – well, I think you should agree. I shall give it my vote.'

Celia feared that LM was driven in part, at least, by the same rather blind devotion to Jack as Oliver; but LM read her thoughts.

'I'm none too sure Jack should be doing it,' she added, with a slightly grim smile, 'but you can keep an eye on him. He'll tire of it in no time, I'm sure, and move on to something else. And meanwhile, he does have some very valuable contacts. And the idea of your great-grandfather's diaries making a book is very sound I think.'

'It's the only one that is sound if you ask me,' said Celia, but she finally gave the project her vote. She could hardly fight three Lyttons.

'My darling!' said Jack, coming into the drawing-room late that night, as she sat reading, 'let me crush you in my arms and show my gratitude. Here – thank you present.'

'Whatever for?' said Celia, although of course she knew, returning his kiss just a little coolly.

'Well, for letting me join your wonderful company. Oliver made it very clear it wouldn't happen until you gave it your approval.'

'Did he?' said Celia. She was very surprised.

'Absolutely. You know how he thinks your opinion on everything is only just below God's. Go on, open your present.'

She opened it: a small box from Aspreys. Inside was a gold brooch, in the shape of a tree, studded with small flowers made of diamonds; it was very pretty and clearly very expensive. She smiled at him, let him pin it on to her dress.

'Darling, that looks beautiful. It was made for you. They must have seen you passing or something.'

'Jack, it's lovely. Absolutely lovely. I adore it. Thank you. But you can't go spending all your money on things like this. If you're going to work for Lyttons, this will represent about five years' salary.'

'Five years' salary well spent. Yes, Oliver named some pittance. Anyway – I'm absolutely thrilled. And I intend to work very hard.'

'You'll have to,' said Celia, 'we're very exacting employers. No more eleven o'clock breakfasts for you, young Jack.'

'Of course not. I shall be there morning, noon and night.'

'I think that might interfere rather badly with your social life,' said

Celia, laughing, 'but it sounds exemplary, nonetheless.' She looked at him. 'Tell me Jack, whatever made you think of this in the first place? This rather late entry into the world of publishing?'

'Oh,' he said vaguely, 'I don't know. It just – came into my head.'

'Oh,' she said, nodding, her expression carefully innocent, 'oh I see.'

She was too fond of him to tell him she had discovered that he had been trying to get jobs in the City for six months, and been turned down by everyone. It was a horribly familiar story, one told by army veterans at every level of society.

She smiled at him; she could afford to be generous.

'I'm going out now, anyway,' he said.

'Out!' She looked at the clock. It was after eleven. 'Oh Jack, you make me feel so old.'

'Yes. Got a girl to meet. Absolute smasher.'

'Really? That's unusual. The lovely Stella?'

'Good Lord no. Got a bit tired of Stella. Bit of a gold-digger, between you and me.'

'Surely not? Well, you're well rid of her then. So – this one – What's her name?'

'Lily. Lily Fortescue.'

'Pretty name. And – let me guess – an actress?'

'Yes. Absolutely wonderful. She's in a new revue.'

'Really? And – is she beautiful?'

'Terribly beautiful. Anyway, I must go, or I'll be late. I'm taking her out to supper. Night darling. Thank you again.'

Celia smiled after him fondly. Whether or not the military list was successful, it would be fun to have him in the office.

Lily Fortescue was in high spirits that night.

'Done an audition for CB,' she said to Jack, 'got a part in his next revue.'

'Oh my darling, that's wonderful. I'm so thrilled for you, so proud. What part will you play?'

'Oh, lots of parts,' said Lily, who found Jack's conviction that she was the greatest star since Mistinguett touching, but rather hard to live up to, 'but a couple of really good numbers. Song and dance. You know.'

'Darling, you are clever. When does it open?'

'Oh, not till the spring. Rehearsals don't even start till after Christmas. So I can carry on with the Follies for now.'

'Splendid! Now come along, darling, you've got to keep your strength up. What do you want to eat?'

'Oh, I don't know. I'm very hungry. Tell you what, I'd love some lobster.'

'You shall have it.'

She had sophisticated tastes, Lily did, for a girl who was born and grew up in a small house in Peckham, in a family of seven. She had met Jack Lytton at a party in the Silver Slipper one night, and she had been very taken by him, with his golden good looks, and his rather dashing, boyish charm. She enjoyed his company very much, and was intrigued to hear that he was related to Lady Celia Lytton.

'She's lovely, isn't she, in all the society papers. I saw a picture of her at the Black Ascot, looking really beautiful. And she's got twins hasn't she, twin girls; yes, I thought so, there was a picture of the three of them in the *Tatler* last week.'

Lily was an avid reader of the society magazines; she read them rather as if she were studying for an examination. As a result she could tell you exactly when Ascot, or Goodwood, or Queen Charlotte's Ball was each year, and what the more prominent society ladies had worn to each one.

She was twenty-four years old and extremely pretty, with dark red hair, brown eyes, and a glorious figure; her voice, with its carefully refined accent was pretty too, oddly musical, and she had very nice manners. She was also very kind-hearted, and after two months, was genuinely fond of Jack; he was fun and he was kind and considerate as well. She wasn't exactly hopeful that their relationship might blossom into something permanent, but she was not unhopeful either; he did frequently express undying love for her, and was waiting at the stage door for her almost every night, whatever the weather. Moreoever, he had not yet proposed any hanky panky, although his kisses were increasingly passionate (and rather good); Lily liked that. In any case, it relieved you of worry; although she had been to one of the new contraception clinics like all modern girls, there was still that gnawing anxiety for two or three days each month.

That night he took her to the Savoy – special occasion he had said. She was looking at him fondly, thinking for the hundredth time how handsome he was, when he said, 'I've got some good news tonight too, Lily.'

'What?' she said.

'I've got a job. In my brother's firm.'

'What, the publishing one?'

'Yes. Isn't that exciting?'

'It is,' she said, 'very exciting. I didn't know you were as clever as that, Jack,' she added, and then realised she hadn't been exactly tactful. He didn't seem to mind.

'Well I am,' he said, grinning at her, 'and I'm going to have my own department as well. A military list it's called.'

'What does that mean?'

'It means I will be publishing books about—'

'War?' she said, 'how boring.'

'Not really,' he said. He did sound hurt now; Lily quickly adjusted her expression to one of breathy enthusiasm. 'I mean, I wouldn't understand them,' she said quickly.

'Oh, I'm sure you would. And not just about war. About regiments and battles, and – well things like that.'

'Oh well,' she said, 'yes that does sound very interesting. That's exciting, Jack. Congratulations. Will you earn lots of money?'

'Not lots. Not at first, anyway. But a fellow has to start somewhere. And it's better than nothing. All I've been doing up to now is spending my army pension and my inheritance. Both of which are pretty puny.'

'Yes. And it is the family firm,' said Lily, 'so I suppose you'll be a part of that from now on. I seem to have got a young man with prospects.'

'You have indeed. So – raise your glass to me, Miss Fortescue. A successful London publisher sits here before you. Aren't you proud?'

'Very,' she said.

'And the best thing is, I think I'll be able to afford my own place pretty soon now. So—' he smiled at her, his intense blue eyes, with their long, feminine lashes, gazing into hers, 'so we'll have somewhere to go to be together. If – if you think you'd like that.'

Here we go, hanky panky, thought Lily, but she smiled back at him. She did quite think she'd like it, and it was about time, she was beginning to miss it. Still, no point in being easy to get; she certainly wasn't having him thinking she was going to be a pushover.

'Don't be cheeky,' she said, 'and don't you believe all you've heard about actresses, either.'

'Darling, of course I don't. Not all of it at any rate. Anyway, here's to us. Cheers.'

'Cheers,' said Lily.

It was Lily who introduced Jack to Guy Worsley; and Jack who introduced him to Oliver. Guy Worsley was among the friends with whom she went to the Silver Slipper, one night after the show; he was going out with one of the other girls, a pretty blonde called Crystal. Lily had met him once before; he was clearly very well connected, although without a title of his own, and seemed to know everybody. He was quite young, only twenty-five; he had left Oxford in 1916 with a First in classics, then tried to enlist, but failed because of what he called a slightly dicky heart. He spent the next two years at the War Office and was now working, with very little enthusiasm, in his father's stock-broking firm. When Lily first met him she thought he might be a fairy, he had rather girly looks, soft brown, wavy hair, and large dark eyes. He was also, which confirmed this view, full of all the latest gossip, and took an inordinate interest in what everyone was wearing, including himself. The girl he was with however, said he was certainly nothing of the sort, quite the reverse indeed.

'Very enthusiastic darling; can't get enough.'

He had told Lily when she met him that he was writing a book; she remembered it now – it was one of her more endearing characteristics, and indeed one of her social graces, that she did remember such things – and asked him how it was going.

'Oh, pretty well,' he said, smiling at her, 'in fact I've finished the first volume.'

'And is it published yet?'

'No,' he said, 'no I'm afraid not. I haven't even tried for that. It's a saga you see, it's going to go on in several volumes and I thought any publisher would want to see more than one volume. So I'm struggling away on the second.'

'You must meet my friend, Jack Lytton,' said Lily. 'He's a publisher. Come on, he's over there, talking to that girl. Much too pretty for my liking. Jack, Jack, come and meet Guy. He's written a book you can publish.'

'Only if it's about the army, Lily, remember,' said Jack, grinning, shaking Guy Worsley's hand. Guy Worsely said it wasn't exactly about the army, although it did cover the war. 'Crucial point, actually, girl's fiancé gets killed, so—'

'So it's fiction?' said Jack, and yes, Guy said, it was, and did Jack really only publish military books?

'Well I do,' said Jack airily, as if a large shelf-full was already being eagerly bought by the reading public, 'but my firm publishes all sorts.'

'And what's your firm?'

'Well, it's not actually mine,' said Jack, 'but my brother's. In fact, it's the family firm. Lyttons, you know.'

Guy stared at him for a moment then said yes, actually, he did know.

'Well, I'm sure they'd like to have a look at your book. I'll tell them about it. It sounds jolly good.'

Guy said he wasn't sure how good it was, and he would very much appreciate an opinion on it.

'You must bring it in, show it to my brother,' said Jack, 'I'll telephone you on Monday when I've had a word with him. Now come on Lily, on to the floor, I've asked them to play "Whispering" for us, told them it is our song.'

★

369

'This is really rather good,' said Celia looking up at Jack and smiling, 'this book your friend sent in. I'd like to take it home and really get my teeth into it tonight. Did you say he's writing several?'

'Yes. Said they were a – a saga. I think that was the word he used. Lots of books about the same people.'

'Interesting idea. There's this book called *The Forsyte Saga*, you know, that everyone's talking about. I was thinking we should try and find one of our own.'

'Oh, I must tell him, he'll be awfully bucked,' said Jack, 'he's a frightfully modest chap, wasn't expecting to get it published at all.'

'Jack, there is no question at the moment of our publishing it,' said Celia severely, 'I simply said I'd like to read it properly. You mustn't raise his hopes, it would be most unfair.'

'Oh – all right. Now can I just show you this outline Teddy Grosvenor's done about the Mutiny, awfully exciting, Celia, we'd sell a lot of copies I'm sure.'

'Just leave it on my desk,' said Celia, 'I'll look at it later today if I have time. Better still, show it to Oliver. It's much more his bag than mine.'

'Righto. I won't say anything to Guy Worsley for a day or two, then?'

'Not for a week or two. If I want to talk to him, I promise you'll be the first to know.'

The Worsley book was actually extremely good. She found it hard to believe that it was a first novel, and that the author was so young. She felt the slight crawling of her skin that always greeted the discovery of a new talent: it had never failed her that sensation, it was an excitement, a thud of the heart and in the head, a rush of power that was almost sexual. All editors dream of making such discoveries; it is what empowers them, gives them authority and status. Celia had made several major discoveries in her time, spotting talent with a sureness and swiftness which sometimes surprised even her; since Oliver's return and the onslaught of his interminable criticism, however, her shining confidence had been dulled, her judgement become diffident. But that day, reading the first chapter of Guy Worsley's saga, she knew absolutely that it had to be acquired by Lyttons, and as quickly as possible.

'It's really quite wonderful,' she said to Oliver. 'It's about a family living in Oxford and London, during and after the war. Buchanan they're called; he's the master of an Oxford college, rather eccentric, wears silk dressing-gowns, you can imagine the sort of thing, and the wife is rich in her own right, not an attractive figure exactly, but a very interesting one, leading her own life really. There's a daughter whose fiancé has been killed in the war, and who decides to forge a career for herself in music, and a son who went through the war as a conscientious objector, working for the ambulance service, and is now studying medicine. All very topical: lots of strands, lots of cross-currents. And it's beautifully written and extraordinarily well-plotted. Please read it, Oliver, it could be our answer to the Forsytes.'

Oliver said he was very busy but he would try to find time to read it; a couple of days later he told Celia he would like to make Guy Worsley an offer.

'You get him in, Celia, you spotted him. I agree, it's marvellous stuff. I think we should make him an offer. But I'd like to meet him first, make sure this isn't just a flash in the pan, that there really are more in the pipeline. Does he have an agent?'

'No. No, Jack said he didn't. We have Jack to thank for him, really. He met him and told him to send his manuscript in.'

'Good,' said Oliver briskly, 'I'm glad he's making a contribution. Has he talked to you about his book on the Indian Mutiny by the way?'

'Yes, just a bit,' said Celia.

The meeting between Guy Worsley and the Lyttons took place the next day; it was an extremely happy occasion. Guy was put under contract with immediate effect: two hundred and fifty pounds was offered for the first book, with an option on the next two. After the meeting, Jack joined them all for a champagne lunch at Simpsons in the Strand.

'Awfully jolly it was,' he said to Lily that evening. 'Honestly, my darling, there really isn't much to this publishing lark. I'm having huge fun with it already.'

It was very odd: being forced through this essentially happy time without the one thing which made her properly happy. Celia sat in the chapel at Ashingham on Christmas Eve, thinking about Sebastian, and about how much she missed him, thinking that there were five more days to go before she could even speak to him, and trying not to think about what might have happened by next Christmas. She had moved into the next stage of adultery now; past the first rapture, past the initial guilt and fear, past settling into some kind of acceptance of it, had found herself in the new, hugely dangerous one, of wanting more, more time, more commitment, wanting some kind of progress.

She saw her mother's eyes on her and smiled brilliantly; forced herself to concentrate on the service. Such a lovely service, with the crib and candlelight. All the children were there, Giles looking terrifyingly grown-up, Barty sitting beside him, sweetly serious, and the twins, giggling, whispering and nudging each other, silenced now and again by their grandmother. Jay was sitting next to Barty, who had her arm round him. He looked very well, and very much a little boy. He would start at the village school after Christmas; he could hardly wait, he told Barty.

'I'm going to be a doctor, I've decided, when I grow up. So I can make sick children better, like they made me. And like you did,' he added, for LM had told him about what Barty had done for him.

Besides, he had never forgotten her sitting there, reading to him in hospital that night. He had no idea what the story was; it was all a fuzzy memory, only that he had gradually felt better and better, until he went to sleep. Since then, though, his mother had read him the book herself; it was the best story he'd ever heard.

Billy was there, too, sitting at the back of the chapel with the other staff; he had his new leg now, was managing well on it. He had wanted to go home for Christmas until he had heard that Barty was coming; then he changed his mind. His mother had seemed relieved; she was going to Frank's girlfriend's house, she told him in her letter, it would save her a lot of work. The girlfriend was called Gwen, 'a lovely girl and so good to me'. It was generally assumed, Barty said, that they would get married as soon as Frank was earning a bit more. He was doing well, though: he had at last got a proper job, as a clerk in an insurance office, went to work in a white collar every day. Sylvia was very proud. If only Ted could have seen him.

After church, after supper, when the children and an exhausted Oliver had gone to bed, after LM and Jay had gone home to their cottage and when Lord Beckenham was asleep in the library, Lady Beckenham looked at Celia.

'What are you up to?' she asked.

Celia looked at her as blankly as she could.

'Nothing. I don't know what you mean Mama.'

'Of course you do. You're all jumpy. And not with us half the time. Got yourself a lover, have you?'

'Mama!'

'I don't blame you. Not in the least. Oliver looks completely washed-out. And he's been very difficult, I realise that. Be careful, though, won't you. Who is it?'

'I – well, that is—' Celia relaxed suddenly. It would be a relief to talk about it. And her mother was the only person she could totally trust.

She told her: as much as she dared. Her mother listened in absolute silence; then she said, 'Sounds all right so far. Don't let it get out of hand. Lovers are no substitutes for husbands, Celia, except in bed. And that gets tedious in the end. You could end up losing everything.'

Celia didn't answer.

'You think you're in love with him, don't you?'

'Mama, I know I am.'

'Yes, well, love affairs do that to you. Always remember though, that you cheat. Oh, not in the obvious way. Of course you're doing that. I mean you cheat on life. Always nice to one another, always amusing, always looking your best. But reality isn't about that, it's about running the house and organising the servants, and disciplining the children. Don't forget that, Celia. There's more to life than flowery words and orgasms.'

'Mama!'

'Well, it's true. What sort of a chap is he?'

'You'd approve. At least I think you would. He went to Malvern.'

'I don't know that I would,' said Lady Beckenham, grinning at her, 'but I'll give him the benefit of the doubt. Not that I expect I'll meet him. Certainly shouldn't.'

'No,' said Celia sadly, 'no you certainly shouldn't. But I wish you could.'

'Just try to enjoy it,' said her mother, patting her shoulder, 'enjoy it for what it is. Don't ask too much of it. You'll spoil it if you do. And don't feel too guilty about it either. Now I'm going to bed. Barty looks wonderful doesn't she? Sweet child.'

'You don't mean you think you were wrong about her?' said Celia, grateful for a change of subject.

'Certainly not. You've got a long way to go yet. But she's getting very pretty. Mind you, that's going to be a headache.'

'No more of a headache than the twins.'

'Oh, Celia. Of course it is. You can't be that stupid. Goodnight.'

Sylvia enjoyed her Christmas Day with Gwan and her family; but after it, when the weather became colder and wetter and the swirling London fogs thicker, she became very unwell. She contracted a form of influenza, not the dreadful septic variety, but it led to one of what she called her chests, and she spent most of January in bed. She was so ill that Marjorie even suggested they should get the doctor; Sylvia scolded her. 'We can't afford it, Marjorie. It's only my chest. I'll be all right.'

She did what she always did; put on a brave face when the family were there, went to bed for the day as soon as they were all out, and struggled up at the end of it to make their tea. By the end of January, she was on the mend, she said; her chest was better, but she had developed an intermittent pain in her stomach, not unlike when she got her monthlies, only sharper, and more severe.

'I'm all right,' she said almost fiercely to Barty, when Barty suggested she should see Dr Perring. 'I'm much better. Now don't you fuss.'

'When we all go down to Ashingham next month for Billy's birthday, maybe you could see someone down there. I'm worried about you, Mum, I hope you'll be well enough to come.'

Sylvia smiled at her. 'I'll be all right, and if you think I'm missing that, you've got another think coming. Can't wait. Billy twenty. Who'd have thought it?'

'I'm thirteen this year, you know,' said Barty.

'I know you are, dear. And very grown-up you look too. A real young lady. Lady Celia must be very proud.'

'Aren't you proud?' asked Barty anxiously.

'Of course I am,' said Sylvia, 'but it's Lady Celia who's done it, turned you into a lady.'

'Mum, she hasn't turned me into anything. I'm still me.'

'Now Barty,' said Sylvia severely, 'that's just silly. You wouldn't talk like you do, know what you do, you wouldn't even look like you do without Lady Celia. You walk so nicely Barty, it's those dancing classes I suppose.'

'Maybe,' said Barty doubtfully. The classes at Madam Vacani's, attended by half the well-born little girls in London, escorted by their nannies, were a weekly torment for her.

'You have to be very grateful to her. And never forget it.'

'I know,' said Barty, 'and I know I'm very lucky. It's just that—'

'Just that what, dear?'

'Just that I get so tired of being grateful. And whatever you say, and whatever I talk like and everything, I am still me. The same me who started out here. You're my mother, and Dad was my father. That hasn't changed. And it's important. Well, it's important to me, anyway.'

'It's important to me as well,' said Sylvia, patting her hand, 'of course it is.'

She was looking forward to the trip to Ashingham with the usual mixture of excitement and dread. It would be lovely to see Billy, to get out of London, and see the countryside, breathe the nice clean air. Even in February. But she was petrified of Lady Beckenham. Petrified of all the animals, of the noises that filled the country darkness. And then there was her coughing. Once she started she couldn't seem to stop. It wasn't very nice, not at all lady like. Suppose she did that in front of Lady Beckenham? And she always felt so sick in the car driving down. Last time she'd had to ask Lady Celia to stop. She'd been very nice about it, but Sylvia had felt dreadfully embarrassed. Still – it would all be worth it. To see Billy. He was doing so well.

★

'Oh, for some proper time together,' said Sebastian. He sighed heavily. They were lying in his enormous bed; Celia had just said she must leave.

'I really have to be back at Lyttons by four. I can't help it, Sebastian, don't look like that.'

'How you can even think about work, about going back to Lyttons, about anything at all, after that performance I cannot imagine. Look at you—' he extended a finger, wiped the sweat from her stomach, licked it gently. 'Rain. Rain of Celia. Sweet afternoon rain.'

'I know.' She smiled at him rather shakily. It had been an epic occasion: even for her. On and on she had gone, thinking it would never end: climbing and climbing, soaring, swooping almost into relief, then climbing again, shouting, loudly, with triumph as well as joy, as her body gripped the pleasure, clung to it, shaped it, and then, finally, released it in a huge explosive flood. And then, as he had come too, drowning into her, she had come again, shocked and surprised by it, and had heard herself, through the violence, utter a different sound, raw, primitive, like the pleasure itself.

'Don't go,' he said, 'stay here. Stay with me. My love. My beloved.'

'Sebastian I can't. Really, I can't.'

That was when he said they needed more time.

It became an obsession: how, when, where. A night, he said, imagine a whole night. Lying together, actually sleeping together. And then a day she said, think of a day, time to talk, to think to walk, to eat together.

'What about your mother's place? I would love to meet her. She sounds so utterly splendid.'

'She wouldn't allow it.'

'I thought she approved.'

'She approves of adultery. Of sex. But not of involvement, not even of love.'

'That won't do then. I love you, Celia.'

She was silent; she still hadn't said it.

'How about a conference somewhere? A literary conference?'

'Oliver would know it didn't exist. And if it did, he would want to be there too.'

'An invitation to speak somewhere?'

'He'd know about that too. I wondered—'

'Yes?'

'I wondered about my sister. She lives in Scotland. I could say I was going to visit her. She'd understand.'

'That might do. That might do very well.'

'But—'

'But what?'

'Still hugely risky.'

'And this isn't, I suppose?' he said laughing. 'We're only a mile or so from your husband.'

She laughed too, began to climb out of bed. 'Yes, I know. How silly.'

'I love you, Celia, Say you love me.'

'I – can't.'

'Why not? Oh, I know. You're frightened of it, aren't you? Why?'

She kissed him, disappeared into the bathroom without another word.

But, 'I'll speak to my sister,' she said, as she kissed him goodbye.

Caroline was amused. 'Of course. I wondered how long you'd be able to stand it. Dear old Oliver: talk about a shadow of his former self.'

Celia felt oddly defensive. 'I think he's a little more than that, Caroline.'

'Glad to hear it. Anyway, just tell me what you want me to say and to whom, and I will. Goodness, it doesn't seem a minute since you were so shocked when I told you about Mama and George Paget.'

'I know,' said Celia and sighed.

'How about the first weekend in March?' she said to Sebastian later. 'Or—' her voice tailed away.

'It sounds perfect. What's the matter?'

'I – just wondered about weekends.'

'Why?'

'You know. Weekends are for – for Suffolk, I thought.'

'Nonsense. Weekends are for love.'

'Don't say that,' she said, her voice suddenly forlorn.

'Why not?'

'Because – well because I – oh, Sebastian, don't be stupid. Surely you can see what I mean.'

'My darling, I do see what you mean. Is it really so painful for you?'

'Yes,' she said very quietly, 'and I know how absurd that is, when you have to think of – of Oliver, and – and—'

'I devote an enormous amount of emotional energy,' he said, kissing her, his face rather sad, 'to not thinking of that. As for Millicent, I truly cannot remember when we last made love.'

'Oh,' she said, 'oh, I see.' The day suddenly became brighter, the room warmer.

'We're nearly there,' said Barty excitedly. 'Look, there's a sign to Ashingham Village. Are you all right, Mum? You look a bit pale.'

'I'm all right,' said Sylvia. She spoke with difficulty; the combined effort of not coughing and not vomiting over the past hour had been almost too much for her. She felt dreadfully sick.

'I'm perfectly all right,' she said again staunchly and managed a smile.

'Good. Oh, it's so lovely to be here.'

Barty and Celia, had picked Sylvia up quite early in Line Street, in the huge car driven by the new chauffeur, a dazzlingly handsome young man called Daniels. Barty, who had loved Truman and wept with genuine grief when she heard of his death at Mons, nevertheless had something of a crush on Daniels, who was just slightly cheeky, and called her Milady Miller when Celia was not around.

Barty was in high spirits; Celia, recognising her academic potential, and ambitious for her, for more reasons than one, had entered her for St Paul's Girls School. She had passed the examination with flying colours.

'Barty!' Celia said at breakfast, her eyes scanning a letter, 'Barty you've won an award. That's a minor scholarship you know. Well done. It's a great achievement.'

Barty had been excitedly disbelieving, had demanded to see the letter for herself; but there it was, the proof. 'We are pleased to inform you that Barbara Miller's work in the English paper was of a very high standard; consequently we would like to offer her one of our foundation awards. We look forward to welcoming her to the school in September and feel confident she will do well here, and will in due course be going on to further education.' Further education: Barty knew what that meant. University. She shut her eyes briefly; it was almost too exciting.

She loved the school when she went for the examination, loved the buildings, the atmosphere, the staff, so clearly not preoccupied with ladylike behaviour as they were at Miss Wolff's. No doubt her other problems would follow her there, but she had been encouraged by something the head, or rather, the high mistress had said about there being girls at the school from every background.

'The only elitism we recognise here, Lady Celia, is intellectual.'

Even the twins had been impressed by the scholarship, and told her they wished they were going to St Paul's.

'And getting away from horrible Miss Fauncey,' said Adele.

'And beastly Miss Barker,' said Venetia.

Celia had told them briskly that there was very little chance of their ever getting away from Miss Fauncey and Miss Barker and certainly not into St Paul's if they didn't spend a little time at least of each school day doing some work. They were not coming down to Ashingham; they had a party, and a dancing class, and were going to keep Oliver company.

'Somebody has to,' said Adele, by way of revenge.

'And we want to anyway,' said Venetia.

'Now here we are,' said Barty, 'and look, Mum, look, there's Billy, isn't it? No it can't be, surely he can't be on that huge horse.'

'Oh dear,' said Sylvia, 'oh my goodness – it can't be, it's enormous.'

But it was: Billy was in one of the paddocks below the drive, astride a horse which could only be described as vast, cantering amiably round on a lunge rein held by Lady Beckenham. One foot was in a stirrup, his other leg was minus its addition, and there was an expression of absolute concentration on his face.

'Keep your bloody hands down,' Lady Beckenham was roaring, 'you look like some sort of poodle on a circus horse. And grip with your legs, you've still got two thighs for God's sake.'

They got out of the car and watched, transfixed, Barty biting her fist as she always did when she was nervous, Sylvia with her hand on her heart, her face white. Even Daniels seemed worried, removed his cap and wiped his sweating forehead. Only Celia stood relaxed and smiling, seeing that Billy was actually perfectly happy and safe, and knowing what her mother was doing for him.

'Hallo,' called Lady Beckenham when the lesson was finally over, 'not doing so badly, now. Absolutely pathetic at first, weren't you, Billy, but he'll get there in the end. Now, what do you think of the horse?'

'He's heaven,' said Celia, ducking under the fence, going over to the horse and patting its huge neck. 'I haven't seen him before, wherever did he come from?'

'France,' said her mother, 'old battle horse; we've called him Major, they were all going for horse meat, auctioned at Waterloo. I couldn't bear it, bought three of them. Peppered with shrapnel, but it worked its way out. Billy and I never stopped picking it out, cleaning out the wounds, did we, Bill?'

'No we didn't,' said Billy. He had picked up the historic Beckenham crutch from the ground near the horse, and hopped over to them.

'Hallo Mum, hallo Barty. Morning, Lady Celia.'

'Billy, you're so brave,' said Barty.

'Not really. He's an old sweetheart,' said Billy, 'isn't he, Lady Beckenham?'

'He is. Marvellous animals all of them. Sweet as pie. You only have to shout halt, and they stop dead. Poor darlings, they could tell a tale or two. Beckenham's going to take that one out next autumn, says he could jump anything.'

'They're sweet,' said Celia, 'what a marvellous idea.'

'Yes, well a few of us thought it worth trying to save what we could. Poor things, they deserve it, doing their bit for king and country. Tell you something really amazing, every so often they form a line and canter down the field together. In a sort of charge. Brought tears to my eyes the first time we saw it, didn't it Billy?'

Billy nodded. Celia looked at him. He was rosy-faced in the biting wind, and looked very strong; he had always been big, even as a child, but he actually seemed to have grown since Christmas, he must be at least six foot four, she decided, and broad with it. He looked wonderfully happy too, his grin wide, his blue eyes, Sylvia's eyes, brilliant. It was odd, she thought and then crushed it again, that her mother's adoption of Billy, along with her determination to keep him in his proper place socially, might turn out to be more successful than her own efforts with Barty.

'Right, well you can go and get on with your work now Billy,' said Lady Beckenham, 'we'll do this again on Monday. Sylvia, you look terrible. I hope you haven't got this dreadful flu. You can go right back to London again if you have.'

'Mama!' said Celia.

'No, I'm sure I haven't, your ladyship,' said Sylvia, her face scarlet as she suppressed a fit of violent coughing.

'Well it sounds like it. You'd better get into the house. This wind's beastly. Want to get back into the car?'

'No I'd rather walk, thank you, your Ladyship.' Anything would be better than getting back into that rolling thing.

'Right. I've put you and Barty in the Dovecot. Barty, you're growing up much too fast. Getting rather pretty. I shan't be able to let Beckenham near you soon.'

'Mama!' said Celia, again.

'It's much better she's prepared for him. Less of a shock that way.'

'Barty's won a scholarship,' said Celia hastily. 'We heard this morning. To St Pauls Girls School. Isn't that marvellous?'

'How absolutely extraordinary,' said Lady Beckenham.

Sylvia got through lunch somehow: it was served in the housekeeper's room, which was just about the warmest place in the whole of Ashingham, being small, with a wonderful roaring fire. Celia put Sylvia next to it, noticing her shivering, and fetched one of her mother's shawls to put round her shoulders.

'Are you all right?' she whispered, knowing how much Sylvia hated a fuss.

Sylvia nodded rather weakly, and tried to enjoy the roast lamb which she could see and even smell to be delicious, but she still felt terribly sick. She managed a few mouthfuls, but each one was a struggle to swallow and turned in her mouth to a dry, almost dusty texture, rather like the stale bread which Mr Phelps sent her from time to time. It seemed a dreadful waste; it would be a very long time before she was offered roast lamb again.

The pain in her stomach was bothering her too; she sat, feeling rather hot now instead of cold, smiling politely as the chatter ran on and on, round the table, Billy so excited about his riding, Barty about her scholarship, Lady Celia rather quieter than usual, and looking a bit tired, she thought. Lady Beckenham didn't eat with them, but she came in at the end of the meal to say she was going for a ride she'd see them at tea time, and that Cook had made Billy a birthday cake.

'We'll have that in here as well. Four sharp, then you can get down to the yard after that, Bill. I'm taking Major out, thought a gallop would do him good.'

'Yes, your Ladyship. I'm sure it will.'

He spoke to her so naturally, Sylvia thought, he wasn't at all afraid of her, although obviously respectful; indeed he seemed very fond of her. She stood up; she really needed to find a lavatory, she hadn't liked to ask before, and it had been a long journey. The pain in her side stabbed at her; she closed her eyes briefly, a small gasp escaping her.

'Sylvia, you're not well are you?' said Celia, 'what is it?'

'Oh – just a bit of a stomach ache. Nothing serious. Could you show me where the toilet is, Lady Celia?'

'Of course. I'm sorry I didn't think of it before, in all the excitement. Come along. It seems a bit serious, your pain. If you're not better tomorrow we'll get old Dr Greer to look at you.'

'Oh I couldn't allow that.'

'I'm afraid you're going to have to.'

Sylvia fell asleep in her room in the Dovecot; she loved it there, it was such a sweet little house, so much less frightening than the big one. She could have stayed there forever, but Barty arrived at ten to four saying they must go over to the house for Billy's birthday tea.

'Or don't you feel up to it, Mum?'

'Of course I do,' said Sylvia, and she did feel better for her rest. 'Think I'd miss that Barty? You need your head examined.'

Lady Beckenham had organised a wonderful tea party for Billy. There was a really big cake, beautifully iced, and candles, even though he was twenty. LM joined them along with Jay, Billy's fellow grooms, and all the house staff, for Billy was very popular. The head groom, a tiny Irishman who had once been a jockey, and survived the war without a scratch, had been heard to say quite frequently that he'd rather face the Hun any day than Lady Beckenham in a temper. He said it that day as they waited for her.

'Me too,' said Lord Beckenham, who had come along, 'you can shoot the Hun.'

Billy blew out his candles to much applause.

'Now you must wish,' said Barty.

He looked at her, then at his mother and Lady Beckenham. 'To be quite honest,' he said, his round face flushed, 'I ain't got nothing to wish for. Excepting a leg of course, and I wouldn't be here if I had that.'

There was much applause and laughter: Lady Beckenham blew her nose loudly on one of the enormous and slightly grubby handkerchiefs she always carried about with her, and then said that was quite enough, and if Billy didn't get down to the yard pretty damn soon and do evening stables, he'd wish he was somewhere quite different.

Sylvia went to bed almost as soon as she got back to the Dovecot; the relief of just lying down and keeping still was wonderful. She lay with her legs curled up; it eased the pain and Barty brought her a hot water bottle which helped as well. She was pretty sure now it was her monthly coming on: of all the times for it to happen. But at least she didn't have to do anything else, until the next day. Probably by then it would be better.

'Are you sure you're all right, Mum? Shouldn't I ask Aunt Celia to get the doctor?'

'Gracious no, Barty. It's nothing, I've had it before and it passes.'

She didn't like to explain any more; Barty was much too young to understand such things.

'Oh. So is it – well, you know, to do with your periods?'

Sylvia was shocked; 'Barty, really! How do you know about that?' she said.

Barty looked surprised. 'Aunt Celia told me,' she said, 'she said it was important to know in good time. So it wasn't a horrible shock. It doesn't sound very nice at all,' she added.

'No, well it isn't,' said Sylvia briskly, 'but it has to be endured, and that's all there is to it. We'll say no more about it now. I feel much better anyway. You go off and see Billy, he'll be waiting for you.'

Barty tucked her up in bed, made her a cup of very sweet tea and went off to have supper with Billy and the other grooms. Leaving Sylvia feeling oddly unsettled at the thought of her daughter being instructed in such intimate matters by someone other than herself. It made her realise how wide the rift was between her life and Barty's, how impossibly far apart they had become, for all Barty's affection and loyalty. She hadn't often felt jealous of Celia over the years, for being so close to Barty; but that night she did. Jealous and something close to resentful.

'And how are you?' said Lady Beckenham to Celia after dinner. They had dined alone with Lord Beckenham and he had gone off to bed. 'And I daresay to try and persuade that pretty new young thing to bring him a nightcap. She probably will as well, she's quite intelligent, likes the status of his attentions.'

'Mama,' said Celia laughing, 'you are amazing. Don't you really mind at all?'

'Good God no. I'm deeply grateful to them. Otherwise I'd have to be on the receiving end, and really I can't think of anything worse these days.'

'Yes, I see.' Celia was silent, trying and failing to imagine herself in such a position, with Oliver over-enthusiastically pursuing her, rather than almost visibly gathering his courage and indeed his strength, albeit it with a little more success lately.

'Well?'

'Oh.' She had briefly forgotten the question, 'oh, I'm all right.'

'That's not what I meant. As you very well know.'

'Nothing's changed,' said Celia.

'Nothing at all?'

'No.'

'Good. Glad to hear it. I'll tell you something, when it's all over, you'll only remember the good things. Bit like having children really.'

'Oh, I see,' said Celia and sighed. She would give a great deal, she thought, for her mother's pragmatism. It was such an essential ingredient in the conduct of an extra-marital affair.

CHAPTER 20

There was something about Guy Worsley that attracted publicity. He had always been the centre of attention, even at school. It was hard to analyse exactly why; he was clever to be sure, and charming and wonderful company, and he was certainly very good-looking – but none of it was exceptional, none of it out of the ordinary even. There was, of course, his rather frail health, his much discussed weak heart – the stuff of women's fiction Oliver said slightly contemptuously, when he heard about it – and that certainly added to his charm for women, alongside the talent for gossip and the love of rather female-oriented conversation about frocks and house decor.

The fact that he had had several well-documented love affairs did not stop rumours that he was homosexual. It didn't mean a thing, people said, lots of them liked women as well as men. Guy himself never went out of his way to deny the gossip, indeed it was said he rather enjoyed it; but the fact was that he was heterosexual, and apart from a rather famous episode at his public school when he had been found in flagrante with both the head boy and his housemaster on the same evening – or so the story went – there was nothing to support the rumours, although they did add considerably to his glamour.

But none of these things quite explained how it was that wherever he went, whatever he did, people talked about him. And the story of the *Buchanan* saga and its purchase by one of the most important and interesting publishers in London made for very good talk indeed. It was almost too good to be true, like a story in itself, as Lily Fortescue, who felt she had played an important part in it, had been heard to remark more than once. Everyone knew that Lady Celia Lytton had discovered him, had made him part of her famous literary social set indeed, that the publishing world had been fighting over the books for months, and that Oliver Lytton had paid a record sum of money for them: all these things made him still more popular, yet more desirable, everyone wanted to know him, to hear about him, to have him at their parties.

And the books were much talked about too; *The Buchanans* became the subject of literary gossip too, at places like the Garrick and the

Reform, it was an early example of what came to be called 'talking up'. Items about it appeared in the weekly papers, speculating as to the content, the likely publishing schedule – and the extent of its ultimate success. Long before copies had even reached the editors, it was described as one of *the* books of 1920.

Sebastian Brooke was very slightly irritated by it.

'You're just jealous,' Celia told him, kissing him fondly to show that she didn't quite mean it, although she also knew that there was enormous professional jealousy between authors. 'You've been knocked off your throne for a day or two.'

'Absolute nonsense,' said Sebastian, 'it's quite a relief in a way. I just don't think it's that remarkable.'

'Well it isn't. Not like *Meridian* is, of course. It's not original, and it's not even particularly literary. It's just a wonderful yarn, which is what people want, and it's also going to be a continuing saga, which is what we want. Years and years of *The Buchanans*, if we're lucky. And there are some very clever bits of plot in it. The slightly sanctimonious, eccentric academic, with his little bit of fluff on the side – I love that. And the poor daughter, robbed of her sweetheart, turning to music for succour – it's terrific stuff.'

'Well, let's hope you're right.'

Kyle Brewer was not doing well; he knew it and he suspected that his father also knew it. In this he was right.

'He tries hard,' John Brewer said to Felicity one night over dinner, 'but he makes some extremely stupid decisions and misjudgements. And he's inefficient as well, inclined to forget things. I really can't trust him completely with anything, even now. It's extraordinary, because he's not stupid, far from it. Clearly we were wrong to push him into the firm; I don't know what to do about it.'

Felicity said they hadn't really pushed him into the firm, and that it had seemed the best idea at the time; 'And don't forget, he did try to get a job in journalism. And publishing. So I don't think we should blame ourselves. Perhaps we should suggest he tries again.'

'Well, we could. But then he'd be earning a pittance, and I don't know if he can afford that luxury. He's taken that apartment, he's seems to enjoy spending his salary. He's got responsiblities and he has to meet them. Maybe I should give him a pep talk, perhaps that's all he needs. To realise he's got to grow up, work a bit harder. God, I wanted to be a professional football player when I was his age.'

'No, you didn't,' said Felicity, getting up and giving him a kiss, 'you always wanted to get into real estate. "I want to see New York twice its size," you said to me one night, over dinner, "and I want to be personally responsible for at least some of that".'

'Good Lord,' said John, 'how extremely prescient of me. Well, it impressed you, obviously.'

'It certainly did,' said Felicity, 'I just wish poor Kyle could impress someone, that's all.'

Kyle wished he could impress someone, too. He felt depressed and anxious about himself and his performance, and that in turn led him into more foolish mistakes. But he didn't see what he could do about it. The newspaper and publishing world didn't want him. And he was blowed if he was going to crawl to Oliver Lytton, or even Stuart Bailey, and ask them for personal favours. So he seemed to be stuck with bricks and mortar. He kept telling himself it could be worse.

LM was oddly happy these days. Her great fear had been of boredom; but she found, much to her surprise, that she was managing to fill her days quite satisfactorily. She read a great deal; she walked long distances; she was developing an interest in archaeology and taking a correspondence course on the subject. Celia had also started sending her manuscripts to read, and publishing plans to consider, and there were the monthly board meetings to keep her in touch. She supposed that in a few years' time and certainly if Jay went away to school, she might very well return to Lyttons during the week. She was quite vexed about the school situation; Jay was clearly very clever, he could virtually read already, he enjoyed doing his letters and he had an extraordinary, almost photographic memory. He loved her to read him poems over and over again, which he then remembered perfectly. He would sit at the table, or walk beside her as they strode across the countryside, reciting them. He was a particularly charming child; even allowing for a great deal of maternal prejudice, LM knew that to be the case, everyone said so, even Lady Beckenham.

He was self-assured without being cocky, friendly but not pushy, independent but in no way precocious. He was also exceptionally self-reliant, perfectly happy with his own company, and like all only children, very much at ease with adults. At five and a half he could easily have been seven, he was tall, and very strong, with his father's rather wide face and Celtic colouring, dark blue eyes and almost black hair, and his mother's sudden smile and bursts of joyous laughter. He loved helping Billy in the stables; he also adored Lord Beckenham who took him around the estate, visiting the farm, talking to the tenants. He spent quite a lot of time with the gamekeeper, who allowed him to collect pheasant eggs and place them in coops, along with extra eggs. 'So the pheasant blood gets changed,' he explained earnestly to LM. He watched in fascination as hundreds of broody hens were put in the coops.

'I want to be a keeper's boy when I grow up,' he announced.

But LM, observing his love of books, the pleasure he took in writing, and even in learning his times tables, knew that his ambitions would ultimately rise beyond that.

She knew Jago would never have countenanced boarding school for him; not at an early age, at any rate. She still struggled to keep faith with Jago, as far as Jay's upbringing was concerned; it was difficult, because they had never even had so much as an 'I'd want a child of mine to play the piano/have a bicycle/his own dog' kind of conversation, and certainly nothing of a serious nature. But she thought she knew at least what kind of life, in the broadest sense, Jago would have wanted for his son. It would certainly include a good education. And, boarding or not, if he were to go to a good school, even at thirteen, he would need a better grounding than the village school could provide.

There was quite a good boys' preparatory school in Beaconsfield which she planned to inspect for an eight-year-old entry; after that, perhaps he might go to a grammar school, rather than to public school. She knew Jago would have approved of that. On the other hand, public school would open professional doors to him in later life that even the best grammar school would not: it was all very difficult. And she had no one to share her anxieties with; Oliver was always too busy, too distracted, to talk to her about anything except Lyttons; Lady Beckenham and Celia both thought that he should go to prep school when he was eight; it was as inevitable as exchanging milk teeth for adult ones, short trousers for long. Dorothy, on the other hand, would have liked to keep Jay safely at home, even to do his lessons until he was eighteen. And there simply wasn't anyone else.

Dear Miss Lytton,

I so enjoyed our teatime meeting the other day, and I am writing also to thank you from the bottom of my heart for the book you sent me. I shall value it always: such a superb piece of writing and the fact that is is a First Edition, and the book is already in its seventh printing, makes it quite extraordinarily valuable. It is so extremely kind and generous of you.

I do very much hope that on your next trip to London, for the monthly board meeting which you mentioned, you will allow me to buy you tea once again. I look forward to hearing from you.

Yours sincerely,

Gordon Robinson

The letter had come that morning; she read it smiling, thinking how nice it was to be able to give such pleasure with such ease. He really was a very charming man. A little dull, perhaps, slightly old-maidish even, but considerate, thoughtful, and so very courteous. And really, she was happier in the company of such people: the glittering crowd with whom Oliver and Celia tended to surround themselves, the Beckenhams' dreadful hunting and shooting lot – she preferred quietly-spoken, unpretentious Gordon Robinson any day. Then she started thinking about Jago and what Gordon Robinson would have made of him, and indeed what he would have made of Gordon Robinson, and sighed heavily. She sometimes thought she must be a very odd person.

'This is very early in the day to be behaving like this,' said Sebastian. 'Ten o'clock indeed!'

'I know, I know. But I have this meeting in Hampstead, and I couldn't resist it. I just looked up the Finchley Road and thought I could see you for an hour or so. So here I am.'

'I might not have been here.'

'Sebastian! When are you ever out of the house early?' Sebastian was a late riser; for a person of such consummate energy, it was surprising.

'Well come on, shall we go upstairs?' They had been kissing, with some fervour, in the hall. He stood back, holding out her hands, examining her. She was wearing a dark pink crepe dress with one of the new very short skirts half way up her calf, and a dropped waistline, her dark hair hidden under a small-brimmed cream straw hat. 'It seems almost a shame to take that off, you look so lovely in it.'

'I'm not going to take anything off. Except, perhaps, the hat. I haven't got time. I just wanted to see you, Sebastian, see you and touch you and hear you. Nothing more.'

'Oh my darling. Oh dear. You've made me feel quite – well emotional. Come into the kitchen then, let me make you a cup of tea.'

She followed him in, sat on one of the wooden chairs, watching him in silence.

'I do love you, you know,' he said abruptly, 'so very much.'

'I know you do. I know, Sebastian.'

'It's beginning to make me unhappy.'

'Don't say that. There's no point in any of it if we're unhappy,' she said, thinking of her mother.

'I suppose not. And – when a man is in love he endures more than at other times.'

'That's very profound.'

387

'Not original I'm afraid. Nietzsche. I was reading him this morning. Anyway, here you are. Nice cuppa. I've got something else to tell you.'

'What?'

'I've told Millicent about you.'

'You – what?' She stared at him, jolted physically.

'Yes. Well not exactly you, of course, that would have been unwise, dangerous for you even. But that there was a you. I told her this weekend. I can't go on like this, married to her, loving you so much, pretending . . .'

'But Sebastian that's—' she paused, then – 'that's so cruel. Why do it, when she's perfectly happy? You said so yourself and there's no possible future for us—'

'Oh, she doesn't really care. She took it rather well, actually. She doesn't see much of me these days, after all, and she rather enjoys her status, of marriage to a famous man who's more or less deserted her. It suits her rather romantic turn of mind. It also turns out she has an admirer. So in any case I won't even have to turn up at her side for hunt balls in future.'

'Oh,' she said. She sat there staring at him, envying him more than she would have believed, this swift, easy exit from his marriage.

'But,' he went on, sitting down opposite her at the table, taking her hand in his, gazing at her very intently, 'but however she had reacted, I would have had to do it. I love you too much to go on like this, travelling up and down to her every weekend, pretending. Far too much. I am still fond of her of course; I always shall be. I shall see that all goes well for her. But I cannot continue to live with her. Even for two days a week. It is as wrong for her as it is for me. And for you.'

'Sebastian—' her voice was heavy with fear: fear and regret, 'Sebastian, you know—'

'Yes, I know. Of course I know. But at least I am entirely yours now. Even if you cannot be entirely mine. I feel – easier about it. Cleaner. As if I can let my emotions go.'

'Oh,' she said again, She looked down at her hands, twisting her rings; she felt dangerously close to both grief and joy. At the knowledge that for her, for a totally unpromised, unhopeful future, Sebastian should have left his wife, even though he no longer loved her. She no longer loved Oliver – did she? – but the severance of all the ties was still a terrifying prospect. Of course, Sebastian and Millicent had no children; but they had those other marital offspring, memories, shared intimacies, hopes, fears, laughter, friends, had lived together through grief and joy, separation and reunion. Together they had shaped his ambition, overcome her breakdown, recovered from the disappointment of a child lost, and no more conceived; more than half their lives had been joined.

What he had done for her and his feelings for her had required great courage: and great love.

'Oh, Sebastian,' she said, and realised she was crying. 'Oh, Sebastian, I—'

'Yes?' he said, looking at her very intently. 'Yes, Celia?'

'I – love you,' she said, very slowly and then faster, savouring the words, savouring the relief of saying them as well as the fear. 'I love you. Very very much.'

After she had gone – much much later, Sebastian sat staring out of the window at his garden. It had been a defining moment that, when Celia said she loved him. Until then, she had always shied away from it, and he had sometimes wondered if he was not simply a diversion for her, a diversion from her increasingly unsatisfactory marriage. Which had hurt, for he loved her very dearly, she had become the centre of his life, and he would have done anything for her. On the other hand, it seemed unlikely that he was only a diversion, for he was aware that he had achieved something rather remarkable in seducing her.

She was famously beautiful and desirable and equally famous for her fidelity to her husband. No one had heard so much as a whisper of scandal about her; even her own enemies, rather more in number than Sebastian's, could find nothing more damaging to say about her romantic life than that she was a flirt. Other aspects of her life provided grounds, to be sure: she neglected her children, people said, she was drivingly ambitious in a most unwomanly way, she had shown Oliver very little consideration when he came back so ill from the war, leaving him at her mother's house while she continued to run Lyttons in London.

But her virtue was unquestionable and throughout the war, when infidelity had been so commonplace, all during Oliver's long absence, she had never done anything that would occupy more than a half sentence of malicious talk. Sebastian was aware of this; it had added – albeit modestly – to his sense of triumph in having finally seduced her, in having accomplished something of rare, indeed unique, distinction, but until that morning he had not known for certain that it was more than a seduction. Now he did know; and moreover, that in time it would be possible to move forward yet again.

Jack was taking Lily out to lunch that day; she had no matinee and they were celebrating their anniversary. 'Three months exactly, darling, isn't that quite something?'

He had bought her a present, a small gold watch which she had admired in the window of Garrards, and he had told her to come and collect him from the office.

'I'd like you to see where I work. Where I earn my crust.'

'Lot of jam on that crust,' said Lily briskly, giving him a kiss, and then said she would like to come in, and if she could meet the legendary Lady Celia Lytton, that would be a big bonus.

Jack wanted to talk to Celia himself; he needed her opinion on General Gordon's manuscript. It seemed pretty good to him, but it was a bit short. He wasn't very experienced yet, of course, but he did know there wasn't enough there to make up a full-sized book, even with the lavish illustrations planned for this one. It was his first book, and it was very important to him. He wanted it to be good, to be as right as it possibly could be. Oliver was very pleased with what he called the trade reaction; several of the big bookshops, including Hatchards, Bumpus, Blackwells of Oxford and James Thin in Edinburgh, had all expressed interest in the project.

'I told you,' he said to Celia, 'it's a minority interest, but it's a very real one. The British love anything in uniform. And the Mutiny is a marvellously emotive subject, I think it's going to do very well. As for that stuff of your great-grandfather's – superb. Quite superb.'

Celia said she had to see a couple of bookshops that morning; 'But I should be in about eleven. I'll have a look at it then.'

She was not in by eleven; nor by half past, or even twelve. Jack sighed; he really had wanted to get the book sorted before Lily came in. And besides, he thought it would be an idea to tell Celia how much Lily wanted to meet her. She might be too busy for such an encounter. She did work terribly hard; and she could be quite difficult when she was feeling harrassed. She might even object to his inviting Lily into Lyttons, if she was in a really bad mood. In which case, he would have to tell Lily to stay down in reception.

He thought of talking to Oliver about the book, but that didn't seem a very good idea. Last time he'd tried to discuss its structure, he'd just said he didn't have time for that kind of detail, and to talk to one of the editors. But the editor who was dealing with the book, a rather highbrow young man called Edgar Green, wasn't actually being terribly helpful about it, had just told Jack to get some more text done, if he thought that was necessary. Jack got the impression Edgar rather resented his presence at Lyttons. Anyway, the real point was he couldn't work out where exactly the extra text might be needed. That was the sort of thing Celia was so good at.

At twenty-five past twelve, the girl in reception telephoned him to say that Miss Fortescue had arrived; Celia was still not back. Lily would be so disappointed. And he'd had a wasted morning. Still, he could show Lily his office. He was rather proud of it. He went down to collect her.

'And this is what we call a proof,' he said airily, pulling out a set of proofs of *Meridian*, which Celia had given him. 'These funny squiggles in the margins are the printer's marks, they're how you correct the proofs. Always in the margins, you see.'

'They do look complicated,' said Lily respectfully.

'Oh, you learn them quite quickly. First the proofs come up in long sheets from the printers, they're called galleys, and then like this, the page proofs. And – oh, there's Celia now. Celia, hallo, please do come in. I've been waiting for you.'

'Have you, Jack? I'm so sorry.' She stood there, smiling in the doorway, looking rather vague, not quite her usual efficient self. 'I got held up, those bookshop owners are dreadful, and then I had to go and see Gill Thomas.'

She was slightly flushed and her blue eyes were very brilliant; she was wearing a loose pink dress and a cream hat. He felt rather proud of her suddenly, proud to be working with her.

'Oh it doesn't matter,' he said, 'it doesn't matter at all. This afternoon will do. Celia, I'd like you to meet Lily Fortescue. She's come in to collect me, we're going out to lunch. We've got something to celebrate. Lily, this is Lady Celia Lytton.'

'How do you do, Miss Fortescue,' said Celia. She smiled again, held out her hand, 'it's absolutely lovely to meet you. I've heard so much about you, and about all your success, getting a part as one of Mr Cochrane's Young Ladies, Jack is so excited about it. Is that what you're celebrating? How thrilling.'

She was talking rather more than usual, Jack thought; well that was all right. It was when she was quiet he felt nervous. He looked at Lily. She was taking Celia in, her brown eyes studying her carefully. She was obviously very impressed by her; well, so she should be. But he was proud of Lily too, she was so pretty and she had such beautiful manners. She was telling Celia that it was only a small part, nothing to write home about, but everyone had to start somewhere, and if Celia would like to come and see the show she would be absolutely thrilled.

'So would I,' said Celia, 'absolutely thrilled.'

A silence fell then; Celia looked between them both, then said quickly, 'Well I'd better get to my desk. Jack we can talk this afternoon about your book. I'm sorry about this morning. Lovely to meet you, Lily. Have a marvellous lunch, both of you.' And then she was gone.

Lily followed Jack down the stairs and out into the street; she was rather quiet until they got to the restaurant.

Then he said, 'Isn't she lovely? Didn't you like her?'

'She is very lovely,' said Lily, 'and yes I did like her. I liked her a lot.'

'We get on awfully well,' he said, pushing her chair in, sitting down himself, 'always have done, I was only a lad when they got married, I'd only just got my commission. I thought she was tremendous then, so beautiful and such fun. And much as I admire old Wol, as the children call him, he isn't exactly fun.'

'No?' asked Lily.

'No, not really. And since the war, even less so.'

'Well she obviously is,' she said.

Jack looked at her. Then, 'What is it, Lily?' he said, 'you don't seem quite yourself.'

'Oh I'm fine,' she said, 'really.'

'Lily, come on. There's something, I know there is. Didn't you like Celia? She didn't say something that upset you did she?'

'No,' said Lily, 'no, of course not. She was utterly charming and very nice to me.'

'Good,' said Jack. He sat back and smiled at her. There was a silence. Then Lily said thoughtfully, 'I tell you what though, Jack. I reckon someone had just been giving her one.'

'What? Oh darling, no. You're quite wrong there. Celia is a pillar of virtue.'

'She might have been a pillar up to now,' said Lily, 'but not any more. I'd put a lot of money on it, Jack. If I had it. I know that look. All sort of flushed and vaguely excited. She'd been with someone this morning, I bet you. Booksellers holding her up indeed! Pull the other one, Lady Celia, I felt like saying.'

'My darling,' said Jack and he looked quite anxious, 'I really can't let you talk like this. Celia would never, ever cheat on Oliver. She just wouldn't. I'd stake my life on it.'

'I'd rather you didn't,' said Lily, leaning forward, giving him a kiss, 'I think I value your life a bit more highly than that, Jack.'

CHAPTER 21

'These sales figures for *Meridian* really are extraordinary,' said Oliver, 'seven editions now, and we are still only in March. That book has legs, as my father used to say. We are going to have to reprint yet again, as soon as possible. We'd better inform the printers.'

'It is amazing,' said Celia, 'Christmas long past, usually children's books fall right off in January. Sebastian will be pleased. Have you told him?'

'No,' said Oliver, 'I think you should do that. He was your discovery, not mine.'

She looked at him.

'That's very – generous of you, Oliver.' She was surprised; he had always found it difficult to acknowledge her successes. And this one—

'Well it's true. Mind you, I think once *The Buchanans* are out there in the shops, I shall give you a run for your money.'

'Oh really?' she said smiling at him, liking the fact that he saw *Meridian* as hers. As it was. As the author was.

'Yes. It's worth a tremendous effort. I'm going to advertise it quite heavily. I'm printing seven and a half thousand of the first volume. I feel extremely confident about it.'

So that was it. He had a success of his own to build up his self-esteem. And it would be a success; it was inevitable. The first volume was superb.

'I think we'll sell more than that,' she said, 'I'd do ten thousand if I were you. It's so marvellous.'

'Really? Well – I'll consider it. You know I did think briefly we might try to publish it earlier, in June say. It would be a scramble, but I'm rather afraid of someone beating us to it, doing something similar. Sagas are so very popular now. Everyone's out to beat the Forsytes. What do you think?'

'I think absolutely not,' said Celia. 'The autumn and Christmas, of course, are the perfect times for big new novels, and you shouldn't rush it. It just wouldn't be worth it. Besides no one could get anything similar out in time now; we'd have heard about it.'

'I expect you're right. I shall take your advice. Certainly we could do with the time. And James Sharpe has done some very good work on the jackets. You do like them, don't you?'

'Yes. Yes, I really do.'

It was true; they were slightly old-fashioned, but all the better for that, it suited the style and the concept: the dust jacket showed a house – the Buchanans' house in Oxford – in loving detail, viewed from the front gate with the door standing just open, inviting the reader inside. It was both charming and clever.

'Good. Well – I have to admit I was wrong about the *Meridian* jacket. It looks marvellous in the shops, and I've lost count of the number of booksellers who have told me how much people like it. Oh, now what on earth is the matter, you're crying, Celia, whatever is it?'

'Oh – nothing,' she said quickly, 'nothing at all. I mean nothing to do with the book. I'm just a bit tired that's all. And you know that makes me over-emotional.' Thinking that Oliver's attitude to the jacket, Gill's jacket, Gill's presence at Lyttons, had been the catalyst which had driven her into Sebastian's bed. 'I'm sorry, Oliver.'

'You do too much, I'm afraid,' said Oliver with a sigh, 'and I'm sorry you had to get involved with the Indian Mutiny as well. Very sorry.'

'Oh – it was all right. It's not too bad. A bit leaden, the writing, but we can liven it up with the editing. I think my great-grandfather's diairies will make all the difference.'

'Well – thank you anyway. I know it's not the project nearest to your heart. But I still think it will do well. And it's nice to see Jack so enthusiastic. Working hard too, I must say.'

'Yes. Yes, that's true, he is,' said Celia. No point in saying anything else: that Jack had as little grasp of publishing as the twins – probably rather less; that his book was going to be extremely expensive to produce and then would find it hard to recoup its cost. Oliver was blind about Jack and – rightly of course – felt he wanted to help him. Well, probably Lyttons could afford it, as Sebastian said. And anyway, he was a Lytton.

'You do look tired, my dearest. You need your weekend away, it will do you good.'

'I – I hope so,' said Celia opening a file on her desk. 'Oliver you will have to forgive me, I have so much to do.'

'Of course. I'll leave you in peace.'

He walked out of her office, shut the door gently. Celia stared after him, wondering how he could possibly be so blind: and how she could be so wicked.

★

They were going to stay at a hotel in Glasgow. Celia felt it was better for everything to be as near to the truth as possible. She left a Great Northern timetable lying about, asked Janet Gould to book her ticket on the sleeper to Glasgow – where Caroline would have met her – made sure Oliver was there when she reminded Daniels to collect her from the office to go to St Pancras, asked Caroline to telephone during the day about the arrangements, so that there would be a written message from her lying on the hall table: all the small, careful deceptions of adultery which, in the case of discovery, make the crime seem so much more heinous, so much greater a betrayal.

She was feeling increasingly dreadful about it, had twice actually cancelled the whole thing. Only Sebastian's passionate importunings, her sister's rather cooler admonitions not to be a fool – 'You have to take happiness where you can, Celia, surely the war taught you that' – persuaded her to proceed. She would look at Oliver over the dining table, at his desk, beside her in bed, Oliver, whom she had once loved so much, still cared for so deeply, Oliver, who deserved not a moment of pain, Oliver, who she knew continued to love her with an extraordinary devotion, and could hardly bear to contemplate what she was about to do to him and to their marriage. Superstitious fears crowded her conscience; something dreadful would happen to the children, her father would have a heart attack, Oliver would become ill – and no one would be able to find her. To increase her wretchedness, Oliver had been particularly sweet to her over the past two weeks, less critical, more appreciative; she found herelf longing for some unjust words, some harsh comment. Neither came. The night before she left he kissed her tenderly and said, 'I do hope you enjoy your few days with your sister. You deserve a holiday from us all,' and she found herself, yet again, in tears of remorse and guilt.

'There you see,' he said, 'you're exhausted. Exhausted with looking after us all. Especially me. Take a few extra days, my darling, why don't you, it's such a long way just for a weekend. Even a long one.'

But she said no, of course not, she couldn't possibly do that, she would be back on Tuesday morning as she had said: promising herself it would be the last time as well as the first, that the whole thing must finish with the weekend, that she would return after it to a life of matronly virtue, would renounce Sebastian as she parted from him, that, in the event of discovery, she would at least be able to assure Oliver that it had been a brief madness which had ended as soon as it had begun. What she felt for Sebastian was an addiction: and addictions could surely be overcome.

She had already left for St Pancras when the printer telephoned to say that he could start work on the new edition of *Meridian* on Monday. At the same time Henry Smyth, the young editorial director whom Oliver had hired to replace Richard Douglas, remembered that Sebastian had particularly asked if he could write a short letter as a frontispiece to the new edition. When Oliver phoned Sebastian at his London home, he was told by his housekeeper that he had gone away for the weekend, but when he rang Suffolk he was told by Millicent Brooke, in more than slightly brisk tones, that Sebastian no longer came down for weekends. Oliver said he was sorry to have troubled her, and told Henry they would have to get the text for Sebastian's letter first thing on Monday morning. And made a note to ask Celia if she knew about the change in Sebastian's domestic arrangements.

'I have decided it's an addiction I feel for you,' Celia said, half-laughing, half-tearful over breakfast on the Sunday: breakfast taken, like dinner the night before in their rooms, for fear of recognition.

He had booked the bridal suite: 'For you come here as my bride, Lady Celia,' a superb set of rooms, with a vast, comfortable bed, a charming sitting-room, and a bathroom which she particularly liked, all mahogany and brass fittings, with a bath large enough for them both. It was their world for the weekend: safe, warm, infinitely luxurious, and they moved into it with delight, and something close to relief at finding themselves properly alone at last.

'An addiction!' Sebastian said. 'I'm not sure I quite like that. It's possible to cure addictions, after all. I certainly don't want you to be cured of me.'

'I can't be exactly cured of you,' Celia said, rather quietly, 'I shall never ever be cured of you. You are part of me now, part of everything I do and feel and think. I shall love you for the rest of my days. But I could manage without you, I suppose. If I had to.'

'Of course you couldn't,' he said, smiling at her over the piece of toast he was heaping with butter and honey. 'You'd be quite, quite lost. And wretchedly unhappy.'

'Sebastian, that's an extremely arrogant statement.'

'It is indeed. I'm an extremely arrogant person. As you know. And therefore given to arrogant statements. But I do know I'm right. You couldn't manage without me because you've changed. You're different. That Celia I first knew, so cool and in control of herself and her life, of course she could have managed very well. But the new Celia – she has an absolute need of me.'

'Absolute?'

'Absolute. And you know why?'

'No,' she said laughing, 'but I do know this is nonsense.'

'It is not nonsense, Lady Celia,' he said, his expression very serious, 'because the new Celia, the vulnerable, uncertain one is my creation. Entirely mine.'

'Of course I'm not.'

'But you are. As I am yours. You must not underrate that. We have transformed one another, by love. You should enjoy that thought, not argue with it. Now eat that fruit. It's good for you. And after that I thought perhaps another short sojourn in that wonderful bath, and thus back to bed.'

'Sebastian—'

'Now listen to me,' he said almost severely, picking up an orange, beginning to peel it for her, 'here we are, in the situation we have dreamed of, rich in time at last, no longer paupers. For heaven's sake let us enjoy every single golden sovereign of it.'

She looked at him; he was suddenly very still, his eyes on hers, his expression serious, almost stern. She felt a shock of desire for him, so violent she could not stay still; she stood up, holding out her hand to him.

'Let us indeed,' she said.

Sex, she thought, as she lay on the bed afterwards, smiling at Sebastian while he ordered champagne on the telephone, was such an extraordinarily complex thing, the physical pleasure threaded through ineradicably with emotion and intellect, so transient but still so enduring, so joyful and yet of a great and solemn importance in the conduct of love.

What she felt for Sebastian was difficult and dangerous, and while bestowing great happiness on her life, was filling it at the same time with fear and potential pain. But while she was making love with him, she found at the heart of the physical turmoil, the throbbing, shaking, violent delight, a most surprising and almost fervent peace.

'I love you,' she said simply now, 'I love you very, very much. Whatever happens, to either of us, remember that.'

'I will,' he said, and his expression was unusually sombre, 'whatever happens, I will remember. I promise you that.'

They ventured out once or twice, walking down the streets, looking into the shops, sitting in the park.

'Isn't it strange?' said Celia, tucking her hand into his, 'people looking at us assume we are simply a couple, a happy, uncomplicated couple.'

'I don't suppose they assume anything at all,' said Sebastian, laughing, 'they have better things to do with their lives. You mustn't aggrandise yourself, Lady Celia, it must be your background.'

She said she wasn't aggrandising herself at all, that people did tend to notice, to look at other people, and remained much taken with the thought: the difference between appearance and reality. It seemed to her

397

very much the stuff of fiction; work, as always, weaving its way into her most intimate life.

'I wonder,' she said suddenly, 'if I had met you at a party or something, if I had not known you were a writer, would I have been quite so − taken with you.'

'You mean you only love me for my genius? Shame on you.'

'Of course I don't mean that.'

'I think you would have been just as taken with me,' he said, 'actually. I would have been the same person, after all.'

'To you. But not to me. What first entranced me about you was − well not your story of course. But your passion for it. And the way you told it. Sitting there, on my sofa, like—'

'Like Scheherazade? Telling tales for her Arabian sultan? What a wonderful idea. I wonder if you will free me after a thousand and one nights.'

'If only we could have a thousand and one nights,' she said sadly, 'maybe I could contemplate it. After only one, it seems horribly unlikely.'

'We have one to go yet. Which brings us down to nine hundred and ninety nine. A much more manageable figure. Now come along. Let's go back to our palace on Hope Street, and I'll try to engage your attention for a little longer at least.'

They dined in their room; it being Sunday there was little choice. They debated braving the dining-room, and rejected it. The risks outweighed the advantages, which seemed in any case extremely limited.

'We are hardly tired of one another,' said Sebastian, 'not running out of things to say. There will be no awkward silences.'

'Indeed not,' said Celia, 'and if there were, then we would have other diversions.'

'Very true. Although I'm not sure I quite like the implication that I am purely a diversion. Any more than purely an author. Or indeed an addiction.'

'Oh Sebastian,' she said, 'how adept you are at distorting what I say to you.'

He looked at her very solemnly then, without speaking.

'Now what?' she said, 'I don't like it when you're quiet.'

'I want to ask you a question,' he said, 'and then I will try my hand at distorting the answer.'

'Very well.'

A long silence. Then, 'Do you think we have any kind of a future together? Other than a continuation of the present?'

It was question so terrifying in its implications, so literally shocking in its unexpectedness, and yet so moving, so heart-shaking that she did not dare even hesitate.

'No,' she said quickly, 'no of course not. We absolutely don't. No kind of future in any way. Other than a continuation of the present that is.'

'Ah,' he said, 'Yes, I thought that was what your answer would be.'

'No room for distortion,' she said, and discovered she was physically breathless with fear.

'Oh, I don't know,' he said, smiling at her. 'You know what Mark Twain said.'

'No Sebastian, I don't,' she said, half irritably.

'Get your facts first,' he said, 'and then you can distort them as much as you please. Good advice. I follow it constantly myself. Now we won't talk about it any more. For the time being at any rate.'

'No we won't,' she said, 'not at any time, being or otherwise.'

'Stop looking so cross. I want to tell you something else.'

'What?'

'I love you.'

Later, lying awake while he slept deeply, while their second night together drifted towards an end and as the reality left so joyfully behind only forty-eight hours earlier began to close in on her once more, she found it impossible not to contemplate, momentarily at least, the shared future he had asked about. And even while knowing the futility, the danger, the stupidity of such contemplation, she found it absolutely irresistible.

'I'm sorry, Mr Lytton,' said Janet Gould, 'but Mr Brooke is still not at home. Not back in London, I mean. What shall we do?'

'I don't know. We can run the edition without his letter, of course, but it's a nice idea and he was very anxious to do it. I like to accommodate him whenever possible.'

'Yes, of course. Shall I phone again later?'

'Yes please, Mrs Gould. If you would. But if it gets to midday we shall have to go without it.'

'Certainly, Mr Lytton.'

An hour later she went back into Oliver's office.

'Still no word from Mr Brooke, Mr Lytton.'

'Oh dear. Well we'll have to run this edition without his addendum. Pity though. She's no idea where he is, the housekeeper?'

'Well – no. I don't think so.'

Oliver felt a flash of irritation. Secretaries were so limited. Even good ones like Janet Gould. They settled for so much less than they might conceivably get.

'I'll phone her myself,' he said, 'thank you, Mrs Gould.'

Mrs Conley, Sebastian's housekeeper, said – just slightly wearily, having been asked the question four times now – that she really had no idea when he might be back.

'But not today, that's for sure.'

'Really? How do you know that?'

'I was dusting his room just now, and I found a letter on his chest of drawers. Just lying around,' she said hastily, clearly anxious lest Oliver think she had been poking her nose into Sebastian's affairs. 'It was from the Great Northern Railways. Saying they were enclosing his tickets on the sleeper to and from Glasgow.'

'Glasgow,' said Oliver. 'Yes. Yes, I see.' His voice was rather loud suddenly. 'And – did it mention the dates of the tickets? This letter.'

'Yes. Up on Friday night, down Monday night. So he might go on somewhere else. But he won't be back till tomorrow morning, whatever happens, will he?'

'No,' said Oliver, 'no obviously he won't. Thank you, Mrs Conley.'

He put the phone down very gently and sat staring at it. Not moving. Feeling – odd. Then he stood up and walked purposefully into Henry Smyth's office and told him to go ahead with printing the eighth edition of *Meridian* immediately. 'Without Mr Brooke's addendum.'

'Is that really all right, Mr Lytton? You don't think he'll be upset?'

'I'm afraid we can't hold up a printing just because Mr Brooke might be upset,' said Oliver briskly. 'There are more important considerations than that, I feel.'

'Yes of course Mr Lytton.'

He stalked out, slamming the door.

Jack was on his way to see Henry Smyth himself; he heard the bang of the door, saw Oliver walking quickly down the corridor. He went in. He liked Henry: far more than he did Edgar Green. Henry didn't seem to think he was nearly so important for a start, which was ridiculous, as he was Edgar's boss. And he had been much more friendly towards him, had had lunch with him several times.

'What was that about?' said Jack.

'Oh – the old man's in a bit of a bait. He's been trying to get hold of Sebastian Brooke and he's gone missing.'

'Doesn't sound very serious.'

'No. But Brooke wanted to write some sort of foreword to the new edition; they've been holding up the printing for days.'

'Oh, I see.'

'And nobody seems to know where he is. Anyway, everything all right with the Mutiny?'

'Oh – yes. Fine. Celia made some suggestions and I've asked the author – it seemed too odd to talk about Sandy as an author – to incorporate them.'

'Good. She's a clever lady. Only I was cursing her this morning, as well.'

'Why?'

'Oh – she's got the Queen Anne proofs. Not her fault, I said she could take them, but it's the master set and she won't be back till tomorrow. I'd forgotten. She's gone away as well, hasn't she?'

'Yes,' said Jack, 'yes that's right. Yes, she's gone to stay with her sister.'

He felt rather odd suddenly. No more than that, of course. Just – odd. It was Henry's choice of words that did it, he thought, walking slowly back to his own office: 'She's gone away as well.'

Sebastian was away; Sebastian had gone missing. And then hearing Lily's voice very clearly: 'I reckon somebody's been giving her one.' Both of them missing: both of them out of London. Only of course that was absolutely unthinkable. Even more unthinkable than that Celia should be – well – doing anything wrong at all.

Janet Gould was worried about Oliver. He looked very shaky; more like he did when he first came back. He was working much too hard, she was sure of it. She wondered if he'd been looking after himself over the weekend while Lady Celia was away. She really shouldn't have left him alone, not while he was still so frail. Like most secretaries, Mrs Gould held a proprietorial, an almost wifely attitude towards her boss. He did need to eat properly, with all the damage that had been done to his stomach. And he probably hadn't bothered that weekend. She decided to make him a cup of coffee and to take him a few biscuits; that would help. When she went in, though, he was looking more like himself, working on a pile of proofs for the new *Dictionary of Music* he had commissioned a year earlier. He had personally contributed several of the entries and had insisted on checking the proofs himself. Yet more unnecessary work for him, that was what junior editors were for. But he was still clearly worried. She longed to be able to help. An idea came to her.

'Should I – that is, would you like me to phone Lady Celia's sister, see if she is there?' she asked.

She was startled by his reaction; he looked up, glared at her, as if she had done something terribly wrong.

'Why on earth should you do that?' he said. His voice was harsh.

'Well – I thought perhaps she might have spoken to Mr Brooke about the foreword. Have the copy for it, even. Also, I believe she has the proofs of the Queen Anne book, Mr Smyth was wanting them.'

'Mrs Gould, as I have already said, we have a business to run and more important concerns than Mr Brooke's feelings. The printing is to go ahead. As for the Queen Anne proofs, they can wait. I really don't want you to waste your time and the company's money, chasing my wife all over the country. Thank you, that will be all.'

'Yes Mr Lytton.'

Poor man. He was obviously feeling terrible.

'Do eat your biscuits,' she said and withdrew, closing the door carefully behind her.

Caroline looked at the clock. Nearly two o'clock. She really wanted to go riding. She'd been awfully loyal, stayed in most of the weekend, fielded a couple of phone calls from Oliver, said Celia was out for a walk the first time, asleep the second, called Celia at once to tell her. She'd instructed her staff to fetch her at once if Mr Lytton phoned: not to attempt to answer any calls from him themselves. In any case they were infinitely discreet, like all good domestic staff, understood the code very well. She hadn't even gone out hunting on the Saturday, Celia had sounded so wobbly. This was clearly very much her introduction to adultery. Amazing, after – what? Fifteen years of marriage.

Caroline thought of the several occasions on which she'd deceived her husband, and felt momentarily guilty. Then crushed it hastily. He'd never known, and indeed the last time he'd gone off to the war, he'd told her how lucky he was to have such a marvellous marriage. Had died, no doubt, thinking that. So what harm had she done him? Absolutely none. And she could hardly blame Celia: Oliver looking so drained and clearly not up to anything much. And Celia still so beautiful. He had been wonderful looking once, she'd envied Celia in those days, still did in a way, not for her huband any more, but for her career. And the new lover of course.

She could do with a lover herself just now; but men of her generation were in short supply. Oh, well. A horse was a pretty good subsitute for a man. She'd always thought so. Less demanding and certainly more rewarding. Yes, she'd go. Oliver would hardly be telephoning now, from the office. He had more important things to do than worry about his wife and where she might be.

★

Caroline's butler, McKinnon, was dozing by the fire in his sitting-room when the phone rang; it took a few rings to wake him properly and a few rings more before he reached it. Everything took longer these days; old age put the brakes on life, not just on yourself.

'Kersley House, good afternoon.'

'Good afternoon. Is Lady Celia Lytton there?'

'Just a moment, Sir. Who may I say is calling?'

'This is Mr Lytton. Mr Jack Lytton speaking.'

'Good afternoon, Sir.'

Now what should he do? The mistress had told him most precisely that any calls to Lady Celia should be directed to her: but she was out riding.

'I'm sorry Sir. She is not available at the moment.'

'Well – when might she be available?'

'I really cannot say, Sir. I'm afraid.'

'Well – has she left for London?'

'I don't believe so, Sir, no. I will ask Mrs Masterson to telephone you when she returns. She is out riding.'

'Oh – no. Doesn't matter. Only an enquiry about a book. Thanks anyway.'

'Entirely my pleasure, Sir.'

It had hardly meant anything of course: if you hadn't been looking for something, it couldn't have meant anything at all. Of course the butler wouldn't know every one of Celia's movements; of course he would refer an enquiry to her sister. Just the same – oh this was wretched. Jack tried and failed to address his mind to editing the last few entries of the fourth Earl of Beckenham's diaries of battle. They were gory enough to distract anyone from anything. Severed limbs littering the battlefield, horses dying in agony, men gagged as the surgeons operated on them in the field – only surely, surely the butler would have known whether or not a guest – his mistress's sister for heaven's sake – had departed from the house after the weekend. Surely. It was the sort of thing they were paid for, for heaven's sake . . .

'Jack? Hallo, it's Celia. I was out for a walk. Is something wrong?' She sounded anxious.

Jack felt terrible. Terribly guilty: at bothering her, worrying her.

'No, no, of course not. I'm so sorry to have bothered you. It was just that I wanted to ask you about the Mutiny.'

'But that can't be urgent. I'm back tomorrow. You know that.'

'Yes. Yes of course. I'm really sorry. Bit of over-keenness.'

'Yes, I see.' She was silent; then 'Well, can it wait? Or is there an army of excited readers out in the street?' She sounded amused; Jack felt better.

'Of course it can wait. It was just that all that gore, in your great-grandfather's diaries you know, I wasn't sure how much to cut.'

'About half,' said Celia, 'or even three-quarters. I must go, Jack, I'll miss my train. 'Bye. Give my love to Oliver.'

'Of course. 'Bye, Celia. See you tomorrow.'

Silly bugger, he thought; ringing her like that. Thinking about her like that. If – when – Lily knew her better, she'd realise it was all a lot of nonsense. Absolute nonsense.

CHAPTER 22

'I wish you could be married to two people at once.'

There was a silence. Don't look at Oliver, Celia, don't.

'Can you be married to two people at once? Does anyone do that?'

Everyone laughed then: the tension was broken.

'I'm afraid not, Maud,' said Robert, 'not allowed. But why do you ask? Who do you have in mind?'

Maud's small face was earnestly intent, her green eyes very large. 'Well, I used to think I wanted to marry Jamie.'

'Maud, Jamie is your brother.'

'My half-brother. That might make a difference. But now I want to marry Giles, as well. Well, judging from his photograph. He's very handsome.'

More laughter: 'It's just as well he's not here,' said Celia, 'he would be very embarrassed. Flattered as well, of course, but he's very shy. You'll have to be a bit careful when he comes on Saturday, Maud.'

'I'm afraid you can't marry your cousin, either,' said Felicity, 'so it's back to the drawing-board, Maud. Or the marriage bureau.'

'You can in England, actually,' said Oliver. 'It's not thought advisable, I believe, purely on health grounds. But it's not illegal.'

'How extraordinary. It's quite illegal in the States.'

'Clearly Americans are more law-abiding than we are,' said Oliver, 'or something like that.' He smiled at her, then frowned and went back to his newspaper.

His attitude towards Felicity was rather odd, Celia thought. He was both edgy and affectionate with her; it was as if he found himself fond of her almost against his will. Probably that was exactly the case; he was increasingly anti-social these days, shying away from any engagement that was not at least semi-professional. 'Oh, I haven't got the time any more for that sort of thing,' he would say or, 'Oh, I really don't have the energy these days to make conversation with those kinds of people.' Anyone who drove him to make an exception to such rules was bound to inspire slightly contradictory emotions.

She could see why he did like Felicity: she was the sort of soft, gentle woman he approved of, living entirely for and through her family, deferring to men in all things. He should have married someone like her, Celia thought rather sadly, not an overbearing, over-ambitious creature who – well he had married her. Or rather she had married him. She often thought that, left to his own rather nervous preferences, Oliver would have quietly removed himself from her wilful, eighteen-year-old self. But he hadn't. And meanwhile, thank God for Felicity; it would help to ease the weekend.

'If you will excuse me,' Oliver said, putting the paper down again, 'I have to get to the office. What are your plans for the day?'

'Oh, we're going to show Maud the sights,' said Robert, 'the Houses of Parliament, Big Ben, try and get her locked up in the Tower—'

'You mustn't do that,' said Venetia, her eyes very large. 'It's horrible there.'

'Venetia, of course we won't. Just teasing. They wouldn't have her, anyway.'

'I wish you two could come with us,' said Maud, longingly.

'We could,' said Adele, 'of course we could, we could miss school, just for one day, Mummy, please, please may we, please . . .'

'No,' said Celia firmly, 'absolutely not. If your last reports hadn't been so bad, I might consider it. But you need every moment that you can get at your desks. Look at you, you haven't even got your boots on yet. Barty, go and get your coat and tell Daniels the twins will be five minutes.'

'Yes, Aunt Celia.' Barty stood up. 'I'll see you all later. I hope you have a lovely day. My special favourite place is St Paul's Cathedral,' she said to Maud, 'right up in the whispering gallery. Be sure to go there if you can.'

'She's nice,' said Maud watching as Barty left the room, 'I really like her.'

'She's enchanting,' said Felicity, 'such a lovely story, Celia. You must be very proud of her. Now don't let us keep you, I know you have to get to the office as well. Kyle dear, are you coming sightseeing with us? Or do you want to go to Lyttons, see around there with Oliver?'

'I'd love to go to Lyttons,' said Kyle, 'if that's all right. With Oliver.'

He had joined their party: it had been Felicity's idea. John had told her that he was performing badly, that he had offered more than once to resign, that he even seemed depressed and she had suggested and John had agreed that he probably should look again at the world of letters.

'But some kind of pride, I suppose, keeps him from using the Lytton connection as a last resort. I know you said Oliver was willing to help, but—'

'Well, he has developed an understandable – and rather admirable –

nervousness about nepotism. But it could be that visiting Lyttons London, talking to Oliver and Celia, might change his mind. Would you mind if I wrote to them and suggested he came with us?'

John said that he would not; and Kyle, presented with the twin delights of a visit to London and what Oliver described as a tour of duty at Lyttons, found himself quite unable to refuse the invitation.

'But I don't want to be a nuisance,' he said with a sigh, 'I'm getting very sick of that.'

Felicity told him not to be ridiculous; 'You are hardly going to be a nuisance over the space of four or five days.'

'I manage it pretty well at Brewer Lytton,' said Kyle gloomily.

'If you will excuse me, Felicity,' said Celia now, 'I should go as well. And I've arranged for you to meet a girl who does a lot of design work for us, Gill Thomas, to discuss your jacket and illustrations on Tuesday. I'll bring your proofs down to Ashingham with me, you can look at them there.'

'I can't wait to see them. Although it doesn't sound as if I'll have much time for proofs,' said Felicity, laughing. 'Your mother obviously has the most wonderful time planned for us.'

'Oh, she's terribly good at house parties,' said Celia, 'she adores them. She missed doing them more than anything else during the war. She turned Ashingham into a convalescent home, you know, so it wasn't possible. It won't be large, probably only about twenty people, including us. You'll have a lovely time, Felicity. I hope so anyway.'

'Won't I have a lovely time too?' asked Robert.

'Of course you will,' said Celia She was very fond of Robert, she liked the way he teased her. He took life less seriously than Oliver. 'How are your charades?'

'Oh – pretty good.'

'Charades!' said Kyle. 'Oh dear.'

'I don't suppose they're compulsory,' said Felicity.

'Not quite. What about jigsaws?'

'Oh – I like jigsaws. Nice and quiet.'

'My mother has a huge table, set with a jigsaw, and people do a bit each time they pass. And quite a lot after dinner. She says more romances have started over that table than anywhere else. Now, I must go. Have a wonderful day all of you. Kyle, you can come with me, that's a much better idea. If you're brave enough to risk my driving.'

'I'm sure it's excellent. What car do you have?'

'Oh, it's heaven. I thought you saw it last night. It's a dear little Morris, I love it to death.'

'She always has small cars,' said Venetia, who had come back into the room, 'so there's no room for her children in them.'

'Quite right. Venetia, do go and get in the car, for heaven's sake. I can hear Daniels hooting. Your father will be late for work.'

'Why does it matter?' said Adele, appearing behind her, 'I never understand, when he's the boss.'

'Because everything depends on him, that's why. So he can't be late. And don't let your grandmother hear you saying anything so vulgar as the boss tomorrow, or she'll send you home again. Last time we were there, one of them started talking about weekends,' she said to Felicity, 'my mother's blood pressure soared. She's a terrible snob,' she added slightly unnecessarily.

'I can see I shall have to be very careful, myself,' said Felicity, 'what's wrong with saying weekend?'

'It's extremely vulgar. Saturday to Monday is what you say in England. God, I'm only teasing, Felicity. Only she isn't, I'm afraid. Come on Kyle. Time to go.'

'And you, Maud,' said Felicity, 'and I think you should wear a hat. It's very cold.'

'The twins have some lovely clothes,' said Maud, 'they were showing me last night. They get them at a shop called Woollands. Could we go to Woollands do you think?'

'Maybe in the morning. Today is sightseeing. Off you go and fetch a hat, it's very cold. And some gloves.'

Celia was writing copy for the autumn catalogue when Sebastian came into her office. She looked at him and tried to smile. He shut the door behind him, leaned against it.

'You shouldn't be here,' she said, 'it's so – dangerous.'

'Of course it's not. You coming to my house, that's dangerous. Us dining in the country, the other night, staying in Oxford, that was dangerous. This is very safe.'

'I – suppose so,' she said. But she didn't really think so. Every day, every risk brought them closer to the final denouement; she was sure it had to come. The close shave that afternoon in Scotland, when Caroline had rung the hotel in a near-panic, to tell her Jack had phoned almost an hour earlier – she'd been scared then. Jack was sharper, so much more worldly than Oliver – but it had been all right, the call seemed genuine enough. Just Jack being over-keen as usual. And it had been good to be able to send her love to Oliver, making sure Jack would tell him that he'd spoken to her. God, she would never have believed she could be so devious.

'I have every right, every reason to visit Lyttons, Lady Celia,' said

Sebastian now, 'I bring you my new oeuvre. Which against considerable odds, largely of your making, I have been able to complete.'

'Sebastian! I don't take up that much of your time.'

'Possibly not my time. But you consume my attention. That is far more disruptive. Anyway, here it is. Don't you want to see it?'

'Yes, of course I do.'

He came over to her, kissed her quickly.

'You look tired.'

'I am tired,' she said.

She did indeed feel it: heavily, achingly tired. The energy, which had been one of her greatest gifts, had deserted her. It was, she knew partly emotional trauma: she was beginning to find herself very unhappy. It shocked her this unhappiness: that something begun so joyfully, as a self-indulgence, a bid for pleasure, should have converted so swiftly into the reverse. All she seemed to feel these days was, at best, a deep longing, a yearning to be with Sebastian all the time, and, at worst, a mixture of discontent and sadness.

When she was not with him, she thought only of when she would be, counting days, hours, until they were together; the moment they were alone, she felt only distress that it was passing too swiftly, and dread at the inevitable parting. Sebastian teased her about it at first, became irritated with it later.

'We are doing this because we love one another,' he said, 'because we want to be happy. What is the point, if all you do is cry?'

She said she was sorry, she would try to be more positive, to enjoy it, thinking of her mother's words as well, so like Sebastian's: 'Enjoy it, there's no point in it, if you don't.'

But it didn't quite work. Guilt was added more and more to her emotions: perversely, Oliver seemed changed, more patient with her, less criticial, increasingly loving.

'It isn't fair,' she said to Sebastian, 'it just isn't fair, I came to you because I felt he didn't love me any more; that made it all right, somehow, or at least not so bad. Now he seems to love me more than ever.'

He wanted to make love more often too, these days; that was difficult. ried to welcome him, to respond, to enjoy him even, but it was difficult, however hard she struggled; and there were times when she simply could not go through with it, would plead exhaustion, distraction, feign sleep. She looked back on the early days of their marriage, the days before the war, when lovemaking with Oliver had been a constant delight, when she had welcomed him into her body night after night, had been not merely responsive but creative in bed with him. Now it was all she could do to accept him, pretending pleasure, feigning orgasm; he appeared content with what she offered him, but that troubled her, too. Was she really so faithless, so duplicitous that she could deceive him, so thoroughly?

'I think he knows,' said Sebastian one day, when she complained to him of Oliver's new sweetness and tenderness. She stared at him.

'Knows? What do you mean, Sebastian? Surely not, he can't.'

'Oh, he doesn't realise he knows. He's only aware of a change in you. A distancing. He doesn't want to examine it, or the causes, but he does know. So he's fighting back. Poor sod,' he added lightly.

'Don't talk about Oliver like that,' she said, 'I don't like it.'

'Sorry. I'm sorry. It's just so hard for me too. Have you thought of that? Thinking of you always with him, waking with him, sleeping with him, talking to him, sharing your life with him?'

'Yes,' she said soberly, 'yes, I have thought of that, Of course. But – he has a right to it, Sebastian. You don't. He is my husband, the father of my children. You can't fight that.'

'I could,' he said, 'if you would let me.'

'No!' she said, the word an explosion of fear. 'No, I won't. You are not to.'

But in the sleepless nights, she did think of it; of letting him. Letting him force things through, of making her divorce Oliver. And then would turn her mind away from it, quickly, fearfully. It was too beguiling a vision, too great a temptation, to allow herelf to consider.

To escape from her unhappiness, she had launched herself into a fever of social activity; went to every party, every dinner, patronised the new nightclubs. Nightclubs were where the new life, the frantic frenetic post-war life was most potently lived. The favourite of that particular hour was the Grafton Galleries which had a negro band and was open until two am; the Prince of Wales was a member – although seldom seen there, I have to admit – Celia said. Anyway, that was where she was going: every night. Or nearly every night. With crowds of friends. Crowds of friends and Jack. And Lily, who very often joined them after her show. Celia liked Lily. She was fun. She was a bit spiky, and very sharp; but she was great fun and seemed genuinely fond of Jack. She had been introduced to Oliver now; he was charmed by her. Most people were; she was very charming.

They also frequented the big London hotels, most notably the Savoy, which had pioneered the latest fad, the dinner dance, and where the non-stop dancing could continue even through dinner, to the horror of the older generation, and where the band was superb, and the cocktails were the finest.

Celia made Oliver buy a cocktail shaker and, when Brunson's skills with it were found wanting, despite tuition from Jack, they made Daniels try. Daniels made superb cocktails. Cocktails were the new thing: along with the endless dancing and the new music sensation from America, jazz.

'We must give a cocktail party,' she said to Oliver, only a day after arriving home from Glasgow, through a haze of sadness.

'Must we really?' he said.

'We must,' said Jack, who seemed particularly pleased to see her, and anxious to please; so Oliver agreed, and a hundred people came to Cheyne Walk that Saturday – short notice for invitations was another new thing – to enjoy Atta Boys and Gimlets and Daniels' finest, a literally heady mix of rye whisky, egg white, lemon juice and absinthe called a Rattlesnake.

'So called because it will either cure a Rattlesnake bite, or kill Rattlesnakes, or make you see them,' Celia expained to her guests. 'You'll adore it.'

They did adore it and the others too, and afterwards went in a large crowd to another new and wildly smart place, the Cecil Club, better known as the Forty-Three, where they danced until two.

Oliver went with them that night, as their host, but usually, and certainly during the week, when Celia went out dining or nightclubbing, he would plead weariness and stay at home. The pleas were genuine, but did not help either her state of mind or her marriage. Sometimes, on those nights, Sebastian would join the crowd; it was a painful pleasure, to be with him, and yet need to to be watchful, terribly, dreadfully watchful, to be in his arms, but only dancing, worse, even still to watch others in his arms, and to kiss him goodnight and then wave him gaily off. He had become accepted now as part of their circle, no one questioned his presence, and besides, he was extremely popular, so good-looking, so charming, with the added glamour of fame and success and the slight air of mystery which surrounded his private life.

'He must have a mistress somewhere,' said one of Celia's friends, Elspeth Granchester, as they watched Sebastian disporting himself, despite his gammy leg on the dance floor at the Savoy with Lily. His energy and creativity had been fuelled by several Old-Fashioneds, his own favourite cocktail. 'He's so desperately attractive, don't you think?'

'Yes, I suppose so,' Celia said, taking a rather large gulp from her own cocktail glass, 'I mean, yes, he's very attractive. But I don't know about the mistress. I don't think he has the time.'

'Darling, one can always make time for sex,' said Elspeth Granchester.

★

'You don't still think Celia's cheating on Oliver, do you?' said Jack, 'not now you know her. Not now you know them?'

Lily looked at him; she was regretting her initial outburst. Jack adored Oliver and he loved Celia; the thought of them being less than perfectly happy with one another was infinitely painful for him. Although how he could think they were perfectly happy, when they were living what seemed to Lily almost separate lives, she couldn't imagine. Still – there was no point in upsetting him. And it was nothing to do with her. Not really.

'No, I think I was was probably wrong,' she said giving him a quick kiss, 'sorry.'

'And you do like her?'

'Course I do. I like her a lot.'

It was true; she did. Liked and admired her. Even if she had got a lover. And she really couldn't blame her. Oliver was sweet, but he was very quiet. Quiet and dull. Lily knew she'd go mad in five minutes, living with someone like that. On the other hand, she was still mildly shocked, she couldn't help it. She was very moral in her attitude towards marriage: her parents had been – still were – wonderfully happy, and she had grown up knowing marriage at its best and with a great respect for it.

She wished Jack would hurry up and find a place of his own. It wasn't just that she was beginning to fancy a bit more than she was getting (and it was every bit as nice as she'd thought it would be, even if it was in rather seedy hotels) but it was a bit undignified, living with your brother and his wife at the age of thirty-five. It wasn't as if he couldn't afford a place either; he went on and on about how little he was paid, but he seemed to her to have plenty of money. He had stocks and shares and in Lily's book, anyone with those had money. She was always offering to help him find somewhere and she had checked out a few places. One dear little mews house in Chelsea was perfect. But he just didn't seem that keen. She supposed it was all too easy for him: meals on tap, no rent, come and go as he liked. Well, she might have to gee him up a bit. She wasn't prepared to put up with this indefinitely.

The one thing Celia couldn't bear was being alone with Oliver; the guilt and the sadness spiralled up in her until she could stay with him no longer and literally had to leave the room. She knew she was behaving altogether badly; she was drinking too much, eating too little, smoking heavily – she had taken it up recently and had a collection of the new, outrageous long cigarette holders – neglecting her children – she couldn't remember when she had last written to Giles – and she found a strange solace in buying clothes, on which she lavished an enormous amount of money.

She had always loved clothes, but the new ones that summer were glorious: the soft, easy knitted jackets and jumpers from Chanel, so simple, so unutterably chic, and for the evening an entirely new glamour, the silhouette slender, dresses which clung to the uncorseted body, with wonderful handkerchief pointed hemlines, swooping, drooping silken drapes. Then there were the long ropes of pearls and of course the bandeaux, sometimes glittering, sometimes silk or velvet, worn low on her forehead, showing off her new, short hair. And the shoes! The pointed, strappy, glitter-trimmed shoes in silk and satin and pastel leather: she could not have enough of them, had more than a dozen pairs she had hardly worn.

'You look very thin these days,' Sebastian said severely now. 'You're not eating properly.'

'I know,' she said, 'I can't. Sebastian don't lecture me, and you really must go away. We're going down to my mother's tomorrow night, for four days with the American lot – you'd love Felicity, she's charming – and I have so much to do before we go.'

'I'm not going to go,' he said, 'until you've read at least one chapter of *Meridian Times Two*,' this was the name they had given the first sequel, after much thought. 'So don't try and get rid of me. I shall sit here and watch you working quietly, until you can find a moment for me.'

'Oh – all right then. It had better be now. Otherwise I shan't be able to concentrate. Sit down there and be quiet, for heaven's sake.'

He sat down on one of her sofas and she started to read; after a few pages she looked up at him and smiled.

'I love it so much,' she said, 'it's just as wonderful. How do you do it, Sebastian?'

'Oh – just natural genius,' he said with a shrug, and then, 'you look quite different suddenly. What is it?'

'It's this,' she said gesturing at the manuscript, 'it's reminded me, as if I needed it, of exactly why I love you.'

That Thursday morning, Jasper Lothian, Master of St Nicholas College, Cambridge, was reading his *Spectator* when he came across a paragraph in the literary section which caused him a stab of concern. He moved on to other articles, and then set the paper aside, expecting the stab to recede, but found it still troubling him at the end of the day; his wife,

Vanessa, finding him rather distracted over dinner, asked him if anything was wrong. Jasper Lothian said there was nothing, but Vanessa knew him rather too well to take this as an answer. Finally, and a little reluctantly, for she was famous for her formidable will and her refusal to accept anything which she did not entirely like, he showed her the *Spectator* article. Vanessa read it in silence, twice and then looked at him; her eyes were hard.

'I think you should speak to our solicitor,' she said.

They arrived at Ashingham at teatime the next day, two cars full; the first was the huge Rolls, driven by Oliver, with Felicity, Celia, Robert and Kyle, and Giles – who they had picked up at Eton. The second was what Oliver called his vintage car, a large Morris Bullnose, driven by Daniels and bearing Barty, the twins, Maud, Nanny and Celia's maid.

'This is just beautiful,' said Felicity, jumping out of the car, gazing around her at Ashingham, its Palladian splendour, enhanced by the sharp-edged light of an early Spring evening, and at the fields sweeping below its high terrace, 'so very beautiful. Just as I imagined it, and never quite dared to hope it could be.'

'How kind of you,' said Lady Beckenham. 'I suppose that coming from your country, you're not used to seeing decent houses.'

It was an odd remark; fortunately, Celia had warned Felicity, about her mother.

In the event, Lady Beckenham took to Felicity rather strongly. She discovered that she hunted in Virginia and that her grandfather was a general, neither of which she had expected and told Celia in a loud voice over drinks before dinner that Felicity seemed to be quite well-bred for an American. The ultimate seal of approval – an invitation to look through the bloodstock records of Ashingham – came when she discovered that Felicity's mother collected Staffordshire china and had had Georgian panelling imported from England to adorn the dining-room in the family house.

'I really hadn't expected to enjoy your visit,' she said, leading her off to the library after dinner, 'but I can see it's going to be rather fun.'

'Good,' said Felicity, 'I think so too.'

She managed, with an enormous effort, not to admire any of the pictures, or the furniture; 'Terribly bad form in English country houses,' Celia warned her, but felt it was probably all right to request a visit to the stables. It was.

'Of course,' said Lady Beckenham, 'I'd like that very much. We could ride, if you like, in the morning.'

Felicity said she would like it very much, but she didn't have any riding clothes and hadn't Lady Beckenham got a great deal to do?

'Not really. Why should I have?'

'Well ten more people arriving – surely—'

'Oh, not really. I've built up a very good staff again, the rooms are done, and Cook is marvellous, I just tell her how many people are coming and she does the rest. I don't plan the meals or anything like that and, of course, Beckenham and the butler sort out the wine. Biggest headache is changing the placement every night, so people don't get bored. Dinner was all right, wasn't it?'

'It was delicious,' said Felicity, 'the pheasant especially—'

'Yes, well, you see that's all so easy, with plenty of our own birds. Cook is an awfully good woman, although she's quite young. She does marvellous shooting picnics, food all in hay boxes, you know. Now then, riding clothes. I'm much smaller than you, so my breeches won't fit you, or my boots, but some of Celia's things are still here. She might like to come with us.'

They were the only guests that evening; after dinner they went into the drawing-room and played games. Not the charades so dreaded by Kyle, but card games, consequences, and a start was made on the weekend's jigsaw.

Kyle found it all rather odd, to be sitting in this immensely grand room, with everyone in evening dress, playing children's games, but he felt happier than he had for weeks. He had enjoyed the day before at Lyttons more than he would have believed possible; he had walked in with Celia, into the untidy, dusty, almost shabby offices, so at variance with their rather grand exterior, where the walls were lined from ceiling to floor with books, the desks piled with books, seen the huge cellar filled with truckloads of books, the loft room in which the archives were stored, packed with books, and felt he had come home. He was surprised by the size of the operation, by how many people were working there: about thirty, Oliver said when he was giving him a tour.

'Well we publish upwards of a hundred books a year, they require a lot of people.'

There were of course the editorial staff, the design office and the accounts department. This was a large room with a glass door, on which the words 'Counting House' were embossed in gold letters. Here men, wearing green eye shades, sat at high desks, looking exactly as if they were working in a newspaper office. Then there were what seemed like an army of office boys and clerks and the lookers out, whose job was literally to look out the books from the warehouse to meet that day's orders. After the guided tour Kyle, looking slightly apologetic, had asked if there was anything he could do. Oliver said would he like to sort out some old manuscripts and proofs that had been in boxes since the war, into date order and re-file them?

'It's a ghastly job, very tedious, but it has to be done, some of them are very precious. I would be grateful and you could see the sort of thing we used to do. It might interest you.'

Kyle settled to it, and was found four hours later, totally engrossed in his task, with a stack of neatly labelled manuscipts in one box: 'And I thought it might be helpful if they were documented in some way, so I started a sort of ledger in date order, cross-referenced alphabetically. I hope that's all right.'

Oliver smiled at him, his weary, sweet smile.

'It's very much all right. I think God must have been listening to me at last. I've been praying for years for someone like you to come along.'

Kyle returned that afternoon to carry on with his task; he said it sounded much more interesting to him than shopping.

On the nursery floor, Giles and Barty, being older than the others, were allowed to stay up after supper in the day nursery; Barty challenged Giles to a game of chess and won fairly effortlessly in just over an hour.

'You're pretty good,' he said, carefully casual, 'I don't get much of a chance to play, of course.'

'Of course not. Wol taught me. He's really excellent. How's school?' she said, packing the pieces back into the box.

'Pretty good, thanks. I'm enjoying it.'

'No more bullying?'

'Good Lord, no. I'll be an Upper next year, able to use Tap and that sort of thing.'

He looked inordinately pleased at this prospect. Barty looked at him.

'What's Tap?'

'Oh, a bar in the town. One can drink beer or cider there.'

'Oh, I see. Aunt Celia was saying she hoped you'd get into Pop. What's that and will you?'

'Good Lord, I shouldn't think so. It's a sort of – well its official name is the Eton Society. Only twenty-four boys, usually the best games players. You have to be elected. I'm sure I won't be.'

'Why not?'

'Well—' he suddenly looked less pompous and grinned at her slightly awkwardly, 'you have to be terrifically popular for a start. Which I'm not.'

'Oh, I see,' She smiled back, 'me neither.'

'Still?'

'Still. But now that I'm going to St Paul's it might be better, I think.'

'I didn't know that, Barty.'

'Didn't Aunt Celia tell you?' She felt hurt.

'No. She doesn't write – much – at the moment.'

'Oh, well. I got a scholarship actually.'

'Barty, that's tremendous. Congratulations.'

'Thank you. Anyway, what are the advantages of being in this Pop thing?'

'Mostly just being in it. But you can wear bow ties, and coloured waistcoats and sealing wax on your top hat. That's about it really.'

Barty looked at him very solemnly.

'I don't know how you can even contemplate not belonging to that,' she said. He looked back at her and they both started to laugh, on and on, until Nanny came in and told them they'd wake the little girls up. After that she asked him to teach her to play gin rummy, got the hang of it at once and after losing the first game, won the next two – and then carefully tactful, allowed him to beat her again.

Afterwards, lying in bed, Giles thought how Barty really was the prettiest and the jolliest, not to mention the most interesting girl he had ever met. He hoped she'd enjoy St Paul's. She certainly deserved it.

Sebastian Brooke had thought he would be grateful for a weekend of peace in London. He had a great deal of work to do, and besides, he liked his own company. But he found himself, early on Saturday evening, feeling both lonely and resentful. It was absurd he knew; Celia was only fulfilling her function as wife and he had no claim on that, but like all lovers, he was beginning to look for more than what had at first seemed so perfectly and joyfully satisfactory. And somehow it was especially painful that weekend; Sebastian was a highly sociable animal, and moreover, as he cheerfully admitted, something of a snob. He would have adored to spend the weekend at a country house party, and a rather grand house at that, to have played tennis and charades and gone for walks and dined in style. The prospect of the solitary meal of poached salmon which Mrs Conley had prepared for him, however delicious, became increasingly unattractive. Indeed, as he sat in his dining-room, contemplating the evening ahead, drinking the first of what he fully expected to be several glasses of a rather good Sancerre, he felt himself becoming almost morose. It was not too surprising then, that when Elspeth Granchester telephoned him on the off chance that he might be able to join her party at the Savoy for dinner and dancing and then on to the Forty-Three, he told her that there was really nothing he would like more.

'Good. Then join us at eight. Don't dress up, black tie will do.'

★

417

For dinner at Ashingham, dressing up was still very much expected; male guests always wore white tie for dinner. Robert looked up and down the long table, and thought that however inevitable it might be, especially in the post-war climate, to question the old social values, it was still very good to see them in action from time to time. It gave life an order, a sense of tradition and his was probably the last generation that would see such wealth, such social power on show in a private house. And it was an impressive show: the huge room, the glorious panelling, the fine fireplace, the long, long table, the lavish flowers, the gleaming silver. And the servants, in full livery, waiting with such infinite discretion and skill: plates placed and removed again, dishes proffered, glasses filled and refilled.

The women, particularly, looked marvellous, flattered by candlelight and jewellery. Lady Beckenham's transformation had slightly surprised him. In her daytime uniform of shabby tweeds, she was scarcely distinguishable from her gamekeeper. At night she emerged as a still beautiful woman, her thick black hair, shot with silver, beautifully arranged with incredible speed by her long-suffering maid, her fine bosom and surprisingly small waist accentuated by the sort of gowns she always wore, rather stiff, in embroidered and jewelled satin.

Celia was looking lovely of course – although tired, she always looked so tired these days – in cream silk, and Felicity equally beautiful in silvery lace, with pearl drops in her hair; she had been placed next to Oliver and had succeeded in making him laugh aloud twice, a difficult feat at the best of times, and was now listening most courteously to Lord Beckenham, as he held forth about the various campaigns he had fought, in the fullest and goriest of detail, finishing each anecdote with, 'Your grandfather would have enjoyed that one.'

The conversation generally lacked the charm, though, of a London or even a New York table, he thought, that was his only reservation; it was parochial, largely concerned with country matters, and its best moments were unconscious. Robert had been ruefully describing how he once turned up at a white tie dinner in New York in a dinner jacket: Lord Beckenham turned to look at him incredulously.

'I hope you dismissed your man at once,' he said, 'extraordinary ignorance. Disgraceful.'

It clearly did not occur to him, Robert realised, that anyone might not employ a valet. At the other end of the table, Lady Beckenham was holding forth about the disgraceful state of modern English society.

'They're diluting the peerage. It's quite dreadful, eight earldoms created in the last three years, and sixty-four baronies. They're just selling them, you know, to the ghastly new rich. A knighthood only costs ten thousand, a baronetcy forty. And in London, the most awful women are coming to the fore as hostesses, Lady Cunard, American, of course, and Lady Colefax, and that appalling Laura Corrigan, no better than when she was a telephonist, well she's American too—'

'Mama, Felicity is an American, you mustn't be so rude,' Celia said.

But Lady Beckenham turned to her and said, 'Oh, that doesn't count. Mrs Brewer is not like an American, she's extremely well-bred. Not many like her.' She said this with enormous authority, as if she had an intimate knowledge of the workings of American society.

Felicity said nothing for a moment, then, 'More than perhaps you'd think, Lady Beckenham.'

There was a silence, then 'I very much doubt it,' replied Lady Beckenham.

Afterwards in the library, during charades, and prompted by Celia, she apologised, but Felicity laughed and said she hadn't minded for a moment, and that to be called well-bred by Lady Beckenham was an honour indeed.

Much later that night, when almost everyone had gone to bed, Lady Beckenham sat down by the fire. Celia was reading.

'Delightful woman,' she said, 'I like her very much. Extremely attractive. Oliver obviously likes her. I saw them with their heads together in the garden earlier.'

'Yes,' said Celia, barely lifting her head, but smiling at her absently, 'yes, he does. It's nice, he hardly ever likes anyone.'

'Well she exudes sex,' said her mother, 'hardly surprising that he should.'

Celia stared at her. 'Felicity! Sexy! Mama, she's a really old-fashioned perfect, submissive wife.'

'And has it never occurred to you how sexy that can be?' said her mother. 'I'm surprised at you, Celia. I thought you were more in touch with the ways of the world than that.'

Celia smiled at her again, and went back to her book.

'Oh what heaven this is. Sebastian, I'm so thrilled you could come. So sweet of you to find a space in your terribly crowded diary.'

'Not very crowded,' he said, smiling down at her; they were dancing, after dinner and before moving on to the nightclub. 'Not this evening anyway.'

'Oh, I can't believe that. An attractive single man like you – you are single, aren't you, Sebastian?'

'Yes and no,' he said.

'Now what does that mean?'

'It means I was once married, and am no longer. And—'

'But you must have another − lady friend.'

'I have dozens,' he said lightly.

'But no one special? No one at all? That's not what I've heard.'

'And what have you heard?' The effect of several Old-Fashioneds and a great deal of champagne, together with a certain sense of grievance, however slight and however unjust, against Celia, was making him less watchful, less careful than usual.

'Oh, that there is someone. And she is − what shall I say − not free. Which is why nobody is told who she is. Oh, now come along, they're calling us over. Taxis must be here.'

Later, in the Forty-Three, another two glasses of champagne working up a bright confusion in his head, Sebastian found himself dancing with Elspeth again.

'Now come along,' she said, 'I long to know. Was I right, about your lady?'

'My lady? And which lady would that be?'

'The one you are said to be in love with.'

'I'm afraid she isn't mine,' he said and sighed.

'Ah − so I was right.'

'Right?'

'Yes. I guessed right.'

'You did?' his head suddenly cleared; panic cut through it.

'Yes, I've thought so for ages. We all have.'

'Oh. Oh I see. But how—'

'Oh, you know. One develops an instinct. Now stop looking so frightened, Sebastian. This is the nineteen twenties. Nobody cares what anyone does any more.'

Celia didn't go riding with her mother and Felicity next morning; she went to visit LM. She missed LM dreadfully; more and more as time went by. Watching her now, as she bustled around her small house, making tea, talking to Celia at the same time as she made up a packet of sandwiches for Jay − 'He likes to go and help Billy on Sundays' − she admired her from the bottom of her heart. She was so competent, so calm: and so settled in her new life. Celia found it almost incredible that LM could have moved, with comparative ease, from her intellectually busy existence at Lyttons into the solitude and emotional torpor of village life.

'Are you ever going to come back properly? I need you so much.'

'Of course you don't,' said LM briskly, 'you don't need anyone, Celia.'

'LM, that's a terrible thing to say.'

'Sorry. But I think it's true. You're the most self-sufficient person I've ever known.'

'I'm not you, know,' said Celia sadly, 'and anyway, I could say the same about you.'

'Well – maybe we're both very good actresses. Anyway, I'll be here for a while yet. I can't disturb Jay now, while he's so happy.'

'You're such a good mother, LM. And I'm such a bad one.'

'Nonsense,' said LM, 'as far as I can see, mothers come in all shapes and colours. You just go at it differently from some. Your children seem pretty all right to me. Oliver looks tired,' she added.

'Oliver's always tired,' said Celia slightly bitterly, and then seeing LM's face, 'sorry, LM. Shouldn't have said that.'

'Of course you should. I'm always flattered that you can talk to me, be honest. Even about my brother.'

Celia said nothing; wondering what on earth LM would say if she were really honest with her.

'It must be very – difficult for you, I think,' said LM, 'when you have so much energy. And you like being out and about so much.'

'Yes, it is. In a way. But at least I have Jack at the moment. He squires me about.'

'I'm glad he's doing something useful. What about his book?'

'Oh – you know,' said Celia carefully, 'it's going to look marvellous, anyway. And the trade like it.'

'Good. So life's all a bit of an uphill struggle is it?' Her dark eyes were thoughtful as she looked at Celia.

'You could say so. Yes.'

'I'm sorry I can't help more. You can always send me more stuff down here, you know. Incidentally, would you earmark an extra First Edition of *The Buchanans* for me.'

'Of course. Why?'

'Oh – I have a friend, who collects First Editions.' Something in her voice made Celia look at her sharply

'A friend, LM? Do you mean a gentleman friend?'

'Well – yes. Exactly that. A gentleman friend.'

'LM! How lovely. Who, where –?'

'It's not lovely at all,' said LM, sounding ruffled, 'not in that way—'

'Sorry, it's nothing to do with me. And I don't usually ask such questions, but you so deserve some – well some fun. Has Jay met him?'

'You could say that,' said LM and then met Celia's eyes and laughed. 'All right. I'll tell you about it.'

★

'It's too lovely,' Celia said to Oliver in the library later. 'She obviously really likes this chap. He sounds eminently suitable. Very charming.'

'Celia, you really are ridiculous,' he said slightly stiffly, 'you talk like one of those penny dreadfuls you were so keen on us publishing.'

'I was not—' she began and then stopped. It wasn't worth arguing with him. Trying to defend herself. 'Anyway, he collects First Editions,' she finished rather feebly.

'Really? Well that sounds more interesting. A man after my own heart.'

'Yes, I thought so. I said he should come in, have the run of the archives. LM was rather pleased.'

'That sounds a little dangerous. We know nothing about him, and there are a great many valuable things in there.'

'Oh Oliver!' said Celia, losing her temper suddenly, 'you're impossible. What harm could it do? He's a highly respectable person. He is a solicitor. He's a friend of your sister's. And he's not going to make off with anything valuable. Why do you have to be so negative about everything?'

She went out of the room, slamming the door and found she was in tears. She was standing in the corridor, staring out of the window at the parkland, trying to control herself, when her mother appeared.

'What's the matter with you?'

'It's Oliver. He's so – so impossible. So down on me and everyone, all the time. It's so depressing.'

Lady Beckenham looked at her. Then she said, surprisingly gentle, 'I think you have some decisions to make, Celia. Come on. Time for a stiff gin, if you ask me.'

'I don't think I shall marry Giles,' said Maud over breakfast when they were all back at Cheyne Walk.

'Why is that, Maud?' said Celia, slightly distractedly. She was pale and seemed tired, Felicity thought. A pity, after such a lovely restful weekend.

'Because I think Jay would be a better husband.'

'Maud, you're obsessed with this thing,' said Felicity laughing, 'and don't you think Jay is a little young for you?'

'No. He's nearly seven. I'm only nine. He's much bigger than me, and he's so clever, and so much fun. He can climb trees like a monkey. He taught me to do it. And to fish. And I do want to get it nicely arranged, so I don't have to worry about it any more.'

'Well, you'll have to see what Jay thinks about that,' said Felicity.

'I already have. He thinks it would be a very good idea, as long as I come to live in England.'

'Fine. Although we shall miss you, of course. And why don't you want to marry Giles any more, what's wrong with him suddenly?'

'Nothing's wrong with him,' said Maud, 'he's really very nice indeed. But he's going to marry Barty, that's the thing. He likes her more than anyone in the world. Any girl anyway. He told me so.'

Celia stood up, pushing her chair back rather violently. There was an odd expression on her face.

'Maud, I am getting rather tired of all this silly talk about marriage,' she said, 'in England, little girls don't think of such things and certainly don't discuss them. Now, will you all excuse me, please, I have a great deal to do at the office.'

Felicity watched her, fine eyebrows raised gently.

'Come along, Maud,' she said, 'we have a lot of shopping to do.'

Howard Shaw, of Collins, Collins and Shaw, took the unusual step of communicating with Professor Lothian at breakfast time at his Cambridge home that Monday morning, and asked him if he would like to come into the offices to discuss whatever it was that was causing him concern; Jasper Lothian, aware that Vanessa was listening to the conversation, because their telephone was in the dining-room, said that yes, perhaps that might be a good idea.

'I would be most grateful for your opinion. And as soon as possible.'

Howard Shaw found a space in the diary for that afternoon, and asked if Jasper Lothian could give him some indication as to what the matter was about.

'Oh – it's rather hard to explain over the telephone. My anxiety was – prompted by an article in a publication.'

'Indeed?' Howard Shaw, who was an ambitous young man, and had developed a particular interest – so far purely theoretical – in the laws of libel, felt a brush of excitement.

'Well – be so kind as to bring the publication with you when you come in this afternoon, Professor.'

Jasper Lothian said he would; and then told his wife that there was no need for her to accompany him.

'I am perfectly capable of dealing with this on my own,' he said.

Vanessa Lothian rather doubted this, but decided for the time being to accept his judgement.

Robert had hugely enjoyed the weekend. Apart from anything else, it had been very good to see so much of Oliver; he had dragged him on to the tennis court on Saturday afternoon, and had gone for a long walk with him and the children on Sunday morning after church. They had then sat with a stiff whisky each in the seclusion of the high-walled Dovecot garden.

'This is the life,' he said, stretching out his long legs. 'Lucky chap, having this for – what am I supposed to call it – Saturday to Monday?'

'Lot of nonsense,' said Oliver, laughing. 'But yes, Celia tells me that is the correct term. How are things over there with you? I've hardly had a chance to talk to you properly before now. Is it really as good as it sounds? I'm very impressed.'

'Oh, pretty good now. We've had a couple of rough patches, but – yes, we're very pleased.'

'Good. I wish I could say the same.'

'Really? Trouble in the literary world?'

'With the finances of it. I won't bore you with the details, but – well we're all up against it. Not just Lyttons. The thing about publishing is, it's hard to cut back. You have to keep publishing, can't afford not to; otherwise you lose books to other publishers, lose ground generally. And at the moment, it's very expensive to do that, and at the same time not quite financially rewarding enough.'

'Sounds like any other business to me,' said Robert.

'I suppose so. Yes, of course. And one has to keep planning forward as well. Anyway, I have a big success – please God – coming up this autumn. A saga, rather like the old *Heatherleigh Chronicles*, remember—'

'Oliver! As if I would ever have been allowed to forget. They were the religion I was brought up with. So what's this one about?'

'Oh – it's rather marvellous. The first volume anyway. A family again, each member with a story of his or her own to tell. The background pulling them all together. It's beautifully written. I'm very excited about. I'm keeping it under wraps for as long as possible; I've actually delayed publication of our catalogue, to keep the other fellows guessing. I'm gambling on it considerably as a matter of fact, put Lyttons' shirt on it, so to speak. I'm printing a very large number of copies.'

'That's very unlike you. Cautious fellow that you are.'

'I know. But I don't think I can go wrong.' He smiled and reached out to touch the table with crossed fingers. 'I may be eating my words in October.'

'And how is young Jack working out? He seems very keen.'

'Oh, he is indeed. Working very hard.'

'I wouldn't have thought it was quite his bag.'

'This area suits him,' said Oliver firmly, 'But anyway, enough of all that. I must come over to New York again soon. They seem to be doing very well over there, but it doesn't do to leave them too much to their own devices. Young Bailey is very ambitious.'

'Yes, indeed. You haven't heard anything from Laurence, I suppose?' Robert's voice was casual.

'Nothing, no. Why?'

'Oh – no real reason. He's a difficult young man, that's all, he might have been trying to muscle in on things.'

'Let him try,' said Oliver. 'No literary instincts of any kind, it seemed to me.'

'That wouldn't necessarily stop him,' said Robert, 'but, with luck, there's not a great deal he can do. Kyle is certainly very excited about Lyttons. He's talked of nothing else all weekend.'

'He's a nice young man. He has a real feeling for publishing. I'd take him on gladly myself, if he was in London. I don't think we have any vacancies in the New York office, it's too small.'

'I don't think he'd take it if you did,' said Robert, 'he's very proud.'

'But miserable at Brewer Lytton?'

'Yes. Very. And not much good either. I'd go so far as to say he was something of an embarrassment. Or will certainly become one. He really would love to move into publishing, but—'

'Well – there are other people he could talk to in New York. Contacts of mine. I could make a few enquiries. Tactfully. God knows, we all need a helping hand. It's a hard world. I'll see what I can do.'

'We would all be extremely grateful,' said Robert. 'Especially Felicity. You like her, don't you? I'm glad, I'm terribly fond of her myself.'

'Yes, she's very – charming,' said Oliver. He appeared slightly flustered. 'We had better go into luncheon now, Lady B gets awfully cross if we keep the servants waiting.'

Robert was amused by the fluster; Oliver obviously admired Felicity. He had been talking to her a lot over the weekend. But he had always been shy with women. It had astonished Robert at the time that he had been so successful with the ravishing Lady Celia. And indeed that the marriage had been so long-lived and faithful.

'Now then,' said Howard Shaw, 'perhaps you would like to tell me what is troubling you, Professor.'

Jasper Lothian, who was half wishing he had left sleeping dogs snoring by the fire, said it was a little hard to explain.

'Take your time. In your own words. Cigarette?'

'Thank you.'

He took one, fitted it into the long ebony cigarette holder he always used, and sat back in his chair.

'As I say, it's rather – complicated. But I was reading this article in the *Spectator*, about a book, or rather, a series of books that are to be published.'

'Ye-es? Are the books fictional or otherwise?'

'Fictional.'

'Go on.'

'They concern a family. Living in Oxford and in London before during and after the war.'

'Yes.'

'The – the head of the family is the master of an Oxford college.'

'I see.'

'He has a wife – and two children. A son and a daughter.'

'As do you?'

'Yes. Yes indeed. In the book the daughter has a fiancé who is killed in the war.'

'And your daughter—' Howard Shaw's voice trailed off tactfully.

'She does – or rather did – indeed have a fiancé. He was not killed in the war. But he was injured, rather seriously, and the engagement was broken off. It was difficult for her, she was dreadfully distressed. But there seemed little future in the relationship—'

'Professor Lothian, this need not concern us now. Or need it?'

'I think not.'

'And the son?'

'No similarities. The boy in the book was a conscientious objector, my son was decorated.'

'I see.'

'But—'

'The wife?' said Howard Shaw carefully.

'The wife is a – a rich woman. In her own right. She has a house in London, where she spends a considerable amount of time.'

'And –?'

'My wife does have independent means. Although she has no house in London, she does spend some considerable time there.'

'I see. Well – forgive me Professor, but so far I see nothing remotely libellous about this. Nothing that could worry you.'

'Ah. Well, but you see – look perhaps I should give you the article to read.'

'That might be helpful. Thank you.'

Howard Shaw read the article carefully, twice. Then he looked at Jasper Lothian.

'You refer, I imagine, to the question of the master's affair?'

426

'Yes. Yes indeed.'

'I imagine, of course, and you must forgive me, that there has been no such impropriety.'

'Absolutely not.'

'Then—'

'But I feel the similarities are enough to attract attention. For those who know us, that is. And the authorities in the university. And could therefore do me great harm. My wife is very much of the same view. Oxford – Cambridge – the link is clear. Master of a college, wealthy wife, two children, the daughter's future ruined by the war—' he stopped, looked at Howard Shaw '—and then he is not unlike me in personality, I feel: a trifle eccentric in his dress, a high-profile figure about the university – but perhaps you think there is no cause for concern.'

There was a long silence; then Howard Shaw said, 'Professor, I have to tell you that I agree with you. This could possibly be actionable. I think we should ask to see the manuscript.'

CHAPTER 23

'I have to talk to you,' said Sebastian. His voice, usually so level and easy, was tense, even on the phone. Celia's heart lurched.

'What about?'

'I – don't want to say on the telephone. Could we meet?'

'I could have a quick luncheon. Very quick. Then I have to go. I've got to see Lady Annabel about Queen Anne.'

'Right. Let's see – somewhere safe. Lyons Corner House? Bottom of the Strand?'

'Sebastian! How romantic.'

'Elspeth knows,' he said.

'Knows?'

'Yes, about us. She knows. She told me so.'

'She what?' Celia felt physically dizzy; the bustling restaurant, with its hurtling conversation, its scurrying waitresses, blurred before her eyes. 'Sebastian, she couldn't have.'

'She did. She said she'd guessed. That lots of people had.'

'Oh my God.' She sat very still, taking deep breaths. This was awful; this was what she had so feared, the thing that had seemed so inevitable. Yet against all logic, they seemed to have escaped. But – how could they? What kind of vanity had allowed her to think that their adulterous liaison would be allowed to escape attention? Attention and discovery?

'Did she say any more?'

'Not much. I shut her up. I was rather drunk.'

'Oh Sebastian! What were you doing with Elspeth anyway? How did it come up?'

'Well – we were at the Forty-Three. On Saturday night.'

'You were at the Forty-Three? With Elspeth Granchester?' Her expression was sharp, irritated; he grinned at her and tried to take her hand. She shook his off.

'So you don't like that?'

'Not very much, no.'

'You were at a wonderful country house party. With your husband.'

'And a lot of dreadful other people. And I could hardly help being there.'

'Celia – that's so unfair.'

'Unfair?'

'Yes. Am I not allowed to accept any social invitations? Am I to remain in solitary confinement in my own house until you graciously condescend to visit me?'

She stared at him, frowning; then, 'Oh this is ridiculous,' she said, 'we have more important things to talk about. Does – does Oliver have any idea? Did she say?'

'Celia, I've told you. She said very little. I didn't want to ask her anything. I don't know any more than that she's guessed. That lots of people have. Those were her very words.'

'Oh God,' said Celia wearily, 'I'll have to talk to her.'

Robert wrote to Oliver: to say that Kyle had been for what was initially a chat, but by some extraordinary piece of serendipity turned out to be an interview: with one of his contacts, a small publishing set up, called Guthries; John Guthrie had interviewed him. Someone had decided to leave that very day, and John Guthrie had jokingly said he didn't suppose Kyle would want his job?

Kyle had said that he most certainly would, and John Guthrie had shaken his head and said he most certainly wouldn't.

'This is a glorified office boy's job,' he said, 'nothing but running errands, and delivering things.'

Kyle had said he would love to do run errands and deliver things; it took about twenty minutes to persuade John Guthrie he meant it. Even then he told him to go away and think about it.

'I'd only be a glorified office boy, apparently,' he had told his father and Robert, smiling at them rather nervously, 'in the promotions department. But it's the best place to learn, they said.'

'It sounds wonderful,' said Robert, 'doesn't it, John?'

'If that's what you want,' said John Brewer, 'it does indeed sound wonderful.'

'And – you would – understand? If I took it?'

John looked at Robert; Robert's eyes met his in absolute complicity.

'We would be very sad to see you go, obviously,' he said, 'but it is so clearly where your heart lies, that it would be wrong to try and keep you.'

The relief on Kyle's face, he wrote to Oliver, was both touching and almost funny.

★

429

'Elspeth? Elspeth, this is Celia. Could I – that is could we – talk?'

'Darling, of course. What about? Our dresses for Ascot? I have been wondering about my hat for Ladies' Day, I'd adore to have your opinion.'

'No, Elspeth. Something a little bit more serious than that.'

'What could be more serious than hats? Sorry, Celia, I can tell you're not in the mood for jokes. Yes, of course. Do you want to come and have tea? Tomorrow perhaps. Or is that too soon for your madly busy life?'

'No. No, that would be very nice. Thank you. About three thirty?'

'Lily, my darling—'

'Yes?'

'I wondered if you might fancy – well, coming back to my place.'

'Your place, Jack? I didn't know you had one.'

'Don't be silly, darling. You know. My rooms at Cheyne Walk.'

'You want me to come to where you're living now?'

'Yes. Yes, I do, awfully.'

Lily stared at him.

'I've never been so insulted in my life,' she said finally.

'What? But darling, why?'

'You expect me to come to your brother's house, where I presume he is at this very moment, asleep. Probably with Celia?'

'Yes, darling, that was the idea.'

'Presumably you're not thinking of just having a cup of tea there?'

'Well – no. Not just a cup of tea.'

'Jack, I think you must be quite mad,' she said.

'I don't understand. You said no more seedy hotels, and of course I respect that. That's why—'

'So instead you're going to smuggle me up the stairs in the middle of the night. Hoping no one will hear us. Like some – some tart. Have a bit of how's-your-father. And then smuggle me out again. Or are you planning to offer me breakfast? With the Lyttons, and all the children.'

'Well—'

'Oh, no, Jack. You've got me quite wrong. I'm not that sort of girl at all. If you want us to go on being together, you're going to have to do a bit better than that. Get a place of your own for a start. And stop treating me like some – some cheap bit of fluff. I'm a career girl. I have more self-respect than that. Now I'm going to go home. Back to my digs. And the answer's no, before you've even thought it. Very strict, my landlady is. Now get me a taxi please. I've got a big rehearsal tomorrow,

430

first one for the new show. I don't want to be worn out before I even get there.'

Jack could see there was no point in arguing with her. When Lily was cross, she was cross. He couldn't see quite why she was so cross, but he'd clearly done something very wrong. He found a taxi for her, and after she'd told him not to get into it, that she wanted to get straight home to a nice peaceful bed, he decided to go home himself. There didn't seem much charm in staying on his own at the Grafton Galleries now. Well not on his own but without Lily. He went inside, back to his table, and said goodnight to everyone.

'Where's Lily?' said Crystal.

'Gone home. I'm in the doghouse. Not sure why.'

'She might have told me, we could have shared the cab.'

'I'll take you home,' said Jack, 'I've got my car.'

'You sweetheart. Would you really? Can you let me have one more dance, I promised Guy Worsley I'd show him the Black Bottom.'

'I could have done that,' said Jack.

'OK. We'll all three of us do it.'

Guy Worsley was not a dancer; he conceded the floor after a very short time to Crystal and Jack. Afterwards, he called them over.

'Champagne?' He was very drunk.

'Yes please,' said Jack.

'How are you, old chap?'

'Oh – all right. Bit of a bust up with Lily.'

'That's a shame. What about?'

'Don't quite understand really. You know what they're like.'

'I do,' said Guy. 'No idea at all what you did?'

'Well – bit of an idea. Tell me what you think.'

He told him; Guy shook his head.

'You can't do that, old man. You're supposed to show that you respect them. I once asked a girl from the town back to my room at Oxford. There was hell to pay. Said I was putting her virtue at risk. What virtue? I asked myself.'

'I thought you could get sent down for having a girl in your room,' said Jack.

'You could, in theory. It was usually the girls who got sent down. No, you don't want to believe all that. Hotbeds of sex, universities are. Not just the undergrads, either.'

'Really? I thought all those academics thought of nothing but ancient Greek or whatever.'

'Don't you believe it. Well, read my book.'

'I thought it was pure fiction,' said Jack, laughing.

'Impure fiction more like it. No, it's based on fact. Very loosely, of course.'

'Really?'

'Really. That's why it's so frightfully good.' He laughed. 'Crystal, lovely angel, come and sit on my knee. How very beautiful you are. Anyway, if I were you, young Lytton, I'd get myself a little place of my own. To take Miss Lily to.'

'I know,' said Jack. 'I do know I've got to. It's just that it's so difficult to find anywhere decent. And it's so – easy living in Cheyne Walk. And cheap. Well, free.'

'Better not let your brother hear you saying that. He might feel he was being taken advantage of. Is the lovely Lady Celia here tonight?'

'No,' said Jack, 'no, she was going to come with us, but she changed her mind at the last minute. Seemed a bit upset. Something had gone wrong with a book, apparently. Hope it wasn't mine.'

'Or mine,' said Guy Worsley.

'Oh my goodness,' said Janet Gould. 'Oh dear.'

She was reading through the morning's post, sorting it into its usual neat piles: one for herself to deal with, one for Oliver's personal attention, and one for discussion between them. The letter she was holding fell very much into the discussion group. Urgent discussion. She picked it up and walked into his office; miserable, already, at having to add to the burdens which seemed to be piling on to his frail back. He always looked so tired these days, tired and worried. Publishing had been so straightforward, so – well, so gentlemanly once. Before the war. Now it seemed to be getting more and more unpleasant every day. Everyone demanding more and more money, the print unions getting so powerful . . .

'I'm sorry to disturb you, Mr Lytton. There's a letter here which seems rather – worrying.'

'Oh dear. Not another demand from the printers?'

'No. Worse than that. Well it might be.'

She handed it to him, watched him read it, watched his face first pale, then flush.

'This is absurd,' he said, 'absolutely absurd. Outrageous even. Mrs Gould, get me our solicitors on the phone, would you? As soon as you can.'

'Celia, darling! Lovely to see you. Come and sit down. Tea? I've had the most hideous morning, had to go to the dentist, horrible drilling, have you ever had it? And then I went to my corsetiere and I've put on half an inch everywhere. Have to do something about myself. How do you manage it, Celia? You're so blissfully thin. Sometimes I quite long for the old days when one could nip the middle bit in and let the bosom and the hips spoosh out. Oh well. Sugar? No, of course not. Cake?'

'No thank you,' said Celia,

'What are you going to wear to Ladies' Day? I know that's not what you want to talk about, but it's still bothering me.'

'I really don't know,' said Celia. 'Elspeth, can we – can I just discuss things with you. About – well you must know what about.'

'Darling I don't, no. I had the most marvellous time with Sebastian on Saturday night, by the way.'

'So I hear.'

'You're not jealous are you? I do hope not, we didn't—'

'Of course I'm not jealous,' said Celia impatiently, 'but I have to ask you Elspeth. As a friend. As a trusted friend.'

'Ask me what?'

'How did you – that is, when did you – find out?'

'Find out? Find out what?'

'Oh Elspeth don't be tiresome. You know perfectly well. About Sebastian and me.'

'About – Sebastian – and – and you –?' Elspeth was speaking very slowly; her face was flushed and her eyes brilliant. 'Celia, what are you talking about?'

The room was very quiet, very still; Celia stared at her, and felt icy cold and rather sick. Then she said, 'You didn't know, actually, did you? You didn't know at all.'

And, 'No,' Elspeth said, and a small nervous smile started to dance round her mouth, 'but – but I do now, darling, don't I?'

'Oliver, don't look like that. Whatever is it, what's happened?'

Guilt, fear, gripped her; she had not expected a confrontation so soon. And wondered why she was still lying, still pretending.

'Look at this,' he said, 'just look at it.'

She took the letter, seeing the heading on the paper: Solicitors . . . Cambridge . . . felt weak with relief. Selfishly, wickedly relieved. At what was, after all, only a reprieve. How long could she stand this, for God's sake. How long? She read the letter, hoping he wouldn't notice her shaking hand. It seemed first unintelligible to her in her confusion, then baffling.

'But Oliver, why should this Lothian man want to see it?'

'I imagine – I imagine because he feels there is something in it that is libellous.'

'But that's absurd. It's fiction.'

'Fiction can still be found to be libellous. If it can be shown that the story too closely mirrors life, and a real person's reputation could be damaged by it. We seem to start with quite a strong coincidence: the books are about the master of an Oxford college, this fellow Lothian is the master of a Cambridge one. God knows how many more there might be.'

'But—' she stopped, desperate to reassure him, 'don't they say there are only three plots anyway, Oliver? It's one of the great truisms, *Cinderella, Macbeth* and—'

'It's the setting for the plots that can do for you,' he said with a sigh, 'and the circumstances of the leading characters.'

'Have you talked to Guy Worsley?'

'I've tried to. He's not at home. I've left a message, naturally.'

'What – what do you think it might be? This coincidence.'

'God knows. The affair of the master's, I can only suppose. There's nothing else.'

'But surely—'

'Yes?'

'I can't believe Guy would have been that stupid. If it actually happened. To have put it in a book.'

'No, I do keep telling myself that. He can confirm it of course. God I wish he'd telephone.'

'What does Peter Briscoe say?' she asked finally.

'He says we don't have to send them the manuscript at this stage, but that it would probably be wise to. So that they can see for themselves that there is nothing to worry about.'

'Well – are you going to?'

'I think so.'

'And – what would happen if – if this man Jasper Lothian thought there was something to worry about?'

Oliver turned a face so raw with misery and fear to her that she felt quite sick.

'They could take out an injunction, apparently. To stop publication. Celia, at this point it would mean disaster for us. For Lyttons. I've already ordered enough paper for over two thousand copies, I don't have to tell you that, I know. Oh God. I had such hopes for this book. Such high, proud hopes.'

He looked down at his hands; she could feel, see his misery. She went round behind him, put her arms round him.

'Oliver don't. Don't be so distressed. Please! It may not come to that. It almost certainly won't come to that.'

'I fear it might,' he said, pulled out his handkerchief and blew his nose. 'And I know Briscoe thinks it might too.'

'Is it not possible to – to change that strand in the novel?'

'It's quite impossible,' he said and sighed. 'It's central to the whole story. Well you've read it, you must see that. The wife's reaction, her leaving him, the daughter's horror that her father could behave in such a way, the repercussions at the college – no, it would mean reworking the entire book.'

'Yes.' Her voice was sober. 'Yes, I do see it. So – what are you going to do?'

'I think I'm going to send him the manuscript. I think the only way is to be open, and hope to gain his confidence. And to pray that there are no other similarities. Such as a son who is a conscientious objector.'

'You bloody idiot,' said Celia, 'you absolute complete fool.'

'What? What are you talking about?'

'Elspeth not knowing, that's what I'm talking about.'

'Celia, of course she knew. She told me so.'

'Well obviously she didn't. She was just hinting. Fishing, even. She had no idea. That it was me.'

'Oh my God,' said Sebastian, 'oh my dear God.'

'I don't think He's going to help much,' said Celia.

'I'm so sorry,' said Guy Worsley, 'I'm so terribly, terribly sorry.'

'So you – did base this character on a real person?'

'Well – yes. Yes, I did. I thought it didn't matter, if it was fiction. And it was so long ago, in the early days of the war, I never dreamed it could matter seven years later . . . oh God.'

'You weren't in this man's college yourself?'

'Heavens no. I went to Oxford.'

'So – how did you hear about it?'

'My cousin was at Cambridge. At the same time. He was rather in awe of this Lothian chap. Apparently he was a terrific character, used to stride about the college looking very dramatic, wore black cloaks and silk dressing-gowns.'

'As he does in the book,' said Oliver. 'Go on.'

'And yes, he did have a rich wife. She paid for the dressing-gowns. I suppose.'

'And did she have a house in London?'

'Oh I don't think so,' said Guy, and then looking more shamefaced still, 'well I don't know, actually. But apparently she was there a lot. She was rather grand, didn't like academic life. Oh God, sir, I'm so, so sorry. After all you've done for me.'

He appeared very upset; his face was pale, his large eyes dark and shadowed. He looked as if he hadn't slept.

'I didn't sleep last night,' he said, 'I lay awake, all night, just trying to remember exactly what I had heard.'

'Did he actually have an affair?'

'No,' said Guy, 'No I'm pretty sure he didn't. There was just a lot of talk about some girl, apparently, one of the undergraduates. Which was hushed up of course.'

'Yes indeed,' said Oliver wearily.

'I've been trying to get hold of my cousin, but he's away. Abroad.'

'Ah.'

'But there are huge differences as well,' he said, slightly desperately, 'I mean, in the book, as you know, the son is a conchie, while young Master Lothian went off to the war. My cousin said he remembered him going, remembered Lothian being dreadfully upset, how they all felt sorry for him.'

'Was your cousin in Lothian's college?' said Peter Briscoe. He had come in for the meeting with Guy.

'No, no, he was at Jesus.'

'Well that's something. Did he know the Lothians well?'

'No, I think he just met him, occasionally. And he knew the daughter. She was very nice, rather plain. He said.'

'She wasn't musical, I supppose?'

'I − don't think so. I don't know. Oh, God.'

Oliver sighed. 'And the wife, did he meet her?'

'I don't know, sir. But I do know there was this constant absence. Not the sort of way the wife of a master should behave. I suppose that was the thing which really intrigued me. The scope for dramatic development through that. My cousin said it was always assumed she had a lover in London. Of course, in the book, she doesn't.'

'No indeed,' said Oliver, 'on the other hand, you have made her a woman of considerable means. As is Mrs Lothian.'

'I know, I know. But—'

Peter Briscoe sighed. 'This seems to be far from straightforward. What about the other masters, was there talk about them?'

'Oh there's always talk. Scandals about students and so on. Obviously. It's part of academic life.'

'Mmm,' said Briscoe, 'well, we can only send them the manuscript and hope for the best.'

'But what can they do? Take out an injunction to stop us publishing?'

'If they feel sufficiently sure of their ground. Feel the similiarities are sufficient for people to notice, to talk about them. The grounds for bringing a libel action, as you should know, young man, are for a character to be brought into hatred, ridicule or contempt by something which is published and thought to be harmful to his reputation. It seems to me there is certainly danger of at least one of those being applicable.'

Guy stared at him. 'I just can't believe this. The book's fiction, it's not biography. And other writers do it, surely. Draw from real life, I mean. James Joyce did it, for God's sake.'

'Yes he did,' said Oliver drily, 'and *Dubliners* was withdrawn three times.'

'Believe me, there are precedents. Rare, but—'

'But surely they couldn't do it off their own bat?' said Celia, 'just get an injunction?'

'Of course not. It would have to be brought before a judge. Only he would have the power to grant it.'

'It just seems preposterous,' said Guy, pushing his hands through his already wild hair, 'that any judge would grant an injunction on this basis. On the book being about the master of an Oxford college. When this chap is at Cambridge and—'

'And is an exhibitionist and has a rich wife and a son and a daughter.'

'Well – yes. But – oh it's absurd. He must be hugely paranoid. To think—'

Peter Briscoe looked at him. 'To think what? That a character in a book has been based on him? I do assure you, large damages have been paid out for considerably less.'

Guy Worsley stared at him for a moment.

Then, 'Oh God,' he said, 'what a hideous mess.'

'Fairly hideous,' said Peter Briscoe.

'Oh God,' said Oliver. He looked very tired.

'What is it?'

'More bad news. Paul Davis is demanding a very large copyright fee for Sebastian's new book.'

'How large?'

'Almost larger than we can afford.'

'Oh Oliver, that's absurd. Lyttons can't be so short of money that they can't find a few hundred pounds.'

'Almost a thousand, anyway.'

'What?'

'Yes. He cites *Meridian*'s great success and the first fee. Which was of course always agreed to be exceptional. And then, you know, other agents hear of these large sums and want them too. It was a dangerous precedent, I told you so at the time.'

Celia was silent; this was a dialogue she had been forced to rehearse a great many times. She was extremely sick of it; had things been different she would have defended herself. Under the circumstances she felt it impossible.

'Things are generally very difficult at the moment. As you know. Even without this Buchanan nonsense. Not only have printing charges and paper costs gone up again, the packers are now asking for more money. I don't think we can give it to them.'

'Could we get a loan?' said Celia.

'No, not advisable. Interest rates are very high.'

'And *Elizabeth* hasn't done very well, has she?' said Celia soberly.

She had published a lavish biography of Queen Elizabeth I that spring. It had cost a great deal of money to print and had hardly sold five hundred of its two thousand copies. It had been one of her few errors of judgement; and she knew why. Her mind had not been properly engaged; other things, were occupying it.

'No, not very. The thing about biographies is that one starts from scratch every time. They sell only on the strength of their subject, whereas fiction sells on the strength of past work. Well, you don't need me to tell you that. But I think Elizabeth just doesn't have the magic of Victoria, or even Anne.' He sighed, smiled at her wearily. 'Still, perhaps she will save us. Anne I mean. But we all make mistakes. And it's very rare for you to do that, I know. Very rare indeed.'

He was wrong there, she thought wearily; her life seemed to be composed entirely of mistakes at the moment.

'The Mutiny book is expensive as well,' he said suddenly.

'Is it?' she said carefully.

'Yes, very. Of course I'm confident it will recoup its costs, but all those coloured illustrations . . .'

'There's something else,' she said cautiously.

'Yes?'

'I think we're going to have to do some fairly heavy re-setting.'

'Why? Why for God's sake?'

'Well, I saw the galleys yesterday. Edgar brought them in to me.'

'And—'

'It just doesn't read very well, Oliver. It's leaden, dull. The only good bits are my great-grandfather's diary. I hate to say that, but it's true. It needs re-writing in parts.'

'In the name of God, why didn't someone show it to me or you before it reached this stage?'

'I'm not sure.' She was; she was fairly certain that Edgar Green, resentful about the book, about Jack's role in it, had deliberately let it go through. He had been evasive when she asked to see the final copy, told her it was too late, that it had already gone to the typesetters. But if that was indeed the case it was unforgivable and a very serious charge to bring.

'Oh, God,' said Oliver, 'dear God in heaven. That is all I need.'

She went to see Sebastian at his house, on her way home; careless of the risks and the danger, furious with him.

He looked at her on the doorstep, smiled.

'My darling, what a lovely suprise.'

'How could you?' she said, walking past him into the drawing-room, 'how could you do that to Lyttons? You and your vile agent.'

'Do what?'

'Sebastian, don't pretend to me. You know perfectly well. Demand another huge copyright fee for *Meridian Times Two*. When you know, you know perfectly well times are so hard. And Oliver has this worry about *The Buchanans*.'

'Who told you that?'

'Oliver. Of course. Paul Davis had written to him today. I just cannot believe it of you, Sebastian, cannot believe you would do that to us, after all Lyttons has done for you. Clearly the publicity and acclaim has finally gone to your head.'

'Celia,' he said, and his eyes were very hard, 'I think perhaps you should check your facts before launching into an attack of this kind. Do you really think I would have instructed Paul Davis to demand a large fee from you? Do you? Because if you do, then we have very little to say to one another from now on. I find it extraordinarily painful that you should lay that charge at me. In fact, I think I would like you to leave my house at once.'

She was silent; panic rising in her. At yet another mistake, yet another misjudgement.

'For what it might be worth to you,' he said and his face was set, his lips white-rimmed with rage, 'I told Paul Davis to tell Oliver I wanted no copyright fee at all for *Meridian Times Two* actually. Given that I do indeed know that times are hard. And that Lyttons need the book. I will of course try to establish why he chose to ignore my instructions; but I think you might have given me the benefit of the doubt, until such time as you were able to establish the facts. In England a man is innocent until he is proved guilty; perhaps, in your usual sublime conviction of your own rightness, you have not troubled to consider that. Good evening to you. I'm sure you can see yourself out.'

He got up, walked out of the room and up the stairs; Celia sat in the drawing-room for some time. Then moving very slowly and heavily, as if she was a old woman, she followed him.

'I think,' she said, 'I have decided to leave Oliver.'

'To live with this man?' Lady Beckenham's face was absolutely expressionless: like her voice. She had come up to London for a few days, to attend a couple of debutante balls and to go to Henley.

'Yes. I can't stand it any longer, Mama. I can't stand the deceit, the endless betrayal. I want a divorce. I'm cheating, all the time, living a lie. It feels so wrong. It's not fair on anyone, least of all Oliver—'

'And I suppose it would be perfectly fair on Oliver to walk out on him. Not to mention the children. Living a lie, as you call it, is the price you pay for the pleasure, Celia. You don't get anything for nothing in this life, as I've told you ever since you could understand anything at all.'

'But it was different for your generation.'

'Oh really? And why is that? Do tell me.'

Her dark eyes, so like Celia's own, were almost amused.

'Well – there isn't the same need for keeping up appearances. For being respectable, doing the right thing. People live more openly now, nobody minds what anyone does any more—'

'I have heard you talk some nonsense in my time, Celia, most notably on the subject of those absurd politics of yours, but that takes the biscuit. I think you would find a great many people would mind what you did, if you actually did it. Walked out on your husband, abandoned your children. Or were you intending to take the children with you?'

'In time yes, obviously. But in the first instance – well I haven't quite decided what to do.'

'It may not be up to you to decide. If you do walk out. A judge might very well say they should stay with their father. Indeed I hope that he would.'

'Mama, that is so unfair.'

'I don't think it is. Why should you remove Oliver's children from him, as well as yourself? What wrong has he done them? Divorce is still an ugly word, Celia, and describes an ugly condition. It is not without reason that divorced people are not received by the royal family—'

'Oh, really—'

'I would suggest, Celia, that you move that stubborn mind of yours forward a few years – only a very few now – when you will want to bring Venetia and Adele out. You would not be able to present them at court yourself. Many of my generation would cold-shoulder you. You would not be invited into the royal enclosure at Ascot. To any garden parties or court balls.'

440

Celia looked at her; then she said, 'If you think I would stay with Oliver, when I no longer love him, simply because I would be banned from the royal garden parties, then you don't know me very well.'

'I know you very well indeed, Celia. I know what matters to you and what doesn't. You enjoy your place in society very much; you enjoy everything it entails. I haven't noticed you actually refusing invitations to court balls, or dropping your title. There is, after all, nothing to prevent you doing that if you really want to. Anyway, let's set that aside. Do you really think this honesty and openness, of which you speak so highly, is going to make up to Oliver for being abandoned, made to look a fool, do you think your children are going to feel happy and secure in the knowledge that you're leading a more honest life, even though you're not living at home with them any more? Or they are being dragged away from everything that is familiar to them, to live with some man they hardly know.'

'They are very – fond of Sebastian,' said Celia.

'Oh Celia, really! The next thing you'll be telling me is that they'll accept him as your lover, say how marvellous for you both and they can't wait to come and visit you. They won't. They'll be angry and bewildered and hostile and with good reason. I'm ashamed of you, Celia, and I want you to be in no doubt about it.'

'I thought,' said Celia, her voice shaking with anger, 'I thought you supported me in this. That's why I'm talking to you about it.'

'Of course you didn't. That's a very dishonest piece of thinking. I supported you in your love affair; I could see life with Oliver was pretty miserable and unfulfilling at one time, probably still is very difficult. Most marriages are from time to time. I wouldn't begin to argue with that. But I told you from the very beginning that the basis for such a thing, if it was to work, was absolute and scrupulous loyalty to what really matters in life: the status quo. For God's sake, Celia, you've got a happy family, you've got money, you've got a very nice house, which, incidentally, your father bought so that you could live with another man you were madly in love with, you've got a career, what are you going to do about that incidentally, carry on working at Lyttons? A little difficult I would have thought. And you've got a good, if rather dull husband who worships the ground you walk on, and another man to go to bed with. What more do you want?'

Celia was silent; then she said very quietly, 'I want to be happy again. I want to live with the man I love.'

'Dear God in heaven. And how long do you think that's going to last? Is this man you love so much never going to bore you at the dinner table? Is he never going to snore, or have bad breath? Or be bad-tempered or lazy, or take less than a one hundred per cent interest in you twenty-four hours a day? Are you going to continue to melt with desire at his touch and want to have intercourse with him at every possible opportunity for the rest of your life? I really do beg leave to doubt it, Celia.'

Celia sat staring at her mother for a moment; then she stood up and said, 'I'm going to leave now. I should never have embarked on this discussion. I thought I might get some help and guidance from you.'

'You've had the help and guidance, Celia. Just think about what I've said before you take any action. That's the only other piece of guidance I intend to offer.'

'Celia, darling—'

'Yes, what is it? I'm just leaving, Jack, I really can't—'

'No, no, I don't want to detain you. I just wondered if you wanted to come to the Berkeley tonight? Lots of us are going, it would be marvellous if—'

'No, Jack, I can't, I'm sorry, I have to work tonight. I've got to visit Lady Annabel about Queen Anne and then—'

'Oh. Well if you change your mind. We'll be there till awfully late.'

'I'm afraid I won't. Change my mind, I mean. But thank you for thinking of your old sister-in-law.'

'Not old at all, darling. Still only thirty-four – just. We're just about the same age, remember.'

'I do find that hard to remember actually,' said Celia with a sigh, 'but anyway, no, I can't. Sorry.'

'It's us who'll be sorry,' said Jack.

He went home to change. Brunson met him in the hall, asked him if he would like a cocktail and whether he would be in for dinner.

'No, not tonight, Brunson.'

'Very well, sir. I will inform Cook.'

Jack went upstairs and lay in his bath, sipping his cocktail. He would miss all this. But he really did have to make the break. He had sent Lily an enormous bouquet of red roses, and gone to see her and told her he thought she was right and that he was already looking at houses and flats.

'Some very jolly places in Sloane Street.'

'About time too,' Lily said; she hadn't been over-enthusiastic, but she had agreed to go away for the weekend with him in between shows, which she'd always refused to do before, so obviously he had done the right thing. Guy had been right. Funny creatures, women. Very complicated.

Poor old Guy; he was in a hell of a state. Worrying about the book. He had been into Lyttons twice more for meetings with the solicitors;

the second time Jack had met him in the lavatory and he'd seemed near tears.

'I never meant to cause all this trouble,' he said, 'I never thought anyone would react like this.'

The manuscript had been sent off to the Lothians now; Jack had read the book and couldn't for the life of him see what they were making such a fuss about. There was a bit about the master of the college, Anthony Buchanan, having an affair with some undergraduate, but if he hadn't really, as Guy continued to swear, what did it matter? Unless he had, and Guy hadn't known about it and even then, it was hardly Guy's fault. And in which case also, it was pretty stupid of the Lothian chap to draw attention to himself.

He came out of his bathroom, whistling and bumped into Barty. She smiled at him and blushed and disappeared into her own room. Sweet kid, and getting so pretty now; she was going to be a stunner. He'd noticed a couple of Giles's friends taking a great interest in her at the Fourth of June this year. When she came out – Jack wondered suddenly if she would come out. If Celia would have her presented. It was a bit complicated, all that. Might be difficult.

'I had to see you,' said Celia, 'I just had to. I feel so – so confused.'

'My darling, there's nothing to be confused about,' said Sebastian, kissing her. 'I love you and you love me. We want to be together. We're going to be together. What could be simpler?'

'I know. I know. But—'

'No buts. We've been butting long enough. We've made our decision.'

'I know. I know.' She was silent, thinking about the making of the decision; the night, after their row, when she had gone up to his room, and found him weeping.

Weeping that she could think so badly of him, weeping at what he saw was the loss of her. She thought about the extraordinary passion which they had found in one another then, the raw tenderness of his response to her, her remorse, her humbling, both so strange to her, so difficult. She had stood there, looking down at him, saying, 'I'm sorry, Sebastian, I'm so sorry,' the words coming out slowly and awkwardly and then there had been his own long silence as he waited, waited to see how he felt, for he had truly been hurt almost beyond endurance, not by her words, but that she could speak them, think the things which had prompted them. And then slowly, very deliberately, she had begun to undress, and had finally stood before him naked, utterly submissive, prepared for rejection. And even as he pulled her to him, reluctant still, in spite of wanting her, angry still, in spite of her apology, he knew he loved her more than anything, that she was dearer to him than he could have believed possible and that he could not contemplate life without her any more.

When it was over, when they had recovered one another, when they lay, shaking, weak, a long difficult climax finally reached, when he was smiling at her through his own tears, wiping away hers, he said, 'Please, Celia. Please come to me. Fully. Join my life. You know it's right, you know you have to,' and she had stared at him, looking shocked and confused rather than joyful and delighted as he might have expected, but finally, through the silence, she had said, 'Yes, Sebastian, I think probably I do.'

'You're not changing your mind are you?' he said now.

She looked at him, looked down at her lap, and said, 'I – don't think so.'

'Celia, please. We've been through this, we've decided, you've decided. We've discussed it all. You said you felt happy about it, that it was the only decision—'

'I know, I know.' She stared at him, trying to smile, to be calm.

Panic engulfed her hourly: at what she had said she would do, at the reasons for saying it; at her own doubts that it was right. Her mother's words had affected her more than she would have believed; in the midst of her turmoil they formed a cool, considered centre. And yet – she knew her mother was wrong. She had never been more sure than the night before; she had come home late, from a genuine meeting with Lady Annabel, walked into the house and found Oliver, apparently collapsed at his desk. In fact he had simply been asleep. And distressed as she was, the dreadful, evil relief had come to her, that he had had a heart attack and died, that she would be free. Lying next to him later, listening to his steady breathing, she had forced herself to confront that relief again, the depths of selfishness and wickedness which she had reached, and wondered how it could possibly be considered right to live with a man she wished were dead.

She lit a cigarette, drew on it hard. 'Sebastian—'

'Celia, no. I can't let you go through all this again. You have said you would leave Oliver and you will leave Oliver. It's right – for all of us. Look at you, you're ill with anxiety over it.'

It was true; she really wasn't well. She had a severe cough – she supposed it must be partly smoking – she had no appetite, but a constant, nauseous stomach pain, and she couldn't sleep. She was dreadfully thin. She looked ghastly, she knew; her hair and skin dull, her eyes heavy and shadowed.

'I have brought you to this,' said Sebastian, reaching out tenderly, stroking her cheek, 'I'm so sorry.'

'No, Sebastian, not you. I've brought myself to it.'

'You do look absolutely exhausted. I suppose you're working too hard as well.'

'I have to. It keeps me sane. Sebastian, what would I do about Lyttons? If—'

'When,' he said firmly, 'when you are with me. I don't know. I've thought about it a lot. I suppose you can hardly go in there every day. It would not be a comfortable arrangement.'

'No,' she said. And thought of her work there, which was so much of her life, much of what was real in her life, thought of being without it, and found it very distressing. For some reason she had not properly confronted it before; before her mother had mentioned it. So central to her, indeed, was her work, that being without it was unimaginable, a life without light or food.

'I thought,' said Sebastian, 'you could set up as a freelance editor. Half the authors and indeed half the publishers in London would come to you. You could still work for Lyttons of course; but not exclusively. You could work from home—'

'From home?' she said stupidly, thinking automatically of Cheyne Walk. 'How could I work from home—'

'We could make you a study. Plenty of rooms. You like that one upstairs, next to my bedroom.'

'Oh. Yes. Yes, I see.' A new home: in a house that was not hers. But that would become hers.

If she was brave enough.

'And – the children?'

'Celia, we've discussed the children. I would love to have the children. Some of the time at least. They are not a problem.'

'But at first—'

'At first you will have to leave them. Until matters have been arranged.'

She was silent; thinking again of her mother's words. 'They'll be angry and confused and hostile . . .'

She repeated them. Sebastian looked at her. 'No doubt they will. And then they'll recover. Resilient creatures, children. And it's not as if they don't know me, don't like me.'

'Oh, Sebastian. That's so unrealistic. They know you and like you as a friend. Not someone who has stolen their mother, hurt their father. I—'

445

'Celia. Consider the alternatives. Realistically. Continuing like this. Can you contemplate that? For very much longer?'

She contemplated it; then shook her head.

'Or – giving one another up. You returning to Oliver. In all its unhappiness. Unhappiness and frustration. For the rest of your life. Could you find that bearable? Is that what you want?'

'No. No, Sebastian, no, it isn't. Of course it isn't. It would be dreadful. But—'

'But?'

'But perhaps that is right. Perhaps—'

'Celia, something that makes you so lonely, so unhappy, so unfulfilled cannot be right. And Oliver is unhappy too, you told me so.'

'I know. But he was not made unhappy by me, but by the war, his own ill-health, his uncertainty about everything—'

'You mustn't see him as helpless, you know. Or dependent. He is neither. He has a formidable will himself, and he knows what he wants. And fights for it. He will survive, believe me. He wouldn't treat you as he does if he couldn't manage without you.'

She was silent again. He took her hand, raised it to his lips, kissed it.

'Come live with me, and be my love. Please, Celia. You know it's right. You know.'

'Yes, I suppose I do,' she said, and then, taking a deep breath, physically straightening, stiffening her back, 'yes, Sebastian, I do.'

She had decided then – yet again – what she must do. But the biggest factor was not Sebastian's words, or even her own wishes; it was remembering again the dreadful moment last night, when she had wished Oliver dead: a moment she could never share with anyone. And in which her marriage had surely, finally died.

CHAPTER 24

There is logic as well as truth behind the old saying the husband is the last to find out. He very frequently is; for the very simple reason that nobody will ever actually tell him. He stands behind a notional door at which the gossip stops. It makes its way most efficiently everywhere else; through windows, doors, down chimneys, across streets, it cuts a swathe through parties, runs round dinner tables, dances its way across nightclubs, drifts around swimming pools and tennis courts. But, somehow, the husband's door is impenetrable; there the gossip becomes silenced, immobilised, impotent.

Gossip about Celia had spread very wide by the middle of that summer; Elspeth Granchester had only told two very close friends, in the strictest confidence, assuring them they were absolutely the first to know, and that it must go no further and they had also only told one or two friends, also instructing silence on the matter and at the end of a week or so, it had covered London, moved into the country, and even – this being the time of the summer holidays – crossed the Channel and made its way down to the South of France, into the hills of Tuscany and on to more than one yacht cruising in the Mediterranean and Aegean seas.

Lady Beckenham had been quizzed about it, albeit in rather veiled terms, both in London and the country (and given the quizzers very short shrift) likewise Jack Lytton professed total ignorance, when people pressed him for details; Caroline Masterson had been very closely questioned on the matter and hinted that there might be something in it, while proclaiming a complete lack of knowledge; Sebastian Brooke himself was not questioned, save by a few old friends, but watched closely for any kind of behaviour which might indicate that it was true. And yet Oliver Lytton, sitting anxious and depressed about a great deal more than his marriage, in his office in Paternoster Row, or staring morosely out of his drawing-room window in Cheyne Walk heard nothing of it at all.

Which was not to say he would have professed that all was well with his marriage had he been questioned and chosen to answer. In fact he felt a constant and growing unease on the matter, feeling Celia becoming lost to him a little more every day, knowing that every time she came home late, or appeared to be absent from him even in spirit at the dinner table, or as they sat in the drawing-room, on the rare occasions when she was at home and not out, drinking and dancing in some nightclub, knowing from her evasive smile when he asked her how she was, from her very slight withdrawing when he bent to kiss her, her emotional and even physical detachment from him, even when he was making increasingly rare love to her, knowing at every turn, at every hour that she was moving further away from him. And yet, he continued to ignore his instincts, to struggle to trust her, to turn his mind absolutely and resolutely away from the truth. For the simple reason that he was quite unable to bear it. Oliver loved Celia absolutely: and he needed her to love him in the same way. The fact that he was occasionally hostile to her, sometimes critical of her, frequently irritated by her, was irrelevant. Without her his life, or at least the point of his life was negated; therefore if he were to carry on as a properly functioning human being, he needed her. It was as simple as that.

'Celia, I'm moving out,' Jack's face was rather pale, drawn; he didn't look at her.

'Oh, Jack. Don't do that, it works so well, you being here, I shall miss you.'

'I – have to. It's high time I made my own arrangements. I'm thirty-five and—'

'Same age as me. As you're always telling me.'

'Yes. Well, anyway, I've found a place.'

'Really? Where, can I come and see it?'

'Oh well – yes possibly. When I've moved in.'

'Where is it?'

'In Sloane Street. A flat.'

'Is it nice?'

'Yes. Very nice. Now you must excuse me, I have to go and meet Lily.'

So he knew, thought Celia, watching him as he left the drawing-room; he had heard. Elspeth had done her work well. She heard him running downstairs, heard the front door slam, watched his bright head moving away from her, down the Walk. She felt a great weight of depression suddenly; she would miss him so much. And miss his affection for her, his teasing, his chatting, his terrible jokes. Miss going out with him after dinner, miss his friends, even miss Lily. Although Lily had never been quite – friendly towards her; had remained cool, distant.

She had probably known for longer; she was smart was Lily, quick, sharp-eyed. A great deal smarter than Jack. She wondered how it would be working with Jack now; difficult. Well, it was probably all a foretaste of the worse that was to come.

Jack had been horribly upset by the news. Lily had told him: one night at the Grafton Galleries. He had been dancing with Crystal and she had been sitting, talking rather intensely to another woman. He went over and asked her what they were discussing.

'Your sister-in-law. Lady Celia.'

'Celia! What about her?'

'I was right.'

'What?'

He was rather drunk; the combination of that and a dread of what she was going to say, closed his mind rather efficiently.

'She is having an affair.'

'Oh, Lily, I don't believe it,' he said wearily, and then, contradicting himself, 'who with?'

'Sebastian.'

'Sebastian?'

'Yes.'

'How – awful. How do you know?'

'Gwendolyn Oliphant just told me.'

'And who told Gwendolyn?'

'Elspeth Granchester's sister.'

'And how does Elspeth Granchester's sister know?'

'Celia told Elspeth herself.'

'Oh,' said Jack. He felt very bleak suddenly and horribly sober. He hated it; hated the thought of Oliver, whom he loved so much and had always looked up to, being deceived, made a monkey of, hated that everyone in London knew, hated that Celia herself should have revealed such a thing to Elspeth Granchester, of all people. Elspeth who would have made gossip out of the news that night followed day. And he hated that Celia, whom he had always adored, whose company he so enjoyed, whose beauty he admired and who had always been, for him, the embodiment of what a wife should be, had proved to be so faithless and treacherous, not merely betraying Oliver, but with someone who was presumed to be his friend. And even experienced a brief, rather ignoble emotion, born of an ignoble memory, a memory of a night during the war when he had tried to seduce Celia, and she had refused. Had refused him: and not Sebastian. The ignoble emotion was jealousy; and it was very uncomfortable indeed.

'Sorry,' Lily said gently, 'maybe I shouldn't have told you. I know how much you like her.'

'Did like her,' said Jack. 'I'm glad I'm moving out.'

'I have to talk to Oliver,' said Celia finally to Sebastian, one hot, bright July evening, when she felt more than usually stifled by her situation and by the unreality of it.

'When?' said Sebastian, with a sigh, for he had heard this before, and more than once; to hear the next day that it had not worked, that Oliver had been too tired, too busy, one of the children had been upset, or ill, Jack had been in all evening.

'Tonight,' she said now, 'it's as good a time as any, he's finally happy with Jack's book, there's no news from the Lothians, it seems they have given up on their foolish case.'

She sat at dinner, unable to eat, watching Oliver push his food round his own plate, refusing the wine she tried to press on him (thinking it might anaesthetise him to a degree at least) talking at great length about Jack's book, about *The Buchanans* – typeset now, for they could not afford to wait – about Giles and how much he was looking forward to coming home from school for the summer.

Finally shaken with fear, but fuelled by the adrenalin of it, she said, 'Oliver, I have to speak to you about something.'

'Yes?' he said, smiling at her rather vaguely, 'yes, what is it?'

'I have to tell you something. Something important.'

'Shall we go upstairs to the drawing-room? And have coffee served there?'

'No,' she said, 'no, I think we should stay here.'

'Very well,' he said, settling back in his chair, 'what is it?'

'I want to talk about – about—' Somehow the words, the right, strong words wouldn't come.

'About what, Celia? The children? The summer holidays? I thought we might all go down to the South of France this year, I don't like the heat very much but the children would love it and so would you, I—'

'Oliver, it's nothing to do with the summer holidays.'

'Oh. Right. Well does that sound a good idea to you?'

'No, not really,' she said.

'Why not? I thought you'd like it.'

'The thing is, I – well, I won't be coming on holiday with you this year.'

'Really?' he said and an expression was moving into his face, a certain wariness, 'that seems a shame. You need a holiday, you don't look well.'

'Yes, but you see, I shall be—'

'Celia, I'm sorry. I think we really should go and sit upstairs. It's such a beautiful evening and it would be so nice to watch the sunset on the river.'

'Oliver—'

'Come along, I'll have the coffee sent up.'

She followed him slowly; for some reason she felt altogether slow, braked, sloth-like. When finally they were settled again, she said, 'It really is rather – difficult, what I have to say.'

'Must it be said?' He looked at her oddly, almost impatient; he knows, she thought, he is making it deliberately difficult. And, indeed why should he not?

'Yes. I'm afraid it must be said. And I don't know how to start. But—'

'Yes?'

'It's about – about our marriage.'

'Our marriage! I would have thought there was very little to be said about that. Getting on in years now, quite well worn, in fact, but – surviving. Wouldn't you say?'

'Well – no Actually. I wouldn't.'

'Really?' He sounded politely surprised; as if she had expressed doubt about the state of the economy, or the lack of progress being made by the labour party. 'Well, that is not how it seems to me.'

'It seems it to me. And I – I want to talk about it.'

'My dear, you must forgive me. I'm terribly tired. Much too tired for a philosophical conversation. I'm going up to bed. Goodnight.'

'Oliver, I—'

'Celia, no. Not tonight.'

It was impenetrable: his determination not to confront it, not to let her make him confront it. It happened again and then again; the last time she said, very loudly, sounding almost desperate – as indeed by then she was, 'Oliver, I am thinking of leaving you. Don't you understand?'

And he had sat staring at her his face absolutely blank and then he said, 'I understand perfectly. But this isn't the time to talk about it. Goodnight, Celia. Sleep well.'

It was checkmate.

'It's checkmate,' she said fretfully to Sebastian, 'he won't listen, he won't answer, he won't discuss it, he won't confront it. I don't know what to do.'

'You'll just have to leave,' he said, 'just walk out. Then he'll have to confront it.'

'I can't,' she said, 'I can't do that.'

'You'll have to.'

She felt increasingly ill with the strain and the distress. Her cough was worse; her appetite non-existent. She couldn't sleep. She could hardly work. Everyone irritated her: the children, the servants, her colleagues at work. She refused to go out, saw none of her friends, took no personal telephone calls, unable to face the prospect of being quizzed, studied, given advice. Her mother had removed herself from her life; LM was equally conspicuous by her absence from it. She prayed that LM did not yet know; she feared that her prayers were not being answered.

LM in fact did not know; there was quite simply no one to tell her. Lady Beckenham would not have dreamed of it; Oliver was incapable of it; and Celia was totally resistant to it. Until she had to, until leaving Oliver was a fait accompli, it seemed unfair to tell LM; to embroil her in the conflict, to invite judgement, to ask her not to judge. LM adored Oliver and she was very fond of Celia; it would be horribly difficult for her. If – when – she was with Sebastian, then she would have to talk to her; their friendship would deserve it. Until then she wanted to keep LM at a distance. Until then.

She felt beleaguered, with no one to talk to, no one to advise her. No one except Sebastian. 'I just don't know what to do,' she said, 'I just don't.'

'So you keep saying. It seems very simple to me.'

'It would to you. He's not your husband. You don't owe him anything. You don't feel guilt or remorse about him.'

'You shouldn't assume that.'

'Oh, Sebastian this is an absurd conversation.'

'I agree. Why don't you just leave?'

'I told you. I can't.'

'It would force him to accept the fact. That you were serious.'

'I know, but—'

'A letter?'

'A letter? Sebastian, you can't mean it. How can I leave Oliver a letter, telling him our marriage is over? It would be cowardly beyond belief.'

'You've tried the brave way. It doesn't work.'

Celia stared at him. 'I don't see how—'

'Leave him a letter. At the house. All right, don't tell him you're leaving for good. Say you're moving out for a while.'

'To be with you?'

'Well – yes. Obviously.'

'I don't see why it's so obvious.'

'It's hardly irrelevant.'

452

'No. No, I suppose not.'

'Say you've tried to tell him. That he won't listen. That you need time to work things out.'

'It seems so brutal.'

'My darling, you can't leave your husband gently.'

'I know. But – what about the children?'

'Well obviously, you will have to tell them.'

'Yes, but I'd thought Oliver and I could talk to them together. Do I – would I – tell them before I leave this letter? Before I go. Or come back and tell them? Oh, God, Sebastian, it's such a nightmare.'

He looked at her. 'Is there any way they could be sent away for a few days? To your mother, perhaps?'

'She's not speaking to me.'

'I see.' He sighed. 'I've caused you a lot of unhappiness haven't I? I'm so sorry.'

Celia looked at him; then she stood up and walked over to him.

'You have given me more happiness, as well, than I would have believed possible,' she said. 'Whatever happens, that is terribly important.' She bent down and kissed him. 'I love you Sebastian. I love you so much. And when I'm with you, I know that what I'm doing is right. I know it. I will – I will ask my mother. It's a good idea.'

Barty was longing for Giles to come home. There was something wrong, and she couldn't work out quite what it was. Nothing had actually changed; Wol spent a lot of time on his own, Aunt Celia was often working late, but that had always been the case. They seemed fairly normal: they weren't even arguing as much as they used to do. Aunt Celia was in a bad temper a lot of the time, snapping at Nanny and very cross with the twins, who had had dreadful reports from school: but even that wasn't really unusual. And she wasn't sleeping at all, Barty often heard her moving about the house in the middle of the night; but then she always had been a night creature. She certainly looked awfully tired and not very well; Barty had even asked her once or twice if she felt all right and she had said yes, she was absolutely fine, just very tired. Well that would be the not sleeping.

But somehow the house didn't feel happy; before, even when Aunt Celia had been really bad-tempered and having noisy rows with Wol, and furious with the twins, everything had been sort of firm underneath. Firm and cheerful. Suddenly, it felt rocky. And miserable.

Jack was moving out, which might have something to do with it; Barty had actually cried when he told her. She loved Jack, he was so funny and such fun, and played Monopoly with her and other games too, sometimes cards and draughts, except she nearly always won those, so they stuck to Monopoly. He seemed rather miserable too. When she asked him why he was going, he said he was too old to live in his big brother's house any more, and he needed to be independent. And that he had a girlfriend, who thought the same. He said he had a very nice flat and Barty could come and see it if she liked; she said she would, but he hadn't asked her yet. Mostly because he seemed so miserable. And he and Aunt Celia didn't seem to be getting on at all; before they'd always been chatting and joking and had gone out a lot together, leaving Wol behind, and nobody had minded. Now Jack went out, presumably with the girlfriend, and hardly talked to Aunt Celia at all. Maybe they'd quarrelled; of course she couldn't ask.

'You're all to go down to Ashingham for a few days,' said Nanny, 'I'll pack your things, but if there's anything you particularly want, be sure to put it out on your beds for washing.'

'Ashingham! When?' said Adele.

'Soon as you break up. Next week, I suppose.'

'Is Giles coming?' asked Venetia.

'I wouldn't know. I suppose so. I haven't been told much.'

'But—'

'But what, Barty?'

'The next week is the concert.' She had been chosen to play a piano solo; she was as excited as she was nervous.

'Well – I wouldn't know about that either. You'd better ask Lady Celia.'

Barty went down to breakfast, feeling upset. Celia and Wol were reading the papers.

'Aunt Celia?'

'Yes, Barty?'

'Nanny says we're to go to Ashingham.'

'Yes, that's right. You are. Next week. Just for a week or two. It will do you all good, some country air.'

'But Aunt Celia, it's the week of the concert. I'm playing in it—'

'Oh, dear. I'd forgotten, Barty, I'm so sorry. I'm afraid you'll just have to miss it.'

'Miss it! But – but I can't, I'm playing a solo.'

'Barty, I can't ask my mother to change all her plans, and change all of mine, because of a concert.'

'Mummy, that's so unfair.' Adele's dark eyes, so exactly like her mother's, were brilliant. 'Barty's been practising and practising. You should have remembered. Anyway, we don't want to go either, we've got a party, and we want to hear Barty play and—'

'Adele, be quiet. Until you and Venetia begin to do better at school,

454

there aren't going to be any more parties, I can assure you of that. Now eat your breakfast, all of you. And be quiet.'

'Celia, I really don't think Barty should have to miss a concert.' Oliver's voice was unusually firm. He never argued with her about the children in front of them. Four pairs of eyes fixed on him. The children almost audibily drew in their breath.

Celia stared at him; then she said, 'Oliver, I'm sorry, but I would prefer that you didn't confuse matters. This is all arranged.'

'Then it must be unarranged. Barty can stay here.'

'Of course she can't. Nanny will be at Ashingham.'

'And where will you be?'

There was an absolute silence; then Celia said 'I – I will be here. Obviously. But extremely busy. That is precisely why I want the children to be in the country.'

Another silence. Then, 'And where will Giles be?'

'At Ashingham. Yes. Once he breaks up.'

'Does he know this?'

'Not yet. Oliver, can we please leave this until later?'

'No. I don't think we should. Barty is very upset and I can understand why. Whatever the twins may or may not do, I think she should stay here. However busy you are. I will be here; Barty and I can look after one another. And I can attend her concert, if you cannot.'

'That's not fair!' said the twins, in unison, 'we want to go.'

'Well, maybe that is too difficult to arrange. When is it Barty?'

'Next Wednesday,' said Barty.

'Fine. I shall put it in my diary.'

'Oliver—'

'Run along now, all of you. Daniels will be waiting.'

As the door closed, and as she pulled on her coat and school beret, Barty heard Oliver say, 'I have no idea what you are planning, Celia nor do I wish to know. But Barty should not have to miss her concert.'

There was a long silence; then the door opened and Celia appeared, slamming it after her and started upstairs.

'Temper, temper!' said Adele under her breath. Not quite enough under her breath. Celia turned and ran downstairs again, raised her hand and struck Adele across the face. Quite hard.

'It's time you learned some respect,' she said.

And then went into the morning room and closed the door, very quietly this time and there was no more sound in the house at all.

Barty sat in the car, trying not to cry, with her arm round Adele who was crying very loudly indeed.

Everything was awful. Absolutely awful. And something was terribly wrong.

★

'I can't go on like this,' said Celia. She was crying; she had taken a taxi up to Sebastian's house at lunchtime, careless of the risk. In any case, what risk? Everyone knew, except for Oliver and he refused to know.

Sebastian took out his handkerchief, wiped her tears away.

'Come on. Tell me about it.'

'I'm just being so dreadful to everyone. Everyone. Turning into a bad person. Well, I am a bad person.'

'Nonsense. I don't like bad people.'

'Don't joke. It isn't funny.'

'Sorry. What have you done?'

'First I told Barty she couldn't play in a concert.'

'Doesn't sound too bad.'

'It's very bad. She's playing a solo and I'd forgotten. And then I said it didn't matter. Sebastian, I would never have done that once. Never. Of course it matters.'

'Well why can't she play in it?'

'Because I've arranged for them all to go to stay with my mother. As I told you.'

'Oh yes. The courageous phone call.'

'It was very courageous. Anyway, she's agreed, that's the point and it's all arranged, and it means I can – well anyway . . . And then Oliver said she must play in the concert, and she could stay, which made me so angry, how dare he interfere?'

'And?' Sebastian's face was a polite blank.

'And then I lost my temper and Adele said something cheeky and I hit her.'

'From what I can gather a few spankings would do those two good.'

'It wasn't a spanking. It was a hard slap across the face. In front of the servants and Barty and – it was dreadful. I shall have to apologise.'

'Well, she'll enjoy that. It'll more than make up for any suffering, I'd have thought.'

'Sebastian, it's serious.' She took a cigarette out of the silver box on his table, lit it, inhaled, and started to cough.

'You should stop that,' he said severely.

'I will. When I – when I feel better.'

'When you're living with me, you certainly will. Now then, listen to me. I do feel sorry. For all of you. But it's simply because you're under such strain, Celia. When this is over, when things are in order again—'

'But will they be? Will that be order?'

'Yes, it will. It's absolutely right, and you know it is.'

'I don't,' said Celia, 'I don't know anything of the sort.'

'Well I do. And if you really don't, then I shall have to know it for both of us. Now come along, let me give you a big hug. It's all going to be all right. When is this concert, incidentally?'

'Next Wednesday. Oliver is going to go. He was terribly angry with me, when he got to the office. Terribly. I said I would like to go too, and he said he would prefer that I didn't.'

'Well in that case,' said Sebastian, 'perhaps that is the ideal day for your departure.'

'Oh no, Sebastian. No, I couldn't possibly do that.'

'I think there are definitely grounds for taking out an injunction against publishing this book,' said Howard Shaw. 'The coincidences could be thought to be too many and too strong. And therefore the material about the affair could very well be argued to be defamatory.'

Jasper Lothian nodded.

'Of course – you must be prepared for some publicity. If they are determined to publish, and I suspect they are, then we must be very sure of our ground. Is that quite clear?'

There was a fragment of hesitation; then Jasper Lothian said, 'Yes. Quite clear. I shall, of course, be seen as standing up for my own good name.'

Howard Shaw looked at Lothian; he wasn't sure that he liked him. He was pompous, he lacked any kind of humour and he was clearly preposterously vain. He dressed rather like an ageing Rupert Brooke, in loose jackets, soft shirts, floppy bow ties; his hair which was silver, fell almost to his shoulders, in what were obviously carefully encouraged waves. Of course academia was full of such eccentricity: more than ever in this rather excessive age. Well, it didn't matter in the least whether he liked him or not; this was an exciting case for him to work on.

'You may have to produce witnesses who can testify as to your moral probity,' he said.

'That can be arranged. Of course.'

'Good. Then I shall write to the publishers.'

'Saying?'

'Saying, in the first instance, that we want the offending passages removed. That is an option they must be offered.'

'Well – that would be the ideal obviously,' said Jasper Lothian. 'Do you think they would agree to that?'

'I would rather doubt it. They are central to the story. But it might be possible. It could be better for them than having to withdraw totally. I would imagine a considerable investment has gone into this book.'

'I see. Well – we shall no doubt see.'

'Indeed we shall.'

★

457

'Oliver, I shall be late into the office in the morning.'

'Not unusual.'

'No. No, I have to go and see Lady Annabel about her book. Foyles want her to do some readings and then—'

'Yes, yes. I daresay Lyttons will continue to run without you for a few more hours. As you know I am going to Barty's concert in the afternoon. I have suggested that Daniels brings her to the office; then we can go there together.'

'I would still like to come—'

'And I would prefer that you didn't. If you don't mind. This is our treat, mine and Barty's. I have promised to take her out to tea afterwards, to the Soda Fountain in Fortnums.'

'But Oliver—'

'We don't spend much time together these days. I am looking forward to it.'

'Very well.'

She made one last desperate effort.

'Oliver I do wish you would let me talk to you about – about everything. Our lives together and so on. It is so very important.'

'I'm sorry, my dear. I have a great deal to do this evening. Especially as I am going to be out of the office for much of tomorrow. I'm sure you will understand.'

Celia gave up.

The twins had gone earlier in the day, with Nanny. Barty was to go down the next day. Celia had said goodbye to them after breakfast. It was horrible. She apologised to Adele for hitting her; told her with raw honesty that she had had no right to do it, that she had been upset about something else. Adele, sensing an opportunity for drama, had started to cry again, and then threw herself into her mother's arms and said she was sorry she had been upset and even more sorry if it had been about her bad report.

Both twins had clung to her that morning, crying, before being put into the car by Nanny, who was not impressed by the performance, having heard them discussing the night before how jolly it would be in the country, with Jay and Billy and the ponies and how much they were looking forward to seeing their dog again. But Celia, who was not to know that, stood looking at their sorrowful little faces, their dark eyes huge and brilliant with tears, remembering the glowing May day when she had brought them home to Cheyne Walk for the first time, two identical shawl-wrapped bundles, seeing Oliver's joyful smile as he ushered them all into the house, thinking how blessed she was – and thinking that she was not saying goodbye to them for a fortnight, but to the life she had shared with them and their father for ever.

She went into her study to write the letter. It was extraordinarily difficult and very painful. She felt she was standing on a beach, watching the tide go out on her marriage, watching it moving relentlessly further and further away from her, out of touch, out of reach; she felt stranded in her misery and loneliness, utterly bereft. And wondered if what she was doing, leaving Oliver bereft as well, could possibly be the right thing. And then thought how intolerable life with him had become for both of them and told herself that in the end they would both be happier for it.

She told him how happy she had been for most of their marriage, how much she had loved him, how much she still loved him.

But I feel we have both moved on, and away from the two people we used to be. Mostly because of the war, but also through our now widely differing views of Lyttons and the direction in which it should be going. And, of course in our personal lives much has changed. I need someone who appreciates me for what I am, rather than what I should be. That is how I feel you view me these days, Oliver, as someone unsuitable in every way, to be in your life − both professionally and personally. I feel criticised at every turn, probably rightly. For a long time, I struggled to do better for you, but to no avail. You make me feel frivolous, selfish, and in no way your equal or your partner any more. This is very hard to bear, and I grow less self-confident every day and increasingly unhappy.

There is someone else in my life now, and it will come as no surprise to you to learn this, I am sure. It is Sebastian Brooke, as you may also have suspected, and as I have tried to tell you many times. I am going to live with him. He is able to accept me for what I am, and consequently I have been able to feel better and happier. If only you had allowed me to talk to you about it, Oliver, we might have been able to avert a lot of pain. Or at least a little.

I am leaving you with enormous grief and regret, for we have shared so much, survived so much. But I know it is the right thing to do. I cannot go on being dishonest with you, because you do not deserve it and I cannot bear it.

I have not yet talked to the children; I felt we should do that together. If you could find that possible, I think it would help them. But that is why I wanted them to be with my mother at this particular time.

Thank you for all the happiness you have given me; and although I do not deserve it, please, please try to forgive me.

I will always love you, very much.

Celia.

She was crying quite hard when she finished the letter; she turned out the light in the study and sat in the darkness, staring at the trees outside the window. Remembering. Just remembering when she had been young and in love with Oliver; when all they had asked was to be together, when to talk, laugh, plan their lives, make love, had been absolute happiness, when finding anyone else, or anything even remotely more important to them had been unthinkable. And wondering that such love, such closeness, such tenderness could disintegrate so hopelessly and so thoroughly, first into indifference and then into despair.

CHAPTER 25

Janet Gould was walking down the corridor when she heard a crash from Oliver's office; startled, she turned and walked quickly back. Oliver was sitting in his chair, his face frozen in despair, staring at a letter; the crash had been his father's heavy cut-glass and silver ink stand which he had hurled across the room and into the corner. Physical violence – or indeed any kind of violence – was so unlike him, that she was shocked. She knocked gently on the open door.

'Is anything wrong, Mr Lytton?'

'Yes,' he said, holding out the letter to her, 'yes, it is. Read this, Mrs Gould. Now, what am I to do?'

Barty woke up feeling very nervous, half wishing she had gone to Ashingham, where she would now be miles away from the concert hall in Wigmore Street where that afternoon she had to play her Chopin Etude. Miss Wetherhill, her music mistress, had told her, that at least two hundred people would be there. It would be absolutely dreadful. Two hundred people, all sitting listening to, staring at her. She felt extremely sick; she went into the bathroom and pulled her toothbrush and toothpaste out of her mug; her hands, as she did so, were shaking violently. How on earth could you play the piano with shaking hands? And there was no one to talk to, no one to distract her. She could never have believed she would miss the twins, but she would have given anything that morning to have them giggling and telling her stupid jokes and stories and saying she'd probably play so badly that everyone would walk out, so there was no need to be nervous. Or to have Nanny saying that as long as she had brushed her hair nicely and was wearing a pretty dress and her shoes were shiny, it wouldn't matter how she played.

She wished desperately that Aunt Celia was coming. She had helped her so much with her piano-playing: perhaps not quite so much recently, but she had always been so encouraging, terribly pleased when she had got distinction for her grade three examination. It didn't seem right that she wouldn't be there, sharing it. She had told her she was sorry about forgetting the concert so many times, that Barty felt quite guilty herself, and had begged her to come. But she had explained that Wol didn't want that. He wanted it to be a treat for just the two of them. That's what they both said, but Barty felt it was because he was cross with Aunt Celia, not just for forgetting the concert, but for something else as well.

Only yesterday at breakfast, which was the last time she had seen him, he had said, 'Our day tomorrow, Barty. How I am looking forward to it!'

And Aunt Celia had picked up the paper and started reading it very intently.

Barty had a bath, put on her old skirt and jersey, for she planned to spend the morning practising and going for a walk, and looked at the clock. Quite late. Nearly nine. Wol and Aunt Celia would have gone. The house was very quiet. She certainly didn't want any breakfast. Although a cup of tea might be nice . . . She ran downstairs; the post had come. There was a card from Giles: 'Good luck,' it said. 'You'll be splendid. I wish I could be there.'

That was so nice of him. He really was such a thoughtful person these days. It made her feel much better. She was so looking forward to seeing him. He had been furious, the twins said, about being sent to Ashingham the minute he broke up from Eton and having to miss her concert; they had read the letter he had written to their mother, which she had left lying on the dining table. They were extremely unscrupulous, the twins, they read everyone's letters if they felt so inclined.

She wished her mother was coming; both she and Aunt Celia had begged her to, but Sylvia had refused. She said she'd feel awkward, sitting there, with all the other parents, worrying about – well about not being one of them. Letting Barty down as she put it. Barty said she wouldn't be letting her down, it was nonsense, but Sylvia had still refused. It seemed so unfair. She still wasn't well; was having a lot of stomach pain. She had promised Barty to go to the doctor, but Barty knew she hadn't been yet. If things had been different at home, she'd have asked Aunt Celia to organise something.

Barty was looking forward to going to Ashingham, to seeing Billy and Giles and LM and Jay, and Lord and Lady Beckenham; it was so wonderful there, they were allowed to do whatever they liked, take picnics off for a whole day, ride the ponies, help on the farm – only they had to help, not play around – 'the tenants have got work to do, they're much too busy to be held up by a lot of tiresome children'. There were scary things as well, of course, like having to dine with the Beckenhams sometimes in the great dining-room, and being made to do what Lady Beckenham called conversing.

'Don't tell me you're shy, Giles,' she roared one night, while Giles sat scarlet and silent, 'find something to say and say it. You can't be that stupid. You owe it to your hostess, not to mention your own friends, to be interesting at the dinner table. You too, Barty. Now come on, think of a subject and we'll discuss it.'

She went into the drawing-room, where the piano was, did some scales and ran through the piece twice; it went quite well, in spite of her shaking hands. Perhaps it would be all right. She decided that after all she was a bit hungry: perhaps a piece of toast would be nice. She got into the dining-room just in time; Mary, the housemaid, was clearing away.

'You help yourself, Miss Barty,' she said, 'you need to keep your strength up for this afternoon. How are you feeling?'

'Oh – sort of all right,' said Barty, 'thank you.'

She sat buttering toast, feeling lonely again; she really would like something to read. She had begun to like reading the newspapers; but they weren't on the sideboard. Cleared away, she supposed, into Wol's study. He liked to read them at length in the evening. Well – maybe she could go in and borrow one. She would put it back afterwards.

She got up, crossed the hall, went in. It was horribly neat; 'You're afraid to breathe in here in case you disturb something,' Venetia had once said and it was true. The papers were lying on his desk, ranged in perfect parallel rows; she went over and picked out the *Daily Mail*. That was her favourite. And noticed that propped up against the big silver desk clock was a letter addressed to Wol. In Aunt Celia's writing. Oliver, it said, Personal and Urgent. She must have put it there before she left; thinking he was still in the house. Barty looked at it anxiously, taking in the word Urgent. Well, it was lucky she was going to his office; she could take it with her, give it to him there.

Celia had left the house as usual that morning; she was indeed going to see Lady Annabel, and planned to come back later to collect some clothes and a few personal things, photographs of the children, a few of her favourite books, her jewellery. Not much of her jewellery, though, only what had been given to her by her mother, left to her by her grandmother. She did not feel she could take anything Oliver had given her; even her engagement ring was placed carefully with the rest in the small safe in Oliver's dressing-room. She felt absolutely extraordinary; the sadness of the night before had gone, leaving her with a mixture of terror and huge excitement. She had promised Sebastian she would be with him by lunchtime.

'I shall feel so odd, rather as if I was a bride, leaving the old home and coming to join you in the new. A rather elderly bride,' she added with a sigh.

Sebastian said nonsense, lots of women got married in their thirties these days, it was an indirect result of the war, and anyway, the youngest bride could not be more beautiful than she was.

She still felt, though, not only desperately worried about Oliver, about how badly he might take the news, but about how he might behave as a result. About how wretched he would be, how he would cope with it, who he would talk to, whether he would feel himself able to talk at all. Or would he shut himself away in his study, grieving and raging silently, pretending to everyone that nothing was wrong? He had become an emotional stranger to her, absolutely changed from the rather tediously predictable creature he had once been; it seemed incredible to her that she had once known, almost to the last phrase, what he would say and how he would behave, right to the final nod of the head, in any given situation. It did in fact, define the vast distance which had formed between them, she thought, that she was totally unable now to predict his reaction, even to this, to something as momentous as the announcement that she was leaving him: it persuaded her that perhaps she was after all doing the right thing. For him as well as for her.

Lady Annabel, charming as ever, was delighted with the editing, with her dust jacket, and even with the title Celia had suggested, *Queen of Sorrows*.

'I know it overstates the case a little,' Celia said, slightly apologetically, 'but it certainly describes her personal life. And her reign was hardly happy in any way, either. I think it is also a very strong title, which we need.'

They parted at eleven: 'Do tell Mr Lytton how happy I am about everything,' said Lady Annabel, smiling graciously from the doorway of her exquisite house, and that I would like to discuss the new book with both of you. Dear Florence; such a very irritating woman, I always think.'

Celia said she would; thinking not only how desperately sad it was that she would not be at Lyttons for what she knew would be a most triumphant publication of *Queen of Sorrows*, but that there would be no discussions between her and Oliver and any third person, with the possible exception of a solicitor, for some considerable time.

She had another appointment before returning to Cheyne Walk: with Dr Perring.

'That cough is really worrying me,' Sebastian had said, 'and you don't look at all well. I don't want to take on some invalid, you have to be fit and healthy if you're going to live with me.'

She had arranged to go to Dr Perring's consulting rooms in Harley Street, rather than call him to the house; sitting in the waiting-room, with so little standing now between her old life and the new, the enormity of what she was about to do suddenly overwhelmed her, together with a wave of such violent nausea that she thought she was actually going to vomit. Even when it passed, and she was lying back rather limply in her chair, feeling shaky and weak, she still felt utterly exhausted, could not imagine ever having the strength to get up again.

'Lady Celia?' It was the nurse, smiling brightly. 'Dr Perring will see you now. Please follow me.'

In the years to come, Celia was never to forget that journey, one of the most important in her life: down the thickly carpeted corridor, with its alcoves set with urns of flowers, its pale grey walls covered with bland watercolours, the sunlight beating through a window ahead of them at the end of the corridor, and nurse in her absurdly elaborate uniform, silhouetted against it, dark and somehow slightly sinister. And Celia following her, still feeling weak and light headed . . .

'I really need time to think about this one, Mr Lytton,' said Peter Briscoe. He had come into the offices, in response to Oliver's urgent summons. 'They're obviously very serious. Is there any way you could do as they suggest, and write out the offending episode?'

'No,' said Oliver, 'it's quite impossible. It is central to the whole book, one of the major strands; it affects everything, the daughter's view of her father, the wife's reaction to the affair, even the son's attitude, a very high-minded young man, the conscientious objector, you know, he is horrified by it. No, it has to remain. There is no book without it.'

'And – forgive me – the book is printed, you say, not merely typeset, or at proof stage?'

'Yes, indeed. I've just had three thousand copies done. It will be appallingly expensive if we don't publish now. Not to mention the loss of face.'

'Then we must fight for it,' said Peter Briscoe. 'I will telephone you in a day or so, tell you what I think we should do next. Test their nerve, I suggest.'

'And how would we do that?'

'Write back and say the chapters cannot be removed and that publication will go ahead. There is bound to be an element of bluff on their part. No one embarks on any legal course of action without knowing they might lose. They are private individuals after all. You have the weight of a large publishing house behind you.'

'Well – a publishing house anyway,' said Oliver with a sigh. 'It won't be very large if we have to pulp *The Buchanans*.'

Peter Briscoe decided to talk again to Guy Worsley. He felt he would like to get further measure of Jasper Lothian. Find out just how tough an opponent he might prove, just how much money and power he had had behind him. Guy had no telephone in his small flat in Fulham, which was tiresome; Peter Briscoe told his secretary to send him a telegram, instructing him to come to see him as soon as possible to discuss the matter of *The Buchanans* further. Arrogant young fellow, thinking he could get away with such a thing. It was blatant folly. That was what came of the young achieving success; they lacked the wisdom and experience with which to temper it.

Meanwhile, he would start drafting a letter to Lothian, telling him that there was no question of removing anything from the text of the book. It was all becoming extremely uncomfortable; and time was running out on them. He had not yet mentioned to Oliver Lytton that if they went ahead, the damages awarded to Lothian could be very substantial, but he would have to do so soon. Pulping the book would certainly be cheaper than that.

'Right, perhaps you'd like to put your clothes on again, and come back into the consulting room. Thank you, nurse.'

Dr Perring had examined her very carefully, questioned her closely as to her general health, listened to her chest – and indeed her heart – for a long time. He had taken some blood for analysis, checked her reflexes and her blood pressure, had looked in her ears and her eyes, and down her throat. Celia was feeling quite nervous by the time she was sitting in his chair again; beginning to think there must be something quite seriously wrong with her.

'Now, Lady Celia. That cough is very nasty.' He looked at her severely. 'I think you should stop smoking at once. For a start. It isn't good for you, in my opinion. You do have some congestion in your lungs, and it could turn into bronchitis very easily. I will prescribe some cough suppressant for you, and I want you to inhale several times a day, with Friars' Balsam.'

'Yes,' said Celia meekly, 'yes, I will.'

She didn't mind taking medicine, nor did she mind inhaling; she would mind not smoking. She had come rather to depend on it; it soothed her raw nerves.

'Now, the other symptoms. The tiredness – well of course you work too hard. And you've always slept badly, haven't you? I expect you would like me to prescribe a sleeping draught.'

'I would – yes. Some nights I don't sleep at all. It's terrible.'

'Of course. Well I can do that. And the indigestion – I've just been looking back through your notes.'

'Yes?' Surely he wasn't going to say she had an ulcer or something.

'You say it makes you feel nauseous?'

'Yes. Yes it does.'

'Mmm. Appetite?'

'What appetite?' said Celia, smiling at him with an effort.

'Lady Celia—' he sat back and looked at her, and he was smiling at her now, a kind, concerned, but indisputably amused smile. She felt irritated; that her ill-health might be a subject of amusement to him. It certainly didn't amuse her.

'Yes?'

'Lady Celia—' another silence, then he said, quite casually, 'there is – there is one question I haven't asked you.'

'Yes?'

'When did you last have a menstrual period?'

'All right Miss Barty?'

'Oh – yes thank you, Brunson.'

'Daniels is waiting with the car. To take you up to Lyttons. If you're ready.'

'Yes. Yes, I am.'

'You don't want any more lunch?'

'No. No thank you. It was very nice, but – well I'm not very hungry.'

'Of course not. Nothing destroys the appetite like nerves. I once appeared in a revue, when I was at my secondary school.'

'Did you, Brunson?' It was impossible to imagine Brunson appearing in anything less solemn than a morality play.

'I did indeed. I was so nervous that I couldn't swallow my supper the night before, never mind my breakfast or luncheon. But you know, the moment I got on the stage, said my first line – I felt quite different. Not nervous at all.'

'What was your first line, Brunson? Can you still remember it?'

'Indeed I can. It was, "Bring in the prisoners, Captain Cook". It was a sketch about some cowardly pirates who had run away. Quite funny, although I say it myself.'

'I'm sure it was. And you were—'

'The magistrate. Although, of course, what a magistrate was doing on board ship, I don't know. Anyway, I enjoyed it in the end, and so will you this afternoon. Cook and I were listening to you practising, we thought it sounded quite beautiful.'

Barty felt very touched; she stood on tiptoe and kissed Brunson on the cheek. Aunt Celia would probably have had a fit, she thought, watching him blush, hearing his embarrassed cough.

'Thank you so much, Brunson. I feel much braver suddenly. I'll tell you all about it later.'

'We shall enjoy that, miss. Don't forget your music.'

'Oh – no. No, I won't. Thank you.'

She took her music case; the letter was in it. As soon as she got to the office, she would give it to Wol. Although probably Aunt Celia would have told him whatever it was herself by now. Still it would be nice to hand it over.

She ran down the steps; Daniels was waiting with the car door open. It was the big car: the Rolls. He saluted her and then grinned.

'Good afternoon, Milady Barty. And what very fine weather we are having for the time of year. Where does her ladyship wish to go? Straight to her concert hall, or somewhere else along the way?'

Barty giggled. 'To Lyttons please, Daniels.'

'I have heard the crowds are already gathering the length of Wigmore Street for your concert,' said Daniels, 'and very wise of them too. Otherwise the seats might all be gone.'

He grinned at her; Barty got into the car and smiled back.

'Your music case, milady. It wouldn't do to forget that.'

'No Daniels, it certainly wouldn't.'

Celia felt as if she were falling very fast and suddenly into a large black hole. A hole filled with such horror and such terror that she gasped aloud, staring at Dr Perring. His expression was amused and gentle.

'I did wonder. Your breasts look rather – swollen. And the tiredness, the nausea – you had quite severe acidity when you were expecting the twins. But as you hadn't mentioned anything . . . You hadn't considered it?'

'No,' said Celia shaking her head, 'no.' And it was true, she hadn't; such a possibility, absurdly, had not entered her head. Of all her anxieties, this was one she had not considered, not contemplated even.

She sat there, her head whirling with dates, with events, trying to force some semblance of order into them. She had been so preoccupied, so absolutely absorbed in what was happening to her, on every level, that she had simply stopped taking note of the one most ordinary, most important, most crucial thing. When had it been, when had she last had a period? Since Glasgow? Yes, definitely since Glasgow. Since Oxford, that wonderful glorious night in the hotel in Woodstock? She had run absurd risks in getting away. Dreadfully reckless, in more ways than one. Think Celia, think. What had she done since then? Worked herself into the ground, gone to a lot of parties, and nightclubs, given a birthday party for the twins – and – yes, she'd had her period then, had thought it was the last straw with all those little girls coming. But since then – surely, surely – but no. Nothing. That had been the last time. And that had been May 6th. And now it was July. The middle of July – well nearly the end, actually. Oh, God. Dear, dear God. She was – or could be – over two months pregnant.

'I just never thought of it,' she said, and felt her eyes fill with tears. 'I don't know why.'

'Don't look so upset. It's not so serious, surely. Your husband will be thrilled. Do him good. He's been looking awfully tired and a bit down lately. I would say this will give him a new lease of life. Even if he does say it's the last thing he wanted.'

She was silent, hardly hearing what he said, questions, terrifying questions filling her head. How, when, where – and most terrifying, most dreadful – whose? Whose, whose, whose baby was it? It could as well be Oliver's as Sebastian's. He had made love to her, and a great deal more than once, over the past two months. And she always allowed him these days, never made excuses, never refused: simply because of her guilt. This child could have been conceived as easily in sadness and remorse with Oliver, as in joy and triumph with Sebastian. She had tried to be careful, had always been careful, indeed. But: well, her body and her fertility had betrayed her before. Several times.

She looked fearfully into the future, even an hour into the future, and knew her place in it to be absolutely altered. Forever. Whatever she did now, wherever she went, whoever she was with, it would be under changed circumstances, different rules. She was no long free to leave her husband because she might be carrying his child; she was not entitled to stay with her husband because she might be carrying her lover's. There was no escape for her, no hiding place; she and her baby were helplessly, hopelessly doomed.

'Oh dear,' she said, 'oh, Dr Perring,' and burst into tears.

He was very good, very gentle; he passed her a handkerchief, buzzed the nurse and told her to bring a cup of sweet tea and asked her if she would like to talk about whatever it was that was worrying her.

'I'm not – sure,' she said, leaning back in her chair, feeling so weak now, so shaken that she hardly knew where she was, 'I—'

And then remembered. Remembered the letter. And knew that whatever else she decided or did, she must stop Oliver reading it. It belonged to another life, that letter, another woman; it had nothing whatever to do with the new life and the woman she had so suddenly and dangerously become.

She must get home and get the letter and destroy it; it was the first and most important thing that this new woman had to do.

'Barty, dear, come along in. I'm afraid I have a bit of a disappointment for you.'

Barty was used to disappointment; her short life had had more than its fair share of it. Nevertheless, looking at Janet Gould's kindly face, she felt tears well in her eyes, a large lump in her throat. She knew what it must be, this particular disappointment: Wol couldn't come to the concert. Something had happened, some crisis had occurred, he had had to leave the office. And since Aunt Celia was not to come either, no one would be at the concert to hear her play.

She bit her lip, trying to stop it trembling. 'Yes?' she said carefully.

'Mr Lytton has had to go out for an hour or so. A meeting at the printers with Mr Jack. So he won't be able to travel to the concert with you. But he told me to tell you that he would be there, in plenty of time, and that you were to go ahead. He will be in the audience, in the front row—' she stopped and smiled – 'holding his thumbs, exactly as he promised.'

'Oh,' said Barty and although it would have been nice go with Wol, and although it would add slightly to the anxiety, fearing he might be late as he sometimes was, she felt almost perfectly happy again. 'Oh, that's fine, Mrs Gould. Thank you.'

And then she remembered the letter.

'Mrs Gould, will he be coming back here before the concert?'

'Oh, I think so dear, yes.'

'Well – could you give him this?' She rummaged in her music case. 'It's very important.'

Mrs Gould took the letter. 'Yes of course. And good luck, Barty. I will hold my thumbs too. I'm sure you'll be splendid.'

'Thank you.'

She turned, walked down the stairs, got into the car.

'We're to meet Mr Lytton at the concert hall, Daniels, after all.'

'Righty ho, milady. Off we jolly well go then.'

Daniels was much given to such racy expressions: reserved for the occasions when his employers were not listening. He was also given to admiring pretty girls and to enjoying their new short skirts; had that not been the case, had not one not just come into view at the end of Paternoster Row, had he not been eyeing her intently in the rear view mirror as he started the car and edged forward – perhaps more slowly than if she had not been there – he would not have seen Janet Gould running out of Lytton House and looking frantically after him, waving a letter. He stopped the car with a screech of brakes.

'Yes, Mrs Gould?'

'Oh, thank goodness I caught you. Here, Barty, you had better give this to Mr Lytton yourself. He isn't coming back here after all, he just telephoned. He'll go straight to the concert from the printers. All right, dear?'

'Yes, of course,' said Barty.

Dr Perring watched Celia thoughtfully as she pulled on her coat and hat with feverish haste, told him she had to get home quickly, at once, indeed, and told him that yes, of course she would take care of herself, and would come back in a fortnight for a further examination and she would give up smoking at once.

Finally, as she said goodbye to him at the door, he said, 'Would you like me to arrange for you to have a test?'

'A test?'

'Yes, a pregnancy test. Such things are now available. It seems to me you need to be absolutely certain about this. So that you can make your plans—'

He knows, Celia thought, aware of it, even through her panic and her fear; he knows, he has guessed. And was grateful; without being sure why.

'Yes,' she said, 'yes, pease I would like that.'

'Well, let me have a sample of your urine. A morning specimen if possible.'

She was fascinated. 'And what do you do with it?'

'It goes to a laboratory, where it's injected it into the body of a female toad. Then after twenty-one days, we do a dissection. If she has ovulated, it means that without doubt your pregnancy is confirmed.'

'Poor toad,' said Celia, amazed that even in her anguish she could feel such concern, and then, 'Dr Perring, I have to go. I'll bring you a specimen tomorrow. It would be very nice, as you say, to be sure.'

But driving down Harley Street, rather too fast, energised with adrenalin and panic, she thought that however sure she might be that she was pregnant, she could never, ever, be sure by whom. It was a dreadfully frightening thought.

'Oh – Brunson, hallo.'

'Lady Celia! We were not expecting you.' He sounded almost reproachful.

'No,' said Celia, 'no, I know.'

'A gentleman phoned for you, Lady Celia. Mr Brooke.'

Sebastian! She had forgotten about him. Waiting for her, waiting to greet her, to welcome her. Just forgotten him: had thought only of Oliver. Of keeping the letter from Oliver. How extraordinary.

'Thank you, Brunson. I'll – I'll telephone him. Now – I just wanted to get something. From Mr Lytton's study. And then I think – could you ask Cook to make me a cup of tea? Please.'

'Nothing else, Lady Celia?'

'No. No thank you. I may have something to eat later.'

'Very well.'

He disappeared through the door at the top of the kitchen stairs; Celia went into Oliver's study. The letter was not there.

'Susan! Susan are you down there? Brunson!' She stood at the top of the stairs, calling down to the kitchen.

'Yes, Lady Celia!'

Susan came up, looking nervous. She hadn't been with them very long and she was clumsy; she had already broken a small looking-glass and a china ornament. Lady Celia had been very nice about it but—

'Susan, there was a letter in Mr Lytton's study. On his desk. You haven't moved it, have you?'

'No, Lady Celia. It was there, I remember it when I was dusting. I didn't touch it.'

'Brunson, have you seen it?'

'No, Lady Celia. Here is your tea—'

'Leave it in the morning-room, Brunson. I have to find the letter, it's terribly important. Has anyone else been in there?'

'No, Lady Celia. No one at all.'

'Oh, God,' she felt furious suddenly, with herself, but more so with them.

'It's ridiculous. It must be found. It's terribly important. Someone must have moved it. Susan, would you go and look for it at once. A large white envelope, it must have been knocked on to the study floor – I'll go and look upstairs. Quickly now. I want it found.'

Fifteen minutes later the letter was not found. And Sebastian, telephoning again, anxious about her, heard her voice hysterically informing him that she couldn't talk to him now and that she would not be up at lunchtime as she had said and – and then the phone being slammed down again.

She felt suddenly faint; she sat down in the dining-room, put her head betwen her knees. And then, wearily straightening up, saw Brunson looking at her anxiously.

'Have you found the letter?'

'No. Lady Celia, are you all right?'

'I'm perfectly well, Brunson, thank you.'

'Lady Celia – forgive me. I think perhaps Miss Barty might have taken the letter. It has just occurred to me.'

'Barty! What one earth was she doing, taking my – Mr Lytton's letters? Why was she in his study at all? Why did you allow it? That was terribly irresponsible of you, Brunson.'

'She was in the study, taking a newspaper to read, and she was going to Lyttons, if you remember, Lady Celia.' His face was courteous, but his voice was mildly reproachful. 'It seems to me quite likely that she would have taken the letter to give to Mr Lytton.'

'Oh – yes. Yes, I see. Well I suppose it's possible. It was very naughty of her though, taking a personal letter like that. I'll – I'll telephone Mrs Gould, see what she says.'

They arrived at the concert hall about three quarters of an hour early. There was a small queue waiting outside; Daniels leapt out of his seat, opened the door for Barty with a flourish, half-bowed as she got out, handed her the music case. The small queue stared; Barty wasn't sure if she was glad or sorry.

'Good luck, Milady Barty. I'm sure it will go very well. I shall be waiting here for you afterwards.'

'Thank you, Daniels,' said Barty. If she hadn't felt so sick, she would have giggled. 'You can't see Wol – Mr Lytton anywhere can you?'

'Not yet. I should go in, if I were you. There's a lady there beckoning to you.'

'Oh – yes. It's Miss Harris.'

Miss Harris was her teacher; she smiled and came over.

'Barty dear, hallo. How nice you're in such good time. We can go through, and even have a run-through if you like.'

'That would be nice. Tell Mr Lytton, will you, Daniels, that I've gone in.'

'Of course.'

Celia felt quite calm suddenly; the eye of the storm, she supposed. It was certainly going to get very violent again. She had to get the letter. After that she could allow herself to think, to work out what she wanted, what she might do. But she could not be pressured by Oliver's

473

unhappiness, Sebastian's rage; neither could she even begin to think what she would tell either of them.

The concert started at two thirty; it was only quarter to two now. Oliver would probably get there at the last minute. She could wait outside for Barty and get the letter. It was the greatest luck, Oliver having to go to the printers. She ran down the steps and into her car and drove very fast towards Wigmore Street.

Barty came out on to the platform. She was the last to play before the interval. It had seemed a very long wait; all the others were terribly good. One boy had played an amazing violin solo: another girl a movement of the Elgar cello concerto. Hers was going to sound pretty silly. Miss Harris had kept smiling at her encouragingly, but it didn't help much. At one point she thought she might pass out, her heart was beating so fast and her hands were sweaty with fright. How could she possibly do this? She wouldn't even make it to the piano, never mind manage to play any notes at all.

But she did: she got there, to the piano and bowed, very slightly to the audience. And there, in the front row, was Wol; smiling up at her, looking so proud and yet so calm, so confident in her, and beside him, which was really lovely, was Uncle Jack, who grinned at her and gave her a huge wink. She suddenly felt quite different: calm and confident herself. She sat down at the piano, set her music down on the stand, and began to play.

'Daniels! Hallo.'

'Lady Celia. Good afternoon. Are you going in? The concert's started, I'm afraid. They've shut the doors.'

'Oh – have they?' She felt like crying. 'There was an accident on the Embankment. The car in front of me. The woman was hurt, the police came and I had to give a statement. I thought I'd never get here. Is – is my husband here?'

'He is indeed, Lady Celia. And Mr Jack Lytton as well.'

Jack! what was he doing here?

'I see,' she said. Her voice sounded bleak, even to her.

'Are you all right, Lady Celia? You look a little pale.'

'I – well, no, I don't feel terribly well, Daniels, no. So sorry. Perhaps I could—'

And for the second time that day, she almost fainted; Daniels was there, just in time, catching her as she half-slumped against him, making soothing noises, helping her to the car, easing her into the back seat.

'You sit there, Lady Celia. That's right. Put your head between your knees, gently now. Deep breaths. And again. That's very good.'

Gradually the nausea eased, the faintness passed. She sat up, slowly and cautiously. Daniels was standing by the side of the car, looking at her, very concerned.

'Is that better now?'

'Yes. Yes, thank you, Daniels. Thank you so much.'

'I have some brandy here.' He produced a small flask from the cocktail cabinet in the car, together with a cut-glass tumbler and poured a little of the brandy into it.

'Take just a few sips. Very slowly. It'll do you good.'

'I didn't know you had medical training, Daniels,' she said, smiling at him.

'Well – not exactly. My mother was a nurse.'

'I see.' She took a sip and then another; she felt much better: so much better that she could feel the panic rising again.

She was too late. Oliver was inside the concert hall and so was Barty; Barty would have given him the letter, he might even have read it. Whatever the case, there was no way she could get it now. Short of having a scene and demanding it back. Either from Barty or from Oliver himself. It couldn't be worse. It was a disaster. She was a disaster. Causing dreadful unhappiness whatever she did, wherever she went.

She sat back, leaned her head back wearily against the window. And suddenly saw on the dashboard, in front of Daniels, a large envelope. A large white envelope. With her own writing on it. Her own rather flamboyant writing, in black ink. Oliver, it said, Personal and Urgent.

It seemed to Celia the most beautiful thing she had ever seen. Half-laughing, half-crying, she said, 'Daniels, could you give me that letter, please. It's for my husband. I'll give it to him myself.'

Later, driving herself home, having assured Daniels that she was absolutely fine, she thought, with intense weariness, that in recovering the letter, she might have won a battle in the field of conflict that her life had become. But she didn't see how she could win the war. Or indeed what form winning the war might possibly take.

CHAPTER 26

'I'll tell you anything I can, of course. But I don't know how helpful it will be.'

'Anything would help. Anything that would clarify matters even a bit.'

'Yes, of course. I'm so sorry about this.' Jeremy Bateson picked up his coffee cup. 'I feel rather responsible.'

Peter Briscoe looked at him. He and Guy Worsley were astonishingly alike. They could have been brothers. Almost twins. Their mothers were sisters, of course, and they had grown up together; even so—

'I don't think you should feel responsible,' he said drily, and then managing a rather wintry smile, 'your cousin perhaps . . .'

'Oh don't,' said Guy. 'Please don't. I feel bad enough already. Mind if I smoke?'

'No, of course not. Help yourself.'

Briscoe passed him the silver cigarette box which stood on his desk, lit one himself, inhaled and blew out a line of smoke rings. They both gazed at him in awe. He smiled. 'Party trick. Now then, Mr Bateson. The thing is, we really need to know a great deal about these people. So that we can assess how close the libel might be, and how likely they really are to go ahead with trying to get an injunction.'

'Right-o. Fire away.'

'Well – first of all, this man, Lothian, what was he really like?'

'Oh – rather ridiculous, I'd say.'

'Ridiculous!'

'Yes. Dressed for an audience. All the time. Flowing cloaks, huge bow ties, that sort of thing. Long wavy hair. And he smoked through a long cigarette holder. I tell you, if it hadn't been for the wife and children, you might have thought he was, you know, queer.'

'Yes, I see. And what was the wife like?'

'Oh – rather grand. Very good-looking. Dark red hair, green eyes. Wore marvellous clothes. Even had a little car of her own. Always dashing about. She was the talk of the college. Most of the masters' wives were rather dowdy. Lot of money of her own.'

476

'And in the book,' said Guy, 'she certainly wasn't very attractive. She was rich, and all right, quite well-dressed and so on, but there the similiarity ends. Mrs Buchanan has a rather severe, forbidding personality. Although the students all like her, once they get to know her, especially the girls. Which is how it was this particular one, the one he has the affair with, comes to be at the house so often. And of course, she does leave Buchanan, when the affair comes to light. Mrs Lothian's still there, isn't she?' he added. His voice sounded rather desperate.

'Yes. And I certainly don't think people liked Mrs Lothian,' said Bateson, 'she didn't seem to have many friends. Certainly not in the university. In fact if anyone was having an affair in the family, it would have been her.'

Briscoe looked at him. 'Interesting. I wonder – well, let's get back to the facts. The children? What were they like?'

'Well, the daughter was a very nice girl. She was about twenty, I suppose in 1912. That's when I went up,' he added.

'And you completed your course? Left in 1915?'

'Yes. There wasn't conscription in those early years and I thought I would like to finish, get my degree. I took a bit of stick for it, even then.'

'That's why I made the son a conchie,' said Guy, 'They came under a lot of fire, those chaps, people said they were cowards. I thought it was really interesting.'

'Anyway,' said Bateson, 'Lothian's son certainly wasn't a conchie. He enlisted, went off to the war the minute he could. I remember seeing Lothian in the town, the day he went. He was sitting on a bench, and I said, "Hallo, sir", and he looked at me and his eyes were full of tears. I felt quite upset.'

'Did Lothian have much of a following? Among the students?'

'Yes, he was quite charismatic.'

'Let's get back to the children. This daughter, was she pretty?'

'No, not really. Shame, because both the parents were attractive. She was very shy, too. Everyone was quite surprised when she got engaged. Anyway, they never married, of course. He – well he got both his arms blown off.'

'How appalling,' said Briscoe.

'Yes. Quite early in the war, about 1916, I'd say. I'd gone by then, but we all kept in touch, and a friend who joined up after me, who was still there, told me. She still wanted to marry him, but he absolutely refused, said she'd be sacrificing herself. He went to live with his parents in Scotland or somewhere.'

'How very sad,' said Briscoe. 'What a lot of tragedies the war caused.'

'Indeed. Anyway, she's buried herself in her work, lecturing at one of the women's colleges. Lady Margaret Hall I think.'

'I made her a musician, of course,' said Guy 'and had the boyfriend killed, not injured. It seemed more – appropriate.'

'Mr Worsley, I have read the book. I am aware of the dissimiliarities, thank you.' Peter Briscoe was beginning to find Guy Worsley and his self-justification very trying. 'Mr Bateson, was there any real talk about Lothian having an affair?'

'A lot of talk, yes. He had a rather flirtatious manner. And he was the sort of person who attracts gossip. And about one girl in particular. She was at the house a lot. And he was seen with her, out for walks and in the town and so on. But then, she was originally befriended by Mrs Lothian, as I said.'

'But there was never any real scandal?'

'No. Well, nothing concrete. Not while I was there, anyway. Or afterwards, as far as I know. And – if you were having an affair with a student, you'd be a lot more discreet than that. I mean with hindsight, I'd say he rather worked the whole thing up. Out of a sense of mischief, you know?'

Briscoe looked at him thoughtfully. 'I think I know,' he said.

'So what we're left with,' he said to Oliver later, 'is a skeleton of similiarity. The master is horribly like your hero, and there was talk of an affair: apart from that, and the wife's money, there is very little they could point to. Well, a broken-hearted daughter, but for a very different cause.'

'So are you saying we don't have so much to worry about?' asked Oliver. He sounded hopeful. Briscoe looked at him; he looked weary almost to the point of sickness. The temptation to reassure him was almost overwhelming.

'I'm afraid we do have a considerable amount to worry about,' he said, 'It would be very wrong of me to tell you otherwise.'

'Mr Brooke to see you, Lady Celia.'

'I'm afraid I can't see him now. Tell him – ask him to wait in reception, please, Miss Scott. I'll come down in about quarter of an hour.'

'Certainly, Lady Celia.'

She had scarcely put the phone down when her door shot open and Sebastian came in. Celia could not remember seeing anyone so angry in her entire life: not her father when she had left a gate open to one of the fields and all the cattle had got out on to a main road; not her mother when she had told her she was pregnant and had to marry Oliver; not Oliver when he came back from the war and saw what she had done to Lyttons in his absence. On all those occasions she had felt able to face the anger, accept it, deal with its consequences, defend herself even. Today she was quite simply frightened. He slammed the door behind him, leaned against it. His voice was low, but violent.

'What exactly, in the name of God, do you think you're doing?' he said.

She was silent.

'You tell me you love me. You tell me you are going to leave your husband for me, you tell me you have told your husband the same-thing . . .'

'Sebastian, be quiet. This is no place for this discussion—'

'I am being quiet and this is the place for it. You tell me you are going to leave him, and on a particular day, at a particular hour. I wait for you, all day. For many, many hours. I telephone you and you tell me you will telephone me back. You don't. All day and all fucking night.'

'Sebastian, stop it.'

'—All fucking night I wait for you. Every car, every footstep I hear, I think is you. No message, no phone call, nothing. Absolutely nothing at all—'

'Sebastian, please—'

'And then today, you instruct me through your receptionist to wait another fucking fifteen minutes. Or fifteen hours. It would be all the same to you, no doubt. How dare you, Celia, how dare you treat me like this.'

'I—'

'No, don't. I don't want to hear explanations, or justifications, or pleas for time, or any other fucking, bloody filthy nonsense. Your behaviour is disgraceful, you are disgraceful. You lack courage and you lack integrity and you lack humanity and you even lack courtesy. I am disgusted by you, absolutely disgusted.'

She sat silent, staring at him, looking into the face of rage. He walked over to the sofas, sat down on one of them suddenly.

'I simply do not understand you, Celia. I do not understand you at all. What is the matter with you, how have you come to this?'

'Sebastian, please—'

'I'm going away,' he said, 'I've decided.'

'Going where?'

'To America.'

'America?'

'Yes. On an extended lecture tour. I've had an offer from an

479

American publisher. I've had enough of this. Of this and you. I hadn't told you, because I wasn't even prepared to consider it, thinking in my infinite foolishness that you might mean what you said, that you might actually be intending to come and live with me. There was always enough to discuss – all about you, needless to say. Sweet Jesus, was there a lot to discuss, Celia. Your husband, your children, your career, your life. I don't recall more than a phrase or two being thrown in my direction. I should have taken some kind of hint from that, I suppose. It should have given me some kind of clue to your self-obsession, to your total lack of interest in anything to do with me. Anyway, I'm going. And as soon as I possibly can: I cannot wait to get out of this city, this country, away from you and anything to do with you. Rather fortunate I hadn't actually signed that contract for *Meridian Times Two*. Macmillan have made me a very generous offer, and Collins are waiting with an even higher bid, I'm told. Paul Davis has been urging me to accept it. Of course I had said it was out of the quesiton. I find myself oddly eager to consider it now.'

'Sebastian, you can't do that.'

'Ah! So now we have it. That would be serious, wouldn't it? Never mind losing your lover. Losing your bestselling author, your discovery, your protégé. That would really hurt. Well, I hope it does, Celia. I hope it hurts you horribly and terribly. Hurts and humiliates you as much as you have hurt me.' He looked at her, then said more gently, 'I loved you so much. I would have done anything, anything in the world for you. I would have died for you, if you had asked me. Do you know that?'

She said nothing.

'I really don't think,' he said finally, 'that you know what love is at all. Except for yourself, of course. You are pretty well besotted with Lady Celia Lytton and that's about the beginning and end of it, as far as I can see.' He stood up. 'Goodbye, Celia. I do apologise for having taken up so much of your time. It must have been extremely inconvenient for you.'

'Celia, there is something I would like to talk to you about.'

'I'm sorry?'

She looked at Oliver across the dinner table; the day had passed, somehow, in a terrible haze of pain. She had no idea what she had done in those hours after Sebastian had gone; she had obviously remained in her office for the rest of the day, because Daniels had driven her and Oliver home together, and she must have signed some letters, because at one point a pile of them had been there, and then later had gone again, and she could see she must have checked some proofs for the same reason. She remembered dimly talking to Lady Annabel, and to Edgar Green, and she had obviously smoked several cigarettes, because her ashtray was rather distressingly full at the end of the day. Dr Perring would not have approved.

She had also, somehow, eaten some dinner; she had looked in surprise at her plate as Brunson had removed it and seen that it was at least half-empty, and the same applied to the wine Oliver had poured for her, it was no longer in the glass. But what she had eaten and what the wine had tasted like, even whether it had been red or white, she could no more have said than she could have walked on the surface of the Thames or flown through the air.

She looked at Oliver now, said, 'I'm sorry?' again, trying to make sense of his words.

'I said there was something I would like to discuss with you.'

Not now, dear God, not now, when it was finally too late; not now when the right moments, the proper opportunities had come and gone too many times; not now when everything was so desperately and dangerously changed; not now when she lacked the strength or the courage for any discussion at all, even the likelihood of an improvement in the weather.

'Oliver, I really am terribly tired,' she managed finally to say.

He looked at her intently. 'You look very pale.'

'I'm fine. Really.'

'Good. You must go to bed early, try to get some sleep. But before that, there is something I really think we should consider.'

'Yes?'

Not a holiday, please God, not even a weekend away with him, not time alone with him, misery, loneliness undiluted by work, the staff, the children.

'I think we have to discuss the condition of Lyttons with LM. Urgently.'

'With LM!'

'Yes. We are in considerable difficulties, I'm afraid. As a partner, she is entitled to know. And in any case, her views are always so sound, I would appreciate having them.'

'Considerable difficulties?' she said stupidly, incapable of imagining what they could be. 'What sort of difficulties, Oliver?'

He sighed, looked irritated. 'Well – this action of the Lothians obviously. For a start. That will cost us very dear, unless they drop it completely. Which is highly unlikely.'

'Yes, I know.'

This was better: distraction. Anaesthesia for the pain. It was real pain, like childbirth, coming in waves. Every now and again so bad she thought she must cry out with it, then receding again, leaving her exhausted, but briefly easier.

'And then – well I hadn't liked to trouble you today, you were obviously so very busy. But I fear we are about to lose Brooke.'

'Really?' Keep calm, don't look at him, have another glass of wine. How quickly, how very quickly he must have acted. Oh God. 'Surely not?'

'Yes, I'm afraid so. Paul Davis telephoned me today, Macmillan have made him an offer I cannot match. Certainly not at the moment. So—'

'How unfair,' she said carefully, 'after all that we've done for him.'

'Yes. But – well he has done a lot for us. Made us a great deal of money.'

'Even so—'

'Well, that's the name of the game. Authors do move around, don't they? Especially when they become valuable and powerful. I feel angry and hurt, of course I do, but I cannot, in all honesty, blame him. I am considering the matter, obviously but I don't think we can afford to keep him.'

'I'm so sorry, Oliver.' For it was her fault, in truth. Had she not fallen in love with Sebastian, had an affair with Sebastian, enraged and humiliated Sebastian, he would never have considered leaving Lyttons. Although they had never properly discussed what he would do if . . . Stop it, Celia. Concentrate.

'I'm sorry,' she said again.

'Well. There it is. And then—' he looked down, fiddled with his fruit knife, 'and then there is the matter of Jack's list.'

'Yes?'

'Although the Mutiny book will do tolerably well, I believe, it has been very expensive. Too expensive.' He hesitated, then finally met her eyes. 'An error of judgement on my part, I fear.'

That must have required great courage. She said gently, 'I have made a great many of those, Oliver. Besides, you don't know yet how well it will do.'

'I think I do. A limited sale, inevitably. And I have to say I'm unwilling to allow him to commission further books, for now, at least. A cheaply produced military book is a contradiction in terms. We need to invest in the backlist, and in authors who will sell in large quantities with any money we do have. So a decision must be taken there—' he looked at her, looked down at his wine glass. 'I'm actually talking about Jack's future here, you see. At very best, I'm going to have to tell him that there can't be any more military books for a year or so.'

'I do see. Yes.'

'And LM really must be consulted. Wouldn't you agree?'

'Yes, Oliver, of course I would agree.' And thought that really, LM would not be over-impressed with either of them; one way and another, they had managed to bring Lyttons to a dangerously low point.

'Lyttons have written back to say there is no question of the book, or indeed any part of it being rewritten,' said Howard Shaw, 'and that they intend to go ahead with publication, as planned.'

'I see. So—'

'So I think we should write back and say we are seeking an injunction to prevent them.'

'And you think we'll get it?'

'I'm fairly confident. If we don't, if the judge decides against us, and if they go ahead and publish, then we can certainly sue for libel. And I think we shall get considerable damages.'

There was a moment's hesitation; then Jasper Lothian pushed back his silver hair and said, 'Fine. Please do whatever you think best.'

'But I must ask you again — forgive me, but the judge will — there is absolutely no question of any uncomfortable details of your private life coming out in court?'

'Absolutely none. There was no liason with any girl, at any time.'

'And you are prepared to swear that on oath?'

'Of course.'

'I feel such a wretch,' said Guy Worsley gloomily, 'such a stupid, useless wretch.'

Jeremy Bateson looked at him; he was quite drunk, and he looked very tired.

'Well,' he said, rather helplessly, 'you didn't mean any harm.'

'No. Of course not. But how could I have been so foolish? I don't know, I just thought — it was so long ago—'

'Not so long.'

'I suppose not. But anything before the war seems in another lifetime.'

'Indeed it does.'

'And — I still think — well, I know that most of the book is entirely fiction. It was only the starting point.'

Bateson was silent.

'The girl—'

'Yes?'

'The one who there was talk about. I mean the particular one.'

'Yes.'

'I don't suppose – well, she's still there? At Cambridge?'

'Highly unlikely,' said Bateson with a grin, 'she must be twenty-four at least by now.'

'Yes. You don't remember her name?'

'Briscoe asked me the same thing today. I've racked my brains, but I really can't. I think her Christian name was Sarah. Or Sally. Or even Susan. Something beginning with S. But you know how it is, you always think that and then it turns out to be B or W. But I promised to look up the records. If I saw the name I'd certainly know it. I've got some old newspaper cuttings, details of degrees, you know I'm going to dig them out tonight.'

'Are they at your flat?'

'Yes.'

'I'll come and help you.'

Several hours later, Jeremy Bateson looked up from his piles of papers and grinned triumphantly at Guy.

'Got her!'

'No! Really?'

'Yup. Susannah! That was her. Susannah Bartlett. Graduated in 1915. Absolutely no doubt about it. God, so she's twenty-six now.'

'Fantastic!' said Guy, 'bloody fantastic. God, what a relief. Well done, Jeremy. Where does she live, how soon can we see her? Oh, I can't wait to tell old Lytton.'

'Hold on,' said Jeremy. 'That was five years ago. She could be anywhere. Anywhere at all.'

'How do we find her then?'

'We can write to the college authorities. Ask them if they have an address for her. That's the only thing we can do.'

'Well, come on,' said Guy, 'what are we waiting for? Give me some paper, Jem, and I'll write straight away. They're bound to know, aren't they?'

'The only thing they're bound to know, Guy, is where she was living then. She could have moved, married, left the country—'

'Well if we don't write, we certainly won't find her,' – said Guy impatiently. 'Don't be so pessimistic. This is a huge break, it's bound to help, surely to God.' Jeremy looked at him; he was standing up now, almost jumping up and down on the spot, pushing his hands through his already wild hair, his eyes shining. He was quite literally childlike, he thought, impetuous, impatient, full of endless enthusiasm and excited by ideas and possibilities. The very qualities which made him so brilliant a storyteller; the very ones that had led him and Lyttons into this appalling mess.

'Yes all right,' he said, 'I'll get you some paper.'

Lily looked at Jack; he had an absurd smile on his face, and he was standing on his chair, doing the one-step, really rather better than usual. She checked his glass: it was still almost full. But – he had a look about him that she didn't entirely like. Euphoric. Almost foolish. Brilliant-eyed. Lily knew that look. It was induced by cocaine. A lot of the girls in the show took cocaine; Lily herself had tried it, and thought it was wonderful, until a friend took too much champagne with hers, went into a coma and was rushed to hospital. Lily had never touched it since. Other people could take it if they liked; she didn't want to risk getting into that sort of condition.

But Jack had discovered it recently and was taking rather too much, Lily thought. They had been at a party when he first tried it; it was one of the theme parties that were so much the rage. In fact, you could hardly go to, or give, a party that wasn't a theme. Masked parties, Greek parties, circus parties, Mozart parties, swimming parties, treasure hunt parties, parties where you had to go as someone else. This particular party had been a treasure hunt and had turned into a motor chase across London, ending in a picnic breakfast on Hampstead Heath, where the final clue had been at the swimming ponds. And over breakfast, as the dawn broke, someone had offered somone else some cocaine, 'Just so we don't start feeling sad, now the party's over', and after a while everyone was taking some. Very little. Just a sprinkle in the breakfast champagne. And Jack had found himself feeling rather terrific, he said. And in no time at all was very enamoured of it indeed.

Well that was all right. He was over twenty-one, as he kept telling Lily when she fussed. And laughed at her stories of its dangers. She supposed it was all right, but it worried her a bit, and it was expensive – very expensive. Like most of his habits. And Lily, who was a sensible girl, could see he was spending a great deal more money than he actually had. He talked big, Jack did, about his important job in publishing and his army pension and his inheritance from his father. But Lily knew none of it actually added up to a row of beans. Well certainly not more than two rows.

She had seen the statement from the bank, last time it came; it had been lying on the table, in his flat. Jack was the reverse of secretive. And he had very little money in the bank indeed. He had long ago left Coutts, saying they were expensive; that wasn't quite true, but Lily did happen to know that they required a large amount of money be kept on deposit and that Jack didn't have a large amount of money to keep anywhere.

He was running up bills everywhere; at his tailors, at his bookmakers, at Berry Bros, the wine merchants, at his clubs. When he had been living at home, with Oliver and Celia, he had just about managed; now he had rent to pay and food to buy, and a servant: nothing grand, just a woman to clean the flat and do his laundry, but still her wages meant money that had to be found. He was drifting into debt with great speed. And it worried Lily a lot. She was ten years younger than Jack, but she felt ten years older. She felt responsible for him. Besides, she was terribly fond of him. It was impossible not to be fond of him, actually; he was kind and funny, insanely generous and incredibly affectionate. In fact, Lily had been heard to say, when she had enough champagne to loosen her tongue, which wasn't often, because she knew tongues were safer kept tight, she could, given half a chance, find herself in love with Jack.

She found herself worrying rather a lot these days, and not just about Jack's fondness for cocaine, but about where it all might lead. She had entered into the relationship because she liked and fancied him, he bought her nice presents and she had a great time with him. She had never expected anything more than that; getting so fond of him had been a bit of a shock. She wasn't sure how fond he was of her; he had certainly never said anything very serious about it, and she was quite sure he had never considered anything remotely permanent. Or even if it would be a good idea if he did. Of course, times had changed and class wasn't quite what it had been. Some girls had married into the aristocracy, most famously Gertie Miller who was now the Countess of Dudley and Rosie Boot of the Gaiety was Marchioness of Headfort. But it was still quite rare. And she wasn't sure if it was a good idea anyway.

Lily was a realist; she knew that once the first flush was over, there had to be a lot more than sex to make a marriage work. Her parents had a wonderfully happy marriage and she could see quite clearly why it was: they loved each other, of course, but more importantly, they were alike, they had the same background, they shared views on things, had the same ambitions and anxieties, the same hopes and fears. She and Jack could never be like that. Struggling to define the difference between the two of them, she had finally said to Crystal one night that Jack was rather like a racehorse, all flash and show, but only able to get from A to B when he was told exactly how and when, whereas she was like one of the wild ponies she had seen on a day trip to the New Forest, extremely fond of its freedom and good at looking after itself, and sorting out life without any help from anyone, as far as she could see.

'And I don't see that a wild pony and a racehorse could have much of a future together. Neither of them would really like what the other had to offer.'

Crystal said she could see what Lily meant, but added, with rare insight, that if push came to shove, the racehorse might be quite grateful for the wild pony, telling it where to go and when.

Anyway, for the time being, there was no need to think beyond the present. It was all much more satisfactory these days, with the little flat in Sloane Street to go to whenever they wanted. Or rather whenever she wanted; she'd had to be quite firm about that. Jack had clearly expected her virtually to move in with him, and had been outraged when she refused to go back with him on his second night.

'But you said I had to get a place,' he said plaintively, 'so we could be together and now you're leaving me alone in it.'

'I said you had to get a place because it was high time you did,' Lily said briskly, 'most men of thirty-five have their own homes, Jack, or where I come from they do. I never implied I was moving into it with you. That was not the arrangement at all, and I can't believe you were stupid enough to think it was. I like my independence, and if you haven't grasped that fact yet, then you don't understand me at all. Now I'm off, it's been a long day and I've got a big rehearsal tomorrow.'

She had left without so much as kissing him, and it had actually been quite hard not to laugh, looking at him staring up at her from their table in the restaurant, his mouth literally wide open. But her words clearly found their mark, because next day an enormous bunch of red roses arrived at the rehearsal rooms for her, with a card on them saying, 'Sorry, Jack', and a lot of kisses. He was very good at that sort of thing, Jack was. The generous gesture. But there it tended to stop. He certainly wasn't one for flowery phrases, unlike Crystal's boyfriend, who wrote her poetry and told her the stars shone out of her eyes, and life was empty if she wasn't beside him. If he had been, Lily thought she would probably giggle, rather than swoon into his arms, which is what Crystal was always saying she did.

Anyway, tonight she was clearly going to have to take him home. He was in a dangerous state, and she wasn't going to feel happy about him until he was safely tucked up in bed. With her. That would be fun. That was the other thing about cocaine of course, the thing Jack liked about it, and she liked about it, for that matter, was what it did to your sex life.

Jack was resistant to the idea of going home: 'I'm fine,' he kept saying, 'we're having a good time, what do you want to spoil it all for?'

Lily said she didn't want to spoil anything, but she was tired and wanted to get an early night; Jack said did that mean with him? And she said it might do, but not if he went on being so bloody stupid dancing on a chair that was clearly going to topple over. An hour later he had calmed down considerably and they were in a taxi on the way to Sloane Street. Everything was all right for a bit; he got some champagne out of the fridge and she said she thought they'd both had enough for now and he got quite grumpy with her, which was unlike him, and said he didn't like being told what he should and shouldn't drink, and then he sat down suddenly and stared into the fire, and she said was something the matter and he said no of course not, and she said she could see there was and went over and sat on his knee, and put her arms round him and asked him again what it was.

That was when he told her that his job at Lyttons wasn't working out quite how he had hoped and that there had been a big meeting that day with Oliver and Celia and his sister, and he might even have to think about doing something else altogether.

'And I can't begin to imagine what it might be. Not fit for anything much at all, really,' he said with a sigh and added gloomily that he was even thinking of going back into the army.

'At least I can do that. Do it well. Oh, come on, Lil,' he said suddenly, managing a smile as she kissed him, 'let's go to bed. That's a much better idea than all this serious stuff.'

It was: a much better idea. For hours it seemed to go on, wonderful bright, light, swooping, flying sex; she stopped worrying, stopped thinking of anything, stopped knowing anything but her body and what it needed and Jack's body and how it met those needs, surely and tenderly. Jack was not always the most sensitive person, but in bed he often became so: responsive, imaginative, careful, the near-to-perfect lover. And at the end of it, he fell asleep in her arms, peacefully happy, but Lily lay awake for a long time, her head full of images of riderless racehorses.

'LM,' said Celia, 'you will come to dine with us tonight, won't you?'

'I – can't do that,' said LM slightly stiffly, 'I'm afraid.'

'Oh. Oh, I see.' Celia was silent. She didn't look well, LM thought; the strain no doubt. 'well – if you change your mind.'

'I don't think I will,' said LM. 'I have a – great deal to do. Up at the house.' And wondered quite why she was being so secretive; and to Celia of all people.

Celia had always been so extraordinarily sensitive about LM's affairs, never pried, never so much as hinted she might want to know more than she was being told. But – well, she just didn't want to talk about Gordon Robinson. To anyone. Not even say that they were friends. Certainly not that they were going to the cinema this evening. Of course she hadn't ever wanted to talk about Jago. And that had been an important, a meaningful relationship. Gordon Robinson certainly wasn't anything of the sort. He was just – well someone she had come across.

Whose company very occasionally she shared. There simply was nothing to be said to anyone about him.

'I have a lot to do,' she added, more gently.

'Of course. I understand. Oh dear, LM, are you very cross with us?'

'Not cross,' said LM briskly, 'a bit dismayed. Very little of it is your fault, it seems to me. Rising costs affect everyone. This libel case – who could have foreseen that? But allowing Jack's book to cost so much, against such modest orders – that was foolish of Oliver, I feel.'

'You – you did encourage him to take Jack on,' said Celia.

'I know I did. But then to give him his head like that. Extremely stupid. He has no experience, no feeling for the business. I would have started him on a modest editing job – surely you could have guided Oliver there—'

'Not really,' said Celia briefly.

LM looked at her and sighed. 'Perhaps not. Oliver can be very stubborn. But Celia – losing Sebastian Brooke now – that is a pity. Surely you could have spoken to him? You seemed such good friends. Perhaps we could talk to him together, I could look at the figures, see if—'

She was unprepared for what happened next; Celia stood up, took a deep breath and walked over to her sofas, leaned down on one of them, her head bowed. Then she appeared to slump, and half fell on to her knees. LM shot forwards, caught her, and helped her round to the front of the sofa, laid her gently down.

'Celia! My dear, are you all right?'

She was a ghastly colour; greenish-white. 'Yes. Yes I'm fine. Just a little – airless in here. It's so hot at the moment.'

'You look terrible. I'll get Oliver.'

'No,' The word blazed out, 'no, LM, he is not to know.' And then more gently, 'He's got so many worries, he's such an old fusspot, please don't. But – well you could help me down to my car. In a minute. I might go home.'

'I shall drive your car,' said LM, 'you're not fit to drive yourself.'

'LM, no.'

'Celia, yes. And I shall tell Oliver we are going to talk through the Brooke problem in peace at home. All right?'

Celia nodded feebly. 'Yes, all right. As long as we don't actually have to. There's – well, there's nothing to be done about it. I'm afraid.'

LM drove her home in silence; she was concerned for her. But she was as unwilling to pry as Celia herself, so she said nothing except to comment on the weather, and to tell her how Jay was not only reading fluently now, but was showing a great interest in English history.

'Extraordinary, I think, for a seven-year-old, don't you?'

'Extraordinary,' said Celia, 'yes, LM, he's very clever. Very clever indeed'. And managed a half-smile.

When they reached Cheyne Walk, Celia said, 'I'll be fine now, LM. I know you've got things to do. Thank you.'

'I shall see you to your room,' said LM firmly.

It was very quiet in the house; the children were still at Ashingham. She went up to Celia's room, with her, helped her to the bed. 'You lie there quietly for a while. You probably just need some rest. You never get any. Anything you want?'

'I – well, a cup of tea would be nice. With sugar, please.'

LM went down to the hall; Brunson was waiting, looking anxious. 'Is everything all right, Miss Lytton?'

'Perfectly, Brunson, yes thank you. But Lady Celia would like a cup of tea. With sugar. She – she didn't feel very well in the office. So I brought her home. I'll take it up to her myself.'

'I'm sorry to hear that, Miss Lytton.'

While LM was waiting for Mary to appear with the tray, the telephone rang; Brunson took it. It was Oliver; a long conversation ensued. LM looked at her watch. It was getting late. And she wanted to see Celia again and to have her tea, before she left to meet Gordon Robinson. She decided to go down to the kitchen and get it herself. She went through the servants' door, started down the stairs.

And heard Daniels saying, 'Not well again, eh? What do you reckon, Mary?'

Mary said she was sure she didn't know what he meant.

'Course you do. Twice the other day, once today. Terrible, she looked, in my car, green as grass. Only one explanation for that sort of thing, if you ask me. I reckon we'll be hearing the patter of tiny feet in a few months.'

'Mr Daniels, that's quite enough from you,' said Cook. 'Mary, take this tray up to Miss Lytton and—'

LM went swiftly back to the hall, sat on the chair in the corner, pretending to read the paper. When she got to Celia's room, she said, just as Celia had said to her, all those years ago, 'Why didn't you tell me?'

'Don't tell Oliver, LM, please.' She sat, flushed now, sipping the tea, her eyes brilliant, almost feverish-looking. 'He doesn't know yet. He's so worried about everything, and he does fuss about me so much. Which actually doesn't help.'

'Of course not,' said LM, 'of course I won't. When – when is the baby due?'

'Oh – I'm not sure. It's such early days. I mean I might not even be pregnant. Dr Perring is doing a test. Even he couldn't be sure. But if I am, it would be February, I suppose.'

LM looked at her. 'It's unlike you to be so vague.'

'I – I know, but with all the other worries, somehow—' her voice tailed off.

'I won't say I envy you,' said LM smiling at her, 'but – well, I'm sure everyone will be pleased. And you like having babies, don't you?'

'Yes,' said Celia, 'yes, LM, I like having babies. Now off you go, I'll be fine.'

But as LM turned from the doorway to smile at her, she saw Celia wiping her eyes with the back of her hand.

The film was very good, a comedy with Charlie Chaplin, but it didn't properly distract LM. She sat, while everyone else – including Gordon Robinson, – laughed uproariously, worrying about Celia. Afterwards he suggested they went out to supper: 'Just a quick snack, some smoked salmon perhaps. At the Regent Palace.'

LM thanked him, but said she really ought to get back.

'Then I shall escort you home,' he said. She smiled at him; he was so nice. So gentle, so unselfish; he was obviously disappointed in the way the evening had gone, yet all he was concerned about was seeing her safely home.

'You mustn't think of it,' she said, 'I always see myself home.'

'Let me hire you a taxi.'

'No,' she said, 'no, of course not. I shall go on the train.'

'On your own! At this time of night?'

'Mr Robinson—'

'Gordon, please.'

'Gordon. And you must call me LM.'

'An unusual name.'

'I know. The letters stand for something too embarrassing to tell you.'

'Oh dear. Then I shan't ask. Now come along, my car is near here; I shall drive you home. I have no intention of letting you go on your own, and neither do I want you to go on the train.'

'But—'

'No buts. Come along. This way.'

They drove up to Hampstead in silence; but it was an easy, friendly silence. LM felt very happy suddenly. As they reached Fitzjohns Avenue, she said, 'Please do drop me off here. It gets complicated, all the little streets.'

'No,' he said; and then, 'you walk through these streets on your own? Late at night?'

'I used to,' she said, 'but of course now I'm mostly safe and sound in the country.'

'Thank God for that. Which way now?'

He refused to come in for a nightcap; he was clearly rather shocked that she even asked him. LM fell asleep, feeling less happy now, almost anxious. Their worlds were so far apart; he was so respectable, so very rigid in his vews and she – well she was an unmarried mother. This would never do. She would have to end it quickly. Before it all got any worse.

In the Westminster laboratory, the young woman bent over her specimen on the dissection bench, adjusted her spectacles, peered into her microscope for a second careful check and then filled in her report sheet very carefully and clearly. Precision was essential, in this work. Absolutely essential. Good news which might be bad: bad news which might be good. You could not afford to make a mistake. Well, this ought to be good news for someone: even if not for the toad.

CHAPTER 27

'Well, Lady Celia.' Dr Perring smiled at her.

She swallowed. 'Yes?'

'Good news.'

'Ah.' That was it then. Bad news. No room for hope, anywhere.

'You are indeed pregnant. From what you told me, about two and a half months. Perhaps a little more. Congratulations.'

'Thank you.' She tried to smile. She felt dull, heavy, utterly weary. He met her eyes, and something passed between them, something gentle, a kind of rapport, a sympathy.

'You must take care of yourself,' he said, 'given your history and if you will forgive the lack of gallantry, you are no longer – very young.'

'No,' she said, with a sigh, 'indeed I am not. Thirty-five.'

'Well – it won't be easy. But you are fortunate, you have a great deal of help and support. And I'm sure the other children will be delighted.'

Would they? Not if they knew that the baby was – might be – only a half-brother or sister, only half-related, that its father was not – might not be – their own beloved father. They would be hostile, angry with her, angry with the child, would take against it, on their father's behalf.

'And – your husband.'

'Yes?'

'Have you told him yet?'

'No. No I haven't.'

'Don't leave it too long,' he said, 'he deserves to know.'

Now what did that mean? So that Oliver could get rid of her, divorce her, throw her out? So that she could tell him she was leaving him, quickly, get it over? And – Sebastian? He deserved to know too. Or did he? Maybe not. Whatever she did, whatever she said it was wrong. Wrong to tell, wrong to keep silent: wrong to stay with Oliver, wrong to go.

'Mr Lytton isn't – very strong you know,' said Dr Perring.

'No, I know that.'

'Given his medical history, he achieves a great deal. I'm constantly surprised by him.'

'Yes,' she said, wondering where this was leading.

'A happy family is the greatest gift a man can have. You have given that to your husband, Lady Celia. You have made him very happy.'

'I – hope so.'

'You have. And happiness is the best medicine. This baby now could be a very large dose of it.'

'Yes,' she said and in that moment, from that word could, she knew he did realise, did understand. Was giving her some advice even; valuable, wise advice.

'I don't altogether like the way the world is going,' he said, beginning to pack up his bag. 'It seems to me we have lost a lot of the old values.'

'I – suppose so.' Don't start lecturing me, Dr Perring. Don't.

'Of course, everyone of my generation talks like this. I am a great deal older than you, nearer your father's age. I should be thinking of retirement in five years or so.' He smiled. 'But – the old ways still seem to me best. Marriage, the family, as a foundation for happiness. It can take quite a lot of punishment, you know, a good foundation. You can kick it around a fair bit. But knock it right away, or rather dig it right up, and the house falls down. On everyone inside it.'

She sat silent, staring at him. He thought she should stay: remain silent, go on with things as they were, pretend.

'Anyway, I must get on.' He smiled at her. 'I have always admired you, Lady Celia. The way you combine your career with your family. The courage you showed through the war, keeping Lyttons going. Your generosity to Barty—'

'Oh that,' she said and sighed, 'there are a great many people who criticise me for that.'

'I daresay there are. People love to criticise, to say what you should have done, what they would have done, when they usually do nothing at all, for anybody. Of course the situation isn't perfect for Barty. But you have given her a life and opportunities she would never have had. And when a charming and clever young woman takes her place in the world, a place she would never have dreamed of without you, then you will have enormous reason for pride.'

'Do you really think so?' Why was she crying? What was the matter with her now?

'Well, of course I do. Left where she was, she would probably be a mother herself by now. Buried beneath the struggle against dirt and exhaustion and poverty, like her own mother. Don't listen to others. Be pleased with yourself. About what you have done. As for those twins of yours – well—'

'My husband says they'll either end up in prison, or as the first women prime ministers,' said Celia, smiling at him through her tears.

'I'd say the latter. They're wonderful girls. Beautiful too, like their mother. And Giles, a young man now. You've made a marvellous family, my dear. It's not easy. And now you mustn't—'

'Mustn't what?' she said, 'tell me, Dr Perring, I need advice.'

'Oh dear me. Dangerous stuff, advice,' he said, 'All I was going to say was, you mustn't let yourself down. You must recognise how well you've done and go on doing it. That's all. Good morning. Now lots of rest, throw those cigarettes away, and come and see me in a month's time. Unless you want a consultation before that, of course. I'm always here.'

Celia went over to him and gave him a kiss.

'Thank you,' she said, 'I'm so grateful to you.'

Dr Perring's face was pink with pleasure. 'Good gracious,' he said, 'no need for gratitude. I just want you to be happy. Remember that. Really happy.'

Now who else had said that? Oh, yes, her mother. Be happy, or there's no point in it. Only she wasn't happy; she was dreadfully unhappy. And whatever she did, more unhappiness lay ahead, a frightening, forbidding thing.

Perhaps she should get rid of it. Rid of the baby. Perhaps that was the solution. It wasn't impossible. In fact it was quite easy. Provided you had money. It could be properly done, by a skilled surgeon, there was no need for old women in back streets with knitting needles. Now who could tell her about that? Bunty Winnington, she knew had had at least one abortion; Elspeth too, she thought. But – oh God, if she asked either of them, they would know. Know it was her, know why she had to have one. Know it was Sebastian's baby. No use saying a friend of hers needed to know. And the gossip would be worse, more horrendous than ever.

And as so often before, during the past few weeks, she wondered yet again how it was possible that Oliver had not heard the gossip, not been outraged by it, not confronted her with it. Why, why not?

'Oh, God,' she said aloud, resting her head in her arms on her desk, 'Dear God, what have I done? What have I done to everyone?'

The Secretary's Office
St Nicholas College
Cambridge
Dear Mr Bateson,

Thank you for your letter. It was good to hear that you survived the war so well, and that you are enjoying your teaching career.

I am able only to give you Miss Bartlett's family's address; she was not one of the students who remained in touch with the university and she has never returned for reunions. Her parents will presumably be able to redirect your letter and after that it will, of course, be up to her. The address is 42 Garden Road, Ealing, London, W5, and her father's name is Mr WE Bartlett. I do hope this is helpful and I look forward to seeing you at the next college reunion. Perhaps if you manage to locate her, you will be able to persuade Miss Bartlett to join you!

Yours sincerely,

W Stubbs

(Secretary, St Nicholas' College)

'Marvellous,' said Guy when Jeremy showed him the letter, 'bloody marvellous. Well done, old chap.'

'It was nothing. Let's just hope that Mr Stubbs isn't too friendly with old Lothian.'

'Even if he is, what interest could he possibly have?' said Guy, 'it's such an innocent request, after all.'

'It is indeed,' said Jeremy, 'now shall I write, or will you?'

'You actually knew her, didn't you?'

'Yes I did. Not well, but she'd remember my name.'

'Then you write. That way the letter can sound perfectly – or almost perfectly – innocent. You could say you just wanted to see her, in connection with a reunion. And then we could go along and see her together. If that's all right with you. I feel much more hopeful already.'

'Well – hold your horses,' said Jeremy, 'she might not agree. And even if she, does, and even if she talks openly, which is quite unlikely, she might have the worst news of all.'

'Which would be?'

'That the rumours were true. That she did have an affair with Lothian.'

'Oh God,' said Guy. 'I hadn't exactly thought of that.' There was a silence; then he rallied; 'I'm quite quite sure she didn't, though. I feel it in my bones.'

'So far,' said Jeremy, 'your bones haven't proved too reliable, have they?'

'Not so far, no,' said Guy humbly.

The children were all going back to London; Jay was outraged.

'It's not fair, why can't I come too?'

'You don't live there,' said Barty, 'lucky you.'

Giles looked at her. 'Don't you like London?'

'Not specially. I prefer the country. When I'm grown-up and a famous writer, I shall live somewhere near here.'

'You could live here.'

'No I couldn't, Giles. Don't be silly.'

'I'm not being silly. Why not?'

'Because I don't belong here. That's why not.'

She sounded and indeed felt irritable, as she often did when the question of her background was raised, however indirectly.

'Well—' Giles hesitated. She was flushed, visibly ruffled.

He felt awkward, sorry for her. He could see why she became upset; her position, as she got older, was so complex.

He often wondered if his mother had actually thought for more than five minutes before taking Barty home with her: probably not, she never seemed to think about anything properly. It would have seemed a good idea to her at the time, the right thing to do and she would have scooped Barty up, rather as if she was a stray puppy and set her down again in her new surroundings and expected her to be happy in them. Of course, in some ways, she was, but there had been some nasty moments, not least when she had been so ill that day: Giles could still remember how outraged he had felt, hearing Nanny lying about her, and telling her she was a guttersnipe, and his parents going off without knowing about any of it: well, they would have done, if he hadn't told them.

And the other children at school, being so beastly to her, that had been very hard. What would happen, and it was only a few years now, when she really grew up? Would she stay with the Lyttons, as another daughter, or would she finally go home to her own family? Surely not: although she often spoke of it with a sort of longing. It just wouldn't work, she wasn't like them, not any of them any more. Billy was a jolly nice chap, but there were light years between him and Barty in terms of education and – well just manners and the way they spoke. And what sort of person would she marry, someone who his mother would approve of, or someone her own mother and brothers and sisters knew? It would be terribly difficult for her. Anyway, lots of people would want to marry her, that was for sure. She was so pretty now and so jolly, Giles couldn't think of any girl whose company he enjoyed more.

This summer had been superb, he had taught her tennis and she played really quite well, and his grandmother had given them both some riding lessons. She was obviously scared at first, but she had gritted her teeth and got on with it, as Lady Beckenham had instructed and after a week or two, was trotting and even cantering quite competently. She wasn't as good as the twins, who might have been born on horses, so blithely brave were they, so easily and gracefully did they sit on the pony: so good indeed, that Lady Beckenham had bought another pony, so that they had one each. She entered them for all the local gymkhanas,

497

and at the end of the month, a row of red rosettes hung on the bridle rack in the ponies' stables.

'Anyway I want to get back,' said Barty now, 'because my mum isn't well.'

'Isn't she? I'm sorry.'

'No. She wasn't before I came down here. I had a letter from Frank the other day, and he said she's been rotten, and I want to get her to see a doctor.'

'She hasn't even seen a doctor?' said Giles incredulously, 'and she's been ill for weeks. Why on earth not?'

'Because, Giles,' said Barty with rather weary patience, 'she can't afford it. That's why.'

'Good Lord,' said Giles, 'how absolutely appalling.'

'Lily, get your coat.'

'What for? I'm quite happy here.'

'Treasure hunt. Really big one.'

'Jack, I'm a bit tired of treasure hunts.'

'No, but this one is special. Thirty of us so far, thirty cars that is, first clue is at Buckingham Palace. Come on, darling, we'll be last.'

'It's not a race is it?'

'Of course it's a race. No point in a treasure hunt if it's not.'

'Lily looked at him; he was flushed, he'd had too much to drink – and she had a busy day next day. She shook her head.

'No, Jack, I'm sorry, I really don't want to come. You go.'

It was the first time she had said that, had refused to go anywhere or do anything with him; he stared at her for a moment, his face shocked. Then he said, slowly and very reluctantly, 'No, I don't want to go without you, Lily. If you won't come, I'll just have to give it a miss.'

Lily hadn't expected that; she'd thought he'd just go, off like a small, sulky boy. She was profoundly touched.

'Well – well maybe I will. Just this once. Wait till I go to the cloakroom, get my coat. It's quite chilly for August.'

'Lily, you're a great girl,' said Jack.

'Good Lord,' said Oliver, 'Look at this.'

Celia took the paper; it was the *Daily Mail*. There was a picture on the front of what looked like fifty cars jammed in front of Buckingham Palace, and another photograph of a lot of young people, hanging out of several of the cars, all looking as if they had had very much too much to drink. The picture was captioned *Bright Young Things put in the dark.*

'Isn't that Jack's friend, Harry Cholmondley?' said Oliver.

'Where? Oh yes, I think it is. Jack was probably there, then.'

'He was lucky not to be in jail,' said Oliver, 'if he was. Listen, "The commotion at one in the morning outside Buckingham Palace as forty cars arrived, tyres screeching, had to be heard to be believed, a passer-by reported. Crowds of young people then jumped out and began rushing up and down the railings, shouting and pushing into the sentry boxes, looking for clues in a treasure hunt. The captain of the guard turned out all his available men and called for reinforcements, believing the palace to be under siege. The young people finally dispersed, after the clue they were looking for was found at the foot of the Queen Victoria memorial and sent them off to Trafalgar Square instead: but not before several had been arrested. Among them was Viscount Avondean, Lord Forrester, the Hon Henry Parker and" – oh God—'

'Jack?' said Celia, seeing his face.

'"And Jack Lytton, a member of the distinguished publishing family, accompanied by his friend Lily Fortescue, the well known actress".'

'Well known!' said Celia. 'Really—'

'Celia, please! "A senior policeman commented that they might all have been expected to know better, although conceding that for the most part it was obviously an expression of high spirits and that no great harm had actually been done". God, what do you think I should do?' said Oliver.

'Nothing,' said Celia wearily, 'he's a complete idiot, but he's thirty-five years old, for God's sake, and it's not as if you're his father.'

'I find it hard to believe he's that age,' said Oliver, 'when I think—'

Celia stood up. 'Excuse me, Oliver, please. I must get something from my room before we leave for the office.'

She just made her bathroom in time; this was awful. The nausea was getting worse. Well – it wasn't for much longer. She sat on the bed for a while, pulling herself together; then went slowly downstairs. Oliver was standing in the hall, looking very black, pulling on his gloves.

'He may be thirty-five, as you said, and I may not be his father, but I have to put up bail for him. His solicitor just telephoned.'

'Bail! How absurd.'

'Not really. There is such a thing as the law of the land. Jack has broken it, and rather publicly. Certain formalities have to be followed. So I'm going to Bow Street and you had better make your own way to the office.'

'Yes, all right.' That was a relief; if she was sick again, at least he wouldn't know. She felt too weak and wretched to give more than a moment's consideration to Jack. 'And I have an appointment later this morning. With – Gill. I'll be back at lunchtime.'

'Fine.'

She had finally decided to get rid of the baby. She had to: it was the only thing that made sense. She had telephoned Bunty Winnington, in spite of her misgivings, asked her for the name of her doctor, for a friend. Bunty had been very helpful, given her not only the name, but a telephone number as well.

'Tell your friend not to worry, darling. He's marvellous, absolutely the highest possible medical standard, and no fear of any comeback. As long as you're discreet, of course. Pricey though: seven hundred pounds now. Tell your friend he likes cash. Naturally.'

She was going to see him that morning; his consulting rooms were in Bayswater. Normally, Bunty had said, you were in the nursing home a week after that. 'Sooner sometimes. And home next day. Bit washed-out, tell your friend, but perfectly all right. Like a bad curse really. Good luck, darling. To your friend, that is.'

So in a week, it would be – could be over.

'Ten pounds! Oh all right. Here – I think that's right.'

'Thank you very much, sir. I'll have your brother brought up now, sir.'

'Is – is Miss Fortescue still here?'

'Who? Oh, the actress. No, she went hours ago. Sergeant, bring Mr Lytton up will you. There will be a charge, Mr Lytton, disturbance of the peace.'

'Yes, I see,' said Oliver. 'Well, thank you.'

He felt quite sick.

'I feel quite sick,' he said to Jack, 'it's an appalling way to behave. Drunk, I have no doubt—'

'Oh Wol, don't you start,' said Jack gloomily. He had adopted the children's name for Oliver years earlier. 'It could happen to anyone. Just bad luck.'

'Bad luck! Making so much commotion the royal guard had to be called out, getting thrown into jail, your name in the papers—'

'Is it? Good Lord!'

'Yes, it is, and it's nothing to be proud of. You're thirty-five Jack, for God's sake, not fifteen—'

'I know, I know. I'm sorry. If I say it was stupid and I'll never do it again, will that help?'

'I'm afraid I wouldn't believe you,' said Oliver. 'Why do you do it, Jack, what's the matter with you?'

'Probably being thirty-five,' said Jack gloomily, 'thirty-five and nothing to show for it. Getting drunk and having fun, that's just about all there is. Life isn't exactly rosy at the moment.'

'Isn't it? What's wrong? You've got a job and a decent place to live, and a very nice girlfriend—'

'I'm about to lose the job, aren't I?'

Oliver hesitated; then he said, 'Not lose it, of course not. But maybe it will – change a little. Anyway, I feel bad about it. Responsible. I shouldn't have entrusted you with so much so soon.'

'Well, never mind about that. And I may not have the girlfriend any more. She was pretty bloody furious with me—'

'I expect she was. Sensible girl, Lily.'

'And as for the place to live – well it's damned expensive. I'm always worried about money—'

'So you conserve it carefully,' said Oliver drily. 'Well you can always come home, you know. If you really can't afford your flat.'

'No thanks.'

Oliver looked at him. 'Why not? We miss you.'

Silence.

'Jack? Is something wrong? I do assure you, you would be very welcome to come back to Cheyne Walk. For a while, at least. Celia would love it, she misses you particularly, you cheer her up and—'

'Oliver, no. Thanks all the same.'

'Well, at least come to supper tonight and let's talk about it.'

'I'd rather not.'

'What, come to supper?'

'Yes. Since you ask.'

He was staring down into his coffee cup; Oliver looked at him intently.

'I don't understand. You used to be so happy with us—'

'Oliver,' said Jack in a sudden rush of words. 'Oliver, you've got to understand. I can't live with you any more.'

'With me?'

'No. With – with—'

'Celia?'

A long silence. Then, 'Well – yes.'

'But why? You've always been so fond of one another.'

'Let's just say we're not any more. Oh – it doesn't matter. I shouldn't have said anything. Sorry.'

Oliver looked at him very steadily across the table; then he said, 'No, Jack, you shouldn't. Shouldn't say harsh things about Celia.'

He was silent: Jack sat staring at him. 'You must know,' he said finally, 'you must.'

Oliver was silent.

'Oliver, why do you put up with it? How can you stand it?'

'Jack,' said Oliver, 'I really don't know what you're talking about. And I think it would be a good idea if we talked about something quite different. Like how you might deal with your debts.'

The doctor, whose name was Blake, was obnoxiously, smarmily polite, nauseatingly sympathetic. Celia told him, as instructed by Bunty, that she could not face another pregnancy.

'Of course I understand your dilemma Mrs, – ah yes, Mrs Jones. Several bad pregnancies, difficult births, severe post-natal depression. No, you certainly shouldn't have to go through it again. Your husband has no idea you're here, of course? No, I thought not. Good, good. Absolute discretion is our byword. Now, our nursing home is in Surrey. Near Godalming. It was a convalescent home in the war and is still used for that. Plus there is a small wing for minor surgical cases. The removal of ovarian cysts, fibroids, appendices, that sort of thing. Nothing too serious. I would like you to be there this Friday, at eleven. If the dates you have given me are correct, then we have very little time. After three months, as you will know, this sort of thing is impossible. You will be home by Saturday midday. I would prefer you to come in your own car, or a taxi of course. We find third parties on these occasions are simply – upsetting. For all concerned. Now – do you have the fee with you – good. In cash? Yes, excellent. Well good morning, Mrs Jones. I shall see you on Friday morning.'

Jasper Lothian was sitting on a bench in one of the lovely quadrangles in Cambridge, reading the *Times Educational Supplement* when he was interrupted by one of his least favourite voices.

'Professor Lothian! Good morning, sir. What a lovely day.'

'Indeed,' said Lothian, delving physically deeper into his paper.

'I hope I find you well, sir.'

'You do, Mr Stubbs, thank you. Very well.'

'I'm pleased to hear it, sir. And Mrs Lothian?'

'She is also in the best of health.'

'Good. Is your son enjoying his life—'

'Yes, thank you Mr Stubbs, I don't mean to be rude, but I have a great deal of reading to do this morning; perhaps you would—'

'Of course, sir. I do apologise, sir. Would you remember Mr Bateson?'

'Dimly,' said Lothian, 'but—'

'He was here at the beginning of the war. Nice young fellow.

Anyway, I heard from him a few days ago. Expressed an interest in the next college reunion. Just got the letter off to him now.'

'Really? Mr Stubbs, I—'

'I thought you might be pleased, because I know you used to tutor him. And he hasn't been up since the war.'

'That applies to a great many young men. Whose absence will be permanent. Unfortunately.'

'Indeed, sir. Most unfortunately. A whole generation wiped out. Dreadful. Dreadful.'

'Yes, indeed.'

Lothian gave up, put his paper down.

'Was there anything else you wanted to say Mr Stubbs?'

'Oh, not really, sir, no. I just thought you might be interested. Would enjoy seeing him. Strange he should have written now. After so long. And he was also trying to contact Miss Bartlett.'

A student of what was later known as body language would have found Lothian's speaking volumes at this point; he became very still, and his eyes focused intently on Mr Stubbs.

'Miss Bartlett?'

'Yes, sir. She was in your tutorial group, wasn't she?'

'No,' said Lothian. Very firmly.

'Oh, I apologise, sir, I thought she was. Well, anyway, he wanted her address. Mr Bateson I mean.'

'And – you've given it to him?'

'Well, of course, I only had her parents' address, sir. I gave him that, yes. They can forward the letter if they so desire. If she is no longer living with them. Of course she may be. You wouldn't know, I suppose, sir?'

'No, of course not,' said Jasper Lothian. 'Of course I don't know. Excuse me, Mr Stubbs. I have to get home.'

He walked very quickly back to his house in the college, went straight up to his study, wrote a letter, stuck a stamp on it and went out to the nearest letter-box. Then he sat down and, although it was still only just after eleven, had a very stiff drink.

'I would like to get home tomorrow,' said LM. 'The other children have gone and Jay will be miserable without them. And, of course, I miss him.'

Celia looked up at her wearily. It had been so good to have her in the office for a few days, receiving her wonderful, brisk common sense, knowing she was passing it on to Oliver, saying the kind of things that she would never have dared say. That Jack should not have been given his head, or allowed to waste so much money; that James Sharpe was spending far too much on coloured illustrations when simple line drawings would have done; that perhaps Oliver should consider taking out libel insurance, as several publishers were doing now. 'Too late for this time, but in future, I would propose it very strongly'; that perhaps Peter Briscoe, with his slow, careful ways was not quite the match for the cut-throat young fellow the Lothians were clearly employing; and that the editors should be trawling the agents energetically for a possible alternative work to *The Buchanans*.

'Of course we can't manage the autumn, but that is no reason for inertia. Christmas is just about possible.'

Celia knew she should have been doing that herself, but she felt too ill, was too wretched to do more than go through the motions of each day. Well, this was the last day; she was off in an hour. Then it would be over.

She had been trying, and had for the most part managed to overcome the sense of blind panic and searing misery which attacked her whenever she actually faced what was going to happen. She had kept her mind somehow turned away from the violation not only of herself, and of her uterus, but of everything she believed in and cared about. From the fact that she held within her all that remained of her love affair, her joyful, ecstatic exquisite love affair, or perhaps – and it had to be a real possibility – the last sad shreds of her marriage. She could not think about the fact that she was wilfully destroying it, brutally, savagely, destroying it, tearing it out, throwing it away; denying it its chance, its future, its potential for happiness. Of any pain to herself, any danger, any misery, she was quite careless. That would be her penance, almost welcome. And in an hour – no less than an hour now – the process would begin. In the name, she kept telling herself, of sanity, of common sense, of pragmatism. So that when it was over, she could begin again. It was the only possible decision to make, the only possible thing to do, the only possible way to be free.

'Mum? Mum, hallo! How are you? Oh, it's so nice to see you.'

Sylvia looked at her daughter with an odd blend of sadness and pride; she was growing up so fast, was so tall, so pretty. Her figure was developing now she couldn't help noticing that; her hair was beautifully cut in a long, curvy bob, her skin had turned a golden brown in the summer sun, her small, straight nose was covered in tiny freckles. No longer a child; almost a woman; a charming, clever, pretty woman. And she had had almost nothing to do with it herself; Barty might be her daughter, but she was Celia's creation. It was hard. But – Sylvia shook herself mentally. She didn't begrudge Barty any of it. She couldn't. And there was still room for pride.

'I'm fine, love,' she said, 'really, I am.'

'You don't look it.'

'Well I am.'

'Frank said you'd been bad again.'

'I am – sometimes. You know.'

Barty nodded earnestly. 'Yes, I do know. I remember when – well anyway, Mum, you are to see Dr Perring. Aunt Celia's doctor. It's all arranged. Daniels is coming for you on Monday and we're taking you to his rooms. In Harley Street.'

'Oh, Barty, not Monday, dear.'

'Why not? Why ever not?'

'Well because – because—' Sylvia stopped. 'It's just not a good time,' she said. 'Because of – well, you know, what we just said.'

'Oh. Oh I see. But – I thought that was when it was so bad. When it hurt so much.'

'It is, Barty. But I can't go to the doctor then. Can I?'

Barty thought for a bit. Then she said, 'Well, you could talk to him. And he could see how bad it was then. I mean that's quite good, I would have thought. In a way.'

'Barty—'

'No, Mum. I think we should go. He's a doctor, after all, Aunt Celia says they're never embarrassed by anything. Now, come on, let me make you a cup of tea. Cook sent you this lovely cake, and a pork pie for our lunch. And it's a nice day, we can sit outside in the sunshine, and I want to tell you all about what I've been doing. I can ride, Mum, ride a horse now. Lady Beckenham taught me. And Giles taught me to play tennis. And at the end of next week, we're all going to the seaside. To Cornwall. Come on, let me help you up the steps. Goodness, you're thin. I'm going to make you eat all that cake all by yourself.'

The two letters arrived at the Bartlett house on the same day; 'This one's from Professor Lothian', said Mary Bartlett.

'Well open it, then.'

'I will. It's to us both.'

'Give it to me.'

He slit it open, read it. Then he said, 'I'm not sure about that. It sounds a bit complicated.' He passed it to her. 'What do you think?'

She read it very slowly, twice. 'I don't know. I certainly don't want her upset.'

'No, of course not. But I never like opening her mail.'

'Nor do I. But if it is what Professor Lothian says – we should check it.'

'You think so?'

'Definitely. Yes. We can tell her it was a mistake. She won't mind.'

'All right,' said Mr Bartlett, 'here goes. If it is from this man – well, it could upset her.'

He opened the letter, read it carefully. Then he looked up.

'It is. So I think – don't you?'

'Oh I don't know,' said Mary Bartlett worriedly and went out to the kitchen to wash the floor.

'LM, I'm off in about quarter of an hour. I did hear what you said about going home, but I wish you'd reconsider it. Just for a few days.'

'Celia, I can't, I'm sorry. I'm worried about Jay.'

'Of course. But it's so wonderful having you here, like old times. I hadn't realised how alone I feel till you were here with me again. But anyway, can you stay at least until the end of the day?'

'Of course. As you won't be here. Where are you going?'

'Oh – to a meeting with some booksellers. In Guildford. And then to stay with a friend overnight. I'll be back in the morning.'

'You really don't look well,' said LM quietly, shutting the door behind her, 'do you really have to rush about like this? You should be taking things easy.'

'LM, it doesn't suit me to take things easy,' said Celia, managing a smile, and then, suddenly, she burst into tears. LM looked at her, then sat down on one of the sofas, patted the seat beside her, held out her arms. She was such an undemonstrative woman normally, that even in her misery, Celia was surprised. She sat down obediently beside her.

'I'm sorry,' she said, 'so sorry.'

'It's all right,' said LM. She put her arm round Celia's shoulders.

'Something's wrong isn't it? Something more than just being pregnant, I mean?'

'Yes,' said Celia, blowing her nose, 'but – well, I can't tell you about it. I'm sorry.'

'Why not? I hope you don't think I'd be shocked. Or even judgemental.'

Celia looked at her very steadily. Normally, she knew, LM would be neither. She longed more than anything at that moment to talk to her, to tell her, to get a brush of her pragmatic wisdom. But this was LM's brother, a beloved and much revered brother moreover, whom she had betrayed. It was impossible to talk to her about it.

'Of course not,' she said briskly, sitting up, blowing her nose. 'Of

506

course I don't. And it's nothing very – serious. Honestly. Now I must go. My car is downstairs.'

'You're not driving yourself?'

'Yes, of course. LM, I'm not ill. I hope,' she added carefully, for she had thought this through, as well. LM knew she was pregnant, would know she had gone away. She just might suspect something. Certain seeds needed to be planted. God, this affair had made her a mistress of deception.

'What do you mean?'

'Oh, I don't know. I just feel slightly odd. I was terribly sick this morning, I expect that's it. Anyway, I must be on my way.'

Somehow, once she had left the office, was in her car, she knew she would feel better. It would be irrevocable. No turning back. And there was no other way. No other way at all.

'Bye, dearest LM. I'll see you very soon. I'm hoping to come down to stay with my mother soon. Possibly when the children are in Cornwall.'

'Fine.'

Go on, Celia, walk out of the door. Then you've only got to get downstairs and into your car and then—

'Lady Celia.'

'Yes, Mrs Gould?'

'These page proofs have just come in. Mr Lytton said he particularly wanted you to see them.'

'I can't. Not now.' She felt an odd outrage that something should be managing to detain her.

'They're Lady Annabel's proofs. Mr Lytton did say I had to make sure you saw them.'

'Oh—' she hesitated. They were indeed crucially important. There were a few things which she had been worried about: chapter headings, the typesetting of the index, these needed the sort of attention only she could give. And it would only take half an hour. She hadn't got to check the whole damn book. She'd just have to do it now. Otherwise, there'd be terrible trouble next week. Life would be going on. Well most of it anyway . . . Resigning herself to thirty more minutes of churning misery, she sat down again and reached for her pencil.

'Is there anything we can do to speed up this action?' said Jasper Lothian.

Howard Shaw looked at him; he appeared extremely agitated. His always wild hair looked as if it had not been combed for a week and he was very pale. Even his hands looked pale, pale and clawlike. He really was not a very attractive man Still – he was the client.

'Well, we're giving them the full ten days if you remember. To reply to my last letter.'

'Which said?'

'That I was applying for an injunction, unless they gave me their written assurance that the book had been substantially rewritten or pulped.'

'Yes, I see. Well, I would prefer we didn't do that. Did you tell them they had ten days?'

'No. But it is usual to give a little grace.'

Lothian looked at him. 'But they haven't come back to us? There is no word?'

'No.'

'This is no occasion for grace, Mr Shaw. I want that book stopped.'

'Well,' said Howard Shaw, 'If we have representatives from both sides along, it could take quite a few days yet. A judge will want to read the material, will demand persuasive grounds for the action.'

'And if neither side is there? Wouldn't that be quicker?'

'Well—' Shaw hesitated, 'well, we can apply for an ex parte injunction'

'What's that?'

'A hearing when only we are present. But it's very unusual for a case of this sort and usually only used in emergencies, so that the other side doesn't have time to prepare, or attend court.'

Lothian frowned. 'That sounds attractive. But how would it be arranged?'

'It would be – arranged by applying for a court hearing to take place almost immediately.'

'But why should the court agree to that? I find that very hard to imagine.'

'If they hadn't been told about it.'

'Is that legal?'

'A letter could be held up. We could claim there was great urgency, and that the other party has still not come back to us. That much is true.'

Lothian hesitated. Then he said, 'I think that is what we should do.'

'Fine,' said Howard Shaw. 'I'll get to work on it straight away.'

Celia was sitting, trying to concentrate on the proofs, when she felt the first punch of pain. She ignored it, frowned, shifted; it came again.

Slightly stronger. She sat back, trying to analyse it; the third time she knew. She had felt it before. It was a miscarriage threatening. A miscarriage! The thing she had prayed for, longed for, fate's own solution, requiring no wickedness on her part, no brutal action. All she had to do was ignore it; there would be no need to do more, no need to drive to Godalming, to submit herself to Dr Blake, to have to live with that for the rest of her life. All she had to do was to stay here, to go on working, then perhaps walk round the block, before driving home, driving quite a long way round to get home, and then not go to bed and lie down, but busy herself there, maybe even turn out her desk as she had been promising herself she would, perhaps take another short walk before finally being forced to go to bed and call the doctor. Then she would lose the baby, and neither Oliver nor Sebastian need ever know, and she could decide what to do about her marriage and her future, untrammelled by this complex, confusing thing, that had to hurt someone almost unbearably and would at the same time make no one properly happy.

Here was her salvation; the god of women and female crises had heard her prayers and responded to them. She should thank him – or her – on bended knee.

Oliver saw Dr Perring's car outside the house as he parked his own. He looked at it fearfully, wondering what it signified. He slammed the door of his car shut, half-ran up the path and in the door. Brunson greeted him, took his coat.

'Why is Dr Perring here, Brunson? Who is ill?'

'Lady Celia is in bed, Mr Lytton. She instructed me to telephone Dr Perring. He has been here for about fifteen minutes.'

'And you don't know why?'

'No, sir. I don't.'

'Are all the children all right?'

'Perfectly well, Sir, yes. As far as I know. Miss Barty has gone to see her mother, Master Giles is upstairs and the twins are at a party.'

'Right. Good. Well – I'll be in my study, Brunson. If Dr Perring wants me.'

Dr Perring appeared a few minutes later.

'Ah, Oliver, Good to see you. Your wife asked me to tell you to go up as soon as you can.'

'Is she all right?'

'She's – fairly all right. I hope. But she'll tell you all about it.'

He was smiling: Oliver took heart from that. And went upstairs, two at a time, to see Celia. She was lying on the pillows, looking pale, but oddly happy. She patted the bed beside her and took his hand. 'Oliver,' she said, 'I've got something to tell you.'

It had been a moment of absolute revelation. That she could not, would not, was quite unable, indeed, to encourage that baby to miscarry. Any more than she would have been able, she could see quite clearly now, to keep her assignation with Dr Blake. She had sat there as one more pain came and went, thinking or rather trying to think, how pleased she was, what a sweet agony of relief it was, and then found herself gripped by panic. At the thought of losing the baby. For all the problems with which it presented her, all the decisions she would have to make, all the pain she would have to inflict, she wanted it fiercely and passionately. She wanted it and she wanted to keep it safe, wanted to care for it, wanted to love it. She could not have explained for a moment why: except that if a baby was an expression of love – and it was – then this one was a very loud and forceful one.

She had not acted at all honourably over the past few months; by forcing herself to go through this particular trauma, she would feel at least a little penance had been done. It was illogical in its own way; both Sebastian and Oliver might arguably have preferred to know nothing about it. About this child, this odd, half-legitimate, child. But neither would they have wanted it to be deliberately destroyed. She had no right to do that: to either of them. They had a claim on it – or one of them did – and it was not for her to renounce that claim. Even while shrinking from the moment of revelation to Sebastian, she knew now that it had to be done. It was the only good that could possibly come out of the whole thing.

'Dr Perring says I have to stay here for at least two weeks. Complete bed-rest. The – the pain is stopping already. And—'

'And no other signs?' he said delicately.

He was always embarrassed by anything remotely intimate. It was one of the reasons he never suspected any of her pregnancies. In the early days she had teased him about it, had talked frankly – country girl that she was – about her body and its functions, but it had never ceased to distress him, so she had given up. Even childbirth remained a mystery to him and although she was baffled, and sometimes even irritated that he turned away when she breast-fed a baby, she allowed him to do so without comment.

'No. Nothing. But there was definitely a danger. Well, there still is. But—'

'I'm so glad,' he said, leaning over and kissing her, 'so very glad.'

And even as she allowed him this happiness, not sure how long-lived it would be, she wondered, with a thud of panic if she had actually done the right thing. But shortly after that, she fell asleep; and although still anxious for more reasons than one, she slept better than she had for weeks, deeply and dreamlessly, and woke refreshed and feeling strong again.

CHAPTER 28

LM picked up the phone and dialled Sebastian's number. It could do, she reasoned, no harm and it just might do some good. She found his defection baffling; he had expressed such loyalty to Lyttons, had been so delighted with the way he had been published, and had even, Celia had said, been planning to waive his copyright fee on the second book. So why, suddenly? – Of course the male ego, combined with the author ego, was a capricious thing. But he had seemed such a friend of the family as well, part of Oliver and Celia's social set. Barty talked about him and his books endlessly. There was probably nothing she could do, but she felt it unlikely that Oliver, who was famous for his pride, would have put in a personal plea.

'Always remember, the authors come first,' Edgar Lytton had said to both her and Oliver as they learned their trade under his guidance. 'They are our treasure. Guard them carefully, cherish them. Without them we are nothing.' LM had a strong feeling that Sebastian had not been sufficiently cherished.

She was rather enjoying herself: it was Monday morning and she had the office to herself. Well, the main floor anyway. Oliver had gone to a meeting with some other publishers, to discuss whether or not they might band together to defeat the printers' outrageous demands and Celia was still at home in bed. She had been there all weekend: surprisingly docile. The children had been told simply that she was not very well, and Oliver had accepted LM's congratulations briefly, but refused to discuss it further. He had seemed rather tense; but then it was natural. There was considerable anxiety over Celia, she had miscarried before. Dr Perring called each day, twice on Saturday when she had complained of cramps. But this morning everything was feeling steadier, she said, smiling at LM; 'And no bleeding to talk of. So I'm – well – hopeful.' She reached out and touched the bedside table. 'I'm so grateful to you for staying, LM. It's very good of you. And with Jay coming up with Mama tomorrow, you shouldn't feel too anxious. He can stay here, he'll be perfectly happy, not lonely at all. He can even go to Cornwall with them all, if you like.'

'Oh I'm not sure about that,' said LM quickly. Visions of rising tides, giant waves, swirling currents, spun before her eyes. 'I think we'll be back at Ashingham by then.'

'Well, as you wish. Anyway, don't worry about him.'

'I presume your mother is coming to see you because she's heard about the baby,' said LM.

'Well – yes. Something like that,' said Celia.

LM had actually had a rather nice weekend; she and Gordon Robinson had gone to the theatre on Saturday night, and seen Lewis Casson and Sybil Thorndike in *Richard III* and then out to supper. On Sunday afternoon, they had taken a walk on Hampstead Heath and had tea at Jack Straw's Castle. She enjoyed his company increasingly; he was extremely cultured, compared the *Richard* with another at Stratford he had seen a year earlier, 'But I did prefer this one, without a doubt. It had more humour. Or should I say wit.' And it was so good to have someone to talk to: as an equal, an interesting equal. She had even managed to discuss – in very broad terms – Jay's schooling, in all its complexity. He had agreed with her that prep boarding schools were inhumanly cruel, that Jay should not be sent away.

'But I would have thought at thirteen, if he is as clever as you say, and if you can afford it, then he should have the opportunity to go to public school. I was at a day school myself: fee-paying, but still, it carried none of the cachet of public school. I have no doubt it held me back. I am sure Jay's father would not have wanted that.'

LM said that perhaps he would not, and thanked him for his thoughtfulness.

'It's so very hard to decide such things on one's own.'

'Of course,' he said, 'I'm no stranger to loneliness. I understand and sympathise.' It was an oddly poignant remark.

They had had supper at the Trocadero, and he actually agreed to a couple of glasses of wine: 'But no more; it goes to my head extremely fast,' and he raised his glass to her and said, 'to us,' in a way which was in no way coy or embarrassing, but entirely charming and rather serious.

The next day as they walked across the Heath, she had stumbled, and he had put his hand under her elbow to steady her and left it there for quite a while. So absurd, LM thought, to be so girlishly, so foolishly delighted by such a thing; but it was a long time since anyone had even looked at her, never mind admired her. She had been troubled, particularly in the early years of her solitary life, by physical frustration; had missed Jago's lovemaking, almost as much as she had missed his company, had found her body at times fretful and uncomfortable. But time and a solitary existence had almost removed such considerations; now, suddenly, in her pleasure and happiness, she was reminded of it, of the intense, warm, passionate pleasures of sex, found herself – although considerably against her will – imagining physical contact with Gordon Robinson. Imagining it and even longing for it, and dreading that he might in some way sense it. The only cloud over the weekend had been when he told her he had particularly enjoyed morning service that day.

'I try to go to a different church at least once a month. Today I went to Chelsea Old Church. A wonderful sermon, on the testing of faith. Such a very stimulating subject, I always find.'

LM lacked the courage to say she no longer had any faith to test; nor that she had not been to church for years, except for at Christmas. She worried about it for a few hours, then put it behind her. It wasn't as if she was going to enter into a proper relationship with Gordon; they were just friends, enjoying one another. And friends did not have to share views on everything.

The phone was answered. 'Primrose Hill 729.'

'Ah. Is Mr Brooke there?'

'No. No, I'm afraid he's not. You've just missed him as a matter of fact. He's gone to pick up his ticket.'

'His ticket?'

'Yes, he's off on a trip on Friday. To America.'

'America!'

'Yes. On a lecture tour. Anyway, I'll tell him you called. Shouldn't be long. What name shall I say?'

'Lytton. Miss—'

'Oh, Lady Celia, I didn't recognise your voice. Silly of me. You sound different. Very well then. Soon as he gets in.'

'I'm not—' said LM, but the phone went dead.

'Still nothing from Miss Bartlett? Or her parents?' said Guy.

'Nope. Nothing. Sorry.'

'Damn. Damn, damn, damn. What can have happened?'

'God knows. God only knows.'

'I have found a judge,' said Howard Shaw, 'and we can see him on Wednesday morning, for the hearing.'

'Excellent. And—'

'Well, I have written to Peter Briscoe, the Lyttons' solicitor, informing him, naturally. We can only hope now that the secretary gets it typed and into the post in time. And that the address I have given her is absolutely correct. But I daresay it is.'

'Excellent,' said Jasper Lothian, 'I'm most impressed, Mr Shaw.'

'Oh, Mr Brooke, there you are. Got your ticket all right?'

'Yes,' said Sebastian abruptly. 'I'd like a coffee. Straight away, if you please. In my study.'

'Yes. Mr Brooke—'

'Mrs Conley, I said straight away. If there are any messages, I'll hear about them later.'

He walked out of the room; Mrs Conley watched him and sighed. He was very bad-tempered these days. She'd be quite glad when he'd gone. Maybe the phone call from Lady Celia would cheer him up.

'I wondered,' said Harry Cholmondley, 'if you'd like to be my best man.'

'Like it? My dear old chap, wonder no more. I'd be thrilled. Thrilled and proud. Who's the lucky girl? Daphne, I presume?'

'Oh – yes. Yes, of course. She accepted me last night. Everyone seems pretty pleased.'

'I'm sure they are,' said Jack. 'Well, congratulations, old man. Well done. I envy you, I must say.'

'Well – you too could be a bridgeroom, Jack. If you wanted.'

'I don't think so,' said Jack. He sounded rather subdued.

'Why on earth not?'

'Oh – I'm a bit off the idea of marriage,' said Jack, 'actually.'

'You are? What on earth for?'

'I – just am. I'm not sure that it works. Oh good Lord—' he stared at Cholmondley, went rather pink, 'now I've upset you. Sorry, old man. Didn't mean anything of the sort, really.'

'That's all right. Anyway, I'm sure you're wrong. Most people seem to find it the best thing.'

'Yes, I suppose so.'

'You should marry Lily, you know. She's such a great girl, one in a million, I'd say, even if she is – oh Lord.' He cleared his throat, took a large slug of whisky, 'sorry old man, didn't mean any offence.'

'None taken,' said Jack, 'I know what you mean but I simply couldn't care less about it.'

'Good man. Fearfully old-fashioned that sort of thing. Look at Rosie after all. And Gertie. And Lily obviously loves you.'

'Do you think so?'

'Of course I do. You can marry Lily and I can marry Daphne and we'll both be very happy. Bet you.'

'I'm still not sure,' said Jack

'Well think about it. For my sake.'

'Yes. All right, I will. Anyway,' he added with a sigh, 'I haven't got any money.'

'Nor have I, old man.'

'Harry,' said Jack, 'you have an estate of three thousand acres in Scotland, another of two thousand in Wiltshire and a very nice house in London. How can you say you haven't got any money?'

'I know, I know, but it all costs a packet. All the servants in London, you know, eating their heads off all year round, and the farms hardly showing any profit, and—'

'You sound like Lady Beckenham,' said Jack.

'Do I? I like her. Awfully jolly old trout. You should talk to her about getting married. She'd set you right.'

'I don't think she'd exactly approve of Lily,' said Jack.

'Are you sure it was Lady Celia?' said Sebastian.

Mrs Conley sighed. 'Of course I'm sure. She said it was. And to ring her the minute you got in.'

'Oh. All right. Well thank you. I will.'

'I'm sorry, Mr Brooke, Lady Celia isn't here. Could it have been Miss—'

'It couldn't have been anyone else. I had a message to ring her. My housekeeper is hardly going to make a mistake of that sort. Please put me through.' Then, as Margaret Jones hesitated, he said, 'Oh for God's sake. This is urgent.'

He sounded furious; Margaret Jones considered what to do. Lady Celia certainly wasn't here, and was unlikely to have phoned anyone, she was at home in bed, resting. Then she realised: It must have been Miss Lytton who had left the message. She could put Sebastian through to her; she was a sensible person, she would calm him down.

'Just a moment, please, Mr Brooke,' she said.

LM was working on the costings of *Queen of Sorrows* when the phone rang; she was so engrossed that she left it for a couple of rings before picking it up.

'Mr Brooke for you, Miss Lytton.'

'Oh – thank you. Put him through.'

'Celia? Sebastian. What is it, what's happened, have you finally come to your senses, have you overcome your wifely principles? Come on, you'd better tell me, and it had better be good, I've been through two weeks of hell waiting for some word from you—'

There was a silence; then LM said carefully, 'Mr Brooke, this is not Celia. It is Miss Lytton. It was I who called you.'

Celia lay in bed, looking rather warily at her mother. Lady Beckenham had arrived, demanded coffee and toast, handed Jay over to Nanny and the delighted twins, instructed Mary that they were not to be disturbed and settled in the large chair by the window, all in the space of rather less than five minutes.

'I thought,' she said, 'you would need someone to talk to.'

'I – do,' said Celia, 'yes.'

'How are you feeling?'

'Sick. Terribly.'

'Baby still in place?'

'Yes. Very firmly so, I'd say.'

'Good. Or is it?'

'What?'

'I said is it good? Or would you have wished it away?'

'I thought I would,' said Celia simply, 'but when it seemed to be going, I knew I wanted to keep it.'

'Right. And now I suppose you're wondering whose it is.'

'Well—'

'Oh come along, Celia,' said her mother impatiently, 'I'm not a fool and neither are you. Of course you are. You're thinking it could be Oliver's and it could be this other man's. Am I right?'

'Well – yes.'

'And you don't know what to do, or what to say?'

'Yes. That's exactly right. I simply don't know what to do. About any of it.'

'Oh Lord,' said Sebastian. There was a very long silence. 'I'm so sorry, Miss Lytton. I didn't mean to sound rude.'

'You didn't exactly sound rude,' said LM. 'Just a little abrupt.'

'Well, I'm sorry for that, too.'

'That's perfectly all right.'

'But someone did phone me. I thought it was – Celia.'

'Someone did. It was I.'

'Oh, I see.' Another silence. LM could hear him thinking. And saw the shadowy shape which had been troubling and puzzling her slowly form itself into a clear outline.

'Er – what about?'

'About what, Mr Brooke?'

'Oh sorry, I'm not making much sense. You telephoned me. What was it about?'

'Ah yes.' She cleared her throat, wished she could clear her mind. 'It was about – about your leaving Lyttons.'

'Ye-es?'

He sounded wary now. She paused. It had seemed such a simple conversation; now it was very complex.

'It seems such a pity,' she said, finally.

'It is a pity, It is indeed. But – Macmillan and Collins made me extraordinarily generous offers; and now Dawsons have topped both of them. I'm sorry, Miss Lytton, I found them too tempting.'

'Yes,' she said, 'yes, well, I can understand that. But I thought you were so pleased with Lyttons.'

'I was. Desperately pleased.'

A funny word to use; but then she supposed they were both talking in riddles now.

'Well then – long term surely—'

'Miss Lytton, there seemed to be no long term with Lyttons any more. It is hard to explain but—'

'I don't think you have to,' she said, 'actually. And of course money is very important. Well, if I really cannot persuade you . . .'

'No,' he said, 'no, I fear you cannot.'

'A pity.'

'Yes. A great pity and I do appreciate all that Lyttons have done for me.'

'If you did,' she said, and her voice was cooller now, 'if you properly appreciated it, you would not be leaving.'

'Well there are you wrong, Miss Lytton. There you are terribly wrong. I'm sorry.'

She was silent.

Finally he said 'Is – is Celia there?'

'No,' she said without thinking, 'no, she's ill.'

'Ill?'

'Yes.' Damn. That was a mistake. She really, really didn't want to tell him in what way and why. Not now. Didn't want to think about it, even.

'Is it serious?'

'Oh no. No it isn't serious. Just – just a cold.'

'Oh. Her cough. She did have a cough.'

'She did indeed. She does still.'

'Yes. Well give her my best wishes.'

'I will. thank you. And enjoy your new publishers, won't you?'

'I'll try to.'

Sebastian rang off; he felt rather sick. There was no doubt the old girl had worked it out. She was very sharp. Now what? Oh, what did it matter? It was over, everything was over. People could think what they liked. He didn't care. Life was so hideous already, it couldn't get worse.

He was sorry Celia was ill, though; she hadn't seemed well for a few weeks. She smoked too much. He'd told her she had to stop when she came to live with him. He hated smoking. Especially women who smoked. She'd gone to the doctor that morning; the morning she was supposed to arrive. That was when all the trouble had started – with that visit to the doctor. She'd been coming straight on to him and she'd never arrived. She—

A sharp shard of suspicion suddenly pierced Sebastian's brain. More than suspicion, revelation. Bright, hard revelation. Revelation and anger. That was it: of course. It all made sense. The sudden withdrawal, the refusal to talk, to see him. The panic, the near-fear in her voice. It had baffled him at the time; but – would she have done that? could she have done that? Not told him, hidden herself and it away? Surely, surely not. It was unforgivable. If it was true. He picked up the phone again, dialled Lyttons' number, asked for LM. She answered, sounding wary.

'Yes.'

'Miss Lytton,' he said, and his voice sounded very strange, even to him, 'Miss Lytton, is Celia – is she pregnant?'

'I'll tell you whose baby it is,' said Lady Beckenham.

'Oh Mama, don't be absurd. How can you tell me, how can you know?'

'It's Oliver's. And I do know.'

'But how?'

'He's your husband. He's lived with you all these years. He's kept you, looked after you, fathered all your children and oh, yes, I know, bored you to death, criticised you, all those things. This is his baby, Celia. There can be no doubt about it.'

'Mama—'

'Celia,' said her mother and her blue eyes were very hard, 'Celia, Beckenhams don't have bastards. Well—' she added, with a rather cool smile, 'Beckenham women don't have bastards.'

'This is ridiculous,' said Celia. She reached out, took a drink of water.

'It is not ridiculous. It is common sense. It's about values and standards and society and keeping your family intact. So you think this child might be your lover's. What are you doing to do? Rush off to him with it, bring it up illegitimate, break up your own family, tear your chidren apart.'

'Well—'

'For God's sake. Pull yourself together. You've had your fun, Celia. Now get back to real life.'

Celia sat staring at her; her eyes filled with tears. She bit her lip, took a deep breath.

'You don't know—' she said, 'you just don't know how bad I feel.'

Lady Beckenham looked at her and her face softened. She went over to her, sat on the bed, took Celia's hand.

'Listen,' she said, 'I'll tell you something. I never thought to, but this is the time for you to hear it. I was once – in your situation. Well, you know about Paget, but – it went further than that. I was pregnant. But I didn't even consider that it might be his. Not for a moment. I just put it out of my head. And when you were born—'

'Me!'

'Yes, you. I knew I was right. I looked at you, Beckenham to the last black eyelash – Paget had those awful pale things – and I knew I'd been right all along. You were Beckenham's child and this child is Oliver's. Whatever happens. Now you put the rest behind you and just get on with it. It's not just good advice, Celia; it's the only advice. Oh, Lord, I can hear those dreadful children of yours. What are they doing?'

'Sliding down the bannisters,' said Celia. Her voice was so thick with tears she could hardly get the words out.

'Oh, for heaven's sake. You can't allow that. It's dangerous. I'm going to stop them. Venetia! Adele! Get off there at once. At once do you hear me. You know I don't allow it at Ashingham, and your mother shouldn't allow it here. Where's Jay?'

'Up there,' said Adele. Lady Beckenham looked up and saw Jay's sturdy backside descending towards her at a great rate from at least fifteen feet above her head. She closed her eyes briefly and thanked God that LM was several miles away.

'I think we should all go out for a long walk,' she said, when he was finally safely down. 'Come along, I'll tell Cook to make up a picnic.'

Sylvia sat in her chair, quite literally doubled up with pain. She had never experienced anything like it: not ever. It was like fire – no more like hot blades – inside her. She felt dreadful altogether, terribly sick and she had a bad headache. And she was hot. Barty was coming with the car to take her to the doctor. Well she couldn't go. She just couldn't.

She shifted slightly and even that small effort made her groan aloud; it was terrible, truly terrible and—

'Mum! We're here. You all right?'

'Not – not too good,' said Sylvia. Even speaking somehow hurt.

Barty appeared in the doorway. 'Mum, you look awful. Oh, dear, what can I do, how can I help—'

'Oh I'm all right' said Sylvia, 'but Barty, I don't think I can go today. I told you it was bad timing.'

'Yes, but I can't leave you here. Like this. Look, everything's changed anyway, Aunt Celia's at home in bed, she's not very well, so Dr Perring is coming this afternoon and he can see you there. That'll be much better, won't it? And he'll know what to do, I'm sure he can help. Oh, Mum – you're so hot—'

Daniels came down the steps. 'Everything all right, Milady?'

'No. Not really. My mother's not at all well. But I still think we should take her home, don't you?'

'Oh, rather.'

'But I can't move,' said Sylvia, 'I really can't.'

'I'll carry you,' said Daniels, 'come on, Miss Barty, hold the door open, and now the car, that's right. There you are, Mrs Miller, let's lie you down on that seat. That's the way. Here, use this rug as a pillow. Brandy?'

Sylvia shook her head feebly.

'Right then, off we go.'

'You ought to have been an ambulance driver, Daniels,' said Barty.

'Funny you should say that. I've often thought of it. My brother was one in the war. Money's bad though. And I'm trying to save for a place of me own.'

'Are you Daniels?' said Barty. She sounded quite upset. 'I hope you won't be leaving us.'

'Don't worry, Milady. If I leave, I'll take you with me.'

'Lady Celia, there's a gentleman to see you.'

'A gentleman?' Who was it, Jack, Dr Perring?

'Yes. A Mr—'

Mary was interrupted; Sebastian appeared in the doorway. He looked completely dishevelled, his hair wild, his eyes shocked, his tie loosened, his jacket undone. It was over three weeks since Celia had seen him; the violence of what she felt made her literally faint.

She lay back on the pillows, briefly closed her eyes.

'Lady Celia if you're not feeling well—' Mary looked anxious.

'It's all right, Mary. Really. Mr Brooke may come in.'

'Shall I bring you anything?'

'Oh – no. No it's all right, thank you. Unless Sebastian, you'd like something to drink?'

'No,' he said, impatiently. 'No, nothing. Thank you.'

Mary withdrew; Sebastian closed the door behind him. He stood looking at her for a long time; his face absolutely tender, totally concerned.

'Why didn't you tell me?' he said.

Then he came over to the bed, and took her hand and kissed her on the forehead.

'I love you,' he said, 'I love you so very, very much. More than ever now. So much more than ever.'

For the second time that morning, Celia started to cry.

CHAPTER 29

'Ovarian cyst,' said Dr Perring, examining Sylvia's abdomen as gently as he could. And adding in a lower voice to Celia, 'infected, I would say. She should really be in hospital.'

Sylvia's eyes, already wide with pain, filled with terror as well.

'Oh no,' she said, 'not hospital, please not hospital.'

'Well – we'll see.' He patted her shoulder gently, pulled the bedcovers up. She had been put to bed in Jack's old room; Barty sat outside, waiting while he examined her. 'Lady Celia, you should be in bed.'

'I know. But she seemed so ill and so upset, I thought I should be with her for a bit. And Barty.'

'Let's go outside and talk about it.'

He led her out to the landing; Barty jumped up. 'Is she – all right?'

'She's not very well, I'm afraid. But we shall make her better. Now, the best thing you can do is sponge her down for a little while and get her to drink plenty of water. Can you manage that?'

She nodded. 'Of course.'

'Good girl. I'll come up again before I leave. Don't worry, your mother's very strong.'

'Which you are not,' he said sternly to Celia, following her to her own room, settling her back into bed. 'I told you, any exertion and you'll lose that baby.'

'I'm sorry.'

He looked at her; she seemed very upset, had obviously been crying. She was pale, and her eyes were heavy and shadowed.

'You must try to be calm,' he said gently, 'it's important. Nothing matters more than this baby, you know. Try to rememer that.'

'I will,' she said, 'really, I will.'

'Good. Now, any more pains?'

'No. None.'

'No bleeding?'

'No.'

'Backache? Headache?'

'No, really.'

'Good. Well, we seem to be keeping him there for the time being.'

'Him?'

'Or her. Actually if it's her, there's more of a chance, you know. Girls are tougher.'

'They certainly are in this family,' said Celia.

'I think I would agree with that,' he said, smiling at her gently, 'Now then, Mrs Miller. I'm afraid she is very ill.'

'I was afraid so, too.'

'She has a very large ovarian cyst. Infected. And I fear, indeed I suspect, peritonitis developing. The abdomen is very hard. She has a high temperature. Really she should be in hospital. Although there is little that can be done, except possibly draining the abdominal cavity. I would like another opinion on that ideally.'

'She's terrified of hospitals. Always has been,' said Celia 'Couldn't she stay, at least a little longer?'

'It could be dangerous. But I suppose if she's frightened and upset it won't help. I think at the very least she should have a nurse here, I could arrange it if—' he paused.

Celia smiled at him. 'Of course. Whatever she needs. Please. Just organise it. And do get a second opinion, by all means.'

'Well,' he said, folding up his stethoscope, smiling down at her, 'I was afraid we might have to get a gynaecologist for you. That is beginning to seem unnecessary, at least. So let us be thankful for small mercies.'

Mercy! That was the word Sebastian had used to her.

'For God's sake,' he had said, 'show me some mercy.'

And she had lain there, crying, staring at him, telling him she could not.

'I don't understand,' he kept saying, 'I don't understand why you didn't tell me.'

'I couldn't, Sebastian. Really, I couldn't. I didn't know what to think, what to say to you.'

'But – it might be mine? It surely might be mine?'

She was silent; willing the words out. They wouldn't come.

'Celia! Tell me. Don't retreat from me like this, I can't stand it. You're pregnant, quite possibly, quite probably, indeed, I would say, with my child. How can you just – desert me like this?'

'I – don't know,' she said and the effort, even of saying that, was intense.

She had until Friday. Then Sebastian was leaving for the United States. 'I will be at home until then,' he said, 'and you can come to me. In which case I will stay here and take care of you. Otherwise I shall be gone and you will not see me again. For a very long time, at any rate.

But obviously this is your decision, although I find it very hurtful that you should have tried to keep it from me.'

She had said nothing – again. And now she was entirely absorbed in her indecision; waiting for something to help her end it.

'I was wondering,' said Guy, 'if there was any point in going to see the Bartletts.'

'How could there be?'

'Well – they might not have got the letter.'

'Very unlikely.'

'Or she might not realise how important it is.'

'That's true. Although you did say it was urgent.'

'She might be away. The girl, I mean.'

'In which case, there's nothing to be done until she gets back. Is there any great hurry?'

'Huge. Publication is in less than a month. A decision has to be made, whether to pulp the books or not. Whether to risk it, or not. Oh, Jeremy, it's such a beast of a thing. My hour of glory: my first novel – all come to nothing. I – I know it's mostly my own fault. But it's not fair.'

'No,' said Jeremy, looking at his tortured face, 'no it's not fair.'

'So – what do you think?'

'I think,' said Jeremy slowly, 'that we just have to wait. It's quite a delicate situation. We can't afford to antagonise them. Here, have another drink.'

'Thanks,' said Guy.

Jack had made his decision. He was going to do it. Ask Lily to marry him. Somehow talking to Harry Cholmondley had cleared his mind: made him realise what he really wanted. All right, so, he didn't have any money and he was lousy at publishing and he behaved like a spoilt child, just as his brother had said. Getting married, having Lily with him, would sort all that out. She'd set him straight, tell him what to do; she might even agree that he should go back into the army. Although he didn't want to. He just needed something steady in his life. Seeing what had happened to Celia and Oliver had shaken him badly. He hadn't realised how badly. He'd believed so much in their marriage; it had been there practically all his life. He'd felt very lost suddenly. But – well, at least Celia was still there. That was something. As long as she stayed, he could just about cope with it. Oliver's attitude to it was so strange. Either he didn't know, which he must surely, or if he knew, he was just ignoring it. How could you do that? When you loved someone as much as he knew Oliver loved Celia. It was really strange. Well that was their marriage. It didn't mean it would happen to him and Lily. Of course not.

He had gone out that afternoon, down to Hatton Garden and bought a nice little ring; nothing special, but it would do for the occasion. It looked quite impressive, in its square leather box. He'd get her something better later, something she could choose herself. He tidied his desk, feeling quite cheerful and went out to meet Lily.

'Are you in for dinner?' said Oliver. 'I'd like to talk to you.'

LM had got back to Cheyne Walk to find that Jay was engrossed in a game of spillikins with the twins; he refused even to consider going to the house in Hampstead.

'What for? There's no one to play with there.'

'Where's Barty?' said LM, trying to ignore the criticism implicit in this remark.

'Upstairs with her mother,' said Venetia.

'And a nurse,' said Adele.

'She's very ill,' said Venetia.

'She might even die,' said Adele.

They were both enjoying the drama hugely.

'Nonsense,' said LM, 'she's a very strong woman. I'm going down to see your father.'

As she walked past Celia's room, she heard her call; she had hoped to avoid a confrontation.

'How are you?' she said abruptly. She felt dreadfully upset, disturbed by her discovery, her lifetime's loyalty to Celia badly shaken.

'All right, thank you,' said Celia with a sigh. 'It seems to be all right. Touch wood,' she added, reaching out to her bedside table.

'Is your mother still here?'

'No, she's gone to Clarges Street.'

'I see.'

'LM, is something the matter?'

'No, nothing,' said LM, 'I'm just a little weary. That's all. How is Sylvia?'

'Not at all well. But the nurse is very good, and a gynaecologist is coming first thing in the morning. She's sedated now and in less pain. Poor Sylvia, she hasn't had much of a life.'

'No indeed,' said LM, 'well, I hope you continue satisfactorily. Is there anything you need?'

'No,' said Celia, 'LM something is the matter?'

'No, really. I'm a little weary that's all. Good night, Celia.'

She saw Celia's hurt face, ignored it. She really didn't care. Celia was inflicting a great deal of pain on a great many people.

She didn't want to spend the evening talking to Oliver; she knew what the conversation would be about. Celia and the state of their marriage. Yet she supposed, it would all be, in a way, a relief. She was no use at dissembling, and besides, she needed to know how Oliver felt about it, what he planned to do, his attitude towards the baby. She wondered if any of them knew whose it was: it was an extraordinary and very complex situation. And then what about the future of Lyttons, how was that going to be affected? If Celia were to leave Oliver, and it must be a consideration, she could hardly stay at Lyttons. Yes, it was an essential discussion.

Nevertheless, she would have given a great deal to have a genuine alibi to save her from it. But Gordon Robinson always had supper with his mother on Mondays and Jay was here, so she had no reason to go anywhere.

'Yes,' she said now, mentally squaring her shoulders, 'Yes, Oliver, I'm in for dinner.'

Celia stared after her, a new curl of panic rising inside her. Sebastian had said he'd been rather tactless to LM. She was very sharp; clearly she'd guessed. The thought of losing LM's friendship was almost worse than losing Sebastian.

'Oh God,' she said aloud, 'oh, dear God.'

There was a tap at the door; it was Barty. 'Aunt Celia, Mum's very bad. I'm worried.'

'What does the nurse say?'

'She says there's nothing we can do for now. Just wait. If she gets worse, she says we can get the doctor back.'

'Well, we can. Of course. Is she lying quietly?'

'No, she keeps talking, but it doesn't make any sense.'

Delirious, thought Celia. Oh, dear. 'Well, Barty darling, she is in good hands, honestly. Look, you go and have supper with the others, and then pop up and see her again. If you're still worried, come and get me.'

'I don't want any supper.'

'Now, you must try and eat. You need to be strong yourself, to look after your mother.'

'All right.' She walked out of the rom slowly. Celia watched her, wondering how on earth she would cope if her mother died. Stop it, Celia, you're being morbid. She supposed it was hardly surprising.

Jack had taken Lily for an early supper to the Trocadero; she was appearing in a late-night cabaret at the Piccadilly Hotel, until her new revue opened.

'You work too hard,' he said.

'I need to,' she said briskly, 'I have to earn money.'

It sounded rather like criticism to Jack; he was silent.

They ordered supper: Lily wanted fish. 'I can't cope with much food if I've got to work later,' and only drank water. Jack was sorry; he had ordered some champagne to suit the occasion. He set to drinking it anyway. The atmosphere was rather strained.

'How are things at Lyttons?' asked Lily politely.

'Oh – pretty bloody. This libel case is getting worse. And it's going to cost thousands and thousands. Which Oliver keeps saying we haven't got. Partly due to my book,' he added gloomily.

'Is it really serious? For Lyttons I mean?'

'I don't know exactly. LM – my sister you know – has been called up to London.'

'Oh yes.'

'To discuss things. So it must be quite bad. And Sebastian's gone to another publisher.'

'Has he now?' said Lily, 'I wonder why that should be. What does Celia have to say about that?'

'I have no idea. She's ill, anyway.'

'Ill? Doesn't sound like her. What's wrong?'

'I don't know. She has to stay in bed for a bit.'

'Has to—' Lily stopped in mid-sentence. She stared at him, flushed.

'What, Lily?'

'Nothing. Really.'

'Yes, there is. I can tell.'

'No there isn't.'

'Lily, come on. I'm not that stupid.'

'Well – when women have to stay in bed – well usually—'

'Yes? Usually what?'

'Oh Jack. Usually they're in the family way.'

'Oh,' he said. He felt very bleak suddenly.

'Yes. My God. What a mess.'

'Yes. What a mess.'

'Oh – come on,' she said, 'let's not worry too much about them. Perhaps it isn't that at all. Let's talk about you. Or me.'

'Yes,' he said pulling himself together, 'yes, let's. Let's talk about you and me. Lily, there's something I want to ask you.'

'Now then,' said Oliver, 'we must talk.'

528

He poured LM a glass of white wine. 'Sorry, I can't drink red. Would you like some?'

'No thank you. This is very nice.'

He was silent for a moment, clearly putting off starting the discussion. Then,

'This is all rather – difficult,' he said.

'Yes, I can see that.'

'Can you?' He looked surprised.

'Yes of course. I'm not stupid, Oliver.'

'No. Well there are so many things to be taken into consideration—'

'Yes, I know.'

'It's very complex.'

'Of course. Of course it is.'

'But there's still a chance. I think.'

LM looked at him. It was extraordinary, she thought. That he should let himself be walked over in this way. Just put up with it, swallow his pride. Such a public humilation. And with the baby—

'I think you're being marvellous,' she said.

He looked surprised. 'You do?'

'Yes, I do. It can't be easy. Especially now—'

'Why especially now?'

'Well, with the baby.'

'The baby? What's the baby got to do with it?'

'Oh Oliver,' said LM impatiently, 'a great deal, obviously. Your wife having an affair is one thing. Being pregnant is quite another.'

There was a very long silence; the room was icy-still. Even the ticking of the clock seemed an intrusion. Then: 'I simply don't know what you're talking about,' said Oliver. 'I wanted to discuss Lyttons, its future, whether it is actually viable any more. I would still like to do that. If you don't mind.'

Lily was out of step; she knew she was. Damn. Once it happened, it was so hard to get back in, All the other girls were on the left foot, she was on the right. Do it double time Lily, just once, then you'll be all right. No, it hadn't worked. Still out. Again. Phew. That was it. She saw Crystal's eyes widen from her place at the back of the stage; she had noticed then. Which meant everyone would have done. It was so unlike her. So terribly unlike her. She just didn't make that sort of mistake. She knew why of course: it was Jack. Asking her to marry him. It had thrown her completely. She felt totally confused, almost shocked. It was one thing to speculate idly, quite another to be confronted with it: forced to make a decision. What, what in the name of heaven was she to do? Cripes! Nearly did it again. Stop it, Lily, don't think about it yet. Concentrate on what you're doing.

But what should she say? What could she say? She knew what she wanted to say. Yes. She really did. She loved Jack and she knew now he loved her. But marriage. How could she marry him? Just thinking about the wedding made her worry: with all his posh relations, not just the Lyttons, but Celia's parents, on one side, and hers on the other, her grandpa who'd been a coalman, and her gran who belched all the time once she'd got a glass of anything inside her. And her dad, imagine Celia's mother the countess or whatever she was, asking her dad what he did for a living and him telling her about his fruit and veg stall.

But it wasn't just the wedding; it was ever after. Whatever they did, wherever they went, they'd be different. Her friends, all dancers and actresses, and the odd model and shop assistant, and his, all army officers and gentleman farmers and stockbrokers. It was all right in nightclubs and at parties, but in real life . . . And then there was the thing about houses: Jack liked everything simple and a bit battered-looking and she liked it all prettied up. She'd noticed the expression of shocked amusement – hastily covered up – when she'd suggested she make him some pretty curtains to replace his scruffy old ones. And when she'd asked him when he was going to be able to afford a carpet to cover the wooden floor. 'I'm not,' he'd said, sounding quite pained. That sort of thing mattered in the end.

And when they had children, then what? Would they be posh little buggers, sent off to school at eight like Giles had been, and Jack himself come to that, bullied to bits, which was supposed to be good for them, God knew why, or would she be allowed to keep them at home with her, looked after, nice and safe and happy?

No. As the number finished, Lily decided. No. It had to be no. It would be very painful for a while, but after that they'd both be happier. Much happier. She'd have to tell him that night, after the show; she'd asked him for time to think, he'd obviously been surprised and hurt, had thought she'd just say yes right away. And then they wouldn't see one another any more. It was the only way. It really was . . . Lily suddenly realised her eyes were full of tears; she ran to the dressing-room, slammed the door buried her face in her arms and cried for quite a long time. Then she cleaned up her face, changed, and went out to meet Jack.

'Is it really that bad?'

LM had forced her mind on to Lyttons with an effort; she looked at Oliver and saw from his face that it was.

'It is extremely bad. The figures are dreadful. The Mutiny book has hardly sold fifty copies and it's cost a fortune. This action of Lothian's is going to cost us thousands and thousands. We just don't have it. And Brooke leaving is the last straw.'

'What about the backlist?'

'Modest at the moment. Certainly not enough to save us. These high printing charges and now the new wage demand – well, we simply can't cope financially.'

'So now what?'

LM had a sudden vision of their father, the last time she had seen him in the office, sitting at his big desk, surrounded with proofs, still totally involved with everything, his gentle old face stern as he pointed out to her a record number of typographical errors.

'It's detail that matters in publishing,' he had said, 'remember the horseshoe and the nail and the kingdom which it lost. Let your typesetting charges go up, and then you're overspending on your printing budget. That has to be allowed for in your cover price and that has to come out of your profits. Every tiny thing is important; always remember that.'

Well, they had forgotten it; forgotten a lot of tiny things. And big ones. And they were all to blame. Even she. She should not have buried herself down in the country, she should have kept a much stricter eye on things. She should have known that neither Oliver nor Celia would have any kind of a sense of detail or be properly concerned with the minutiae of finance. It would have been perfectly possible. If she could spend time on her wretched archaeology, she could spend it on Lyttons' administration and accounts. Oliver was clearly to blame; he should have taken a much closer interest in the Buchanan affair, her father had always closely questioned any new author, especially a young one, about his sources. And she had advised him to take out libel insurance many times. As for Celia: well, Celia's only crime – against Lyttons that was – was bringing about the defection of Sebastian Brooke. A huge money-maker for them gone. His sales would have easily counter-balanced the Buchanan losses. Certainly would have bought them time to find another saga.

'Father would have been very cross with us,' she said, trying to lighten the occasion a little.

'Don't talk about Father,' said Oliver. 'I've thought about him every hour of every day, since this wretched business all began. And – although I may have a solution, he wouldn't like that either.'

'A solution? What?'

'Brunnings have made me an offer. They would meet all our debts, keep us viable.'

'And take us over?'

'Yes.' His face was very drawn. 'Take us over completely. We would simply become one of their imprints. We would be allowed to continue with the reference book list as Lyttons, but that would be all. Everything else would be published under the Brunnings imprint. Not,' he added, trying to smile, 'not that it would be a great deal.'

'Oh God,' said LM, 'Oliver, we can't do that. We just can't.'

'I don't think we have a lot of choice,' he said, 'except to close down altogether. Anyway, we have until Friday. To make up our minds. I'm sorry to spring it on you, but I had a long meeting with Brunnings today.'

'It seems very pressing of them.'

'They can see they're in a strong position. That we don't have much choice.'

'It isn't very gentlemanly.'

'LM, publishing is no longer a gentlemanly profession, I'm afraid.'

'What does – what does Celia think?'

'I haven't troubled her with it' he said, and he did not meet her eyes, 'not when she is unwell. I thought we would spare her.'

'Oliver,' said LM, and it was a moment of absolute revelation to her and the beginning of an exoneration of Celia and what she had done, 'Oliver how can you possibly not involve Celia in this? Celia is Lyttons as much as you or I. It would be outrageous of you to keep it from her.'

'I don't agree,' he said, his pale blue eyes very hard suddenly, 'I don't agree with you at all. And I would prefer that you did not discuss it with her. Dr Perring said she should be spared any extra strain. It would be terrible if this caused her to lose the baby, LM.'

LM stared at him. Everything was beginning to become rather clear. If Oliver wanted a revenge, he could hardly find a better one.

'I'm sorry, Oliver,' she said, 'I think I know Celia rather better than that. If anything caused her to lose the baby, it would be seeing Lyttons sold out over her head. Apart from anything else, she is on the board. You have no right to keep it from her. And if you don't tell her, then I most certainly will.'

Jack sat staring into his glass. The glass of champagne, filled from the bottle he had bought to celebrate his and Lily's engagement. Only there was no engagement and nothing to celebrate. Lily had said, very sweetly and gently, that she simply did not feel able to accept his proposal.

'It's not that I'm not very fond of you, Jack. I am. But – I just don't want to get married. Not to anyone. Not yet. And not for a very long time either,' she had added, seeing his face, thinking he was going to propose a long engagement, believing that she would marry him in the end. 'I'm really sorry.'

'But Lily—'

'And anyway,' she said, her voice growing more determined, 'anyway, I may be going to Broadway next year.'

'Broadway!'

'Yes. CB is taking the show over there, he's rather keen for a group of us to go with him. And I really don't think I could resist that.'

That had hurt more than anything. To think that Lily, his Lily, should set aside marrying him, just for the chance of being in a Broadway show. It was almost unbearable, it hurt so much. He sighed heavily, refilled his glass.

'Jack, hallo. You look as if you've lost a shilling and found sixpence.'

It was Gwendolyn Oliphant. He liked Gwendolyn, even if it was she who told Lily the rumours about Celia. She was fun and she was pretty. But she was engaged to Bertie Plumrose. Engaged. Everyone was getting engaged. As he would have been by now. He looked at Gwendolyn's finger; a large ring sparkled on it.

'Where's Bertie?'

'Getting the car. We're going down to the coast. Why don't you come?'

'The coast?'

'Yes. We'll be there in a couple of hours. It's so hot, and we thought it would be awfully jolly down there. We could swim. Come on, Jack. Join us.'

He was tempted; anything was better than just sitting here. 'Is it just you and Bertie?' he said. He had no desire to play gooseberry. Tonight of all nights.

'Heavens no. About ten carloads. Last one in the sea's a cissy. Look, finish that drink — where's Lily?'

'I have no idea,' said Jack.

'Oh. Oh, I see.' Gwendolyn looked at him thoughtfully. 'Oh dear.' She put her arm round him. 'In that case, you must certainly come. Cheer yourself up. We're going to have a picnic on the beach. Champoo and cocaine, Bertie's got loads, plenty enough for you, it'll be such fun.'

'Weell—'

'Darling Jack! I knew you would! Bertie, darling, over here. Jack's coming with us, aren't you Jack?'

'Yes I am,' said Jack firmly, 'and won't you help me finish this bottle before we go?'

'No, you have it,' said Bertie, 'I've had a skinful already. Glad you're coming though, old chap. See you on the road.'

★

There was a knocking on the door: gentle at first then louder. Celia sat up.

'Come in.'

It was Barty; she was white-faced and shaking.

'Please come,' she said, 'Mum's so bad. The nurse says she thinks we should get her to hospital.'

'I'll come at once.'

She pulled on her robe; looked at the clock. Two in the morning. Crisis time. The worst possible. She followed Barty upstairs; the nurse was bent over Sylvia, bathing her forehead. She turned as they came in.

'She's very poorly,' she said.

Sylvia was tossing on her pillows, her eyes brilliant in her flushed face. Her hands were twisting together and she was pulling at the sheet.

'It's very bad. Very, very bad,' she said, in a harsh, low voice. 'Can you give me anything for it, for the pain?'

'You've had as much as you can for now, Mrs Miller. Dr Perring hasn't given me any more for you.'

She seemed to accept this. Then, 'Can you get Lady Celia? I want her, I want to talk to her.'

'I'm here, Sylvia,' said Celia, sitting down by the bed, taking her hand. 'I'm here.' She turned to the nurse. 'Go and telephone for Dr Perring quickly. The phone's in the hall.'

'Of course.'

'Need her here,' said Sylvia. 'Need her to help me. Get her, please.'

'Need who, Mum?' said Barty. She sounded dreadfully frightened.

Celia wrung out a cloth in cold water, bathed Sylvia's forehead. She kept pushing it fretfully away.

'How much longer?' she said. 'How much longer now?'

'She keeps saying that.' The nurse had returned. 'She thinks she's in labour, I just realised, they always say that.'

'Yes we do,' said Celia with a sigh, 'and what did Dr Perring say?'

'He's coming, and he's sent for an ambulance.'

'Good. Barty darling, don't be so frightened. She'll be better in hospital.'

'But—'

'Nearly over,' said Sylvia, 'the pains are so bad. It must be nearly here.'

'There, there,' said the nurse soothingly, stroking her forehead. 'There, there, Mrs Miller. Yes, it'll soon be over now. It seems best to humour her,' she whispered to Celia.

'Yes of course.'

'Lady Celia, are you there? Are you there?'

'Yes, Sylvia, I'm here—'

'I want to look after this one. Whatever's wrong. I don't want to do that again.' A silence: then, 'Don't tell Ted. Don't.'

The nurse looked at Celia. 'Poor thing, what's she on about?'

'I – don't know,' said Celia quickly. This was becoming a nightmare in more ways than one.

Sylvia was tossing and turning on her pillows: then, 'Is it all right,' she said, 'is she breathing?'

'She's fine, Mrs Miller. Fine.'

'Lady Celia, be quick, quick. Oh God—'

'Oh Mum,' Barty looked up at Celia in terror.

Sylvia was biting her fist now, her eyes staring. 'Do it quickly. Quickly. Before anyone comes in. Poor baby, the poor, poor baby. She's died now, she's died—' She stopped talking, groaned, clutching her stomach. Her pain was obviously extreme.

'What can we do for her, what can we do?' said Barty. She started to cry. 'There must be something.'

'Nothing, darling. Until the ambulance gets here. It won't be long.'

'I'm rather afraid of septicaemia,' said the nurse under her breath to Celia.

She nodded. 'I know but—'

'Oh God,' Sylvia's voice was low, very fast. 'God, dear God, help me, Her poor little legs, all twisted look. Help me, please, please, take the pillow.'

'Sylvia, hush. Lie still. Everything is all right. Let me sponge you down again! And stop talking, Sylvia, please stop talking.

Her stomach was absolutely iron-hard; the infection was clearly spreading. The nurse took her pulse again. 'It's faster,' she said to Celia, 'I wish the doctor would come.'

'I'm sure he won't be long. It always seems forever when you're waiting.' She felt quite frightened herself. Panicky almost.

'It's over now,' said Sylvia suddenly. 'It's done. All for the best. All for the best really. She's gone.'

'Yes,' said the nurse gently, 'yes, it's all for the best. There there, Mrs Miller. Lie still. Doctor will be here soon. Oh heavens, where is that ambulance?'

'Where is that ambulance? It must have gone via Scotland—'

'Coming now. I can hear it. Here, wave your torch. That's right. Over here.' The ambulance pulled up; the driver got out.

'Is this – oh yes. Ah. Right.'

'Looks bad doesn't it?'

'Not too good.'

They had seen it all, Jim and Dot Everett. They had been asleep in their small house on the outskirts of Lewes, when the noise of all the cars woke them. One after another, hooting wildly as they came round the corner and down the hill, enough to wake the dead, Jim said. And then this one had somehow shot across the road, on to the wrong side, hit a lamp-post, spun back on itself and turned right over. Just like that.

'It was like slow motion,' said Jim to the policemen who had now arrived. 'Over on to its back. And then over again. And then sort of drifted into that tree.'

'Yes. Yes, I see.' One of the policeman walked over to the ambulance men; they were bent over their stretcher, strapping the body on to it.

'How bad?' he said.

'Not good. Too soon to say for sure.'

'Any identity?'

'Can't find any yet. Might be a wallet or something in the dashboard. Only it's all folded up. Like a concertina. One of these stupid young people isn't he? Look at him, dinner jacket and all. What do they call them? Bright young things. None too bright if you ask me. Champagne bottle open on the seat beside him. And this little ring box as well, look. Dear oh dear.'

Dr Perring had diagnosed acute peritonitis; the ambulance had come, and Sylvia had been taken off in it with the nurse. Barty, crying bitterly, stood on the steps in front of the house, with Celia's arm round her shoulder, waving her mother off. Oliver had awoken, and so had LM; they all went down to the kitchen.

'I'll make a cup of tea,' said Celia.

'No, you mustn't,' said LM, 'you should be in bed. I'll do it.'

'I'm all right.' She rubbed her eyes wearily. 'Barty darling, you really must try not to worry too much. Your mother is very strong. And Dr Perring says they will be able to do all sorts of clever things in hospital. She'll be all right. Truly.'

'We should have made her go earlier,' said Barty, wiping her nose on the back of her hand, and then, seeing Celia's face, 'sorry, I haven't got a hanky.'

'Here,' said Oliver, 'take mine. That's better. No, Aunt Celia's quite right, they can do wonders in hospital.'

'Yes, but the doctor wanted her to go this afternoon and we – we—' She started to cry again. 'Oh, Wol, it was so awful, she was in so much pain, and saying such strange things.'

'Very strange,' said Celia quickly, 'she was delirious, none of it made sense.'

'It sort of did,' said Barty, 'she thought she was having a baby, and first it was alive and then it was dead. It was so horrible.'

'Poor Sylvia,' said LM, 'how dreadful. Didn't she have a baby that died, Celia? I seem to remember something—'

'Yes,' said Celia quickly, 'yes, she did.'

'How old was I?' said Barty.

'Oh, tiny. About two, not even that.'

'What happened?'

'Barty, it's such a long time ago, I really can't remember.'

'Poor, poor Mum,' said Barty, starting to cry again, 'I'm so afraid she'll die.'

'Barty, she won't die,' said Oliver firmly, 'I'm quite sure she won't.'

'I wish I could go to the hospital with her.'

'Well, you can't. They wouldn't let you in. But in the morning, first thing, we'll telephone, and see when you can visit her. Now what about bed? It's – goodness gracious me, it's nearly four o'clock. Celia, come along, my dear. You really should be in bed. You look terrible. As if you'd seen a ghost.'

'Do I?' said Celia. She felt she had seen exactly that.

They telephoned the hospital at eight; the news was not good. Mrs Miller had acute peritonitis, a ward sister informed Oliver, her temperature was extremely high and there could be no question of visitors. Beyond that, she offered no information; Dr Perring was more successful.

'They have inserted a drain into the abdominal cavity, as I rather hoped they would. That's all that can be done to fight the infection at this stage. The cyst should be removed, but of course while the infection is so acute, surgery is out of the question. She must have been in dreadful pain for months, poor woman. Dear oh dear.'

Later that morning he telephoned again.

'Between you and me,' he said to Celia, 'I don't think there is very much hope. Septicaemia has set in. I don't quite know what to think about Barty. Or the other children—'

'Oh God,' said Celia, 'well – Billy works for my mother; he'd have to come up on the train. The others are all in London, as far as I know.'

'Would Barty know how to contact them?'

'Oh yes. Poor little girl.'

'Well – maybe it won't be necessary. How are you today?'

'I'm fine. But Barty will want to visit. If only to say goodbye. She's a very clever child. I couldn't fool her for long.'

'No. Well, I think you should be as honest with her as you can. Just tell her her mother's no better, but that there is room for hope. I'll be in touch if it's thought that – well, Barty should be taken to the hospital. And the others . . .'

'Yes. Please do. Thank you for everything Dr Perring. Once again.'

'Where on earth is Jack?' Oliver put his head round LM's door. It was extraordinary how quickly she had become part of the establishment again. 'Do you know?'

'I have no idea, no.'

'He's often late, but not this late. I've telephoned his flat, he's not there.'

'Might his girlfriend know?'

'Well possibly, but I have no idea where to find her, either.'

'I'm sure he'll turn up soon. Is there anything from the Lothian tribe this morning?'

'No, nothing. So – another day's breathing space.'

'Yes. For which much thanks.'

'Dear oh dear,' said Howard Shaw to his secretary, 'is there still nothing from Lyttons?'

'Nothing, Mr Shaw.'

'Extraordinarily remiss of them. Well, if they don't get in touch today, we may be forced into an ex parte hearing. Mr Justice Berryman will not be at all impressed.'

'No, indeed, Mr Shaw. You did post the letter on Friday, didn't you?'

'Of course. It was very urgent, that is why I wanted to do it myself. I told you that.'

'Yes, of course. Mr Shaw. Shall I phone Briscoe's?'

'Certainly not, Angela. If they are so inefficient, or even discourteous as to ignore anything this important, they don't deserve to have us running round after them.'

'No, Mr Shaw.'

It was a very beautiful morning: the slightly harsh end of summer just tinged with the softness of autumn. Susannah Bartlett was reading the newspaper in the garden when the postman arrived.

'Good morning, miss.'

'Good morning.' She smiled at him.

She was a pretty girl, he thought. Woman, rather She looked very young for her age. She must be over twenty. Well over. She seemed younger. Of course, living with her parents as she did, and not working much, just doing her translation or whatever it was, she seemed more like a student than anything. So it was natural to think of her that way. He liked her; she was a bit odd of course – the milkman said she was slightly touched, but that was rubbish. His wife, who did for the vicar at St Stephen's knew the Bartletts' cleaner and she said it was just the drugs she was on. She had nervous problems; she'd had a bad nervous breakdown while she was at university and she was very highly strung anyway, so she had to be kept quiet. It was a shame, the Bartletts' cleaner said, because she'd been ever so clever, still was, she translated books from the original Greek and Hebrew and the Lord knew what else, but she couldn't cope with a proper job. Not in an office and that.

She had wonderful long hair, hanging in a thick plait down her back; he liked to see long hair on a woman, didn't approve of all this bobbing. Nor the short skirts. Unfeminine, that's what they were. Funny, when they all thought they looked so attractive in them. He parked his bike, went through the gate and up the short garden path to the front door.

'You're late, this morning,' she said.

'Yes, I know. It all got held up at the depot.'

'Got anything for me?'

He flicked through his pile.

'No, sorry.'

'Oh dear. I was expecting something. From the translation agency.'

'What about the one that came the other day?' he said.

'I didn't get a letter the other day. You must be thinking of someone else.'

'Course I'm not.' His professional pride was hurt. 'I always remember who gets letters.'

'Well – there was one a couple of weeks ago.'

'No,' he said, 'no, Friday it was. I remember, because I had hardly any for this whole row of houses that morning, I don't like that. Doesn't feel right. None in the second post, either. So I noticed yours. And there was one for your mum and dad as well. Someone's still writing letters, I thought. Thank goodness for that.'

'Oh, I see.' She looked rather tense suddenly.

Oh Lord. Now he'd done it. Upset her. Maybe the drugs affected her memory. They were funny things, drugs were.

'Maybe I'm mistaken,' he said quickly, 'maybe it wasn't Friday.'

'Don't worry about it,' she said. She managed a smile. 'We all make mistakes. I certainly do.'

She went into the house.

'Mother! Mother where are you?'

'In the kitchen, dear.'

Susannah went into the kitchen; her mother was standing at the sink with her back to her, wringing out some washing.

'Mother, was there a letter for me on Friday?'

She saw her mother's back tense, watched her hands go still.

'I'm – not sure, dear. Maybe.'

'Was there?' she heard her voice shake; damn. Keep calm, keep calm.

'Now, Susannah.' Mrs Bartlett's face was anxious, her voice carefully soothing, 'You mustn't get upset.'

'I won't get upset, Mother. If you give me my letter.'

'But I don't know what letter you mean. You get so many.'

'I get very few. And one came on Friday, and I think you didn't give it to me for some reason. Please give it to me now.'

'I'll – I'll have to ask your father about it. He'd know where it was. If there was one.'

'But he's at work. Please be kind enough to have a look through the desk. Or I will.'

She felt herself getting hot; she took several deep breaths.

'No, no, dear. I'll go. You sit down there.'

'I'll come with you. Help you.'

That was better; she felt calmer already.

She watched her mother going through the desk, carefully and methodically. There didn't seem to be anything there.

'Upstairs? In his wardrobe?'

'I don't think so, dear. But we can have a look, if you like.'

'Yes, I would like.'

No letter.

'I'm really not sure there was one, dear.'

Susannah felt her temper rising.

'Mother, please don't lie to me. I may be a depressive; I may be on permanent medication, but I am not a fool. Clearly there was a letter and you've chosen to keep it from me. Why?'

'Well—'

'Mother, if you don't tell me, I shall allow myself to get upset. All right? I'm trying very hard at the moment but I could – let go. So—'

'We thought the letter would upset you, dear.'

'You thought so. Why?'

'It was from a young man who wanted to talk to you About your time at Cambridge. He's a journalist.'

'Well, what's wrong with that? I'd rather like that, I—'

'Professor Lothian didn't want you to talk to him.'

'Professor Lothian! Why on earth not, why should he care?'

But – she knew. So did her mother.

'Now you can imagine why, dear. Although how he knew about it, I really don't know. Anyway, that's why we thought it best to – well leave it for a while. You haven't been very well lately and—'

'I've been perfectly well, Mother. Rather better than usual. What I want to know is what you were doing opening my letters anyway. And how did you know Jasper Lothian didn't want me to see him?'

'He – he – wrote to us. About it.'

'He what? But that's outrageous.'

She felt herself getting edgy now; she sat down. Her mother looked at her.

'Susannah, please.'

'I'm going to get that letter,' she said, 'now where is it?'

'I really don't know, dear. Your father had it.'

'I know. You said.' She could hear her voice shake again. 'Mother I don't like this at all. Not at all. I think I'd better go and find Father now.'

'Oh, Susannah, no.' And then clearly seeing that Susannah meant it, she said, 'well have a nice drink first. And perhaps you should take your second tablet early.'

'Yes, all right,' said Susannah, 'I will. If that will make you feel any better. Now tell me more about this letter. Please.'

My darling Celia,

I know I said I would leave you alone but there was so much left unsaid yesterday, I thought I must write to you.

I love you. That is the first thing. Not unsaid, I know, but so important that you have to hear it again and again. I love you unimaginably, beyond thought, beyond reason.

I want you with me. Forever. I want to love you and care for you, I want to live with you, wake with you, sleep with you. I want to see the world with you, come home with you. Be with you. You, and now, it seems, our child.

The thought that we have created a child is almost unbearable. Not a happiness I had thought to know; and an extraordinary and precious one. That child is ours: yours and mine. I know that, with absolute certainty. We made it, our love made it; we must share it, we must love it.

Without it and without you, I have nothing, nothing at all. I love it tenderly, and deeply already with all my heart. As I love you. Absolutely.

Sebastian

'Oh God,' said Celia.

She lay back on the bed, tears streaming down her face. This was awful; this was unendurable. She would have to go; go with Sebastian.

Anything else was madness. She explored the decision for a few minutes, waiting for uncertainty to return. It didn't. She remained sure, calm and suddenly and astonishingly happy.

She would leave now, today. She could, easily. She could get up, get dressed, there was no one about, she was perfectly all right now. And just go to him. She got out of bed; went to the wardrobe, pulled out a dress and some shoes. She began to dress, slightly shakily. She must keep calm, must be quick; suppose Mary came in, suppose her mother arrived—

She brushed her hair, picked up her handbag, started down the stairs. There was her car: good. She had been half afraid LM might have borrowed it. She opened the front door; she felt a sudden rush of exhilaration. She'd done it. She'd escaped. Escaped from Oliver, escaped from her old, dead life. She was free.

She half-ran down the steps, pulling her car keys from her bag. Above her head, over the river, seagulls wheeled and screeched; a tug hooted. The air felt warm, wonderfully sweetly warm, on her face, a breeze lifted her hair. She smiled, opened the door of her car. Just for a moment, her happiness was pure; there was nothing else. It would not, could not last like that; but just for now, she was safe, encased in it.

'Lady Celia!'

It was Brunson. He'd seen her. Damn, damn, damn.

'Yes, Brunson, I can't stop I'm afraid. I'm in a terrible hurry.'

'It's Dr Perring, Lady Celia. The hospital has phoned him. Mrs Miller is worse. He wants to speak to you.'

Sylvia! The one person she could not fail, the one friendship she would not deny. Slowly, unwillingly, she got back out of the car, walked up the steps, in through the door. Picked up the phone. It felt very heavy.

'Yes. Dr Perring?'

'Lady Celia, Mrs Miller is dying. There is no hope for her. I think you should send Barty over straight away. And the other children too – if it can be arranged. Before it's too late. Can you do that?'

'Yes,' she said, and heard the loss of hope in her own voice, 'yes, of course I can. I'll bring Barty myself. I won't be long.'

'Is that Mr Lytton?'

'Yes. This is he.'

'It's Lily Fortescue. I – wondered if I could just speak to Jack.'

'I'm afraid he's not here. I'm sorry.'

'Oh. Well, do you know where he is, then?'

'I'm afraid I don't. I rather wish I did, as a matter of fact.'

'Oh, I see. Well – if he does appear, could you tell him I telephoned? I was looking after his wallet last night, had it in my handbag, and I went off with it. He'll be needing it. It hasn't got much in it, but just the same—'

'Yes, of course, Miss Fortescue. Thank you for telephoning. And if you do hear from him, would you let us know? Thank you.'

Roger Bartlett was the accountant at the Westminster Bank, South Ealing. He was very proud of his position; it was the result of many years' hard work. He didn't earn very much, of course, and indeed such things as university fees could not have been managed without the help of a legacy from Mary's godmother; but it was nonetheless a salary, rather than a wage, and for a profession. That was what he was proudest of, having an important job locally. He knew everyone in the community and they knew him; he was someone. And it was a very respectable job. Respectability was everything to Roger Bartlett; he had a horror of anything that he labelled unsuitable. Causing a commotion; making a noise; being improperly dressed.

The appearance in the foyer of his daughter, wearing only the casual shirt and shabby skirt in which she worked, with no hat or gloves, her hair unbrushed and her face wearing the tense expression which often heralded one of her fits of hysteria, was one of the worst moments, therefore, of his life.

'I want my letter,' she said, very loudly and clearly, walking over to his counter, 'I want my letter, at once, please.'

'Barty, darling, I want you.'

Barty was playing snap with the twins; she went white and stood up immediately, dropping her cards sharply on the table. The twins, sensing the drama, were silent also, their eyes large, their faces solemn.

'Come along,' said Celia, 'come with me downstairs. To my room. Girls, you stay here.'

It was a measure of the moment that they did not even attempt to argue.

'Your mother—' Celia stopped.

'I know. She's going to die Isn't she?'

'Yes,' said Celia, quietly. 'Yes, I'm afraid she is. I'm so sorry. So terribly sorry. But we must go and see her now, and you can—'

'Say goodbye. Yes, of course.'

She was so composed; Celia could not believe it.

543

'What about the others?'

'We can send Daniels for them. If you give me the addresses. I know some of them, of course but—'

'Yes. Yes of course. And Billy—'

'I've telephoned Ashingham. He's coming on the next train.'

'I hope he's in time,' said Barty. Still so calm.

'Yes. Well, I expect he will be.'

Billy wasn't in time. Nobody was, except Barty. Barty and Celia. Sylvia had been moved to a small ward on her own; she was heavily sedated with morphine and was quite calm and still; there was none of the dreadful agony and trauma of the night before. She lay, already somehow in another place, her breathing fast and dreadfully shallow, her face pinched and fallen in on itself. A nurse sat by her bed, holding her hand; as they came in, she stood up and left the room.

Barty stood looking at her mother in silence for a while, holding Celia's hand very tightly; then she moved forward, and bent to kiss the changed, lost face.

'It's Barty, Mum,' she said quite clearly, 'I've come to say goodbye.' And then, 'You mustn't worry about me. You mustn't worry about any of us. We'll be all right.'

And somehow the words pierced Sylvia's consciousness and her eyelids flickered, even though her eyes did not open. She licked her dry, cracked lips, almost smiled and lifted her hand just a little from the bed. Barty took the hand, kissed it and said nothing more; there was silence, then, for a while. Celia stood very quiet, very still, watching the two of them, mother and daughter, together, absolutely close, despite all the years and the circumstances of their separation and found it profoundly difficult to bear; she moved forward once, herself, to say goodbye to Sylvia, kissed her other hand, smoothed her hair: then went back to her vigil at the back of the room.

Suddenly there was a rough, rasping breath, then absolute silence and Barty turned to Celia and said, her voice very low, very steady, 'Is she – is she dead?'

'Yes,' said Celia, coming over to her now, looking down at Sylvia, thinking of the long years and their strong, strange friendship, hoping, praying even, she realised, that she had done something to make her sad, difficult life a little better, 'yes, Barty she is dead. She's gone from us now.'

And Barty laid down her mother's hand gently on the bed, and turned and walked out of the little room. Celia waited a few minutes, looking down at Sylvia, released from pain, thinking how brave and how good she had always been, uncomplaining, loving, optimistic, infinitely loyal and thinking how unfair life was, that she should have so much and that Sylvia should have had so little it counted for almost nothing at all. She went out and found Barty, sitting on a chair in the corridor, crying silently, her face white and her eyes full of something she did not understand.

Barty said, 'Now I'm quite alone,' and then Celia did understand, and it hurt more than she would have ever believed.

CHAPTER 30

'She's written. She's written at last. I can't believe it.'

'Who's written?'

'Susannah Bartlett, You total idiot. It came this morning. She says she'll see me.'

'When?'

'Um – not till Thursday. She's not very well, apparently. But I've got a telephone number, I can phone tomorrow. Isn't that marvellous?'

'It is. Absolutely marvellous. Are you going to tell Oliver Lytton?'

Guy thought for a moment. Then he said, 'No I don't think so. It might not help, as you said, it might even make things worse. So he'll just get his hopes up. And we have a fortnight after all, another day isn't going to make much difference. Oh, this is so exciting.'

'What does she actually say?'

'She says, Dear Mr Worsley, Thank you for your letter. I apologise for the delay in replying but I haven't been very well. I will be very happy to see you and talk to you about my time at Cambridge, although I don't know how helpful it will be. I don't know how much hurry there is, but I would prefer to leave it a couple of days yet. Perhaps you would like to telephone me tomorrow morning, on Ealing 459, and we can arrange a mutually convenient time. Yours sincerely, Susannah Bartlett.'

'Fantastic. Absolutely fantastic.'

'Isn't it? And there can't be anything for her to hide, surely, or she'd be a bit more cagey. Don't you think?'

'Well I'm not so sure about that,' said Jeremy, 'all she knows is you're writing something about Cambridge in the war years. It probably hasn't even entered her head that you want to know about her and Lothian.'

'No. No, I suppose not. But even so – I'd have thought she'd be a bit wary, at least. Oh go on, Jeremy, allow me a bit of triumph. I think it looks as if everything might be all right after all. Won't you agree even to that?'

'Yes,' said Jeremy, 'yes, all right. I'll agree to that.'

Jack lay in a haze of pain; everything hurt. His leg of course, but it was broken, so you'd expect that; but also his stomach, encased in bandages. Three broken ribs, they'd said. And his head: that was really bad. He'd tried to sit up a couple of times, but he just felt so sick and dizzy, it hadn't seemed worth the effort.

Worse than all the physical pain though, was his misery. Lily's rejection. It had been the first thing that came at him, through the sick, black blur as he slowly came to, next morning; the memory of her face, gazing into his, of her brown eyes, very sad, and of hearing her awful words. He really hadn't expected them; he'd been sure she'd say yes, having had time to think about it, she had said, 'I'm sorry, Jack, I really don't think I can marry you.'

And now here he was, laid up in some awful hospital, not given enough dope for the pain; life was pretty bloody, it really was.

'Do my family know I'm here?' he asked the nurse who was taking his temperature and his pulse; she said she really couldn't say, but she knew the police had been round, asking if they could interview him.

'Interview me! What about?'

'I don't know,' said the nurse, 'time enough for you to find out when they get back.'

She prodded his stomach. Hard. 'That hurt?'

'Yes,' said Jack.

'How's the headache?'

'Terrible. Can I have something for it?'

'You've had all you're written up for, for quite a while.'

'But it's bl – absolutely terrible.'

'Well, you can tell the doctor that, when he comes to see you.'

'Look,' said Jack, 'look, could you get someone to come and talk to me, so I can ask them to contact my family?'

'I'll try, but everyone is extremely busy,' said the nurse, 'including me.'

Which meant, he reckoned, that she wasn't even going to try. Well, maybe it didn't matter. Maybe it would be better for everyone if he just died here, without bothering anyone further. No one would care. Least of all Lily.

'A car crash! Oh, God. Is he all right, where is he? Oh, dear, when did you hear, has anyone seen him—'

'He's perfectly all right,' said LM briskly. 'Well, he has a broken leg, several fractured ribs and mild concussion, but he's very much alive. Silly boy. It really is time he grew up.'

547

'I know, but he must be feeling absolutely awful,' said Lily. 'I mean, it can't be much fun—'

'Possibly not. Anyway, I'm going to see him tomorrow. He's in a hospital in Sussex, Lewes General. Do you want to come with me?'

'Oh – I don't know.' Lily felt confused. Should she go? It would be different if he was in danger, but since he was comparatively all right, maybe it would be best if she stayed away. He might get the wrong idea if she turned up at his bedside, think she hadn't meant what she'd said. It was terribly difficult.

'Well, let me know,' said LM. 'I'll be leaving London at about ten. You can telephone me later today, or early in the morning at my brother's house. I'll give you the number.'

'Yes. Yes, thank you' said Lily. 'I'll let you know today.'

Rum sort of girlfriend, thought LM; not rushing to Jack's bedside. Well she was an actress, Celia had said. She was probably just using him, getting what she could out of him, and then moving on.

'Billy, do you know anything about Mum's baby that died?' said Barty.

They were sitting in the garden at Cheyne Walk; Billy had arrived several hours too late to see his mother and had been very upset, far too upset to go back again. Celia had said he should stay until after the funeral; it would help Barty, she thought, as well as him. Barty was in a very odd state: withdrawn, almost cold, she couldn't get near her to comfort her, or even to talk to her. Distressed by Sylvia's death herself, she found it very hard.

Billy turned to look at her. 'Not much, no. It was born dead, far as I know. I mean it didn't die after.'

'Oh. Oh I see. But—' she was silent.

'I was only six. Six or seven. Can't remember much. What I do rememer is that Lady Celia was there.'

'There! When it was born?'

'Yeah. It was Christmas, and it come early. The baby I mean. We was all sent next door to Mrs Scott and I remember the big car coming, and Dad asking her to go in and be with Mum.'

'Yes, that would make sense,' she said slowly, 'and then—'

'And then what?'

'Well, what happened?'

'Barty, I don't know. She come in next door and told us the baby was dead. The midwife took it away—'

'The midwife!'

'Yeah,'

'But Mum never had midwives, I thought Mrs Scott always helped her.'

'Well, I don't know. But there was a midwife, I know that. Anyway, what does it matter?'

'Oh – it doesn't really, I suppose. But the night before she – died, Mum was very ill, rambling and she kept talking about it. About the baby. She thought she was having it. Oh dear.'

Her lip quivered at the memory. Billy put his arm round her.

'It was so awful, Billy. She was in such pain. And Doctor Perring said she should go to hospital and I—'

'Yes?'

'I said she was frightened of hosptials, and did she have to go? And maybe if she had – then – oh Bill—'

'No,' he said, gently, 'it wouldn't have made no difference. There was nothing they could do. The doctor told me.'

'Yes, I know then. But the day before – maybe—'

'You could ask the doctor. Set your mind at rest.'

'Do you think so?'

'Course. He seems a nice chap. Why's he here all the time, anyway?'

'Aunt Celia isn't very well. He comes every day to see her at the moment.'

'What's the matter with her?'

'I don't know. She's got a bad cough. Billy, this baby that died – was there anything wrong with it?'

'Barty, do give over about the baby. I don't know. If you want to know more about it, why don't you ask Mrs Scott. She might be able to help.'

'Oh God. Dear, dear God.'

'What Oliver? What is it?'

'Look at this.' He held a piece of paper out to LM with a shaking hand.

'What's that?'

'It's an injunction.'

'What?!'

'Yes. It just arrived. By special messenger who insisted on handing this to me personally. It says – let me see – yes, the judge has heard an application for an affidavit submitted by Messrs Collins, Collins and Shaw and the injunction on the publication of the work known as *The Buchanan Saga* is – is hereby granted and served. So that's it. Oh, LM. How did this happen?'

'I don't know,' said LM. 'How could it have happened? We didn't know about any hearing, we weren't told, we haven't been able to put our case—'

'Oh God,' said Oliver. He rubbed his hands across his eyes; he looked absolutely exhausted. 'Well, whatever the reason, we're done for now. This is the end of Lyttons.'

'Are we? Are we really? It seems so unfair. Can't we contest it at least, demand the judge hears our side of the story? Can't we find out how this happened, there must be some mistake, surely—'

'I'll get on to Briscoe at once. See what he says. But – I don't have a lot of hope, I must say.'

'Yes, this is Susannah Bartlett. Good morning, Mr Worsley. Yes, I feel much better, thank you. No, I'm still happy to talk to you tomorrow. If that's soon enough. Apart from everything else, I have an urgent translation to do today. That's what I do for a living, you see.'

She had a pretty voice, Guy thought. She sounded nice. Very nice.

'I'm not sure quite how much I can help – if you tell me the sort of thing you want to know, I can be thinking about it. Just university life in general, or what it was like for a woman or—'

'Yes,' said Guy, seizing on the latter as being both true and sounding quite likely. 'Yes, that, certainly.'

'Right. Well, it was quite – interesting. As you can probably imagine. There weren't many of us. I'll see you tomorrow then. Here, at eleven. There's a train that comes to Ealing Broadway station, then you just walk across the green, anyone will help you.'

'Yes. Yes, thank you very much indeed.'

'Well,' said Susannah Bartlett, putting down the phone, 'I wonder what you really want, young man. And why. And what on earth it's got to do with Jasper Lothian.'

Wednesday: Wednesday already. Only two days left to decide. She had retreated into limbo again, Sylvia's death, the arrangements for Sylvia's funeral absorbing her. It was very frightening, this deadline. When the time for decision was infinite, or when at least there had been no stop on it, it had seemed quite easy. One day, she had told herself then, she would decide. One days things would be decided for her. Something would happen and then she would know. But – in forty-eight hours? Less than forty-eight hours now. What could possibly settle it for her now? And if she decided to stay, the decision was irrevocable. There would be no changing, no going back. Or rather going. No saying to

Sebastian, I've made a mistake, I'd like to come to you after all. He'd be gone, sailing to America for months.

She had heard of animals in traps, biting their own legs off in order to escape. Otherwise they starved. She felt a bit like that. Either way was agonising. But there were no half-measures: the decision had to be made. The clear, happy certainty of the moment she had almost gone had died: died with Sylvia. She was lost again and worse than before.

She thanked God for the instruction to stay in bed; it had afforded her a degree of privacy, at least. Dr Perring had actually said she could get up for meals, but she had not told Oliver that. In any case, she couldn't swallow, and unless a question was put to her directly, neither did she seem able to talk. Not coherently. She couldn't follow the simplest conversation, the most basic argument. She would manage perhaps one sentence and then, as the reply to it came, her mind raced, unchecked, back to her dilemma and she had no idea what that reply might have been. She pleaded anxiety over Barty, distress over Sylvia; but all that occupied her, in truth, were the scales of injustice, tipping this way and that, in favour first of her husband and family and a duty in which she could see no pleasure and little point, and her lover and her love in which she could see a great deal of both, but immeasurable pain for many people she cared about. And time passed for her and waited, in its inimitable way, no one.

'Daniels?'

'Yes, milady.'

'Daniels, would you take me down to my mother's – to Line Street. I want to get a few things from the house. Would you mind? I'd be so grateful.'

'It would be a pleasure, Miss Barty. Sorry about your mum. Very sorry. She was a nice lady.'

'Yes, she was a very nice lady,' said Barty, 'thank you Daniels.'

She went down the steps and into the house; there was no one in the two small rooms. The two younger children were with Frank, and Marjorie was with her young man. A pasty, spotty youth who did what Marjorie told him without argument; poor thing, little Mary had said, he must be mad. Barty silently agreed with her.

She stood there, looking round the room: so small, so dark, so shabby, yet imprinted with her mother's presence, with the small defiant touches of charm and prettiness which she had brought to it: the stone jug, filled with dried grasses and flowers that she had saved from a visit to Ashingham, the large photograph of all the younger children which

Celia had had taken for her one Christmas and framed, two paintings by Barty in papier mâché frames that Barty had also made, the picture of her wedding day, with Sylvia looking up trustingly at Ted, Ted's medal, pinned to the mirror over the chest of drawers, the brass oil lamp given to her by her own mother, shining as it always did. Barty could never remember a time when that lamp had not been brilliantly polished, a gleam of light in the dim room: her mother must have done it even in those last few days when she had felt so ill.

And then the sadder things, the shabby coat, hanging on a hook behind the door and Sylvia's black hat, the worn-out boots, the old cradle, which again, Celia had given her, used now to store clothes in – all neatly folded and clean. The threadbare curtains, the unravelled doormat. Barty thought briefly, angrily of the rooms in Cheyne Wall, refurbished year after year, rugs, curtains, covers, all changed in the name of fashion: it was all so unfair. So dreadfully dreadfully unfair. She blinked hard, brushed away the tears.

'Barty, hallo dear. What are you doing?

'Oh – Mrs Scott. I just came to get a few things. Things that Mum was specially fond of.'

'Of course. I'm so sorry, dear. Oh, I shall miss her myself. She was the best friend and neighbour anyone could have. Such a shame. If only she'd gone to the doctor earlier. But she was so stubborn. I don't want you to go thinking it was your fault, she told me you tried lots of times to persuade her, and the lady too. Proud, she was, your mum. So proud. And so brave.'

'Yes,' said Barty, 'yes, she was brave.'

'You'll let me know about the funeral won't you dear?'

'Of course I will. It's going to be next Monday, I think. We were going away this week, but we're staying now till it's over.'

'Billy up here, is he?'

'Yes. He came up to say goodbye, but – well – oh, dear—'

'Come here, my lovely. That's right. Come and have a cuddle. There we are. That's right. You come on in to my place, I'll give you a nice cup of cocoa. And a bit of cake, just baked it is.'

Two pieces of cake and a cup of cocoa inside her, Barty suddenly said, 'Mrs Scott can I ask you something?'

'Course you can. What about?'

'Mum had a baby. One that died.'

'Oh yes?' Mrs Scott's face had changed, become wary. 'What about it?'

'Well – could you tell me about it?'

'Nothing much to tell. Born dead, it was. She was. It was a little girl.'

'Yes. Um – she was definitely born dead was she? She didn't die – afterwards?'

'No,' said Mrs Scott firmly, 'she was born dead, your mum said.'

'Oh. Because you see she was talking about it the other night, when she was so ill. It all sounded a bit – odd somehow. Aunt Celia was there, it seems when she was – when she was having the baby.'

'Yes, I think I knew that.'

'And she said some very strange things. Like – well like – "don't tell Ted", and, "be quick, be quick", and, "I want to look after this one." And then she said, "It's all over now, she's gone." I just – well I just couldn't understand it.'

'No, well nor could you,' said Mrs Scott, 'nothing for you to understand, Barty, the baby was not right, and it was as well it didn't—'

'Didn't what?'

'Didn't live.'

'So it was alive? Was it?'

'Barty, don't keep on about it. It's not important.'

'It is to me,' said Barty and she was very flushed, 'it's terribly important to me. I think something happened. I think there was something strange about that baby and what became of it. And why did she have a midwife? She never had a midwife, you always looked after her.'

'Because there was complications,' said Mrs Scott, 'no need to go into them now.'

'But I want to, really I do, what sort of complications?'

'Barty,' said Mrs Scott firmly, 'there's no point raking it all over. Really. It was all for the best what happened. Your mum was very upset at the time, but afterwards she said she knew it was for the best.'

'Yes, but what? What was for the best?'

'Well, that it – she – didn't live. Your poor mum and dad had enough problems, you and five more already. It was before you went to the lady, don't forget; another one, and crippled too she was and a lump on her back as well, how would they have managed?'

'I don't know,' said Barty. She clearly wasn't going to get any further with this just now. She put down her cup. 'Anyway, I think I ought to be going now, Mrs Scott. There's Daniels hooting. Thank you so much for talking to me. And for everything you did for Mum. And of course we'll let you know about the funeral. And everyone else in the street who'd like to come.'

'That'll be most of them,' said Mrs Scott, 'everyone round here loved your mum. Very special she was. Very special indeed.'

'Yes, I know she was,' said Barty.

★

553

'They are claiming,' said Peter Briscoe, 'That we didn't reply to correspondence, so they were forced to seek a hearing at short notice.'

'But we didn't know about it.'

'I know that. But they wrote a letter. It did, in fact, arrive this morning. Second post. Asking why we had not come back to them. They were able to show a copy of it to the judge, who was, not too surprisingly, displeased. And they could put their case unhindered by any contradictory evidence.'

'I see,' said Oliver.

'I have written to the judge, protesting, and applied for a further hearing to be inter partes. Which would take place in ten days' time. If he grants it. Which I think he will,' he added.

'By which time our own deadline will be long past,' said Oliver. He ran his hands through his hair. 'This is a nightmare. An absolute nightmare. We can't win now, LM. We really can't. I had a call from Matthew Brunning today. He has some provisional contracts drawn up for Friday's meeting.'

'Well he may have them drawn up,' said LM, 'but I shall certainly not be signing anything.'

'LM, we don't have any choice. Whether we completely rewrite or pulp *The Buchanans*, or go ahead and fight to get the injunction withdrawn, we shall be as good as bankrupt. So it's Lyttons as an imprint of Brunnings, or no Lyttons at all. Oh God. For the first time, I'm deeply relieved that Father is dead. What would he have said to all this?'

LM was silent. Then she said, 'Have you talked to Celia yet?'

'No. Not yet.'

'Oliver, you must.'

He sighed. 'But whatever she says, or thinks, we have to sign with Brunnings.'

'Well, Celia and I don't actually know that. And, if you don't talk to her, I will.'

'Very well. I'll do it this evening.'

'I'm glad to hear it,' said LM.

'Will you be in?'

'No, I have an appointment,' said LM. She looked rather pink.

'I see.' Oliver almost smiled. 'Well I won't keep you. Have a good evening.'

The Bartletts were all sitting down to supper when the telephone rang. Roger Bartlett answered it; he was gone quite a long time. He came back into the dining room, looking rather harrassed.

'It's Professor Lothian,' he said to Susannah, 'he wants to talk to you.'

'Roger,' said Mary, 'is that a good idea?'

'He seems to think it's essential.'

'Oh, I see. Well – don't be long dear,' she called to Susannah.

'I hope he'll be gentle with her,' she added, as the door closed behind her.

'He promised he would.'

Susannah wasn't gone for long; when she came back she was looking quite calm. 'I understand much better now,' she said, 'what this is all about. I can see why he was so anxious for me not to talk to this young man. Who has been rather – underhand, I must say.'

'Well, dear you don't have to talk to him.'

'No, of course I don't.'

'Good,' said Mary Bartlett, 'well, why don't you let me telephone him and tell him not to come. It will be far better, and then everything can get back to normal.'

'Yes. What a good idea. I'll go and get his telephone number now.'

She left the room.

Mary Bartlett smiled happily at Roger.

'Thank goodness. What a relief. I really was so worried. I—'

'So stupid,' said Susannah, coming back into the room. 'I can't find his number anywhere, I've got an awful feeing I threw his note away. I wish I wasn't so scatty. Why don't you intercept him for me, Mother, when he gets here in the morning. I'll stay up in my room. Or, better still, I'll go out for a little walk. That might be better.'

'Of course, dear. I think you've been very sensible. Now why don't you go and sit down with your father and have a read, and I'll bring you some coffee. And, if I were you, I'd go to bed early, you look terribly tired.'

'Yes, I think I might,' said Susannah, 'it has all been a bit of a strain.'

'You're going to sell out to Brunnings? Just – sell out?'

'I don't have any choice, Celia. Really. You have to believe me.'

'You don't have a choice!' Her voice was hostile, scornful. 'It's not your decision, Oliver alone. As I understand it.'

'Very well, we don't have a choice. Does that suit you better? Don't you understand? We are virtually bankrupt. We will be bankrupt, even if we get this injunction lifted. Lothian can still sue for libel. Or, alternatively, we don't publish. The cost of printing those books, plus the cost of losing Brooke, the loss of—'

'Yes, yes, you've said all that before,' said Celia impatiently, 'but you must have considered other things. What about a bank loan?'

'It would have to be extremely large. And we're not exactly a good bet at the moment.'

'Have you tried?'

'I've made enquiries, The responses I've had were not encouraging.'

'Your brother? He has plenty of money. Couldn't he help?'

'I wouldn't dream of asking him.'

'Well I would. I will, if I have to. To save Lyttons. He'd want that surely, he's a Lytton too.'

'Celia, no. I forbid it.'

She ignored him. Then! 'Why Brunnings? They're a miserable house. No style, no vision. If we have to merge with someone, what about one of the others, someone we could live more happily with—'

'But Brunnings have the money. They may be miserable, as you put it, but they're also very rich. And successful. In their own way. Their offer is the only one worth considering.'

'And why,' said Celia, her voice very hard suddenly, 'why have I not been involved in all this? How long has it been going on?'

'A couple of weeks.'

'A couple of weeks! And you've kept it from me.'

'Not at all,' said Oliver. He sounded angry suddenly, 'you knew all the problems. About Lothian, the Mutiny book, Brooke's defection. The only thing I haven't discussed with you is a merger.'

'Oh really! Such a small thing. The end of Lyttons. Nothing really. Hardly worth mentioning, even. Good God, Oliver, how could you? When Lyttons is everything to me; you know it is, when I've spent my entire life working for its success, when I am a Lytton – you betray me, keep me out of the decision—'

'It's not your decision,' he said icily, 'it's mine. I shall make it. And you are not a Lytton. Not in that sense of the word. Goodnight.'

If he wanted revenge, Celia thought, too angry, too outraged even to cry, he had surely found it. And wondered if this, finally, was the sign she had been looking for.

Up on the nursery floor, Giles and the twins heard the angry voices, the slammed doors. Giles tried to ignore them, but the twins hung over the bannisters, struggling to hear more.

Barty was not there; she was spending the night in Balham, with Frank and his family and Billy. She had accepted the invitation without a great deal of enthusiasm, since Frank's wife was wary of her, difficult to talk to. But Frank had wanted her to go, and so had Billy and besides, she had thought, if she was there, she could easily, first thing in the morning, go and see Mrs Scott again. And talk to her about what was becoming an obsession, troubling her almost as much as her grief over her mother's death.

★

'LM—' said Gordon. He looked nervous, uncomfortable. He ran his hands through his white hair.

'Yes, Gordon?'

'I – wondered if we – that is if you – could – oh, dear, I'm finding this very difficult.'

LM smiled at him.

'Would you like me to help? Or would that be presumptuous of me?'

'No. No, of course not. I mean—'

'You wondered if we could be more than friends. Is that right?'

He blushed bright red. His forehead was damp. His expression was almost desperate. Then he said, 'Well – yes. If we could consider that. One day.'

'One day! Do we have to wait such a very long time?'

He looked embarrassed.

'I'm not sure. I wouldn't want to rush you in any way. But if you could think about it—'

'Gordon,' said LM, 'I don't need to think about it. It would be marvellous, I think. Really.'

'Oh. Oh well. Oh, I say. My dear—'

Even in her happiness, LM was struck by how absurdly different he was from Jago, how extraordinarily different his courtship had been. She had made love with Jago that first night; Gordon Robinson was proposing it after many weeks – months. Well – it was perhaps as well. It would avoid comparison. Of any kind – She allowed her mind to roam forward a few hours and felt a pang of such violent pleasure and delight she could hardly bear it. She lifted her wine glass, took a large sip and leaned forward to tell him.

'I – have no idea how we should proceed—' he said after a while, but he reached over the table and covered her hand with his. 'Whether you would agree to an actual engagement straight away. A formal one, that is—'

LM's heart lurched uncomfortably. She had not expected this. 'An engagement!'

'Well, yes. Oh, now I've worried you. Clearly we should leave it a while longer. But I would—'

'I hadn't thought of an actual engagement,' she said carefully. Wondering how she felt.

'Not yet, of course. I can see that now. Well, it can wait. If I know you are willing to consider it, that is happiness enough for me. I—'

'Gordon,' said LM, 'Gordon, have you ever been engaged before?'

'No. No, I haven't. There was only one young lady, with whom I felt myself very much in love, but – well it was all rather unfortunate—'

'What happened?' She smiled at him, reached out and touched his face. It was such a sweet, kind face. 'Tell me about it.'

'Well – it transpired that she – well that she had had a relationship before—'

'What, you mean she'd been in love before?'

'No, no, that wouldn't have troubled me. One can hardly expect to be the first and only love of a woman's life. I would not be that to you, of course. I realise that.'

'No. No, indeed. There is Jay, after all—'

'Yes, and you have had a husband. But—'

'Gordon, there is something—'

'No, no let me finish. It's important. My – my dear.' He was clearly very pleased by this endearment. He said it again. 'My dear LM.'

'My dear Gordon. My very dear Gordon,' she said, smiling at him. She reached for his hand, pressed it; he became scarlet again, looked around the restaurant anxiously, as if fearing some kind of retribution.

'Anyway,' he said, after a while, 'I discovered that she had had a – a – physical relationship. With a man.'

LM suddenly felt rather sick.

'Yes?' she said, 'and—'

'Well, you see – as you know, I am a Christian. To me, marriage is sacred. The only way to consummate a – a—'

'Physical relationship?'

'Well – yes.'

'So you broke it off?'

'Yes, I did. I felt I had to. I couldn't respect her any more. And therefore could not—'

'Could not love her?'

'No. Well, certainly could not respect her. Which to me is an essential part of being in love.'

'Yes. Yes, I see. Gordon, forgive me for asking this but – since we are talking of intimate things – are you – that is have you ever had a close relationship with anyone?'

He stared at her; he was pale now, and very agitated.

'I have not,' he said, 'no, I could not. Having not married. How could I? It would have been very wrong.'

'Yes,' said LM, 'yes I see.'

Suddenly her joy was quite gone. She felt very near to tears. Wretched in every way. This would not do. It could never do. It could never work. She was a woman of considerable passion and experience: even though she had been celibate for many years now. She had had several lovers, and one of them had fathered her child. She no longer believed in God; she did not actually believe in marriage. And here she was, contemplating a serious relationship with a man who was, at fifty years of age, a virgin, committed to strict Christian rules and beliefs. It could not be; it could never be. And there had to be a reason to give him: a good one—

'I – I do thank you,' she said, stuggling to keep her voice steady, 'for the great honour you have shown me. But I think – well I think it is probably – for the foreseeable future at least – not the best idea. I still feel a great loyalty to Jay's father. It would seem a betrayal.'

'Oh,' he said and he looked so dejected, so absolutely downcast that she almost relented, tried to tell herself it would, after all, be possible to make it work. But it would not. It really would not. And the sooner it was settled, was put behind them both, the better. For both of them.

'So – I have to say no,' she said. And it was one of the most difficult things she had ever said. 'I'm so sorry.'

'Yes,' he said, 'yes, I understand. Of course. But – well, should we continue as we have done? As friends. And maybe in time—'

'No, Gordon,' said LM, dredging up the courage from she knew not where – God perhaps – 'no, I think not in time. Not ever, really.'

'But you said – earlier—'

'I know. But I've been thinking about it, even as we talked and—'

'Very well,' he said standing up, and she thought she had never seen anyone look quite so sad, 'of course I appreciate what you have said and your honesty. You must let me take you home now.'

'No, really,' she said, 'I couldn't. I will get a taxi. I promise I will,' she added, 'don't look so worried. Good – goodbye, Gordon.' She held out her hand. 'And thank you again. For everything.'

'Goodbye LM,' he said.

She looked back as she reached the door of the restaurant; he was sitting, with his head down, just staring at the table. It was all she could do not to rush back over to him and tell him that she was wrong, that she would like to consider an engagement. But she knew she could not. It would never, ever do.

CHAPTER 31

LM put the phone down; in its own way that call had been the last straw. This little slut of an actress, saying no, she wouldn't come and see Jack, she was very busy with rehearsals, but to send him her best wishes.

'It might cheer him up,' LM had said and the girl had said she didn't know about that, but she really couldn't come.

'But I've still got his wallet,' she said, 'I meant to bring it round this morning before you went, but—'

'Oh, I wouldn't expect you to get up early for something so unimportant,' said LM coldly. 'No doubt you were up very late last night, dancing—'

'No, actually I—' said Lily, but LM had put the phone down.

In her misery, her sense of despair at the new emptiness of her life, the clear knowledge that she would not, at her age and in her situation, find another man to love her and whom she could love, in that dull aching misery, speaking at all was an effort: speaking to someone she felt innately hostile to was impossible. She picked up her coat and hat and rummaged in her bag for the key to Celia's car, which she had borrowed for the day; she couldn't find it, tipped the contents of the bag out on her desk. A note from Gordon Robinson, thanking her for the first (signed) edition of *Meridian* was amongst them; she stood staring at it, watching it blur with tears.

Lily made a face at the phone. Old witch. Well, she'd certainly had a lucky escape from acquiring her as a sister-in-law. Maybe if she'd only let her explain about the wallet, that she'd stayed with Crystal last night, that the wallet was at her parents' house in Bromley and it was impossible to get it before Miss Lytton left for Lewes, she'd have been a bit nicer. Anyway, it didn't matter. She could just leave it at Lyttons this evening; or maybe give it to the old girl then. She was sure to be going to visit Jack again. Dear Jack. God, she missed him. God this was difficult.

Mary Bartlett felt quite sorry for Guy Worsley. He really did seem a nice young man, pleasant-faced and very polite. It was a great pity they hadn't been able to find his telephone number, so that he'd had to make the journey for nothing, With his hopes so high. Still, he shouldn't have embarked on this in the first place. If, indeed, Professor Lothian was right about his motives. It was underhand and – well – wrong.

Just the same, his face as she told him Susannah wasn't there, that she had had to go out for the day, and wouldn't be able, in any case to see him after all, was very crestfallen. Very crestfallen indeed. In fact his whole body seemed to droop in disappointment and despair. Poor young man.

'I really am very sorry,' she said, 'sorry you've had to come all this way for nothing. Can I get you a drink of lemonade or something? It's terribly hot.'

Guy Worsley thanked her courteously, said it was quite all right, that he didn't want anything and set off down the path, drooping more than ever.

Giles was looking out of the window when Barty came back. She was walking down the Embankment and looked very upset. Poor Barty. It must be dreadful for her: she had no mother now and no father. And she had loved her mother so much. In spite of the rather fragmented nature of their relationship, she had loved her more than anyone. It was a great credit to his own mother, Giles thought, that she had worked so hard to ensure Barty saw her so often. He might not approve of what she had done exactly, but he did admire that. He decided to go down and meet her. Perhaps she'd like to go for a walk. Or even – go up to Sloane Square, where they could have a lemonade in the cafe at Peter Jones.

He ran down the stairs and opened the door. She stared at him, as if she hardly knew who he was. She looked dreadful. Utterly dreadful. White-faced and shocked, her eyes huge and dark-ringed.

'Barty,' he said, 'whatever is the matter?'

'I – don't feel very well,' she said. And was extremely sick, all over the hall floor.

The last day. Inside the final last twenty-four hours. Sebastian was leaving at ten on Friday morning. It could be that she would never talk to him again. Certainly not as a lover, not as a beloved. Perhaps cool chat at literary parties, cold exchanges over contracts, and in many years' time, it was possible there'd be friendly reminiscences at other people's houses. And she would be herself again: happy, whole, in command of what happened to her. Even that hurt: that love in all its anguish might ease to such a degree.

He had kept his word: he had not telephoned, had not written. Several times she had picked up the phone, asked for his number, for what purpose she did not know: certainly not to tell him anything, for there was still nothing to tell. And had then rung off before there was an answer. And returned to her wrack, her solitary torture.

She had hoped that Oliver's behaviour over the merger would settle her mind; the way he had set her aside, ignored her wishes, denied her position in the company. It did: for a while. But after her first brief rage, she lapsed back into a strange inertia, an inability to move away from her own intense concerns. It had become almost self-perpetuating, that inertia; unfamiliar to her, but overpowering. She felt very unfamiliar altogether; she could hardly recognise herself.

'You don't look too good, I must say,' said LM. She sat down by Jack's bed, began to unpack the bag she had brought him, sweets, biscuits, fruit, the kind of things she would have packed for Jay.

'Well thanks. I haven't had much access to barbers or tailors,' said Jack plaintively.

'Of course not.' She managed a smile.

'You don't look too good yourself,' he said, studying her, 'is anything wrong?'

'No. I'm a little tired, that's all. What happened, Jack, what did you do?'

'I honestly don't know. Came round a corner, trying to catch up with the others, hit a tree or something, don't remember any more. Quite a bit of champagne inside me, I'm afraid.'

'Jack! You are a fool. You might have killed someone.'

'I might have killed myself. I suppose you wouldn't care.'

'Of course I'd care.'

'Not many people would.'

'Now Jack, that's absurd.'

'No it's not. I've helped to wreck Lyttons for Oliver. Lost touch with all my old regimental friends. And then – Lily.'

'What about Lily?' she said carefully.

'You – haven't heard from her?'

'Well – not really. She has your wallet by the way.'

'Ah. I wondered where it was. I'm afraid that means it's over then.' He sighed, pulled miserably at a loose thread in the bedclothes.

'You're better off without her, I would say,' said LM, 'she doesn't seem a very caring sort of person to me.'

'Oh, you're wrong there, LM. She's very caring, very kind. And I could have sworn she cared about me. She's been so loyal, such a brick, always interested in what I was doing. We've been – close for quite a long time. She's jolly pretty too,' he added, 'and a terrific actress.'

'Really?' said LM drily. 'Altogether a paragon then.'

'Yes, actually. That's why I don't understand any of this. I mean it all ended so suddenly. I asked her to marry me and—'

'To marry you?' This was a huge step; Jack had seemed the eternal bachelor.

'Yes. Well, I – I loved her, LM. Still do. And I thought it was time I settled down. Anyway, that was what did it. Seemed to put her right off me.'

'Well – obviously she didn't feel ready to settle down herself,' said LM carefully.

'No. No I suppose that's it. She said she might be going off to Broadway, or some such nonsense.'

'There you are then. Obviously she's married to her career.'

'Obviously.'

'We don't seem to be very lucky in love,' said LM, 'any of us.'

He looked at her. 'You too?'

'Well – you know.'

'Yes. And – Oliver?'

'The less said about Oliver's marriage, the better I should like it,' said LM.

'You know too?'

'Yes, I know too. Dear oh dear. What a mess that is.'

'I don't know why he doesn't throw her out on the street,' said Jack.

'That would seem a bit harsh. But he does persist in being excessively saintly about it all. It – it irritates me. And I don't understand it.'

'I'll tell you one thing,' said Jack, grinning at her almost cheerfully, 'it's very hard being younger brother to a saint.'

Guy Worsley felt almost as if he might burst into tears as he trudged back down the road towards the station. So much for cracking the case, saving *The Buchanans*, saving Lyttons. What a beast this girl must be. Not even having the courtesy to phone him. Raising his hopes, sounding so friendly and so helpful: he still couldn't believe it of her. Well: that was that. Absolutely that. No more hope. He might as well go back to teaching. No one would look at anything he wrote ever again. Thank God he hadn't said anything to Oliver Lytton, raised his hopes. At least he was spared the humiliation of having to tell him he was back at square one.

He sighed. It was terribly hot. He looked round to see if he could see a shop anywhere that might sell him some lemonade: he almost wished now that he'd accepted Mrs Bartlett's offer. There didn't seem to be anything. Just rows and rows of over-neat houses. God he hated the suburbs. Well he would probably have to live in one himself. And not even as nice a one as this. He'd thought he'd be rich on the strength of *The Buchanans*, be able to buy himself a really good house in the country. Fine chance of that.

'Mr Worsley?'

Guy turned round. A young woman stood behind him; rather Bohemian-looking with long, fair hair and unfashionably long skirts. She was breathless; she had obviously been running, trying to catch him up.

'Yes,' she said, 'yes, I'm Guy Worsley.'

She held out her hand. 'Susannah Bartlett. I thought you must be. I was watching you from behind a bush. Sorry about all that,' she said, smiling at him, at his bewilderment. 'Look, let's get a train a little way up the line, shall we, maybe to Kew or something, have a coffee. I don't want there to be any chance of my parents or their friends seeing us.'

'But – I don't understand,' said Guy, 'I thought you didn't want to see me.'

'I didn't want anyone to know I'd seen you,' she said, smiling at him again, 'and I really had lost your phone number, so I had to get you over here. I'm rather good at losing things. Come on, here's the station now. Only I haven't got any money on me, can you stake me for the fare to Kew?'

Guy would have gladly bought her a ticket to Australia at that moment if she'd asked him.

Barty was in her room now; Giles had led her upstairs, helped her off with her shoes and laid her down on her bed. Then he went to ask Cook for some tea for her, and to apologise for the mess in the hall.

'That's all right, I'll see to it,' said Mary. 'Bless her, she's just upset, poor lamb. Horrible for her, losing her mum like that. You get on back up to her, Master Giles. Nanny and the little ones are all out, otherwise I'm sure she'd take care of her.'

Giles knocked gently on Barty's door, went in with the tray. She was lying on the bed, staring up at the ceiling, dry-eyed now, but she was shaking and her teeth chattered in spite of the warmth of the day.

'Barty, you've got to tell me what the matter is, you've really got to,' said Giles. 'Is it just about your mum, I don't mean just, of course, but is there something else, can I help in some way?'

She shook her head silently and took a rather reluctant sip of the tea; then she said, 'Thank you, Giles, but I really want to be alone now, if you don't mind. Sorry.'

'That's all right,' he said, 'I'm in the garden if you want me. I'd stay in my room if it wasn't so hot. Would you like me to get Mother to come up to you—'

'No,' she said sharply, so sharply he was quite shocked. 'No I don't want to see her.'

'All right. Well, try to have a sleep. That'll do you good.'

He turned to look at her from the doorway; she had pulled the covers over her, right over her head and had turned to the wall. Something was obviously very wrong. He wondered if Billy might know. He'd be back later; he could ask him.

'You don't really want to hear about life as a woman undergraduate during the war, do you?' said Susannah.

Guy flushed; 'Well – I do. Yes, of course. But—'

'But – shall we say, rather more about my life in particular. In some detail even.' She smiled at him. 'Mr Worsley, I may seem a little odd to you. Eccentric, even. But I'm not in the least stupid.'

'I didn't think you were,' said Guy. 'You seem extremely clever to me.'

'I am quite clever,' she said simply, 'but I – well let's say I have certain problems. Of an emotional nature. You don't want to know about them, though.'

'I do actually,' he said. He smiled at her. 'If you want to tell me.'

She was so nice; so very nice. They were sitting in a cafe by the river near Kew Bridge; the sun was shining on the water, and on her long, fair hair; the air was very gentle and warm. Rather like her personality. *The Buchanans* notwithstanding, he couldn't think of anyone he would rather have been with at that moment.

'Well – I had a very severe nervous breakdown. The year I graduated. It meant I did much less well than everyone had hoped. Including myself. Afterwards, I was terribly depressed. I – well I did something rather stupid.'

Tried to kill herself, he supposed.

'I had to be in hospital for a long time. In the end. I was able to leave, lead a comparatively normal life. But – I – well let's say I have to be on permanent medication. And it is agreed I couldn't cope with a normal job. Or very much stress of any kind.' She smiled. 'So I have to live at home with my parents. Treated rather like a child. Which is why we're here, and not talking in the garden. Well, it's one of the reasons.'

'I see,' he said.

'The other reason,' she said, 'is Jasper Lothian. He told me not to see you. Would you like to tell me why that might be?'

Celia, lying on the sofa in her room, trying to read, had heard the commotion when Barty came in, heard Giles running up and down stairs; she peered out of the door and intercepted Giles with a look as he came down the second time.

'What's wrong?' she asked quietly.

'I don't know. She's terribly upset.'

'Shall I go up?'

'No,' he said, 'no I think she wants to be alone At the moment. Perhaps later.'

She tried not to think about it, to leave her; but after an hour or so she couldn't bear it any longer. She went upstairs, knocked on Barty's door.

'Barty? Can I come in?'

No answer. She knocked again, then opened the door gently. The room was very stuffy: Barty was in bed with the covers over her. She must be terribly hot.

'Barty, darling, let me open the window. What's wrong, can I do anything?'

She was not prepared for the reaction. Barty turned over suddenly, sat up, looked at her. Her face was contorted with what Celia could only describe as hatred.

'No,' she said and it was very loud her voice, loud and harsh. 'No, you can't. I don't want to talk to you, I don't want to see you even. Get out of my room, please.'

Celia felt as if she had been physically struck.

'Barty—'

'I said get out of my room,' she said more quietly, but with the same absolute dislike in her voice. 'Now.'

Celia left.

'Now come on, Mr Worsley. I'm not going to tell you any more if you don't tell me something. What is all this about? And why does Jasper Lothian want me not to talk to you?'

'Well,' said Guy, 'it's like this—'

He talked for quite a long time; she listened quietly, without interrupting, except to say, 'I think I remember your cousin. He looks very like you. I couldn't think why I felt I'd met you before.'

When he had finished, she sat for a while, looking at the river. Then she said, 'Lothian is a charismatic man. He was very powerful. His students were hugely influenced by him. Including me. I fell completely under his spell. His mind is — extraordinary. He is the most wonderful tutor. He makes you feel you could break new boundaries.'

'In what way?'

'In every way. Intellectually, of course. He made us argue, struggle, propound outrageous theories, support them. He made us examine everything we thought and thought we knew, and go back to first base and start again. It was a great privilege to be taught by him.'

'And Mrs Lothian?'

'We hardly ever saw her. She was always away somewhere or other. She was very beautiful, great fun, wonderful clothes. But a most unsuitable person to be a Master's wife. Totally uninvolved in his work, in his life there—'

'So — did you like him?'

'Very much. Very much indeed. I adored him. We all did. We would have done anything for him.'

'Yes. Yes, I see.' Guy felt a great fear closing in on him; it was becoming clear that fiction had indeed mirrored fact. That she had even perhaps—

'Miss Bartlet,' he said. He had to get it over with.

'Please call me Susannah.'

'Susannah, please forgive me for asking this. But — did — did you have a — a relationship with him? With Jasper Lothian?'

There was a very long silence. He could hear people laughing in the background, gulls crying overhead, a tug hooting; the waitress came out, asked them if they would like anything else. They both shook their heads.

'Lovely day isn't it?' she said and disappeared again.

Finally, Susannah Bartlett said, 'No. No, I didn't have an affair with him. But — my brother did.'

LM got back to Lyttons at three o'clock. She felt exhausted: exhausted and depressed. Everything seemed wretched. Her own future, Lyttons' future, Oliver's marriage; there seemed no joy anywhere. She phoned the house, to hear that Jay and the twins were having a picnic tea in Kensington Gardens with some other children and their nannies, sent up a silent prayer that no psychopath might lurk behind the bushes, nor indeed beneath the grey and brown uniforms that the Norland and Princess Christian nanny colleges saw fit to clothe their graduates in, and went to see Oliver.

'Any news? Of anything?'

'No. Nothing. Nothing has changed. Unless you count Matthew Brunning having sent over the draft contract. You might like to look at it. It ensures us employment, if that is of any interest to you. You and me, and Celia, that is.'

'I expect it does,' said LM tartly, 'some of the major talent in English publishing, you could say. Oh, Oliver, I do wish you wouldn't rush into this.'

'I'm hardly rushing. And over this injunction on *The Buchanans*, there something else, you should know, we've had a letter from their lawyers demanding we pulp all existing copies and destroy the printing plates since we won't completely rewrite as they wanted. They would send a representative to witness that this has been done.'

'Oh,' said LM. 'Oh, dear. Yes, I am aware of that procedure. There are precedents, of course.'

'The cost of this whole thing is absolutely crippling. And the publicity will not be good. It makes us appear careless, at best. It is not good publishing.'

'No. Even so, I still think there might be someone else, some other way. I wish you'd fight.'

'I'm weary of fighting, LM. I've been fighting since 1914. In various ways.'

'I know, but–' She suddenly wished passionately that Celia was there: fighting. But she seemed oddly defeated; no longer part of things. She seemed to have abdicated responsibility. Well, she had other things to concern her.

'I feel so – ashamed,' he said suddenly, 'so desperately ashamed. To have brought Lyttons to this. I'm so glad—' he stopped.

She didn't say anything, merely patted him on the shoulder and left him. But she was glad too. That their father wasn't here to see it.

LM went into her office. Her father's office, as it had been in the early days, which she remembered and Oliver did not: when Lyttons was partly printer and bookbinder, with publishing only a rather small, unimportant sideline. Her father would go down to the type-room himself every day, and put his cotton cuffs on to protect his shirt sleeves and set type himself, run off proofs and then look at them, considering them with infinite care. He had a great love for and understanding of typeface, 'No, no,' he would say, 'this is a book of poetry, it needs a romantic typeface, set it in Bodoni.' or, 'That's marvellous, LM, you can't beat Times New Roman for authority and clarity.' He was skilled at binding too, inexhaustible in his search for exactly the right materials, his slender fingers pushing and pulling parchment smooth, leather corners tight. He loved doing that almost more than printing; he had been, above all, a craftsman. A painstaking, devoted craftsman. And all his work was going to be thrown away: the result of some careless groundwork, some foolish nepotism and—

'Miss Lytton?'

'Yes.'

She looked up; a very pretty girl stood in the doorway. Slightly flashy, but undeniably pretty. She had dark red hair and dark brown eyes, long eyelashes, creamy skin and a very sweet smile. And an extremely attractive voice, light and clear. LM warmed to her immediately.

'Yes,' she said again.

'I'm Lily. Lily Fortescue.'

The warmth cooled. Swiftly.

'Oh yes?'

'I've brought Jack's wallet.'

'Ah, thank you. A pity you didn't get it here before, I could have taken it down to him.'

'I'm sorry. I – well – I couldn't have got it here in time. I could send it, if you like.'

'No. No. I'll take it next time. He doesn't have a great deal of use for it at the moment.'

'How – is he?'

'Oh, he's all right,' said LM briskly, 'a few broken bones and a bad bang on the head. He'll recover. To do it again, no doubt.'

'He'd better not,' said Lily.

'I fear no one is going to stop him. He's not exactly a – responsible person.'

'He could be,' said Lily.

'Indeed? And what gives you the authority to make such a judgement?'

'Well – I was his girlfriend. For quite a long time.'

'I am aware of that. But no longer, as I understand it.'

'No,' she said and her voice was very low.

'Well, thank you for bringing the wallet. I am very busy, Miss Fortescue, your really must forgive me.'

'I wondered if it might be a good idea to – send him some flowers, or something,' she said, 'just to cheer him up, you know. And if you'd give me the address of the hospital.'

'Miss Fortescue,' said LM, pulling a pile of letters towards her, picking up her pen, 'I really think the less Jack hears of you from now on, the better.'

'Yes,' said Lily, with a sigh, 'yes, I expect you're right. Anyway – next time you see him, just give him my best wishes.'

She seemed to be lingering rather too long. Weariness, her own depression, made LM sharper than usual.

'I doubt if even they will be welcome,' she said, 'and I think in the long run my brother will be a great deal better off without you. Now, I suggest you get back to your music hall or whatever. Some of us have work to do.'

'I don't think there's any need to be rude,' said Lily.

LM stared at her. 'I rather disagree with you there. I certainly don't feel any compunction to be specially polite to you.'

'Oh, stop it,' said Lily crossly, 'stop being so hostile. You don't understand.'

'Oh, but I think I do.'

'No, you don't. You think I'm just a cheap little actress and I've been using Jack. Don't you?'

Silence. 'Don't you?'

'Well—'

'You're you're wrong. I love Jack. I love him very much.'

LM stared at her. 'You have an odd way of showing it, Miss Fortescue.'

'Oh, stop it,' said Lily again and then suddenly burst into rather noisy sobs.

LM was alarmed; she was not used to histrionics.

'Now then,' she said gruffly, 'now then. No need for that. Here, you'd better sit down.'

'I don't want to sit down,' said Lily. Large tears rolled down her face.

LM wondered briefly if they were genuine. She was, after all, an actress. Then she pulled herself to order. That was unkind. The girl seemed upset.

'Oh don't be absurd, 'she said. 'Here, come along. Sit down here. How would you like a cup of tea?'

Lily nodded between sobs.

'He – had asked me to marry him,' she said suddenly.

'Yes, I know. He told me so. And you refused.'

'Yes. But I didn't want to.'

'So why did you? Oh, I remember, Jack said something about you going to America.'

'Oh, I made that up.'

'Made it up?'

'Yes, I had to have some good reason to give him. No the thing was – well,—'

Janet Gould came in with the tea. 'And there are some biscuits, Miss Lytton. Oh, hallo, Miss Fortescue.'

'Hallo,' said Lily through sniffs.

'You mustn't worry about Mr Jack. He'll be fine, I'm sure, won't he, Miss Lytton?'

'Absolutely,' said LM. She had not realised that Lily was so familiar a figure at Lyttons.

'I know how fond of him you are,' said Mrs Gould, 'But he's quite a tough character. Anyway, you drink your tea. Nothing like a nice cup of tea, I always say.'

'That's what my mum always says, as well,' said Lily. 'Thank you, Mrs Gould.'

'Right,' said LM, when Janet Gould had rather reluctantly gone, and the door was closed again. 'Tell me why you turned Jack down.'

'Well – well I know it sounds stupid. But – it just wouldn't have done, wouldn't have worked.'

'But why not? Exactly?'

'You're—' she hesitated, 'you're all so posh.'

'Posh!'

'Yes. Look at this room for a start, it looks like something out of a mansion, the marble fireplace and the wood panelling and that. And the house in Cheyne Walk, that is a mansion, more or less. And Jack was a colonel in the cavalry. And Lady Celia, and her parents, whatever would they make of me?'

'I don't think it would matter in the least,' said LM, 'what they made of you.'

'Yes, it would. After a bit. You should see where I live—'

'Where do you live?'

'In a terrace house in Bromley.'

'I grew up in something very similar in Peckham,' said LM calmly.

Lily ignored her. 'Three up three down it is. I mean, it's very nice and comfortable and everything, but – well – It's a terrace. And my dad's got a greengrocer's stall. I left school when I was twelve. Jack went to some posh school – where'd he go?'

'Wellington,' said LM.

'Is that where Mr Lytton went?'

'No, he went to Winchester. Jack wasn't clever enough, he didn't get in.'

'Oh. Well anyway—'

'So you turned Jack down, purely because you thought he was too posh? Is that right?'

'Yes. Because I just don't think it would have worked.'

LM looked at her. Her expression was very solemn. Then she smiled: the sudden, wide grin which so transformed her face. 'Miss Fortescue,' she said, 'my father was a jobbing bookbinder. He arrived in London from Devon, with nothing but a very small suitcase and his apprentice-ship papers. He went to work for a Mr Jackson, who had a bookshop and a small printing press on which he printed educational pamphlets. He taught my father typesetting as a second skill. My father married the boss's daughter – my mother – and slowly worked his way up in the world that way. Now then. Does that sound very posh to you?'

'No,' said Lily. She smiled rather reluctantly back at LM. 'No, it doesn't.'

'And,' said LM, wondering why she was revealing all this to a complete stranger, 'My – that is, Jay's father was a builder. He was killed in the war. As for Celia: well, yes, her parents are rather posh. As you put it. But I think we outnumber them rather satisfactorily. Although I have to tell you that her father would be extremely pleased to have you in the family. Anyway – if Jack has been giving you the impression that he's in some way socially superior, then I can only say it's time he was brought back down to earth with a bit of a bang.'

'Oh, no he hasn't. Really. Honestly.'

Lily was still crying; but she was smiling at the same time.

'I think I might get on down to Lewes now,' she said, 'I should be able to get a train, shouldn't I?'

'Of course you will. Good luck. And send my love to Jack. Tell him he's a very lucky chap. To have you, I mean.'

'Thank you,' said Lily, 'thank you very much, Miss Lytton.'

'I didn't realise for a long time,' said Susannah Bartlett. 'I was rather naive, I suppose. I loved my brother very much; he was only eighteen months younger than me, and a year behind me academically. When he arrived at Cambridge, I introduced him to all my friends. And to Jasper Lothian of course. We used to go to his house a lot. And we invited him to our rooms. He was often alone, you see, Mrs Lothian being away so much. He was so theatrical, so much larger than life. Very generous and hospitable.

'And amusing. He just attracted gossip. People used to tease me, ask was I in love with him? Ask if he was in love with me. I'm afraid I rather encouraged it, I enjoyed being the centre of attention. I hadn't had any men friends before, I'd led a very sheltered life. Anyway – well, I did find out. My brother told me actually.'

'And – how did you feel?'

'Oh—' she smiled, 'actually rather excited. Once I got used to the idea. Certainly not shocked or anything. It all seemed rather splendid and decadent. Light years away from Ealing and my father's job at the bank. But then – well then Lothian began to get rather – unpleasant. For all his unconventional talk, he was terrified of the truth getting out. He said he would like to encourage the idea of our having an affair, to put up a sort of smokescreen. That did shock me; I said I didn't want to do that and he said he thought it would be in my interests, that if it did get out about Freddie being homosexual, it would be dreadfully distressing for my parents and so on. It was a sort of blackmail.'

'How frightful,' said Guy.

'Yes. He is frightful. But then I couldn't see it, of course. I was literally dazzled by him. And, as I said, it all seemed rather exciting. Anyway, I went along with the fiction, for about a term and a half. Then he got tired of Freddie, dropped him just like that. Freddie was heartbroken. He threw it all up, said he didn't want to finish his degree. He was nearly nineteen by then; he went out to France.'

'And?'

'And he was killed,' said Susannah. Her voice shook. 'After only about three months.' There was a very long silence; then she said, 'But before that, when he first went away, things became very unpleasant. One of the other masters had heard rumours about him and Freddie; Jasper came to my room one night and said he wanted me to tell this man that it was quite untrue, that my brother was completely heterosexual, and that nothing of the sort had ever happened. That I would know if it had, and that Lothian and I had been having – not an affair, exactly, but a relationship. I said I didn't feel I could do that and he said if I didn't, he would tell my parents about Freddie. And implied that I wouldn't do very well in the exams. So I – I did. I don't know if this other man believed me or not, but anyway, I did. I hated doing it, I felt depraved myself. The irony was that I never minded about that sort of thing, homosexuality I mean. I could never see anything wrong in it. Freddie and I talked about it endlessly, he said he'd known he was – well that he was one since he'd been quite a little boy—'

'It is terrible to think,' said Guy, 'that it is a criminal offence.'

'I know, isn't it?' She was silent. Then, 'Anyway, just before I did my finals, the news came that Freddie had been killed. I did very badly, and Lothian was the opposite of supportive. He said I'd let him down, let the whole college down. And I don't know, it was all too much for me, the whole thing was so horrible, and that was when I had my breakdown. I was in hospital for months.

'He came to see me several times, ostensibly to see if I was all right, but actually to make sure I wasn't talking about him and Freddie while I was in analysis, or with the drugs, or anything. He kept telling me over and over again I must never tell anyone. I honestly think he was trying to drive it into my subconscious. While presenting himself to my parents as a kind, concerned father figure. Showing a huge interest in my illness, the management and treatment of it, suggesting friends who were psychiatrists, who might be able to help. My parents are very simple people. Very impressed by authority and terribly impressed by someone like him. They knew he'd had been very influential in Freddie's life at Cambridge, and he told them what a brilliant boy he'd been, how he would have got a First, And he sort of implied that I just wasn't up to it, that university, the course even, was all too much for me. He really belittled me in their eyes.'

'But why? And why did you let him get away with it?' said Guy.

Susannah smiled at him. 'I really was quite ill. I couldn't fight him. They thought he was wonderful, kept saying how lucky we were to have him as a friend. I have come to loathe him. *Loathe* him. Anyway, I haven't had to speak to him for a couple of years now. I've kept well away from the college, never go to reunions or anything like that. He's kept in touch with my parents, always asking how I am, sending them Christmas cards, that sort of thing. But when I found you'd written to me, and that he'd told them not to give me the letter, I knew it must be pretty important.'

'Yes, well it is,' said Guy, 'pretty important.' He looked at her; 'it's so very good of you to tell me all this. I don't know quite why you should.'

'Two reasons,' she said, 'I don't like being manipulated by anyone. Least of all by Jasper Lothian. And I liked your cousin, and I liked your story. I wouldn't have told you if I hadn't. I'd just have said it was wonderful at Cambridge and left it at that. The only thing is,' she added, 'I don't want Freddie's name dragged into this, publicly I mean, It would break my parents' hearts.'

'It won't be,' said Guy, 'I promise. Golly, look at the time. Look, let me escort you back.'

'No, really. I'll be fine,' She smiled at him again. 'I'm not mentally deficient, you know. I'm perfectly capable of finding my way from Kew to Ealing. If you give me my fare, that is.'

'But I'd like to,' said Guy, 'really.'

'You're very kind. But you mustn't get off the train with me. I'm quite serious; if my father, or my mother saw us, they'd guess. And I really don't want that.'

'Well – I'll just come to Ealing with you, then.'

'What – what do you think you might do,' said Susannah, 'about it all?'

'I'm not sure. Talk to my cousin first. I swear I won't tell the publishers. Not about your brother, anyway.'

'Thank you,' said Susannah, 'I do trust you not to.'

CHAPTER 32

Celia sat in her room, on the edge of her bed, with one arm round each
of the twins and looked at them through a haze of tears. They looked
back at her and smiled uncertainly. She had been crying for a while;
Venetia had heard her and summoned Adele; they had come in,
alarmed, to comfort her.

'You never cry,' said Ventia, 'whatever is the matter?'

'You mustn't cry,' said Adele, 'please, please stop.'

Celia stopped: with a great effort.

'What is it?' said Venetia, 'please tell us.'

She couldn't; how could she? She looked at them, thinking how
much she loved them, wondering how she could possibly leave them
and began to cry again; then stopped once more and wondered whether
children could be a cure for grown-up grief.

'It's – nothing,' she said finally, 'nothing important.'

'It can't be be nothing,' said Adele, 'people don't cry over nothing.
Has someone been unkind to you?'

'No,' said Celia (if only they would be).

'Are you feeling ill again?'

'No.' (She almost wished she was).

'Where's Daddy?'

'At the office, I suppose.'

'Shall we telephone him?' They liked doing that; it made them feel
important.

'No, Adele, certainly not. He has a great deal to worry about at the
moment.'

'Is that why you're crying?'

'Sort of.'

'Poor, poor Mummy. Would you like a drink of something?'

Poison perhaps? That would solve things. 'No, thank you, darling.'

'Cigarette?' said Adele.

'She's given them up,' said Venetia, 'haven't you?'

'Yes, I have.'

'That's why you're crying,' said Adele, her face clearing. 'When

575

Nanny made us give up sweets for Lent, we cried all the time. It's horrible, not having things you really like.'

'Maybe it is,' said Celia, managing to smile.

And perhaps it was not having the thing, the one thing she really liked. The one thing that could make her happy: the thing which was leaving the country in about twelve hours' time. Still waiting for her; still not knowing if she was going to come.

She heard Nanny calling. 'Run along. It's teatime. Thank you for looking after me.'

'That's all right,' said Venetia. 'I should have a cigarette, if I were you. We won't tell. Barty's not well,' she added, turning from the door. 'She won't come out of her room.'

'I know. Now she really has got something to be upset about.'

In his house in Primrose Hill, Sebastian continued to pack. It was an act of superstition: if he was all ready to go, everything packed, put away, then he would be required to stay. It was a simple as that. He grew increasingly confident that she would come to him. She would have told him by now if she was staying. She would have made her decision in her clear, brave way, and informed him of it. The indecision was good: a sign that he had changed her. Changed her permanently. Made her frailer, less independent. He had fractured her self-sufficiency, her toughness; he had made her love him, and he had made her need him. She would come to him; he was quite certain.

'I don't believe it,' said Jeremy, 'I just don't believe it.'

'Isn't it marvellous? Isn't it superb? We've got him. We've really got him. The bastard.'

'Yes, we have. Well you have. What a story. My God. It's much better than yours.'

'Thanks. Well, never mind.'

'What are you going to do? Tell Oliver Lytton?'

'No. Not yet. I promised Susannah I wouldn't involve her brother and I can't. I'm going to see him. Lothian, I mean.'

'When?'

'In the morning. It's a bit late now.'

'Yes. I suppose one more day can't make any difference.'

'No. I did think of just telling Oliver. I thought it would be all right, but then he'd start asking questions and it would get so complicated. Better to present him with a *fait accompli*, I thought. God, he'll be so thrilled.'

'He will indeed.'

'She's so nice, Jeremy. Susannah, I mean. Do you remember her?'

'Yes, I do now. I think I liked her.'

'She liked you. She said she only talked to me because I reminded her of you. She's pretty, too.'

'Is she? All those bluestocking girls looked the same to me, a bit severe and – sort of pale.'

'Susannah's neither. Certainly not severe. Very thin, wouldn't eat anything. I tried to buy her lunch, but she wouldn't hear of it, nibbled at a sandwich. Anyway, I'm off to Cambridge first thing in the morning. Can I stay here tonight? It's so near Liverpool Street.'

'Of course. Shall I open a bottle of champagne?'

'No. Let's keep that for the real celebration. Anyway, I want to have a very clear head in the morning.'

'Very wise. I'd come with you, only school starts again in a fortnight and I have so much preparation to do. Anyway, I think you'll be better on your own.'

'I think so too. Have the champers on ice for when I return.'

'You're on.'

Staff Nurse Thompkins was growing very weary of Mr Lytton. He was nothing but trouble. He complained constantly, about the pain in his leg, his nausea, the inadequacy of pain-killing drugs. He wouldn't eat his meals, saying they were disgusting and increased the nausea, and then complained that he was hungry. He kept demanding to see the doctor, and to be told how his treatment was progressing and when he could go home. He appeared able to set aside both his nausea and his pain every time any pretty young nurse appeared on the ward, and flirted disgracefully. He kept refusing to answer questions about his basic bodily functions and then demanded the bedpan or the water bottle when he could see she was at her busiest. His sister had arrived out of visiting hours and had insisted on being allowed to see him, in a very overbearing way; and now, as the last straw, a young woman, a rather showy-looking young woman, clearly no better than she should be, had arrived well after supper time and said she wanted to see him as well.

'I'm afraid,' said Staff Nurse Thompkins, 'that is quite out of the question. Supper is over.'

'Well if it's over,' said the girl, 'I'm not interrupting it. Am I?'

Nurse Thompkins glared at her. 'After supper,' she said, 'patients need to be quiet, preparing for the night.'

The girl looked at the fob watch, pinned to her unfashionably large breast. 'At – half past six?'

'There are important things to be done for them. It all takes time.'

'Like what?'

Staff Nurse Thompkins sighed. 'I am not prepared to discuss medical matters with you. Please leave. You can come back tomorrow. At two o'clock. That is official visiting time.'

'But I've come all the way from London.'

'I'm afraid that is your problem, not mine. Please leave.'

She escorted Lily physically to the Reception area of the hospital.

'This young lady,' she said to the porter on duty, with a strong and ironic emphasis to the word lady, 'is leaving. She naturally will not be able to return until tomorrow.'

'Right, Staff,' said the porter. He leered at Lily; she didn't like the look of him.

She went out; it was a lovely evening. She thought of Jack, cooped up in bed in a hot stuffy ward and could hardly bear it. Well, she wasn't going to take this lying down. She looked around her; various people came in and out of the hospital all the time. Surely she could sneak in with one or other of them. But the porter knew her; he had her number, as her dad would say. She sat down on a bench, just out of sight of the door and waited. Lily's dad had always told her there was much to be said for waiting, when all else failed.

'Something usually turns up,' he said, 'sooner or later.'

She had never put much faith in it till now, but it seemed worth a try. Certainly in the absence of anything else.

Something did turn up. In the form of a young, and very good-looking doctor. He was in a small car; Lily watched him. Initially she had thought he was a visitor, but then she saw him reach into his car for his bag. Right. Here was her chance. She dropped her face into her hands and began to cry. She was very good at crying. Not loudly, but absolutely noticeably. When she was a child actress, she had once played Little Nell in *The Old Curiosity Shop*. Her heart-rending tears were mentioned in more than one review.

She heard the doctor's footsteps slow; then stop.

'Excuse me. Are you – all right?' he said.

Lily looked up at him; her large brown eyes surprised to see him, her tears and her sobs momentarily halted.

'I – I'm sorry,' he said, 'I must have startled you.'

'Only a little.'

'Is there something wrong?'

She fumbled in her pocket for a handkerchief, failed to find one. 'Oh dear,' she said.

'Here,' He offered her his. That was good. Men were always moved, for some reason, by the sight of a girl using their handkerchiefs. It seemed to give them a proprietory feeling. She took it, wiped her eyes, smiled at him gratefully.

'Thank you. Thank you so much.'

'What is it?'

'Oh – well you see – no, I mustn't keep you, I'm sure you've got important patients to see.'

'I have. But they can wait.'

She shifted on the seat slightly, so that her skirts slipped up, showed more of her legs. She could see him looking at them. She sighed again.

'Well – the thing is, my fiancé is in the hospital. I've come to see him, he's had a terrible accident, and I've been travelling all day. And the nurse won't let me in.'

'Won't let you in?'

'No. She says it's not visiting hours. Of course I understand you must have rules, but—'

'Well, that's absurd. Does she know you've had such a long journey?'

'Yes, I did tell her But she said – she said I must come back tomorrow. And I've nowhere to stay, and it's cost me a lot to to get here and – oh dear.' More tears. Welling up. She'd better stop after this, or her eyes and nose would start looking red. She swallowed. 'Anyway, thank you for listening to me. For being so kind.'

'Come along. Rules are made to be broken. I'll take you to your fiancé. What ward is he in?'

'H Ward.'

'Ah,' he said, 'Staff Nurse Thompkins. She does take her duties very seriously.'

Jack was trying to decide whether cocoa or tea would be preferable, or rather, less disgusting, when Nurse Thompkins appeared at his bedside with a doctor. She looked furious, red in the face with a white line round her taut mouth.

'Ah, Mr Lytton,' said the doctor, 'I was just coming to see how the leg was.'

'Bloody awful,' said Jack, 'I need more painkillers.'

'Sorry old chap. Not till bedtime.'

'But—'

'I also wanted to make sure you were respectable and not using the bedpan or anything.'

Obviously the consultant was coming; well that was something. He might be able to—

'Your – fiancé is here,' said the doctor, 'and owing to the very long journey she's made, Staff Nurse Thompkins has kindly agreed that she may visit you now. Even though it is out of visiting hours.'

'My fiancé?' said Jack. He felt rather faint. Must be hallucinating. Must be the drugs.

'Yes. I met her outside. Some chaps have all the luck. Do come in, Miss Fortescue. Mr Lytton is ready to see you now. Only thirty minutes, Staff. Mr Lytton mustn't be over-tired. Or over-excited,' he added with a wink at Jack over Nurse Thompkins' head.

'Hallo Jack,' said Lily. He must be hallucinating: this couldn't be true. She was looking glorious, in a sort of light-coloured dress he hadn't seen before, her red hair tumbling down as she pulled off her hat. 'It's lovely to see you Jack. You don't look too bad. Thank you so much,' she said turning to the doctor, 'you've been so kind. Um – may we?' She indicated the curtains.

'Of course,' said the doctor, 'don't want to be upsetting the other patients.' He winked again and drew the curtains carefully round the bed. The last thing Jack saw before Lily bent over him and kissed him was Nurse Thompkins's furious face, redder than ever.

'What's this about a fiancé?' he said, he still felt he must be dreaming.

'Well,' said Lily, 'I like that. Have you forgotten already? You only asked me two nights ago.'

'I know I did. I know. And you said—'

'Oh, I said a lot of silly things. What I meant was, I'd love to marry you. As soon as possible, Actually. Well, as soon as you've got yourself organised, doing a bit better with that job of yours, and paid off a few of your debts. Oh, and you've got to promise me to give up cocaine.'

'I promise,' he said, reaching up, taking her hand. 'I do promise, Lily. I'll promise you anything. Anything at all.' He stared at her. 'I still can't believe this.'

She smiled at him. 'Yes, you can.'

He lay there smiling up at her foolishly in return, occasionally kissed her hand, not saying anything; then he suddenly turned away from her and started rummaging through his bedside cupboard.

'Damn,' he said, 'damn. Where is it?'

'What? If it's your wallet you're looking for, I've got it. I've brought it with me.'

'No. No, it's not—'

'Whatever's that?' she said, staring at something in fascination.

'Oh – oh, don't worry about that.'

'No, what is it?'

'It's a pee bottle,' he said, 'here, take the bloody thing will you? Ah, now here we are. Lily, give me your hand. Your left hand. There. I hope you like it. It comes with all my love. If you want something better, I'll get it for you the minute I get out of this wretched place. But it will have to do for now.'

And Lily sat, staring down at her left hand, still holding the hospital water bottle in her right, staring at the small, modest diamond ring Jack had pushed on to her engagement finger, and said, 'It's absolutely perfect, Jack. I love it, and I love you. Thank you. Thank you so much. And I certainly don't want anything better. Not now, not next week, not ever.'

'Really?' he said, 'it's not very grand, I'm afraid.'

'That's exactly why I like it,' said Lily and bent to kiss him again.

Giles hesitated outside Barty's door; it was hours now since he'd left her there. It was – he looked at his watch – half past six. She'd been lying there nearly all day. He couldn't leave her any longer. He couldn't. He knocked gently. No answer. He opened the door, looked at her. Lying there, almost as he had left her, on the bed with the covers pulled over her head.

'Barty,' he said gently, 'Barty, it's me, Giles.'

'Hallo,' she said. Her voice was odd: unfamiliar. Sort of heavy.

He went over to the bed, looked down at her. She pushed the covers down; her face looked awful. Red and flushed and sort of sweaty; and her eyes were terribly swollen. She had obviously been crying and crying.

'Can I open the curtains? It's awfully stuffy in here.'

She nodded. 'Yes, if you like.'

He pushed the curtains back, opened the window. The light fell on her face; she winced.

She saw him looking at her, tried to smile.

'I must look awful. Sorry.'

'You don't look awful. You never look awful.'

This time she managed a proper smile.

'Of course I do.'

He sat down on the bed. 'Poor old you. Poor Barty. Want to – want to talk about it?'

She shook her head violently. 'No. No I don't.'

'All right. Well can I get you anything?'

She shook her head again. 'No, thank you. Well – I might have a bit more of that lemonade.'

'All right. Here.' He poured a glass out for her, held it for her. She took a few sips.

'That's nice.'

'Good.'

He smiled at her. Perhaps it had just been her mother. Perhaps she'd be all right now. After she'd had what Nanny called a really good cry.

'I'm so sorry,' he said again gently, 'so sorry. Whatever it is.'

She looked at him. He thought she was going to smile at him. But she didn't. She suddenly started to cry again, sobbing, like a small child, her arms folded across her body as if she was in some kind of terrible pain, saying, 'Oh, Giles, Giles,' over and over again.

'Barty,' he said, 'Barty, don't. please don't.'

And then, he didn't quite know how, he was lying on the bed beside her, holding her in his arms, and she was still crying, her head turned to him, clinging to him, as if he was a lifeline, and he just went on holding her, saying stupid meaningless things, like he couldn't bear to see her so upset, and that she must try not to mind so much, whatever it was. And then, that he loved her. Loved her very much indeed.

'Home?' said LM. She had put her head round Oliver's door; he was still sitting at his desk, Just as she had left him, poring over pages of figures.

'I keep hoping I'll find something,' he said, 'something that I've forgotten about, some asset that will save us. I can't.'

'I've been doing exactly the same thing,' said LM. 'How absurd we both are.'

'Any luck?'

'No. None. I'm afraid.'

'I'm afraid we've run out of it,' he said, 'luck, I mean.'

'It seems so. In every way.'

She hadn't meant to say that; he looked at her.

'Anything wrong?'

'No. Well – a bit. Yes.'

'You can tell me about it. If you like.'

'I know but—' She hesitated.

It was delicate. LM found it hard to talk about anything more personal than how she had slept at the best of times. She might, had other circumstances been different, have told Celia. But – Oliver. Her younger brother. Self-protective, uncommunicative. Like her. As their father had been. It had probably not helped any of them.

She sighed.

'Go on' he said, 'it might take my mind off my own troubles. Think of it as a kindness to me. We could have a glass of sherry, if you think that might help.'

Perhaps she could. Perhaps it would help.

'Well, it will probably all sound very – foolish,' she said.

Oliver looked at her; he reached into the cupboard by his fireplace and pulled out a bottle of sherry and two glasses.

'Go on,' he said.

★

She would go. She would definitely go. She had decided once and she had decided again. That decision had simply been interrupted. She couldn't stay here, held in this prison, any longer. It was stifling her, incapacitating her. In every way. She felt enervated, diminished, hardly able even to talk any longer. The last straw, she realised, had actually been Oliver telling her she was not a Lytton. If that was the case, then what was she doing here? Her rage at his saying that had passed, leaving only a terrible misery. She had spent her whole life being a Lytton. How could he deny her that? Whatever she had done. No, she must go. However much unhappiness it caused, that was what she had to do.

She would telephone Sebastian and tell him, and then when Oliver came home, she would tell him and try to explain to the children and then she would leave. She went into her study, picked up the receiver and asked for Sebastian's number.

'So you want to – well, let us say, have a relationship with this man.'

'Yes, Very much.'

'And he with you.'

'Yes. But he wants it only within marriage.'

Oliver smiled at her: a rather wintry smile.

'An interesting reversal of the usual state of affairs.'

'Yes. I know.'

'Well is marriage so horrific a prospect?'

'I don't believe in it.'

'But you would have married Jay's father?'

'Yes. Yes, I suppose I would. He—'

'Yes?'

It was so difficult talking about all this.

'He did ask me. When he knew about Jay. But – then he was killed. As you know.'

'Yes, I do know. You had a lot of unhappiness. So many did. Caused by the war.'

'Yes. And that's another thing, Oliver, he assumes, of course, that I was married to – to Jay's father. He would be so horrified, if he knew.'

Oliver looked at her. He poured himself another sherry.

Then he said almost impatiently, 'Oh for heaven's sake, LM, why tell him?'

'He's not here, Lady Celia. No. He's gone for a meal with his agent. He said to tell anyone who phoned, he'd be back at about nine. He won't be late, because he's leaving tomorrow, quite early. On this trip. You know?'

'Yes, Mrs Conley. I do know.'

'I'm just off home myself now. But I'll leave a note, saying you rang.'

She felt desperate, near to tears. She needed to speak to him so badly. To have her courage boosted.

'Well – yes. Thank you, Mrs Conley. But he will be back – later?'

'Oh, yes, Lady Celia. By nine thirty I'd say. At the latest.'

'So you think I should lie?'

LM was shocked; Oliver, who was a by-word in the family, in the publishing industry, for honesty, for absolute integrity. Advising such a course of action, taking the side of pragmatism, of economy with the truth.

'Well,' he said, 'no need for that. Just silence. Valuable stuff, silence. I've great respect for it, personally.'

'But—'

'Look, LM. You've had many years of loneliness, not a lot of happiness. If you have a chance of it now, why, in the name of heaven, not take it? And if, in the process, you have to allow this man to assume you were married to Jay's father – as you would have been, you say – well, what is so wrong with that? Come on, let's go home now. I could do with a bit of peace before tomorrow.'

Celia decided to go up to the nursery. If she were not to see her children for a while, then it would be good to spend a little time with them. In any case, there were Sylvia's funeral arrangements to discuss with Barty; however upset and hostile she was, that had to be done. She went up to the top floor; she could hear the twins chattering, telling Nanny in between shouts of snap, what they were going to do in Cornwall. It sounded rather alarming, involving cliff-climbing and underwater fishing. She went in, smiled at them.

'Are you all right now?' said Venetia.

'Yes, I'm fine. Thank you.'

'We want you to come to Cornwall,' said Adele, 'we just said, didn't we, Nanny?'

'You did,' said Nanny.

'I'm afraid that really is out of the question,' said Celia, thinking just how much out of the question it would be. 'I have too much to do here. Now – where's Giles?'

584

'Don't know.' They turned back to their game; Nanny stood up, followed her out of the room.

'I'm worried about Barty,' she said, 'she's been in her room all day. Crying a lot. She sent me away. It doesn't seem right.'

'No. No, it isn't,' said Celia. 'No, I'll go in and see what I can do, Nanny. Although I was sent away as well.'

She sighed; she didn't relish this encounter at all.

She knocked very gently. No sound. Obviously, Barty hadn't heard her. Maybe she was asleep. Well, that would do her good. Very slowly and carefully she opened the door, looked in. And saw them. Saw them lying on the bed together, in each other's arms. And felt violently, dreadfully angry. 'Giles! Giles get up. Get out of this room. Go to your own and stay there. Until your father comes home. You are disgraceful. Disgraceful. How dare you! How dare you behave like this. And you Barty, what are you thinking of? In this house, how could you? After all—'

She stopped. Just. Just in time. She turned, walked out of the room, ran down the stairs. She was half-crying again. She had just reached the main landing when she heard Barty's voice behind her; she turned and saw her standing, a few feet away. Her eyes were blazing, her face working, her fists were clenched. She stepped forward and Celia thought she was going to hit her.

'How dare you speak to me like that,' she said, her voice very low, 'how dare you. I know – what you thought, and you had no right to think it. As if I would, as if Giles would. In this house. And to me. He was being kind, comforting me. He is my friend, my best friend—'

'Barty,' said Celia, her voice absolutely cold, 'Barty, friends of different sexes do not lie on a bed together holding one another like that. I have obviously failed to make some important things clear to you. I blame myself.'

'Oh, shut up!' said Barty.

'Barty!'

'Just shut up. Shut up, shut up, shut up. It's you who are disgusting, you who are disgraceful.'

'What did you say?' Did she know, had she heard something?

'I said you were disgusting. I know what you did, and it was horrible. Horrible!'

This came out more as a scream than anything else. Celia looked up, realised the twins were hanging over the bannisters, their eyes enormous.

'Go to your room at once,' she shouted at them. 'And you, Barty, get in there.'

She half-pushed her into her bedroom. Barty ducked, ran down the stairs, into the drawing-room. Celia followed her; she was standing by the fireplace, her fists clenched, breathing heavily.

'I'll say what I want to say and I don't care who hears me. All right? But you might care, you will care, I know what you did, you killed our baby. Killed my mother's baby. Well, didn't you? Didn't you?'

Dimly, Celia was aware that Oliver and LM had come into the house, that they were standing in the hall, listening; thought, and was amazed to find that she could think at all, that the servants might be listening too, and closed the door behind her. It opened again; Oliver came in.

'It's all right,' he said quietly, and stood against it, so that no one else could enter.

Barty ignored him; her eyes, her wide, brilliant eyes, were fixed on Celia.

'Well – didn't you? Don't deny it, because I know you can't. Mrs Scott told me, she told me what happened, my mother told her, that the baby was alive, and you put a pillow over her face and she died.'

'Barty—' said Celia, stepping forward, feeling only at that moment, dreadful pain for her, 'Barty, you have to let me explain. Please.'

'I don't want you to explain,' she said, but she was silent, nonetheless, stood staring at her, with her fists still clenched.

'The – the baby was alive. That is true. But she was dying. When she was born, she didn't breathe at all. She was two months' premature, she had dreadful deformities.' She looked at Oliver as if for support; he nodded imperceptibly. 'Her legs were horribly twisted, and she had something called spina bifida, a terrible open wound on her back. She seemed to be dead, but suddenly she did breathe – once or perhaps twice. And – and your mother asked me to help her. I think – I know – she felt it must be ended quickly. Rather than letting her suffer any more.'

'I don't believe you. It would have been your idea. Everything has to be your idea. Everything you want to do, you do. My mother had just had the baby, she couldn't have even thought of such a thing, I know she couldn't. She was my mother, she was good and kind and gentle. It was you, taking over, like you always do, making things go your way, doing what you think is best. Like you brought me here. I didn't ask to come, I didn't want to come, it's been horrible, I should have stayed at home with my own family. Giles is the only person who's been my friend, and now you have to interfere with that, as well. Why shouldn't he like me, be fond of me? I suppose I'm not good enough for him. After all you've done for me, that's what you were going to say, wasn't it?'

Celia was silent.

'*Wasn't* it? I know it was. After all you've done for me, brought me

586

from the slums, just so you could feel pleased with yourself, your own little guttersnipe, that's what they used to call me at school, you know. Well, it was murder, what you did and I'm going to tell the police. And I hope you get put in prison, and hanged. I hate you. *I hate you.*'

Celia stood staring at her, absolutely bereft of words. Or even feelings. Then she sat down abruptly, and buried her face in her hands. Oliver moved forward, put his hand on her shoulder.

'Are you all right?'

'Yes.'

'Barty,' he said very gently, 'Barty, come here.'

'No.'

'Please.'

'I don't want to,' she said, but she was sobbing now, and more quietly.

'Come along.' He sat down on the sofa, by the fireplace. 'Please. Come and sit down here, with me.'

She shook her head; then very slowly, moved towards him. He held out his hand. She reached out her own; he took it, as if he was rescuing her from some dreadful physical danger and pulled her gently towards him.

'Come on. Come and sit down with your old Wol. That's right.'

He kissed her gently on the top of her head; still sobbing, she leaned it on his shoulder. He put his arm round her.

'There. That's it. That's better. Come on. Cry as much as you like.'

Slowly she stopped; sat hiccupping quietly,

'Now,' he said, 'now, listen. It was a very dreadful thing, you learned today. Very dreadful. I feel desperately sorry for you.'

'Don't tell me I was wrong. I know it was true.'

'Of course not. I know it was true.'

Celia stared at him, her eyes startled. He looked back at her very steadily.

'I knew about it. And I knew why it happened. Barty, life is very cruel. Very cruel indeed. Your mother of all people knew that. She had such a struggle and she managed so terribly well. And she had a wonderful family and we are very proud to have a member of it as part of ours.'

'I'm not part of yours,' she said, but she sounded less angry. She started picking at a thread on the sleeve of his jacket.

'Of course you are. That's ridiculous. An important, special part. We are all changed because of you. The twins love you—'

'They don't.'

'Oh, but they do. They were crying the other night, when your mother died. They respect you and they love you. They're just very

587

badly behaved a lot of the time, I'm afraid. And you are an important example to them. If they become even half as hard-working, as clever, as beautifully mannered as you, I shall be very happy. As for little Jay – try telling him you're not part of the family. He'd put you right very quickly. And Giles is desperately fond of you, and I am proud that he is.'

'But—'

'And I love you very, very much. You were so special to me, when I first came home from the war. Who had me taking my first proper food, who read to me, hour after hour when everyone else was busy, who played the piano for me, when I couldn't sleep? Eh?'

She was silent.

'Now. The baby. Yes, it's true. Your mother and Aunt Celia did what you heard today, but it wasn't the dreadful brutal thing you imagine. It was kindly, gently done. They were easing her on her way. Your mother couldn't bear it, couldn't bear to see her suffering, and she did indeed ask Celia to help her. Celia told me, when she got home, how peaceful and beautiful the baby looked, how she wrapped her in the shawl she took for her, and gave her to your mother, so that she could hold her and kiss her goodbye. And how your mother thanked her. For everything. Everything Barty. Understand that.'

'It was wicked,' she said staunchly, 'it was a crime.'

'You can think of it like that, of course. Or you can think of it as it really was, an act of great courage and of kindness to a small creature in terrible pain, who could only live for a very few hours at the most.'

More silence.

'And Barty, Celia loves you too. So much. She would never do anything wittingly to hurt you. She has only ever wanted to do her best for you? I know things have gone wrong for you at times: they do for all of us, you know. Giles had a dreadful time at school, as well. So did I, as a matter of fact. But things have gone right, too, you must admit that. No, Barty, Celia is one of the bravest – no the bravest – and the most truly loving person I have ever met. Except for your own mother perhaps, and I didn't know her very well.

'And Celia is a wonderful person to have on your side. Ask her one day what she did for LM, after Jay was born. Well, ask LM. She'll tell you. It was remarkable. She cares for you and for all of us with – well with passion. Although she is very – bossy,' he said and half smiled, 'I grant you that. But we would be nothing without her, any of us. Nothing at all. I know you're angry with her, and probably you should be. I know you're shocked. Of course you are. But you will feel better soon. I know you will. And you'll forgive her. I hope so anyway.'

He kissed her; she was slumped against him now, sucking her thumb like a small child. She looked up at him and almost smiled.

Then she said, 'Can I stay here for a while? With you?'

'Of course you can. As long as you like.'

Celia stirred; she cleared her throat. 'Would you like me to go?' she said.

Barty looked at her; her large hazel eyes thoughtful. Then she said, without smiling, but in a different voice altogether, 'No. Don't go.'

What seemed like many hours later, there was a knock at the door. Celia opened it. It was Brunson.

'Telephone, Lady Celia.'

'Thank you, Brunson.'

She went up to her sitting room; picked up the extension. It was Sebastian, as she had known it would be.

'Celia?' he said.

'Yes. Yes, it's me.'

'Why – why did you ring?'

'To tell you I wasn't coming,' she said, 'that's all. Goodbye, Sebastian. Goodbye.'

CHAPTER 33

'You're looking very grim.'

'I'm feeling very grim. I wouldn't have thought you'd expect anything different.'

'I don't see why.'

'Then you show a complete lack of grasp of the situation. I'm very surprised.'

'Oh Jasper really! You've got the wretched thing banned, or whatever—'

'I don't think, Vanessa, you quite realise what a strain this has been for me. Quite appalling. And it's not over yet, and besides they may apply to have the injunction withdrawn.'

'How could they do that?'

'Oh – it's a legal technicality.'

'Well, clearly I lack a grasp of that as well. Anyway, since you're so wrapped up in your problems, I expect you've forgotten I'm going away this morning.'

'I had actually. London?'

'Yes. Only for a few days.'

'And where are you staying?'

'At the Basil Street Hotel.'

'You love that place, don't you?'

'I do. Such charming people there always. No one in the least vulgar. And so beautifully kept. Not for nothing is its telegraphic address Spotless.'

'Is it?' said Lothian, amused. 'I didn't know that. I might come with you. I could do with a break from this place.'

'Oh, I don't think that would be possible,' said Vanessa quickly. 'I'm leaving in – oh, in about an hour.'

'I don't see any problem with that. Unlike you, I take about five minutes to pack. Probably less.'

'I would actually take issue with that, Jasper. I seem to remember an appalling fuss about your shirts last time.'

'All right. Ten minutes. Certainly less than an hour.'

'Yes, but—'

'My dear,' said Lothian, 'you need not worry. I won't interfere with your plans. I'll stay in another hotel, naturally.'

Vanessa looked at him thoughtfully.

'It – probably would be better.'

'Very well. But at least we could travel down together. I just have a couple of telephone calls to make and then I'll get my things together.'

'I can't think why you want to go to London,' said Vanessa, 'in August.' She sounded fretful.

'I could say the same to you. I need to get some books from Dillons, there are a couple of Promenade concerts I'd like to go to next week. We might even have dinner together one evening. But I promise I won't cramp your style.'

'Well – all right.' She gave him her quick, dazzling smile. There was clearly no point arguing. And as long as he wasn't at the Basil Street Hotel with her and Dick Marlone, who was quite the best and most inventive lover she had ever had, she really didn't care. 'You'd better go and start looking out your thousand and one shirts, my darling.'

'So – this is the last day of Lyttons' life. If you have your way.'

Oliver looked at her and smiled.

'It's nice to have you back,' he said.

'Oliver, don't change the subject. This is too important to joke about.'

'I'm not joking. I do feel you are back. In fighting form.'

'Well, I'm glad you think that.' She smiled at him briefly; she looked exhausted, pale and heavy-eyed. But LM looking at her across the breakfast table could see what Oliver meant. The lethargy, the remoteness was gone: the essential Celia was there again.

'We're going now.' The twins stood in the doorway, dressed in identical sailor dresses with straw boater hats. Nanny was taking them and Jay to London Zoo. LM had given her permission slightly reluctantly, fighting off fears of escaped rogue elephants and rampant tigers, of Jay breaking the glass of the python's cage.

'Thank you,' said Adele, 'um – have you seen Barty this morning?'

'Yes,' said Celia, 'she's staying in bed for a while. She's a bit tired.'

'Why?' Venetia's expression was carefully innocent; they had both heard the beginnings of the row, were desperate to have details.

'Because she's had a very difficult time, that's why. She'll be all right soon. Especially when the funeral's over.'

'Should we go and see her, cheer her up a bit?'

'No, Adele, you are not to disturb her. Do you understand?'

'But she'll be alone all day. And if she's upset, she'll need cheering up.'

'Billy is coming over later. He'll cheer her up.'

'Yes, but he's not here now. She might be crying again, she—'

'Venetia, I said no. Barty is perfectly all right. She just needs a rest.'

A rest and some time. She had gone up to bed very quietly at about ten o'clock, having fallen asleep, finally, on Oliver's knee. He had taken her up and tucked her in and then came back down to the drawing-room.

'She wants you to go and say goodnight to her,' he said.

'Are you sure?'

'She's sure.'

She had gone into Barty's room; she was lying, half-asleep, her lids heavy.

'Goodnight, Aunt Celia,' she said, formally polite.

'Goodnight, darling. I'm – I'm sorry you had such a horrible day.'

'Well, it's a bit better now.'

'Are – you a bit better now?'

'Yes. Yes, thank you.'

A silence; then she said, 'It hasn't all been horrible. Being here. I didn't mean that.'

'Good,' said Celia, 'I'm glad.'

She waited a minute or two, but that was clearly as far as Barty was prepared to go. It seemed to Celia quite a long way. She didn't kiss her; it seemed presumptuous.

'Goodnight,' she said, 'I'm so sorry I – I misjudged you and Giles.'

'It's all right. 'Night.'

Celia had apologised to Giles: 'It was stupid of me. Wrong. I just thought—'

'Not that stupid,' he said. She thought at first he was being generous, then realised there was another interpretation to be put on it. He was extremely fond of Barty; and they were at a vulnerable age.

She suddenly remembered her mother saying, 'She's getting very pretty. It's going to be a headache,' and misunderstanding. Now she knew what she meant. Well – there was nothing to be done about it. Not at the moment.

'Is she all right?' he said.

'Yes,' she said, 'I think she's all right now.' She didn't elaborate; it was not for her to do so. If Barty wanted to tell him about it all, she would. There was nothing to be done about that either.

'Your father was wonderful with her,' she said.

'They are very fond of each other.' There was an edge of reproach in his voice; well, no doubt she deserved it.

'Yes. Well, goodnight, Giles.'

'Goodnight, mother.'

She had gone to bed after that. Oliver put his head round her door. 'Are you all right?'

'Yes. Yes. thank you. And thank you for – well for everything. I don't know what would have happened if you hadn't been there.'

'Oh, she would have calmed down, I daresay,' he said lightly.

'I don't think she would have. Poor little girl.'

'Well, it was a dreadful shock for her.'

'Dreadful. I hope – I hope she can come to terms with it. It won't be easy.'

'No. But she's still a child. Children are very resilient.'

'Not quite a child,' said Celia, the image of Barty and Giles, lying together on the bed, suddenly rising in front of her, 'she's maturing very fast. Physically.'

'Yes, yes, but she's a child emotionally.'

'I suppose so. Oh dear.' She sighed.

He looked at her. 'You must try not to take to heart all that she said. It was designed to hurt.'

'It did. And I deserved a lot of it, I'm afraid. And I certainly didn't deserve all those – those nice things you said about me.'

'I think I should be the judge of that.'

She was silent; then, 'Oliver,' she said, 'I – I didn't know you had guessed about Sylvia's baby.'

He looked surprised. 'I didn't. Not until then. But it all seemed very clear suddenly. I do remember you being dreadfully upset. Odd about it. I only wish you could have told me about it at the time. It must have been terrible for you.'

'It was. Terrible. But I still don't feel it was wrong. Taking in all the circumstances. Well, the wrong thing, for the right reasons. Like so much of what I do.'

He smiled at her rather sadly. 'Goodnight, my dear,' he said, 'I expect you'd like to be left in peace.'

Peace? When had she last known that?

'Yes, it might be best.' She looked at him, hesitated. Then she said, 'Oliver—'

'Yes?'

'I – I know you don't like talking about these things. That they embarrass you. But – this baby—'

'Yes?'

His face was politely interested.

'For reasons which I won't trouble you with, I do know when it was conceived. With absolute certainty.'

'Indeed?'

'Yes. It was that night, after the opera, at Glyndebourne. There is absolutely no doubt that it was then. I wouldn't make a – a mistake about anything so important.'

He flushed slightly, smiled at her.

'Good. Well, that was a good omen, wouldn't you say?'

'Yes, I would.' She looked at him. 'You do know – what I mean, don't you?'

'Yes,' he said, 'of course I do. And I'm very pleased you told me.'

At that moment, she realised, she absolutely believed it herself.

She fell asleep immediately: too exhausted to feel anything, even remorse, even grief. But she woke later, crying bitterly, and lay awake for hours. Feeling absolutely and dreadfully alone.

And yet in the morning, she did feel something more like herself again. Strangely energised, and determined, absolutely concerned about Lyttons.

'There must be something,' she said, 'something we can do to save it. Save us.'

'Celia, there isn't. Please believe me.'

'LM, what do you think?'

'If there is anything,' said LM rather sadly, 'I can't find it.'

'Well, we should go on trying.'

She was going, she said, not only to the office, ignoring Oliver's protests, but also to the meeting with Brunnings. 'I'm perfectly well, it's quite safe. The pregnancy is past three months now, there's very little danger.'

'Perhaps you should ask Dr Perring.'

'I have,' she said untruthfully, 'and he said I could go if I wanted to. And I do. I still think we can fight this.'

'There is nothing to fight. Except bankruptcy.'

'Well, we will fight that then.'

LM had to smile; Celia was never better than when she had not only her back to the wall, but several knives at her throat as well. It was good to have her back; whatever distant grim place she had been in for the past weeks, she had left it now. In spite of everything, in spite of LM's distaste for and disapproval of what she had done, it was impossible not to admire her today.

'I don't see what the rush is. Why can't we wait a few more weeks? We're not on the breadline yet.'

'Because the offer from Brunnings is a good one. Because we should be grateful for it. And take it before it's withdrawn again, before things get worse.'

'Well I'm not grateful for it.'

'And because this injunction has come from Lothian. They will be in London next week to witness the shredding of the books and the type.'

'I thought you were going to appeal. Get an inter partes hearing.'

'Well—'

'Oliver, why not? While we still have a chance. Give in now, pulp those copies and we're really done for.'

'To be honest,' he said, 'I don't think there is the slightest point. You know the facts as well as I do. The similarities between the book and Lothian's real life are quite simply unarguable. No judge in his right mind is going to withdraw that injunction. We have no defence, as far as I can see. And Briscoe agrees with me.'

'But I don't. Can't we talk to Guy again?'

'What on earth for?'

'I'm not sure. I just think we should. It's his book that's going to be destroyed. It seems very harsh to do it without warning him.'

'He shouldn't have done what he did,' said Oliver heavily. 'It was foolish, unprofessional.'

'Oliver, he's only a boy. It was his first book. We should have been more watchful ourselves.'

'Well, I don't feel any great sense of loyalty to him.'

'Not loyalty perhaps. But professional decency. One day he may write another book—'

'Not for Lyttons,' said Oliver.

'Obviously not for Lyttons, if you have your way. No one will be writing books for Lyttons. There won't be a Lyttons.'

'Oh Celia—'

'I'm going to talk to him somehow. Before we see Brunnings. I absolutely insist.'

'It can't change anything.'

'You don't know that.'

She looked at her watch. Nine o'clock. In an hour Sebastian would be gone. Then she would feel calmer. Still in pain, the raw, awful pain: but at least less tormented.

'What time is this meeting with Brunnings?' she said to LM.

'Midday.'

That would be better. He would be well away by then; probably on the ship.

'Is Peter Briscoe going to be there?'

'I believe so.'

595

'Well – shall we go? We have a big battle to fight. Legions to draw up, campaigns to plan. Come on.'

As long as she kept moving, physically, she seemed to feel better.

Guy had caught the milk train to Cambridge. It left Liverpool Street at five thirty; it was a fairly fast train, due in at eight. He had Lothian's address; he could be on his doorstep by half past. He had considered telephoning him to warn him, but he decided against it. He wanted to surprise him totally. He knew he was at home, had not gone away. The worst that could happen was that he would be out. In which case, he would just wait. All day if he had to. There really was not that much of a hurry.

It was a nice journey: surprisingly pretty, along the edge of Hertfordshire and up into North Essex. It was a glorious day, and the English countryside was almost absurdly perfect, golden and slightly misty.

Guy had made himself a picnic, a cheese roll and a flask of coffee; he sat, enjoying it, as they crossed a superb viaduct near Colchester, looking down almost as if from the sky at the suddenly small fields and trees and river below him, and thought of the day when he would be a famous and successful author, travelling Pullman, eating his way through a four course breakfast. Well, it might happen quite soon now; and when it did, he would take Susannah Bartlett out for dinner at the Ritz. She certainly deserved it.

He didn't feel remotely nervous; quietly confident in fact. He knew exactly what he was going to say. And how he was going to say it: very courteously, respectfully even. And then leave again. Then he would go straight to Lyttons and give them an absolute assurance that the book could go ahead. It all looked very simple suddenly.

And then the train stopped.

LM sat in the car, listening to Oliver and Celia talking easily, discussing the day ahead, wondering yet again how he could endure it: her duplicitiousness, her infidelity – it was extraordinary. She had heard only the raw edges of the row with Barty, had no real idea what it was about, but clearly Oliver had been defending Celia. And very vigorously. How could he do that? She had even seen him, as she emerged from her room on her way downstairs, give her a kiss, take her hand. She was baffled; she had thought she knew Oliver absolutely, in all his transparent honesty and straightforwardness, but clearly she didn't at all. She thought again of his advice the previous evening, and wondered at that as well. She still wasn't sure what to do about it: if she should take the advice. Had it come from Celia, in all its worldly pragmatism, she would have been more sure, but from Oliver—

And then if she did, how should she approach Gordon Robinson? Her proud, independent spirit shrank from going to see him, from telling him she had reconsidered his offer. Her personal history had made her nervous of letters and their capacity for being delayed, or failing to arrive altogether. She supposed she could go to his house and push a missive through the letterbox herself; but that seemed rather dramatic and even undignified. She couldn't telephone him, because he had no telephone at home and he would certainly be horrified by a call at his office. But something would have to be done, and she would have to take the initiative. It had probably taken Gordon all the courage he possessed to say what he had. Wounded and rebuffed as he had been, he was not going to come to her on bended knee, begging her to reconsider. She still wasn't sure that she should do anything. Oliver could be so wrong. His own behaviour over personal matters was hardly – well, hardly worldly.

'Jasper, if you're not ready in five more minutes I'm going without you. The train leaves at ten and we have to get tickets. I wish I'd never agreed to this.'

'I'm sorry, Sir, I really couldn't say what time we'll be in Cambridge now. Signal failure, that's what it is. But I'm told it shouldn't be more than another half hour.'

'Another half hour!' said Guy. 'That's appalling.'

'I'm sorry, Sir. Really very sorry. We don't like this any more than you do. We pride ourselves on our punctuality on the Great Eastern. But of course the safety of passengers is paramount. Could I get you a cup of coffee, Sir, from the restaurant car? Compliments of the management.'

'Yes, that would be very nice, thank you,' said Guy. His calm confidence had somewhat deserted him. He kept telling himself that there was no great hurry, that time was not quite of the essence, but it was dreadfully frustrating. And Lothian might go away for the weekend or something. God, why hadn't he thought of that before? He wished now he'd listened to Jeremy and telephoned him. Jeremy'd told him he was mad, that it was an appalling risk. Well, it was too late now.

★

'Is that Mrs Worsley? This is Lady Celia Lytton here. From Mr Worsley's publishers. Good morning to you, I wondered if your son was there? If I might speak to him. Oh. Oh, I see. Well – yes, it is quite urgent. Do you know? – Ah, ah, yes, thank you. I'll try Mr Bateson straight away. And if you do hear from Guy, would you ask him to telephone me please? At London Wall 456. Thank you.'

Jeremy was engrossed in his work when the phone rang. He had decided to set his brighter pupils on a rather ambitious reading course that year, to include Dickens and Trollope, and he was anxious that the children should see both authors in the context of the time in which they lived and the hugely differing circumstances of their backgrounds. It was extremely complicated; he had embarked on the work too late in the holidays and he felt hugely irritated by the interruption.

He picked up the phone said, 'Yes?' rather abruptly. Hearing it was Lady Celia Lytton made him feel no better: the combination of Lyttons, *The Buchanans* and his cousin having been largely responsible for his delay.

Hearing that she wanted Guy made him feel worse; either he had to explain, which was extraordinarily difficult, or not explain, which made him less than honest. He decided on the line of least resistance.

'I'm very sorry,' he said, 'I have no idea where he is.'

It was, he reasoned, going back to Trollope's Barchester with some relief, perfectly true. After a fashion.

Barty got up in a silent house. Everyone was out, it seemed. She was relieved. She felt completely incapable of talking to anybody. Probably ever again. She probed her feelings carefully, rather like she might probe a sore tooth. The shock and outrage of her discovery about the baby were easing now; it was still a dreadful thing, almost impossible to contemplate, but she had managed to believe much of what Oliver had told her. It had been done for the best; the baby's life would have been dreadful and pain-filled. Besides, it was true, if she was two months early she would almost certainly not have lived. And her mother would not have been able to cope with her, and the dreadful problems she would have brought. Just the same: it hurt. It hurt dreadfully. That her gentle mother, whom she had loved so much, could have done such a thing. Or rather, asked Celia to do such a thing. That Celia could actually have done it. It was a crime, and Celia had committed it: Barty had meant it the night before when she had theatened to go to the police. She still could. In some ways, she felt she ought to. But, she supposed she

598

wouldn't. What would be the point? She started to dress, thinking about the other things Oliver had said, about her being an important part of the family. She would like to believe it, but – it wasn't really true. They might be fond of her, might admire her, love her even, but she didn't belong to them, she wasn't a Lytton. She would never be a Lytton. And she wasn't a Miller any more, either. She was – she was a no one. The thought hurt dreadfully. She sighed, looked at herself in the mirror as she started to brush her hair.

And then there was a knock on the door. It was Giles.

'LM,' said Oliver, putting his head round the door, 'We need the deeds of this building. Before we go to the meeting. You don't have them do you? I thought I did, but I can't find them anywhere. Could you just check your files?'

'Of course.'

She was fairly sure she didn't have them, but . . . She went through all the files where the deeds might be, moved on to the ones where they should not be, finished with the ones where she knew they could not possibly be. They weren't there. She went along to Oliver's office.

'I don't have them. I'm sure you did; you asked me for them, before the war, said they should be put in your safe. In fact, I remember putting them in there.'

'I know, but I've looked again and again, and they're not there. Well – we can get duplicates, I suppose. Just doesn't look very efficient. Par for the course, I'm afraid.' He managed a smile.

'Excuse me, I have to see James Sharpe about something.'

'Of course.'

LM looked at the safe: the old, heavy safe Edgar had bought when they first moved into Paternoster Row. 'Now we're not living over the shop,' he said, 'we have to have somewhere to store valuables. It's very important.'

She knew she had put the deeds in there: she knew it. She suddenly realised why Oliver might not have found them: she had not placed them with the company documents, but with the personal ones which had also been kept in the safe during the war: the old family records, going back to Edgar's childhood, birth certificates, marriage certificates, documents of that kind. She would look; she knew where Oliver kept the key, in the top drawer of his desk. She unlocked the safe, looked inside it frowning. It was very full and very untidy. Unlike Oliver really; he was as methodical as she was. But she would recognise the big parchment folder the minute she saw it: it even had a red wax seal on it.

There it was. Right at the bottom. She pulled it out; only underneath it was something else. A much more recent package: a big envelope — maybe she should look in that first, it would save a lot of time.

She pulled out the contents; it was a small, a very small bundle of letters. Only half a dozen. All with an American stamp on. From Robert, no doubt. She wondered if she had ever seen them. Idly intrigued, she opened one of the envelopes, And sat there, reading, absolutely frozen with shock. Shock and total disbelief. For the letters were not from Robert. They were love letters. They were from Felicity.

Ten past ten. He had gone. The car taking him to Waterloo, and thence to Southampton, would be — where would it be? She knew the area round his house, the way there from the City, how long it took to travel each tiny bit of it, knew it so well, so painfully well. He would probably be — he would be — at Regent's Park, driving round the Outer circle. And would be thinking — God what would he be thinking? And feeling? She dared not let her mind even drift in that direction. It was too awful, too painful. She got up, went out into the corridor, walked up and down it, went into the ladies' cloakroom, looked at her face in the mirror. Her pale, exhausted face, with its shadowed eyes, which actually betrayed almost nothing of the terrible misery that lay behind it.

But she was safe now. Quite safe. There was no way, no way at all she could contact Sebastian any more. She couldn't see him, couldn't telephone him, she couldn't write to him, for many, many weeks, it was physically impossible. He had moved out of her reach; the dilemma, at least, was over.

She felt tears spilling into her eyes, brushed them away impatiently, blew her nose. And then forced herself, with an enormous effort of will, to smile, smile at herself in the mirror. If she could do that, she could do anything.

'No, I'm sorry, sir. Professor and Mrs Lothian have left. You just missed them, as a matter of fact. What a pity you didn't telephone first. They've gone away for a few days. Would you like to leave a name and address so that they can contact you when they get back?'

'How would you like to go for a walk?' said Giles.
'I — well, I don't know.'
Barty felt awkward with him, embarrassed and she was afraid of him asking her about the row, what it had been about. She didn't want to

tell him: but she knew it would be difficult to lie. And he adored his mother: in spite of being rather overawed by her, half afraid of her, even. It would all be like stepping into some very dangerous new country without a map. She supposed that was what growing up meant.

'Oh, come on,' he said, 'You look like you haven't been out for days.'

'All right,' she said, 'yes, that might be nice. By the river?'

'Well, certainly not to the park. I know how much you hate it.'

She smiled at him. 'Yes, I do. Have ever since—'

'I know. *Titanic* day.'

'Yes. It was so awful. My life – got much better after that though. Thanks to you.' She looked at him. 'I owe you quite a lot. One way and another.'

He blushed. He was clearly feeling awkward after the incident the day before.

'Oh, I don't think so,' he said, 'come on, let's go.'

They crossed the Embankment, went down on to the walkway. He walked carefully, a little way away from her. She was relieved, without being sure why.

'I'm looking forward to Cornwall, aren't you?' he said.

'Yes. yes, I am. I wish Jay was coming. He'd love it.'

'I know. Father says it's because LM worries about him so much.'

'Well, I'm going to see if I can make her change her mind,' said Barty. 'I'll look after him.'

'We both can. I think it's going to be really jolly. The hotel is full of families, and they have treasure hunts and picnics and parties.'

'Oh dear,' said Barty, 'I don't terribly like parties.'

'These will be fun, I think. One or two of my friends from Eton will be there. I'll look after you, don't worry.'

'You'd better,' said Barty. She managed a smile for the first time: a proper smile.

They walked in silence for a while: then Giles said, 'Sorry about last night. Sorry I got you into trouble.'

'We were both in trouble.'

'Yes. Typical adults.'

'Yes.'

He looked at her. 'Mother apologised to me though. Said she'd misunderstood. Did she to you?'

'Yes, she did,' said Barty, 'actually.'

'Good. She does think the world of you, you know.'

'I really don't think that's true,' said Barty.

'Yes, it is. I swear. When you're not there, we get sick of hearing about you and how wonderful you are, how hard you work and what wonderful manners you've got,' He grinned at her. 'It's really nauseating. The twins find it specially so.'

'I expect they do. Oh, dear. I must tell her to stop.'

'When did my mother take any notice of anyone telling her anything?'

Barty looked at him seriously. 'Not often,' she said.

'And while we're talking about it, I know you think everyone sees you as different, as not part of the family. You're wrong. They do.'

'Giles, they don't. And I don't see how you could think that.'

'Because – it's true. The other day, Grandmama asked mother if she'd thought of sending you to boarding school. And do you know what she said? Mother, I mean?'

'No.'

'She said, "I wouldn't dream of sending any of my girls away to school. I want them growing up at home with me." There now. Does that sound as if she thinks of you as different?'

'Heavens,' said Barty. She felt rather odd suddenly, as if someone had just come up to her and given her a very big hug. As if she were warmed and safe again after the cold, chilling danger she had felt herself to be in. 'Heavens,' she said again.

'Yes. So you see, you really do imagine a lot of it. Not surprisingly really, I know,' he added hastily, 'but you shouldn't.'

'No. No well, maybe – maybe I shouldn't.' They walked in silence for a while; then Giles said, 'You don't have to tell me, of course. But – there was something else last night. Wasn't there? Some other row. What was that about?'

Barty took a deep breath. Then she said, 'Oh – I was just going on about how I wished she'd never brought me to live with you all. I was just terribly upset altogether. About Mum and everything, you know . . .'

'Yes, of course,' said Giles.

'I felt awful afterwards, really guilty. I said I was sorry. I think – well I'm pretty sure she understood. Wol certainly did.' She smiled at him. 'I feel even worse now. After what you just said.'

He grinned back at her. 'Don't be. Not many people stand up to her. Probably did her good.'

'Well – I hope so.'

He looked immensely relieved, started whistling, threw a stone into the river. Barty watched him, feeling much happier. Happier and rather grown-up.

LM was sitting at her desk, finding it difficult to think even where she was, let alone what she was supposed to be doing, when Celia came in. She was holding something. One of the copies of *The Buchanans*.

'I thought you might like this,' she said, 'it could be valuable one day. I thought we'd keep a couple whatever happens, just pulp four thousand nine hundred and ninety-eight of them. I'm sure they won't be counting that carefully.'

'Oh – yes. Thank you, Celia.'

Celia stared at her. 'LM, are you all right? You look rather – odd.'

'Yes, I'm all right,' said LM, 'thank you.'

She smiled at Celia. Her discovery had changed rather a lot of things. She felt too confused to work out properly what, or indeed why, but one of them was that she could like Celia again. Stop feeling outraged about her and her behaviour. It was illogical, she knew, but that didn't seem to matter.

'Thank you,' she said again. 'It's very kind of you.'

'That's all right. I'll see you in the board room for this vile meeting.'

'Yes. Yes, I won't be long.'

LM wondered if Celia knew. About Felicity. Presumably she did. It certainly explained a lot. But – was that affair still going on, were Oliver's increasingly frequent trips to New York, his expressed desire to have an office there, all cover for it? Surely not. He just wasn't capable of it. Of such treachery. No, LM, stop deceiving yourself about him. He is. He most certainly is.

Her view of Oliver had been suddenly and almost totally changed. All at once he seemed both less admirable and more so: human she supposed. And a great deal more worldly-wise. With worldly-wise advice to offer. Advice that seemed suddenly irresistible. What exactly had he said? If you have a chance of happiness now, why not take it? He was right: she did have a chance. And it might not come again. It probably wouldn't come again.

She sat looking at the book: a first edition. Gordon would love to have that; it had real rarity value. A first edition of a book that was never published. Of course most people could not be entrusted with it, but he could. Especially if he had some kind of relationship with the publisher.

LM pulled a piece of Lyttons' writing paper towards her and wrote a short letter on it in her neat, careful hand; she put it into a large envelope, together with the book and sent for one of the messengers. She asked him to deliver it personally and as soon as possible to Mr Gordon Robinson at Messrs Oliphant & Harwood, Solicitors of Fetter Lane, London, EC4.

Then she went to join Celia and Oliver in the board room to have yet another meeting over the future of Lyttons. Or rather, as she greatly feared even Celia was going to have to agree, the lack of it.

★

603

'There you are,' said Jasper Lothian, 'Plenty of time. Train isn't even here yet. You get a porter, I'll buy the tickets. I knew there was no need for all that fuss.'

Vanessa directed the porter to the down-train platform, hoping the train would come in and that Jasper would miss it. She feared there was little hope of that; and wondered, as she so often did, how she had stood living with him for almost thirty years.

'Right,' said Oliver, 'I think we should gather our things together. We have to collect Peter Briscoe on the way.'

'Brunnings are in Regent Street, aren't they?'

'Yes, in a rather beautiful building. That will be nice, at least.'

'You mean – we won't be able to stay here?' Celia felt suddenly close to panic.

'No, of course not. The upkeep of this place, with the huge rise in rates since the war, is astronomical. Since Brunnings do not propose to take more than half a dozen of us on, and since we shall be using their distribution system, our stock can merge with theirs. It clearly makes absolute economic sense for us to move in with them.'

'Oh,' she said, 'oh, I see. I hadn't realised that.'

'Well it's fairly obvious,' said Oliver, 'you must see that.'

'I – hadn't. How stupid of me. Will you excuse me a moment? I have to fetch some – some papers from my room.'

'Of course.'

She went into her office; her beloved office, where she had spent so much of her life. The kingdom within a kingdom she had created for herself. The huge, leather-topped desk looked just as it always did, heaped with letters and books and diaries and files, every one of which she could lay her hands on in a moment, organised chaos of the finest kind; there were the booklined walls, the piles of dusty proofs and papers, some of them undisturbed for years, but the cleaners still forbidden to touch them; the two vases of always fresh flowers, one on the fireplace, one on the low table which she had managed somehow even throughout the war, to maintain and on either side of the fireplace stood her two beloved sofas, where she had read far into the night, slept from time to time, where authors sat while she studied their manuscripts and received her congratulatons, where she had been when the news came that Oliver was safe, and where Sebastian had first read *Meridian* to her, on that same extraordinary morning – and where he had often held her, and kissed her, where he had raged at her on that day when she had misunderstood his behaviour over the copyright fee. It held her whole personal history, this room, it was home in the truest sense, the only place she had ever felt completely safe, fully in control of her difficult, tempestuous life. And now she was to lose it, just as she had lost Sebastian: forever.

'London! London! All passengers for London. London train leaving now from Platform Four. Platform Four for the London train. All classes for London, Platform Four.'

Guy climbed on to it. He felt infinitely weary.

Remorse slowly wormed its way into Jeremy Bateson's consciousness. He shouldn't have done that. Said he had no idea where Guy was. The Lyttons didn't deserve it; Guy didn't deserve it. It was hardly their fault that he had been so busy. Well, only very remotely. He decided he should ring Lady Celia back. Tell her where Guy was. Tell her he had gone to see Lothian. There was no need to go into any kind of detail. Just exactly that.

He picked up the telephone, asked for Lyttons' number.

'Oh, no, Mrs Gould, no more calls now. We're late already. Come along, Celia – are you all right my dear?'

'Yes, I'm fine. Thank you.'

She looked dreadful, Mrs Gould thought. She had obviously come back to work much too soon. Well, at least it was Friday. She smiled at them, turned back to the telephone.

'I'm so sorry. Mr Bateson. They've just left, I'm afraid.'

The name pierced Celia's misery; she felt as though she had been physically struck.

'Who is it, Mrs Gould?' she said.

'A Mr Bateson. He wanted to speak to you.'

'Oh. Oh heavens, Oliver, I must speak to him. Please.'

'Well, be quick, I'll go and tell Daniels you're on your way.'

Oliver and LM went down the stairs; he was holding the door open for her when he heard Celia calling him. Her voice sounded odd: raw, excited.

'Oliver. We must wait. Guy has gone to see Lothian, in Cambridge.'

'Celia, we can't wait. Nothing is going to change Lothian's mind now. Certainly not a last minute plea from Guy Worsley. If you won't come, we shall have to go without you.'

'Can't you delay the meeting? Jeremy really seemed to think this might be important.'

'No, I can't delay it. I'm sorry. What are you going to do?'

'Stay,' she said after a moment's pause. 'For a bit anyway. And don't sign anything without me.'

Oliver left the building and slammed the door very loudly behind him.

Gordon Robinson was finding it hard to concentrate. The depression which had invaded him as LM left the restaurant two nights earlier had not lifted, indeed it was haunting him. It felt rather physical, a combination of a dull headache and bad indigestion. He had not realised, until she had turned him down, quite how much he had hoped she would accept him. And how bleak the prospect was of life continuing along the solitary, old-maidish lines which had seemed so oddly satisfactory until a few months earlier.

He decided to take an early luncheon. He informed his secretary, picked up his umbrella – a constant companion, even on days of such brilliant sunshine as this one – and walked through the outside office, through the reception area of Oliphant and Harwood. As he reached the front door, a messenger came in with a package. He was not a boy, but a rather elderly man; he looked tired and uncomfortable. Well, it was very hot.

Gordon Robinson was a courteous man. He stood back for the messenger, then said, 'If you want the desk, it's over there.'

'Can't leave it at the desk,' said the messenger. 'Got to deliver it personal.'

'Oh. Oh, I see. Well, the desk will inform whoever it is for and ask them to come down.'

'Yes, thanks.'

He looked round; the reception area was large and rather daunting, the desk behind one of the vast marble pillars. Gordon felt sorry for him.

'Here, I'll come over with you. Who is the package for, I might even know the person in question.'

'It's a Mr—' the man looked at the package – 'a Mr Robinson. Mr Gordon Robinson. From Lyttons Publishing.'

'Good Lord,' said Gordon Robinson. 'Well, that's me. I say, how extraordinary. Good Lord.'

The train was terribly crowded. The main one of the day to London, Guy supposed. He finally found a seat between two extremely stout ladies, and opposite a rather tall man with very long legs. He was dreadfully uncomfortable and thirsty. And bored. He had long finished his newspaper and the journey seemed a lot less appealing this way round, and with the early gloss gone from the day. There was a limit to how much interest there lay in the various illustrations of Cambridge and Frinton and Skegness. He wondered if he could afford a drink, or even a coffee. With great difficulty, anxious not to poke the two fat ladies in their well-padded ribs, he eased his hand into his pocket, pulled out the change.

Ninepence. The taxi to the Lothians' house had been very expensive. Hardly a king's ransom, but it would probably be enough to buy him a coffee. He eased himself up from between the padding, off the seat, climbed over the very long legs, and went out to the corridor. God he felt depressed. Depressed and foolish. How could he have done that? Jeremy had told him he was an idiot. Expecting Lothian to be there, just waiting for him. Now it could be days. Weeks even. He sighed, started making his way down the corridor.

There were suitcases all the way along it. People sitting on some of them, disgruntled because he had disturbed them. He felt pretty disgruntled with himself. The restaurant car was right at the front of the train; it meant going through the first class carriages. It was rather different in there. Lots of room, arm-rests betwen each seat, linen head-rests, meshed luggage racks, brass fixtures on the doors and windows. Really nice. Bit like a gentleman's study. There was no one sitting on suitcases in the first class corridors, either. Guy moved along it quite easily; then met a steward with a tray coming in the opposite direction. He stood back against the glass door of one of the compartments to let the man past.

'Thank you, Sir. Very kind.'

As he went past, Guy turned idly to look into the compartment; it was empty. Presumably they were in the restaurant car, having lunch or a champagne breakfast or something, before coming back to their comfortable seats. He felt quite resentful. It wasn't fair. It really wasn't. Still, they could probably afford it because they were clever and successful; they wouldn't do something stupid like going to see someone a hundred miles away without first checking that they were going to be there.

Nice luggage too: very nice. That was a lovely pair of matching leather holdalls up there. With wonderful matching leather labels. Superb. When he was a successful author, that's what he'd have. When he'd finally got the better of Jasper – what a ridiculous name, like the villain in a pantomime – Jasper—

'Oh my God,' said Guy, aloud, 'oh my God.'

And blinked furiously and rubbed his eyes to make sure he wasn't dreaming; then read again, the magical, incredible, truly unbelievable words: Lothian. Basil Street Hotel, London.

'Right,' said Matthew Brunning, 'I've looked over the figures, Oliver. They appear to be just as you said. Not – good. But nothing that we can't sort out for you.'

Oliver managed to smile. LM didn't try. This was hideous. Sort out for them. As if they were junior employees. She felt sick.

'Now, let's just run over this again. The modus operandi, as it were. Brunnings would take over Lyttons, in its entirety. Take on all its debts—'

'And its assets,' said Peter Briscoe.

'Ah, yes, its assets.' He spoke as if they were negligible, of no import.

'We would acquire the backlist, and those with the Lyttons imprint would take on the new combined logo – I've had our art department draw something up, I'll show you later – as each edition expired. The dictionaries and the other reference works would remain as your own imprint. I would insist on that.' He smiled as if this were an act of extraordinary generosity.

'We would retain certain key members of staff: you, Miss Lytton, and Lady Celia, of course. The rest would be open to negotiation. There will have to be some what shall I say – economies made on the staff front, as I'm sure you would agree. Your costs are – quite high.'

'We employ very high-calibre people,' said Oliver, 'they don't come cheaply.'

'Of course not. But you know, we have found here that the high-calibre people, as you call them, are not necessarily the best. Heads of department can direct quite junior people very satisfactorily.'

'They can indeed,' said Oliver, 'but you know, they can also direct them into conformity, away from ideas, from lateral thought, from questioning.'

'Really?' said Matthew Brunning. He sounded impatient.

He was a dreadful man, LM thought; what were they doing here? Oliver was right, one of the things which had given Lyttons its excellence, given all the great houses excellence, was allowing people to question. To say why not? To push boundaries back. And to make mistakes. And waste money.

'What about the art department staff?' she said. 'Our editors?'

'Well, we have our own art department. I would see that as a major area for rationalisation. Frankly, I do consider your studio costs are very high. As to the editors, as I say, I would consider each man on his merits. Again, we have many extremely competent people here.'

'Yes,' said Oliver, 'yes, I see.'

Competent was exactly what they were, thought LM: competent and no more.

'And, of course, all your administrative staff would probably have to go. With the exception of one or two, not necessarily senior people. Our finance director, for example, would not be looking for any assistance from yours.' He smiled slightly grimly. 'Especially in the light of − forgive me − a certain lack of attention to detail.'

'I am Lyttons' finance director,' said LM mildly.

Matthew Brunning looked at her. He flushed very slightly. 'Ah. I had thought − well—'

'But you're right. There has been a lack of attention to detail. For which I blame myself entirely.' She did not attempt to explain further. There seemed little point.

'Anyway,' said Matthew Brunning, 'clearly these are matters which can be resolved in the fullness of time. The main point of this meeting is to reach heads of agreement. To provide a formal launching point for the new publishing house.'

'Indeed, yes,' said Peter Briscoe.

'Now, I wonder if you'd like to look through this draft contract, Mr Briscoe. There are copies for you, Mr Lytton and you, Miss Lytton. Er − is Lady Celia joining us? I had thought—'

'I hope so yes,' said Oliver, 'she has been delayed. She − she said she would be coming on to join us shortly.'

'How long might she be? I have a luncheon appointment and . . .'

'Oh, I'm sure she won't be much longer.'

'I'm going straight to the hotel,' said Vanessa Lothian. 'Are you going to your club?'

'Yes, I think so. You wouldn't like to have a quick luncheon with me first?'

She looked at him, appalled. Dick Marlone had already outlined in great detail what he had planned for the two of them at lunchtime.

'No, I don't think so. I'm not hungry.'

'Very well. Can you take my wallet a moment? I want to sort out some papers.'

'Of course. Nearly there, look, Romford already. We should arrive easily by twelve thirty.'

And at the hotel by one, and in her room with Dick Marlone by one fifteen. Excellent.

Celia was pacing up and down reception, waiting with diminishing hope for a phone call from Guy Worsley, telling herself at the end of each five minutes that she would wait five more, when a very tall man with white hair came in at the door. He raised his hat to her.

'Good afternoon to you. I – I wonder if I might leave this letter for Miss Lytton. Miss LM Lytton.'

'Of course,' said Celia, 'I'll give it to her myself. I'm about to see her. Thank you.'

'No, thank *you*. How very kind.'

Celia smiled at him graciously. 'Would you like me to give her a message? As I am going to see her personally?'

'Oh no, no,' he said, 'no, the entire message is contained within that note. Er – do I have the pleasure of addressing Lady Celia Lytton?'

'You do,' said Celia, 'yes.'

'Good Lord,' said the man. 'Good heavens. This is indeed an honour.'

He appeared rather overcome. He held out his hand, half-bowed over Celia's. 'I had not thought to meet you today.'

'Well, I'm not usually hanging about in reception,' said Celia, briskly, 'but it's extremely nice to meet you too. And you are—'

'Robinson is my name. Gordon Robinson.'

'Ah,' said Celia carefully. This was difficult territory indeed. 'Mr Robinson, how do you do. How very nice to meet you. I've heard—' No, don't say you've heard a lot about him, Celia, possibly not a good idea, 'I've heard you rather like books.'

'I do,' he said, and his rather pale face flushed. 'I do indeed. And I have been most grateful for all the first editions you have sent my way.'

'It was our pleasure. Really. And you must come in one day and browse through our archives. If you'd like that.'

'I say!' he said, 'I most certainly would. How absolutely marvellous. Yes.'

'Well, you will be very welcome. Although,' she added, and she could hear the sadness in her own voice, 'they may not be here for very much longer.'

'Oh really?' he said. He sounded alarmed. 'I had not realised that.'

'No,' she said, 'no, nor had I. Not properly. But while there's life there's hope. And all that sort of thing.'

'Indeed,' he said. 'I've just had that brought home to me very forcibly.'

'You have? That's encouraging. Now, I shall give your note to LM. Thank you. And no doubt she'll be in touch with you.'

'I very much hope so,' said Gordon Robinson. He smiled at her; an amused, almost conspiratorial smile.

He has a sense of humour thought Celia; he's absolutely delightful. Very attractive too, in spite of his shyness. Exactly right for LM. Tall enough, even. Who would ever have imagined that Jay being run over and nearly killed would have led to this? Funny thing, fate. She watched him walking back along the street, swinging his umbrella. He looked as if he might be about to break into a dance.

Guy had watched, fascinated, from the end of the carriage as the Lothians returned to their compartment. Lothian was exactly as he had imagined him, tall, eccentric, distinguished-looking. His wife was extremely glamorous; with her dark red hair, her beautifully cut tweed suit. They were actually a very glamorous couple: far more so than he had made them in the book. God this was interesting. He moved up as soon as they had closed the door, stood in front of the next compartment, so that he could still just see them. She lit a cigarette, smoked it through a long cigarette holder. Lothian regarded her with what Guy could only describe as dislike. He couldn't hear what they were saying, but it appeared to be discordant; she finally stubbed out her cigarette, took a copy of *Vogue* from her case and sat reading it, ignoring Lothan totally. It was excellent theatre.

He hung back at Liverpool Street; he knew where they were going after all, and he didn't want them to notice him, to suspect he was following them. They were gone very quickly; they hired a porter and presumably got into a taxi. Well that was fine. He could follow them. He looked at his watch; only twelve forty. The problem was that he had no money and he was miles from his bank. He would have to go to Jeremy's flat, get the taxi to wait and ask him to lend him some. This was all getting very expensive. Well, it was worth it. He felt quite sure of that.

Jeremy greeted him with patent relief.

'Thank God you're back. The Lyttons are running out of time.'

'Out of time? How?'

'Too complicated to explain. You must get on to them straight away. Tell them what's happened. How did you get on?'

'I didn't. I haven't seen him yet. Well I've seen him, but—'

'What? What on earth are you talking about?'

'I can't explain now, but I have a date with him at the Basil Street Hotel. Only he doesn't know yet. Lend me five bob, old chap. I've got a taxi outside, with the clock running. I'll pay you back later today, I swear.'

'Only if you also swear to go straight to a telephone when you've seen him and tell Celia Lytton what's happened. She's in a fearful state. Lyttons are about to sign themselves over to another publisher, literally.'

'Oh God,' said Guy.

'Goodbye Jasper. Telephone me, maybe on Monday. We might do a theatre or something. I'm not sure of my plans.'

'I will. Have a good time.'

'I intend to,' said Vanessa.

'Look I'm sorry, Oliver, but I don't think I can wait very much longer. I have an appointment, as I said to you. I'm already late. I do think it's rather – inconsiderate of Lady Celia to fail to appear like this.'

'She's very busy,' said Oliver feebly.

'Well, we're all busy, aren't we? I think perhaps we should go ahead and sign without her – since it's only heads of agreement.'

'Let's give her a little longer,' said LM. 'I really think she should be part of this.'

Guy's taxi pulled up at the Basil Street Hotel. He paid it off, almost ran inside.

'Yes, Sir.'

'I'd like to see Professor Lothian, please.'

'Professor Lothian, sir?'

'Yes please.'

'Professor Lothian is not here, sir. We are not expecting him. Mrs Lothian has arrived and has instructed us that she is not to be disturbed. So I'm afraid we are unable to help. I'm extremely sorry.'

'Oh God,' said Guy Worsley. For the second time in two days, he felt like bursting into tears.

Jasper Lothian had actually arrived at the Reform Club when he discovered he hadn't got his wallet. He felt violently irritated. He knew where it was: he'd left it with Vanessa. Damn. Well, he'd have to go and get it. He wasn't spending three days without it, however occupied she might be. He went into the office of the Reform, and borrowed a five pound note, then went out into Pall Mall and hailed a taxi.

'The Basil Street Hotel, please,' he said.

Guy stood outside the hotel, looking up at it, thinking how rum it was to build a hotel literally on top of an underground station, and wondering what on earth he should do next. He was out of money again. He seemed to be no nearer Jasper Lothian, or to saving his book than he had been a week ago. And now Lyttons were apparently going to go under entirely. All because of him. What a nightmare. What a filthy bloody mess.

'Well, I think yes, perhaps we should go ahead,' said Oliver with a sigh. 'I'm so sorry about Celia.'

'But presumably you are able to sign on her behalf?'

'Oh yes,' said Oliver, 'in this case. Two out of three board directors – perfectly all right.'

He looked very unhappy, LM thought: as unhappy as she felt. It was dreadful. Absolutely dreadful. She could hardly bear to look at the heads of agreement document.

'I trust this is all quite clear. Mr Briscoe, are you happy with it?'

'Perfectly,' said Peter Briscoe. 'Oliver? LM?'

'Hardly happy,' said LM. She saw Matthew Brunning frown at her; she didn't care. She might be going to sign the damn thing, but she owed it to all of them, she felt, certainly to her father's memory, to make it clear she didn't want to. She wondered if there might be one last delaying tactic she could use, one last query she could raise. Just in case Celia arrived. Just in case. Something complex, something time-consuming.

'I wonder if we might look again at the paragraph on contracts,' she said.

Guy had just started to walk away from the hotel, down Basil Street, towards Harrods, when a taxi drew up behind him. He turned round, mildly interested; another fortunate person, arriving at the hotel. And then stared and stared harder. It was Jasper Lothian. No. It couldn't be. He must be hallucinating. Or dreaming. Or something like that. Having thought about no one else for so many hours. Only – it was him. Absolutely no doubt about it. Looking determined, and slightly cross. He told the cab to wait, walked into the hotel. Guy didn't even hesitate; he turned round and followed him.

★

613

'You see, I just don't think that is legally correct,' said LM. She had no idea whether she was talking sense or not. But it seemed a very good arguing point.

'What do you think, Mr Briscoe?'

'I'm not at all sure,' said Peter Briscoe. He looked annoyed. He clearly thought it was irrelevant to the discussion: which it probably was. They were not signing a final contract, after all: merely heads of agreement. But LM did know that, although this was not actually legally binding, it did form a very clear statement of intent, a commitment on both sides. It could only be reneged upon with difficulty. It would be a great deal better to avoid it.

'Well, you see, I do think we should try and hammer this out now. Otherwise we may have a lot of very upset authors when the news breaks. They might even seek other publishers. Their contracts are with us; therefore do we renew them, with the new, merged company? Or with Brunnings, negotiating through us? It's really very complex.'

'Dear oh dear.' Matthew Brunning pushed his hair back wearily. He looked at his watch. 'Do we really have to settle it now? It doesn't seem very central to me. Central to our agreement.'

'Perhaps not to our agreement,' said LM, 'but to our authors – extremely so. And you know, Matthew, my father always said authors are the only true assets we have. Without them—'

'Yes, yes, LM,' said Oliver. Even he sounded exasperated. 'I'm sure Matthew doesn't really want to hear what Father thought about authors.'

'Then he should,' said LM sharply. She suddenly felt angry; very angry. This was their father's company they were in the process of signing away; a fine, important publishing house. What he had thought about authors was hugely important. Matthews Brunning would have nothing to buy without it. If he didn't want to hear it, then he was a fool.

'I really think this is crucial. Let's just look at it from the authors' point of view, shall we? How they are going to feel, suddenly being published by a completely different firm. You see, I think—'

She was actually enjoying herself suddenly. It was rather like that party game. Talk on this subject for two minutes without repeating yourself. Only she was going to try to talk for a lot longer than that. And get Oliver talking, too.

Jasper Lothian looked at Guy.

'Who are you and what do you want?' he said.

'I'm Guy Worsley and I want a conversation with you,' said Guy, 'that's all. Not a lot to ask, I'd have thought.'

Lothian's eyes were very hard, very hostile. But there was something else behind them: it was fear. Guy recognised and welcomed it; it meant that Lothian knew he might be dangerous. It meant he was going to win. He had no doubt about it. They were sitting in the lounge of the Basil Street Hotel. It was an odd setting, Guy thought, with its air of discretion and elegance, its fine furniture and paintings, its smattering of patently well-bred guests, for a scene which might well become violent.

'Well,' Lothian said, 'I'll give you—' he looked at his watch – 'two minutes.'

'Fine. I can do it one. Easily. I don't want to take up your valuable time. Now then. I know about your relationship with the Bartletts. If you persist in trying to get an injunction on my book, I shall have to tell my lawyer. That's all. Good afternoon.'

He stood up, smiled the particularly sweet smile at Lothian that he normally reserved for pretty young ladies and just occasionally rich older ones, and picked up his paper. 'I'm afraid you'll have to pay for the tea, I only have half a crown left.'

'No. Wait. Just a moment.'

'No, honestly, there's no need. There's no need for anything more to be said. Any more time to be wasted. It's perfectly simple. We shall look forward to getting your letter on Monday morning, giving the go-ahead to publication. Naturally, when we do, I shall consider the matter closed, and I will never speak of it to anyone. You have my word.'

'Your word! For God's sake. I'm supposed to believe that?'

'Well, I think you should. Who would be interested, if the book does go ahead? You should be pleased if anyone does associate you with it, the master's affair is highly heterosexual. Well you've read it. It's awfully good, don't you think?'

Silence: then, 'Did you see Susannah?'

'Susannah?' Guy put on what his mother called his puzzled look. He wore it whenever he was protesting his innocence. She said that was how she – and she alone – knew he was guilty. 'No, of course not. I did try to see her, but her mother sent me away; she'd gone out for the day. Ask her, if you don't believe me.'

'And why should anyone believe this preposterous story of yours?'

'I don't know. Why should they read anything into the one in the book? Equally unlikely, it seems to me. But someone might. A good journalist. Someone might look into it. You're a very well-known figure in the academic world, after all. There must be people who were around at the time, who'd have suspected, and then – well, it wouldn't look very good for you, would it? I think you should do what I suggest.

Let the book go ahead. I honestly think you're making a mountain of a molehill about it. I don't think there's the slightest danger that anyone will connect it with you. Not really. I think you're being over-anxious. Guilty conscience, perhaps. Anyway – I'll leave you to think about it over the weekend. No great rush. But we will want a letter. By Monday morning. After that – well I have a great friend on the *Daily Mirror*—'

'Jasper! There you are. I thought you were going to wait in reception. Oh—' Vanessa smiled at Guy. 'Who are you?' She was flushed, her green eyes brilliant. She really was a very beautiful woman.

Guy smiled back, held out his hand. 'Mrs Lothian? I'm Guy Worsley. I wrote the Buchanan book.'

'Oh, did you?' She looked at him and her expression hardened. Less beautiful suddenly.

'Yes. I'm sorry it's caused you such a lot of worry. Absolutely not intended.'

'Really?' she said coldly.

'No, of course not. My cousin, Jeremy, he was at St Nicholas you know, in 1915, he was a huge admirer of your husband. Huge. He said he became a sort of role model for him. He got to know all his students, tried to find out as much about him as he could. He told me he was a sort of blueprint for the perfect academic.'

He smiled at her: the innocent smile. She didn't smile back.

'I see. I'm afraid I don't remember him. Jeremy who?'

'I do,' said Lothian. 'Jeremy Bateson. Not very bright, as I recall.'

'No?' said Guy. 'He's doing awfully well now,' God, he was enjoying this. 'He's a teacher, very successful. But he does a bit of writing here and there. Under a pseudonym, of course. As a result he knows an awful lot of journalists and so on. Anyway, I mustn't keep you. Thank you for tea, Professor. I'll look forward to hearing from you. On Monday. By – shall we say – ten?'

'Wait!' Lothian was standing up himself now. 'Just a minute.'

'I can't, actually,' said Guy, 'sorry. I'm in a fearful hurry. I thought you were, too. Now—' he walked over to the reception desk, 'I wonder if I could possibly use your phone.'

'Excuse me, Mr Brunning. Lady Celia Lytton is on the telephone. She would like to speak to her husband. Just for a moment. She says she is really terribly sorry to interrupt your meeting, but it's very important. Very important indeed.'

'But suppose,' said Oliver, sinking down into his chair, pushing his hands wearily through his hair, 'suppose Lothian doesn't deliver. Doesn't write this letter.'

'Guy is absolutely certain he will.'

'Guy was absolutely certain it wouldn't matter if he took a slice out of Lothian's life and turned it into fiction.'

'I know. But this is different.'

'But how, why?'

'He wouldn't tell me. He says he can't. But he says he is absolutely convinced, indeed that he knows, that Lothian will write the letter. By Monday morning. I really think we can trust him.'

'Well,' said Oliver with a sigh, 'I certainly hope so. We've lost Brunnings anyway now. They'll never come back to us.'

'Good,' said LM, 'they're insufferable.'

'Insufferable and rich. Well, I shall believe it all when I have Lothian's letter in my hand.'

'You will. On Monday morning. By ten at the latest, Guy says.'

'How on earth does he know that?'

'I have no idea. But he sounded totally confident. Please, Oliver, please don't fret. I know it's going to be all right. Oh, talking of letters, LM, there's one for you. I took delivery of it personally. From a very nice, very tall, very attractive man. Here it is.'

'Thank you,' said LM. She flushed slightly, took the letter and walked out of the room. Oliver raised his eyebrows at Celia; she smiled at him.

'Totally suitable. Too good to be true.'

'Excellent,' he said and smiled. Rather complacently, Celia thought. 'She must have taken my advice.'

She went back into her own office and sat down at the desk. She felt terribly tired. She looked at her watch. Almost three. The ship would have sailed. Sebastian was gone.

Reaction hit her; her courage suddenly failed. She felt the tears rising again, a great lump of pain in her breast. She got up, strode round the room, sat down again. It didn't help. Nothing helped. Nothing could ever help. She buried her face in her hands, began to cry; and having begun, could not stop. The pain overwhelmed her, possessed her. How was this to be borne, how was she ever to recover, to be herself again?

'Celia! Celia, my dear. There, there,' It was LM's voice, gentler than usual, tender even. Celia took a great breath, threw her head back, looked at her. LM's eyes, watching her, were no longer accusatory, no longer hostile. Just full of sympathy and affection.

'I'm – so sorry,' she said.

'Thank you, LM. I don't deserve it, I know. But it helps.'

'Well,' said LM, stroking her hair, 'well, we don't always get what we deserve. Either the good or the bad.'

'No, I know. Poor Sylvia certainly didn't,' she added irrelevantly.

'No. Poor Sylvia. You were such a good friend to her. As you have always been to me.'

'Oh – I don't know, I stole her daughter—'

'Celia! Don't you think she would have fought you for her, if she'd wanted her?'

'I don't know,' said Celia with searing honesty, 'possibly not. She was very – in awe of me.'

'She seemed a pretty strong character to me. I think she would have done. Anyway, you've—'

'Don't tell me I've done wonderful things for Barty, because I don't know that I have.'

'All right. I won't tell you. I'll keep it to myself.'

Celia managed to smile. 'It's over, you know,' she said, 'the – the affair. I – just wanted you to know that. That's why I was crying. Why I keep crying.'

'I see. Well, thank you for telling me. I appreciate it. Obviously I'm glad. For—' she hesitated, then went on – 'for the family's sake. All our sakes.'

'You were going to say for Oliver's sake, weren't you? I did it only for him actually. Not the family. He's so good, so loyal, he loves me so much. I don't deserve him.'

LM was silent. Celia looked at her. 'I feel so guilty about him,' she said, 'so desperately guilty, LM. Even now, I can't begin to forgive myself. His loyalty is absolute. I – oh God. I feel so ashamed. So – disgusted with myself. To think I could have done that. All in the pursuit of my own happiness. Self-indulgent happiness.'

'Well,' said LM carefully, 'well, he is very – difficult. Oliver, I mean. Especially since the war.'

'No, no,' said Celia, 'I mean, I know he is. But it's no excuse. Not really. I used that, but I was deceiving myself. Telling myself it made it all right. Of course it didn't. Of course not. I'm a rotten person, LM, through and through, I'm afraid.'

'Celia, you are not rotten,' said LM. She sounded stern. 'I can't let you think that.'

'I am, I am,' said Celia. She had begun to cry again, felt it getting out of control. 'I go through life hurting people, look at the damage I've done to Sebastian as well as to Oliver. How long will he take to recover from my – selfishness? Self-indulgence.'

'A fairly self-indulgent person himself I would have thought,' said LM drily. She hesitated. 'Celia—'

'Yes?'

'I think perhaps, there is something you ought to know. That might help you. It's not for me to tell you, really, I'm not even sure if I should but – well the circumstances are very extreme. And it can't do a lot of harm.'

Celia's tears were staunched. By curiosity. She sat back in her chair and looked at LM.

'Well,' she said, 'well go on. Tell me.'

It was extraordinary how much it helped. Eased the guilt, the self-loathing. She sat there, thinking about it, about the fact that her husband, who she always supposed totally faithful, absolutely committed to her and in love with her, had had an affair with another woman and she felt a great rush of relief. She was not the shoddy, cheap adulteress she had thought: well, she was of course, but there was at least some excuse for her now. She could go back to Oliver, ask his forgiveness, albeit tacitly, knowing that he had something to be forgiven for as well. Possibly more important, she could forgive herself. A little at least. It felt very sweet. Absurdly so. And it explained so much: his refusal to discuss things, to confront her situation; obviously thinking, fearing indeed, that it would lead to confession, revelation, increased hostility, to a greatly increased chance that she would leave him. And of course it would have done; she would have seized her excuse, her permission for adultery and run with it. That hurt: but oddly, not for long. Oliver would still have loved her, unquestioningly, unreservedly; she would have found that out, too, through the storm with Barty, and stayed with him just the same.

She thought about Felicity: Felicity, with her sweet face and gentle ways, her devotion to her family. Celia had liked her so much. She would have been the last person she would ever have suspected. But her mother had said how sexy she thought she was. God, her mother was clever.

Frightful nerve, though, when she had given her hospitality, published her poetry, offered her her big chance. Fairly bad behaviour. She suddenly found herself angry with Felicity. That helped, too. She wondered if it was still going on. Surely not. It couldn't be: she would know. But – she hadn't known. Hadn't suspected. Well, it certainly wasn't going to go on any longer now.

She smiled at herself, at her absurd indignation and tried to remember how Felicity and Oliver had seemed together that time at Ashingham. Certainly Oliver had seemed very taken with her. But no more than that. It must have been going on then. It must have been. When had it started though, when could it have—

'Good God,' said Celia aloud, 'Dear God.'

It had been after that first trip to the States, that Oliver had come home able to make love to her again. Felicity had obviously done that for him. For her.

'Well, Oliver,' she said aloud, 'you are a dark horse. A rather wonderfully dark one.' She found the thought moving: almost exciting. How odd she was. How very, very odd.

The door opened. Oliver looked in.

'Are you all right, my dear?'

'Yes, yes thank you.' She smiled at him.

'You look better.'

'I feel better. Thank you.'

'You should go home now. Get some rest. You've had an exhausting time, and none of us can do anything until Monday. God, I hope this is going to be all right. This thing with Lothian.'

'It will be, Oliver. I know it will.'

'I hope so. Oh, by the way, this just came for you.'

He put a package on her desk.

'Thank you,' she said, 'I'll look at it later.'

'All right. I'll tell Daniels to take you home, shall I?'

'Give me a bit longer.'

She picked up the package, took it over to one of her sofas. It was large – very large. It seemed to be a manuscript. It was a manuscript. A letter fell out. A letter on heavy, white vellum paper, covered in black, scrawling handwriting . . .

'My beloved,'

By the time you get this, I shall be on the high seas. Quite possibly feeling sick. I'm a rotten sailor. Well, it will take my mind off my misery.

I enclose the manuscript of *Meridian Times Two*. I want you, and Lyttons, of course, to have it. I could not, in the end, even contemplate another publisher. No one else knows and understands *Meridian* as you do; no one else can do it justice. No one else deserves it.

This must not be a long letter, for if I really begin to tell you how much I love you, and what extraordinary happiness you have given me, I shall never stop.

I wanted only to say goodbye: lovingly, tenderly, with all my heart. And to allow *Meridian*, which, after all, brought us together, to make sure that we are not quite apart ever again.

Thank you for everything that you are.

Sebastian

Celia sat on her sofa for a long time, holding the manuscript to her, the manuscript which was all that she had now of Sebastian. Then she stood up and walked into Oliver's office and put it on his desk.

'Here,' she said, 'here you are. No matter what happens now, Lyttons is safe.'

EPILOGUE

'LYTTON. – On 17th March, at the London Clinic, to Celia, wife of Oliver, a son.'

'I bet you're glad, Giles,' said Venetia, as the car rolled towards Harley Street, and their first meeting with their baby brother. 'Suppose it had been another girl?'

'I'd have left home,' said Giles. He grinned at her.

'Well, you did that years ago,' said Adele, 'you're so lucky, I wish we could go to boarding school, it's so dreary at Miss Wolff's.'

'You should work a bit harder, get into St Paul's, like Barty. She loves it there don't you, Barty?'

'Yes,' said Barty, 'I really do.'

'Yes, well we're not clever like Barty,' said Venetia.

'That's rubbish. You're both terribly clever.'

'No we're not.'

'Oh, all right,' said Barty equably, 'you're not. But you're much better at dancing and reciting poetry and talking to people and riding, than I am.'

'That's true. We're going to be racehorse trainers, aren't we, Venetia?'

'Yes, and live at Ashingham. So there's no point working at school anyway. Oh, look, we're here. Thanks, Daniels.'

Oliver came out of Celia's room, smiling. 'You'll have to wait a minute, she's got too many visitors, matron says. Jack and Lily are about to leave.'

'You mean they saw the baby before us? That's not fair.'

'I know. I'm sorry. But they're off later today, on their trip to New York, and they have such a lot to do.'

'New York! Lucky, lucky them. I don't see why they couldn't have taken us with them' said Adele.

'I do,' said Giles.

'But why? They were always saying they would before it was fixed, and then the minute it was, they said they wouldn't.'

'Well, I think Lily's agent thought that a husband was quite enough of a hindrance on this trip. Anway, it's a belated honeymoon really, they haven't had a proper one yet, and so that Lily can meet some casting directors and—'

'I wonder if she'll have to lie on a casting couch,' said Venetia.

'Venetia! What do you know about casting couches?' said Oliver. He sounded rather shocked.

'Quite a lot,' said Venetia airily. 'Someone at school told me about them, so I asked Lily. She said they're sort of really lovely sofas, and the actresses lie on them, and the film-makers decide whether they look beautiful enough.'

'Oh,' said Oliver, 'oh yes, I see.'

The door opened, Jack and Lily came out.

'Hallo you lot,' said Lily, 'How are you?'

'Jealous,' said Adele.

'Cross,' said Venetia.

'We want to go to Hollywood with you.'

'I know, darlings. I wish you could come. But it's very expensive getting there you know, and—'

'Daddy would pay, wouldn't you, Daddy? He's so rich now, that *The Buchanans* has broken every record, and the new *Meridian* as well. He wouldn't mind, he'd—'

'Adele, you are not going to New York,' said Oliver, 'so can we please hear no more about it. Now, do you want to meet your new brother or not?'

'Yes, please.'

'Come on, then.'

Jack and Lily waved kisses to everyone and disappeared down the stairs. They looked very happy: they were very happy. Unbelievably so, Jack thought. Everything had worked out just splendidly. They had had a marvellous wedding at Chelsea Old Church and a reception at the house in Cheyne Walk; Celia had begged to be allowed to do it for them, and Lily had persuaded him to accept. They had had one slightly difficult conversation, he and Celia, but once that was over, somehow they had slipped back into their old, easy relationship. He was still a bit disappointed in her, but everything did seem to be perfectly all right again. Sebastian had gone to America, Celia was having this new little sprog, and that, combined with saving Lyttons from bankruptcy, had made Oliver very happy. It had probably just been a moment of madness on her part. Well a moment or two. Jack was no stranger to moments of madness himself. And old Oliver was, after all, a bit dull. So, he couldn't entirely blame her. And when he was so happy himself – well it was easy to forgive and forget.

Apart from Lily agreeing to marry him, he had had the most marvellous bit of luck. Lord Beckenham, with whom he had always got on awfully well, and who had certainly taken to Lily in a big way – rather too big a way but Lily had said she could handle his lordship perfectly well and in fact was enjoying it – had mentioned that the Royal Angling and Gunsports Club was looking for a secretary and would Jack like him to put a word in. He'd got on splendidly with them and been offered what was really a jolly good and interesting job. Much more his bag really than publishing.

And now they were off to New York. On the *Mauretania*, which would be very jolly. And all the American Lyttons, whom he liked a lot. Including Kyle, who was doing very well at his publishing firm; Oliver had told him, apparently, that he was planning to get him on board at Lyttons New York, which was also doing very well. The only problem was the wicked half-brother, Laurence, who owned forty-nine per cent of it and was, Oliver said, more than capable of causing trouble. But so far, he had kept very quiet. Jack wondered if he and Lily might manage to meet Laurence. He sounded intriguing. Like something out of a novel himself.

'Come along, my darling,' he said, as they reached the street and hailed a taxi. 'we have a great deal of packing to do.'

Lily said he might have a great deal to do, she'd done hers and if he thought she was going to help with his he had another think coming; she was going shopping.

Celia was lying back on her pillows, holding the small, befrilled baby in her arms. She smiled at them.

'Hallo, all of you. Come and say hallo to the baby. We thought we'd call him Christopher, Kit for short. Do you like that?'

'Yes, it's quite nice,' said Giles. He grinned at her, slightly embarrassed. The whole thing had been slightly embarrassing, he thought: his parents being so old, well past all that sort of thing, suddenly producing a baby. Still, they'd seemed very happy about it. And at least it was a boy.

'Oh, he's so sweet,' said Adele, 'so tiny. Look at all those fingers, waving about.'

'Only ten I hope,' said Barty. She put one of her own out; the baby gripped it tightly, squinted blindly at her out of his blue eyes.

'We thought, Wol and I, that you might like to be his godmother,' said Celia to Barty. 'As you're not – strictly speaking – related to him. How would that be?'

'It would be – wonderful,' said Barty. She flushed with pleasure, and smiled at Celia: a rapturous smile. 'I couldn't think of anything I'd like more.'

'Good. Well that's settled then. You can keep a really close eye on him.'

'Yes, on his spiritual welfare,' said Giles, 'that's what godparents do, isn't it?'

'Yes,' said Celia.

'Can we hold him, Mummy? If we're really, really careful?'

'Yes. One at a time, perhaps. Go and sit down in that chair over there.' Sister put a disapproving face round the door.

'More visitors. Miss Lytton. I shouldn't really let her in—'

'Try and keep her out,' said Celia, laughing, 'LM, come in. Meet Kit. Where are Gordon and Jay?'

'At home, playing with the trains,' said LM. She looked slightly disapproving. The discovery that Gordon Robinson had an entire, large room in his house devoted to a Hornby train layout, set at waist level, with stations, tunnels, signals and points, had been a considerable shock to her. It had also greatly eased the absorption of him into Jay's life: this combined with Jay's discovery that Gordon's other passion in life, apart from books, was birdwatching. The two of them spent whole weekends roaming the countryside around Ashingham, sitting in hides, peering through binoculars, collecting and chronicling birds' eggs. When Jay was eight, Gordon had promised to take him to the Highlands of Scotland, to watch the eagles; Jay was keeping a chart of the three hundred or so days until then and ticked one off every night.

'Well, there's young Kit, as we have decided to call him. Being shared by your bridesmaids.'

Venetia smiled at LM. 'We had a fitting this morning. The dresses are lovely.'

'I'm glad you like them,' said LM. That had been the other shock: that Gordon had insisted on a proper wedding. Not large, but quite formal, in the small church at Ashingham.

'He's going to find out now that I wasn't married to Jago,' she had said to Celia, 'it's bound to come out. What am I going to do?'

'Stay vague,' said Celia, 'an awful lot of churches and so on were bombed. Records destroyed. I think the wedding was in one of those, don't you? And anyway, the only thing the vicar will actually need is Jago's death certificate. Which you've got.'

'No,' said LM decisively, 'no, I don't think I can do that. I've never actually lied to Gordon and I don't want to start now. I'm – I'm going to have to tell him, I'll do it tonight.'

She had turned up the next day at the hospital, looking quite cheerful. 'You won't believe this,' she said, 'but he'd guessed.'

'Really?'

'Yes. He just started laughing when I told him. He said he hadn't liked to embarrass me by telling me before, when I was obviously so eager to keep it concealed from him. That seemed to make it perfectly all right.'

'Men are very odd,' said Celia.

Later that afternoon, the Beckenhams arrived. Lady Beckenham looked at the baby and nodded approvingly.

'Very nice,' she said, 'well done, Celia. Looks exactly like his father. Exactly. More than the others do.'

'My dear, what a thing to say,' said Lord Beckenham. 'Here, let me hold him a minute. Yes, he does look like you, Oliver. Jolly nice-looking.'

A young and very pretty nurse appeared.

'I'm sorry, Lady Celia, but Mr Drummond is here, wants to have a look at you. I wonder if your visitors could wait outside for a moment or two?'

'Certainly, certainly,' said Lord Beckenham. He handed the baby back to his daughter. 'Very fine, Celia. Lovely little chap. Now where would you like us to wait, my dear?' he said to the nurse. 'You just lead the way and I'll follow.'

'Beckenham—' said Lady Beckenham. But he had already disappeared.

Celia lay back, grateful for a little peace and quiet. She smiled down at Kit; he looked back at her, unseeingly. He did look exactly like his father. That, at least, was perfectly true.